PENGUIN CLASSICS

The Penguin Book of Polish Short Stories

THE
PENGUIN BOOK
of
POLISH
SHORT
STORIES

Edited and introduced by
ANTONIA LLOYD-JONES

———

With a preface by
OLGA TOKARCZUK

With translations by Tul'si (Tuesday) Bhambry, Stanley Bill,
Sean Gasper Bye, Jennifer Croft, Bill Johnston, Madeline Levine,
Antonia Lloyd-Jones, Eliza Marciniak, W. Martin,
Jess Jensen Mitchell, Ursula Phillips and Anna Zaranko

PENGUIN BOOKS

PENGUIN CLASSICS

UK | USA | Canada | Ireland | Australia
India | New Zealand | South Africa

Penguin Books is part of the Penguin Random House group of companies
whose addresses can be found at global.penguinrandomhouse.com

Penguin Random House UK,
One Embassy Gardens, 8 Viaduct Gardens, London sw11 7bw

penguin.co.uk

Penguin
Random House
UK

First published in Penguin Classics 2025
001

Introduction, selection and editorial material copyright © Antonia Lloyd-Jones, 2025
Preface copyright © Olga Tokarczuk, 2025

Pages 561–565 constitute an extension of this copyright page

Set in 11.25/14.75 pt Adobe Caslon Pro
Typeset by Jouve (UK), Milton Keynes
Printed and bound in Great Britain by Clays Ltd, Elcograf S.p.A.

The authorized representative in the eea is Penguin Random House Ireland,
Morrison Chambers, 32 Nassau Street, Dublin d02 yh68

A cip catalogue record for this book is available from the British Library

HARDBACK ISBN: 978–0–241–56339–7

Penguin Random House is committed to a sustainable future
for our business, our readers and our planet. This book is made from
Forest Stewardship Council® certified paper.

MIX
Paper | Supporting
responsible forestry
FSC® C018179

Contents

Contents

COUPLES

MEN BEHAVING BADLY

Contents

WOMEN BEHAVING BADLY

MISFITS

SOLDIERS

Contents

SURREALISTS

SURVIVORS

Preface

Novels are good for inducing a state of trance, immersing you in an alternate reality; while short stories are good for gaining insight, situating you in reality. That would be my most concise functional definition of the short story.

Writing a solid short story requires discipline, clear thinking and self-control. To write a short story you must cast aside everything that's superfluous in favour of a precise message and a distinct main point, reining in excess of any kind: of words, images, or the temptation to introduce too much of yourself. It means constantly asking yourself the question: 'What's the point I'm trying to make?' and assiduously finding the most perfect form of expression possible. In good hands, the content of a short story alone can map out and define its form. The short story is the haiku of fiction; it is the concentrated spirit of the narrative.

For the reader a good short story can be a hallowed experience. It can change our perspective, it can amaze us, move us, or make us laugh. It can sink so deeply into our memory that it starts to function as a model of literary experience. We can read a short story in a discrete, tangible space of time, in one unbroken sequence – on our way to school or work on the bus, for instance, or over dinner or at bedtime. Reading in this way helps us to understand that the short story is a psychological whole, integrating the conscious and unconscious. Short narratives can have great force, and are sometimes far more powerful than long novels, because they focus on things and bring them closer, giving us a view of reality as if through a microscope. I use 'reality' very broadly here – meaning everything we take part in psychologically, even if we 'only' imagine it. A short story acts with force: it releases energy, accumulates and brings that energy to a climax, and finally quenches it therapeutically, creating a minor catharsis. A good short story stays in the memory, and sometimes can be recalled just as intensely as a personal recollection.

We can all remember several short stories of this kind, even if we read them years ago. The image and memory of them remains invariably strong and fresh, and the denouements still prompt a shiver. Sometimes we've forgotten the author's name, which gives the stories the character of universalizing parables in the reader's reception of them. Perhaps this is the greatest compliment we can pay to a literary text – to forget who wrote it, but have a perfect memory of its mood and content. Great literature can be anyone's; it can be the voice of a generation, of the general public, the community, society or even the collective unconscious.

Short stories are sometimes unfairly regarded as a less refined form of literature. We're usually waiting for our favourite writer to 'finally' produce a novel. Compared with a novel's heft, a short story seems flimsy, inconspicuous, nothing but literary frippery. But that's not true. These small pieces have dazzling strength, and their power relies on the fact that they can shock us and change the synaptic connections in our brains.

I'm pleased that publishers and readers have been returning to short stories lately. Perhaps it's to do with our love of scraps, this new skill we've been taught by the internet – stopping on details, crumbs, and miraculously combining them into a network. I'm seeing more and more short stories in bookshops, not just collections by a single author, but various kinds of anthology, resulting from the intellect and creativity of the editors of these collections and proof of the publishers' courage.

In this selection of Polish short stories compiled by Antonia Lloyd-Jones we won't find the ones that are studied at school and regarded as the flag-bearers. This original, detached view of Polish short-form fiction offers us a completely different perspective. Lloyd-Jones has chosen texts that show us a very wide variety of literary excellence, presenting a range of aspects from a sensibility that I don't want to call 'Polish' because of its universal human qualities.

Lloyd-Jones has also given up on schoolbook chronology or boring alphabetic order, and has introduced an order of her own, far from stereotypes and officious historical associations, far from martyrology and mechanical patriotism. Here the leading players are animals and children, human couples and inveterate individualists, soldiers and survivors of the horrors of war. This is a rebel order, but one that alters the standard view of my country in a wonderful way. In this constellation the power of literature is revealed, capable of changing the smallest and most trivial events in our lives into an expressible particle of universal human experience.

I am particularly drawn to the fact that Lloyd-Jones has accepted a seemingly impossible challenge. For this collection she has chosen stories by authors that were written over a space of almost a hundred years, and thus cover periods in the history of Poland and of the Polish language that differ greatly from each other; they were created under different legal, political and ideological systems, and also to some extent within different linguistic environments, demanding of the translators unusual contextual knowledge and a good ear for language. The texts in this anthology tell us about times of great change, brought about by the First World War and the realia of the Second Republic (the short, almost twenty-year period of Polish independence between the two world wars); they also survey the events of the Second World War and the occupation of Poland, as well as the Holocaust. Others are set in the postwar reality of the communist era, and finally the most recent explore the democratic transition that took place after 1989 and our modern times. Lloyd-Jones and her cohort of translators have the magical power to understand all these eras and voices, offering the English-language reader one of the most intrepid journeys imaginable – across many styles of the Polish language and through the history of Central Europe – something that really would be impossible to relate in any other form than this sort of miscellany. It's worth knowing that these radically separate, objectively short periods that I have mentioned are in fact entire epochs within the history of Polish statehood and literature. As much happened in these one hundred years as in several centuries in the history of other countries and geographical regions less tried by fate. And that, as a result of these rapidly changing circumstances – fundamental in effect for the average resident of these lands – borders, ideas and languages were constantly undermined and invalidated for altogether four, or maybe five generations of people living here. At a meta-literary level, the stories in this collection refer to a time of constantly changing reality, which is hard for the British or American reader to imagine. They immerse us in a Poland (or, as some would say, a nowhere) that's multinational and multilingual, far from unequivocally defined identities and statehoods.

They also employ many linguistic forms and draw on many experiences. It's quite impossible to compare the vision-like, oneiric fiction of Bruno

Schulz, a Polish Jew murdered in Drohobych (in today's Ukraine), with the documentary language of Tadeusz Borowski, an Auschwitz prisoner who committed suicide a few years after the war. Nor can one find parallels between Stanisław Lem, a writer who created extraterrestrial worlds, and Miron Białoszewski, a great innovator in literary Polish, whose works rarely move beyond a small flat in a remote district of Warsaw. There's also nothing in common between the works of Marek Hłasko, the depraved, tragic tough guy of the communist era, and the socially committed attitude of Irena Krzywicka, one of Poland's first feminists. The classical and positivist writers, Maria Dąbrowska and Jarosław Iwaszkiewicz, cannot be compared with the farcical Sławomir Mrożek or Witold Gombrowicz, for whom nothing was sacred. How can one think of the presence, in one and the same place, of authors as diverse as Zygmunt Haupt, in whose lifetime just one collection of stories appeared and whom we have been rediscovering after several decades of almost total obscurity, and the famous Tadeusz Różewicz, poet, dramatist and prose writer, who for many years was tipped as a candidate for the Nobel prize? Can you place the work of authors canonical for my generation and much younger authors – some still labelled 'promising' – alongside each other in a single volume?

I could carry on leading you along this historical-and-biographical path for some time, because this anthology includes thirty-nine stories in all, but, as I tried to show at the start, Antonia Lloyd-Jones has managed to create such an unusual and, in a very subtle sense, representative work, that it is not its apparently mutually exclusive qualities that determine the unique nature of this undertaking. You may have random and unrelated cause to remember these stories many years from now, even if you've forgotten the names of their authors, and the impressions they leave will allow you to see Polish literature as an integral, rather than a peripheral part of the world's humanist-and-cultural heritage. This is thanks to the universality of these texts, their literary impeccability in an infinite variety of tones, like the unbridled imagination of their creators, their multiplicity of themes, and the originality and precision of their expression.

Hold tight, here we go – welcome to Poland!

Olga Tokarczuk, March 2025

Introduction

This is a book for any English-language reader who likes short stories, and who is interested in exploring Polish short stories in particular. No knowledge of Polish literature is required. It aims to be entertaining, thought-provoking and informative. Polish literature, and especially fiction, is not very familiar to English-language readers, despite three Nobel prizes in literature since 1980. Olga Tokarczuk's Nobel in 2018 has improved the landscape, but there is much more yet to be discovered.

I was asked to compile this anthology because I have been translating Polish literature for the past thirty-five years. But I haven't made an academic study of the Polish short story, I simply know what I enjoy reading. I started reading Polish literature in 1983, when, in an effort to teach myself the language, I bought Polish novels and their English translations to read in parallel. I also read *The Modern Polish Mind*, an anthology of fiction (including extracts from novels as well as short stories) and essays in English translation, compiled by the writer Maria Kuncewiczowa and published in 1962 – the year I was born. I had only heard of one of the twenty-eight writers in the collection, Stanisław Lem. Ten of these writers' stories are in the anthology you're now reading, and there is also one by Maria Kuncewiczowa. Forty years on, I'm still drawing inspiration from her anthology, which steered me towards many outstanding authors at the start of my career. In turn I hope this anthology will inspire readers to explore the work of the authors they find here, and in particular that it will encourage present and future translators to investigate the unfamiliar or little-translated authors.

The Stories

Editing this anthology was a huge responsibility: here was a rare opportunity to showcase the best of Polish writing and to promote deserving

Polish writers. It would have been impossible to read every short story ever written in Polish, so I started by setting a few criteria.

First I set a time limit: the oldest story in this book ('A New Love' by Jarosław Iwaszkiewicz) was written a century ago, in 1925, and the newest ('The Isles' by Dorota Masłowska) was written especially for this anthology in late 2023. Thus the collection bridges two periods of Polish independence, with the Second World War and the communist era in between.

Then I made a very long list of authors whose work I thought should be included; it was a good starting point, though the final, much shorter list would eventually include some writers of whom I was ignorant at the outset. Next I consulted people who were well placed to advise me, including Polish literary critics, other translators, writers, scholars, publishers and librarians. And of course I read every anthology and individual collection of stories I could find, which gave me an excuse to explore second-hand bookshops and book stalls in several Polish cities.

The authors included in this book are a diverse group: there's a contemporary reggae star, a pioneering 1930s women's rights activist, a 101-year-old Holocaust survivor (among several others), a wild child of Polish literature who wrote a bestseller aged nineteen, a Nobel laureate, two former Home Army partisans, authors who were banned or censored and many more.

The thirty-nine stories I eventually chose consist of nine that were already in translation, and thirty new translations, by myself and other translators. Only two of these thirty had ever been translated into English before. Of the nine previously translated stories, seven are by classic authors who couldn't be omitted, such as Stanisław Lem, Bruno Schulz and Witold Gombrowicz; all or at least some of their stories or novels have already been translated. The other two are by living authors Maciej Miłkowski and Julia Fiedorczuk. Most of their work has yet to be translated.

Reading the existing Polish anthologies showed me that women writers are badly under-represented, so I made an effort to redress the balance; one third of the stories in this book are by women. I discovered that during the communist era their short stories were rarely published, let alone translated.

Beyond that, I purposely chose excellent authors whose stories have hardly been published in English at all. Some of the remaining thirty authors are known in translation for their novels (e.g. Jerzy Andrzejewski,

Marek Hłasko, Magdalena Tulli, Paweł Huelle, Olga Tokarczuk, Michał Witkowski and Dorota Masłowska), fiction and poetry (Tadeusz Różewicz and Jacek Dehnel), plays (Sławomir Mrożek) or non-fiction (Margo Rejmer). But even if a story or two of theirs has appeared in translation, most of their short fiction is unfamiliar to the English-language world.

Inevitably, in any anthology there are limits on word count and budget, and there must be omissions. For readers who are familiar with Polish literature, and who are disappointed not to find their favourite in here, I'm truly sorry. Early on, a friend asked if I was including Polish authors who wrote in languages other than Polish: Yiddish, for instance, Silesian, or Kashubian, among others. But the commission was for stories written in Polish, so these stories were not included., though it would be an interesting project to compile an anthology of Polish authors writing in other languages.

The short story is not the most widely practised genre in Poland, which is a land of poets and novelists; and generally publishers tend to prefer novels to short-story collections, which they find hard to promote unless the author is already an established novelist. But recently Polish literature has produced plenty of good collections of short stories. I was obliged to be selective in my choice of stories by contemporary authors, and was sorry not to have the space to include more of the well-known novelists and poets who also write short stories. I have listed a number of the existing translations of their story collections in the Further Reading section at the end of this book. I hope readers will want to read more by the authors whose stories catch their imagination.

Story Categories

Rather than list them chronologically, I decided to group the stories under loose headings, to help readers who are unfamiliar with Polish literature to find their way around. Researching the book showed me that a large proportion of the most powerful Polish short stories written from the 1940s to the late 1970s and beyond are about the Second World War and the Holocaust, as literature tried to make sense of the nation's appalling experiences. Every Polish home has a personal story to tell from this period, every one is different, and they are all shocking and moving. Nothing could matter more, and the stories, whether true memoir or fictionalized experience, need to be told. That said, it worries me, as a promotor of contemporary Polish literature, that the general perception among English-language readers is that Polish books are about nothing but the Second World War.

So I was determined to make sure this anthology would illustrate a much wider, more respresentative range of Polish literature over the past one hundred years. I have placed most of the stories about the war and its consequences within the categories called 'Soldiers' and 'Survivors'. In some cases, I found excellent stories of survival – by Irena Krzywicka, for instance, whose wartime wanderings were extremely dramatic, but I preferred her delightful sketches about the animals she had lived with at various points in her life, and chose one of those instead. I found many stories about childhood or from the point of view of children, most of which are grouped under the heading 'Children'; these and the ones in the 'Animals' category probably say something about my personal taste. I wanted to include plenty of comedy, both abstract and realistic, love stories, stories about family life, village life and society. In any case, the categories are designed more for amusement and as an aid to exploration than to give any individual tale a label. The stories are arranged chronologically within each group, and each one has an introduction that will provide literary and historical context.

The Translators

It is a joy to be able to display the work of some of the world's best translators of Polish literature in this book. I am sorry not to have been able to include more of them. Translators are key to the publication of literature written in little-known languages. To me it is tragic that many readers rarely venture beyond the safe and well-promoted zone of books written in English, or translated classics. Translators from less familiar languages often champion their favourite authors, seeking English-language publishers for their work and then producing superb translations with the same power as the original. I sincerely hope that this anthology will be a source of ideas for both readers and other translators, now and in the future.

Acknowledgements

I would like to say a huge thank you to the many people who helped me to research this book, providing suggestions and special knowledge of particular authors. They include: Daniel Bird, Mikołaj Gliński, Maciej Hen, the late and much-missed Jerzy Jarzębski, Elżbieta Kalinowska, Bronisław Maj, Michał Nogaś, Dobrosława Platt and Małgorzata Pogorzelska at POSK (the Polish Social and Cultural Association) Library in London, Justyna Sobolewska, Tadeusz Sobolewski, Beata Stasińska, Wojtek Szot and Konrad Zieliński.

Many thanks to the translators, some of whom did all the research for their particular authors: Tul'si (Tuesday) Bhambry, Stanley Bill, Sean Gasper Bye, Jennifer Croft, Bill Johnston, Madeline G. Levine, Eliza Marciniak, W. Martin, Jess Jensen Mitchell (thank you for finding all those wonderful female and Jewish authors), Ursula Phillips (thank you for your thorough and invaluable exploration of several women writers) and Anna Zaranko. It's a great pleasure to work with you all.

I'm extremely grateful to all our living authors, who in many cases answered my questions about the inspiration for their stories, and provided some corrections to them too. Many thanks to Anna Pawlikowska for her help with Beata Obertyńska's very difficult text, and to Mariusz Tukaj for his help with Adolf Rudnicki's story. And to Jan Chodakowski for his expert help with the historical timeline.

A big thank-you to Beata Górska at the Polish Book Institute for her help with copyright permissions. Many thanks too to the Polish Cultural Institute and the Polish Embassy in London, in particular Bartosz Wiśniewski, Marlena Łukasiak and Clarinda Calma, for their generous support for this book. And for the kind and touching contribution of Stefan Ingvarsson and his late mother Elżbieta Gieysztor Ingvarsson.

Finally, I am deeply indebted to my editor at Penguin Books, Ka Bradley, who has been the epitome of patience and midwifely support through the long gestation and birth of this book, my copy editor Louisa Watson, whose enthusiasm for these stories makes all the hard work worthwhile, and our tireless editorial manager, Ruth Pietroni.

Historical Timeline

Polish literature has often had to serve a national cause, and is frequently caught up in the machinery of political events. Once a large and powerful country stretching from the Baltic to the Black Sea, by the end of the eighteenth century Poland had been carved up by the neighbouring empires who took advantage of its fractures.

1795–1918   Poland was partitioned by the neighbouring empires and disappeared from the map of Europe. Warsaw and the east were engulfed by Russia, Poznań and the west by Prussia, and Kraków, Lwów and the southeast by Austria-Hungary. Each partition suffered repression, to which the Poles responded with regular insurgencies. This was a period of Romantic literature, when poets such as Adam Mickiewicz and Juliusz Słowacki rallied to the cause of independence and were forced to live in exile. Polish culture fought back doggedly, as the Poles refused to lose their identity.

1918–1939   Following the First World War, Poland regained its independence and returned to the map as the Second Polish Republic. The interwar period was a boom time for literature, when many writers could finally express themselves and be published freely. The earliest stories in this anthology appear at the start of this new resurgent period, and several of the authors featured here belonged to Warsaw's lively literary environment.

1939–1945   When the Second World War began, Poland was invaded and occupied by Nazi Germany and the Soviet Union. Few nations suffered as badly; Poland's many Jews were herded into ghettoes before some three million were annihilated in Nazi concentration camps. About two million non-Jewish Poles were incarcerated and murdered too, while others were forced to work as slaves in German labour camps and factories.

   To the east, the Soviet invaders arrested many members of the Polish officer class, imprisoned them inside Russia, then assassinated them at sites remembered collectively as Katyń Forest; their families and hundreds of thousands of other Poles, including escaping Jews, were deported to labour camps and primitive collective farms in remote parts of the Soviet Union. When Germany attacked the USSR in 1941, the Soviet occupiers released the Poles and allowed them to gather in the south of Russia. Some 125,000 emaciated Poles made perilous journeys to join what became 'Anders' Army' (the Eighth Army under Polish officer General Anders), which travelled through Iraq, Iran and Palestine, ultimately to fight the Nazis in Italy, notably at the Battle of Monte Cassino. These Poles were given refuge in Western Europe, and a large number settled in the United Kingdom.

The Poles who remained in Poland included members of the dominant resistance movement, the Home Army (Armia Krajowa), who fought as partisans. Many civilians conspired against the Nazi occupation in other ways (e.g. by hiding Jews and other victims of repression). Many Polish military personnel who left at the start of the war fought with the Allies, including as pilots in the Battle of Britain.

In spring 1943 the brave but doomed Warsaw Ghetto Uprising was followed by the liquidation of the ghetto. In August 1944, as the Red Army stood at the gates of Warsaw, the desperate citizens staged the equally doomed Warsaw Uprising, after which the Nazis destroyed most of the city before withdrawing.

By the time of the Yalta Conference in February 1945, communists backed by the Soviet Union had already established a Provisional Government of the Republic of Poland. The Allies agreed to shift Poland's borders westwards; Poland lost land to the east to the USSR, and gained an area of formerly German territory to the west. A great migration took place as Poles from the eastern Borderlands were transferred to the so-called Recovered Territories, from which the Germans were deported. Poland lost the cities of Wilno (now Vilnius in Lithuania) and Lwów (now Lviv in Ukraine), and gained Wrocław (formerly German Breslau) and Gdańsk (formerly the Free City of Danzig).

1945–1989   The Polish People's Republic (PRL) was Poland's official name in the era when it was dominated by the communist Soviet Union.

This meant a new form of oppression: under Stalin, many who had fought for Poland in the Home Army were arrested and imprisoned as opponents of the new communist regime. Culture was expected to extol the virtues of communism as ruined cities were reconstructed. The Palace of Culture and Science, Stalin's 'gift' to the Polish people, would soon dominate the Warsaw skyline.

Stalin's death in 1953, followed by the political thaw of 1956, brought the worst repression to an end, though censorship continued throughout the communist era.

In 1970 poor living conditions prompted public protests, including strikes by shipyard workers. Dozens of protestors were killed in the streets by the state militia. A new communist government then boosted the economy, but did so by relying heavily on foreign loans.

In 1980 soaring prices and political iniquity led to a wave of strikes, culminating in the foundation of the nationwide Solidarity trade union movement and wide-ranging demands for democratization. In December 1981 the Soviet-backed authorities responded by imposing martial law; many people were arrested, but the effort to restore the unlimited power of the communist order failed. Despite repression, Solidarity was never entirely crushed.

1989 to the Present Day   The fall of the Berlin Wall in 1989 heralded the Third Polish Republic, and Poland became an independent democracy again. In the 1990s, economic 'shock therapy' (measures designed to arrest hyperinflation and liberalize the economy, but with tough consequences in the short term) and freedom for private enterprise gradually turned the country's fortunes around, though not without public hardship. In 2003 Poland was economically stable enough to become a member of the European Union. Since democracy was restored, the country has been politically divided, and is now split between the conservative, Catholic right (represented by PiS, the Law and Justice Party), and the progressive, liberal, centre-right and centre-left (represented by KO, the Civic Coalition, which combines three parties). In 2023 the Civic Coalition won the parliamentary elections and took power by a narrow margin.

ANIMALS

IRENA KRZYWICKA

1899–1994

In the words of her biographer, Agata Tuszyńska, Krzywicka was a woman of action; if she wanted to do something, she just did it. This freedom of spirit resulted in a colourful life story – retold in her 1992 memoir, *Wyznania gorszycielki* (*Confessions of a Scandalous Woman*) – just as it ensured her legacy as one of the loudest and most risqué feminist voices of the interwar period.

Krzywicka, née Goldberg, spent most of her childhood in a tolerant, socialist and highly cultured household in Warsaw. While a student, she began publishing poetry and essays in prominent journals, orbiting within and around the Skamander group of experimental poets and other artistic circles of the interwar period. She inspired not one, but four, portraits by Witkacy, which she criticized with honest charm (publicly, in the literary magazine *Przekrój*, in 1956).

Then as now, Krzywicka was identified as a pragmatic advocate for sexual freedom; she openly advocated for polyamory, family planning and abortion. Shortly before her 'marriage of friendship' to Jerzy Krzywicki, she converted to Lutheranism to guarantee her right to a divorce. While expecting her first child, Krzywicka interviewed the celebrated translator and literary critic Tadeusz Boy-Żeleński for the journal *Wiadomości Literackie*, leading them to form a romantic partnership that would last until his death in 1941. While happily married to other people, they appeared together publicly and even opened a non-profit women's health clinic.

'Life and Love in the Hen House' is taken from *Mieszane towarzystwo* (*Mixed Company*), an impressionistic short-story collection from 1961 inspired by various domestic animals. Inseparable from the author's bold enjoyment of life's incongruities and (non-)human foibles, the collection is likewise informed by the tragedy of the Second World War; it is impossible not to detect hard-earned wisdom in tales of perverse ducks, beloved squirrels and cats on heat. A year after the collection's publication, Krzywicka left Poland with her son, and spent her later years drinking coffee, eating almond cake, and listening to audiobooks in Bures-sur-Yvette, France.

Jess Jensen Mitchell

Life and Love in the Hen House

Translated by Jess Jensen Mitchell

If you think that poultry lead boring, monotonous lives, entirely focused on their eventual ascension to the platter, surrounded by potatoes and spinach, and seasoned with dill – you'd be wrong. A fowl's life is like any other life, full of fuss and bother, and romance, either ordinary or bizarre. That solemn moment of hatching from an egg, that moment at which a domestic bird exerts a strong effect on the human imagination, is quite unparalleled. It's not at all ugly, bloody or painful, as it is for mammals, it's nothing but fun, a surprise, a sort of silly but charming joke. A live creature coming out of an egg – a little oval box – is almost like pulling a rabbit from a hat. It's basically a circus. Just holding a warm egg to your ear to hear if there's any tapping, if there's life in there, has something supernatural about it, something like what Pygmalion must've felt when a living being started to appear to him from sculpted stone (in fact she came to life later on, but no matter). Knock-knock, the delicate pink mineral of the beak emerges from the mineral of the shell – a toy from a toy – and then here it is, first a little embryo, wet and crumpled, then a little ball, a puffed-up dandelion clock, something between a hairy fruit and a flower. How much prettier, more tasteful and more charming it is than for mammals, who . . . but again, never mind about that. And if hatching from an egg is at once mysterious and infantile, are these two things really contradictory?

Then comes a period of great beauty and grace, of inspiring examples of motherly love and the hatchlings' equally inspiring obedience. Yellow, black and fluffy, the little nestlings maintain an egg-like shape for a long time. They stay yellow, but get bigger, with long necks, flat beaks and webbed feet, clumsily plodding to the pond, where they will soon blossom, like giant marsh marigolds – there is nothing edible or useful about them yet, everything is still within the realm of aesthetics. Let's not talk about what will happen later, though isn't it all the same? Death in a roasting pan or death in any other form?

In the hen house, the days go by with sobriety and foresight; the greatest attention is devoted to food, some to love, and besides that to trifles such as pecking the weak and warding them away from the trough even when it's full, or a sand bath, or dividing into groups that either tolerate or loathe one another. Nothing new there. There's nothing new when it comes to love, either. Some birds stay in pairs, but usually polygamy prevails. And, from time to time, there are strange kinks. One of the pigeons fell in love with a cockerel, a big one, with long, thin legs, a dumb face, and a rump covered with sticking-up feathers. The pigeon would fly down to the cockerel and coo, overcome by passion, walking in circles around him, puffing out his feathers, spreading his tail like a fan, and circling, circling. The cockerel would stand in the middle of the pigeon's magic circle, his neck extended, crazy-eyed, understanding nothing and afraid to move. And the pigeon would keep on circling, ever closer, ever more magically, ever more irresistibly, droning hypnotically, his outstretched wings scouring the earth. And I don't know what would have happened if mortal fear had not forced the cockerel to pull himself together, break the magic spell, and take off, head over heels, blindly, tossing his long, naked legs high behind him. Nothing came of their love, the gulf between them was too deep, because it was, after all, a mismatch of species, age and maybe even gender. But love, whatever the obstacles, is love, and the pigeon would always fly down to the same cockerel to try his charms. In vain. Death – as it always does in great tragedies – soon settled the matter: the cockerel was browned in a skillet and the pigeon lost his dream lover, then either got married, or died of despair.

More successful was the duck's equally bizarre love for the rooster. Despite everything, this love proved mutual. The enamoured duck promptly became the favourite, the maharajah's most adored wife, and she always walked just behind the triumphant, crested rooster, just behind his splendid, fluttering tail. She'd follow him, quacking, dragging her rump over the ground and waggling her hips, which must have depressed the hens. None of them dared to give her a stealthy peck; they advanced meekly in a dense, dull flock awaiting their master's favours, a crumb of love. But his favour was always bestowed on that outsider, that harlot, that home-wrecker. The rooster would pounce on her like a conqueror, from above, in a cloud of dappled feathers, like a sort of avian Zeus, while she, flattened to the ground, quacked lovingly and let him do as he wished. The hens, petrified, stood meekly to one side and waited their turn. But after this lightning blast of pleasure, the rooster would shake down his feathers, step aside, scratch his lowered head with a claw, and ravenously start to eat grain. The wives had to wait. Finally, after a long period of procrastination, the rooster would fulfil his marital duties, but it was clear that they were only duties, and nothing more. As for me, I was waiting impatiently to see what would emerge from the eggs laid by the perverse duck. None of them hatched. In terms of production, it was a total flop.

So, to conclude the deviancy – which as we can see, is something that affects not just humans but also animals – there was another hen who crowed and had the stump of a rooster's tail, but still laid eggs. There was also a shy, bashful rooster who stuck to the sidelines, steering clear of the chickens, and delighted in sitting in a basket reserved for laying hens. He would sit there for no more than a few hours, then he'd get up, look for a time with displeasure and shame at the basket's empty straw bedding, and sometimes even investigate with his beak to see if one of his imaginary eggs might be hidden somewhere. And then he'd leave, pensive and sad, to stand by the fence and crow in a brief, anguished falsetto, though he had already reached adulthood. His sorrows and uselessness were so abundantly clear that his young life ended in a broth.

Anyway, the hens were hopelessly, totally stupid, if you can put it that way; reaching any sort of an understanding with them was out of the question – they came when they were called, and that was all. It's just there were those heartbreaking moments when my housekeeper, Marynia, would chase after a hen or rooster destined for slaughter. 'What a base creature!' she would shout. 'What villainy! It refuses to be butchered.' To someone who didn't know what she was chasing, her exclamations might have sounded strange.

So to finish with the chickens, here's a nice story: once upon a time, one of the speckled hens disappeared. Either she was stolen, or a dog tore her to pieces. She was long gone. But then, suddenly, two months later, in the strawberry patch, by then fully exploited and overgrown with weeds, a charming parade appeared: the missing hen followed by sixteen little chicks. Greeted enthusiastically by the household, she marched at a dignified, matronly pace to the hen house, apparently having decided she'd had enough rough living and sleeping under the stars, and that the kids needed some comfort. Plenty of crushed egg shells and a carefully lined nest remained among the strawberries, which restored my respect for domestic fowl as natural birds, and not just potential roasts grubbing around in the hen house. You have to appreciate her strength of character: after laying an egg, a hen, as we know, lets out a hysterical scream, announcing her extraordinary good news to the world. Spotty, however, didn't scream, or wail, or yell, or else she'd have been discovered. She suppressed her joy and triumph, she refused to undersell herself, disdained the easy advertisement, and then showed the world her ultimate, monumental accomplishment. She proved she could choose a life of freedom, outside the hen house, in primitive conditions, in hunger and rain, without any help, encouragement or conveniences. At the end of the day, you could say she hadn't done anything new because, well, she was just a chicken, but she did it on her own, and that is why the name Spotty lingers in my memory and why I will always utter it with respect.

But that's enough about chickens. *Basta*. More than one kind of poultry has passed through my life. A turkey and a gosling proved especially memorable. They tried to live human lives, but such ambitions are unhealthy for poultry.

Thirteen baby turkeys hatched, so there were fourteen of them including their mother. All of them survived, which was no minor feat of animal husbandry, given that young turkeys are unusually delicate. They're afraid of the damp and they die if their legs get wet. Only in their youth, of course, then they toughen up, forget about their exotic origins and bravely withstand every downpour. But while these ones were small, we – as well as their mother – diligently protected them from the damp. Whenever it started to rain, she would race into the bushes, huge, her wings and warty neck extended, the little ones racing after her, stretching out their long, dark, girlish legs in skimpy knickerbockers, tensing their sparsely feathered bodies. They were terribly ugly, and haughty too, they kept their distance from the other fowl. Besides, they couldn't stand the hen house or the barnyard, so first thing in the morning they'd go, solemnly, all their ducks in a row (turkeys in a row, we should say instead), to the wooded part of my garden. Eventually they got tired of that too and took up residence on the main patio, where we also spent most of the day. The house was in the modernist style with a round patio, encircled by a low wall of three different heights. The turkeys would sit along the wall and watch our life in silent contemplation. We had fourteen witnesses of our joys and sorrows, arguments and reconciliations, work and idleness. Twenty-eight eyes glued on us without a break. It was enough to send you mad. Nothing could drive them away. Those shooed off the lower wall settled on the higher wall, while those on the highest wall closely followed what was happening beneath them. Black, shining, rather blue, with wispy clip-on earrings and beads decorating their heads and necks, they watched us like ravens, like vultures, and were just asking in no uncertain terms to leer at us and say in a funereal tone, 'Nevermore'. Except we were the ones threatening them with slaughter, not the other way round. Staring, motionless, they contemplated their inevitable, tragic fate. And we looked so innocent, so happy, so cheerful, we were definitely more interesting than the chickens and ducks, and yet we were so ominous. I envied the turkeys their blissful ignorance, their illusions, although I was just as stupid as they were, just as unaware of my future. They didn't know they'd end up on a platter because it didn't enter into their ways of thinking, and in much the same way, I couldn't have known at the time that the Nazi occupation lay ahead of me, something just as inconceivable to a civilized person as a platter to a turkey. But, full of typical human pride, I looked down on them with pity, envy and an appetite. Here begins a sad tale, my most shameful moment.

You'd be wrong to think there aren't individual differences between animals – there are, even among birds, even among the carp swimming in the bathtub, awaiting their central place on the Christmas Eve table. There are vigorous and enterprising carp who perform a range of leaps in the tub, jumping above the water's surface, and who swallow chunks of bread roll with gusto. There are others, indifferent and lifeless, who lurk at one end of the tub, barely moving their fins, with a look of distaste on their wide mouths, utterly tired of life. There are also ... but never mind. We were talking about the turkeys. So here's the story: it cannot be denied that one of them distinguished herself by a remarkable individualism, by her capacity for independent thought and by getting up to extraordinary mischief. Having broken free of the motionless circle of her brothers and sisters who would sit for days on end observing us from the walls of the round patio, one day she let out a hoarse scream – although it came out like a gurgle – awkwardly waved her wings, jumped into the middle of the patio, ran up to the table where a guest was sitting and eating cake, snatched a piece from his hands, and wolfed it down, googly-eyed, as if she were about to choke. And she never returned to her family again. She was alienated from her species, race and class, she went rogue, she became human. Generously rewarded with cake for her nonconformist relationship with the other poultry, she never went back to the wall, from where her family would watch her, astounded. Instead, she took up a regular post at the table, and whenever I headed for the garden, she would follow me, rhythmically bobbing her warty neck and spitefully jabbing with her beak to keep away the dog, who – in her opinion – offered us entirely unnecessary company. 'Turkey, Turkey!' we'd call out, and eventually she understood we were talking to her. Unfortunately, her bird brain was not capable of anything more than following a human step by step and snatching food from our guests, which prompted everyone to feign their delight, as at the high-jinks of insufferable children, in order to make the parents happy. In any case, she stood out positively from the company of the other young turkeys and even won a certain renown for herself within literary circles.

One by one her brothers and sisters disappeared, like people in times of tyranny. Every Sunday, every holiday, there'd be one fewer of them, simple as that. When autumn came, we'd return to the city for the winter, and the summer house would be locked up tight. It's a shame to say it, but one day, Turkey's time came too. What could we do? We couldn't possibly take her to Warsaw . . .

The moral of the story is: don't make friends with fowl.

'*Stosunki w kurniku*'
Published as part of the collection *Mieszane towarzystwo* (Czytelnik, 1961).

ANNA KOWALSKA

1903–1969

In Poland, Anna Kowalska is perhaps best remembered for her long-term relationship with the more famous novelist Maria Dąbrowska. But Kowalska was a gifted writer of novels and short stories herself. Published in 2008, the diaries she wrote from 1927 until her death in 1969 have re-established her as a notable literary figure. This frank self-portrait is an intense testimony to historical events and literary life, and to Kowalska's love for Dąbrowska as the object of fascination as well as fear and torment. 'How unusual, beautiful, singular and tragic our friendship and life together was,' she wrote in 1967. At the time of writing, an edition of their prolific twenty-five-year correspondence is due to appear, heralded as further evidence of Kowalska's writing talents.

As a student of classical philology at Lwów University she fell in love with her professor, Jerzy Kowalski, and began her literary career co-authoring novels with him. Her close friendship with Dąbrowska developed in Lwów and in Warsaw during the Second World War, and was marked by complications arising from their existing liaisons with men and their own strong personalities. Although Kowalska and her husband had formerly devoted themselves to travelling for research and other creative work, in 1946 Kowalska gave birth to a daughter; according to Kowalska's biographer, Dąbrowska felt betrayed. After her husband's death Kowalska and her daughter went to live with Dąbrowska, an inevitably complex domestic arrangement.

Kowalska came into her own as an author in 1949, with the publication of *Opowiadania greckie* (*Greek Stories*), followed by autobiographical fiction about her youth in Lwów, historical fiction and other short stories and novels on themes including the emotional life of the Greek poet Sappho.

Kowalska preferred short narrative forms, and wrote in a restrained, lucid style, often about love and passion as a destructive force. The story that follows illustrates her head-on presentation of runaway emotions and their effects, but also shows her sense of self-irony.

Antonia Lloyd-Jones

Horses

Translated by Antonia Lloyd-Jones

I have weak lungs, I explained. Could I have said I'd come to this village in Podlasie to cure myself of jealousy? No one believes the truth unless they've been prepared for it well in advance. I know something about it: for twenty-five years I've been a teacher. I should say: a teacher by vocation. In my boyhood I used to say: I am a human being by vocation. Now I avoid big words. Anyway, I do have weak lungs. So what I'm saying isn't a lie, but it's not the relevant truth.

On my first day here, I wondered what my dear Doctor Grącki found so delightful about the place. Pine trees, sand, a long way to the river. And that stream beyond the village? It's horrid! It flows through the middle of some boggy meadows, among alders, it's black and teeming with leeches. The village is very large and rich, the houses are well kept. It's strange there's no lighting and no pharmacy. They say they're going to have both. As it is, it could be 400 years ago. Those ten kilometres from the railway station do their bit. It's the back of beyond, buried in the woods. I should add that it's one of those villages inhabited by the impoverished gentry – a 'noble backwater'. The phrase sounds comical nowadays, but that's exactly what it is.

It's not just the woods that preserve the local antiquity, but the lack of roads too. Unfortunately, every car gets bogged down. Unless you drive straight after a downpour. Otherwise the wheels get stuck in the sand and you're immobile. Only a horse can manage it.

I spend whole days in the woods. I pick mushrooms, bilberries and juniper. Some of the locals recognize me by now. They know I'm strapped for cash and that I have 'weak lungs'. One time I got lost. Far from human habitation, the forest is quite different. There are no broken branches. The amanitas and russulas are intact, not crushed or kicked. The moss is star-studded with orange chanterelles. Lovely penny buns with dark-red caps. Dead silence, then a whirr and a wail in the silence. The pine boughs creak in a creepy way. I was beset by fear. And those monotonous tree trunks, black and tan, eerie in their monotony. I turned and fled back along my own tracks. Eventually I was relieved to see a hay wagon. The horses were driving themselves home. A boy was asleep on the hay. I shouted with all my might, but I couldn't wake him. He was fuddled by the scent of hay. Finally he sat up in shock. He didn't know where he was or what was happening. He looked at me mistrustfully.

I can't understand how I failed to see how beautiful it is here immediately. If I'd only happened to spend a single day here, I wouldn't have known what it's really like. So I'd only have been here on the surface. You don't just have to be prepared to recognize the truth, but to see beauty too. Perhaps that applies to everything, including every relationship with another person.

I revel in the silence, except that I can hear my own heartbeat more clearly in it, and the whistling in my chest. I can also hear my own thoughts. Sometimes I stop on the path and say to myself: 'I'm not going to think. I want to rest. I want to be rid of the anger that's tormenting me.'

There are moments of great sweetness. Yesterday I sat out on the balcony for a couple of hours, feeling a rare sense of peace. The moon illuminated nothing but the sky, the garden was drowning in darkness, and just the tops of the birch trees beside the house shimmered. Cows lowed and sheep bleated *fortissimo*. It was an unlikely concert. At the neighbours', below, there was hustle and bustle, nailing things and pouring water, as if everyone were washing and scrubbing themselves. Someone came slowly along the road, loudly singing an unfamiliar song to an unfamiliar tune. To the right, in the garden undergrowth, owls wailed insistently in a summoning tone. Then dogs replied to each other from various ends of the village. It felt good, I desired nothing, I awaited nothing.

Almost every day I go and visit the pines around the sand dune. They grow in isolation, and have done for ages. I don't think I've ever seen such beautiful pine trees before. Giant, elegantly shaped. And each one is different. And what luxuriance, what vivid colours. A truly heavenly corner of the world (if it weren't for the ants). Everyone I encounter there says: 'You've chosen the right spot for yourself. The air here is good for you.'

And the people are nice-looking. Especially the men. Well-built, tall, narrow-hipped and broad-shouldered. They bear themselves with dignity. There are surprisingly few children. That's why the village is quiet. For so many generations they've intermarried. Perhaps that leads to infertility. So says my landlady, Miss Marta Terlikowska.

I bought some liquid paraffin, for burning. If I have tea, bread and butter, I need nothing more for complete happiness. Good old Grącki gave me his spirit stove. He knew what he was doing. Miss Marta doesn't like me entering the kitchen. I make my own tea and it does me good. We hardly see each other at all. But she keeps an eye on me, the rascal. Whenever I go to the well she spies on me from the veranda, and when I go to the WC she watches, hiding behind her myrtles.

I can't say I find this overzealous attention particularly pleasant, and at first I wondered whether to move to the teacher's house, but I would be sorry to lose the balcony. In fact it's scary to sit on it for long, because the beams are rotten, but for all that I'm almost in the crowns of the birch trees, and I can see the songbirds close up. It's their favourite place. At the top of the birches, even long after sunset, the pink afterglow takes forever to fade. Every day I look out for this moment. Teresa always accuses me of preferring to be where I am, as that's where I happen to be. She regards it as naivety, banality, in short, something truly awful. She mainly prefers to be where she is not at the present moment. Oh, Teresa, Teresa. I'm still mentally in dispute with her, trying to explain things to her, or to justify myself. Mainly I justify myself. It sounds funny, but I feel guilty. Feeling guilty means admitting that the other person is right, not that they're in a stronger position. It's one of a teacher's professional skills to be able to distinguish being right from having the advantage.

I've aged so much with Teresa that none of my newer acquaintances could possibly guess that I'm fourteen years younger than she is. It was my fault that I felt my youth to be an advantage. I was so sure of myself: that's to say, sure about Teresa. When she dropped Tadeusz for me, I thought it obvious. Now that Teresa has lost her head over Jacek, I'm stunned. Stupefaction, fury, laughter, tears. A hundred times I've killed them both in my mind, a hundred times I've committed suicide. I can honestly say: the melodrama is me.

The funniest thing is that actually I have nothing to be jealous about. Nothing has happened. *Non est consummatum.* Teresa only sins visually. But the way she looks at him! And the way she says: 'Jaceeek . . .' At the thought of it I feel acute pain in my left lung. I only exist to hear about Jacek, his virtues and his charm. I've come to hate the French language. I hate so many things. My entire life with Teresa, our work, the books we read, the walking tours, even the friendships are now tasty morsels to feed to Jacek whenever he comes for his lesson.

'Emil, tell Jacek what it was like in Grenoble, Emil, tell the joke.' Emil this, Emil that. Whenever there's a damned French lesson I sit in the kitchen reading the papers. Sometimes I'm summoned by Teresa to perform a minor task and after the lesson I serve them tea.

Teresa persuaded me ages ago that I liked cooking, serving at table and going shopping. For years I thought I did too, but now I have no idea what I like and don't like. Teresa was horrified when I tripped and poured boiling water into Jacek's lap. And the crockery, the most valuable kind we had, was scattered all over the room. Teresa turned to stone, then began to shake and gasp so hard that I felt ashamed. Meanwhile Jacek, like the gentleman in a comedy, started apologizing to me. I had tripped over his bloody briefcase. I had to pull the trousers off him. He wasn't too badly scalded. The worst thing of all is that I'd really like Jacek if Teresa weren't so infatuated with him. The lad does indeed have lots of fine qualities. So what, when his gentility has come to sicken me, and his grinning civility has driven me to sadism. I fell so low that I kicked his dog, Mars. I, who love animals and have longed all my life to have a sheepdog like Mars. Teresa has always refused to hear of having any dog at all. The animals in books by Colette are enough for her. When I kicked Mars, I realized there was something wrong with me. And good old Grącki said: 'Run for it, brother, while there's still time!' And that lady doctor of nervous diseases of his was horrified. I'm curious to know what sort of a face she'd make if I were to tickle the sole of her foot like that.

When I was young, I couldn't imagine wanting to be alive after the age of fifty. How different it looks now!

So far I've been lucky with the weather. I rest and I walk about. I want to walk off all the nonsense. 'Neurosis,' says Teresa. I feel ashamed when I hear that word. Teresa likes elegant expressions. The last time I heard it, I was afraid I'd do her an injury.

Sometimes Miss Marta Terlikowska, whom I think of by the name Klara, breaks the rules of her enclosed order and, simpering and sniggering as if she were being tickled, comes up to me with a blade of grass and asks its name. I don't know why, but she has assumed I'm a botanist. She encourages me to pick the black berries in the garden. They really are huge and sweet. I plucked a few, out of politeness.

'*Myrtalos, myrtalos,*' she cried over my head as I was picking them. She giggled as she said it; for her it was an indecent word.

Miss Marta starves herself. But she feeds up the birds. The garden is huge and has gone wild. There are few places with as many birds as this garden. In fact there are weasels, martens and squirrels too. There's a family of squirrels nesting in the attic. Miss Marta puts out bowls of water for them in the garden. She's done it ever since one of them drowned in the well. All day she talks aloud to herself, to the birds and the squirrels. She's a bit like a squirrel too – ginger-and-grey, timid and brazen.

Since her sister's death she has lived in complete isolation. Sometimes in the summer one of the family comes to visit. It must be hard to keep going here in winter. Being alone is a shock. When you live among others, you think being alone is the same as your present state, except free of people tiring you. But being alone is disastrous. Suddenly there's no one there. There's nobody looking at you, so you too cease to exist. Nature becomes hostile through its indifference. The earth is lying in wait to swallow you, so are the maggots and the little blades of grass. The birds don't stop. They fly away to places you won't reach. Whatever once connected you with others starts to seem an illusion. You remain in suspension – it's a dreadful state. Only after some time does an isolated man start to keep himself company as if he's someone else, but by then he has gone across – to the other side. To the other side of what? There is a border of this kind, but I don't know what to call it. The man becomes an oddball, a lunatic. He'll talk to a bucket, a spade or a candle. He communicates with things, with trees. Once he has personified everything around him, he's not himself any more. That's when animals start to come to him. The loner is occupied all day long, passionately interested. Especially if he's poor and has to save on clothes and equipment, in other words, must keep repairing them. Mending things becomes an obsession. It gives him the satisfaction of being a sportsman and a collector. The perfect loner changes into the perfect miser. He's like an ant tirelessly building an anthill – for himself, that's to say for nobody.

Whenever someone visits the loner, especially someone from the 'outside world', the loner impatiently waits for the visitor to clear off as soon as possible. Nothing that the visitor says is of any use to the loner. The guest's presence merely prevents him from carrying out hundreds of his favourite, and at the same time agonizing, duties. Loners come across as bigheads who take revenge by ignoring the world to which they've lost access. Above all, they have filled the void with themselves. And something that's full can't be filled any further.

I don't have much contact with Marta-Klara, but I seem to know quite a lot about her. Once, when her bucket fell into the well, she declared that she'd sell the property and move to Warsaw, she'd live like a human being. Poor thing! She loves every little pine tree here, every clump of moss. Her father was a teacher in Warsaw. He came from this village and built the house here for his old age. Miss Marta is comical, unbearable, a real fright, but she moves me. I ventured to tell her never, ever to sell the place, and that it's beautiful here. After this conversation, when I returned from my walk to my room in the garret, I saw a pot of myrtle on the windowsill by the bed. I don't like pots of myrtle, but I appreciated the meaning of this botanical gesture.

Once a week, at first light, a cart appears outside our house full of fresh bread. They're off to the market in town. The smell of loaves, rolls and croissants is so strong and delicious that it'd satiate all Olympus. Meanwhile it feeds me instead of all those defunct gods. I'm fond of that aroma, and I rejoice as I run downhill to the gate. On the spick-and-span cart, covered with new tarpaulin, sit a very neatly dressed, robust-looking woman and a splendidly youthful farmhand. I didn't need Miss Marta's meaningful looks to guess that these two are lovers. Once laden with bread, I don't leave the gate immediately, but gaze after them as they drive along the wide forest road. I stand and watch, and I envy them so badly. I'd like to be that lad, or even that oldish woman. I watch, and my heart aches with sorrow.

Teresa and I were happy. Poor, but so happy. There would be long months when we had no dinner. We hadn't the time or the money. Tea, bread, something to go on the bread, and that was it. Now with irony, oh, with flirtatious irony, Teresa is telling Jacek about our happiness. But our happiness looks like my eccentricity. Teresa and I are no longer a couple. I have become a harmless witness to Teresa's new happiness. Now Teresa says happiness is a misconception. It's Jacek who has converted her to this new fashion.

I can't stop thinking about Teresa. It's so exhausting. Sometimes when I'm in the forest it's as if Teresa and Emil are walking ahead of me. I can see them. I'm halted in my tracks when I remember that Emil is me, watching them. And that those two no longer exist and never will.

Our nearest and in fact our only neighbours are also called Terlikowski, but whenever my Miss Marta mentions them it's as if her mouth were full of vinegar. She regards herself, poor wretch, as being infinitely superior. She doesn't like seeing me drop in on our neighbours, not just for milk, but for a chat too. The housewife is named Bogusława, and her husband is Bogusław – Bogusia and Boguś for short. There are lots of families with the same surname in this village, so first names matter here, in the old-fashioned way.

I like Bogusia very much, though I'm not attracted to such ginormous women as she is. Nor do I like those large, buck teeth and her noisy laughter, which rolls around the yard like whinnying. And yet she emanates something that delights me.

I've no thought of love affairs. All I can dream of now is someone who was Teresa, but who's not like today's Teresa. Bogusia delights me the way trees or horses delight me.

This morning it rained, and Miss Marta took me to the woodshed to search, in her presence, for a nail. It's full of awful junk, but in incredible order. For a while I was shocked: only insanity can force someone to collect and sort out torn leather straps, little bits of metal, the caps off tubes and broken clay pots. Sometimes the quantity shifts – into insanity. I began to heap praise on these collector's treasures.

'I'm not mentally ill,' she said calmly. And I felt so dreadfully ashamed that instantly I was twelve years old, and there before me stood my uncle's cook, a good, saintly woman, who had caught me scoffing the jam.

'I'm not mentally ill,' she repeated. I can't remember how we came to be sitting in the woodshed on a small bench, gazing at a moving curtain of rain.

'Does Bogusia please you?'

'I like her,' I replied simply.

'Nowadays Bogusia's a woman like any other, but . . .'

'I don't think she is like any other.'

'Mr Emil, I know what I'm saying. You should have seen her five or six years ago before she got married! Lie down, Kruczek!' she shouted at her dog, who had put his head on my knee. 'From childhood Bogusia has always loved horses. I've never seen anything like it. Everyone here likes horses, I used to in the past,' she said, sighing. 'But to like them as much as Bogusia does is . . . Lie down, Kruczek! Bogusia can't walk past a horse without patting it, and there's no horse that won't look round at her. If you were here for longer you'd understand what I mean. Not that there's anything wrong with it . . . Why are you looking at me like that?' she giggled, and I got goosebumps. 'Polikarp Lipko's son was in love with Bogusia. His name's Maciej. Probably the best-looking boy in the village, though he's small. Cheerful, skilful, one of us, so to speak. He and Bogusia were often seen together from when they were tiny, and mainly around horses. Maciej was poor, Bogusia wasn't rich, Maciej was little, Bogusia was large. But they were oddly well-matched. Old Boguś – he was her great-uncle, well, not quite, but almost – lost his wife. Great wealth; in fact Maciej didn't just help Boguś with the horses, but did what was needed in the house. But you can't get by without a woman. Nowhere are a master and a mistress, a husband and wife, as necessary as in a peasant household.'

'But they're gentry,' I said, laughing.

'They are, my dear sir,' she replied through clenched lips. 'But the household is a peasant one. Anyway, the Lord God groomed Adam to be a serf. Lie down, Kruczek!'

I bent over to do up a shoelace.

'You can laugh all you like. I'm not bothered. I know I'm laughable, but I understand myself, which isn't true of everyone, you must admit.'

'I'm very sorry, Miss . . .'

'Marta,' she prompted angrily.

'So what happened to Bogusia?'

'Everyone in the village was wondering who would be a suitable wife. There were two widows and some girls a little older. One day Boguś asked Bogusia if she'd marry him. And just for a laugh, she said that if he gave her his chestnut mare, Jaskółka was her name, then maybe she would. That very afternoon he brought the horse to Bogusia's father's stable. They were married. At the wedding Boguś said: "I know I'm old and sad. Bogusia loves horses, and I love horses. Maybe life won't be unkind to us." The priest from town said that for a Catholic wedding there was too much talk about horses. And that they weren't pledging their love to horses. And he was right. But the priest himself has the soul of a cavalryman.'

'What?'

'He's a decent man. A native of Podlasie.'

'And then what?'

'Bogusia respects her husband, Boguś takes care of his wife. Sometimes people marry out of great love, and then hate each other. It's different for Boguś and Bogusia. They weren't in love, but they thrive on their love of horses. They talk about horses. The only worry is that they haven't any children.'

'What about Maciej?'

'Haven't you heard of him? He became a jockey. He's famous.'

I thanked her for the chat and went to my room. I was feeling rather restless and couldn't decide whether to read or go for a walk. I took off my sandals and lay on the bed, if that flat box on wobbly legs can be called a bed. On my very first day I had an exchange of views with Miss Marta on the subject of what defines a bed. I did not emerge victorious from this attempt. The famished patron saint of squirrels looked me up and down, then her gaze stopped on my belly. She'd have been a good actress! Well, well, so I stopped wondering what defines a bed. On the sly I set out four mouse traps and hung up six fly papers. My Marta-Klara defends the life of the tiniest midge. She's afraid the birds won't have enough flies. I feel guilty for disturbing the natural order. Anyway, now it's quiet in my little room, there's no more buzzing, no more scratching. So I fell asleep almost at once, as soundly as if I'd taken a miraculous drug.

'Mr Jurasz? Emil Jurasz?'

I opened my eyes and replied mechanically: 'Emil Jurasz, teacher.'
Beside the bed stood the postman.

I heard Miss Marta's indignant voice: 'Professor, not teacher.'

'He probably knows what he is,' the postman scolded her.

'Bah,' snapped the old maid sneeringly.

'Please sign here. No. Below.' A blue-eyed boy with a lovely, tanned face was looking at me suspiciously. My hands were shaking. I'm like that these days – whenever I'm suspected of something, I actually become suspicious, or at least anxious. Dr Grącki laughs at me. He says that if anyone were to accuse me of eating my own grandmother in tomato sauce, they wouldn't have to torture me to get a confession of guilt out of me, or at least readiness to analyse my feelings for my grandmother. Teresa said of me with pride: 'Idiot.' I am an idiot. Of the plainest kind, not some literary hero.

With a copying pencil I signed: 'Jacek'. And did so under the intent gaze of the young postman, for whom the art of writing is not a banal, soulless function, a mechanical habit, but a feat of which he and his family are proud.

'Are you making fun of me? Jacek or Jurasz?' he cried in an offended bass and frowned like a militiaman reminding you of the penalty for obstructing him in carrying out his important duties.

'Jacek or Jurasz?' he repeated.

'He's got a lung disease. Leave it. I'll vouch for him.'

'Thank you,' I said, and burst into tears, to my own immense surprise.

'You see, the poor fellow's ill,' said Miss Marta indignantly. 'Mr Emil, I'll bring you some wild strawberries. Please calm down. Everything's going to be all right.' This was the voice she used to address a squirrel with an injured leg, or an owl with a broken wing.

I turned to face the wall, holding the envelope, on which in huge red letters was written 'Registered Express'. I didn't sleep any more, but I daydreamed. It happens to me. For a year I've had sub-febrile states. At any rate, whenever I'm tempted to take my temperature, it turns out to be 37.5.

I finally hauled myself out of bed and opened the balcony door. The most innocent of azure skies appeared before my eyes. The world looked heavenly, enticing. I went out, having eaten the bowl of delicious wild strawberries with cream and sugar and a thick slice of bread fragrant with fennel seed. I was in such a light-headed mood that I kissed Miss Marta on the hand. It would seem to be nothing. But I held her hand to my lips for too long. I saw her eyes and felt afraid she was ready to set out with me.

'Off to the forest?' she asked.

'There's too much rain dripping off the trees. I'll go towards the meadows.'

'Good luck,' she quipped through clenched lips.

'Goodbye!' I called from the doorway, and only then did I hear that 'Good luck' of hers. I'm often so scatterbrained that I only hear what's being said to me a moment later. As my mother used to say: 'For Emil, the bells are behind time.'

It must have been the most beautiful afternoon since the world began. The colours and radiance were a thrill to behold, and my heart was full of joy. Every pine needle, every little bilberry leaf, every blade of grass shone, bathed in celestial dew. Not a soul in the vicinity, so I started to hum my favourite song:

> How am I to see you, lassie,
> How am I to see you,
> When from the sunlit cottage
> The fathers will not free you?

At first I hummed, and then, feeling the desire, I 'shattered the silence of the forest' with loud singing, something we always forbid our pupils to do. I only stopped singing when I saw Kruczek. Several times I've treated him, behind Miss Klara's back – I mean behind Miss Marta's back – to the sausage that I brought with me.

'Off you go, Kruczek. That'd be better for both of us.' And when he didn't go away, but just gazed at me beseechingly, I stamped my foot and shouted: 'Go home!'

I crossed the footbridge over a drainage ditch, jumped two more, and found myself on a large common where horses were grazing. I leaned against a fence and rested, drinking in the brightness of the sky and the pure green of the common. A light wind carried a bitter scent of willows, fanning my brow with pleasantly crisp air.

On seeing Bogusia, who appeared beside me out of nowhere, I pointed at a foal and said: 'It'd be nice to be a horse.'

Bogusia turned her eyes on me, and a blue flame flashed across to me.

'You too?' she whispered in terror and joy. 'You too?' she said in amazement. 'And all my life I thought it was just me.'

For some time we said nothing, staring into space, no longer seeing anything. And I couldn't tell if it was a dream or reality, if it was I, or someone I was dreaming about. Bogusia took me by the hand and led me to a grove where her favourite mare, Jaskółka, was grazing. Bogusia laughed that laugh of hers like whinnying. Bogusia, Bogusia, you wonderful force of nature.

I almost forgot to say. In that express letter of hers Teresa wrote that Jacek has won a scholarship and is going abroad. He has given us his sheepdog, Mars. Teresa writes that she's pleased my wish will finally come true: I'll have a dog.

I'll write back to her. I don't know what I'll write. My poor old lady. How badly I've treated her!

'Konie'
Published as part of the collection *Kandelabr efeski* (Państwowy Instytut Wydawniczy, 1960).

KORNEL FILIPOWICZ

1913–1990

Writer, poet and screenwriter Kornel Filipowicz has been called the bard of the Polish provinces and a master of the short form. He grew up in the small, provincial town of Cieszyn and went on to study biology in Kraków. He was a keen fisherman and kayaker – his expeditions involving family and friends were organized, to their amusement, with military precision.

During the war, Filipowicz had been imprisoned in Gross-Rosen and Sachsenhausen, and the experiences of that time, and of the wartime fates of those known to him, certainly form part of the themes that he takes up in his short stories. Filipowicz was adamant, however, that he was not a writer who explored human psychology; he felt that the inner person was almost impossible to access. He never moralized, but approached human beings through their relationships with other humans, with objects and, as in the story that follows, with animals. His training as a biologist made him a careful observer; in this particular story, the cat's point of view is consistently foregrounded, though in his writing more generally Filipowicz closely examines the decisions made by human beings. He does it with such formal restraint and discipline that the reader often feels compelled to reread the story, as the balance of the scales clearly tipped somewhere, but when exactly did it happen? Filipowicz has been called an existentialist writer and is sometimes compared to Camus; it is true that the existentialist project – human existence as a drama of freedom, with the human being in a constant act of self-creation in which each decision counts – is an underlying feature of his work. There is also a clear sense that human beings do not live apart from their environment and that the real danger is not so much in the face of external pressures as in internal acquiescence, so that the loss of liberty is ultimately barely noticed or even a matter of concern.

Filipowicz's own cat, Mizia, appears in his stories and was also immortalized in poems by Tadeusz Różewicz and, perhaps most famously, by Wisława Szymborska in her poem 'Cat in an Empty Apartment'.

Anna Zaranko

Cat in the Wet Grass

Translated by Anna Zaranko

It rains and rains and rains. It rains by day and by night. And it's cold to boot. Old tomcat Murder – with his great square head, small, somewhat battle-mauled ears, and thick, short tawny fur that always manages, despite everything, to remain carefully groomed – naps deep in a cellar window. Unobserved himself, he can at any moment see everything that goes on around him. He sits in the position that takes up the least space, ensuring him the most perfect stillness, to pass as something wholly unmenacing, and on days as cold as today, to best keep himself warm. Murder the cat is perfectly still, but he is not a brick, a stone, a log. Nor is he a pigeon, a crow, a dog. He has a very strong sense that at this moment he is precisely this cat and no other. What's more – he does not lose awareness of who he is even when faced with a human being. He has, then, a very strong sense of identity.

I called Murder an old cat. It's true. Murder has a few years under his belt, but that means nothing, for Murder does not age. Admittedly, he was once, long ago, a small, quietly miaowing kitten, but later, when he grew up, he came to a halt and ceased to change. He did not moult, grow bleary-eyed or fat, he didn't bulge around the belly, unlike many of the neighbourhood dogs, for example. His body remained lean and lithe, his fur stayed smooth and shiny. The pupils of his eyes are pure as the sky at sunrise. Murder looks with those eyes and sees everything, by day and by night, from an ant walking along the ground to the owl that has perched on the edge of a roof. Murder devotes a lot of time to looking. He looks when he hunts, but he looks too for the sake of looking. He looks as if, for all the world, what he saw – the grass, the houses, people, trees – were also his sustenance.

Who knows why, in the house of a certain university professor where Murder had lived for several years and where life was pretty good – he'd been dubbed a 'murderer'? Murder the cat is no more a murderer than anyone else. How many times had he witnessed the professor's wife, with the help of the servant, killing a great fish, wrestling with it and shouting all the while at the top of her voice! Murder saw it all from where he sat under the sideboard. And not just once or twice. And where did those mountains of red meat on the kitchen table come from, those chickens and broilers, rabbits and pheasants? The heaps of white bones? The bloody little livers sizzling in the pan? Ever since the professor and his wife and servant had disappeared from the house and their furniture, smelling of cedar, had been arranged on a great horse-drawn cart and departed – the door of the house where Murder lived had been closed to him forever. Forever? Murder often sat at those doors, waiting for them to be opened and attempting to slip inside, but every time he was chased away. He tried to endure this change of fortune and could be seen peacefully dozing, for days at a time, on the windowsill in the stairwell, but the professor's furniture never returned. It was a most distressing business, but Murder considered it a temporary state of affairs. He never ceased to consider the professor's flat his own, just momentarily inaccessible – not to speak of the building and its immediate vicinity. He would not have relinquished them at any price. That was badly put: nothing, not even the highest price could come into play, since such an intention had never entered Murder's head, not even the thought, not even the whim. If there was some force capable, against his will, of transporting him 500 kilometres from home – he would have done everything possible to return to this house and his neighbourhood. He would have walked day and night, through rain and scorching heat, across country and forests, sneaking past the edges of towns and housing estates by night. And he would have got there. And if not, then only because he had perished, torn apart by dogs or run down by cars on the great highway, but in any event on his way home.

Murder cannot bear din and bustle and above all the screech and scrape that iron vehicles produce. The endless noise the town emitted, striking iron against stone from morning until evening and even into the night, this he'd grown used to – of necessity. Because he had to live in this town, because he'd lived here since he was born. He'd learned not to hear these nasty sounds. Or, to put it better: he had the ability to separate and isolate them from the ones that he found pleasant or simply needful in life:

human footsteps, the quick scamper of rats, the chirping of nestlings, the scratching of mice, the rustle of leaves.

So here is Murder, who did not need to return from somewhere because no one had taken him anywhere by force, sitting inside the cellar window and seemingly deeply happy with the fact that he is who he is, and with the precise place in which he has found himself. Could he have been happier still, if the place he was in had first been taken from him – and if he had then regained it? Who knows. It seems to me that he would be just as happy, neither a little more nor a little less. Because Murder the cat's aim was, is, and always will be to return to the very same place – no matter if the return should be from next door's garden or from the next province, or even country. For it is his greatest joy and satisfaction to constantly check that the principal elements of the world surrounding him – trees, stones, bushes and fences – are, so to speak, in their proper places. Only with the sense that he is who he is and in familiar surroundings can Murder the cat live and function. Against the background of the unchangeable, and without changing himself – he can see and understand better what changes persistently, grows, moves, repositions.

The rain was slowly beginning to ease, the cold wind too was dying down. It gave a final gust as though just to shake the drops from the trees, to stir and part the stalks of grass, to agitate the tiny leaves of bushes – and then came silence. Murder went on sitting in the window frame a long while yet, but at a moment entirely of his own choosing, he made a decision and acted upon it at once: he jumped lightly and very carefully onto the ground. As carefully as though he were jumping not from a height of half a metre, but from the first floor. He stood a moment, looking and listening, to make sure that his movement had not caused any commotion hereabout. But nothing was happening. Peace reigned, with only occasional dripping from the trees. As was his habit, to provoke any change that might be lurking somewhere under cover of peace and quiet and unexpectedly threaten him, he himself energetically swished his tail two or three times. Then he stood, looked, and listened. It took some time, but Murder was patient. Patience was his chief attribute. Murder never had the feeling he was wasting time, a feeling that accompanies even the most patient people at times of waiting, for example for a train that has been delayed, or when engaged in some dull, monotonous activity. When, sitting or standing motionless, he would stare into the dark mouth of a burrow from which a mouse might emerge at any moment – the time never dragged for Murder. Immobility, endurance, waiting was the same to Murder as running, flight, pursuit, battle, and therefore no waste of time. It was simply a slightly different but equally valuable way of being in time and space.

Now Murder was moving through the grass, which reached to his back; he went slowly, at a lazy pace, as though he were very tired. He skirted the tall clumps of weeds to avoid rubbing against the wet leaves, which he did not like. Murder generally disliked any contact with water. A great drop had fallen onto him a moment before, unexpectedly, from a tree, the pain of it piercing him like an arrow. Murder twisted his head and licked his coat on the spot where the drop of water had struck him. Murder disliked water intensely – but he succumbed to something more powerful: a great passion for fishing. Had Murder been born near a river, he would have hunted fish for sure. True, it's hard to imagine, but it's common knowledge that many of Murder's relatives fished with great success. Let us not be surprised, then, that when hungry, Murder hunted in all conditions, even in wet grass. Lo and behold: suddenly, his head still twisted half around and tongue out, from the corner of his eye Murder saw, or perhaps only surmised, some movement at the foot of the fence. He turned his head, froze to the spot, looked. His mouth remained half-open, the pink tongue protruding slightly. His ears, too, were cocked in the same direction as his watchful eyes, attempting to assist them. Along the fence, from the side of the wall, a great grey-brown rat ran in the direction of the concrete litter bin. He moved none too quickly; he was busy sniffing. Near the concrete he turned, ran back the same way, and disappeared. Murder stood as though turned to stone, but only on the face of it; inside, he was raging, agitated, trembling. An encounter with a rat was something more than hunting. It was a battle, sometimes a matter of life and death. Once – it was winter at the time – while hunting mice in the cellar, Murder the cat had been attacked out of the blue by several rats and had been close to death. He was still very young then, and inexperienced. He fought desperately, rolled about among the rubbish, coal, broken bottles, trying to jettison his attackers, to push them away with his legs, shake them off. He killed two or three. But other rats were clinging to his ears, his tail, pouncing at his throat. He was saved by a sudden light and the entry of a human with a spade. Rats feared people; he, Murder, feared them too, but a little less. To tell the truth, Murder the cat had suffered much at the hands of humans: children threw stones at him, adults set their dogs on him. But on the other hand, he'd also met much kindness from humans. There were those who gave him saucers of milk, tossed him meat or a bone. At the professor's flat, as mentioned before, he'd led a perfectly comfortable life. Murder preferred, however, to keep out of humans' way. He observed them, rather, from a distance and tried to guess their intentions in advance, since they were as a rule unclear, inconsistent, difficult to predict. Of rats he remained wary from the time of his youthful escapade. When he had the advantage – he fought and killed them, bit them to death (but did not eat them, they disgusted him). He fled them when they had the upper hand, when he noticed that they were trying to creep up from behind, to surround him, cut off his retreat. Murder generally learned to be vigilant in all circumstances, by day and by night, awake or asleep. There was only one place in which Murder felt secure and slept in safety (not counting the smack across the head with a cloth which he got after bringing in a mouse, but that was a long time ago): the home of the university professor. After sleepless spring nights, after hunting, wandering and brawling, he could curl into a ball on the wardrobe, on a chair, sometimes even on the desk, and sleep like a log, oblivious to conversations, clattering, or sing-ing. Touched occasionally by a hand, or even stroked, he'd raise his head, look at the human, then arrange his head even more comfortably on his own fur and sleep on. But unfortunately, the cedar-scented furniture was no more. Someone else was living in the professor's house. Murder would sometimes raise his head and look at the windows on the second floor, but he saw strangers there, alien faces, other shapes and colours. Murder never stopped believing, not for a moment, that he'd return there someday. Believe? It wasn't faith; it was a deep conviction that the familiar-smelling furniture would be moved back into the apartment on the second floor and that the people who called him 'Murder' and were kind to him would enter once again. Kind meant that they were not mean – nothing more. That was enough for Murder; anything more would not be to his liking. Because Murder did not wish to feel obliged in any way to people. Though, pardon me: one fine day he did bring a mouse in his mouth and placed it carefully, half alive, on the floor. The offering presented by Murder to the professor's household was not well received, however, and Murder never repeated it.

Murder the cat stood still a long time, staring at the place where the rat had run past – but the rat did not appear again. The tiresome sounds of the town had completely abated, as though all the windows opening onto that alien world had been tightly shut. Another moment's waiting, and Murder moved on, deeper into his world. He advances, moving noiselessly. He lifts his left forepaw to step over a twig lying across his path, a twig which, had he touched it, would have made an unnecessary sound. Then he steps across the twig with his left back paw, without touching it, without looking around, as though that paw possessed an eye. Of course, one cannot see with a paw, but what of it? Murder the cat's back paw executes precisely the movement necessary in order not to touch the twig – and that's that. Because in each and every movement – stepping, stopping, a turn, a leap – Murder the cat must be absolutely perfect. Murder's world, in its constancy and immutability that Murder values so highly, is nonetheless very diverse, so diverse that it seems always to be changing. In order to exist in this world, Murder must be soft and supple, his movements must be fluid, they must never repeat themselves. Each movement must be different, but always precise. Murder's body cannot be hard and angular like the edge of concrete steps, like a window frame, like an iron handrail. Murder was not made by a human, whittled of wood or sculpted in stone. On the earth and under the sky, among plants and animals, Murder is a part of the whole world (and perhaps the universe?), but a concentrated, self-contained and enormously independent part, and this precisely is Murder's existence. But does Murder the tomcat know anything of this? Murder doesn't need to know, because he is this life, he is precisely this existence. It's enough, as I've said already, if he retains the sense that he is nothing and no one other than himself. That he is authentic, as people say. That at any moment, whenever he likes, he can do what needs to be done. Here, for example, out of the grass right beside Murder, a small four-legged creature suddenly jumped, rose into the air and fell back into the grass. Murder froze, but only for the blink of an eye; this was not a creature that Murder hunted. He let it slip away. It was simply a frog, a slightly comical being (when he was younger, these creatures used to put Murder in a good mood, he'd lie in wait for one, pretend to attack, and toss it up with his paw). Besides, it was soft and slippery, but so tightly encased in such tough skin that neither claw nor tooth was any use. So, Murder let the frog quietly depart. He glanced once more in its direction: it was squatting in the grass, propped on its front legs, and watching him with bulging wide-set eyes. Murder turned his head and continued on his way, in the direction of the brick and stone rubble. He kept to the tall wet grass all the time, flinching, giving a shake, but on he went. He was approaching the place where the grass was short and sparse, the ground strewn with gravel and tiny stones, overgrown with scanty yellowed chamomile. Something would often happen in this place and before he approached, Murder habitually observed it from a distance for a moment. One should never be too hasty with expectation, but nor should one rule anything out. One should be ready for anything. Lo, Murder sees, hears and senses: in the very middle of this bare clearing there is indeed a mouse. It stands on its hind legs and in its forepaws holds a piece of bread, the crust, and nibbles it. It looks around constantly as it does so, but it doesn't see Murder. Murder, meanwhile, sees it perfectly, though hindered a little by the blades of grass. Murder is hungry, he hasn't eaten anything for three days, maybe four. To get close enough to the mouse to execute a leap, Murder must submerge himself in still thicker and wetter grass, he must circle the mouse from behind. Murder turns his head to the right and then to the left, he checks what is happening all around, takes in the world surrounding this most important event of the moment: the mouse nibbling bread. Murder, turning his head in both directions, wanted to see everything surrounding this scene which at this moment was after all the very centre of the world. And perhaps the universe? Murder the cat was also looking about, while unobserved by the mouse, to confirm that nothing in turn was threatening him. Was he, while hunting, simultaneously the object of someone's observation and desire? The mouse, too, darts glances to the left and right, because while eating it wants to know, must know, if it is in danger. Murder the cat had one more, seemingly comical reason for turning his head away from the mouse: he wanted to be sure the mouse was not an illusion. The mouse was no illusion, it was a real phenomenon: without relinquishing the bread in its paws, it was looking now to the right, in the direction of the lilac; something had clearly alarmed it. But it was no more than an instant; the mouse resumed eating its bread. Murder pressed on, then, half his usual height, almost crawling on his stomach in the cold wet grass whose touch made him shiver. In this position he was absolutely invisible and only someone looking from above could see him, but at that moment Murder didn't care. He was also inaudible, for he moved so cautiously as not even to hear himself. If he could not hear himself – would anyone hear him? Murder was hungry and perhaps for someone else in his place impatience would have long since prompted a mistake, a carelessness – some impatient movement, a premature leap. But that would not be Murder the cat. He grew more cautious as he drew nearer, more intent, his movements were now so slow that they ceased to be movement. He was very close now. Just two more steps, muscles readying for the leap, just a pause, finding the best position to push off from the hind legs – when suddenly something happened: the mouse disappeared, as though in a puff of wind. But it was not he, Murder, who had frightened it. Something trembled, clattered in the air; Murder paid no great heed to the sound, but the mouse had seemingly heard it a fraction of a second sooner – and Murder saw the discarded bread crust, the empty ground, the motionless stones, the still trembling blade of grass. A woman was walking across the garden with a pail in her hand, approaching the concrete bin. She tipped out her rubbish and returned in the direction of the wall where there was a door. She paused in the doorway, switched the bucket from one hand to the other, and closed the door behind her.

Murder the cat stood there a long time yet, without moving, then he ventured onto the open space, to the place where the mouse had been a moment ago. He shook off the drops bedewing his fur. He was cross and agitated and twitched his tail nervily. From the city, from the alien world, came sounds that Murder could not bear: whistling, jangling, grating. Murder had to restore some order to the world before he could move on, immobilize the trams and cars, separate uproar from tranquillity. It took some time. The failure he had suffered just a moment ago was gone from his mind. Failure, anyway, is nothing more than something that brings success closer. Even if he fails ten times, or twenty – Murder the cat will not stop hunting. For hunting is his passion and necessity.

I've said that Murder the cat is old. But Murder will never die, or at least he won't die of old age, like those ugly, fat and indolent dogs who will eventually have to be put to sleep at the vet's. Murder will never die, unless somebody kills him or a car runs him over. If Murder does not die a violent death, no one will ever find his body. Not a single bone of his will be left behind, nor a scrap of fur. Murder will simply disappear. One day I shall not see him sitting deep in the window or slowly traversing the orchard. No matter how hard I stare, I shall not see that place where earthly matter is so miraculously concentrated and so perfectly formed into a mobile, living, sentient and seeing being. In the deserted air I shall see only ground, stones, grass. If I cease to see what I previously saw, it will be as though something that I previously had has been taken from me. And I shall be sad.

'Daddy, cats are evil, devious and bloodthirsty, aren't they?' Andrzej said to his father. He stressed the word *blood-thirs-ty*, lingering over the sounds . . .

'What's that?'

'Cats are devious and bloodthirsty,' Andrzej repeated, turning his head to look at his father. To move his head, he had to tear away his cheek momentarily from the butt of the airgun propped on the windowsill. His eye stopped seeing the front sight, rear sight and target. His father sat in the armchair, newspaper on his knee, watching the television screen where a newsreader with a parting in his hair was talking about the catastrophic fall in pound sterling, the slight rise in the rate of the dollar and the boom in gold. The newsreader turned over his sheet of paper and began to talk about something else, the war in Africa. The father looked at the son and said:

'Be careful where you shoot, my boy, don't hurt anyone!'

'There's no one there,' replied Andrzej. He looked into the garden again. From the second floor, it was visible in its entirety: trees, bushes, ground covered in grass, clumps of nettles, a heap of rubble at the foot of the fence. But the target at which he had been aiming had moved and Andrzej had to adjust the barrel of the gun likewise, a centimetre or so.

'Kot w mokrej trawie'

Published as part of the collection *Kot w mokrej trawie* (Wydawnictwo Literackie, 1977).

PAWEŁ SOŁTYS

1978–

Long before becoming a published writer, Paweł Sołtys made his reputation as a singer, songwriter and musician known by his stage name,
Pablopavo. Starting in the early 2000s, he was part of several bands,
including Vavamuffin, a Polish roots reggae, dancehall and raggamuf-
fin group. Since embarking on a solo career in 2008 and widening his
musical range to include a variety of styles, he has recorded over a dozen
albums, most of them with his regular band, Ludziki. Overall, he esti-
mates that he has written about 400 songs, played over a thousand
concerts and had his work featured on approximately fifty albums
recorded by other artists.

Sołtys's debut short-story collection was published in 2017 to widespread critical acclaim, and he is one of the very few people to have been
nominated for the prestigious Polityka Passport Award in more than
one category: music and literature. His compact, highly concentrated
stories – like his song lyrics – transform the closely observed details of
everyday lives into quietly powerful meditations on the passage of time,
memory, storytelling, love, ageing and death. Most often, his protagonists are ordinary inhabitants of Warsaw, living on the margins both
physically and metaphorically. Subtle, layered storytelling, an eye for
detail and the blending of past and present are among the key features
of his style.

Asked about the source of his inspiration, Sołtys says, 'Like most
writers, I rely on the mish-mash that results from the shuffling of memories
and fabrications. These are the two wellsprings from which I drink. The
wellspring of truth usually brings with it more surrealism than the one of
invention.' The story 'Rysio the Cat', which comes from Sołtys's second

book, published in 2019, is no exception. 'My grandfather didn't have a cat,' he explains. 'But I remember the melody of his stories. Melodies are what matters most.'

Eliza Marciniak

Rysio the Cat

Translated by Eliza Marciniak

Grandpa Rysio and Mittens were in collusion; more than that, they were like the twin stars I'd read about in Marek's book, the one with the black and white illustrations so blurry they looked like abstract gouaches, though the word 'abstract' didn't mean much to me back then; it had only a flavour and a melody, almost no substance, and in fact the word 'gouache' was only sour too, a single mouth-puckering bite. Mittens the cat and Grandpa were allies in skirmishes with my grandmother, in a sluggish war against time and the confines of their flat in Bielany; more than that, they were like a man and a kite on an invisible string, seemingly separate yet tightly connected. They didn't look at each other much, just as twins don't need to look at each other, though their resemblance was more of a metaphor than a real likeness, but of course back then the word 'metaphor' didn't mean much to me either; it just had a metallic aftertaste and a melody similar to that of 'abstract', and it tasted like the door handle I licked in secret one evening because Grandpa Rysio had said: this is aluminium. Who wouldn't want to know what aluminium tastes like? Surely only an utter fool.

As Grandpa cleaned his pipe with a scraper and I mentally repeated the harsh, grating word 'scraper', Mittens washed one of his back paws, lifting it like the girls dancing the can-can in the film Grandpa and I were watching, though my parents would have ordered me to go to bed long ago, but Grandpa Rysio didn't order me to do anything, he just laughed soundlessly, probably to avoid waking Grandma. He didn't smile, he laughed, his chins shaking, but as if someone had turned the volume knob all the way to the left, and the black and white girls danced on the black and white Amethyst television, and Mittens sat on the windowsill chattering at some nocturnal birds perched on the window ledge outside, telling them, I'll break your necks, you plucky nightbirds, but to me it seemed as if he were playing along with Grandpa looking at those can-can girls, though I'm sure in my head I called them 'ladies', since I was eight years old and they were eighteen, since I was in colour and they were black and white and from a different world, though when I looked at myself, in my pyjamas, in almost total darkness except for the flecks of light from the picture tube and two street lamps outside, when I looked at myself, I was black-and-white too, or at best black-and-white-and-grey. And I remember thinking that maybe someone was watching me too, on a television screen somewhere, and that I had no idea whose eyes were looking at me, and I felt frightened, but the twins must have sensed it with their human-and-feline instinct because the balding one stroked my head and ruffled my black-and-white hair, and the fluffy, bouncy one jumped down from the windowsill and onto my camp bed to lie on my thin shinbones, and the camp bed squeaked, or I did, relieved that the fear had vanished, I can't remember.

As the cat lay sunning himself on the floor, bright patches appearing on his grey flank, Grandpa would sit reading on the sofa. He'd scratch his ear more calmly than Mittens and not with his hind paw, but he'd purr and growl to himself just like the cat, and then without warning he'd raise his eyes from his book and say to me: How would you like to change your first name, Wojtek? Or better yet, both your first name and surname? Listen to this: your namesake, Wojciech Bobowski, changed his name to Ali – Ali Ufki! Would you like to be called Ali or Mehmed? Changing one's name has gone out of fashion, hasn't it? And he'd laugh soundlessly, though I had no idea why, since nobody was sleeping and it was just the three of us, including the cat. Or maybe the four of us, because something would light up in Grandpa's weary eyes, and there was Wojciech Bobowski, alias Albertus Bobovius, alias Ali Bey, and this alias would start weaving itself in my head like an arras, because I knew the word 'arras', Grandpa had explained it to me earlier, and there, on that arras, was this crazy Ali-Wojciech captured by the Tatars, a slave who became a translator, a diplomat, a confidant of the sultan, a man who had travelled through Egypt, Arabia and Europe and half the world besides, because he could speak fifteen human languages as well as the language of horses and naturally the language of camels, which is as hairy as their humps, and sand was blowing into my eyes, though we were sitting in the flat in Bielany, as I contemplated expensive gemstones, Turkish sabres, parchments written in Arabic, Turkish, Latin and Aquitanian, and all the letters shimmered before my eyes, some looking like our own and others as if they were cut out of upside-down horseshoes, and of course I believed it all, though I knew perfectly well that it was only a story, and meanwhile Ali Ufki really did write down Ottoman songs, and really did translate the Bible and touch the world in so many places that he could be on first-name terms with it. In fifteen languages. And Grandpa Rysio, a retired middle-ranking civil servant who loved books, women and cats, would finish his tale with a loud mwah, as if blowing a kiss towards long-extinct harems, and Mittens would answer him with a meow that meant the sunshine is good, the story is good, but it's time to eat something, and they would follow each other down the narrow hallway, their bellies quivering and eager for swift satisfaction, and in the kitchen the old man would open a tin of fish livers, which made me feel ill but made the cat feel well, and as for Grandpa, I don't know how he felt, because he would stand still in front of the kitchen window gazing out for a long time, attentive or absent, as if he had really turned into a five-foot-four cat who had been taught by some Ali Ufki to stand on his hind legs, wear a cheap suit and smoke a pipe.

Grandpa Rysio wasn't effusive, and he'd use up his year's supply of a dozen affectionate gestures on Mittens and me. They were alike in this way too: I had never seen the cat sit on anyone else's lap except his or mine, just as I never saw Grandpa hug anyone except us, not even Grandma or Mum. To say goodbye, he would peck Grandma on the cheek, like a mother-in-law, sending her out into the world, or he'd go out himself with a bouncy step, though his legs were plump and seemingly ill-suited to marching. I remember once asking my father: Do Grandpa and Grandma love each other? Of course, he replied; after all, it was for him that she . . . But then he broke off, as if realizing that what she had done for him was not suitable for underage ears or thoughts. Grandpa, by contrast, treated me almost like a grown-up and often read or told me stories nobody else would have dared to. Listening in the doorway, Grandma would sometimes mutter to herself, silly old fool, but even though he was certainly old, he was by no means silly. His stories, fairy tales and anecdotes were always about other people, never about himself, as if the world was so wondrous and interesting that he had written himself out of it, so as not to spoil the effect with his baldness and corpulence. I don't know if any other eight-year-old knew the story of Countess Báthory, but I did. I also knew which American actress was a knockout and which was, pfft, too skinny, and why Elżbieta Czyżewska had more sex appeal than Beata Tyszkiewicz. Of course, I didn't understand a thing, but he didn't seem to mind. He would show me photos in *Kino*, the monthly film magazine Grandma subscribed to, and smack his lips, mwah, as if he'd just eaten something delicious, and the cat would raise his head to see if it might be tomatoes by any chance, because he adored tomatoes, as long as they didn't have any salt or onions on them. Both of them had bizarre culinary tastes; apart from fish, Grandpa rarely touched meat, which in the 1980s smacked not just of extravagance but possibly stupidity. He ate things in order from best to worst. Both of them gulped down their food quickly, with loud swallows, after which Grandpa would fill his pipe while Mittens cleaned his shiny fur, twisting comically, and Grandpa would laugh soundlessly even though he'd seen it a thousand times before, and he'd pretend to lick his own hand and clean his ears with his forearms, until I started to laugh too, and Grandpa would cry out as if to egg me on: You laugh the way Rubinstein plays the piano! He would rush over to the record player, his belly flapping under his summer shirt, to put on an album of mazurkas, which I pretended to enjoy because I loved him very much, though I couldn't understand why sometimes those mazurkas made tears roll down his face, and in those moments I tried to remember something terribly sad to make myself cry too, but of course nothing came to mind, despite the fact that at home and at school I cried more often than was seemly and I had to be really good at football to not have other kids laugh at me. Maybe those mazurkas were somehow harmonized with his tear ducts, or maybe Rubinstein recorded them specially for Grandpa Rysio and Mittens the cat, who sometimes licked those Chopin tears off his face, and that was strange, but it was not, after all, the strangest thing in their alliance.

In the 1980s the bathrooms in all flats looked alike, except maybe at some rich person's house, but fortunately we didn't know any rich people. In these bathrooms there were always too many pipes, gurgling or creaking, and all sorts of devices had screws sticking out of them, screws that seemed redundant and were there only so that one could bump into them or, like me, cut one's head open after slipping in the bath. In Grandma's huge mirror the stitches over my temple made me look like a pirate, and I even liked them, except they itched terribly and I wasn't allowed to scratch. That's why Grandpa kept calling out, Wojtek the Sea Dog mustn't scratch! If you scratch, out the hatch! – at which the cat would flatten his ears and hiss, because he didn't like shouting, and to this day whenever I hear a cat hissing I can't help reaching for the barely visible mark under my hairline. The bathtub was enormous and could have easily fitted three Wojteks and two cats or more, provided they liked water, of course, but Mittens limited himself to strolling along the edge as I tried to sink a French admiral's flotilla by discharging salvos from my sponge, until Grandpa would shout: All clean? Come out, there's a storm brewing. I wasn't afraid of storms, though I didn't particularly like it when thunder was rumbling nearby or lightning struck close to us; one hundred and twenty-one, one hundred and twenty . . . Boom! Not even two kilometres away. That was another thing he taught me, that counting. He and Mittens disliked storms, and I was embarrassed to realize they were a bit afraid of them, though they put on a brave face, the cat only briefly, because he'd soon crawl under the bathtub and fail to respond to me calling, kitty, kitty! as I dried myself with a shoddy towel that didn't absorb water and functioned only because of friction and the heat that it generated. So when I put on my pyjamas I looked ruddy like an Iroquois or Shoshone chief, and I'd rush over to Grandpa to have him tell me one of Fenimore Cooper's tales, and as he patiently told me the story, even though by now I could have read it myself, he'd get absorbed in it and talk away the storm, so it was only when Grandma, standing by the window, would say, it sounds like a war out there, that he'd cast her a quick glance out of the corner of his eye. Before long Grandma would sit at the table to play Patience, drinking tea from a glass in a metal holder, and Grandpa would point to that holder, decorated with coloured beads imitating precious stones, and say, that's from Tula. And I had no idea what or where this Tula might be and wondered if it had anything to do with *tułaczka*, which meant wandering, because this wandering was in a poem we were studying at school, and Grandpa would laugh, but it was only a brief laugh, a couple of chuckles, a couple of shakes of his couple of chins, and he'd tell me about Tula, about the famous Tula master craftsmen and samovars, and even more famous gingerbread, and soon Tsar Ivan the Terrible was slaughtering the residents of Novgorod, *oprichniki* were galloping down the narrow hallway towards the kitchen, with severed dogs' heads strapped to their saddles, followed by that Orthodox priest with his workman Balda, and the golden fish, and Pushkin, who was in fact Black. Pushkin was Black? That's right, and I would fall asleep, despite the loud peals of thunder and flashes of lightning that turned Grandma's cards on the table silver, and every king had Grandpa Rysio's face, every jack was whiskered like Mittens, and every queen waved at me, whispering, Sweet dreams, Wojtek the Sea Dog, may you dream of the tsar's golden samovars being blown to bits by a gingerbread flotilla.

Grandma and the cat gave each other a wide berth, and only rarely was his tail wrapped around her calf, its tip lifting up the hem of her skirt. She didn't feed him, but sometimes she forgot to clear the last slice of ham from the kitchen table, or a scrap of fish would fall after being dipped in batter. Mittens waited until he could approach with dignity, like royalty, and casually snatch the morsel before licking himself and looking at me as if to say, I hate things going to waste. In the evenings, Grandma would play Patience or sit down with a book protected with a newspaper cover, and I would read snippets of articles from *The Express* or *Warsaw Life* that broke off abruptly, so that I had to invent their endings or beginnings, and that's how the four of us got on together whenever I went to stay with them during the school holidays, or just for an evening, because my parents were going to a name-day party or an anniversary celebration or a ball, or wherever adults who are not yet old usually go. And sometimes when I began to nod off, Grandma would sing to me softly. She would sing in Polish and in languages I didn't understand, but it didn't matter because dreams are international by nature and a few drops of a foreign song can do them no harm. So I dreamed about faraway lands and fathomless oceans, and if ever my dream turned bad, she would pull me close to her ample bosom in her old-fashioned nightdress and take off her thick ring, to avoid scratching me as she stroked my head. Or that's what I thought she meant, although instead of the word 'scratch' she used a Russian-sounding word I didn't quite understand.

One day that ring went missing, and naturally suspicion fell on the cat.

But the cat wouldn't confess and instead watched with feigned surprise as wardrobes were moved about, the rug lifted and the parquet blocks tapped one by one, and I thought that this ring must have been made of platinum, because not long before Grandpa had told me that platinum was even more expensive than gold, and Grandma was swearing, swearing for the first time in her life, exclaiming, Bloody hell! over and over, and I imagined blood dripping onto the floor from the bare space on her finger as she walked to and fro, and Grandpa kept saying, It'll turn up, it has to turn up, and he got down on the floor to shine a torch under the book-case, which nobody could ever make budge, and poked around underneath with a walking stick, which he'd inherited from someone I never met, and then got up all out of breath and stared at me for a long time, but it really wasn't me who had hidden the ring, it really wasn't me. In the end, the ring was found under the threadbare runner in the hallway, at which point Grandma looked at Mittens but didn't say a word, and Grandpa poured himself a nightcap of lemon vodka to calm his nerves, and I wondered if hot liquid platinum wasn't exactly the same colour.

Looking the cat straight in the eye, he would mutter, So, which one of us will go first, you or I? – though normally this was a dangerous thing to do because prolonged eye contact with Mittens usually led to the use of claws or teeth, both potentially terrible weapons, but the cat just tilted his head and answered him telepathically, and Grandpa muttered, Ah yes, of course, how else, and then switched on the television, because Argentina was about to play West Germany in faraway Mexico. Ah, Mexico, I wouldn't go to Mexico, there once was a man who'd gone to Mexico, muttered Grandpa, before whistling appreciatively and saying, That Maradona, he's got real pluck, he can beat them all on his own, and that little Batista is good too, even if his name isn't promising, Wojtek, not promising at all, and I loved Grandpa all the more, because when someone loved Maradona, it was as if they loved me extra. And then the Germans scored to make it two-all, though it had seemed like the match was long over, and I hated Rudi Völler, I hated him for the way he played and the way he looked, I even hated his name, my head full of television war dramas like *Four Tank-Men and a Dog* and *Polish Roads*, and I waited to see what Grandpa would say about this Völler, but he said nothing, he didn't even mention the players from West Germany, as if they weren't there at all, on that black-and-white pitch, he just clenched his fists, his bald head beaded with sweat that glistened like a diadem, and his pipe puffing like one of the steam engines from *Polish Roads*, so much so that Mittens jumped down from the back of the armchair, though usually he didn't mind smoke. If he could have, he too would have clenched his fists for Argentina, but he just sat in front of the screen following the ball with his eyes, like a true predator. Then all of a sudden we were on top again, because Maradona had run, feinted and passed in such a way that Burruchaga couldn't help but bury the ball in the net, and for the first and only time in my life I saw Grandpa Rysio dance, and I suspect Mittens was also seeing it for the first time because instead of running away he bounced between Grandpa's thick calves, and I danced too, while from the corner of my eye I could see Carlos Bilardo, the Argentinian coach, who looked like Grandpa except slimmer, and he was dancing as well, and I realized that Grandpa and Mittens were like Carlos Bilardo and Maradona, that the M in the cat's name was not a coincidence, because we start believing in coincidence only when we stop being children, and in that moment what I wanted most in the world was to remain a child, to be the grandson of Grandpa Rysio alias Carlos Bilardo and Mittens the cat alias Diego Armando Maradona, because after all Mittens could run as nimbly and beautifully as the Argentinian, and if he ever wanted to play football he'd be the feline world champion, and Grandpa would stroke him after a match and feed him fish livers and unsalted tomatoes, and to top things off they would drink milk from the shining World Cup trophy, ignoring Grandma's and FIFA president João Havelange's scandalized glances. Then the match was over; we were eating wafer cake, Grandpa was drinking liqueur, and my parents were going to pick me up soon. The calm after a storm, said Grandpa, and added, idling in the doldrums, and I didn't ask him what 'doldrums' meant, I just savoured the word, but it was like the paper I once ate for a bet, except that it had no edges, it filled my mouth too much, it was scary, and I think that was the only time Grandpa said something about himself: Before the war I used to play football too. And that was like an extra goal for Argentina. For which club, Grandpa: Legia, Polonia or Gwardia? Oh, the club doesn't exist any more.

*

This wasn't long before Grandpa went to Łódź to 'meet with a doctor', and I guess nothing good came of that, but that's another story. I just remember him saying to Grandma, I really must go, it's not like I'm doing it for my health. And I didn't understand a thing, because why go all the way to Łódź to see a doctor if it's not for one's health, but there were many things I didn't understand back then, yet I could always go and ask that balding, tubby man who knew everything and had more time for me than all the other adults put together. But this time he just snorted at me like a cat.

It was quiet. Grandma had gone out to do some shopping, probably for that trip to Łódź, there were no leaves rustling outside since it was already November, Mr Rubinstein was not playing mazurkas, and even the television was silent. Out of boredom I stared at the large map of the world on the wall. It was old and black-and-white, a reprint, he had once told me, then explained what that meant. 'Reprint': that word was like a spring, you pressed it down and it bounced right back, it tasted of rust, but maybe I got that wrong. Reprint, old, rusty, that was the sequence, and unfortunately once you know something, you cannot unknow it, not when you're eight years old and you can still remember everything, because everything is still worth remembering. I put on my slippers, though I disliked wearing them, because somehow it didn't feel right to disturb that silence with my bare feet. They were in the kitchen: Mittens on top of the windowsill, Grandpa leaning against it. I stood there for ten minutes, trying to breathe as quietly as possible; the grey light of the autumn morning had turned them into two dark silhouettes, and they looked as if they'd been cut out of crêpe paper, a huge roll of dark crêpe paper. Only the tip of Mittens's tail was moving, ticking like an old metronome. Finally the cat sensed my presence. And since he turned around, Grandpa's head followed. Come and join us, he said, and when I did, he lifted me up onto the windowsill. And I thought that now I looked like I was made of crêpe paper too, that from the hallway you could see three black silhouettes against a white background, though of course nobody was looking at us. The kitchen window gave onto a square, and now that the trees were bare you could see all of it clearly, the whole couple of hundred metres. Along the paved path running diagonally, a disabled man dressed a bit like a child was walking with his father, their arms linked. He was around forty and not in full control of his legs; every few steps his head was thrown back and we could see him grimace. The father had a walking stick and was old; maybe he wasn't even his father but his grandfather. His steps were unsteady too, and in fact it wasn't quite clear who was holding up whom. They were probably going to church, the one on the far side of the square, their progress slow and dangerously wobbly. Every now and then the old man would say something to his son with a shy smile. Of course we couldn't hear what, and then we could no longer make out their faces. It took them about twenty minutes to walk those couple of hundred metres, while we crêpe-paper silhouettes watched them. When they had nearly reached the end of the path, Grandpa said, My God, how I hate going away and leaving him behind! And he stroked my head or the cat's, what's the difference?

'Kot Rysio'
Published as part of the collection *Nieradość* (Wydawnictwo Czarne, 2019).

CHILDREN

JAN PARANDOWSKI

1895–1978

Jan Parandowski is familiar to every Polish schoolchild through *Mitologia* (*Mythology*, 1924), a beautiful retelling of the Greek and Roman myths that has been required reading for decades. He wrote novels, short stories, essays on world literature, travel books about Greece and Italy and translations from ancient Greek, Latin and English. His lucid prose translation of the *Odyssey* was a contemporary bestseller.

Born in Lwów (now Ukrainian Lviv, then a Polish city within the Austro-Hungarian empire), he studied classical philology and archaeology at Lwów University. During the First World War he was interned in Voronezh and Saratov, where he worked as a teacher. His experiences in Russia during both revolutions led to his first book, *Bolszewizm i bolszewicy w Rosji* (*Bolshevism and the Bolsheviks in Russia*, 1919). This incisive analysis of the state of terror then prevalent in communist Russia was not reissued until 1996.

On graduation he wrote about classical literature for the leading contemporary journals, and edited a series of classical translations for the Altenberg publishing house in Lwów. He taught literature at a drama school, where among his students he met his future wife, Irena. In 1929 he moved to Warsaw, where he produced literary radio broadcasts. He had many friends among the famous writers of the time, who would meet at their favourite haunt, the Ziemiańska Café. From 1933 until his death in 1978 Parandowski was president of the Polish PEN Club.

'The Phonograph' is from *Zegar słoneczny* (*The Sundial*, 1953), a collection of short stories describing Parandowski's childhood. Several relatives are vividly portrayed, but the author's father is never mentioned. Parandowski bore his mother's surname, and claimed she was widowed early, though according to speculation he may have been the illegitimate son of a Uniate priest. His novel *Dysk olimpijski* (*The Olympic Discus*, 1933), which reimagines the attitudes of the ancient Greeks towards their Olympic games, won him an Olympic bronze medal in the arts competition held in parallel with the infamous Berlin Olympics of 1936.

Antonia Lloyd-Jones

The Phonograph

Translated by Antonia Lloyd-Jones

Even when he arrived from his little hole of a town, as he jokingly described it, Uncle Stefan looked more urbane than anyone else we knew. He was scented with eau de Cologne and the best soap, he wore a gold pince-nez on a string of silk, and whenever he saw fit to comb his moustache and long, fair side-whiskers, from a waistcoat pocket he would fetch out a tiny, silver-backed brush, stored in a small kid-skin case, while for his hair he had a tortoiseshell comb that folded like a penknife, kept in a tortoiseshell cover.

I would stare at his hands and pockets with the same burning curiosity with which I had watched the magician I'd had the fortune to see twice. Those pockets were full of surprises and dazzling trinkets. Now a little key would appear, so fine and neatly shaped that at once one could see in the mind's eye the exquisite casket that it opened. Here were an ivory toothpick and ear scoop combined, folding together like the wings of an insect. The top pocket was home to two or three frequently animated amber cigarette-holders, each the size of a little finger.

From a large leather cigarette case Uncle Stefan would take out a cigarette and press the holder into one end of the tube; then, having extinguished the cigarette, he would fetch the case out again, light a new cigarette, and press the holder into its tube. With these few repeated gestures he wove a steady path between his jacket pocket, his little waistcoat pocket and his lips, which looked pale red beneath his nicotine-yellow moustache. He made his own cigarettes using 'Abadie' rolling paper and, needless to say, 'Pursiczan' tobacco, a large tin of which stood on his bedside cabinet whenever he stayed the night with us.

One could be sure that every new invention would reach him first. It was in his fingers that for the first time in my life I saw a cigarette lighter, of which he was very proud. Giving it a cursory glance, my grandmother shrugged and said: 'That is flint. In my young day, before there were any matches, one lit the fire by striking flint against steel. The Swedish match seems to me greater progress. Aren't you ashamed to waste money on such a thing?'

These words did not have as strong an effect on Uncle Stefan as the hemming and hawing that accompanied them; he dropped his gaze and, looking troubled, said nothing in reply. I enjoyed gazing at his broad, wrinkle-creased forehead, and ardently wished I had his cares and could be so nobly lost in thought. But I was not allowed to have his cares – never. My grandmother told me so most plainly, and repeated it so many times, always with such a menacing look, that throughout my life I really have steered clear of Uncle Stefan's cares.

It was they that drove him in pursuit of my mother as soon as my grandmother left the room. My mother would be whirling about the flat with a plume of multi-coloured feathers fixed to a cane, sweeping away the dust without listening to what he was telling her. His brisk gestures and rapid words detracted from his innate gravity. Finally he would take a long, narrow piece of paper from his pocket and twirl it overhead, while crying: 'For the love of God, Julia, this is the last one ever!'

'One sin is enough, why are you adding another?' my mother would say reluctantly, but in the end she always took the wretched piece of paper, while from his enchanted pockets Uncle Stefan would extract another extraordinary thing: a gold fountain pen that worked without an ink-well, and hand it to her with a bow, as if presenting it to her. But hardly had she signed than he hastily took both pen and paper from her hands, sighed with relief, and half the wrinkles would be gone from his brow. He would kiss my mother on both hands, and shortly after he'd be seen outside, waving his walking stick, the handle of which was carved into the shape of a horse's head.

'What was that piece of paper, Mama?'

'Oh, don't ask! It's an abomination!'

I would see this abomination many a time in Uncle Stefan's hands, but in the name of his wonderful pockets I always forgave him; moreover I had noticed that days with a piece of paper would end with a dazzling gift for me. So it was that one evening, following the usual morning scene with the feather duster, the paper and the gold pen, I was given a magic lantern. This was a black metal box with a rounded, glazed snout at one end. At the other there was a small oil lamp, and inside there was a gap, into which one slotted long, thin glass slides with little coloured pictures on them.

Set going in a dark room against a white door, they showed boys throwing snowballs and building a snowman, and girls picking apples in an orchard, with one of them falling off a ladder. On another plate there were boats on a lake, and I was most astonished to see that this image was exactly like one of the pages in my picture book, with the same lilies on the water, about which a little poem at the bottom said: 'Lilies too are seen aplenty . . .'

Most dramatic of all was the fire. A two-storey house with a crest of flames on the roof, its windows red from the conflagration, was burning from cellar to attic, and here was the fire brigade, pouring on water, the firemen in their helmets were climbing ladders, and on the upper floor one could see a woman wringing her hands. Grandmother took this picture to heart. It reminded her of something familiar.

'If it weren't two-storeyed, I'd say it was the Wicherskis' house. But it also reminds me of Kalina's house, which burned down . . . hold on, when exactly was it?'

She couldn't make up her mind, and in the morning, as she was dressing me, she'd say: 'You know what, it's probably the house on Trybunalska Street, where two children burned to death.'

And in the evening, to make sure, she would light the magic lantern herself and project the burning image on the white door, where because of its uneven surface the picture shuddered and bent, intensifying the impression of motion and tumult.

One day when Uncle Stefan appeared in the company of an unfamiliar man who was carrying a large box, my mother exclaimed: 'What? Not another lantern! The first one has already given me a headache, the lamp produces so much smoke.'

But with the words: 'Just a moment, Julia,' Uncle Stefan left the stranger in the dining room, and gathered us all in the drawing room.

'I'd like to ask you a favour,' he began, took off his pince-nez, ran his puffy eyes over us and greatly deepened our amazement.

He gave a lengthy speech. I would not know how to repeat it, and did not understand much of it. One word dominated: *phonograph*, and one name: *Edison*, which he uttered with reverence, raising an index finger. As he spoke his final words he drew a large circle in the air, which was meant to signify the world. The phonograph had already conquered the entire globe, and could not be resisted any longer. What a fabulous invention! It recorded voices, human words, and for us it would provide an everlasting memento. My mother disliked the adjective 'everlasting', which smacked of the graveyard, and cast a glance at my grandmother, but on her it made no impression.

After this preparation Uncle Stefan led us into the dining room, where on the table stood a shiny horn, the inside of which looked like quicksilver, with a box underneath it and a cylinder, of a dark yellow colour, I think. Uncle Stefan behaved exactly like the magician at the fête in Lubień. He gave explanations, touched objects, and circled around the table.

'You have to speak loud and clear into here,' he warned, tapping a fingernail against the horn, which responded with a soft clang. His assistant bustled about even more, tinkering with something on the cylinder, occasionally dropping this activity to look at us in the manner of a photographer trying to arrange a group, then smiled, and made faces at me.

'Let's start with Granny,' said Uncle Stefan, and kissed her on the hand.

'No, darling, I'll go last. First I must watch and learn.'

For a while there was some bickering, then finally it was agreed that Uncle Stefan would speak first, and his assistant announced: 'Pay attention please, ladies and gentlemen, we are about to begin. As soon as I set the cylinder in motion, every word will be recorded.'

It was so quiet you could hear a pin drop. Uncle Stefan tiptoed to a chair in front of the horn, sat down, straightened his back, and in an emphatic tone of voice, the one he must have used at his office, said: 'Today is the second of June, 1900. We are at Granny's house, number eighteen Chorążczyzna Street. This is Stefan speaking, in a moment little Dunek will say something, followed by his mother, our dear Julia. Granny wants to speak last.'

He stood up, and with an urgent gesture signalled to me to approach the horn. I was seized by blind panic. With no idea what to do, I pressed the trumpet I was holding to my lips, and blew it, but in response to my mother's impatient gestures I dropped it on the floor, and barked into the silvery orifice: 'Bow wow!' My mother held her head in her hands.

'Say a poem,' she whispered.

My picture book flashed before my eyes – I knew it by heart, and hastily began to chant: 'In summer when the sun is hot, How nice to be aboard a yacht . . .'

At that point the technician removed me from my post by lifting me up, and Uncle Stefan brought my mother close to the horn.

Instantly she burst into sincere laughter, through which she said: 'I'm laughing at my silly little son, for whom I wish the best of health, and am just about to kiss.'

And she skipped away from the silvery funnel to grab me in her arms. Meanwhile my uncle bowed before my grandmother, who slowly approached the table, sat down in front of the phonograph, and in a tone quite unfamiliar to me, at the sound of which everyone froze on the spot, as if presenting each word separately she carefully uttered: 'If it is true that my voice will be recorded here, that it will outlive me and that you will be able to hear me when I am no longer alive, then I shall tell you that I love you all: you, Julia, my mainstay; you, Stefan, you old scapegrace; and you, my darling Dunek, whom I tuck up in his little quilt each night. And I bless you.'

At her very first words my mother burst into tears, Uncle Stefan fetched out a handkerchief, and the technician was so moved that his hands were shaking. My grandmother was moved too, but not wishing to show it, she quickly took some snuff and gave a great sneeze. We all cried: 'Bless you!', and in a hoarse voice the technician said: 'May you live to a hundred!'

'I'm not far off it,' said my grandmother, smiling at him.

'Is that all there will be?' said Uncle Stefan anxiously.

'The cylinder came to an end on the good lady's sneeze, if you please, your worship.'

Once the technician had gone, for a long time we sat immobile and in silence, staring at the empty space on the table. Uncle Stefan got up first.

'Apparently,' he said, preparing to leave the room, 'in a week it will all be ready.'

'Meaning what?' asked my mother.

'The cylinder. Something will be impressed on it, something will be cast on it, then it'll be preserved, we'll be given the cylinder, and we'll be able to play it whenever we like.'

The cylinder did appear at our house – not in a week, of course, but even so, it made quite an impression. It was inside a case, wrapped in many layers of tissue paper and tied with blue string. We spent half a day seeking a quiet place for it, safe enough from my curiosity (I took an honest part in the search), until finally losing patience, my grandmother grabbed the cylinder and tossed it into her chest of drawers.

Now and then someone remembered it, and the matter was discussed of whether to borrow or actually acquire an 'apparatus' that would enable us to play the cylinder and summon up our voices.

'And pigs will fly,' said my mother one day, and that was the epitaph for the whole adventure, which was finally forgotten.

But a time came when the days dragged on in silence, and the snow that never stopped dropping from the grey sky heightened the hush enveloping our house. My mother did not know what to do with herself, and now and then she wept. No one dared approach the closed door of the room where my grandmother no longer resided. There was no sound of her crinoline-like skirts rustling, the snuff box wouldn't ring anymore, no drawer would ever rasp again on opening.

Since my grandmother's death no one had moved anything in her room. It was merely cleaned with the greatest care, and the untouched objects gazed at each other in the yellow sheen of the polished floor, then chatted at night in the language of creaks and crackles. The keys lay on the chest of drawers.

One day my mother picked them up, put one in the lock and opened the top drawer. She slid it half open and stared at the jumble of random items that had been gathering in there for years. Suddenly – as if she had had a revelation – she seized a longitudinal object wrapped in tissue paper. She banged the drawer shut, then only on the threshold slowed her pace and tiptoed out.

A couple of days later I was sitting over the Latin first conjugation when my mother came in wearing her fur coat and told me to get dressed. The whole way she said nothing; she was lost in thought, and also seemed anxious. We slowed down outside the house on Sykstuska Street that was home to Bilbel, who made my trousers and uniforms, but the day was not about him. In a gateway my mother took hold of my hand and said swiftly, in a whisper: 'I don't know if it's good or bad. I've found a shop here, or rather an office, on the first floor, where one can listen. You know, to the cylinder. I've got it with me.'

I understood. I slid my hand into hers and we went up to the first floor.

My mother's greatest fears evaporated at the first words of the bald gentleman who led us into a cold, empty room where there was a table, a couple of chairs and a mirror on the wall. In another wall there was a hole, through which a grey-metal shell-shaped horn emerged.

'Our workshop is in there,' said the bald gentleman, 'but you and the boy will sit here. And we shall play the disc right away. Oh, it's not a disc, it's a cylinder. No matter. It is a little antiquated, and if you wish we can transfer it onto a disc. But first let's do a test.'

And he pointed at the horn on the wall.

'I was so afraid there would be people present,' said my mother.

In the wall something began to hiss and whistle, and all of a sudden Uncle Stefan spoke. My mother seized me by the hand. I heard the trumpet, 'Bow wow', and a childish voice trilling the words of the poem. Was that me?

'My voice is so altered . . .' whispered my mother, when her words and her laughter issued from the horn.

'Not at all.'

'Hush!' said my mother, embracing me with an arm that was trembling, and pressed me to her breast, where her heart was beating violently.

'If it is true that my voice will be recorded here . . .'

It was true. Her voice had been faithfully recorded. A little hazy, wreathed in parasitic murmurs, but it was hers, unmistakably.

'. . . I bless you', the words resounded.

My mother smiled through her tears, waiting for the chance to hear the sneeze. But it wasn't there. Some noises, something like wings beating the air, began to whirl on top of the final word, and then something closed with a bang – a door or a lid.

'*Fonograf*'
Published as part of the collection *Zegar słoneczny* (Czytelnik, 1953).

JOANNA RUDNIAŃSKA

1948–

Joanna Rudniańska is well known as the award-winning author of children's books. These include *Kotka Brygidy* (*Brygida's Cat*, 2007), which describes the events of the Holocaust from the viewpoint of a little girl whose parents try to protect their Jewish friends. They're not always successful, and the book aims to show children the reality of life for the Jews who were confined to the ghetto before transportation to the death camps. It also shows how some of them survived. Inspired partly by the wartime experiences of family relatives, it is not Rudniańska's only book to present difficult topics to children in a realistic but sensitive way.

Her fiction for adults is equally challenging and thought-provoking, expressed with the same light touch. 'Her Sovereign Decision' comes from the collection *RuRu* (2019), compiled over a twenty-year period. Rudniańska has a particular talent for writing through the eyes of a child, and an ear for the way children express themselves, as this story shows.

'"Her Sovereign Decision" is taken from life,' she says. 'There used to be a fashion, perhaps it still exists, for parents to pretend their small children enjoyed the freedom to make important decisions for themselves. My daughter-in-law would prepare two sets of clothing for my granddaughter to choose from, and her friends did it too. The full story occurred to me when I heard an interview on the radio with a woman who'd been putting pressure on her daughter to cut off her hair and donate it to a charity that made wigs for children with cancer, but the child couldn't make up her mind. "But she's sure to decide soon." Of course the word "pressure" wasn't said. From that interview, or possibly from Facebook, where I looked at some posts by parents putting their children on show, I took the monstrous sentence: "What other sacrifice can a little girl make to the world?" Either way, I didn't make it up. And there I had my story.'

Antonia Lloyd-Jones

Her Sovereign Decision

Translated by Antonia Lloyd-Jones

'Don't worry. I wouldn't dream of suggesting anything to her. It'll be her sovereign decision,' says Itta's mother.

'Won't you mind?' asks Henryk.

'You don't understand. It's the one and only sacrifice a little girl can make to the world,' replies her mother.

Henryk laughs out loud, but it's not a symptom of hilarity. Henryk is quite capable of laughter that's sad.

Itta knows who they're talking about. She's the only little girl in this house. She doesn't know what 'suggesting' or 'sovereign' mean, but she knows all the other words. She's especially fond of the word 'decision'.

Whenever she lives here, with her mother and Henryk, each morning there are two sets of clothes ready for her.

'It's entirely your decision what you put on today,' says her mother.

The clothes are laid out on the sofa in the sitting room in such a way that, if you ignore the lack of heads and hands, they look like two large, flat dolls, or like two little girls who've been run over by a lorry. Sometimes Itta chooses the girl on the left, and sometimes the girl on the right. One day when she put on a top from one set and trousers from the other, her mother said that red clashes with pink, and she should have chosen either red trousers with a black top or dark-blue trousers with a pink top. At the time Itta had imagined the red trousers and the pink top literally clashing, growling like dogs, and she was pleased she wasn't wearing them.

'Hurry up, Itta,' her mother urges her on. 'The fact that I give you a choice doesn't mean you can make a silly one.'

'At Daddy's I fetch my clothes out of the wardrobe myself,' says Itta.

'I can see that whenever you come home. You look as if you'd got dressed in the dark,' says her mother.

'At Daddy's I'm at home too. Even more than here.'

'Don't be cheeky,' says her mother, ending the discussion.

Although she's only seven, Itta has already realized that the decisions she can make cannot be about important matters. Even when she's asked her opinion, her answers aren't taken into consideration. Just like the time during lunch at her grandparents, her father's parents. It was her grandfather who asked her that question.

'Who would you like to live with permanently, with your mum or your dad?'

'Most of all with Róża and Henryk,' Itta had replied, prompting general mirth.

Grandma Martyna laughed the loudest.

'Do you think Róża and Henryk are a good match?' she asked.

'Don't laugh at her. Don't ask the child that sort of question,' said Róża, her father's girlfriend.

'What do you know about children?' said Grandpa Krzyś indignantly.

'Róża works at the Children and Cancer Foundation. You know that,' said her father.

'Well, so what? We know what those foundations of yours are for,' said her grandfather.

'Well, what are they for?' shouted her father, getting up from his chair.

'Krzyś, off you go to the kitchen and bring the white wine from the fridge,' said her grandmother to her grandfather in a raised voice.

'Come on, Itta. Let's go and play on the swing,' whispered Róża, taking Itta by the hand, and they went outside into the garden.

Róża looks like a princess. She has chestnut shoulder-length hair curled at the ends and large, very green eyes. Itta wants to look like her when she grows up. The swing in her grandparents' garden is a gondola that rises up to the branches of the apple tree and higher into the sky. They sit facing on the little wooden benches.

'What you said was nice. That you'd like to live with me and with Henryk. That means you've grown very fond of us, although we're not your real parents. I like Henryk too, he's great. But I love your dad. And Henryk is your mum's husband. We can't live in a threesome, you, me and Henryk, because Henryk lives with your mum and I live with your dad. But I'm always very pleased when you come to our house. I know it might be hard, you have two homes and in each one it's as if you had completely different parents. But perhaps it's more interesting than living in the same house all the time with the same people,' says Róża. 'For now you have no control over it, but when you're grown up you'll be able to live with whomever you want.'

'Including dogs?'

'Of course.'

'Then I'll live with dogs,' says Itta.

'Do you know what kind?'

'Dogs like Ficek. But there'll be lots of them. When one dies there will still be several left.'

'And what will they be called?'

'Ficek. A whole pack of Ficeks!' cries Itta.

The swing rises and falls, the apple trees blossom around them, and Itta and Róża laugh out loud. The woman's floating chestnut hair and the little girl's long, fair, almost white hair – it's a lasting moment.

When Itta was four years old, the river of her life divided into two separate currents. In one current she still lives at her old home on Puławska Street, where she has always had her own room, with all her toys and furniture in it. Her father and Róża live there. In the other current she lives in the suburb of Kabaty, in Henryk's large apartment, into which her mother moved. There she shares a room with his sons, Błażej and Romek, who during the week live with their mother and her husband, and who spend the weekends in Kabaty. Their room is so huge that you can ride around it on a skateboard. Full of nooks and dark passages, the apartment is like a house in the country, even though it's located on the fifteenth floor. From the sitting-room and kitchen windows you can see trees growing in pots on the terrace. A lame magpie often flies onto the terrace. That's Henryk's girlfriend, jokes her mother. She plainly doesn't like it.

The magpie usually flies down when they're having lunch. It sits on the branch of a small tree, staring angrily through the window and squawking, until Henryk jumps up from the table and runs to the fridge.

'I must give her something to eat,' he says.

With a large knife he cuts up some red meat; the blood stains his hands and dribbles onto the tabletop.

'We're vegans,' Itta's mother reminds him, as she eats her buckwheat and vegetables.

'She's carnivorous,' says Henryk, wiping his bloody fingers on his trousers.

Itta is carnivorous too. But she only gets meat at her old home, at her father's house.

It was Henryk's older son, Błażej, who taught her to read before she started going to school. He taught her some other things too. Such as how to go onto Facebook. At the age of eleven Błażej already had his own Facebook page; he gave a date of birth that made him look two years older so he wouldn't be rejected.

'You can go on it using my account. I'll tell them I let you use our computer when we're not here. Just don't add any comments and watch out they don't catch you,' he said.

Błażej and Romek always used to bring their dog, Ficek, with them to Henryk's. Ficek was an old Pekinese. One Sunday morning Itta and the boys were lying on the rug in front of the laptop, watching YouTubers fooling around, and Ficek was lying in between them with his head on Itta's lap. Suddenly he started to bark in a terrifying way, and when the children tried to get up, they realized he was dead. At the funeral, which was held in a meadow next to Kabaty Woods, Romek played the violin, everyone took turns to say something about Ficek, and Itta's mother took photos. The boys' mother and her husband Antoni also showed up at the funeral, and then they all drove to Kabaty together. On the way they dropped in at Leclerc for wine, cheese and crisps. We'll have a wake for Ficek, said the grown-ups. Itta didn't know what a wake was. That night she couldn't sleep. She kept thinking of Ficek, how he used to jump onto her bed and lay his sweet little head on her pillow. She burst into tears. The grown-ups were still sitting on the terrace, chatting and listening to music, so she tried to cry quietly. From the top of the boys' bunk bed Błażej climbed down with his iPhone and told her that if she stopped bawling he'd show her something interesting. It was a photo: in the foreground Itta was holding Ficek wrapped in an old pink blanket, next to her Romek was playing the violin, past them Błażej was looking at his phone, Henryk and the boys' stepfather were holding spades, the boys' mother was holding a large cup from Starbucks, and behind them all there was a sunset and the railway line that had been disused for years. Ficek looked as if he were alive, like a sleeping puppy in the blanket. Before taking the picture, Itta's mother had come up to Itta, ruffled her hair and uncovered the dog's head. Super, the setting sun provides excellent light, she had said.

'Where did you get that photo?' asked Itta.

'Can't you see? Your mum posted it on Facebook.'

'My daughter is coming to terms with death. We're about to bury her beloved dog,' read Itta. 'Ficek wasn't mine, he was yours,' she said.

'So what? Look how many people have liked that post. A hundred and fifty-three,' said Błażej. 'People on Facebook really like animals. Read the comments underneath. Go on, you know how to read.'

'Poor child. What a brave little girl. I hope you'll go to the shelter and choose a new one. A trauma like that could affect her for life. It's very important to experience mourning,' read Itta, and looked at all the little blue hands, red hearts and weeping faces.

'This is the best one: How can you make a child cuddle a dead dog? Do you know how quickly the bacteria multiply in corpses?' read Błażej in a deep voice, pretending to be a grown-up guy, and began to laugh.

'Children can't go onto Facebook,' said Itta.

'I can. But I only do it for them. So they think they know what I talk to the boys about. Well, you know, we just pretend we're on Facebook. In fact we're on Instagram. I have to be on Facebook because I want to know what's going on. When Mum and Antoni wanted to send us to tennis camp, they didn't tell us about it, I found out from Facebook. Hey, fabulous Facebook friends, who organizes great tennis camps for kids?' screeched Błażej in his mother's voice. 'I hate tennis. Luckily they didn't register us in time. I told my dad and he agreed we could go to our granddad's instead. Better to keep your finger on the pulse. That's a saying,' added Błażej, seeing the look on Itta's face. 'You keep your finger on the pulse too. You never know what they'll come up with next.'

Błażej speaks so fast and unclearly that not everyone can understand him. But Itta always understands him perfectly.

The boys have a large, old laptop they inherited from Henryk. Itta scrambles onto the top bunk with it and goes online. If anyone asks what she's watching she says '*The Pink Panther*'. In fact she has two windows open, one showing a Pink Panther film, and the other is Facebook. It was Błażej who taught her how. Every day Itta's mother posts several updates, usually about what she and Henryk are doing, ordinary things, such as that they went for a bike ride, or to the cinema, or they ate something delicious. Henryk appears in her posts as 'my man'. What about Itta? She's often there too, but it's not Itta at all, it's a little girl called 'my daughter'.

Itta envies that little girl. Of course she knows it's her, but at the same time 'my daughter' is someone completely different, a nameless little girl whom Itta only knows by sight. How can that be? She doesn't give it much thought. That little girl is better than Itta, and her photos are liked by lots of people. 'My daughter and me at a picnic', 'My daughter on a field trip', 'This is a very important moment in my daughter's life . . .' That's how her mother captions the photos, and Itta understands her, because she doesn't like the name Itta either. The double 't' often leads to a misunderstanding – whoever reads that name thinks it's a spelling mistake and that she's really called Ita or Ida. Her father gave her the name despite her mother's protests; Itta has heard the story many times.

Her mother's Facebook daughter always looks very pretty and whatever she does prompts general applause. She even gets away with being naughty. One time when Itta addressed her mother in a commanding tone: 'Today I want a soft-boiled egg, but make sure it's exactly right, not hard and not snotty, with frothy cocoa and two slices of toast, slightly burned', her mother said: 'You're going a bit far, aren't you?', and Itta was given porridge for breakfast, which she can't stand, because it has even more snotty lumps than an undercooked egg. But for the same remark her mother's daughter on Facebook got thumbs-ups, hearts and smiles, as well as praise for knowing what she wants, and 'is sure to grow up to be a great leader'.

The daughter is a lovely little girl, she has long legs and wonderful hair, and lots of people express the view that she's going to be a beautiful woman. Whereas Itta has legs like sticks and her long hair is nothing but trouble, especially as she can't stand having it brushed.

Reality is like a jigsaw puzzle. It's cut into pieces that don't fit together, but then at some point it turns out to be cohesive and logical, so almost the whole picture is visible. Jigsaws usually show a landscape, or a castle that you can see on the box. In life things aren't that foreseeable. It's like at the cinema – unexpected, loud and scary.

Her mother chose to follow the Children and Cancer Facebook page. It was a very important piece of the puzzle, but Itta didn't know that. There were at least a dozen photos on this page. The first showed a little girl of Itta's age with ginger hair cut very short. Her name was Marianna, according to the caption underneath. She was looking with disgust at the narrow reddish belt she was holding in both hands. It was a plait of braided hair, and it looked real, but Itta had to study the pictures that followed to guess how very real it was. More than that – she realized that beforehand that plait had belonged to the little girl, Marianna. In each of the pictures a child with short hair (usually a girl, but there were two boys as well) was holding their own cut-off plait! It was very odd, and Itta didn't know what to think about it; most of the children seemed happy and proud, but Itta could understand Marianna's disgust – her cut-off plait looked like a fox's tail, or the body of a small animal, killed and dead, a squirrel, a kitten, or maybe a bird.

One Sunday the pieces of the puzzle start to fit.

Henryk's not here, he's away. Breakfast is delicious: soft-boiled egg, spot on, cocoa with milky froth sprinkled with little bits of chocolate, and slightly burned square pieces of toast with melting butter.

There's a large mug of black coffee in front of her mother, and that's all.

'I'm going straight to yoga,' she explains. 'You know your dad's girlfriend Róża runs that foundation, Children and Cancer? You know that, right?' she asks.

Itta doesn't answer because her mouth is full. She nods. She knows, but it's of no consequence. What matters is that she loves Róża.

'She makes wigs for children who've lost their hair after chemotherapy.'

Itta crunches a piece of toast. If you crush this sort of toast with your teeth it makes a very nice sound.

'You know what,' her mother continues gently, 'I'm sure you'd like to give up your hair for this noble aim.'

Itta hasn't heard the word 'chemotherapy' before. It reminds her of another word her mother often uses, 'psychotherapy'.

'I don't want chemotherapy,' she says.

'You're not going to have any chemotherapy. Chemotherapy is for children with cancer. And it makes their hair fall out. That's why they wear wigs. But to make the wigs you've got to have other children's hair.'

At this moment the puzzle suddenly comes together. All by itself. As if the bizarrely shaped pieces had raced in from all directions and fitted onto each other.

'Róża would be proud of you,' says her mother.

'Róża has lovely hair,' says Itta very loud. 'I don't want to cut my hair. I want to have hair like Róża. Chestnut.'

'I see. You're not ready for it. But have a think about it. Once you're ready, we'll go to the hairdresser's. But don't say anything to Róża or your dad. It'll be a surprise.'

That same day, late in the evening when her mother has said goodnight to her and shut the door, Itta goes onto Facebook and sees the daughter running across the park. The trees are yellow, orange and red, and the daughter's hair is golden-white. The wind is blowing and the hair is floating in the air, like the wing of a large bird that's flying just above her but doesn't fit in the frame. The film ends and starts again, as if it were to continue forever. This time there's a record number of likes – two-hundred-and-three. And nothing but sighs: that's wonderful, incredible, sweet, so beautiful, really cool . . .

At the top she sees her mother's comment: 'I'll be sorry when my daughter cuts off her hair. But what other sacrifice can a little girl make to the world?'

Itta goes into the kitchen. It's dark but she doesn't put on the light. Through the window, her mother and Henryk are sitting on a bench under the Christmas-cypress tree. They're kissing. The flames of lights in coloured glass jars set out on the terrace look like votive candles at a cemetery. A light twinkles on the kitchen table. A telephone. She picks it up and presses the receiver icon under a photo of Błażej.

'Dad, will you drive us to school tomorrow? Mum's in the bath, drinking wine and crying, and Antoni's gone away. She definitely won't get up tomorrow. And I've got a test,' says Błażej.

'It's me,' says Itta quietly.

'Where's my dad?' asks Błażej.

'They're on the terrace, kissing.'

'Let them. It's their anniversary. I'll send him a text instead.'

'I saw a film on Facebook. There have only been photos before now.'

'She must have done it with her iPhone. Dad bought her a new iPhone. I went to the mall with him because he didn't know what to choose. He wanted to get her some perfume, but I told him better get her an iPhone because her smartphone is hopeless.'

'She wants me to cut off my hair.'

'Don't do it. You've got the nicest hair in the world.'

'For the children who are sick with cancer. They haven't got their own hair.'

'What if a sick girl joins your class? And she's got your hair? And you're bald as a coot?'

'She said it's to be a surprise for Róża.'

'Then cut it off. What's the problem?'

'But what if someone puts on my hair?'

'You won't even notice. I was joking.'

'I don't want to.'

'All right, then don't. Bye now, I've got a test tomorrow.'

Her father and Róża are going to Japan to climb a mountain called Fujiyama. And when they get back they're getting married. So said Grandma Martyna. Itta is to go to the wedding with her grandparents.

Her mother has bought Itta a little white dress with a high lace collar.

Itta tries on the dress. She meets her mother's gaze in the mirror. Her mother sends her a smile.

'Beautiful. I had one like that for my wedding to your father. But that one had nylon lace because the real kind was terribly expensive.'

'I don't want it. The lace scratches my neck,' protests Itta.

'You look lovely in it. The high collar will suit short hair. It emphasizes the oval of your face.'

'But I've got long hair. And I haven't got an oval.'

Her mother laughs, goes up to Itta, gathers her hair in both hands and twists it in a knot behind her head.

'Look how beautiful you are now.'

'It's you that's beautiful,' says Itta.

'Do you think so?'

'The skating teacher said so. "Where's your beautiful mum?"'

'Aha. Go on, take a look.'

Holding Itta's hair from behind, her mother bends her knees and brings her face close to Itta's, very close, just like in the photo of two identical girls, much older than Itta. Those girls always had to be together because they had conjoined heads. One was smiling, and the other was showing her tongue. The faces in the mirror are like each other too, but one belongs to a little girl, the other to a grown-up woman. Itta scowls, sticks out her tongue and abruptly pushes her mother away.

'What are you doing?'

Itta runs out of the room and races down the passage. She stops in the sitting room. Through the window she spots the magpie, sitting on the branch of a small tree. Itta moves up to the window, but the magpie doesn't fly away, it just stares sternly at Itta with its piercing avian eyes. Itta has never seen it so close up before.

'I'd like to stroke you,' she says, but the magpie shakes its head.

My daughter is running across a meadow full of brightly coloured flowers. She's wearing a little white dress and has very short hair that's stuck together in pointed peapods, huge eyes and narrow, sneering lips. She's different from usual. She has the face of a boy from manga. This isn't a film on Facebook. It's a dream.

Henryk drove Itta to Puławska Street, to her father and Róża's place, and then he went to fetch Błażej and Romek to bring them home for the weekend. Itta was hungry, but it didn't look as if there was going to be any lunch. Her father wasn't in, and Róża was sitting on the floor by the wardrobe putting clothes into a backpack. Itta went to her own room. In here were all her old toys, headless Barbies, moth-eaten teddy bears and a shabby doll's pram. She sat down at her little red table and got down to some drawing. She drew various little girls, some bald, others with hair. She was sorry she hadn't stayed at Kabaty, where at least she could have played Minecraft with the boys. She had come here because her father was also entitled to her company. But he wasn't here anyway – he was at work, as usual.

'That's nice,' says Róża. She's standing behind Itta looking down at her drawing. Itta didn't even notice when Róża entered her room. 'What sort of girls are they?'

'With hair and without.'

'What are they called?'

'They haven't got names,' says Itta and goes on drawing, while Róża watches over her shoulder. There are more and more little girls on the sheet of paper.

'May I?' asks Róża.

'Uh-huh.'

Róża picks up a blue crayon and gives the two bald girls blue hair, long and curly. She gives some others green hair, and gives the next ones pink hair . . . Until all the little girls have hair.

'Would you like to have coloured hair?' asks Róża.

'I don't want to have hair any more,' says Itta.

'Why not?'

'Just because,' says Itta and tears the drawing in half.

Róża sits on the bed.

'You know what, I'm worried. We're going to fly in a plane,' she says.

'I know. You're flying to Japan, you're going to climb a mountain that's not called a mountain but a yama, and when you come home you're going to get married.'

'How do you know?'

'It doesn't matter,' says Itta.

'I have no idea if I will climb Fujiyama. But next time you'll come with us. And maybe with someone else too.'

'With Mum?'

'No. With your brother. When he's born.'

'Is Mum having him?'

'No, I am. In five months' time.'

'Where's he going to live?'

'With us. Here.'

'In my room?'

'First in our bedroom, and then maybe in this room. Would you like to choose a name for your brother?'

'No,' says Itta.

'Well, have a think. What names do you like?'

'Błażej.'

'You've already got a brother called Błażej. Well, he's almost your brother,' says Róża, laughing.

'I want to have another one. Or maybe Romek,' says Itta.

'Well, I don't know.' Róża shrugs. 'Shall we order a pizza?'

'With ham and pineapple,' says Itta. 'This is my room. I don't want Błażej or Romek to live here.'

'We'll see what happens. We might sell this apartment and buy a bigger one.'

'But don't sell this room. This is my room. And I won't give you my hair.'

'What are you saying, Itta? I don't want your hair. What's got into your head?'

'Never mind,' says Itta. 'I'm going back to Henryk's. Call him and get him to come.'

The form teacher has told the children in advance that they're going to have a new classmate. He said the new girl is sick, and asked the children to be kind to her. Itta was expecting the new girl to have cancer and not to have any hair. The new girl is small and slight, she walks on crutches, hopping comically, and she has two long ginger plaits. She's like Pippi Longstocking. She's seated next to Itta. Her name is Ola. She tidies up Itta's school bag and offers her a sandwich. It's ciabatta bread with Italian ham, delicious, she says. It really is delicious. Itta is living at her mother's right now and in her lunch box she has buckwheat bread with fried celeriac. Yuk, says Ola, and she's right. During the form period she announces that she's planning to cut off her plaits and donate them to children with cancer.

'That's very nice of you,' says the teacher and explains why children with cancer need other people's hair.

'It's the only thing a little girl can give to the world,' says Ola, looking at Itta.

'The only thing?' wonders the teacher.

'What else can she give?' asks Ola, still looking at Itta.

'I'm going to cut off my hair too and donate it to the sick children. I've been thinking about it for ages,' says Itta.

'Me too! Me too! Me too!'

Two girls expressed their intention too, and one boy who had almost waist-length hair.

'They won't want your hair. It's too short and thin. I know what kind they need,' says Ola to one of the girls. 'Itta's hair is the most suitable. It's even better than mine,' she adds.

Now the whole class is looking at Itta.

That day, after supper her mother takes Itta to the new ice-cream parlour where there are sixty-five flavours of ice cream. Itta asks for Salt Caramel, Chocolate Poo and Bloody Mary with lime.

'I'm so pleased you've finally made your decision. It'll be a great day,' says her mother, eating her ice cream, which is called Coffee and Cigarettes.

'What great day is that?' asks Itta.

The Bloody Mary ice cream looks the best. As if real blood were dripping down it.

Her mother's spoon stops half way to her mouth.

'You finally decided to donate your hair,' she says. 'You told everyone during the form period.'

'How do you know?'

'Oh, I have my ways,' says her mother, smiling.

'How do you know?' Itta repeats the question, raising her spoon full of Bloody Mary as if to hit her mother with it.

'But you know we have our page on Facebook. Parents of the pupils in One B.'

'Ah, yes.'

'It's buzzing with the news. Your new classmate Ola is nice, isn't she?'

'No, she's not. And I don't want to cut off my hair. I was joking,' says Itta.

Her mother puts down her spoon on the table. She says nothing. Itta eats her ice cream very slowly, relishing it. The Coffee and Cigarettes in her mother's bowl changes into grey gloop.

Magpies don't go to sleep like other birds. If you walk across a park or a housing estate at night you can hear their conversations. They have hoarse voices, as if they always had laryngitis.

Itta is falling asleep. Suddenly she hears the magpie. She doesn't know if it's a dream that has appeared ahead of time. She gets up and runs onto the terrace. The magpie is sitting on the table next to a lamp. It looks at Itta, tilting its head as if trying to ask a question.

'I don't want to give up my hair,' says Itta.

The magpie opens its beak wide and screeches horribly, making a noise like someone ripping a sheet of tin apart.

'I don't want them to take away my hair.'

The magpie squawks even louder.

'All right. I'll go and get you some ham. You don't have to scream like that,' says Itta and goes into the kitchen. She opens the fridge and takes out a packet of ham on cardboard covered with gold plastic. And then in the gloom she sees her mother sitting motionless at the table. 'Mum,' says Itta. 'Don't worry. I'll cut my hair tomorrow.'

'Oh, my darling daughter!' cries her mother, jumps up from her chair and hugs Itta. 'That's wonderful. Because I've invited lots of guests to celebrate the occasion. It'll be your special day!'

'It'll be my special day,' says Itta, freeing herself from her mother's embrace, and goes back to the terrace to feed the magpie.

Next day she wakes at dawn. She gets up, puts on her dressing gown and takes a pencil case out of her school bag. She crosses the apartment slowly, avoiding squeaky floorboards. She gently opens the balcony door and goes out onto the terrace. She has never been here at this time of day before. The sky above the houses is pink, it's quiet and as fresh as in a garden or by a river. Itta takes some red plastic scissors out of the pencil case. She stands by the railing and winds a strand of hair around her finger. Below she can see the cube-shaped block of Tesco's, and further on the woods, all the way to the horizon. The scissors are sharp and cut her hair easily. Itta holds out her hand and opens it. The hair rises in the air like gossamer. Itta cuts off another strand, then another, and another. Suddenly the magpie appears, grabs a cut-off lock in its beak and flies away. As Itta keeps throwing her hair into the wind it whirls and ripples.

The magpie returns and lands on the railing.

'Take it,' says Itta. 'Make yourself a nest.'

'Suwerenna decyzja'
Published as part of the collection *RuRu* (Wydawnictwo Nisza, 2019).

OLGA TOKARCZUK

1962–

Olga Tokarczuk's parents were teachers, and her father ran the school library. Surrounded by books from an early age, she has been a voracious reader ever since. Her interests and erudition are wide-ranging. She studied clinical psychology, and seemed set for a career as a psychotherapist, but her natural urge to write fiction proved stronger.

Tokarczuk has a vivid imagination and an inquiring mind, resulting in novels that vary enormously. She plays with form and generally steers away from conventional structures. Two of her best-known works, *House of Day, House of Night* (1998) and *Flights* (2007) are what she calls 'constellation novels', each a collection of loosely related texts that, if viewed the way we look at the stars, join to form a complete image. While all the stories and ideas in *House of Day . . .* relate to the remote Kłodzko Valley in south-west Poland where Tokarczuk lives, *Flights* takes the reader on long journeys away from home, and deep inside the human body. In Jennifer Croft's translation, *Flights* won the 2018 Man Booker International prize.

Her magnum opus, *The Books of Jacob* (2014), which took her eight years to research and write, is a historical novel about Jakub Frank, the self-proclaimed Messiah and leader of a heretical eighteenth-century sect. Many of the characters are based on real people, including the priest Benedykt Chmielowski, author of *New Athens*, one of the first Polish encyclopaedias. This was a source of inspiration for 'The Green Children'. 'Chmielowski told a similar story,' says Tokarczuk. 'I developed it and transferred it to the Belarusian marshlands. The theme of feral children is as old as the world and probably features in every culture.'

Her genius won her the 2018 Nobel Prize in Literature, as the jury put it, 'for a narrative imagination that with encyclopaedic passion represents the crossing of boundaries as a form of life'. In 2023 the British theatre company Complicité made her ecological murder mystery, *Drive Your Plow Over the Bones of the Dead*, into a successful drama that toured Europe.

Antonia Lloyd-Jones

The Green Children, or: A Description of Bizarre Events in the Region of Volhynia, Drawn up by William Davisson, Physician to His Majesty King John II Casimir

Translated by Jennifer Croft

All this occurred in the spring of 1656, when I was lingering in Poland. I had arrived a few years earlier at the invitation of Marie Louise Gonzaga, wife of John II Casimir Vasa, the Polish king, who wished me to take up the role of King's Physician as well as Director of the Royal Gardens. The invitation was not one I could decline, in part due to the eminence of its issuers, and for certain personal reasons, too, which need not be mentioned here. As I was travelling to Poland, I felt ill at ease, knowing nothing of that country that was so far removed from the world that was familiar to me, conceiving of myself as a sort of ex-centric, a person who ventures out past the centre with its recognizable set of expectations. I feared the foreign customs and the violence of these eastern and northern peoples, but above all I worried about the unpredictable local weather, the damp and the chill. At the forefront of my thoughts, of course, was the fate of my friend René Descartes, who a few years earlier had, on the invitation of the Swedish Queen, set out for distant Stockholm, and catching cold there in her frigid palaces, was struck down in his prime and at the height of his intellectual powers. What a loss to all the sciences! Fearing some similar happenstance, I took with me several of the finest furs; and yet already in my first winter these French things were revealed to be too light, too delicate for the Polish clime. The King, to whom I took an immediate and sincere liking, gave me a wolf's fur that extended all the way down to my ankles, and from October to April, I would not remove it. I was in fact wearing my wolf's coat during the expedition here described, and that was March already. You should know, Reader, that winters in Poland, and in the North in general, are wont to be severe – just imagine, people make the crossing to Sweden via short-cuts on the ice over the Baltic Sea; and on many of the ponds and lesser rivers, carnivals are held. Because that season lasts so long here, concealing every plant under a thick blanket of snow, not much opportunity remains to the botanist. Like it or not, therefore, I turned my attention to people.

My name is William Davisson, and I am a Scot who hails from Aberdeen, though I spent many years in France, where my career culminated in the office of Royal Botanist, and where I published my most important works. Few had read them in Poland, but I was treated with respect regardless, for anyone arriving from France is there received uncritically and with deference.

What caused me to follow in Descartes' footsteps and set out for the very edge of Europe? It would be difficult to respond to such a question directly and succinctly, but since this story isn't about me, and I am but a witness in it, I shall simply pass over it in silence, trusting that you will be more drawn in by the tale itself than you would be by its insignificant teller.

My service to the Polish King coincided with the worst possible incidents befalling that realm. The Kingdom of Poland was war-torn, ravaged by the Swedish armies, besieged meanwhile by Muscovites in the East. Unhappy peasants had already risen up in White Ruthenia. And the King of this unfortunate Commonwealth was, as though by way of some mysterious symmetry, tormented by ailments as numerous as the attacks upon his country. His bouts of melancholy could often be cured with wine and the proximity of the fairer sex. His contrarian nature required him to be ceaselessly in motion, although he was endlessly repeating that he hated to be on the road and longed for Warsaw, where he would be awaited by his beloved wife, Marie Louise.

Now our retinue made its way north, where His Majesty the King was to conduct an official visit to assess the conditions in that region and to try and establish coalitions with magnates. The Muscovite forces had already come in and set about attempting their conquest of the Polish-Lithuanian Commonwealth, which, when combined with the actions of the Swedes, who were tyrannizing the west of the country, made it seem as if dark forces had conspired to make the Polish lands the main stage for the cruel *theatrum* of war. Given that it was my first foray into this wild, peripheral land, around the time we left the outskirts of Warsaw, I began to regret my decision, and had it not been for my curiosity as a philosopher and a botanist (as well as for – I see no reason to deny it – the lavish guerdon), I certainly would have stayed at home and spent my time on quieter inquiries.

Yet even in those vexing circumstances, I did dedicate myself to research. Since my arrival in Poland I had taken an interest in a certain local phenomenon that was admittedly known to the world, but in Poland it was widespread beyond measure, so much so that if one merely walked the poorer streets of Warsaw, one would witness it on people's heads – the *plica polonica*: a strange object made up of twisted hair in a variety of guises, on some persons a set of thick, strong ropes, on others spooled hair balled, while others still wore it as a sort of braid reminiscent of a beaver's tail. These plaits are considered to be brimming with good and evil forces, to the extent that those who wear them have sometimes chosen death over removing them.

As I often sketched, I had already amassed a number of drawings and descriptions of this phenomenon and intended upon my return to France to publish a brief work on the topic. The affliction is known by many different names around the whole of Europe, and it is perhaps rarest in France, for people there attach great significance to their appearances and are ceaselessly arranging their hair into curls. In Germany, the *plica polonica* occurs as *Mahrenlocke* or *Alpzopf* or *Drutenzopf*. I understand that in Denmark it is called *marenlok*, *elvish knot* in Wales and England. When I once travelled through Lower Saxony, I heard such hairstyles referred to as *Selkensteert*. In Scotland people believe it is the ancient hairstyle of European pagans, common enough among Druid tribes. I have also read that the origins of the *plica polonica* are thought to be with the invasion of Poland by the Tatars, under the rule of Leszek II, the Black. There have even been suggestions that the fashion travelled here all the way from India. I have also encountered the idea that it was the Hebrews who first introduced the custom of interweaving the hair into felted pods. *Nazarite* was the term for the holy man who vowed never to cut his hair for the Glory of God. The combination of this vast quantity of opposing theories and the limitless white snow initially plunged me into a kind of intellectual torpidity, but at some point I emerged into a state of creative excitement, and in every village we went through, I researched the *plica polonica*.

My work was greatly aided by a young man by the name of Richivolski, a consummately capable fellow who was not only my butler and interpreter, but also helped me conduct my research, as well as providing me with the moral support that I needed – I shall not pretend otherwise – in that alien environment.

We went on horseback. The March weather was wintry one minute, almost springlike the next. The mud on the roads alternated between freezing and unfreezing, turning into swampy slush into which the carriages bearing our luggage would sink their whole wheels. The penetrating cold transformed us into something like furred bundles.

In this wild swampland overgrown with forest, human settlements were situated far away from one another, so that we were forced to overnight without complaint in any mouldy old shack – once we even spent the night in a tavern, when snowfall slowed our progress! His Majesty went incognito then, passing himself off as an ordinary noble. At each stop I would apply His Majesty's medicaments, for I carried with me a veritable pharmacy, and though it sometimes fell to me to let his blood on hastily thrown-together beds, wherever possible I would at least arrange a salt bath for him.

Of all the royal maladies, the most harmful one seemed to me to be that courtly one His Majesty had apparently imported from Italy or France. Although it produced no visible symptoms, and was thus easy to conceal (at least in the beginning), its outbreaks were dangerous, treacherous – it had been demonstrated, after all, that it could get into the brain and mix up a person's senses. Which was why as soon as I arrived at His Majesty's court I attempted to persuade him to take a mercury treatment, lasting three weeks, but His Majesty never could find the time to take the mercury in peace, for on the road such a treatment was unlikely to have any real effect. Of the king's other ailments I was also concerned about podagra, or gout of the foot, though this was easy enough to prevent as it was caused by immoderation in food and drink. It would be sufficient, then, to head it off with abstinence, although while travelling it wouldn't do to fast. Thus did I accomplish little on behalf of His Majesty the King.

The king was travelling to Lviv. Along the way, he would meet with local nobles, currying their favour and exhorting them to recall they were his subjects, for the loyalty of these nobles was much in doubt, as they were always looking out for their own interests, and not for those of the Most Serene Commonwealth of Poland. We were always received with seeming generosity, and with great pomp and ceremony, but I sometimes felt that some of them took the king for a sort of petitioner. But then again what kind of kingdom is it where the king is voted upon and elected to office? Who had ever heard of such a thing?

War is a frightening, infernal phenomenon – even if human settlements go untouched by the battles themselves, the war still spreads into everything, steals in under the humblest thatched roof, with famine, disease, universal terror. People's hearts get harder; people grow indifferent. Human thinking itself changes – everyone cares for and takes care of himself alone, simply to survive. And man thus grows cruel and insensate to the suffering of others. How often on our way from Lithuania to Lviv did I look upon human evil, how much violence, murder, unbelievable barbarity? Whole villages burned, fields torn apart, turned fallow, gallows scattered everywhere, as though the art of carpentry were only in service of this – building instruments of death and destruction. Human bodies unburied, ripped apart by wolves and foxes. Only fire and sword found gainful employment there. I would gladly forget all of this now that I have returned to my homeland and am writing these words, but the images remain before my eyes, and I cannot rid myself of them.

Worse and worse news began to reach us. The February defeat of Czarniecki's regiment in the Battle of Gołąb so impacted the king's health that we were obliged to stop for two days, so that the king might have his Egerbrunnen waters in peace and drink his decoctions to regain his strength. It was as though all the ailments of the Commonwealth were reflected in the body of the king, a mysterious mirroring that was at that time much to his detriment. After the battle with the Swedes was lost, before the notice even reached us, His Majesty had an attack of podagra with a fever and such terrible pain that we barely got it back under control.

Some two days before reaching Lutsk, as we passed by Lyubeshiv – which had been burned to the ground by the Tatars – and as we were travelling through thick damp forests, I understood fully that there was no land on Earth more cursed, and I regretted agreeing to go on this expedition. I had a deep conviction that I would not make it back home, and with these omnipresent swamps, with this damp forest, low sky, standing water covered in thin ice that looked like the wounds of some giant lying prostrate on the ground, I recognized that everyone, whether dressed poorly or richly, whether king or soldier, is nothing – that we are all no more than nothing. We saw the charred walls of a church where the Tatars had locked up all the inhabitants of a village and burned them alive, forests of gallows, and the blackened scorched earth littered with human and animal corpses. It was only then that I truly comprehended the King's reason for travelling to Lviv: at this terrible time, when external forces were ripping the Commonwealth apart, to place the country under the care and protection of Mary, Mother of Christ, who was most revered and glorified there. I had at first found this veneration of Mary somewhat odd. It frequently seemed to me that they were worshipping some pagan goddess while – and let this not be read as blasphemous – God Himself and His Son Christ humbly bore Her sash along behind Her. For in that country every shrine was dedicated to Mary, and I had become so accustomed to images of Her that I, too, began to pray to Her on miserable evenings, when, cold and hungry, we lay down for the night, believing in my heart of hearts that She *was* the ruler of this country, as Christ reigned among us. In any case we were left with no choice but to give ourselves over completely to a higher power.

The day the King had his attack of podagra, we stopped at the estate of a Mr Haydamovich, chamberlain of Lutsk. It was a wooden manor house, built on a dry promontory among the swamps, surrounded by huts belonging to the woodsmen, a few peasants and the servants. His Majesty did not take supper, retiring immediately instead, but as he could not sleep, I was called upon to guide him into slumber with the aid of my elixirs.

It was a pleasant enough morning that shortly after dawn a few of the King's armed men, wishing to cut down the waiting time before we set out again, ran out into the woody undergrowth as though hunting for some game and vanished from our line of sight. We were expecting, upon their return, deer or pheasants, but the prey our hunters brought us was so extraordinary that we were struck speechless, including the still-drowsy King, who instantly came to.

It was two children, both scrawny little things, poorly dressed, or even worse than poorly, for they wore only coarsely woven linen that was torn and smeared with mud. Their hair was stuck together into cords, which fascinated me as perfect examples of *plica polonica*. The children were tied up like deer and strapped to saddles – I worried this had harmed them and particularly feared their thin bones might have been broken. The King's guards explained that there had been no other way, for the children had bitten and kicked.

When His Majesty had finished breakfast and then taken the herbs that gave some hope of lifting his spirits, I went out to the children and, having ordered their faces washed, examined them closely, making sure, however, that they did not bite me. Judging by their height, I would have said they were about four and six years old, but their teeth made me think they were older, despite their diminutive size. The girl was bigger and stronger, while the boy was frail, waif-like, albeit lively and active. But what interested me most was their complexion. It was a strange shade, one I'd never seen before – something between that of a baby pea and an Italian olive. Their hair, hanging in those plaits over their faces, was fair, but it looked as though it, too, was covered in some greenness, like stones covered in moss. Young Richivolski told me these Green Children, as we soon began to call them, were likely war victims who had survived until now by grace of the forest, a story not unheard of – to take just one example, there is the famous case of Romulus and Remus. Nature's field of action is vast, far larger than man's modest patch.

The King once asked me – as we were driving through the steppe, from Mogilev, where scorched villages were still smoking on the horizon and were already beginning to be reclaimed by the forest – what nature was. So I answered according to my view that nature is all that surrounds us, excluding what is human, i.e. ourselves and our creations. The King blinked his eyes as though to test them, though what he saw then, I know not. What he said was: 'One great nothing.'

I think this is the way people who have been brought up in court view the world – those who are accustomed to gazing upon the flourishes of Venetian textiles, the elaborate weavings of Turkish kilims, puzzles made of tiles and fine mosaics. When their eyes are exposed to the complexities of nature, they shall glimpse there only chaos, only one Great Nothing.

All catastrophes allow nature to reclaim that which man has robbed it of, and it will even reach for human beings, attempting to restore them to their natural state. But looking at these children, one might have been forgiven for doubting whether there was any idyll in nature at all, so wild and haggard were they. His Majesty took a particular interest in them – he ordered them included in our luggage, so that they might be taken to Lviv with us and there thoroughly examined, though in the end he gave up this idea because circumstances suddenly changed. It turned out that the king's big toe had swollen so much that His Majesty could no longer force on his boot. His pain was intense – I could make out the drops of sweat forming on his face. A shiver ran down my spine when I heard the ruler of this great country begin to issue plaintive wails. There was no question of departing. I placed His Majesty near the stove and set about preparing compresses, ordering the removal, too, of anyone who might unnecessarily witness His Majesty's discomforts. As the unfortunate children caught in the woods were carried out, tied up like lambs, the girl somehow miraculously escaped the servants' grasp and threw herself at the King's aching feet. She began to rub his big toe with her matted hair. The astonished King permitted her to do so. After a moment, His Majesty said in amazement that it hurt less, and then he ordered the children to be well fed and clothed like people, which was done. Nevertheless, as we were packing our bags, and I innocently reached out my hand to pat the boy on the head – as is done with children in every country – he bit me on the wrist so hard that it bled. I rushed to wash the wound out in the nearby stream, fearing rabies, but there, by the water, on a muddy, boggy bank, I slipped and, falling badly, I hit the little wooden bridge with my whole body, knocking loose a pile of wood that all fell on top of me at once. I felt a terrible pain in my leg that made me howl like an animal. I had just enough time to understand that this particular turn of events was not a good one, and then I passed out.

I came to as young Richivolski was patting my face, and I saw above me the chamber ceiling, and all around me worried faces, including His Majesty's – all of them were oddly elongated, shaky, blurry. I comprehended then that I was feverish and that I had been unconscious for quite a while.

'For God's sake, Davisson, what have you done to yourself?' cried His Majesty, leaning over me. The curls of his travelling wig brushed against my chest, and even that delicate touch was painful to me. Even at such a moment, it did not escape my attention that His Royal Majesty's face had brightened, and that the beads of sweat had gone from it, and that he was standing before me in his boots.

'We must move on now, Davisson,' he said to me with worry in his voice.

'Without me?' I moaned, shaking from pain and from horror at the prospect of being left behind.

'You shall soon have the best doctor in Lviv . . .'

My sobbing arose more from despair than it did from physical suffering.

I bade a tearful farewell to His Majesty, whose procession moved on. Without me! Young Richivolski was left to me as a companion, which alleviated at least some of my pain, and we were placed under the care of Chamberlain Haydamovich. Perhaps in an effort to cheer us up, the Green Children were also left behind – perhaps in order to ensure I had some occupation until such a time as I could be rescued.

As it turned out, my leg had been broken in two places, and the fractures were complicated, too. In one place, the bone had pierced the skin, and it would require great skill to set it back. I wouldn't be able to do it myself because I would lose consciousness at once, though I had heard of certain persons who could even perform amputations on themselves. Before his departure, however, the King had sent ahead an order for the best doctor in Lviv to set out at once for the chamberlain's estate, though I assumed it would take at least two weeks for him to arrive. In the meantime, my leg had to be set as soon as possible, for in that humid climate, had gangrene taken hold, I would never have seen the French court again – that place I had so repudiated, but which seemed to me now the centre of the real world, a lost paradise, the most exquisite of all dreams. Nor would I ever have seen the mountains and hills of Scotland . . .

For several days, I administered to myself the same pain-relieving preparations I had previously given the King for his gout. Finally, a messenger arrived from Lviv, but without a doctor, as the doctor had been killed along the way by a band of Tatars, the likes of which were so numerous in these parts. The messenger assured us that another physician would be dispatched soon. He also brought us a report of the pious words spoken by the King in a Lviv cathedral. His Majesty had entrusted the Commonwealth to the care of the Virgin Mary, that she might protect it from the

Swedes, Muscovites, Khmelnytsky and all those who had set upon Poland like wolves on a lame deer. I was aware, of course, that His Majesty had myriad troubles, so it was even more wonderful to me that not only had we news of the King, but also an exceptional eau de vie, several bottles of Rhine wine, a fur hat and French soap – though it was perhaps this last that pleased me most.

It is my view that the world is made up of concentric circles originating from a single place. And that this place, known as the centre of the world, changes over time – it was once Greece, Rome, Jerusalem, and now it is undoubtedly France, or rather Paris. You might draw the circles around it with a compass. The rule is simple: the closer to the centre, the more real and tangible everything seems, while the farther away, the more the world seems to fall to pieces, like a faded canvas in the damp. And furthermore – the centre of the world is as though raised above, so that ideas, fashions, innovations, everything flows down in all directions from it. First the closest circles absorb it, then the next ones, but less so now, and the farthest places are reached only by a small portion of the contents. I realized this while lying in Chamberlain Haydamovich's manor, somewhere out there among the swamps, no doubt in the final circle, far from the centre of the world, lonely as the exile Ovidius in Tomi. And such was my delirium in those days that just as Dante wrote his *Divina Commedia*, so I could have written a great thing about circles, not in the afterlife, but in the world, about the circles of Europe, and each of them would be struggling with a different sin, each subjected to a different punishment. It would truly be a wonderful comedy of hidden games, broken alliances, a comedy in which the roles alternated over the course of the performance, and right up until the end it wouldn't be clear quid pro quo. A story about the mania for grandeur in some and the indifference and selfishness of others, about the courage and sacrifice of the few, though perhaps they are more numerous than it might seem. The heroes operating on that stage called Europe would not be united by religion at all, as some might wish – because religion is likelier to divide, a fact that is difficult not to acknowledge, taking into consideration the quantity of corpses felled for religious reasons, even in the wars being waged this very day. But they would have something else in common in this comedy – since the finale would need to be a happy one – namely trust in sense and reason, in this great divine work. God gave us our senses and our reason to explore the world and multiply our knowledge. That is Europe, where reason is at work.

Such things were swirling around in my head in brighter moments. Yet I spent the majority of the next few days in a malignant fever, and when the Lviv doctor continued not to appear, my hosts, with the consent of young Richivolski, sent to the swamps for a certain woman. She arrived along with her mute helper and, after first pouring a bottle of eau de vie down my throat, she pulled out my leg and set the bones that were broken in it. All of this was related to me with some considerable excitement by my young companion, for I myself remembered none of it.

When I came to after this procedure, the sun was already high. Easter would be coming soon. A priest arrived at the manor to celebrate the holiday Mass, and on this occasion, he baptized the Green Children, which my friend reported with glee, adding that some in the house had been talking about a spell that must have been cast upon me by those creatures, to bring me such misfortunes. I did not believe in such nonsense, and I forbade the repetition of it.

One evening, Richivolski brought that girl to me, now clean and neatly dressed, and in addition quite calm. And he had her, with my consent, rub my injured leg with her matted pods, as she had previously done for the King. I hissed, as even the touch of her hair was painful, but I endured it bravely until the pain slowly subsided, and the swelling seemed to decrease. She did this three more times.

After a few days, as it grew warmer, it being spring, I attempted to rise. The crutches that had been carved for me were quite comfortable, and so I went out to the porch. There, desirous of light and fresh air, I spent the whole of the afternoon. I eyed the bustling of that chamberlain's somewhat impoverished household. That is to say, the manor was rich and large, but the stables and barns appeared to have come from a much more remote circle of civilization. It was with some sadness that I realized that I should be stuck there for some time, and that in order to survive my exile, I really did need to find some occupation, as that would be the only way to avoid falling into melancholy in this damp, swampy country, the only way to keep alive the hope that the beneficent Lord would still let me return one day to France.

Richivolski brought me those wild children, whom the Haydamoviches had taken in, not knowing what to do with them in this out-of-the-way place, especially in wartime, and also probably expecting that His Royal Majesty might eventually reclaim them. The children were kept under lock and key on the ground floor of the granary, where the Haydamoviches kept many things unnecessary and necessary. As its walls were made of wooden planks, the children could follow the members of the household through the gaps between them. They relieved themselves in front of the house, squatting; they ate with their hands, very greedily, but they wanted nothing to do with meat and spat it out. They had no beds, nor water bowls. When frightened, they would throw themselves on the ground and, walking on all fours, try to bite, and when scolded, they would cower and remain perfectly still for a long while. They communicated with each other via hoarse croaks, and as soon as the sun was shining, they threw off their clothes and exposed themselves to its warmth.

Young Richivolski determined that these children would be both entertainment and employment for me, because as a scientist I should want to study and write about them, which would help me not to think about my broken leg.

And he was right. I had the sense that these little freaks felt something like remorse when they saw my hand bandaged from their biting, my leg immobilized in its splints. Over time, the girl started to trust me and sometimes allowed me to examine her more closely. We sat in the sun in front of the warmed wooden walls of the lumber room. Nature came alive; the omnipresent smell of damp subsided. I gently turned her face to the light and took a few cords of her hair in my hands – they felt warm, as if made out of wool, and when I smelled them, I noticed that they smelled of moss; it looked like some lichen had grown into them. When seen up close, the girl's skin was covered in tiny dark-green dots, which I had previously mistaken for dirt. Richivolski and I were very surprised by this – we thought there was something vegetal in it. We suspected that this was why she would undress and expose herself to sun, because, like any plant, she required sunlight, which she fed on through her skin, and she didn't need to consume much else – breadcrumbs were enough for her. She was already being called Ośródka – a difficult name for me to pronounce, but it sounded pleasant, quite like Osh-rude-ka. It signified the soft centre of bread, and therefore also someone who ate the centre out of a slice, leaving the crust behind.

The manor's inhabitants had varying opinions about what to do with the children's *plica polonica*, or matted hair. More so because these ones were green! It was commonly believed that the mats were the extrusions of an internal illness, and that if they were to be cut, the illness would go back inside the body and kill the person whose body it was. Others, including Chamberlain Haydamovich – as he considered himself a man of the world – insisted that we must cut it as it was a habitat for lice and other vermin.

Once the chamberlain even ordered sheep shears to be brought to chop off the children's greenish pods. The terrified boy hid behind his sister (I assumed she was his sister), but the girl herself seemed bold, haughty, even – she stepped forward, fixed her eyes on the chamberlain and would not take them off him until he grew sufficiently bewildered. At the same time, a growl came from her throat, a growl like a wild animal's, and her lips parted, revealing the tips of her teeth. There was something incongruous, separate in her regard, as if she simply had nothing to do with what we wanted, as if she saw us as an animal might – seemingly straight through us. On the other hand, there was an unexpected and grown-up self-confidence in it, so that for a moment I glimpsed in her not a child, but a stunted old woman. Chills ran down our spines, and in the end, the chamberlain told us to forget about cutting their hair.

Sadly, some time after their baptism in the wooden church that looked more like a hen house, it happened that the boy fell ill in the night and, to everyone's great surprise and horror, suddenly died. The servants took this as a sign of his devilishness – for who but a devil could be killed by holy water? And as for it not occurring right away, well, just proof that evil put up a good fight . . . *Summa summarum*, it was judged that higher powers were involved in the matter of those Green Children.

And that very day the marshes around the manor were filled with strange sounds, not birds, not frogs – more like a funereal orchestra. The child's tiny body was washed, dressed and placed on a bier, and candles were arranged around it. As a doctor, I was permitted to examine the body once more during these preparations, and for a moment, my heart sank at the sight of such a poppet. Only when I saw him naked and still did I truly see him as a child and not just some strange creature, and I thought then, too, how, like any living being, this child must have had a mother and a father – and where were they now? Did they miss him? Had they been worrying about him?

Having quickly mastered these emotions, so unbecoming in a learned physician, following a thorough examination I concluded that the child had obviously been harmed by bathing too soon in the icy water of the stream, and that this was what had prompted his death. I also found that there was nothing strange in him, but for the colour of his skin, which I attributed to his long stay in the forest, among nature's potent forces. Evidently the skin had become like its surroundings, just as the wings of some birds became like tree bark, as grasshoppers resembled grass. Nature is full of such correspondences. So, too, was it designed so that for every ailment there would be a natural cure. This was written by my personal master, the great Paracelsus, and I now repeated the same to young Richivolski.

The very first night following the young boy's death, the body vanished. It happened that the women watching over it grew dazed by the smoke from the incense and just after midnight went off to bed, and when they rose at dawn, there remained not a trace of the body. We were roused, the lights were lit all around the manor, fear and horror resounding in us all. The servants instantly spread the news that the little green devil, thanks to its magical powers, had but feigned death, and when no one was at his bier, had come straight back to life and returned to his own kind in the forest. Others added that he might want to take revenge for his captivity, and they began locking their doors – great anxiety pervaded, as though we were under imminent threat of a Tatar invasion. Once more we placed Oshrudeka under lock and key. She was oddly indifferent, in her torn, dirtied clothing, which aroused certain suspicions against her. Young Richivolski and I carefully examined all the traces: in the room itself there were only a few streaks on the floor, as if a body had been dragged, but outside, panic had taken its toll and nothing could be distinguished, as all had been trampled. The funeral was called off, of course, the bier cleared, and the candles put away in trunks, where they would await the next occasion. Let it not come too soon! For several days, as mentioned, we lived in the manor as though under siege, but this time it was not because of the Turks or the Muscovites that we were terrified – it was some strange fear, leafy greenish, smelling of mud and of lichen. A sticky, wordless fear that muddied our thoughts and sent them towards the ferns, towards the bottomless swamp. The insects appeared to be watching us, and we mistook mysterious sounds from the forest for calls and laments. And everyone, the servants and the masters, gathered in the main room to eat a modest supper without appetite, drinking spirits not for rejoicing, but out of worry and fear.

Spring was arriving with ever greater strength from the surrounding forests, pouring into the swamps, which soon turned yellow with flowers on thick stems, water lilies of unusual shapes and colours, and large-leafed floating plants, the names of which I did not know, which felt shameful to me, as a botanist. Young Richivolski did his best to entertain me, but how much entertainment could be devised under such circumstances? We had no books, and the small supply of ink and paper only allowed me to sketch the plants. More and more often, my eyes wandered to that girl, Oshrudeka, who, now without a brother, began to cling to us. She became particularly attached to young Richivolski, following him around, so that I began to suspect that I had misjudged her age. I therefore tried to detect in her some signs of early womanhood, but her body was childish, thin, without any kind of curves. Even though the Haydamoviches gave her a nice outfit and shoes, she circumspectly removed them as soon as she left the house, placing them carefully against the wall. Soon we started teaching Oshrudeka how to talk and write. I drew animals and showed her, hoping she would make some sound at the sight of them. She looked on attentively, but it felt to me that her gaze slid off the surface of the paper without noticing its contents. When she took up a piece of charcoal, she was able to draw a circle with it, but she soon grew bored of this.

I must write a few words here about young Richivolski. His first name was Felix, and the name described him well, for he was a happy man in all situations, always in good humour, filled with good intentions, despite all that befell him. And what had befallen him was that the Muscovites had slaughtered his whole family, disembowelling his father and brutally raping his mother and sisters. How he managed to retain his sanity in the face of this I could not understand, for he never shed a tear or gave in to any melancholy. He had already learned much from me, so that His Majesty's efforts to place him with a good teacher – if it could be considered appropriate to speak of oneself in this way – had surely not been in vain. This man, petite, slight in stature, agile, fair, blue-eyed, would have had a chance at a great career had it not been for the events I shall relate presently. In the meantime, however, young Richivolski, unable to venture further than the yard, made sluggish by the Polish diet, was even more interested than I in the phenomenon of *plica polonica*, which here, at the Haydamoviches', had become synonymous with Oshrudeka.

In the summer, in the July heat, we learned from letters that Warsaw had been taken back from Swedish hands. I thought all would be restored to its previous order, and that I would recover enough that I would be able to rejoin His Royal Majesty and treat his gout once more. For now, another doctor was charged with tending to His Majesty's strained health, which filled me with anxiety. The method of mercurial treatment that I wished to administer to the King remained little known. The art and practice of medicine in Poland were imprecise. Doctors were unaware of the latest discoveries in anatomy and pharmacy, relying on old methods that were nearer to folk medicine than to science. But it would be dishonest of me to conceal my belief that even at the magnificent court of Louis the Great, there were few physicians who were not de facto charlatans, pulling their findings out of thin air and fabricating all of their research.

Unfortunately, my leg was not healing well, and I still couldn't stand on it. I received a visit from that woman – the whisperer, they called her there – who rubbed my flabby muscles with some stinking brown liquid. It was around that time that we received the sad news that the Swedes had captured Warsaw yet again and were plundering it mercilessly. I thought about my lot, then, about the fact that there might have been a reason why I had been forced to recover there in those swamps – that surely God had intended all this for me to hide in safety from violence, war and human madness.

Meanwhile, some two weeks after Saint Christopher's Day, solemnly celebrated there in the swamps – understandable, given that that saint had carried Christ as a child across the water to dry land – we heard for the first time the voice of Oshrudeka. First she spoke to young Richivolski, and when he, astonished, asked her why she had not spoken until then, she replied that no one had asked her a question, which was true, in a sense, since we assumed she could not speak. I really regretted my poor knowledge of Polish, because I would certainly have asked her about all sorts of things, but even Richivolski had trouble understanding her, as she spoke some local Ruthenian dialect . . . She would utter single words or short sentences and look at us, as though testing their power or demanding we give her confirmation. She had a voice that did not suit her – low, masculine; it was above all not the voice of a young girl. When, pointing at the thing, she said 'tree', 'sky', 'water', I felt very strange, because it sounded to me as though her words for those simple elements flowed from somewhere else, maybe somewhere in the underworld.

Summer was in full swing, so the swamps had dried up, but no one was particularly happy about it because they were now passable to all, which meant that the Haydamoviches were exposed to ceaseless attacks by scoundrels and bandits emboldened by the never-ending war – at such a time it was difficult to figure out who was with whom or whose side anyone was on. Once we were attacked by Muscovites; the Haydamoviches had to make a deal with them and pay them off. Another time we repelled an attack by a marauding band of soldiers. Young Richivolski took up a gun and shot several of them, an act perceived as quite heroic.

In every new arrival I hoped for a royal messenger, wishing His Majesty would call me back, but nothing of the sort was to be, as the war was raging on, and the King was bravely following the troops, no doubt forgetting his foreign doctor. I fantasized about setting off without any summons, so what if I couldn't even mount a horse. Buried in such sad thoughts, I watched from my little bench as, day by day, Oshrudeka was surrounded by an ever greater number of the very young servants of the manor, peasant children, and sometimes both the young masters and young ladies of the Haydamovich family, all listening to her talk.

'What could they possibly be talking about? What are they saying?' I asked Richivolski, who first eavesdropped, then openly joined this strange group. He then reported it all to me as he put me to bed and, with his delicate hands, rubbed the stinking ointment from the whisperer into my slowly healing wounds; it had turned out to be quite helpful.

'She says that in the forest, far beyond the marshes, there is a land where the moon shines as brightly as a sun that is somewhat darker than ours.' His fingers gently stroked my skin, then kneaded my thigh in an attempt to make the blood course better. 'In this land, people live in trees and sleep in hollows. During the lunar day, they climb up to the very tops of the trees and expose their naked bodies to the moon, which turns their skin green. Thanks to this light, they do not need to eat much and are satisfied with forest berries, mushrooms, and nuts. And since there is no land to cultivate or houses to build, all work is done for pleasure. There are no rulers or lords there, no peasants or priests. When they are about to embark upon some project, they gather in one tree and confer, then do whatever comes out of that conference. If one of them differs, they give them their space, knowing they'll be back soon enough regardless. When someone takes a liking to someone else, they stay with them a while, and when the feeling wears off, they leave and stay with someone else. This is where children come from. And when a child does appear, everyone is that child's parents, and all are happy to take care of them. Sometimes, when these people climb the highest tree, our world looms in the distance, and they see the smoke of scorched villages and smell the stench of burned bodies. Then they quickly conceal themselves under the leaves, for they do not wish to ruin their eyes with such sights or ruin their noses with such smells. The brightness of our world disgusts and repels them. They consider it a kind of Fata Morgana, for no Tatars or Muscovites have ever reached them. They think we are unreal, that we are a bad dream.'

Once Richivolski asked Oshrudeka if her people believed in God.

'What is God?' she asked him in response.

It seemed strange to everyone, yet it also seemed attractive, a life without any awareness of God's existence – it could be simpler, and we would not have to ask ourselves tormenting questions like, Why does God allow such great suffering in all His creations, though He is good and merciful and almighty?

I once asked how those green people spend their winters. That same evening, Richivolski brought me the answer and, caressing my poor thigh, told me that they do not even notice winter, because as soon as the first cold weather comes, they gather in the largest hollow in the largest tree and there, clinging to one another like so many little mice, they go to sleep. Slowly they are covered by a thick moss, which protects them from the cold, and large mushrooms overgrow the entrance to the hollow, so that they become invisible from the outside. Their dreams are such that they are shared, meaning that when one of them dreams something, someone else will 'see' it in their mind. In this way, they never grow bored. They lose a lot of weight during the winter, so when the first warm spring moon rises, everyone goes out to the tops of the trees and exposes their pale bodies to its rays for lunar days on end, until they have healthily greened again. They also have their own way of communicating with animals, and since they do not eat meat or hunt, the animals befriend and help them. Apparently they even tell them their animal stories, which enables these people to become wiser and to know nature better.

This all sounded like a folktale to me, and I even wondered if Richivolski himself wasn't making these things up, so one day, with the help of a servant, I sneaked in to eavesdrop on Oshrudeka. I was forced to admit that the girl spoke quite fluently and boldly, and everyone listened to her in rapt silence. I couldn't say whether Richivolski had somehow embellished her story. One time I asked that she be asked about death. Richivolski brought back this response:

'They consider themselves to be fruit. Man is a fruit, they say, and the animals will eat him. Therefore, they tie their dead to tree branches and wait until the bodies are eaten by birds and forest animals.'

In mid-August, when the swamps dried out even more and the roads became harder, the long-awaited messenger from the King finally appeared at the Haydamoviches'. He came in a comfortable carriage, with several armed men and letters and gifts for me. There were new garments and fine spirits. I was so moved by this royal generosity that I began to cry. My joy was immense, for in a few days, we were to go back into the world. Limping and hopping, I kissed Richivolski again and again, so sick of this manor house hidden among forests and swamps, this rotting foliage, these flies, spiders, worms, frogs, beetles of all kinds, the omnipresent humidity, the smell of mud, the thick, intoxicating fragrance of greenery. I was so sick of it all. I had just completed my little work on the *plica polonica* and felt that I had successfully exhausted the subject. I had also written about several of the local plants. What else could there be for me there?

But young Richivolski was not as pleased as I was about our impending departure. He acted restlessly, disappearing, and in the evenings he only reported that he was going to the linden tree to engage in some discussions, claiming he was conducting his own research. I should have surmised something then, but I was so dazzled by the prospect of leaving that I could make out nothing else.

The full moon fell on the first day of September, and I had always had some trouble sleeping well during full moons. This moon rose above the forests and the swamps, so huge it was terrifying. It was one of the last nights before our departure. Although I had been packing my herbariums all day and felt tired, I could not sleep and tossed and turned. It seemed to me that somewhere in the house I could hear whispers, the pitter-patter of small feet, shuffling, the warning creak of door hinges. I thought it must have been some sort of hallucination, but in the morning, I found out how wrong I was. All the children and young people had vanished from the manor, including the chamberlain's children, four girls and a boy – in all there were thirty-four of them, all the young people of the settlement; only infants at their mothers' breasts still remained. My sweet young Richivolski, whom I had already been imagining by my side at the French court, had also disappeared.

It was Judgement Day at the Haydamoviches' house. Women's laments rose high into the heavens. It was suggested that this was the work of the Tatars, who, as is known, abscond with children, but this suggestion was quickly thrown out – for it all happened too quietly for that. Then they began to wonder whether some impure force was at work. The men, sharpening whatever they had – scythes, sickles, swords – crossing themselves many times, set out at noon in tight formation to search for the missing. They found no trace. In the evening, in the forest near the manor, the farmhands discovered the body of a child high up in a tree, a finding that elicited horrible screams as everyone recognized the body as that of the Green Boy who had died in the spring, though there wasn't much left of it now, the birds having done their duty.

All youth, all promise had gone from the settlement – the future itself had disappeared. The forest stood like a wall around the Haydamovich family, as if it were the army of the most powerful kingdom on earth and as if its heralds were now announcing their retreat. To where? Into the last, infinite circle of the world, beyond the leafy shadow, beyond the patch of light, into an eternal shade.

I waited for young Richivolski to come back for three more days before finally leaving him a letter: 'If you return, no matter where I am, come find me.' After those three days, we had all understood that the young people of the Haydamovich manor and surrounds would never be found again, that they had crossed over into the lunar world. I cried as the royal carriage started to roll away, not because of my still-painful leg, but because I was so profoundly shaken. There I was, leaving the last circle of the world, its disgusting, damp borderlands, its nowhere-recorded pain, its blurry, uncertain horizons, past which lay only a Great Nothing. And I was heading towards the centre again, where everything made sense at once and formed one coherent whole. And now I have described what I saw in those borderlands, honestly, exactly as it was, without adding anything, and without taking anything out, and my hope is that my reader might help me understand what happened there then, as it remains hard for me to comprehend, for the peripheries of the world mark us for all time with a mysterious powerlessness.

'Zielone dzieci'
Published as part of the collection *Opowiadania bizarne* (Wydawnictwo Literackie, 2018).

JULIA FIEDORCZUK

1975–

Julia Fiedorczuk is a poet, novelist, translator and literary critic, and the recipient of many awards. She is a professor at the Institute of English Studies at the University of Warsaw where she is also one of the founders of the Environmental Studies Centre. An important topic in Fiedorczuk's work is the relationship between human beings and their planetary environment, and both her fiction and poetry address issues of climate change, the loss of biodiversity, anthropocentrism, the upheavals of migration, the notion of borders in all their forms and, in her most recent poems, the return of war to Europe.

Her poetry collection *Psalmy* (*Psalms*) won the prestigious Wisława Szymborska prize in 2018. Fiedorczuk learned Hebrew to study the psalms more closely, and even took singing lessons with a synagogue cantor. Her own beautiful and elegiac poems correlate biblical poetics with modern discourse, singing hauntingly of the lost and excluded: animals, landscapes, people and ecosystems.

Fiedorczuk has a strong interest in scientific disciplines and in how the imagination responds to our developing environmental situation. She aims to place the human being within the landscape as an integral part of it, rather than as an external observer of nature. Her fiction is often set in the primeval Białowieża Forest in eastern Poland where she was raised and where she takes students as part of the innovative ecopoetics programme that she teaches.

'Like much of my writing, "Moss" is an attempt to write human time into more-than-human time (planetary, cosmic, whatever you want to call it),' says Fiedorczuk. 'It is about wisdom and the passing on of wisdom, which happens outside any formal "teaching" – indeed, outside words and formulas. It is about the fact that wisdom is a quality of one's entire being, not just some intellectual content. It is about a happy old woman who dies a happy death. And a little girl who receives a treasure. It is, as always, about "the Way" (in the sense of "tao").'

Anna Zaranko

Moss

Translated by Anna Zaranko

But I'm still a child, then, who doesn't know how to read yet.

I'm five, maybe six years old, in a purple flannel dress with little green roses. That child's thin legs are sticking out from under the dress. Scratched and bruised like seventy sorrows. I'm sitting on a high stool in front of a mirror, legs dangling in mid-air. She's standing behind me. Brushing my hair. I have long hair, the colour of ripe corn. Fine hair; it won't survive adolescence: it'll have to be cut when I hit fifteen.

It doesn't hurt. It hurts when my mother does it, but not when she does. She touches me delicately, like an angel, like a good witch. I see her veiny hands in the mirror. I see how they tremble. I say 'veiny' now, because now, that is four decades later, I think in words; but at the time, as a child, I thought in images. 'Granny,' I say, 'your hands look like spiders.' Granny smiles at me and so do all her wrinkles. I watch the spiders dance in the mirror: one is holding the comb, the other divides my hair into strands and presses them against my scalp, so as not to tug. Then the first one puts the comb down on the dresser and both together they plait my hair into two thin braids on my head.

The flannel dress has gone. I don't know what happened to it, but I imagine it went the way of all flannel clothes: cut up for cloths – first to dry the dishes, then to wipe the dust, till finally they end up washing the floor. I imagine the material gradually darkening along the descent through these various incarnations until it ends up a uniform brown. The little roses vanished, absorbed into their clothy background. By the time the rag landed in the garbage it barely differed from earth. And later, it became earth.

The trembling hands – the spiders – tie my braids with two green ribbons.

We wore big bows in those days with ribbons bought by the metre at the haberdashery shop. While the shop assistant was wrapping them in grey paper and Granny was paying, you could look at the pins with different-coloured heads because in her world, that is my world, there was no pink plastic yet. Anything that wasn't white, or grey, or brown was a thrill. I look at the spools, balls and skeins of coloured threads, the silks and yarns, and I imagine another world, woven or knitted entirely in these colours. There'd be more reds, more blues. And yellow. I think of a saturated yellow verging on orange, like the yolk of an egg or – sometimes – the sun, just before sunset. It would be a light world, a not completely serious world. Lacy. A bit transparent. Knitted by ten spidery legs for that girl I am then, the one who will hatch me.

Granny has pink hair. She pins it up in a little bun like a sparrow's nest or, if she's put in rollers the night before, she leaves it down. She has thin grey eyebrows. Since Christmas, she's been outlining them with a black pencil. Sometimes I ask her: 'Granny, let me colour in your eyebrows.' Then she leans over so that I can reach her face and I concentrate so hard, my forehead is all furrowed. These were my first initiations.

From time to time we go to feed a dog. The dog belongs to someone else, but those people are often away. The dog's chained up or runs about the neglected yard, overgrown with nettles, surrounding a wooden house with pelargoniums and little pictures of the Mother of God set in low windows that look out onto the street. He climbs out easily through the holes in the fence and greets Granny joyfully. He jumps about, squeals, fawns and whimpers. The people in that house don't like us visiting the dog. They get really mad if they catch us at it. Then we pretend that we don't understand what the problem is and we're just walking by without a care.

The dog is big and lean and black and greying like Granny's eyebrows. I think he's called Son-of-a-bitch, because when the people from the house call him, they shout: 'Get back here, Son-of-a-bitch.' The dog doesn't want to go back, but he does as he's told – he's more attached to his owners than to us. So he goes, glancing at Granny apologetically. He knows that Granny will understand. She understands everything. Granny puts the sausage back inside the violet bag embroidered with beads; we turn back like we haven't a care, or go down to the river.

The river is wide and grey. I dream about the other side. On the other side there are villages whose names mean almost nothing to me; they have only some vague dream-like associations. I imagine another world. Haberdasheries, ice-cream parlours, the homes of people I don't know, whom I'll probably never meet, and who have no idea – how is that possible? – that I even exist. Girls I'll never play with and never quarrel with. The pink ribbons in their hair, more beautiful than mine. I envy them those ribbons, if I end up imagining them too clearly. I imagine the girls' parents too: farmers, fishermen, milkmen. They seem wonderful professions to me, not like the boring office work my parents do. I tell myself that when I grow up, I'll be a fisherman. I won't sit my life away in libraries or tap at the keys of a typewriter. I'll sail out to the middle of the grey river before dawn and wait in the silence for the sun and the birds. I imagine how, for those girls with the pink ribbons, the town where my parents live, where I live, is just as exotic as the other side is for me.

But in the winter, when the river freezes, that other side becomes less inaccessible. Sometimes, the ice is so thick, you can cross to the other bank, wading through snow up to your calves. The fishermen hack blowholes in the ice and light fires, maybe to make it melt more readily, or maybe just to warm their hands.

Then the dog died. I don't remember when, but it must have been before I cut my hair. I don't know if it happened out in the yard beside the little wooden house, or if he went off somewhere to die alone, as animals do. It doesn't matter, because he's just earth now.

I'm five, maybe six, and Granny is teaching me to use the telephone. I know most of my letters, and I'm slowly learning numbers. I count. First there's the delight of counting up to ten, then somehow, before you know it, up to a hundred. Like all children, I love the astonishment of adults, their praise and applause. It incubates a vanity which grows. It will come in useful, but in the end, it has to be overcome; that is, I shall have to overcome the vanity, the applause, my own self, and measure up to life – measure up to death. Granny shows me how to dial the number of my house in town – the place I live when I go to pre-school and where my parents live. This amuses me. I wait for the praise. I stick my finger into the round space with the right number and I turn the dial. Then the next one. The number has five figures. I have to concentrate and apply some force because my fingers are still very small. We practise lots of times and finally I manage to do it by myself. 'Hello?' my mother's voice answers in the receiver. They both applaud, Granny and my mother.

There are lots of records and books in Granny's house. The records were left by her second husband, who wasn't my grandfather, because my grandfather died in the forest at the beginning of the war. No need to explain which one. When I'm a child, there is only one war. Apart from the records, Granny has lots of different knick-knacks and bits and bobs; so many that there's always new treasure to find. There's a plaster figure, half standing, half lying on the chest of drawers – it's an angel with a broken hand and a wire protruding from the stump; Granny hauled it back from an old church. By the wall there's an openwork wooden music stand and part of a piano found in some barn. 'Mice were nesting in it,' says Granny. At the bottom of the wardrobe, under the coats, I find a piece of pale-coloured stone with strange letters that make you think of bird tracks. And little pictures – I recognize a candelabra, a bit of a hand. When I ask about the stones, Granny explains that they're old headstones for which there was no room left at the cemetery. For a while, I'm convinced that this is simply what you do – that old headstones for which a place can't be found at the cemetery for whatever reason are kept in the wardrobe under coats. Granny gathers these stones on the overgrown hillside by the river, in the tall grass under the junipers. Like mushrooms.

Granny is queen of her house; me – I'm a page. The queen's page is a butterfly. So, I'm a butterfly. And Granny is the house. Granny fills the house with the smell of paint – she paints pictures, which seems to me then the most natural thing in the world. The other smell comes from herbs: basil, thyme, sage, parsley. I'm not keen on herbs, but Granny says that each of these leaves has some information meant for the parts that make up my body, for me. So I learn to eat scrambled eggs with sage, sandwiches garnished with parsley, tomatoes with basil. In this way, the mysterious force that makes things grow, seek the sun and produce fruit, is on our side.

In the mornings, I jump into Granny's bed. She sleeps well and long and soundly. She goes to bed late. I hear the shuffle of her slippers across the kitchen floor as I doze off. She keeps watch as I sleep. Those fathomless dark hours, when I'm no longer among those keeping watch, all belong to her. I envy her that time, or maybe I envy the time having her – the granny I don't know and never shall. I know that before I fall asleep and before I cease knowing anything, she'll light a cigarette and begin mixing paints by the light of the lamp in the kitchen. And then, on boards or bits of plywood, she'll paint grass, trees, flowers. Much later, I realize that she rarely painted anything but plants.

'Look,' she says sometimes, 'this leaf looks like a hand, and the veins like rivers. Life flows like rivers.'

'Where to?' I ask. 'Where is it flowing?'

'To the sea,' she says without hesitation. 'Everything came from the sea and everything returns to it, but sometimes in a roundabout way. Sometimes very slowly. Sometimes quickly.'

But I still hadn't seen the sea then.

So, I jump into her bed, and she is still sleeping. I tug her pinkish hair, she doesn't react. I tickle her under the chin, she smiles. She starts to snore very loudly, pretending. Finally, she says: 'Fetch yourself a book, Granny needs three more minutes.' But I've got a book already, because this is our usual ritual. I look at the pictures, I touch the letters and words; at first they're mostly opaque and strange, but with time, with the flow of weeks and months, they become more and more readable. At last, Granny gets up, she yawns, stretches, complains about her aching back. For an instant, I see that she's fragile, but it's barely a moment: she's quickly queen again. And me – who will I be today?

Just after the war, Granny lost a child. Luckily not my mother, or I wouldn't be here, unless someone else had me, but then I wouldn't be me. My mother told me about the child who died; Granny never mentions it. It was a long long time ago. Granny's dead child is just earth now.

Sometimes, rarely, at special moments, Granny takes me to the forest. The forest begins just beyond the meadow and goes on for miles. I'm convinced then that it goes on forever. I imagine what a misfortune it would be to get lost in that forest and wander about between the thick resinous stumps, under the needle-leaved crowns which deprive the sun of its power and extinguish the moon. I wonder what it would be like to spend the night in a forest like that. I want to and I don't want to. Want to and don't want to.

Granny teaches me the word: 'sanctuary'. It's a place in the middle of the forest where animals live. A wild place which is needed to maintain life on earth. Including the life of the imagination. And then she shows me some twisted roots.

'Look,' she says. 'They look like my fingers.'

She spreads out her spider-hands and smiles.

'This tree is old,' she says. 'As old as your grandmother.' She laughs. 'When it dies, it will turn into moss. It will be so tired it will fall asleep for a thousand years. A thousand thousand.'

'A thousand thousand thousand,' I add.

Soon, we really do find a fallen tree. It's sleeping on the moss, leafless, with its bark come away. Its tangled roots stick up.

'There's someone living in those roots,' says Granny.

'I don't believe you,' I answer, slipping easily into my role.

'You'll see.'

Granny takes a penknife out of her pocket, cuts off a piece of dead root, and starts to whittle. I get it. I'm not sure if it's a trick or not. A few minutes later, I hold a roughly carved dwarf in my hand. He's got a head, a pointed hat and a bit of a trunk. He still has.

Only one photograph of my granny has survived. I don't like it. She's badly dressed, looks old and her smile looks fake, made awkward in the role of model.

During one of our trips to the forest she tells me about the war – only once. She talks about the people who were driven through the village, thin and bloodied. About how she looked at them through the gaps in the wooden fence, after she'd shut her children in the house. Then she'd take milk and bread out to the forest. But so that the village headman didn't find out because if he had, they would all have been done for – the ones in the forest and she and her children too. I find it hard to understand. Granny says – and it's the only time she says such a thing – that I'll understand later. In the end, someone took the people away; she never found out where.

'Did you look for them?' I ask her.

'Yes. I look for them in every forest.'

And then we discover fairy rings; toadstools growing around a big pine stump in a near perfect circle, as though someone had planted them specially. Granny explains that they're growing out of the mycelium, under the ground. The mycelium is one great big branching body from which individual pericarps grow.

One morning I jump into her bed. I look at her for a moment: when she's sleeping, her wrinkles almost completely smooth out. Then I tug her pink hair – nothing. I tickle her under the chin – nothing.

'Granny!' I call.

Nothing. She doesn't smile. she doesn't snore.

For a moment it's as though I'm paralysed. I can't move; it's like I've frozen solid. Then, slowly, I walk to the telephone. Very carefully, I dial the number of my house in town. My hands are shaking. I hear the tone, three, five, seven long notes. Eventually:

'Hello?'

My mother is hoarse, sleepy, I've woken her up.

'Granny's fallen asleep,' I say, straight to the point. 'Get some moss.'

'Mech'
Published as part of the collection *Bliskie kraje* (Wydawnictwo Marginesy, 2016).

DOROTA MASŁOWSKA
1983–

Dorota Masłowska has been dubbed the wild child of Polish literature. At the tender age of nineteen she caused a literary sensation with her first, revolutionary novel, *Snow White and Russian Red* (2002). Set on a housing estate, its low-life characters take drugs and misbehave, but in ingeniously inventive Polish; Masłowska's secret weapon is her way of making the language her own, using the conventions of hip-hop and rap, as well as a parody of street talk. Her novels are cynical, about the disappointments of life in the modern materialistic world where success is always out of reach.

Her second novel, *Paw królowej* (literally *The Queen's Peacock*, 2005) won Poland's biggest literary award, the Nike, and is written in a rap style that defies translation without substantial rewriting. She is also a successful playwright and singer-songwriter.

Believing that she had a place in this anthology, I wrote to Dorota to ask if she had any short stories to offer me. She said no, but then, as she relates:

'I wrote "The Isles" while on a scholarship in Switzerland; my rooms were within a monastery, a short way outside a boring little town, so I'd had no one to talk to for days on end. As a result, I had a build-up of energy that normally I'd be wasting on meetings and conversation, but now the silence and lack of interaction was causing an unnatural logjam, and I felt an urgent need to write. I should add that as a professional writer it's unusual for me to feel like that. So I sat down, and remembering that you had asked me for a story, though I've never written any, under pressure I started to spit out sentences that began to form images, which in turn spawned further images. Then I took the train to Zurich, and when I saw the great sliver of the moon multiplying in the passing lakes, I realized it was full; its magnetism made my brain tip up and spill its load like a crashed lorry.'

Later on, the story 'The Isles' developed into a novel, *Magiczna rana* (*The Magic Wound*).

Antonia Lloyd-Jones

The Isles

Translated by Antonia Lloyd-Jones

It's not really my name but a sort of nickname my mum's friend gave me, then it caught on. Eventually she started calling me that herself, and she's probably forgotten by now that my name is Kamil, just like her brother who's not alive any more – Gran always leaves the room whenever he's mentioned. That's why everyone avoids saying my name if they can, and that must be why the family has taken to calling me Junior, because as soon as Mum says: 'Kam . . .' she sees Gran, and instantly says: 'Come here and I'll give you five zlotys, all right?'

'Really?' I gladly reply. And although she's only got three zlotys seventy, a lucky carp scale and a 50-pence piece in her purse, the cash comes my way, but Gran has left the room anyway, and there's silence, though everyone knows she's secretly crying in the bathroom so nobody will notice. And so Mum and no one will shout at her.

'All right then,' says Mum's other brother, who's alive, extracting from under his bum a packet of Marlboros that's fallen out of his pocket, 'How's things, how's it going at school, Junior?'

But before I have a chance to reply . . .

'He doesn't go to school,' says Mum automatically.

'What do you mean?'

'He has one-to-one teaching for special needs.'

'What, he sits there all on his own?'

'No, he's got mates,' says Mum.

'No, I don't!' I say.

'There's that girl.'

'What girl?'

'Niki.'

But before I have a chance to say what I think about that, Gran's back from the bathroom, all red and smiling, and with a stuffed-up nose she'll say something like this to Mum's other brother: 'Are you smoking again?' and to me: 'Come here, Bubba, come to Granny,' as if she's counting on this spell to change me back into a baby, she'll finally manage to turn back time, and everything will be the same as in the past. But it doesn't work, and everything's the same as it is now; it shows on my face, though at this point I'll feel sorry for Gran, who's so old and grown-up but so childish; I can smell her powder, scent, lipstick and despair, by now I'm drowning in her rising and falling bosom and it's like I'm in a warm, living swamp. She's probably not so old at all, she goes everywhere as normal, to the hypermarket and the shopping mall like everyone else, and to Nordic walking, yet she often says things like: 'Oooh, my legs aren't what they used to be, times have changed,' or 'Look at this for me, you've got strong young eyes', and she shows me her battered smartphone while bringing her gold-rimmed specs closer, then moving them further away, though they're covered in greasy grime anyway.

Then Mum chops up the food with her fork on our plates, separating the pancake from what's inside it for me and for herself. It's some sort of tomatoey gloop, and the whole thing looks like the remains left by gladiators that have been dragged around the Colosseum by vultures, so the only hope left is that there'll be something sweet for dessert.

'No sweets,' says Mum.

'Why are you hacking up your food like that?' asks Gran. 'There's no meat in there.'

'I've told you one-thousand-five-hundred times we can't eat this stuff.'

'Why not?'

Mum leaves the room, clanging the cutlery, before her eyebrows fly off her face to a place where people aren't so dumb. At that, Gran picks up her glass of wine, stares at it a while doubtfully, and instead of getting sidetracked, drinks the lot and puts it down empty. Then she gets up and pushes me towards this, like, woman in a wheelchair, who's been sitting next to us the whole time.

'Auntie! Say hello, Auntie, this is Wika's son.'

'Who?'

'Wiktoria's son, you know him!'

'The one that's not normal?' shouts the auntie out of the blue, briefly surfacing from herself. But after this effort her bald bonce sinks back between her shoulders, as if that were the peak of her potential and now she must instantly sleep off this sudden spurt.

'Do you want some cake, Auntie?' Mum bellows in her ear, making lots of noise with the plates, as if auntie's remark could be drowned out in reverse.

'Lay off Junior, eh?' says my uncle. 'These days it's in to be one fag short of the pack, ain't it, Junior? The main thing is he's not saying he's a girl. Eh? My mate's son buggers around in a dress. And makes them call him Leto.'

'Let him bugger around if he wants to.'

'He's round the twist, to put it mildly.'

But that was yesterday. And today is a completely different day, today's today.

'Hey, Junior, pass the Rizlas,' says that friend of Mum, who's just arrived. 'The short ones, not the long ones.'

He makes two roll-ups, keeping one lovingly stuck to his tongue while dexterously rolling the second, winking at me, but Mum comes into the kitchen and in a single fluid movement takes the finished one out of his mouth.

'Do you want your lunch now?' she asks me, leaning against the kitchen island, though we've only just had breakfast. She raises an eyebrow at her friend – it's like the time I put Buzz Lightyear in my pocket at the hypermarket, and she raised an eyebrow, and just using her eyebrows she took my hand, removed Buzz from my pocket and put him back on the shelf; so now, invisibly, with nothing but her eyebrows, she takes her friend's hands, makes them put everything away in a tin, screw it shut and put it and the lighter down on the kitchen top next to a cookery book.

'Siano's playing a concert today, at the Coconut club. I can get us onto the list,' he says.

'Did you hear me? Do you want lunch?' she asks me.

'I don't want any,' I say, and in my head I hear: 'The word is thank you.'

'The right word is thank you,' says Mum, like a jammed being-Mum machine to me, the being-her-kid machine, and for the one-thousand-two-hundred-and-seventh time she puts on the kettle for tea that never gets made because she no longer has the strength or the desire for it. It's one of those days when she woke up feeling great, but somewhere around breakfast, as she was getting the ketchup and the mayonnaise out of the fridge, she felt as if it were all a big mistake, as if she were sliding into an endless swamp, and by the time she was slicing the bread she was lying among the waterweeds at the bottom of it. But soon after, her friend pressed the entryphone; for this event she has briefly crawled to the surface, and even rapidly used some air freshener as he was coming up the stairs. He's brought us a four-pack of beer as a gift, and without looking Mum puts it in the fridge.

'Do you want to go for a sleep-over at Niki's today?' she asks.

That must be addressed to me, because how could he know Niki? Frankly, Niki's only plus is that she's got a PlayStation, but last time, when I trod on some poo in their garden, her parents wouldn't let me come in the house but told me to stay outside, off the terrace, until it cleaned itself off somehow, while everyone else was tucking into the best ramen. Unfortunately it was raining and I got sinus trouble. Mum was super angry about it and said no way, I'd never go there again, 'cause someone must have got something pretty wrong there.

Meanwhile the friend puts one hand on his hair, as if he's about to shake off his dandruff, and hooks the other one where Mum's jeans begin, where she's got a tattoo of a fly, where the skin looks like live glass, with little blue and green veins emanating from it like the rays from the wound of the Jesus in the picture Gran keeps in her *Crosswords* mag. She says those rays are the love of our Lord, our man Jesus, but I don't know what sort of a man that is – I don't want no bloke to love me; Mum's come out of it badly so many times before. Gran says Mum's only got herself to blame, because the ones she finds ain't got no money, no job or nothing, and she shouldn't fool herself with this new one either, because he won't be any better than the rest.

'This new Jesus?'

Then Gran gets cross. Jesus isn't about that sort of love – he was done in on the cross because of our sins, and now he and that mother of his called Mary, if you ask them really nicely, come and help people, and they might help me too, if Mum agreed to it. But Mum categorically disagrees, shouting: 'Are you off your rocker?'

'Maybe I am,' says Gran proudly. Because apparently Gran's friend's daughter was helped a lot by exorcisms. When she had bad migraines.

So Jesus won't help me, and no one will help me, they'll just send me to Niki's so's I'm not here, and then they'll be late picking me up, and her mum'll call five times in a rage.

'No, I don't want to,' I say, remembering Niki's charming family and their garden mined with dog shit next to the trampoline. Luckily, when Mum calls, Niki's parents say I can't come anyway, because they're taking her to the Aquapark today. And when Mum tells them I adore the Aquapark and I'd love to go there with them too, they say sorry, but Bruno's coming, so's Latrina, Lavina and Bogina, and their entire car is full.

'Can't you take your van?' asks Mum helplessly, looking around for her friend, who's fiddling with his phone, while chewing his cuticles until they bleed and not looking at her, but they say their van is having its AC cleaned right now.

'Ah, OK,' says Mum, pretending that's fine for her, but hearing this, the friend leaps up from the couch as if he's just remembered something of vital importance, though seconds later he makes a face as if he's forgotten what it was. He goes up to the kitchen island, takes the tin from the table top, reads the label, the contents and weight of the crap that was once in it, then juggles with his lighter, which isn't that clever a trick, seeing he's only got one.

'*Life to the Full, Gluten-Free?*' he asks, picking up the cookery book. Mum takes it out of his hands and puts it back where it was.

There's something written on his arm like 'reality – isn't – reality' or a similar sort of message; I told Dad when I went to see him last month and he said it's probably secret code for 'I smoke lots of dope and that's why I've got shit for brains, you muddafukkas', but Mum says he was just joking because none of that is true.

She does know how to cook, all I can say is that the things she cooks aren't always very good, so sometimes she makes something, then just shoves it in the fridge and we order a *tricolore* pizza, then the gluten trashes our body cells, destroys our stomachs, thyroid glands and brains, though I'm told that even so it's paradise compared with how bad and unhealthy the food is in the British Isles.

'Maybe that's what Uncle Kamil died of.'

'Not because of that,' says Mum.

'So what did he die of?'

'Not because the food was bad.'

'Then what of?'

'Because he had some problems.'

'Like what?'

'Various.'

As she said this, Mum's eyes became absent. As if somewhere deep inside she could see those problems, and in the background those Isles, distant and dreadful, hurricane-tossed, full of rats drowning with a squeal, thorny black palm trees torn out by the roots and wet, broken parasols; innumerable and hostile. At once she realized that I was looking over there too, and she quickly destroyed the image so I wouldn't see it. But she seems to go on seeing it somewhere inside, because when they called from the consulate to say they'd fished out the body and someone from the family had to fly there to identify it, apparently Gran went doolally and ran around the flat as if trying to catch a ball as a thousand angry drunken-red Brits threw it to each other over her head. There was no talking to her, they had to call an ambulance, and finally Mum had to fly to the Isles on her own, because her other brother, the one who's alive, couldn't get time off work.

And I had to stay behind and sit with Baldy, watching episode after episode of *The Piasts*, where just about nothing ever happened, except those Piasts all dressed up in crowns and robes and things stood in a chamber blathering on at each other. Meanwhile Gran got some very good pills and wasn't bothered about anything after that.

I go to the bog and try to crap, but the dry shit gets stuck in my arsehole; I have to sit there a long time waiting for it to loosen up, and meanwhile there's an awkward silence in the lounge. When I go in there Mum and her friend are sitting side by side on the couch in a cloud of smoke, choking; Mum has a red mark on her neck and a look on her face as if she were sailing on a toilet seat lid to nowhere, but all right, if no one else applies, she'll take the guy on the voyage with her.

'You can keep playing until five, then have a break,' she says to me aimlessly with her eyes half-shut, as if in a hurry to prove she's still herself. Meaning Mum.

'Who touched my phone?'

'No one.'

'It's not how it was. Not like this, but like that.'

'Kam . . . Kamil, calm down. We don't shout,' says Mum.

'So the point is, the latest research has shown that the disturbances he has might be to do with not absorbing gluten, see?' I overhear her say in a hushed tone. The entry phone buzzes. Panic.

Mum shouts from the hall that she hasn't got a tip for the guy who's brought the pizza because she happens to have given me all her change yesterday, and at most she can give him a fifty-pence piece or a carp scale, unless . . .

'Got any cash?' she suddenly asks.

'Who?' asks her friend, coughing.

I definitely ain't got any.

'Kamil, slow down! You're about to fuck up your T-shirt,' she shouts at me. 'He's more nervous after he's had gluten and he starts behaving like that,' she tells her friend. 'He might not have to take all those pills if he doesn't eat it.'

'I guess it's too late for this.'

'Where'd you get a hundred-dollar bill? Go on, tell me, seriously.'

'Seriously? I found it.'

Meanwhile a dollop of hot cheese lands under my shirt, at first scalding, but then exuding a nice greasy warmth.

'Those are strong drugs,' says Mum. 'I don't want him to take them. They give him weird ideas.'

'I get weird ideas too,' mumbles the friend, as if he had something in his mouth, and from the corner of my eye I can see it's her ear. Smoke rises from the pizza boxes. He pins her bodily to the kitchen island, she's a bit sulky, but finally she stretches out her arms and wraps her entire self around him, like around a pillar or a stake. It's like they're drowning, but at the last moment they've clambered onto each other, you can't tell who's on top of who, and somehow they're trying to ride out the storm on each other. The friend has got a tight grip on Mum's breasts and she's holding on with her mouth latched onto his neck, while the waves toss them up and down.

I'm off. I don't know where. I'm on my way somewhere. I think I'm on my way to my favourite room, meaning the bog, I shut the door firmly behind me and I turn the lock.

It stinks a bit inside, but there are walls, and I can't hear all that slurping and moaning. I sit there a pretty long time.

'Kamil?' I finally hear Mum's worried voice in the distance. I can hear her knocking, then pressing the door handle, but I can't open it because I'm occupied.

I put a foot into the toilet bowl.

'Kamil!' she shrieks, banging her fist on the door.

But now I'm putting the other foot in. The water in the bog spins and whirls.

'Calm down,' says the friend, and I can hear him start to show off, fiddling with the lock. 'Get me a knife.'

Success. I wait until they manage to open the door, and then at the last moment I press the flush and let down the lid with a bang after myself. Mum runs up, but it's too late, the flying water is already pushing me through, dragging me down the pipe. A roaring roar is the only sign by now that I was ever me. While they run around the entire toilet, despairing, that's to say mainly Mum does, the friend less so, because he's so wasted he's seen some nice moving patterns on the tiles. Meanwhile I'm travelling down the pipes through the entire block faster than on the slides at the Aquapark, because Niki's sister isn't there who's a pain, or her mumsy who's stuck her spongy bum in the pipe with a kiddy on her lap, and has her legs against the sides for safety, creating a logjam, so everyone who falls on top of her shouts fuck off, you fat pig, you're in the way, and she kicks them with her heels and calls them fucking country bumpkins living off the social.

Like this I reach the sea and beyond. The crossing takes quite a long time, but gradually the murky water gets clearer and clearer, and at last I surface over there, on the other side. There are palm trees everywhere, but they're snapped, they look as if they've had a mighty kick in the belly. I can hear seagulls crying and ships wailing. The hurricane seems to be over and the weather's bright. Just then someone nudges me.

'Uncle Kamil!' I cry with all my might, very joyfully.

My uncle is pleased too. He looks almost exactly like in the photo in Mum's purse: South Park T-shirt, tattoos, hair styled with gel, pits left by acne, except that on one eye he's got a strange bump, and his whole nose looks as if it's on just one side of his face, and not the other.

Uncle is a bit grey, all damp and waterlogged; no wonder, seeing as he arrived on the Isles some time ago; there are various bits of crap on his clothes, waste matter and seaweed. But he doesn't look at all bad. I don't understand why Mum threw up when she saw him at the morgue, and didn't get out of bed for a whole week after she got back from the Isles.

I don't think Uncle Kamil knows anything about it, and he's so pleased someone from the family has finally come to visit him here that he's pretty much jumping up and down for joy. And by staring and moaning he tells me to pull off the masking tape stuck to his mouth – he can't because his hands and feet are bound.

'*Wyspy*'
The opening story from *Magiczna rana* (Karakter, 2024).

COUPLES

POLA GOJAWICZYŃSKA
1896–1963

Gojawiczyńska came from an artisan background and was self-taught, working initially in kindergartens and libraries. She made her debut in 1915 with the novella *Dwa fragmenty* (*Two Fragments*). Her literary career, however, only flourished from the early 1930s onwards, when her more established colleague, novelist Zofia Nałkowska (1884–1954), arranged a stipend so that she could devote herself to writing. Gojawiczyńska lived most of her life in Warsaw except for the period 1931–2 which she spent in industrial Silesia, the setting of her first collection of stories *Powszechni dzień* (*The Working Day*, 1933) and novel *Ziemia Elżbiety* (*Elżbieta's Land*, 1934).

Her novels and short stories portray the daily struggles but also inner lives and aspirations of impoverished working-class people living mostly in cities, especially women. In 1933 Helena Boguszewska and Jerzy Kornacki founded the group of left-wing prose and reportage writers known as 'Przedmieście' ('Outskirts'), which also included Nałkowska and was dedicated to portraying workers' neighbourhoods; Gojawiczyńska was not a member but was close to its ideology and principles.

Her protagonists are invariably burdened by unsurmountable barriers related to class, poverty and unemployment as well as to biology and sexual discrimination; her conclusions are often pessimistic. Her most popular novel is *Dziewczęta z Nowolipek* (*The Girls from Nowolipki Street*, 1935) which portrays an interconnected group of Catholic and Jewish young women from the eponymous street in Warsaw on the eve of the First World War as they strive for fulfilment and happiness. It was twice made into a film (1937 and 1985). After being imprisoned during the German Occupation in the women's section of the notorious Pawiak Prison, she wrote *Krata* (*Grille*, 1945), a combination of reportage and memoir.

The story 'W raju' ('In Paradise') is from the collection *Dwoje ludzi* (*Two People*, 1938), portraits of lonely individuals living in small towns, workers' settlements or the countryside that explore difficult relationships from alternately male and female perspectives. Despite the misunderstandings and material hardships, a ray of hope shines through.

Ursula Phillips

In Paradise

Translated by Ursula Phillips

They wanted at long last to have a wash and had to hurry, because before eight they were opening their kiosk on the corner of Plażowa Street. Mr Peterek had set them up without any guarantee, as a better deal had just arisen for him: a small shop in a booth in the port city. It was a feverish time, the height of the season, boat trip after boat trip was calling in at the port, so Mr Peterek did not take long to make up his mind. He was a businessman. 'Here's the goods, so get cracking. Once I've seen to the other one, I'll drive over and we'll come to some arrangement.' Needless to say, with this speech, the heavens shone on them, since their bones were already aching from hours spent sitting on roadside benches by the main street leading to the harbour. Pangs of hunger often made themselves felt. Szymon had begun running to the harbour and railway station to hire himself out as a courier while Śliwka roamed from cottage to cottage offering her services to summer holiday-makers. Then they would come together on a bench at the corner of Plażowa Street. Competition was fierce at both the station and the harbour, while Śliwka's crushed appearance failed to inspire confidence. The fishwives simply chased her away.

Yet all of a sudden – one word from Mr Peterek and they'd begun trading.

There were also other reasons for taking a bath so early. When you've been out of work for a long time, you lack everything. Szymon, who in his role as salesman was often on the beach before noon, felt the whole impropriety of his appearing with Śliwka among the beach robes, bathing costumes, swimming caps, sunshades and so on. Their shirts were in a lamentable state, not to mention anything else. They could venture here only on the sly, shamefacedly, so as not to offend people's eyes. They still had an innate sense of decency: weren't they human beings after all?

On the previous day, in the evening, Szymon had bought soap from the neighbouring stall for thirty groszy, fragrant pink soap. He presented the soap to Śliwka. It was not just a question of cooling the body, but of scrubbing it clean. They'd already been cooped up for a fourth day in the kiosk on Plażowa Street, where passing cars raised clouds of dust, and the sweltering heat extracted the last drop of sweat. Excited, therefore, they made certain preparations: Szymon bought soap, while Śliwka hastily cut the legs off some old drawers, producing something akin to a pair of men's bathing trunks. She laid it next to Szymon's pallet in the cubicle where they slept behind the kiosk. Her outfit was to consist of a towel which she would wrap around her hips.

Szymon awoke in the night and said: 'I wonder if other people will be there too? Because if they are, nothing will come of this bath.' Śliwka, who was planning, when they returned, to make potato soup on their makeshift cooker with plenty of root vegetables, muttered scornfully: 'Well, so what? We'll go in a little farther.' Szymon burst out laughing. 'What, so we can drown? Farther out it's not fenced in! So deep it's terrifying!' Śliwka, cross that the great strapping fellow did nothing but caw and caw, turned onto her other side and pretended to be asleep.

They really did set off as soon as it was dawn. At such a time the beach was empty. Not a soul in sight. Dense forest separated it from the village, summer camp and the whole human disarray. Their spirits rose at once and Szymon shouted: 'Come on, let's go!' Sunlight was already basking on the yellow sand and they immediately felt hot. Szymon pulled off his clothes. They'd imagined themselves dark with filth; whereas pale bare flesh appeared, deathly white compared to their suntanned faces and hands. Scraggy ribs appeared; it was possible to count them. Szymon's shoulder blades were crooked and protruded like wings. Such posture stemmed from the days when he was 'every inch a gentleman', when he sat at school and then in some hole at a post office before they sacked him because he did not have the required 'education'. With Śliwka it was better, because she'd had dark skin since birth, which was why she was called Plum.

Szymon, as befitted the man, was first to take the plunge. He stopped at a spot where the waves rushed in fast and withdrew, leaving darker traces.

Their white fringes, foaming and noisy, unexpectedly touched Szymon's feet. Szymon yelped and jumped.

'Water's deuced cold at night!'

He retreated further. Looked not at the vast expanse of sea, but only at the shore, at the nearest waves, which drew themselves up high so as to collapse and splash gently onto the sand. Śliwka was struggling with the towel and cried: 'How long are you going to stand there like that?' Szymon, in fearful panic lest she push him into the water, withdrew. She glanced at him as he stood hunched and trembling in his cut-off drawers, and snorted laughingly. They felt somewhat ashamed and sad. With arms crossed over her breasts, clad in the towel fastened by safety pins, Śliwka moved ahead.

'Listen, here's a rope.'

The rope was swaying, low down, tossed on the surface of the waves, supported by short stakes almost hidden beneath the water. In order to reach it, Śliwka had to bend forward. At that moment, she was covered by an oncoming wave. Szymon shrieked: 'Careful!' but she was already clinging to the rope for dear life, unable to utter a cry of terror as she felt the sand slip away from under her feet. Before her, she saw a side stake and dreamed of reaching it, because the slender rope didn't seem sufficient support in that roar, onrush and inevitable return of the waves. She caught a glimpse of one such wave: huge, like a wall of glass, as it moved right on top of her. She leapt up and grabbed the stake with fingers spread. Her flesh stung from the freezing water. She was wet from top to toe, even her hair was wet. She had conquered her fear: 'Are you coming or not?' she yelled.

Szymon pretended that he was quite happy on the sand and wasn't thinking of budging at that moment. 'I'm coming, I'm coming, there's no hurry!' he muttered reassuringly. Śliwka, holding on to the rope, was jumping up and down to keep warm, already accustomed to the water. Then, as she stood calmly in the crystal-clear water, she inspected the even surface of the sand around her and the dark fish flitting swiftly about her legs. Szymon was jealous that she'd conquered her fear; he got up and approached the edge.

'Listen, is it still so cold, eh?'

She was standing facing the sea and did not respond immediately. She was gazing at the coloured bands of water, farther and farther, farther and farther away; there was no end to them in sight, as one's eyes passed over that blue, green and silver path, shifting on its surface and white with foam, meeting in the far distance the azure of the sky. Śliwka turned around and asked absentmindedly: 'Well, what?' Her straight dark hair, wet through, clung tightly to her cheeks; her eyes shone with a bright streak from the glare of sky and sea, while her short upper lip revealed sharp teeth. Szymon was both scared and entranced: never had he seen her so pretty, so mysterious.

'If you'd give me a hand, I'd come in.'

'Take the soap.'

Without knowing why, they now spoke in hushed tones, as if in a church, so as not to ruffle the silence. Clasping Śliwka's hand, Szymon stepped into the water with heroically gritted teeth. He too grabbed hold of the salutary rope and then with an elegant gesture handed Śliwka the soap. 'Give my back a scrub.' He longed to find himself back on the sand as soon as possible. Śliwka soaped her palms, but at that moment the pink bar slipped from her hands and came to rest on the sandy bottom.

'Damn!'

Bending over, they watched as their celebratory purchase crumbled into tiny flakes. Szymon judged this to be the effect of the salty sea water. From out of the distance, along the shore, a kind of trembling white trail was drifting. 'Butterflies, look, look!' Śliwka exclaimed.

A whole throng of them, all white, fragile and trembling, a veritable migration. They were dancing above the waves and soon the waves cast the first victims onto the beach. Śliwka stared in dismay: 'But how stupid!'

Szymon, moved by sorrow and anger at the needless loss of life, said with emphasis: 'If people don't buy up the greengages today, they'll go completely rotten.' Śliwka, a thousand miles from their kiosk, business and greengages, whispered: 'Perhaps they'll dry out in the sun.' She was thinking of the butterflies, so beautiful, now lying motionless on the sand. Then, sighing, she came out of the sea onto the beach and rubbed herself down with wet sand since she no longer had any soap. Snorting like a horse, Szymon lay down on his back in the sun. Suddenly, the earth fled from under him, and he found himself beneath the empty cupola of the sky in terrifying stillness and silence. He raised his head in fear, but for a time saw nothing; coloured blotches flickered before his eyes. Had he gone blind or something? He cried out. Eventually, he caught sight of Śliwka, his little Śliwka, gaunt and totally black against the backdrop of sea and sky.

'Come here! Come!'

She came running, parting the waves to either side with a roar, and squatted on the sand, soaking wet. As it trickled off, the water formed little patches around her. With a rapturous sigh, she sank onto her back and stretched to the full. Safe in her warmth, Szymon reached over and whispered: 'Oughtn't we to get back?'

'Oh, forget it! It's still early!'

They fell silent. And to think that once upon a time people lived like this, naked, in forests and beside waters, knowing nothing of unemployment, harbour benches and cities where there was nowhere to sleep and nothing to eat. Śliwka pulled herself up and sat in a squatting position again, gazing at the sea. The waves spilled constantly onto the shore. Their monotone roar created something akin to a type of never-heard music. Śliwka froze, with eyes motionless. She felt a vague sense of eternity and greatness. 'Do you hear?' she whispered.

'Aha.'

'And that constant ebbing and flowing, ebbing and flowing, and the roaring?'

'A thousand years is no joke,' Szymon replied gravely.

From somewhere off to the side, a black fishing boat appeared with people on board. Long poles slowly sank into the water. They were checking the seabed in order to mark places where it was safe to bathe that day. Szymon leaped to his feet as if scalded. Far away, at the very start of the beach, a commune employee was trundling his rubbish cart.

'Let's go, d'you hear, Śliwka, let's go!'

His hands were shaking; he was expecting any moment an invasion of summer holiday-makers, beach pyjamas and robes, coloured sunshades and bodies so beautiful they were terrible. But Śliwka, smiling and revealing her sharp teeth from behind too-short lips, gathered up their ragged clothing in a single sweep and seizing him by the hand, dragged him deeper onto land. The sun was already scorching and the forest steaming with the scent of resin. Sharp seagrass stabbed and slashed their bare feet. As though bewitched, Szymon followed Śliwka as she strode boldly ahead. The pine trees seemed to part and then close behind them. The roar of the sea could still be heard, but now a different and higher note joined in: the piercing whistle of birds. Endless woodland paths, demarcated by the ruddy trunks of pines, led into the forest depths; their feet trod on something soft and velvety as they sank in blissful tenderness towards the beautiful earth. And Śliwka, pale and solemn, slid onto her knees, pulling her companion with her. They rested their heads on each other's shoulders, rubbing neck against neck like forest beasts, in a gesture of endearment and fortifying comfort in this great world, full of voices yet mute, of earth, trees, birds and water.

'*W raju*'
First published as part of the collection *Dwoje ludzi* (Wydawnictwo Rój, 1938), here from *Opowiadania* (Czytelnik, 1956).

JERZY ANDRZEJEWSKI

1909–1983

Jerzy Andrzejewski is an enigmatic figure in the landscape of Polish literature. One of the country's most prominent twentieth-century writers, his changing literary styles and political views, combined with a knotty personal life, make him difficult to categorize.

Czesław Miłosz wrote about him as 'Alpha' in *The Captive Mind*, claiming his moralistic zeal drove him from pre-war Catholicism to post-war Stalinism. Andrzejewski later broke with the Communist Party and eventually became a card-carrying oppositionist, publishing his books underground or abroad. Whatever his political permutation, he remained a literary leader, playing an important role in the wartime cultural resistance, as well as in writers' organizations and journals after the war.

This leadership was also artistic – he was a thrillingly pioneering writer. He is best known for *Ashes and Diamonds* (1947), a novel about the power struggle in the immediate aftermath of the Second World War. Published before the introduction of censorship, it went through several editions as political temperatures changed, and was made into a classic film by Andrzej Wajda. Other notable books include *The Gates of Paradise* (1960), an almost single-sentence fever dream set during the Children's Crusade, and *Miazga* (*Pulp*, 1979), whose blend of fiction with Andrzejewski's own journal makes it perhaps the first postmodern Polish novel.

Queer themes occur throughout his work. Though married to his wife Maria for nearly three decades, Andrzejewski's promiscuity with men was an open secret. He experienced major, unrequited infatuations with the poet Krzysztof Kamil Baczyński and the prose writer Marek Hłasko. So much contradiction was perhaps too much for one body: he struggled his whole life with alcoholism.

Among Andrzejewski's firsts, he addressed the realities of day-to-day wartime life early on, sometimes with unexpected humour. Here, in 'The Passport Wife', written in the bleak summer of 1944, he mocks the decadent lifestyle of Warsaw's elite even as their city was laid to ruin.

Sean Gasper Bye

The Passport Wife

Translated by Sean Gasper Bye

A year after the Germans captured the city of Lwów, a certain young man, a radio technician by profession, for many reasons feeling less than safe, decided it was prudent to leave his home town. He did so with a small valise – for he had no personal possessions – and arrived in Warsaw. Soon, another unfortunate coincidence, caused by his obstinate refusal to stop working as a radio technician, forced the man from Lwów to change his name. Aid in this troublesome situation came from an old schoolmate from Chyrów, Tonio, who'd been raised by Jesuits and was the former owner of a landed estate adjacent to Trembowla. This Tonio was now sitting pretty, for in Warsaw he and a graphic artist had jointly launched a business producing false *Ausweise* and ration cards, while also keeping in close contact with another, kindred enterprise dedicated to producing counterfeit dollars.

Soon the man from Lwów received an impeccable, authentic *Kennkarte* issued in Biłgoraj and formerly belonging to a man who'd died a few months earlier in undefined circumstances. Having inherited the deceased's personal information, the man from Lwów was henceforth known as Jan Bielski. His year of birth – 1918 – remained the same, yet he'd changed profession and marital status: going from a radio technician to a lumberjack, and from a bachelor to a married man. The dead man's wife was named Stefania and – his friend from Chyrów assured him – was no longer alive, which dispelled the young man from Lwów's qualms and fears. Thus equipped with new personal data, he returned safely to his former life.

At roughly this same time, a certain woman from Warsaw – young, single and an attendee of underground medical lectures – fell into similar trouble. Soon afterwards her friends provided her with an impeccable, authentic *Kennkarte* issued in Biłgoraj under the name Stefania Bielska, who had died a year before in undefined circumstances. The dead woman's husband was named Jan and was also dead, which dispelled the young woman from Warsaw's qualms and fears. Thus equipped with new personal data, she returned safely to her former life.

For a while the couple, thus united, lived in Warsaw entirely ignorant of one another. Until one day it transpired that the man from Lwów, weary of trading in British cigarettes, and at the encouragement of a society lady, shifted into dealing in paintings and works of art. This lady, fearing the random street round-ups to deport people for forced labour, left her house very rarely and stayed only in her immediate neighbourhood, meaning she handled all business matters in her flat, which had been discreetly and tastefully transformed into an antiques shop. Jan Bielski knew little of paintings, porcelain and rugs, but being a cunning and resourceful fellow, he identified a few of his former recipients of counterfeit Lucky Strikes and Chesterfields who managed to show some interest in the benefits of purchasing works of art.

One of his customers was a long-serving payments collector for the tax office, a certain Mr Mariusz Głowacki, a quiet and hard-working man who would assuredly have perished by now on his insignificant salary had he not followed in his colleagues' footsteps and, by way of undermining the occupation authorities' orders, begun waiving taxpayers' liabilities, in exchange for taking one-half of the required sum for himself. These private and patriotic manipulations had him doing incomparably better than before the war, and since he was a solitary man and sensitive to beauty, with the resourceful man from Lwów as his go-between, he soon became one of the society lady's clients and the owner of two old Persian rugs, an Empire-style clock, some small Chippendale display cases and a writing desk from the famous craftsmen of Kolbuszowa. He took a particular liking to the writing desk and developed the habit of sitting at it every evening to play rounds of patience, which never went in his favour, forcing him to help things along by rearranging the cards appropriately.

The man from Lwów's second client was the ex-owner of a soda-water stand on Wolska Street. This man – Teodor Baścik was his name – shortly after a catastrophe in which his stand was obliterated during military operations, developed an interest in the stock market and – having at that time a private office in the vicinity of Napoleon Square and also numerous agents out in the city focusing on foreign currencies, gold and diamonds – had been pondering for some while founding a publishing firm for magazines and books after the end of the war. Since he was in the midst of furnishing a four-room flat, the man from Lwów had supplied him with many paintings, a Steinway concert grand, a sideboard and two Renaissance chests, a bit of Copenhagen porcelain, a few Turkish tapestries, as well as a pair of old Jewish candlesticks and a collection of English etchings. In spare moments, Baścik frequented establishments where the roles of waiters and bartenders were performed by well-known actors and actresses. In public places of this type he enjoyed performing as a so-called 'big cheese', and he often said to the people from the artistic spheres for whom he would fund lunches, dinners and numerous rounds at the buffet: 'Hold on to Baścik, and you won't sink!' So they did. Presently Baścik began casually maintaining one of the young actresses, and her elegant legs persuaded him to commission a bust of her from a sculptor with beautiful eyes.

Indeed, this future publishing potentate – also at the encouragement of the young actress, who was planning to host artistic gatherings at home – was on the lookout for just the right tea service. The society lady, informed by the man from Lwów of this new profitable commission, immediately launched a search by telephone. There soon arrived at her flat a beautiful set of eighteenth-century blue English delftware for twelve people. Mr Baścik expressed his desire to examine the kit, as he called it, but when the man from Lwów, after discussing the meeting at the society lady's apartment, arrived to fetch his client half an hour before the appointed time, the art patron took one look at him and exclaimed:

'Bother you and your delftware! Your wife has sorted me out some better kit.'

The man from Lwów concealed the impression this news made on him, and after remarking 'Oh, excellent!' allowed himself to be led into the drawing room, whose walls were hung with horses and uhlans by Jerzy Kossak and the pink-and-purple *Arab Women* by Adam Styk. On a small Louis-Seize table, in the shadow of a Jewish menorah with eagles, stood a fantastic Japanese tea service.

'Well?' cried Baścik.

The man from Lwów frowned slightly. 'Who's to say? I have to admit I don't care for Japanese stuff, myself. Too garish.'

'But, but, but!' cried the other man. 'Say what you will. For tea, only Japanese kit will do, as you well know! Your wife has a better handle on good taste.'

'That could be,' muttered the man from Lwów.

'And do you know who the Japs cooked up this kit for?'

Stefania Bielska's husband admitted he did not.

'For the mikado himself!' exclaimed Baścik. 'Just take a look, see how nice they tidied it up . . .'

Indeed, the cups with beautiful painted birds were intended at one time as a gift from some Japanese merchants for the current mikado, when he was still heir to the throne. Twelve brilliant artists had painted one cup each, but whether the service turned out to be insufficiently magnificent or there were other determining factors, as soon as the mikado's son received the new gift, he offered the service to a famous general, one of the victors at Tsushima; while the general, as a gesture of courtesy, bestowed the set on a captured general from the Russian side. He, in turn, passed it on to his nephew as a wedding present. The revolution drove the general's nephew, with the cups, all the way to Rome, where at auction the service passed into the hands of a tinned food manufacturer from Chicago, a collector of Japanese wares. Unfortunately, the manufacturer was presently killed in an automobile crash and the service was inherited by his son, who for patriotic reasons detested Japan and immediately auctioned off his father's collection. Next this would-be gift for the Japanese ruler decorated the flat of a Hollywood starlet. But when a hormonal disorder caused the starlet to put on weight, the service was bought by an elderly English marquess for a very young Parisian danseur. When the marquess dumped the danseur for a German boxer, the Japanese service was bought by a Greek financier, yet as bankruptcy soon drove him to leap out of an aeroplane, the precious set was acquired by an advisor to the Polish embassy in Paris, who'd married wealth, and after a certain time came to Warsaw with the twelve teacups. In September 1939, the advisor hastily departed for Romania and the service was sold by a currently impoverished cousin of the advisor, who was looking after his flat. Admittedly, one cup had broken while the city was under siege, but a nephew of the impoverished cousin, a secondary-school student, had very deftly glued it back together.

While Baścik recounted this long and convoluted story, the man from

Lwów, barely listening, was enduring the rotten experience of one upon whom fate had suddenly bestowed an unknown wife. He was jolted out of this unpleasant reverie by a shout from Baścik: 'So I understand kit! It's got a geology like Prince Radziwiłł himself.'

'Sure does,' confirmed the man from Lwów.

Yet Baścik, tapping his fingers on porcelain as fragile as human happiness, continued: 'Got to admit I didn't even know you had a wife. A bachelor, I thought. But congratulations, you got a lovely gal, a savvy one too.'

The man from Lwów cleared his throat gently, but Baścik continued: 'She comes to my office yesterday, introduces herself and says, "Would you like to buy a tea service?" I go, "Why not, I can." And she says: "Because I've got a service for you." "I know that already," I say, "English delftware". "Why delftware?" she asks. So I tell her: "Well, the one your husband's unloading on me." I see this caught the little lady by surprise. "My husband?" she asks. "Well," I say, "isn't he your husband, Mr Jan Bielski?" And then she laughs and says, "Of course, but what I've got to sell isn't delftware at all, because my husband and I do business separately."'

'Yes, that's right,' mumbled the man from Lwów. 'Completely separately.'

'I forked over the dosh, sure enough,' said Baścik, slapping his knee, 'but you won't find another kit like that anywhere in Warsaw. Am I right?'

Once back on the street, the man from Lwów stepped into a small café nearby, where, jostled by a crowd of people greedily wolfing down pastries and cakes, he phoned the society lady to inform her the deal had fallen through. Because the society lady, relying upon the assurances of her middleman, had made certain expenditures in anticipation of profit, she received the man from Lwów's call with bitter displeasure; while he, irritated by the failure as well as the society lady's moods, replied with a few choice words and slammed down the receiver, thereby closing the door on a further career as an antiques and art dealer. He then tracked down his friend from Chyrów to hold him responsible for the disloyal resurrection of the late Mrs Bielska. But Tonio felt no guilt.

'What are you worried about, mate?' he finally said in conclusion. 'You've got a wife while the war lasts, you don't have to live with her or pay her bills. Is that so bad?'

'That pleasure,' frowned the man from Lwów, 'is costing me at least a grand. And I got made a fool of, which I don't much like.'

'Who does?' replied the false documents dealer. 'But if you got made a fool of, get your own back.'

The man from Lwów considered.

'Oh yeah? How?'

With his mind on the possibility of future payback, he decided to head for City Hall, to get his passport wife's address from the records office, just in case. But along the way, to buck himself up, he stopped to have one vodka, and by the fourth, he'd got the chance to play middleman on a small but lucrative currency exchange transaction. In the next bar, he ran into an acquaintance from Lwów who invited him as an expert radio technician to get involved in installing a secret broadcasting device. The man from Lwów, forgetting his bad experiences in this area, accepted the proposed job, which led him to forget about his wife entirely.

Nevertheless, that very day, the young woman from Warsaw, having learned the true situation of her marital status from Baścik, started telling her friends about her passport husband without delay. Soon two of her closest female friends got hold of the man from Lwów's telephone number and one evening, once the young man had returned home after a full day of work, Mrs Adamska the major's wife, a heavy-set blonde who, during her husband's absence, dealt in wool and tricot garments, informed her lodger of an abundance of phone calls.

'Women,' she added with a trace of bitterness, since the man from Lwów was a handsome and well-built lad. 'They said they'd call again this evening.'

And sure enough, not long after curfew, the phone rang.

'Is Mr Bielski there?' asked a kind, feminine voice.

'Speaking,' replied the man from Lwów.

Mrs Adamska, naturally, was eavesdropping from her room.

'How is Stefcia's health?' the kind, feminine voice continued the conversation.

The man from Lwów grew slightly disconcerted.

'Stefcia? I'm sorry, there must be some mistake. Which Stefcia do you mean?'

'What do you mean *which*? Stefcia.'

'And who would you like to speak to?'

'To Mr Jan Bielski. Why, you just said that was you.'

'Because I am Jan Bielski. But what's this about?'

'Oh goodness!' said the kind voice, 'you're getting cross ... But I just wanted to find out if your wife was home yet. She's not asleep already, is she?'

'She is!' the man from Lwów shouted and smashed down the receiver.

But after a moment the phone rang again.

'Is it true,' spoke a different, but equally kind feminine voice, 'that you're not living with your wife?'

The man from Lwów stifled an oath and replied in the calmest voice possible: 'On the contrary, madam, I've never stopped living with her. You've been misinformed.'

'And do you love your wife very much?'

'Very. I'm unconditionally in love with her. Do you hear, madam? Un-con-di-tion-al-ly.'

'So what's getting under your skin?'

The man from Lwów hung up with a bang. Five minutes later, right when he'd started getting undressed, the phone piped up again.

'Hello,' he said in a voice muffled with passion.

'Mr Bielski, is your wife's hair blonde or black?'

'Ginger.'

'And yours?'

'Ginger as well. And our children will be ginger too.'

'So you don't have children yet?'

The fourth phone call pulled the man from Lwów out of bed. Pale with rage, he dashed out into the entryway in his pyjamas and, no longer caring if the major's wife was listening under the door, roared into the receiver: 'Will you shut up, you silly cow? Get some fella into bed with you so you don't go bananas at night ...'

A splutter came through the receiver.

'How dare you!' shouted a man's voice from the other end, after a moment. 'Who are you? Unbelievable! I wish to speak to Mrs Adamska.'

As it later turned out, this was a long-standing acquaintance of the major's wife, an elderly philanthropist and papal chamberlain.

Over the next few days, the evening phone calls recurred with bloody-minded regularity, plunging the man from Lwów into rage at his passport wife, and giving Mrs Adamska insomnia caused by tribulations of a nature both psychological and carnal.

At this same time, the young woman from Warsaw, ignorant of these matters, managed – thanks to her numerous connections, and in the moments when she wasn't studying or distributing secret newsletters – to sell Baścik an electric gramophone, five bottles of French cognac, a Balochistani carpet, one hundred American razor blades, a length of English flannel, a refrigerator, a Waterman fountain pen and three pairs of warm Swedish long johns. She earned a significant commission on these transactions, and to top it all off, she was invited, along with her husband, to Baścik's flat for the première of their artistic soirées. The party was expected to go on all night. The young woman from Warsaw accepted the invitation, though as for her husband, she raised no great hopes that he would come. She explained that her husband had many different jobs and didn't like large gatherings anyway.

'He doesn't?' said Baścik, amazed. 'Fancy that! A bloke who seems so cheerful . . . in short, is a bore?'

Jan Bielski's wife vigorously protested, but Baścik wouldn't let himself be so easily convinced.

'What are you telling me? How is it that a young, healthy, handsome fellow . . .'

'Handsome?'

'What, isn't he handsome?'

'I'm not saying he isn't . . .' replied the young woman from Warsaw, evasively.

'Well then! Young, handsome, and he doesn't like a good time?'

'Oh, you see,' said the young woman from Warsaw, 'he just adores it at home!'

The next day, shortly before curfew, in front of the Aria on Mazowiecka Street, a long procession of bicycle rickshaws set off towards the Mokotów district, where Baścik lived, carrying his invited guests. Baścik and his young actress led this cheerful cavalcade, and bringing up the rear was a rickshaw holding the cook specially hired for the night. All the riders were already many rounds in, paid for by the art patron in the Aria; and as the distance between the rickshaws was not great, in the early darkness of autumn, just like in a murky and dense forest, they kept calling out to one another with a loud halloo! Once past Union of Lublin Square, Baścik's lady companion felt suddenly moved to lay a bouquet of roses that a friend had offered her by the wall of a house where, a few days before, a dozen or more hostages had been shot. Baścik was not a man insensitive to the noble impulses of the heart, and therefore ordered the rickshaw driver to halt; the rickshaws behind them stopped as well, and the young actress, in floods of tears, staggering very slightly, laid the red roses on the muddy sidewalk.

'Bravo! Bravo!' cried one of the guests, a journalist by profession. 'What a performance!'

Next they continued on. A journalist riding in the second rickshaw along was singing a pre-war tango at the top of his lungs: 'The night is ours, and otherwise we've not a thing . . .' Then, after reaching their destination, the party immediately went into full swing and began to whirl like a colourfully festooned carousel. The cold snacks turned out perfectly, and the drinks were wonderful. There was Martel cognac and original whisky sold by Germans coming back from France, and there was no shortage of home-made liqueurs from a certain aristocratic cellar. The party, initially concentrated in the large drawing room where the *Arab Women* and horses hung, quickly moved on to other rooms as well.

Yet what pen could describe that night of merriment? Just think, dear fellow, why are you shoving your way into this whole crowd? Outside it is a lovely July night, containing greater breath of approaching liberty than any other night of the past five years. Yet why, as I hunch over my sheet of paper, does my heart feel heavy? Freedom, freedom!

An atmospheric, cozy half-light now prevailed in Baścik's spacious flat. Just after the solo dance spectacles and the poetry recitations, the guests, scattered about various rooms, began making reciprocal contacts of a personal nature. Only the journalist who had just been singing on the rickshaw ride 'The night is ours, and otherwise we've not a thing . . .' was able to maintain independence in this situation since, under the influence of alcohol, he was utterly consumed with political issues. Soon, once he'd managed to collect a certain number of listeners around him, he began with meticulous honesty to disclose to them his secret resistance activities. A couple of his listeners, also keenly politically inclined, followed the journalist's example and began to expose and reveal their own relationships and underground activities, as well as those of their friends and acquaintances. Meanwhile those who had no such relationships and conducted no underground activities made up facts, names and addresses on the trot, sparking envy in all the others.

Whilst these lively confessions were underway, Baścik, unable for some time to track down the actress he was casually supporting and who – he presumed – must be secreted away in some cosy spot with the sculptor with the pretty eyes, turned on the overhead lights in each room one by one. This reunified the party, and the young actress, after unexpectedly crawling out from beneath the piano, threw herself round Baścik's neck, right in full view of the gathering, because she was not of a nature to jealously conceal her emotions from others. Baścik, greatly flattered by this turn of events, decided the time had come to take his first steps in publishing, and he purchased on the spot a volume of philosophical sketches from one of the poets in attendance, and a psychological novel from a fiction writer crowned with an honourable prize from a provincial city.

Finally, now, some time after midnight – when many Ukrainian *dumky* had been sung, the mood was growing melancholy and human hearts tender and wistful – it dawned on Baścik that he had not yet paid sufficient attention to the young woman from Warsaw, Mrs Stefania Bielska. He remembered that she had indeed come without her husband, but he was unsure whether the young man had arrived separately. He therefore set about looking for the young woman from Warsaw and, after wandering at some length round his own flat, he finally discovered her in the company of the fiction writer crowned with an honourable prize from a provincial city. Because the man was a psychological writer, his conversation with the young woman from Warsaw was therefore psychological – in other words, he was saying very interesting things about himself. Yet this had now gone on for a rather long time, in any event long enough for the young woman from Warsaw to sadden and begin to regret that her passport husband had not joined them. No wonder, then, that when Baścik stood before her and inquired about her husband, her eyes spoke of a deep melancholy.

'You've had a row!' guessed Baścik.

Mrs Bielska pitifully nodded her lovely little head.

'That good-for-nothing!' raged Baścik. 'I should tan his hide! Where is he, the wretch?'

Yet it turned out Mrs Bielska unfortunately didn't know.

'So that's the sort of chap he is!' replied Baścik. 'The rat's moved out!

Never you mind. You'll make it up tonight or my name's not Baścik. Hold onto Baścik and you won't sink. You don't know where your other half's bolted off to, but Baścik will find out soon enough . . .'

With these words, he searched amongst his guests for one of his trusted men, namely young Jaś Mirski from Mirów in Podolia, who told him that Jan Bielski had at one time been in loose business contact with him and he lived in Powiśle district.

After returning to the young woman from Warsaw with this information, Baścik presented the matter manfully: 'Let's bring him here, eh?'

'Now?' said Mrs Bielska, frightened.

'Why wait?' replied Baścik. 'Hold on to Baścik, now I've set my mind to it . . .'

After declaring this, he climbed onto the Renaissance chest and signalled that he wished to address his visitors. Word of this event winged its way throughout the flat and before long the room where Baścik was standing on the Renaissance chest was packed full of people.

'Friends!' So Baścik spoke once the hubbub in the room had died down. 'Here among us is a lady, I'd even call her a beautiful lady, who has suffered, if you like, certain marital misunderstandings. It can happen, ladies and gentlemen. Life is not a romance, as we know. There's a time for tears in life as well.'

Heavy sighs resounded all round.

'Oh, life, life!' said someone wistfully.

Baścik's young actress was resting her head on the shoulder of the sculptor with the beautiful gaze, and her tear-filled eyes wandered over the ceiling.

'Yes, ladies and gentlemen,' continued Baścik. 'So it goes. Now what about us? What about us, I ask you. Are we going to let this young lady suffer?'

'We won't!' voices rang out. 'Down with suffering!'

Baścik raised a hand. 'Right you are! That's what I mean, we won't. Are we a chivalrous nation or not?'

'We are!'

'Hurrah!' roared Baścik. 'Who'll volunteer to go fetch our friend's husband?'

Here enthusiasm seized the gathering and some of the company instantly resolved to set out into the city, to the address that Baścik gave them, to seek out the husband of the young woman from Warsaw and bring the man they sought back to Mokotów. Soon a small crowd of men and women made its way outside.

In keeping with the air defence rules, it was a blacked-out night, and the streets, appropriately for these severe regulations, were empty and frightened. Only sporadic police patrols slipped along the walls of the houses, shooting periodically to make their presence known. In other places, resistance fighters were doing the same for the same purpose, as their lorries transported grenades, ammunition, machine guns and small cannons. So amidst the scattered popping of gunshots, the company searching for Stefania Bielska's husband wandered the streets of Warsaw blithely and unmolested by anyone, singing brisk military songs interspersed with pre-war tangos.

On Świętokrzyska Street, against a decorative panorama of expansive and fantastical ruins, the poet who'd sold Baścik his volume of philosophical sketches movingly danced the *Dying Swan*, while a little further along, on Teatralny Square, in front of the scorched walls of the National Opera and Theatre, the young actress began reciting the balcony scene from *Romeo and Juliet*. At around three o'clock they finally reached Powiśle district, where Jan Bielski lived on one of the smaller side streets.

It was a broad-shouldered, portly and yellow-lipsticked building. The sound of hammering at the gate sparked panic within the house. A few endangered men ran into the cellars in their nightshirts, and a certain bookkeeper, upon remembering that a few days before he'd told a joke in the office about Hitler, abandoned his sizeable family and crawled through the attic onto the roof to hide behind the chimney.

Yet the man from Lwów, abnormally untormented that evening by telephone calls, was sleeping safely and soundly. Meanwhile the insomniac major's wife, upon hearing bad noises, leaped out of bed and, barefoot, with a dressing-gown thrown carelessly over her nightdress, dashed into her lodger's room.

'Mr Bielski! Janek!' She set about waking up the young man.

Half-revived, the man from Lwów sat up in bed.

'The phone?'

'Worse,' whispered the major's wife. 'The Gestapo. Do you hear?'

Sure enough, coming from downstairs was the babble of many voices already in the courtyard. The major's wife, trembling nervously, sat down on the edge of the bed.

'They're coming!'

'They certainly are,' said the man from Lwów, mechanically.

Since the major's wife was warm and soft, he embraced her and drew her to himself.

'My dearest!' the woman whispered with relief.

The man from Lwów, meanwhile, unhurriedly yet decisively did in the darkness everything it befits a young man in such a situation to do. All of a sudden, the noise, thumping and hurly-burly coming from the stairs yanked the major's wife out of his arms.

'Oh God, it's you they're after!' moaned the doubly unhappy woman.

The man from Lwów, having shaken off the last traces of sleep, leaped to his feet. At the same time there came a mighty pounding on the door.

'What to do, what to do?' said the major's wife, trembling.

'Open the door,' replied the man from Lwów.

His calm, somewhat harsh masculine voice had a very strong effect on the major's wife. She swiftly pulled herself together physically and morally, and once she'd done so – went out to face their destiny. But she had barely got the door open when she was overcome by a joyous, carnival tumult. A swarm of gesticulating and half-dancing figures stormed into the entryway.

'Bielski! Where's Bielski?' cheerful voices cried out.

'Where's the husband?'

'Husband?'

'We're looking for the husband! Give us the husband!'

Meanwhile the bookkeeper burdened with the fatal joke was having a particularly dreadful time on the roof, because he had been a homebody for years and suffered excessively from agoraphobia. Clinging tightly to the attic window, in a nightshirt billowing like a sail in the wind, he slid on feet shod in soft slippers down the steep roof, and over a dark abyss. If there's an air-raid siren now, I'll lose my mind, he thought astutely. Meanwhile the men hiding in the basement and the remaining residents of the house strained to listen.

'We demand the husband!' cried the poet who'd just been dancing the *Dying Swan* against a backdrop of ruins.

'The husband! The husband!'

'Let the husband show himself!'

One music critic hummed the wedding march from *Lohengrin*, and, to one side, Baścik's young actress, gesticulating vigorously, was miming one of Lady Macbeth's monologues. Yet the cunning man from Lwów, immediately guessing what this was about, swiftly locked his door and didn't open it until the cheerful company had left the flat. Yet before this happened, he had to withstand a collective attack on his room.

'Oh lackaday! The husband's squirrelled away!' the poet cried into the keyhole.

'Bielski to his wife! His wife is waiting! His wife is yearning! His wife is weeping!'

At a certain point Mrs Adamska felt it necessary to intervene.

'Ladies and gentlemen,' she announced with an accent of indignation, 'there seems to have been some misunderstanding . . .'

'What misunderstanding?' She was shouted down. 'There's no misunderstanding.'

'Mr Bielski is a bachelor!' she said with dignity.

Her answer was met with a collective roar of laughter.

'And you believe him, silly girl?' said the poet, in exasperation.

Then a mighty spirit possessed the major's wife. She turned crimson and, pointing to the way out, shrieked: 'Get out of my house!'

Slight consternation came over the members of the expedition for Jan Bielski.

'Out!' repeated the major's wife.

The people packed into the cramped entryway automatically began withdrawing towards the door. Luckily Jaś Mirski rescued the situation in dignified fashion.

'Gentlemen and ladies!' he said. 'Calm, above all. We have satisfied ourselves that, it would seem, Mr Bielski is not a man of honour and is not deserving of our interest. Madam!' – here he bowed before the major's wife in her dressing gown – 'please forgive us this nocturnal and unexpected visit, but the fault we bear is truly less than the circumstances might indicate. We were roused, as it were, by a higher calling . . .'

'I understand,' interrupted the major's wife, 'and I request no further explanation, for it is not you that owes one to me. And now, farewell.'

That night, no one slept in the entire house. Apart from the hassle of needing to get the bookkeeper off the roof, an innumerable variety of commentaries on the entire affair kept everyone awake. Since the caretaker had recently got a kilo of sheep's wool from the major's wife, he gave unclear and vague answers to all the tenants' questions. No wonder, then, that early in the morning, following an unpleasant conversation with the major's wife, the man from Lwów left the house in Powiśle with his small valise; and the neighbourhood shops and the nearby market square in Mariensztat were all a-quiver with rumours and speculation. By seven o'clock, word was out in the city about a night-time blockade of Powiśle and hundreds of victims pulled from the buildings. Another current bore a swift rumour about a certain young man shooting heroically for several hours from a roof. Many people heard grenades detonating and saw with their own eyes cars full of police. At nine o'clock, news of a nocturnal orgy of Gestapo officers in the apartment of a certain woman agent quickly carved out a successful course for itself. Before noon it emerged that this agent had been cruelly murdered by the party-goers, while the young man who'd been living with her for some time had been shot.

Whilst this larger-than-life story was thus taking shape, the man from Lwów was on the lookout for a new flat. The difficulties of this activity – specifically, the street round-ups taking place – once again aggravated his blind hatred of his passport wife. Finally, in the late evening he managed to set his little valise down in a dark and dirty box room on Copernicus Street.

The man from Lwów's new flat was a cramped cubbyhole with a narrow little window overlooking a murky and mouldy courtyard. The furnishings consisted of a camp bed, a stool and a nail hammered into the wall that – according to the owner, a retired clerk – was intended as a temporary replacement for a wardrobe. A broken stove meant that this hovel was bitterly cold. But at least the flat had no phone.

After tallying up his significantly enfeebled funds, Jan Bielski threw his coat over his shoulders, sat down on the bed and, staring grimly at the grey wall of the tenement on the opposite corner, began to reflect on the possibilities of getting revenge on his passport wife. Sadly, he didn't manage to come up with anything that night or over the following days. While various ideas did indeed come to mind, he soon rejected them as nonsensical or unachievable. Yet the longer he contemplated revenge, the stronger his desire to avenge himself became. This constant preoccupation caused him to grow thin and lose not only his appetite, but also his innate cunning and resourcefulness. He spent idle and sluggish days in his dark, unheated hovel. If he went out into the city, he did so surreptitiously, carefully avoiding main streets, especially the area of Napoleon Square, as well as public establishments where he might run into Baścik or someone he knew. By thus neglecting his business, he was quickly approaching the total exhaustion of the funds he possessed. Finally, one day, having found himself facing unavoidable material poverty, he decided to return to active life and restart his so unfortunately severed business relationship with the society lady. Sadly, he met with failure, for it transpired that a few days before, in the small hours, the society lady had come down with a bad migraine, and since she was out of headache powder and there was no one to hand in the house to send out for some, she had decided to go herself to the nearby chemist's. As chance would have it, at that very moment some Nazis had arrived with their green police vans, and amid the general round-up, they also seized the society lady on her way out of the chemist's with her powder.

After learning all this over the phone from the society lady's elderly aunt, the young man from Lwów blamed his passport wife for this turn of events as well. Downhearted at this new misfortune and with his need for vengeance still unfulfilled, he didn't leave his flat for two days. His odd behaviour attracted the suspicion of his host, who began to suspect his lodger must be a Jew in hiding. Fortunately, on the third day, and first thing in the morning at that, the young man finally went out into the city, leading the relieved clerk to decide to bear the cost of cleaning the hitherto non-functioning stove in his lodger's room.

Meanwhile, once in town, the man from Lwów headed for the city hall, where he began seeking the municipal address office. He naturally found it without much difficulty and, after acquiring the appropriate form, stepped off a little to the side to fill it out in peace. Yet he quickly discovered he had little to say. He therefore wrote: Stefania Bielska, and very carefully, with a squeaking pen, filled in the blank for the husband's first name. That was unfortunately the extent of his knowledge about the wife he was looking for. At the bottom of the form he supplied, as required, his own name and address.

When, conscious of this embarrassingly paltry information, he somewhat hesitantly passed the completed form to the appropriate clerk, she – a woman of indeterminate years, small and wizened, in a black dress with a white piqué collar at her neck – upon reading the name of the person sought and the name of the person seeking, raised her mouse-like face from over the form and gave the inquirer a particularly sharp looking-over. The young man tried to smile, though he could tell he didn't really manage it. Meanwhile the tiny clerk's eyes were boring ever deeper into him.

'Are you looking for your wife?' she finally asked in a frail little voice.

'That's right,' he replied.

To which she sighed sympathetically:

'Goodness me, everyone's searching these days. People have gone missing, vanished from sight . . . Have you been apart for long?'

Jan Bielski shifted somewhat anxiously.

'Oh, a while now.'

The clerk sighed and suddenly smiled with maternal tenderness.

'And yet isn't it lucky that you're finally tracking one another down! And what a coincidence! Twenty years I've been working here in the address office, and I've never had anything like this happen before. It's a long time since you've seen your wife, is that right?'

'Quite . . .'

'Then I can assure you that your wife is still lovely and charming.'

'Mmh!' murmured the man from Lwów.

'There, you see, sir! We clerks, we know everything.'

Madwoman! thought the man from Lwów. But the tiny clerk with the white piqué collar at her neck smiled mischievously.

'And maybe you'd like to learn who was just here a moment ago, not long, fifteen minutes at most . . .'

The young man could feel his face getting stupider and stupider.

'And stood at this very window,' the clerk continued. 'And was also looking for someone's address. And also hadn't seen her husband in a long time. And who was very, very attractive . . . Well, can you guess now who it was?'

Jan Bielski was not generally prone to blushing, yet at this moment a dark flush descended on his face. Presently, with an affectionate farewell from the beaming little clerk, and his wife's address in his pocket, he found himself in front of the city hall and, humming, walked onward.

On Krakowskie Przedmieście he bumped into Tonio, whom he hadn't seen in quite a while.

'What's got you so cheerful?' asked the forged documents dealer curiously.

'Me?' said the man from Lwów, surprised. 'Cheerful?'

'Have you made a good deal?'

'Me? A deal? Why should I be making a good deal? I haven't made a deal. Though, who knows, maybe I have. I'll see. Maybe there's one deal I will make.'

Tonio peered at his friend suspiciously.

'Admit it, you've been stepping out for a quick tipple.'

'Me? Why?' said the man from Lwów, indignant. 'I never dreamed of it. I'm not stepping out anywhere. That is, I am, but not where you're thinking at all. Anyway, why don't we talk another time, because now . . .'

'What, you in a rush?'

'Am I in a rush? Actually no, though, in fact, yes . . .'

'Good Lord!' moaned the man from Chyrów. 'What's going on with you, mate? Did you fall on your head or something?'

'Me? On my head?' Bielski was honestly astonished. 'How? I haven't fallen on my head at all. Why should I have fallen on my head? I'm in a rush, that's all. You know, I've just remembered that I'm in an awful rush. So I'll see you next time, then. Cheerio!'

And, after bursting into laughter, he strode off humming, having left the astonished man from Chyrów in the middle of the pavement. It was drizzling slightly and an autumn mist was hanging in the air. After a moment, Tonio noticed Bielski had stopped in front of a nearby flower shop and was now urgently looking over the display. Then he went inside, and before long re-emerged on the street holding a bouquet under his arm, and, with a spring in his step, he walked onward.

'Paszportowa żona'
Published as part of the collection *Złoty lis* (Państwowy Instytut Wydawniczy, 1956).

MIRON BIAŁOSZEWSKI

1922–1983

Miron Białoszewski is best known as an idiosyncratic, avant-garde poet of the post-Stalinist 'Thaw' of the 1950s. His work overall, however, is as eclectic as his vision was experimental and includes not only lyric poetry, but life writing, plays, cabaret sketches, short documentary prose and novelistic narratives. What unifies it is his odd-angled attention to the Polish language and everyday life – the 'kingdom of insignificance', as scholar Joanna Niżyńska puts it, which in his unmistakable style is reproduced in cadences of quotidian speech and often whimsical neologisms that activate both familiarity and surprise.

The defining experience of Białoszewski's life was the German occupation of Warsaw during the Second World War, especially the uprising of 1944. His extraordinary 1970 *Memoir of the Warsaw Uprising* (translated by Madeline G. Levine, reissued in 2015) unconventionally skirts the patriotism and heroism of most narratives of that pivotal episode of Polish history. The curiosity it brings to inconspicuous details, interiors, the topography of Warsaw neighbourhoods and the personalities of the author's friends and relatives, especially women, can be found in 'Nanka' too. Published in 1980, 'Nanka' describes the Warsaw life of Białoszewski's family before and briefly after the war. It shares many features of the short-story form, including the conflict between Nanka and Michał and the author's ethical epiphany at the end.

Białoszewski never hid his sexuality, and queerness was integral to his work. The flat on Dąbrowska Square in central Warsaw, where he lived with the painter Leszek Soliński, served in the 1950s and 1960s as a venue for the legendary Teatr Osobny (Separate Theatre), an experimental collective he ran with friends Ludwik Hering and Ludmila Murawska.

His relationship with Soliński has been crucial for his legacy, as Soliński fastidiously collected Białoszewski's manuscripts during his lifetime and later served as his literary executor. When Soliński himself died in 2005, custodianship of the estate fell to his widower, Dutch Slavist Henk Proeme, who has since helped facilitate new editions and translations of Białoszewski's writing.

W. Martin

Nanka

Translated by W. Martin

Her mother (my grandmother) had to make her go to school. She'd get to the gate and turn back. She had no desire to go. She wanted to stay home. Her whole life.

When her mother gave her ten groszy, she would go into town and come back with ten groszy. There was nothing for her to spend it on, nor did she want to.

She said:

'My mother works hard, how can I spend her money?'

She would help her around the house.

This was before the other war. Her mother, my grandmother, Bronisława Białoszewska, would sew quilts in the only room; they would sleep in the nook and the kitchen. A beggar pasted a piece of bread smeared with lard to my grandmother's door since he felt he deserved something better. She would feed the beggars, take them in, put them up. And they often robbed her.

Bronisława's husband, my grandfather Walenty, had an apprentice for many years. Kostek. They'd taken him out of an orphanage somewhere, a child with parents unknown. They said his father must've been an officer and his mother a lady, because when he got called up for the Tsar's army all the way to the Manchurian border, he was put to work in the chancellery on account of his beautiful handwriting. He and Nanka got engaged. He came back on leave. The Białoszewskis had a cousin from Warka living with them then, young and skittish. They'd taken her in to do the cooking, since my grandmother sewed the quilts and had to keep her hands clean for the damask. Kostek arranged in secret to meet that cousin from Warka, and they spent the night in a hotel. Grandma found out everything and showed Kostek the door.

'My daughter won't be marrying a rogue.'

There was no use begging. Nanka lay down in bed and fell ill. My grandma told her:

'My child, if he's done you this way now, imagine what he'll do later.'

Kostek sent letter after letter, but my grandmother intercepted them all. When my grandfather asked her:

'What's happening with Kostek?'

'He doesn't write.'

Nanka remained in the dark until her dying day.

Kostek went off to Russia. Nanka kept his photograph her whole life; now Sabina has it.

The first war wore on, horribly hard. After the war, in 1920, Michał showed up, with his Swedish moustache. A communist, he'd captured the Winter Palace. They wanted to make someone out of him over there, but he saw how one day you're in charge and the next day in the gutter, and ran off to Poland, where he'd been born. I even know where. In Sanniki, which I used to pass through on the way to Płock. It wasn't such a shabby place. But to hear Nanka, Sabina and my mother make fun of it. They'd say he was born in *Sienniki*, 'straw mattress town'. Michał had been born out of wedlock too. What's more – while he was thick-skinned about every other personal matter – in this one area he was quite sensitive. Apparently, someone once alluded to it by mistake, and he flew off the handle.

Nanka and Michał had already set a date for their wedding when Michał got drunk. My cool-headed grandfather Walenty grabbed hold of a chair and chased him out with it. Nanka fainted. My grandfather got over it, the wedding took place. It happened at 99 Leszno Street. A one-room apartment with kitchen.

And then my grandmother Bronia died. On the same bed where four years later I was born. That bed had been made by my grandfather. He'd carved grapevines on it, then died in it himself, a year before the last war broke out.

After I was born, my parents slept in that bed; my wicker crib stood between it and the tile stove, and at the other end of the room stood Nanka's and Michał's bed and, between that bed and the door, the divan where Sabina slept. The sister of Nanka and my father, and also my mother's dearest friend from their girlhood to this day. Inside the divan were coats strewn with mothballs, books and hair extensions with wire headbands that looked like radio headphones. Back then, people talked about falsies and augmented calves. Every now and then Sabina would exterminate the bedbugs. They especially loved to nest in the bolsters, in the pile furrows.

We had a dog, named Lala, I called her Lalunia. The two of us loved to jump around on the divan, but when Nanka called out 'Sabina's coming!', we panicked and jumped back down.

On the wall above the divan hung Matejko's *The Battle of Grunwald*. A large, framed reproduction behind glass. The glass broke once and a shard got stuck at the bottom, sticking out over the frame; I always think of that when I think of the Teutonic Knights' banner and Witold on the horse. And I don't know if it was Witold or someone else who sat facing the horse's tail. There was a patch of damp on the ceiling, large and con-voluted. It was even more interesting than *The Battle of Grunwald*, but even less legible.

My mother was quick, she would slice noodle dough for the chicken soup fast as a catapult. Nanka was never in a rush, she cut the noodles three times slower.

She would sleep late. Then she would read her book. Only later would she start cooking. Patiently she stood in place at the stove, waiting.

Michał came back from work in the carpentry workshop and always found Nanka in the same position.

'What, no supper yet? For crying out loud!'

Nanka muttered something to herself, made a movement forward and then one to the side, shook her leg and let it be. She was unflappable. When she went to get vegetables from the shop downstairs, she could stand there and chew the fat for two hours. She had long hair down to her ankles and every day before the looking glass she combed it at length. They said her hair made her weaker and that's why she was so anaemic. She had headaches almost daily. Often, she sent me down for Kogutek to the pharmacy, which was in our building. Kogutek pills were for the headaches.

Michał made Nanka a cord for her radio headphones that was so long she could peel the potatoes, walk around the kitchen and make the whole dinner while wearing them. The radio was a crystal set. You had to fiddle with the crystal now and then because the sound would go out. Late in the evenings, Michał would pick up Moscow and listen to it reverently.

As late as September, in '39, when the news broke that the Soviets were coming to the aid of Warsaw, he took off with other enthusiasts to decorate Kierbedź Bridge with flowers. He only stopped being a communist after the war, when he got fed up.

He saved up his money for a Catholic burial, although he wasn't religious. That church burial was so important to him that right before he died, in Góra Kalwaria, he agreed to take confession. Apparently, it took a while.

But let's go back to the old days. Nanka took a great interest in her dreams. Oftentimes she dreamed she was being butchered. She said it was from sleeping on her back. Whenever she woke up from a strange dream, she started telling Michał about it at the top of her voice – quiet was not her thing – in bed in the middle of the night. Michał shouted:

'For Pete's sake, would you pipe down? Let a man sleep!'

Michał often drank. In Zawadzki's pub on Wrona Street. Sometimes a drunk would be lying outside Zawadzki's, and a few times that drunk happened to be Michał. When the weather was good, Zawadzki's massive dog, Tumry, would be there outside the bar. He would lie splayed out across the sidewalk, so people had to step down into the cobblestone street to get around him, they were afraid of him. Other times, you'd see Michał draped over the windowsill in the stairwell at night. Michał's footsteps announced themselves the moment he walked into the hallway, drunk. He'd open the door with such a flourish a stray bucket of dishwater in the corner began to tremble. Doffing his cap, he'd say:

'I ran into a Flora in our courtyard.'

Or: 'A single green monkey was coming down Leszno.'

Nanka shouted:

'Quiet! The kid'll hear you!'

And the kid, who was me, was quickly unloaded by my mother or Sabina on Zosia next door.

Some Sunday or other, Michał came home in a cantankerous mood. He shouted: 'Fucking hell, I'll massacre the lot of you!', and started scuffling with the drawer of a sideboard, the rickety one an apprentice of my grandfather had made. The drawer smelled of strewn cloves, and Michał was getting the rusted forks tangled up with old shoelaces. At last, he took out a large kitchen knife and started waving it about. Then from atop the linen chest, where she was sitting in her overcoat, Auntie Józia jumped to her feet: 'Oh, Michał! Michał!' – and ran home to Ogrodowa Street, her apartment on the fourth floor, where she sewed linens to get by. And where she often complained about being a widow twice over and how hardly anyone visited her.

'But when you go to see her,' my aunts would say, 'all you get is her padlocked door in your face.'

And the padlock Józia used was huge. She would make the rounds of her friends, and of relatives near and distant, telling the ones about the others, she knew a lot and could she ever talk.

'A nattering Nelly that one,' they'd say about her.

If she didn't know something, she'd ask. How do you pronounce that? Who painted that picture? When did Mickiewicz write that? She adored historical painting, old buildings, operas. Sienkiewicz's *Trilogy*, the poems of Mickiewicz. She was good at reading aloud, but probably not so good at writing. She only got to second grade in grammar school.

She loved taking public transport with me to various planned destinations, like Wierzbno. We had been talking for weeks about going there, until one sweltering Sunday, Auntie Józia walked in ceremoniously, her purse with the loud clasp under her arm, and said:

'We are going to Wierzbno. We shall walk to Okopowa and Gęsia and take the 9 from there.'

It was terrifically hot on Okopowa Street. Ludwik's sister would go that way to work when she was younger, and she remembers how there wasn't a single tree the whole way, the buildings were low, and the fences provided hardly any shade.

In Wierzbno, on Puławska Street, I remember the branches protruding and ditches full of dust. At one point Auntie Józia exclaimed:

'Oh look, a church, let's go in.'

We went in. It turned out that the Sisters of Saint Elizabeth ran a hospital here. Auntie Józia soon got hold of a nun and had a nice long chat. Afterwards she said:

'Let's go to the tram, but slowly, slowly.'

And we returned home, enchanted.

Auntie Józia said to Nanka:

'It's just your fate to be with Michał. Once, the Lord Jesus pretended to be an old beggar and asked a young lady walking by for a handout. She gave him all the farthings she had. And the Lord said to her: "Here's your reward: your future husband", and pointed to a drunkard in a ditch.'

When Michał got really pickled, Nanka would set a basin of water next to his chair, to wash him and get him tidied up. With all she'd suffered and had to bear, she could afford to be harsh and a little spiteful.

'Your foot! Come on, give me your foot. Now!'

She drubbed him this way and that like a mannequin.

'Now the other one, you son of a bitch!' – and thump went Michał against the wall and Michał's elbow on the table.

More than once, I woke up late at night in the dark room, everyone sleeping, the only light coming from the crack in the door to the kitchen, from where I could hear sloshing water, scuffling, and Nanka's voice:

'Come on, your foot! Just look how plastered you are!'

Michał's drunken scenes were a way to vent his genuine loathing for petty-bourgeois, mouse-like prudence. When he was sober, he would simply say he didn't like that furniture or those things. As for him, he didn't need anything. He'd as soon throw it all out the window. But when he was sober, he behaved. He was respected as a professional carpenter, and if he messed up at one job, he easily found another. He always gave Nanka money, except when he drank it all. But Nanka would search through his pockets each time, and she always turned up something.

Every now and then, Nanka would sew a quilt. First, she would go to the Jews on Dzika Street for cotton or down. And for damask, printed with large flowers. Then she would borrow the key to Mrs Hotkiewicz's 'upstairs' and, with me at her side, walk up to the fifth floor, to the so-called 'upstairs'. There were three doors there locked with padlocks. The doors had cracks in them and through the cracks I could see a dimly lit space with beams that smelled strongly of dust and wood. I never saw the two adjacent attics. In general, I rarely had a reason to be in the stairwell, only when my grandfather ground horseradish out on the landing before Easter, or when Mrs Hotkiewicz had some beef with my mother, or when Nanka would take me upstairs with her to hang out or gather up the linen, or to retrieve or return the quilting frame. The quilting frame had been inherited from her mother, the quilter: my grandmother Bronisława. In the attic, columns of sunlight fell in through the narrow windows, galaxies of dust whirling in them as if they were beams of revelation. The frame was long, dark and squat, with rows of holes running along it for the pegs.

Nanka would set up the frame in a square in the middle of the room, stretch the fabric and batting across it, draw her pattern on top and slowly begin sewing the quilt. Then, beneath the quilt's stretched-out underside, I would make a nest for myself. By the third day, the quilt-roof would be smaller, lower. Nanka would finish her work. Then she carried the frame back upstairs.

She loved sitting at home. Throughout the summer, everyone would go into town in the evening, but Nanka and I stayed in the kitchen. Nanka near the stove, because she liked the warmth, she liked warming herself; when she drank tea, she would warm her hands on the mug. And I would hop across the floor, one floorboard at a time; I pirouetted on the nails or drew maps of invented cities, or else made cities out of building blocks, which I always ran out of, or I would cross the floor by tram, meaning chunks of firewood – at least there were always enough of those – that I attached numbers to. Sometimes Nanka would sit with her elbows on the table, legs tucked under the seat, and read. Ideally until midnight, one in the morning. Behind her back she had the stove and the door with the transom window to the hallway. She once sat like that until three in the morning with her book.

'Suddenly, I get the feeling someone's looking in through that window up there. Immediately I think Czesiek, Uncle Kazimierz's Czesiek, must've died. I was afraid to turn around and look. I backed out of the kitchen and went to the room.'

Then, at five in the morning, Uncle Kazimierz came over. Czesiek did die that night.

Sabina, Nanka's younger sister, would also get so lost in reading that once – and she was alone in the apartment – she was roused only by the voice of a woman begging: 'I haven't even a shirt to my name'.

Nanka and Sabina called my mother 'Mistress Quickly'. Normally they'd say to her: 'Listen, Kacha' – short for Kazimiera.

They had trouble with the dative case – to and for whom – and forgot the softened consonants. Instead of 'Kasze', they came up with: 'I gave it to Kacha'.

When Mama, who had a quick temper in those years, tried to get after me, they defended me. I always hid behind Nanka's back.

All three of them loved to go to the cinema. And I loved hearing them retell the movies. One time, Nanka told us about a ship, how someone was going down below decks; it was night, the sea was stormy. I don't know what happened, but that was enough for me. Another time, Nanka told us a different story:

'That was a scene. He's in a prison cell. In comes his daughter and starts pulling her dress off from the top. He doesn't know what to do. She pulls the dress lower and lower. He thrashes about until he grabs a knife and cuts off his fingers.'

Mostly they would go to the Comet on Chłodna Street. A cinema and music hall. Once they took me with them. I found the variety show interesting, but all I remember is someone sitting blindfolded on a chair in the middle of an empty stage, guessing who had on which coat with what kind of buttons. Coming out of the Comet, my mother and my aunt put on their own act:

'Here's where my geranium will grow' – and they dug their fingers into their palms, imitating the actress who had sung it.

Sometimes all three would be getting ready to go to the movies, Nanka taking the longest. She'd be putting on fancy shoes over her aching corns. In the kitchen, she walked to the window and back.

'No, I'm not going, my feet hurt.'

And to think that after the uprising the Germans took Auntie Nanka far away, to the mountains, where they forced her to walk to work every day in clogs, who knows how many miles. There was a lot of snow then, it would stick to the bottom of the clogs, turning them into wedge shoes, and it constantly had to be scraped off. But somehow Nanka endured it. She wasn't the only one. A tenant of Auntie Józia, a seamstress, walked beside her. They took Józia and my mum away to the same mountains, just farther away.

Auntie Józia had suffered from liver disease for years. Whenever she worried, and she worried over a lot of people, her liver would give her trouble.

'Someone roll me a cigarette,' she would say to us there on Leszno Street and sit hunched over on the trunk, the dirty underwear inside sometimes showing through the cracks. On account of that liver, she was laid up in a hospital in Silesia in the autumn of '45. Pale as tissue paper.

The nurses there were still the German nuns. But she had no problem communicating with them since she could speak Yiddish. She had always lived among Jews. We left her there like that, along with Sabina, because we had to take my mum back to Warsaw. I had a feeling Auntie Józia would soon die. And she did.

During the uprising, when the Germans were seizing and razing the neighbourhood of Wola, Nanka and Michał were in the cellar on the corner of Leszno and Wrona. Bombs were going off. All of a sudden Nanka and Michał started fighting over something. Michał shouted:

'I hope the next bomb takes you out, you shrew!'

At which Nanka grabbed her bundle and went out to the Germans.

As soon as they took Leszno Street, they forced Michał to go to Saint Adalbert's Church in Wola. There was a terrible crowd there. Women were giving birth. Michał delivered babies on the main altar. The church and all the people were supposed to be blown to bits, but the order was revoked at the last minute. Probably on account of General von dem Bach. My mother ran into Michał in Głogów during the deportation.

Nanka returned in May, after the war, with her folks, on foot, pulling carts; on the road she passed other groups, vehicles heaped with bundles, even a horse-drawn hearse full of people and bags, but drawn by hand, since no one had horses. It was sweltering hot. Nanka started hearing a hallucination or howling that kept getting louder, sounding more and more like a human voice, until they came to a shouting cottage. Nanka rushed inside. Empty. Just a paralysed old woman in a chair, crying: '*Trinken! Trinken!*'

Nanka grabbed a pitcher, ran to the well. The well was dry. Nanka ran back into the shack with the empty pitcher, the old woman groaned: '*Trinken*'.

Nanka looked around, she didn't know what to do, her folks kept getting farther away. What would she do without them? She ran off after them. Devastated. Haunted by the desperate '*Trinken . . . Trinken*'.

It haunted her to the end of her life. That's what she told me, in her last apartment, in Praga. One room with a kitchen. She and Michał were allocated that place after their basement apartment in Targówek got flooded. The water often rose as far as Targówek. Michał made Nanka a riser out of boards, a kind of stage, the stove was set on it, and when there was flooding, there Nanka would sit. Until one time something burst on them and water filled the basement up to ground level. Nanka grabbed onto the pipes in the ceiling and hung there like that a few hours until the fire brigade came.

At the new apartment in the old house on Kępna, kitty-corner from Targowa Street, Nanka slept in the room and Michał in the kitchen. They would sit together in the evening. It wasn't their fate to split up. When she got back from the deportation, Nanka stayed with Auntie Władka – a poet – out in Grodzisk. Yet another poet in my family. An amateur, whose husband, a teacher, had mental breakdowns, and she would run off to teach the children for him.

Then, right on Corpus Christi, after all those years, a parade took place on Krakowskie Przedmieście, between the mounds of rubble. I was there. Unexpectedly I ran into my grandmother Frania, who was also back from a sojourn. She was living with her son and daughter-in-law. That daughter-in-law and her two daughters, after the terrible bombing of Miedziana and Towarowa streets, they were transported to Dresden and had to survive the catastrophe of Dresden too. I was living with my father on Poznańska Street then. I was working next door in the main post office. Sorting letters. On Corpus Christi, early in the morning, I had just got home from an all-night shift. Sabina came. She told me Nanka was on her way back.

I saw Nanka for the first time since the uprising. We still had my father's concubine, Zocha, living with us on Poznańska then. At the beginning of the war, after we'd moved back in with Nanka on Leszno Street, Zocha saw my mother leaving the house one morning and she knocked on the door:

'Is Zenek here?'

Zenek, my father, was lying in bed in the room, behind the other door. Nanka told her: 'He's not here'.

'What do you mean he's not there? He has to be.'

'What do you want, lady? You have some nerve to barge in on us like this! Get lost! Get out of here!' And Nanka grabbed a broom and Zocha fled.

And now it was Zocha, who – as hostess, and not having seen Nanka since that incident – was preparing the table, the food.

'Please, have a seat, eat.'

And Nanka sat down and ate. And everyone talked. The thing is, they had all been through the uprising. And that meant something. Zocha, too, had come back from forced labour and digging trenches outside Vienna a few days before. She had come on foot by way of Budapest and Czechoslovakia, pulling a cart with her things behind her, and she kept a diary on the way.

Nanka moved in with Sabina on Złota Street. I was with my father on Poznańska. At the market I ran into Michał in the crowd. He was looking for Nanka. He found her. She told him she did not want to be with him. He came again. Once again she told him no. He came yet again. And she relented. Neither of them had changed. He continued to drink and make scenes. One time, Sabina stopped by when Nanka was visiting me.

'Your drunken husband is lying over on Wspólna Street.'

'So? Let him lie there.'

Later, Michał calmed down a bit, drank less. He had liver disease. Was in and out of hospitals. Behind Nanka's back he was putting money aside for a rainy day and a Catholic burial, although he refused to let the nun who came to see him hang a crucifix over the bed, he even told her off. Nanka, behind Michał's back, was also putting money aside in a little tin box for her rainy day.

One time I went to see them, and we were sitting in the kitchen, I was telling them about my visit to Płock and the new houses there. Michał said: 'New houses in Płock? I built those houses.'

'But when?' Nanka exclaimed.

'Well, I suppose it was some time ago, in 1905.'

It occurred to me recently that as we get older, time starts to warp like that all on its own. In 1945, I moved into a very old, art nouveau building on Poznańska Street. On the wall was an inscription: '1912'. So, it was about thirty-three years old then. That's about as old as the first new post-war houses are getting to be now, the kind of building where some friends were apparently allocated an apartment not long ago.

One morning, Michał had had enough of waiting for Nanka. He was getting worried, why was she so quiet? He got up in his long johns and, leaning on his cane – which was how he was getting around the apartment by that point – he hobbled to Nanka's door. Silence. He peeked in. Nanka was half-lying on, half-kneeling next to the bed. In her nightgown.

Motionless, cold, but alive. She couldn't speak. Michał went out in his long johns onto the stairs and started shouting: 'Help! Help!'

A neighbour ran off for help. They laid Nanka on the bed. The ambulance came. They diagnosed a stroke. Nanka lay there in her room a few days. Sabina and her husband, Julian, tended to her, washing and feeding her.

'Get me Julian,' Nanka mumbled. No one could reposition her like he could.

They took Nanka to the hospital. She was scared. But hopeful still of going back home. She never did. She died a few days later. At the end of March.

Michał lay in his kitchen, groaning on account of his liver. Sabina and the nun took turns looking in on him. They had never got along, Michał and Sabina. Now he trusted Sabina, he adored her, gave her the thousands he'd squirrelled away for his funeral and something extra for herself.

He said to me once, when I was over:

'Lying here like this in the kitchen, staring at that wall. It'd drive anyone crazy.'

They took him to Góra Kalwaria, to the hospital for the terminally ill. There was no other choice. He died there in June. He had a Catholic funeral, in Bródno Cemetery.

But not everything was so transparent after all.

Sabina told me recently how she once watched Nanka tying a knot, then untying it. She asked her:

'What on earth are you doing?'

'I'm practising patience.'

'Nanka'
Published as part of the collection *Rozkurz* (Państwowy Instytut Wydawniczy, 1980).

JÓZEF HEN

1923–

On 8 November 2024, Józef Hen celebrated his 101st birthday. His numerous works include novels, stories, biographies, memoirs, diaries and screenplays.

Born Józef Cukier to a Jewish family, he grew up on Nowolipie Street in central Warsaw, and later wrote a memoir of his childhood, a lively description of the coexistence of Polish and Jewish culture in the interwar years. He began his literary career at the age of eight, when his work was published in Janusz Korczak's newspaper written entirely by children, *Mały Przegląd* (*Little Review*). During the war, Nowolipie Street was part of the Warsaw ghetto. Many of Hen's closest relatives lost their lives. Hen himself survived various ordeals that took him as far as Uzbekistan. There he served in the Polish 2nd Army, became a war correspondent and ran an army theatre. He later described his own and his family's war experiences in the novels *Nikt nie woła* (*Nobody's Calling*, 1990) and *Najpiękniejsze lata* (*The Most Beautiful Years*, 1996).

In 1947 he returned to Warsaw and rapidly developed his career, writing screenplays for films, including *The Cross of Valour*, based on his own stories about young soldiers fighting for the new communist Poland; and *Prawo i pięść* (*The Law and the Fist*), based on his 1964 novel *Toast*, and described as the Polish equivalent of a western as it features a lone hero representing the new regime as he fights a gang of bandits.

Perhaps the best known of his biographies – written in literary, rather than academic style – is *Ja, Michał z Montaigne* (*I, Michel de Montaigne*, 1978), a panorama of sixteenth-century Europe set against the life story of the eponymous French essayist and thinker.

His son Maciej, who is also an acclaimed novelist, remembers that

Józef Hen wrote 'A Long and Speedy Boat' shortly after his wife's death in 2010. 'He distinctly told me and my sister that in a way it was a story about himself and our mother – about her passing.'

Antonia Lloyd-Jones

A Long and Speedy Boat

Translated by Antonia Lloyd-Jones

'Uncle Methuselah,' said the Youth. 'What have you dreamed of lately?'

'Shh!' hissed the old Wizard. He had been trotting around the room with his hands raised, but now he stopped, panting. 'I almost had her, but then you burst in with your question . . . She gave me the slip!'

'Who did, Uncle Methuselah?' asked the Youth, whose name was Japheth.

'Don't say uncle,' said the Wizard irritably. 'You're to call me Your Honour. Those are the Missionary's orders, as you may have heard?'

'Father Nehemiah?'

'Yes, Father Nehemiah. Now sit quietly, son, and don't open your mouth needlessly. I must catch this unfortunate fellow's soul.'

A man Japheth didn't recognize was lying on the ground on a scanty bed of leaves, wheezing.

'Can you hear him, son? He's suffering, though he may be unaware of his own suffering.'

'Can you help him, Your Honour?' asked the Youth.

'That's what I'm for,' replied the Wizard. 'He hobbled here to see me from a village far away. His body has withered and his soul has escaped from it. She's trying to elude me by hovering somewhere close to the roof.' Methuselah the Wizard showed Japheth a small bottle filled with transparent liquid, which had a needle stuck into the cork. 'You see? I'll catch his cunning little soul in this vessel, I'll catch her and she won't give me the slip again. Now squat down and don't get in my way.'

Japheth obediently squatted down.

'I'm going to run around the walls, clapping and dancing. The neatest way to lure a soul is by dancing. And you must watch out, don't open your mouth, for if the soul takes refuge inside you, things will be bad, very bad . . . Both for him and for you.'

The Wizard clapped out a beat on his thighs and began his dance – the kind the People in his village usually dance. Taking small steps he glided around the room, bowing as he passed the bare, shabby cross hanging on the wall, waved his hands overhead some more, and suddenly exclaimed: 'Got her!'

Holding the bottle high, he stamped out a victory dance, crying: 'You're here, you crafty little soul, you clever little soul, you wayward little soul, you're here, I've got you and I'll force you to serve me, just as a soul should.'

Then he turned to the Youth.

'Look, son, here she is!' He showed him the little bottle with the needle. 'You can't see her, because souls are invisible – that's why it's hard to catch them. But now look . . .' The Wizard went up to the sick man, kneeled beside him and stuck the needle into his skinny buttock. Gradually the liquid in the bottle lessened, until finally it was empty. 'I have injected his soul inside him,' said the Wizard, getting up from his knees. 'She will grow in there and fill him entirely.'

'He's not wheezing any more,' noted Japheth.

'He's not suffering. Now he'll sleep,' said Methuselah.

'Will he recover?'

'If his soul doesn't resist. Speak up, son. You had a question for me, didn't you?'

'I wanted to ask what you've dreamed of lately, Your Honour. If it was of a long and speedy boat, I'd buy the dream from you.'

For a while neither of them spoke, old or young. Then Japheth added: 'I've got two packets of Lucky Strikes.'

Methuselah the Wizard remained silent.

'It's not much,' muttered Japheth.

'No,' replied the Wizard.

'Well, then, three packets. OK?'

'Aha, you've grown rich.'

'I hauled some crates for the Missionary. He was very pleased, he praised me and added a can of cola.'

'Three packets, you say . . .' Methuselah the Wizard scratched his head, covered in greying curls. 'Yes, that would be enough. But I haven't dreamed of any boat.'

'That's a pity.'

'Yes, son, it is. Maybe it'll happen. What's your name?'

'Japheth.'

'Japheth. A strange name. Is that another one from the book Father Nehemiah carries around with him?'

'Yes, that's right, Your Honour, it was he who gave it to me. He plunged me in the lake and said this: *I baptize you in the name of our lord* – he didn't say the lord's name – *and I give you the name Japheth*. Japheth, he said, because I'm different from the People, my hair's not black, but golden.'

'It's a little dark in here, but perhaps it is golden. Well, don't worry.'

'I'm not worrying,' replied Japheth.

'If anyone tries to hurt you, I shall defend you.'

'But what I need is a boat.'

'The time comes for everything. Dreams don't just appear when you want them to. You have to wait patiently. And another thing: don't mention this to the Missionary.'

'He knows.'

'Does he?' Japheth thought the Wizard seemed alarmed. 'And?'

'He said it does no harm. "*All right*," that's what he said.'

'All right, aha, good. He, this Father Nehemiah, has immersed many of our villagers in the river, baptized them and given them names. And he sent some People to me who are skilled workers, they came from afar, they knocked new beams into the walls to widen the room, and covered it with thick, new leaves, laying them densely to stop it from leaking. And he hung up this cross and said: *May the spirit of our lord hang here, now he resides in these slats that I have blessed*, and then he said: *May the People come and beg for mercy for their sins, and the lord will have mercy, because he is love.*'

'Love,' repeated Japheth. 'What does he mean?'

'One day I'll tell you.'

'Why not right away?'

'The time comes for everything. What was I saying? Oh, yes, Father Nehemiah also said that he, their Wizard, suffered on the cross, long, long ago, he suffered for our sins. He was a great Wizard.'

'Nobody has come here today,' said Japheth. 'I can't see anyone except the sick man.'

'Look, he's sleeping peacefully.'

'Do People come to beg for mercy?'

'They come to buy dreams.'

'And to catch souls.'

'Yes, that too.'

'They don't sin,' said Japheth.

'*All right*,' agreed the Wizard. 'The People here don't sin.'

'I have no sins. All I need is a long, swift boat. Is that a sin?'

'Those who are unfortunate or sick come to see me, but nobody sinful. Not like those fellows, in their stone houses. The great Wizard didn't have to suffer for us, the People,' said Methuselah, pointing at the cross nailed to the slats. 'His soul is still suffering.'

'Do you think so?'

'I've heard what goes on among them over there. He's definitely suffering.'

Methuselah shook his hands as if casting something off them. End of conversation, Japheth understood. And heard: 'I did have a dream recently that you could buy.'

'But not of a boat.'

'Of a girl. Slender, lithe – I don't know if one like that would suit you. Buy yourself that dream. I can let you have it for one packet of Lucky Strikes.'

'But what do I need a girl for?'

'What do you mean? You can't live without a female.'

'I've got my eye on one already. Jezebel – have you ever seen her, Your Honour? I think she's willing.'

'But it won't be the girl from my dream.'

'That's true, Your Honour. Not from a dream.'

For a while both old and young were silent. Then the Youth spoke.

'She has everything I need. There's something to get my hands on. Except that . . .'

'Except what?'

'I don't know if I should say it.'

'Here you can say anything,' Methuselah reminded him. 'I am a Wizard. A Wizard does not repeat the words entrusted to him in confidence.'

'This future female of mine has decided she's going to cover her breasts.'

'Really? You're not joking?'

'No!'

'Just like those other women?'

'Yes, like them.'

They both knew who they meant.

'That bodes ill, Japheth,' said the Wizard sadly. 'A proper female doesn't cover her breasts. Maybe they're flat?'

'No, they're large and supple. I've touched them. *All right.*'

'So she likes to do that,' said the experienced Wizard. 'She likes hiding them as a way to be arousing.'

'I was aroused anyway.'

'To be even more arousing.'

'That I would expect,' said Japheth, smiling at last. 'Things were different with the last one. Naomi, that's what the Missionary baptized her from his book. This Naomi was like all of them. Proper in every way.'

'So you're not with her any more?'

'No.'

'Did she leave you for another man?'

'No, it was I who told her to leave. She was a chatterbox. I couldn't stand her prattle. She always had something to say.'

'About what?' wondered the old Wizard.

'Anything at all. We'd be walking towards the forest, to get food, and I'd only have my eye on what we were to gather, but she'd say: *Look, a flower.* So what, a flower. And then she'd say: *How pretty it is.* But what's a flower supposed to be like? And she'd say: *What colours! A flower, colours, how pretty, how fragrant* – so it has a smell, what's there to say? I'd spend the whole time thinking how much food to pick from the trees, but she'd be going on about the flowers. She had to keep prattling away. And she'd look at me like this, sideways, she'd stare at me, fixing those dark eyes on me, and meanwhile those twig-like hands of hers would move as if dancing, and when she wanted to ask me to come to her, she'd say: *Come on, Japheth, enter me. It's so fragrant here.* I'd be inside her and she'd say: *Wasn't that flower pretty – just like* – and then: *like your cock* – and more: *Faster, faster, harder, harder, my sweet Japheth,* and why did she say that, as if I don't know what I have to do? And then, when she'd got what she needed, she'd burst out laughing – I have no idea why. She says hello and goodbye to everything with laughter. There'd be a turtle moving along the path, and she'd say: *Look, how funny!* And she laughed like . . . like a stream as it rolls over the pebbles. Anything at all made her laugh.'

'Youth,' said the Wizard with a sigh.

'Honoured Methuselah, I'm young too, but I certainly don't laugh at just anything.'

'When was the last time you laughed?'

'I'm not sure . . .'

'That's not good, son. She lives more wisely. What became of the turtle? Did she cook it?'

'She let it get away.'

'She was fond of it,' said the Wizard. 'Your Naomi was a good female, you just couldn't figure her out. All that babble . . . about flowers, colours, anything – that's their kind of joy. It's magic. And those caressing glances, cast from under the eyelids, peeping sideways, pupils like quivering butterflies, as if whispering: Do you want me? Do you like me? Yes, that's the nicest gift they give us.' Then he added with a sigh: 'While they're young . . .'

The boy looked around the room, as if in search of something, but evidently didn't find it, because he asked: 'But where is Her Honour? Has she gone to fetch sweet potatoes?'

The Wizard sat with his head drooping. Japheth persisted: 'Or breadfruits, perhaps?'

'Rebecca isn't here,' stammered Methuselah. 'They've taken her.'

'They've taken her? Who? How?'

'The Missionary, Father Nehemiah. He said that Lady Rebecca – that's what he called her, Lady – needed treatment. Over there, at their place. And that I could no longer manage. That may have been true, her soul was no longer obeying me, we knew each other too well. First they installed a bed for us here, with a soft base, so Lady Rebecca would not have to lie on a litter of leaves. A white iron bed. But she fell off it, possibly on purpose because she didn't want it, and I went to her, I picked up my lady, and I think she liked that. Sometimes Mrs Missionary came, I can't remember her name, but Rebecca didn't want her, she didn't want either fish or prawns or anything else from her. She'd shout for that woman to leave, there could only be one lady in this house, and that was her. Formerly, when I took care of her myself, things were better for Rebecca. At night I would think about what to give her to eat in the morning; she'd always been fussy, but now she was very choosy. But she praised whatever I offered her. At night she only had to move, and I awoke, I'd get up and go to her, I'd lead her outside, I'd wipe her with leaves and wash her. I never got enough sleep.'

'Always tired?'

'Yes.'

'You should have more respect for yourself, Your Honour.'

'No harm will come to me, I can get tired if necessary. So many years together . . . When I took her for myself she was a girl, just coming into bloom, with breasts like little apples. Then those bubbies of hers grew, they swelled, and when our baby boys appeared, there was always enough milk for them. Now they are far away, all three, drawn to live in those stone houses where souls don't settle; one lives differently there, and one dies differently there too. The two of us were left alone. And how her breasts look now is easy to imagine.'

The Wizard stood before the cross and gazed at it a while in silence, before addressing young Japheth again: 'Oh, Rebecca – how good she was at catching souls! She taught me more than I taught her. This dance is hers.' He knocked out a few bars on his thighs. 'But lately her head had been working more and more poorly. She was like a child again, saying she must return to her daddy, who was waiting for her. *Do you know who my daddy is, Sir?* she'd ask; *The great Wizard Methuselah. People journey to see him from faraway villages, yes, Sir, they do. And he's been so good to me.*'

'And have you?' asked the Young Man.

'Not always. But she couldn't remember that. *We must go there*, she'd say – there, meaning the village I took her from – *back to my daddy, for he thinks I've lost my way in the forest, he thinks I've gone missing in the marshes.* Your father's not here any more, I would try to explain, he's been gone a long time, his soul has taken off. And she would all but scream: *There are no souls! There are no souls! It's all lies!* Yes, son, her head had gone wrong. Her head, as Missionary Nehemiah explained it to me. But without his help I already knew about the head, that the head is to blame for everything. It stops you from sleeping. It causes you to suffer.'

'I can sleep,' replied Japheth. 'I don't suffer. Now you can sleep too, Your Honour.'

'Yes, I can.'

'You don't have to get up at night any more.'

'No, I don't. But I don't sleep and I do get up. I look: she's not here, and there's no iron bed, they took it along with Rebecca.'

'You don't have to think of food for her any more.'

'No. But I do.'

'And you don't have to prepare it.'

'No.'

'No obligations.'

'It's true.'

'So your life's easier.'

'Yes.'

'More comfortable.'

'More comfortable, yes,' Methuselah repeated.

'That's a good thing, isn't it?'

'No, it's not.'

'It's not a good thing that life is easier and more comfortable?' asked Japheth.

'Easier and more comfortable. Not a good thing,' said Methuselah, wiping away tears. 'It shouldn't be easier.'

Japheth didn't ask any more questions.

'Go now,' said the Wizard. 'When I dream about a boat I'll send for you.'

He led Japheth outside, under a sky twinkling with stars, and a full, silvery moon sailing among them.

'Three packets,' the Wizard reminded him.

Twice the silver moon came and went before the Wizard Methuselah could send for Japheth.

'Tell him to come at dawn,' he instructed the serving boy, 'and not to forget the Lucky Strikes.'

The dawn was glowing pink when Japheth appeared on the threshold.

'Your Honour?' asked the Youth. 'You summoned me?'

'Yes, Japheth, I haven't forgotten our conversation.'

The Wizard waited a while, keeping the young man in suspense, before announcing: 'Because . . . I had a dream about a boat.'

'Oh, Your Honour!'

'A long, slender boat. I knelt down in it, I plied its oar in the water, and it raced forwards fleetly. Like an arrow released from a bowstring. Now I know that I dreamed it for you. Exactly the kind of boat you wanted.'

'Long and speedy,' said Japheth, revelling in the words.

'Just so.'

'Will you sell me the dream, Your Honour?'

'Three packets.'

'But Uncle Methuselah, I only have two.'

Methusaleh nodded.

'OK.'

'Thank you, Uncle Methuselah.'

'It was a dream for you. I can let you have it for nothing, without the Lucky Strikes.'

'No, no,' Japheth protested in alarm. 'If I had it for free there would be no purchase. If there's going to be a boat . . .'

'All right,' Methusaleh interrupted him. 'Give me the Lucky Strikes.'

Japheth handed the Wizard two brightly coloured packets. Methuselah opened one of them and asked: 'Would you like one?'

'I don't smoke, Your Honour.'

'OK, then I won't either.'

The old Wizard and the Young Man shook hands.

'So now it's done,' said the Wizard. 'The dream is yours.'

In silence Methuselah hobbled around the room. It occurred to the boy that he should leave, when Methuselah said: 'Rebecca is dead.'

'Over there, at their place?' the boy asked shyly.

'Yes.'

'Couldn't they catch her soul?'

'They die differently there.'

'When did it happen, Your Honour?'

'Before the last moon.'

'Long ago.'

'Yes, long ago.'

'So you've been able to get used to it by now.'

'To her being gone? That is my greatest fear: that I'll get used to it. That "So be it, time for a new life" – without her. Father Nehemiah imparted a phrase of theirs to me: "It's normal". I don't quite know what it means, but I can guess and I don't agree. Fortunately, fortunately . . .'

The old man broke off.

'Fortunately – what?' asked the Youth.

'I haven't got used to it. This room has grown empty, it's too spacious. There are plenty of odds and ends in here that turn out to be unnecessary – they were necessary when she was here. But without her, they're not.'

'What if you were to summon up her soul?'

'She won't come here. No, she'll refuse. There was a time when I would wash her, and she'd understand why I was doing it, because sometimes her head worked, and those moments were the worst, because she felt bad about herself, and she'd say: "Methuselah, get me some curare. Methuselah, why do I have to live?" At first I didn't know what to say, I didn't know how to explain that I wasn't going to give her any curare, because she had to live, and why she had to live, and finally I'd say: "To be beside me".'

'Is that what you said?'

'Maybe I just wanted to say it.' The old Wizard looked around. 'But she is here. In these objects she has left behind. You see? In these necklaces, pendants, rings and bracelets. In the oils and scents. In the coloured powders she used to paint her face and body. In the little sacks and bags. Her eye is looking at me – it's there, in her eye that her soul is hiding. I've no need to summon it.'

The old Wizard wiped his eyes with the back of his hand. Turning his face from Japheth, he whispered: 'Why did I let them take her away from here?'

The Youth heard. He laid a hand on the Wizard's arm.

'Uncle Methuselah,' he said gently, 'you need a new person, a new life companion.'

'Now your head has gone wrong!'

'No, Your Honour, I know my facts, I know you need a female beside you, one that's experienced but not yet withered . . .'

'After Rebecca?!' said Methuselah indignantly. 'Here – some other woman? There really is something wrong with your head.'

But Japheth would not give in.

'But Your Honour, don't forget that Lady Rebecca wasn't the only one – you had relationships with other females, the People noticed, one of them was long-lasting, even.'

'Yes, I'm not saying I didn't care about them,' agreed the old Wizard. 'They were tempting creatures, the effort to win them was as exciting as hunting, because you had to hide, creep up, keep quiet, be cunning – yes, exciting, because of the threat of having your eyes scratched out for them. And Rebecca had long, sharp claws. But now what? There's no threat. I can do anything. The room is empty. I don't have to look round behind me. In fact some of them are already prepared to come here, to scrub my old back and wind their arms around me. But . . .' – Japheth waited patiently for the words that would follow this 'but' – '. . . I don't know why, but they've become alien to me. Maybe because it's not like hunting any more. There's no one lying in wait.'

'Except her soul.'

'Oh yes . . . Her soul, yes . . . If a soul had fingernails . . .'

The Wizard wiped his eyes, and now when he spoke, his voice was composed, low, deep and masterful.

'Japheth!'

'I hear you.'

'You're to go to the Missionary. Got it?'

'Yes. I'm to go to the Missionary.'

'You're to borrow a powerful axe from him. You're to tell him I requested it. Don't delay.'

'I won't.'

'You're to go to the forest and choose a strong, straight, sturdy tree.'

'I will. And what shall I do with the tree?'

'You'll fell it. Maybe someone can help you?'

'My brother Shem.'

'OK. Together you will fell the trunk to a length of at least forty feet. You'll scrape off the bark to make it lighter.'

'And then what?'

'You'll use tools to hollow out the inside of the trunk, and you'll have a boat.'

'Why do I have to do that, Uncle Wizard, I've bought a boat, haven't I?'

'You've bought a dream. A dream about a boat. Now you have to make the boat so that it can sail into your life.'

'But that's hard work.'

'Hard work is needed. Sweat is needed.'

The Youth nodded.

'Sweat, yes. I think I understand.' Japheth thought a while, and then said: 'My brother Shem will help me. He knows more about boats than I do. He's not afraid of hard work.'

'That's good. Don't forget: the more sweat, the better the boat. You'll have the kind of boat that appeared in my dream. A long and speedy boat.'

'A long and speedy boat,' repeated Japheth, as if uttering an incantation.

'Don't forget about the oars.'

'I won't.'

Japheth walked over to the doorway, and was about to draw aside the plaited curtain shielding it, when he remembered that the Wizard had promised to explain something to him.

'Your Honour, I wanted to ask you . . .'

The Wizard wiped his eyes and took a deep breath to stifle his sobbing. Now Japheth wanted to back off.

'But if you don't want to . . .'

'I do,' replied the Wizard.

'It's that the Missionary, that's to say Father Nehemiah, keeps going on about love. What does he mean? Love? What is love? You're sure to know.'

'Yes, I do. Love is . . . Just a moment, let me think . . . Love is . . .'

The Wizard began to weep.

'No, I don't know,' he said through his tears.

He wiped his eyes with the back of his hand and repeated: 'I don't know, I don't know.'

'*Długa, chyża łódź*'
Published as part of the collection *Szóste najmłodsze i inne opowiadania* (Wydawnictwo W.A.B., 2011).

MARGO REJMER

1985–

Małgorzata (Margo) Rejmer divides her time between Poland and Albania, and between fiction and non-fiction. In English translation she is best known for *Mud Sweeter than Honey* (2021), based on conversations with victims of political repression in Albania under Enver Hoxha. Although it is a factual work of non-fiction, among the diverse narratorial voices Rejmer inserts creative texts, told from the point of view of, for instance, a pair of running shoes desperate to escape. Her writing is often profoundly visual, presenting vivid images, and she never shies away from describing her interlocutors' most harrowing experiences.

After initially moving to Albania for six months, she swiftly realized that to write about it convincingly she needed to live there, and six months soon became six years. Albania inspired several of the stories in her most recent fictional collection, *Ciężar skory* (*The Burden of Skin*, 2023, from which this eponymous story is taken). Rejmer's themes include issues affecting social outsiders, and the ways young people feel about themselves, spiritually and physically.

'I wrote this story for an Albanian friend who is a lesbian,' she says. 'We'd been to a stage show in Tirana together, a monologue based on the life of a transsexual activist who ended up committing suicide. My friend complained that this was the only narrative ascribed to homosexuals in Albania: "They always die alone or break up with their partners. It makes me feel afraid my life will be like that. I wish I could read something positive, with a happy end!" So I said: "I'll write a story especially for you, and it's sure to end well." But later a reader told me she finds the story sad, and to her the ending is just the central character's fantasy.

I wasn't surprised, because I designed all the stories in this collection to have ambiguous endings, leaving the reader to interpret them in their own way, depending on their own experiences and the mood they're in.'

Antonia Lloyd-Jones

The Burden of Skin

Translated by Antonia Lloyd-Jones

I watch him from afar as he approaches the small table unsteadily. He has one eye shielded by a black pirate patch; the other is mistily staring at me, trying to find its focus. He has none of the light grace of the other young waiters, greedy for tips, none of their predatory cunning and mercenary charm. He treads heavily, as if his legs are crammed full of stones. Only when he steps under a lamp and the light floods his ebony hair and narrow nose can I see what taut, fine skin he has, peppered with little pink veins on the temples and in the dip of the nostrils, like the body of a soft sea creature.

'Can't you take that eyepatch off now?' I ask. 'It's way past midnight.'

He straightens up, as if he has finally noticed me and realized where he is. In that pirate costume he looks like a miserable child at a fancy-dress party who doesn't know how to have noisy fun and avoids the other kids. I imagine his long, thick eyelashes brushing against the black, satin material that's covering his eye, and at once I feel a rush of blood. Without a word he takes off the patch and puts it in his pocket. He blinks and rubs his eyelid with a finger, as if he's just woken up.

The pirate bar on a ship moored at the wharf in Vlorë is open until one in the morning, and I am one of the last remaining customers, a survivor. It's Tuesday night, and at this time no one else is likely to come in. There are salvoes of noise coming from the neighbouring bars. This place is hideous, with all the lights on and thudding music, but I'd been hoping to meet someone just like him in here.

His neck is long and smooth; my fingertips can remember the firm feel of skin like that.

'It's a pity to hide such a pretty face,' I say.

Nothing in his expression changes, but for the first time he looks me in the eyes, with an attention I wouldn't have suspected him of, and then he sees the deep scar on my forehead. He runs his gaze along the edges of the indentation, while I imagine him exploring it with a finger.

'Do you think I have a choice?' he asks.

As if he'd hooked my cheek with the pirate hook he doesn't have.

'You're a lousy pirate,' I say.

'You're a lousy soldier,' he replies.

'I'm as good a soldier as you're a pirate,' I say.

'Everyone knows you here by now, man,' he says. 'Albin thought you wanted to kill him.'

I shrug.

'Perhaps I went too far.'

Once again, he dips his gaze into the dent in my forehead.

'You speak Albanian with a bloody awful accent.'

I burst out laughing, while he turns away and goes to fetch a menu at a pace of stone. As he tosses it to me, I feel like grabbing him by those long fingers and pulling him towards me, telling him that in another life, as someone else in another country, he'd be just as unhappy, but for completely different reasons.

I ask his name.

'Dritan,' he says, without looking at me.

I know what it means: light.

He disappears. Two other very young waiters are roaming around the room, both in similarly ridiculous jackets, drowsy and tired after a long day catering to the whims of tourists. Perhaps one of them still has a night shift ahead of him. I look round for Albin, but it must be his day off, or else he left with someone earlier. Meanwhile the waiters are leaning against the counter, talking in hushed voices and casting the occasional glance in my direction, or perhaps that's just my imagination.

Near my table, on the windowsill, sits a cage with a red parrot huddling inside, and just behind it on the wall hang at least a dozen more, side by side, full of twitching, multi-coloured birds. Wherever I go, I see them in captivity. A vibrant trill amid the sterile clatter of everyday life in the restaurants and grocery stores, at the seamstress's and the cobbler's. Colourful fluttering and white heat from the sky, which pours in between the cage bars from dawn till dusk. I imagine that the birds end up unable to breathe because of the swelter, and that death brings them relief, filling their fiery throats with cold. If they hadn't cut down so many trees the birds would be singing in the branches. But meanwhile those coloured sparks jump from one perch to another, like wound-up mechanical toys. They're full of life and raring to go.

One day they'll burst into fire. A golden flame, a peach-coloured flame, a pistachio-coloured flame.

A wall of warbling. A deafening beat of wings. The screech of birds mixed with the thudding bass of the disco. Even if I ask, they won't turn down the music.

Boom, as if bombs were falling.

I lean my palms heavily against the edge of the table, gripping it hard so I won't start trembling all over – if I do, I won't be able to stop. I dig my fingernails into the dark, scratched surface coated in peeling varnish, into the brown, fluid mass in front of me, glossy in the middle and matt at the edges, about to start flowing onto my knees.

Dritan comes closer, and I see him as a blurred image where the pixels are black, blue or white, in the shades of his vulture-like, prematurely aged face. Yet he was so beautiful when I gazed at him a short while ago.

'You look like someone who wants to order water,' he says.

I snigger. I look at his ashen, sunken cheeks. My skin is puffy, scarlet from the sun, while his is pale, out of the cellar.

'Do you find that sight intolerable too?' I ask, pointing a finger at the bird cages.

He casts a glance as if seeing me for the first time, with a silver spark in his eye.

'Sometimes, when I'm about to fall asleep, I imagine opening those cages,' he says.

I wait for him to say more, for the chance to grab hold of him at last, to latch onto a sentence, but he falls silent again and seems lost in thought. It's a June night, as warm and noisy as a spring day. I can feel drops of sweat on the back of my neck, and perspiration on my temples.

I order a whisky and water, which he brings almost instantly, as if he had it ready in advance.

For a while I feel better, the music quietens down, I rock gently like a red buoy on a calm sea and forget where I am, or what sort of body I'm in. The boys vanish, and the room seems empty, piercingly ugly. I fit in here. Apart from me there's one other guest in the bar, a Swede or Dane from somewhere in the north; obese, red in the face, he sways at an angle, groaning as he smears his face and forearms with lotion, changing into a cake with whipped cream.

I down the whisky in one. I push back my chair as noisily as a body turning over in its coffin, and walk up to the cages. The twinkling, sparkling eyes of parakeets and canaries, their delicate feathers that weigh nothing, the pink twigs of their limbs, their feeble fluttering. One by one I open them, one by one. Those who want it can have a taste of freedom and die for it. The rest will remain inside, to suffer in silence.

The Swede or Dane is watching me mistrustfully; for a while he's dismayed, but then he picks up his beer, nods to me, takes a deep swig and belches with satisfaction.

Some of the birds timidly emerge, and soon they're whirling against the ceiling, creating a feathery, iridescent cloud, flapping, rustling and warbling. Their excited screeches proclaim freedom. I can see nothing but the flickering fans of wings, and all I can hear is tremulous flapping, unreal quivering, setting my body in motion. One of the birds thuds dully against the ceiling, then falls to the floor at my feet. Long, slender feathers of a golden hue, stiffly stabbing the air, and the curled twiglets of legs ending in pearly talons. When I lean towards it the bird springs up, flutters for a second or two beneath the lamp, flashing the flamelets of its feathers, and flies straight out of the window. A great whirl of wings spins above my head, buzzing and chirping resound, and then, in a matter of seconds, one after another the birds fly out. They're gone. I look at the ones that are still here, immobile in their open cages. They're twittering just as before, as if nothing has happened at all. I can hear chirping all through my body, a shuddering clang. I drop some money on the table, pick up my backpack and leave.

My skin is roasting, my entire outer layer. My red, aching flesh is trembling as it clings to the calcifying bones that form the fragile scaffold on which my life hangs. I stand in the doorway of the bar, stunned by the boom of night-time Vlorë, the cacophony of thudding noises. If one of those young predators wants a fight, I'm ready. I wait for them a while longer, but no one comes down, so I walk to the nearest little store, where the prematurely aged, plumped-up sales assistant is completely incapable of hiding her great interest in the state of my forehead. When she realizes I can speak her language, she fights an internal battle to stop herself from asking me what happened; I can see it in the nervous look in her eyes and her clumsy fingers as they extract the coins from the till compartments.

'Some of the helmets are badly made,' I tell her, as I put six cans of beer into my backpack, and after a long pause she laughs, then as a parting shot she eagerly says 'Goodbye', as if feebly attempting to compensate me for everything.

I go straight to the beach. Behind me there's light and peals of noise, ahead of me blackness and the roar of the boundless sea. I pass a pack of restless, bony dogs in pursuit of a timid bitch. I walk among the animals, but they cast unseeing glances at me and race on, following their sexual urges. Somewhere in the distance there's a bonfire glowing on the beach; I could go there and have a chat or piss on it, depending on my mood. I open a beer and down it in one draught; the chill of the can in my hand gives me a shock, and I wipe my face with my wet hand. The wooden steps sway as I climb the lifeguard's tower. I imagine I'm a lifeguard in the daytime, someone who pulls children from the sea, forces the water out of distended bodies, and blows life into livid blue lips. I imagine I'm a lifeguard who sees a body in the distance, sinking under and breaking through the surface of the water, fighting hard for its life, and yet he turns to look the other way.

Clouds shield the moon and total darkness reigns; the roar of the waves pours into my body through my ears, flooding it. As if I weren't there, and that's neither a good thing nor a bad one. Suddenly I hear someone strike the back of their hand against a post supporting the tower. A small, grey figure in a white singlet – it's Dritan. As the darkness recedes a little, the moonlight picks his boat-shaped smile out of the darkness. As he climbs the steps, first I see his slender hands stretched ahead of him, then the rest of his lithe, boyish body.

'Lucky it wasn't the boss,' he says. 'He might shoot you.'

Without asking, he reaches for one of the cans. The metallic rasp of the ring pull, a long hiss of escaping gas, relief. He sits down so close to me that we're almost touching shoulders. The skin on his forearm is smooth, pale even in the darkness. I can smell his body, like sun-baked herbs, thyme and oregano. I can't remember when I last lay down in a meadow, though I did go hiking in the hills around Vlorë, and they smelled exactly like him.

As he gazes ahead, I can see the harmonious line of his profile and a smile at the corners of his lips. He raises the beer can, turns towards me and says in English: 'Cheers'. '*Gëzuar*,' I reply.

'Don't you know that in the Balkans you must look the other person in the eyes when you raise a toast?' he says, laughing. 'You foreigners always turn your gaze away as if you were afraid of it.'

I look him in the eyes, two diamonds, salt and pepper.

'I feel as if I dreamed it all,' he says, smiling. 'The birds fluttering against the restaurant ceiling.'

'Perhaps all this is a dream,' I reply after a long pause, amazed by how easy I'm finding it to say stupid things in his presence. 'Scraps of my dreams sometimes come back to me,' I continue, in English now. 'An old stone fountain in a garden in Berlin that I've never seen. Dark, multi-lane streets I've never crossed. Being on a flight in a falling plane, the despair of the man sitting next to me. I waste the final seconds of my life trying to reassure him, when all we had to do was to die together meekly, surrender to our fate. Sandstorms, sandy rust burying me entirely. A tornado. Avalanches. A great flood that I won't be able to escape. A pistol barrel at my temple. I don't know how many times I've died in my dreams.'

Although I'm not in the water, I feel as if I were drifting, as if the rhythm of my words were rocking me.

'Sometimes you just have to die,' says Dritan, and smiles.

The sea quietens, the waves flow in at a leisurely pace and shatter against the shore. He lays a hand on my back, and through the material I can feel how gentle and light it is, like a bird's wing. He has seen my forehead, yet he has touched me. The ball of the moon shines in the cloudless, leaden sky. I point out to him the pink light of Venus in the distance. And so life can be like this too. It can have the scent of herbs, the roughness of wood beneath your fingertips, and the softness of his skin.

We hear clamouring voices, then a protracted squeal, like the roar of chaos, a cross between yodelling and Apache war cries. As the howling comes closer, we see three young boyish bodies racing ahead, throwing up sand and stones, and then they hurl themselves into the darkness, straight into the water, in their clothes. One tries to jump on top of another, and from this distance it looks like they're trying to drown each other, although they're playing in the shallows. I can hear squeals and swear words, they're the voices of children, they haven't broken yet. Suddenly one of them whistles, and instantly the other two straighten up, as if on command, and all three emerge from the water. They're barefoot, their T-shirts clinging to their small, skinny bodies, which not long from now will shoot up, making them even skinnier and gawkier, even more menacing. They creep unhurriedly in our direction, without taking their eyes off us.

'*Hajde!*' calls the one who's the leader to the others, and stops facing the tower. 'Where are you from?' he asks.

'I'm from Tropojë,' says Dritan, and smiles at the boy. 'And he's an American.'

'Oh,' says the boy, livening up. 'How are you? What are you doing here?' he asks in English.

'I live here,' I reply in Albanian.

'Have you got a wife? Kids?' he asks.

I laugh.

'No.'

'Why not?'

'I just don't.'

The boy looks at me watchfully. He has long hair, bangs that get in his eyes and fleshy lips. He's completely unaware of it, but one day he'll be beautiful.

'What happened to your forehead?' he asks.

'My father whacked me when I was a little older than you.'

'Aha,' says the boy, as if it were the most normal thing in the world. For a while he says nothing, lost in thought as he shifts the sand with a bare foot, until a new idea rouses him from his torpor. 'Got any marijuana?'

I shake my head to say no.

'Yes, you do!' shouts the boy. 'Don't lie! You've got some!'

So far his pals have been listening to the conversation, but now they're growing restless. One of them tries to touch the leader's arm, but the boy pulls away from him. With both hands he grabs a thick branch that's lying on the sand and starts whacking it as hard as he can against the post supporting the wooden structure.

'Fuck you, man, gimme some money!' he shouts. 'Gimme some!'

I imagine how easy it would be to break his neck. It'd be enough to immobilize his head in the triangle of an arm, then one firm yank. In a matter of seconds stiffness would flood that furious, wriggling body, and the child would finally feel peace.

'Gimme, gimme, gimme!' screams the kid. As he steadily beats the branch against the post, I can feel each blow throughout my body. 'Fag-gots! Fag-gots! Fag-gots!'

Then suddenly he stops shouting, and throws the branch ahead of himself. He takes off and runs after something or someone he has seen. I watch his small body getting further away, and the two other boys as they take off too, struggling over heaps of sand and stones in their effort to race after him.

The wooden boards are digging into my skin. When and how will that boy die? Who will kill him, and in what circumstances? Or perhaps his own frenzy will kill him? What will he manage to do before someone settles his hash? What home will he return to today? Who has heard his scream?

In the semi-darkness of the moonlit night, up on the lifeguard's tower, I feel as if I'm in a shaft of light, on stage. I can feel invisible eyes staring at us, the eyes of the people walking along the promenade at night, the people smoking cigarettes on their hotel room balconies, and the two or three shadows in the distance that are still wandering the beach because they cannot sleep.

Without a word I get up and climb down the steps, and Dritan follows me. I feel the cool velvet of the sand, the sharp edges of the stones beneath my feet.

'You told Albin it was a grenade,' says Dritan behind me.

'I told you, I'm not a soldier.'

'My father beat me up too when he found out. I hoped I'd lose consciousness, but I didn't. I can remember everything.'

I turn to face him. He looks me straight in the eyes, two shining onyx stones in his mild face.

'Albin said you attacked him when he tried to take off your T-shirt,' he says.

I pull off my T-shirt. My broad, firm body is unfurled before him. I close my eyes.

And I feel him drawing a finger over the map of my scars. He lays his hand flat, touching the uneven patches with its entire surface, stroking my skin, as if trying to smooth it out. He runs a finger along the narrow channels between the folds. In slow motion he massages the thickened tissue. I am as if hypnotized. I am just a body that's registering and absorbing every movement of his hand.

'It's as if the frost had drawn flowers on the windowpane of your belly,' he says.

'Where have you ever seen such a frost in Albania?' I say, laughing.

'I told you, I'm from the north.'

I let him undress, and then, both naked, we enter the water, lie down on our backs and let ourselves be rocked by the waves. His body wraps itself around me like a warm blanket. I can feel our bodies losing weight. My skin weighs nothing.

We emerge from the water and fall asleep together on the beach. Two bodies nesting in the cool, wet sand, curled up together.

I awake at dawn, as a golden glow rends the washed-out blue, while a steely stripe of water marks the thin line of the horizon, and I'm shivering. There's no one beside me, all that's left is the outline of a body stamped on the sand. I stare into the deep, dark sea, as rays of sunlight twinkle across it. The pain beneath my skin steadily floods my entire body, moving down to my belly, and changing into a caustic tangle. I embrace myself, the rough insides of my hands stroking the cold skin. Another day of life. Another day.

I turn around and see him walking towards me, holding a white cage with a gold, flickering flame inside it, one of the birds that were afraid to escape.

He walks at a swinging step, treading softly on the sand, as if on tiptoe, and his skin shines like ivory in the early morning sun. His hips are gently swaying, and inside his body there's a calm sea flowing.

As he walks towards me, he is the light.

'Ciężar skóry'
Published as part of the collection *Ciężar skóry* (Wydawnictwo Literackie, 2023).

MEN BEHAVING BADLY

JAROSŁAW IWASZKIEWICZ
1894–1980

Jarosław Iwaszkiewicz grew up in Ukraine, the son of a landowner dispossessed for taking part in the January Uprising of 1867. He spent much of his youth with the family of his cousin and close friend, the composer Karol Szymanowski.

He studied law and music in Kyiv, and in 1918 moved to Warsaw, where he was soon established as a poet, associated with the experimental Skamander group. He was a prolific author of prose as well, including short stories, novellas, novels, plays, memoirs, essays, translations from several languages (of Rimbaud, Gide, Andersen, Tolstoy and Chekhov) and libretti.

As a diplomat in the 1930s, he lived in Copenhagen and then Brussels. He had a lifelong love of Italy, especially Sicily, where some of his stories are set.

'A melancholy affirmation of the world as it is – that is the hidden message, never directly expressed, of Iwaszkiewicz's prose,' wrote the philosopher Leszek Kołakowski, who praised him as 'a very good person'; during the war Iwaszkiewicz provided refuge at his residence for many Jews and Poles escaping Nazi persecution.

After the war his loyalty to the new communist authorities in his role as chairman of the Writers' Union was seen by some as opportunism, but although he avoided taking political sides, he used his position to protect other writers from being banned. *Twórczość*, the literary journal that he edited for thirty-five years, was a cultural oasis within the Polish People's Republic.

Several of his best novellas were made into successful movies, notably *Mother Joanna of the Angels*, directed by Jerzy Kawalerowicz (about nuns who are possessed by devils), and *The Birch Grove*, directed by Andrzej Wajda (about two brothers in conflict).

His short stories are often about unhappy love affairs, lack of fulfilment, a loss of religious faith and a search for meaning amid life's adversities; once revealed, it proves inexpressible. 'A New Love' is an exquisite example of Iwaszkiewicz's outlook, where hope and optimism fall victim to cynicism, and passion proves hollow.

Antonia Lloyd-Jones

A New Love

Translated by Antonia Lloyd-Jones

Everything was ready before the bell rang. On the table stood a huge bouquet of ten pink roses. In full bloom, they looked more like fruits than flowers, or like edible flowers. Each neatly pleated rose resembled a small cream cake, coated in cochineal icing. Their scent floated right across the room, permeating it gently and sweetly. Close to, it was oppressive. If he buried his nose right in the middle of the bunch, he felt dizzy. As he touched these flowers he was reminded of something meaty and over-sensual. He was touching flesh. He took a long, careful look at them: they were already very overblown. The small, round, wrinkled patches in the centre were going a bit white and had half-opened, revealing a few golden stamens. They were very short and shamefaced for having failed to turn into sweet-scented petals before the rose had reached full bloom. The sight of these golden stamens and the white spots surrounding them gave him the grudging thought that they were only ordinary cabbage roses. Just as this occurred to him, the doorbell rang.

It was a strong, confident ring that immediately reminded him of the look in her eyes yesterday. That first look as often as not encapsulates the entire essence of future impressions. There in the light of a new pair of eyes he had found all his old strengths and hopes. Such a fervent portent of unexpected happiness that at first he had been taken aback and had failed to respond with the same sort of look. He could see that what had come crashing down on him was without question a great love. He felt like a chemist at the moment when an experiment confirms the theoretical calculations he made earlier. He had known it was bound to happen again one of these days: maybe today, tomorrow, or a week from now. Once more he was destined to be filled with a fresh, new emotion, to get drunk on it and intoxicate others with it too! Greater than ever before. He hadn't had many such loves, but this one would be greater. He had been waiting a bit too long now for it not to be the greatest. It was coming along to sweep him off his feet. So should he once again surrender to that violent wave imbued with a fragrance of roses? Four years of waiting for just such a ring at the door.

At the first jingle of the clapper his eye was caught by something moving among the roses. One flower appeared to have flexed its muscles among the rest; it had shifted to a more comfortable position, drawing itself up a bit by working its way out from under two small green leaves, which were still gently shaking. The flower had unfurled even further, brazenly showing its pale centre, like a wide-open mouth with golden teeth shining inside. For a moment he hesitated, wanting to hear what the parted lips of the flower would say to him.

It doesn't take much talking to reach an understanding. A night of intense certainty stood between him and yesterday. There is nothing sweeter than a sound night's sleep with the thought of something miraculous growing inside us, gradually filling us up. The sort of night slept by mothers when they have just found out they are pregnant. Deep, peaceful sleep had weighed down on him like a golden sepulchre, but the thought of new happiness had remained alert at his bedside, and as soon as he awoke he had immediately, quite naturally been aware of it. He had dressed quite quickly, revelling in the coolness of the bathtub, the freshness of the eau-de-Cologne and the chill of the autumn morning, fully conscious of fast approaching happiness, soft, deeper than other happinesses. The plural number caused him to stop and wonder. There is only one true happiness, he thought, and that is love. The ashes of a former love, and the sense of a lack of love had been dribbling through his fingers for far too long now, finding no response in him, for they were nothing but ashes. One does a thousand things, travels, walks, thinks and reads, but it takes just this sort of encounter to understand that all this time one has been living on the ash-heap of the past, that the sun looked dead, as if in a haze, the air was steeped in the smog of decay. For all that, there was only one thing he wanted – for her to come and sweep him off his feet at last. She had kindled a new pillar of fire on the ash-heap and had filled the air with easy breathing. The years go by, and the clocks of all cities strike out hour after hour in unison, while there is no one, until along comes just such an evening as yesterday's, and the whole world is revealed anew. Everything that lacked colour takes on a tone, everything that was beyond disentanglement is resolved.

He noticed that the flower, which had recently spread wider among the little green leaves, like a bourgeois lady in a pink dress, had bowed its lower petals downwards as if under the weight of an invisible insect. Instinctively he wanted to stop them from falling and to give it a natural pose. He brushed the tip of his finger against two of the petals from underneath. He felt a velvet touch, but as he let his hand drop, the petals came loose, described a great circle and as gently as two tiny sails, settled nearby on the carpet.

He knew what was coming next. An unexpected discovery, the revelation and devotion of another soul, of an unfamiliar treasure. Something he certainly valued in love was the satisfying of one's curiosity, the boundless world of the human soul and of human life, which gradually throws itself open before a lover, as he grows more accustomed to the presence, existence and memory of his beloved. First there would be that charming novelty of tastes, habits and perceptions. Favourite dishes, one's way of taking one's seat in a carriage, one's way of threading a needle. A thousand little trifles that at first absorb one on the outside, then make their way into conversation and fill one's very voice with a different tone, relating to all sorts of subjects, and taking on a thousand associations. This tone of voice will then colour one's thoughts, which on the surface are abstract and internal, and blend with one's particular philosophical outlook, altering one's entire view of the broad or narrow horizons of the world.

A total change of thought, a new approach to things, to works of art, to ways of working – yes, that was what lay ahead of him. He would have to change his newspaper, his bookshop, his friends, his restaurant, his collars, his philosophy and references. Under her influence he would be sure to start throwing foreign words into his conversation (Italian, or English, perhaps?) and would yearn for travel. They would share reminiscences. The multitude of characters he had encountered in the past would double. Once again new friends would be introduced to his imagination: someone else's childhood would pass before his eyes like an English novel.

The two petals lay at his feet on the green carpet, just by the shiny tip of his unpolished shoe. He gave the pink petal a gentle nudge with his toe, covering a tiny bit of it. The blush of the petal looked pale against the rather commonplace colour of the carpet. He looked up at the bouquet. Another petal was starting to droop, just as slowly, but just as inevitably, turning its washed-out inner face towards him.

How intriguing! Nights spent no longer on endearments, but on telling each other one's life story. One's entire life story. How many such stories he had already heard by now! Of course, each new love pervaded his whole past life with its essence, manipulating it as it fancied. As a rule he had treated all those women with contempt. On each past emotion he had bestowed the label 'not it'. Besides, he only used whatever he regarded as potentially seductive material in his narrative. On the other hand he drank in, he simply drank in women's confidences about themselves (he could listen to them for nights on end). They nonchalantly opened their hearts to him to the depths of their souls, all their greatness and all their weaknesses. He knew about their adventures in motherhood, in love, about their sweetness and their indifference. He could reach directly into the core of their experience and try to get to the heart of their words, even to the heart of everything they hid from him, right into the essence of things they weren't aware of, just as he was able to find pleasures in their bodies that they had never suspected were there. Besides, there had only been four or five such women who counted as his 'great loves'.

The doorbell rang a second time. The shudder in the air caused the drooping petal to fall. With an instant reflex he tried to stop it from falling, caught it in mid-air, weighing it up for a moment in his cupped hand, then raised it to his lips.

'Love!' he thought. He would have to tell his life story all over again, well, at least sketchily. This time it would be just a summary, of course. Why worry about the past when the task of creating the future lay ahead of them? It would be intensive, exhausting work. Shunting his life onto new tracks, into the rays shining from new eyes, different from any others that had ever cast their sunlight upon him. The stones might be heavy, but he would be building new bridges between what was already possible and the yet-to-be-realized. He would be casting bold arches capturing infinities of thought, vigorously shaking himself free at last of all the bitterness that had welled up over the past few years of drought. He had torn himself free of the ensnaring net of humdrum days, so much so that he had ceased to feel the passage of time. Suddenly he was looking around himself, wondering how he could have lived like that until now, amazed that he hadn't rebelled. He would have to move out of this flat – he cast a glance round the room – just as one should move out of a building full of preconceived ideas. The sort of cold cynicism he had wallowed in for the past four years wasn't appropriate for a man in love. He might even have to rebuild his whole system of beliefs. She seemed to have so much enthusiasm in her eyes. He forced himself to think about packing up his books and sticks of furniture into wooden crates, and all that straw – the place would be full of it! But of course true love asks no questions. He wouldn't confide his entire life story in her, and he wouldn't ask her any questions either. But what if she has another lover?

Several more petals had fallen onto the table, all in a rush, as if jostling one another: tap-tap-tap. The rose had spread its remaining petals even wider, as if attempting to hide the loss, yet all the more plainly revealing its whitish centre, like inelegant underwear.

Taking on a new love, he thought further, without doubt means taking on a massive burden. All one's efforts will have to be geared towards making sure nothing can ruffle the harmony of two bodies merging into one, two souls joining in unison. There must be no little niggles, not even the tiniest point of friction. One should be able to look both oneself and the truth in the eye and adroitly juggle the events of one's life to make sure they don't sully everyday conversation. That's quite a tall order! One must constantly keep oneself up at a certain level, like a swimmer, while at the same time never taking one's eye off one's partner. One must direct events skilfully, conversation too, which demands far greater social tact. Frankly speaking, through clever moves one must seize the initiative from the lady's hands. That's all rather tiring, especially at length. He smiled. It's quite simple, really, but love is just a fight for the initiative.

Still smiling, he prodded the remaining petals; off they fell in such a violent rush that in falling they looked paler, like a flock of seagulls illuminated by the setting sun. They sent a subtle fragrance floating into the air. Leaning over the wilting vase no longer made him feel dizzy. Yet the scent in the room was becoming more pungent. There were only a few pink featherlets left on the green stem now, wrinkled like silk after rain. Granules of golden dust from the centre had scattered on the petals.

So what? He was still young. He could boldly take up the battle anew. Take her in hand from the start. No, he wouldn't think of moving house, he wouldn't change his flat or his bookshop. Nor his collars either, nor would he go abroad. That's just pretension. Tough, she'll have to take him as he is, without looking round at the rest of the world. It was she who would have to cast off her usual custom and adapt herself to him. His habits were already set, and it would be hard for him to give them up. However, imposing his will on the woman was bound to involve a fight. That fight would have to be dexterous, in forays. Small but firm remarks at table and in the bedroom. It would mean taking control of her desires, saying no over a few basic points, and a careful effort to conceal his jealousy.

'Well, I'd better open up then!' he said to himself and set off for the door, but just as he reached the hall he stopped.

Conceal his jealousy? Fight? A heavy burden was already starting to oppress him. But then a great love is a very heavy thing, isn't it? How much there is to overcome, how strong one has to keep on being! The bitterness of the first time she was late, the despair after the first tiff, the aimless wandering with a heavy heart after the first quarrel. Pacing the streets (usually in the dark) that first evening not spent together. Oh, it's beyond my strength, he said to himself and leaned his head against the door frame. Accumulating mutual bitternesses that burst into a sulphurous, smoky flame for any reason whatsoever, because of a lost ribbon, or a half-smoked cigarette. Terrible hatred at the most painful moments. How can she be like that? She, whom I love like a goddess, is behaving like someone ordinary, she's crying! Ah! And the burden of tears, which every woman uses to crush, to cast a gloomy, ashen cloud on a bright and cheerful sky, remains for good and all like an indelible shadow, like the dingy, dying pallor of a pearl. This burden of the burn-out to come, which would leave nothing but a heap of ashes.

The bell rang for the third time, not so boldly now, but rather uncertainly; its sound dissolved into *mezza voce*, as if the finger pressing it were starting to tremble and withdraw. But he just went on standing in the doorway, listening intently. He thought he could catch the sound of her breathing on the other side of the door. After a long pause, while his mind went blank, fully occupied with listening, he heard reluctant, ponderous footsteps turning away. He tiptoed up to the door. The footsteps were moving off, at first slowly, but as they got further down the stairs they grew faster, as if gladly. He sighed with relief as the downstairs door gently banged shut.

He went back into the living room. As he drew near, the final rose petal fell. The green stalk, reaching down into the fluted grooves of the vase, gave its empty interior a willow-green glow. A few golden stamens still sat in the small brown centre. He stuck his little finger into the cavity and raised the tiny, sticky granules to the light, golden dust colouring his fingertip. He blew it towards the light of the window and off the stamens flew, leaving a tinge of golden dust, so he carefully wiped his fingers on his handkerchief.

'Nowa miłość'
Published as part of the collection *Nowa miłość i inne opowiadania* (Czytelnik, 1946).

STANISŁAW DYGAT
1914–1978

Dygat was from Warsaw, where he studied architecture and philosophy at the university. His family had French origins, and as the possessor of a French passport, when the Nazis occupied Poland he was arrested and interned in a camp near the Bodensee. His year in this mildest form of prison was the subject of his first novel, *Jezioro Bodeńskie* (*Bodensee*, 1946), a satirical text which set the tone for much of his later work.

Rebelling against the prevailing grim mood of 1942 he sent up his experiences, himself and the Polish Romantic tradition. In this Dygat was following in the footsteps of Witold Gombrowicz, who encouraged him.

'Spitefulness and a passion for debunking clichés led him to transform his adventures into an anti-heroic novel,' wrote Czesław Miłosz. 'The narrator presents himself as uncertain, unauthentic, vacillating between his role as patriotic Pole and his flirtations with French girls in the camp. He is both attached and opposed to his Polish Romantic complex . . . [his] casually structured plots go together with a colloquial, nonchalant language which appropriately conveys his abhorrence of literature treated as a "sacred cow".'

His narrators often sound naïve, helpless and dreamy, with ambitions they will never fulfil, doomed to face up to bitter reality. His best-known novels, written after 1956, when the political mood had changed and socialist realism was no longer the politically required genre, were *Podróż* (*The Journey*, 1958), whose main character's illusions are shattered on a trip to Italy, and *Disneyland* (1965), about a young man who idolizes an elusive girl and who finally realizes that she and his actual girlfriend are the same person. But his writing is often humorous, and it's hard not to feel sorry for his childish characters.

His second wife was the film star, singer and sex symbol Kalina Jędrusik. Their affair caused public controversy, as did their well-publicized open marriage.

Antonia Lloyd-Jones

In the Shadow of Brooklyn

Translated by Antonia Lloyd-Jones

My father caused me a lot of trouble. I don't mean he did it in person, not what we generally understand by someone causing us trouble. What I'm thinking of is his situation, his – what's the right word for it? – position in the world, and – how can I put it? – society's attitude towards him, compared with my own. It's impossible to explain it clearly if I beat about the bush or generalize, and don't just come out with it. All right. I've never liked talking about it. I've never liked facing up to it. My father was a famous and eminent writer, widely respected in society. That might seem a cause for pride and satisfaction. For someone like me, who has their own artistic ambitions, albeit in a different genre, it is not necessarily a joy to have a famous and eminent father. Anyone who has an illustrious father will know exactly what I mean. But in my case that wasn't really the problem. Why fudge it and wrap it up in cotton wool? As a writer, my father was a deadly bore. I've never managed to finish a single one of his books, and in my circle the situation was strange and abnormal, in that my father was never talked about, as if he didn't exist. So he was a deadly bore, but nevertheless he was regarded as an eminent writer, a classic; plainly, at some point in the past, that's how things had panned out, then the idea had been generally accepted, and no one wanted or dared to change something so firmly established. On top of all this he was favoured by the authorities, regardless of changes of political direction, thaws and the like, because his writing made claims to address progressive social issues. Naturally, he was showered with state awards and all sorts of honours, translated into lots of languages and equally well known and respected worldwide. With the caveat of course that only his name was world famous, while here, one must admit, he had hordes of genuine

209

admirers or even fans, because there's no bore on earth who, given the right publicity and credence, will not find thousands, if not tens of thousands of other bores ready to adore him for his boringness. Whatever happens, there will always be plenty of bores. But he was my father, and I sort of loved him, because I remembered how he had cared for me in the past, and bought me presents for Christmas and my name-day. Obviously, it's not that I was obsessed with gifts, but these things provide a touching memory, as I've no need to explain. Everyone knows what I'm talking about, how and why it is that one loves one's father or some other family member. My relations with my father had been stiff and cold for a long time. I was independent of him, I had started to earn a living very early on, and was doing quite well. I usually went to see him for some practical purpose, less often just for a chat. We didn't have much to talk about, and we were always a little awkward together.

Lately two matters involving my father had worried me greatly. More than worried. They were nagging me and poisoning my peace. One of them was his fiftieth birthday celebration. How could he have agreed to a celebration of this kind? Agreed to? I think he had zealously courted it, he'd made sure it happened. It was pitiful. Things that should have been left in peace to draw as little attention to themselves as possible were being brought to the surface and displayed in a flagrant manner – namely, the disproportion between my father's value as a writer and the official recognition he enjoyed. Of course, some might say that this was my personal point of view. And it certainly was. Nor was I going to regard the matter in any other way than from my entirely personal point of view. I longed for my father at least to whisper in my ear that everything he was doing was purely out of opportunism and self-interest, that he saw himself as a swine and a petty schemer, but his life was all right like this, comfortable, so there it was, tough. But of course he did nothing of the kind. The tragedy lay in the fact that he ardently believed in it all – I'm sure he believed he had a sort of mission, though he still had enough tact and restraint not to say it out loud. He also behaved accordingly. He kept his distance from people and overawed them with his heightened sense of his own value. Undeniably he had a certain charm, he could be witty, amusing, affable even, but his sort of affability never seemed to me a natural way of communing with others, but more like condescension prompted by favourable conditions. On top of that he was gifted with great discernment and sharpened spitefulness, a critical instinct towards many of the things that surrounded him. Possibly everything except himself.

The second thing that was bothering me in connection with my father was his surprising flirtation with little Miss Hantz. Of course my father's sex life was of no concern to me. But I was bound to be concerned about him making a fool of himself in public. What could connect an eminent, widely respected writer with a rather average little chanteuse, nice and amusing in her own way, but flitting between bits of drudgery, a tiny part of the bland and dismal (as viewed from backstage) world known as 'Entertainment'? Here I may be accused of inconsistency. On the one hand I am complaining about my father's artificial, sham position in the world, while on the other, in the name of this very position, I'm trying to defend his dignity and honour. I could provide a very simple explanation for this inconsistency, but I don't feel like it. I don't mean to treat anyone with scorn. It's just that you may find some more seeming inconsistencies in my story. If you understand it, fine. If you don't, it's not worth listening to all this blather anyway.

I don't know how and where my father met La Belle Hantz. But apparently he had been seen with her lately. At a lunch party, then at the cinema, then out for a walk. He had gone so far as to take her to a premiere at the theatre. I regarded appearing in public with her before the pitiful little world of theatrical premieres as the height of foolishness. But even sillier was the way he told me one or two confidences about his affair. He did it rather obliquely, but with obvious alacrity, when I dropped in to return the 500 zlotys I'd borrowed a month ago. I was afraid he would talk about the birthday celebration, but he didn't say a word about that. He said nothing at all, while I sat in an armchair, leafing through a year-old copy of *Paris Match* that was lying on the television. I couldn't just drop by, hand over the 500 zlotys and be off. As I was there, I'd have to stay a while and do something. So I was sitting in an armchair, leafing through last year's *Paris Match*, when suddenly, out of the blue, my father started talking about Miss Hantz. It came so totally out of the blue that I was flabbergasted, I dared not tear my eyes from *Paris Match* but listened with my head bowed. At first he stammered a bit, then he began to speak more fluently. Truth be told, I found it easier to bear when he stammered. Actually, in formal terms, he didn't say anything unusual. But he got tangled up in generalities that, combined with the meagre facts, allowed, or rather bade me to decipher the real state of affairs. He did not mention her by name. First he prattled on about loneliness, resorting to banal statements, such as the fact that nature created woman to save man from feeling abandoned and helpless in his battle against adversity. Then, referring to nature again, as if to dump responsibility on the authority of nature for all the hopeless stupidity of his situation, of which he must have had at least some awareness, he declared that sometimes one had to wait long and patiently before finding one's destiny. But it was worth waiting in order to realize that one had found the true shape of happiness. He said lots more nonsense of the same kind, which it'd be an embarrassing waste of time to repeat, then finally he added a few concrete facts, from which it emerged that he was 'very much involved with a certain person', and that it was a quite exceptional matter, because it concerned an altogether very special understanding between two human beings.

All this gave me such a shock that it was hard for me to keep my equilibrium. But I managed it – I just wanted to leave as fast as possible. 'Jolly good, that's nice,' I said, or something of the kind, and got up. My father got up too. I could see that he wanted to say something else, because he had the look of a bashful supplicant on his face. Finally he informed me that the next day, which was the actual birthday, the 'person concerned will be coming to the celebratory lunch', and I shouldn't be surprised because 'it's someone you know well and have met several times before'. I understood that it would be a sort of official presentation at court. The minister would be there, and various other important people – heavens above, what could I do to protect my father from making such a terrible fool of himself? I muttered something and left.

Little Miss Hantz! Well, I never. What did she want in all this? I knew her well, and I couldn't believe she'd fallen in love with my father. True, my father was very handsome, he looked young and was bathed in glory, so perhaps he could still appeal to La Hantz too. But for her to be that much in love with him? For something like that to have occurred between her and my father? It was out of the question, as far as I could tell. Of course she might consider using my father to further her career, but she was perfectly capable of advancing her career anyway; she didn't need my father for that. The next morning I was due to meet her for a television rehearsal. She was going to sing my new song. I was annoyed: the song ('Dreams that Last Longer than a Night') had come out well, and had a chance of catching on, but I didn't think the Hantz girl was the right person to promote it. But what mattered was that the next morning I was going to meet with her. I decided to do something, to take some sort of action. I didn't know what, but I had to do something. The birthday party *and* La Hantz. No! The one followed by the other was really too much.

I left my father's place. It was a fine evening, so I wondered where to go. There was nothing waiting for me at home. It happened to be one of those rare evenings when I had nothing to occupy me. Anyway, I have a confession to make. I'm not one of those people, so numerous these days, who complain of being lonely. I manage perfectly well on my own and I don't need anyone to lean on, nor do I long for someone else to lean on me. But sometimes when I'm at home, especially in the evening, there's been a vague something floating in the air, like a sort of whisper reminding me that nobody loves me, and I don't love anyone either. Occasionally I've found this whisper bothersome. Not because it has stirred yearnings in me. Nothing of the sort. I see it as a sort of mockery, like a vague threat, and I find that annoying. I haven't wanted to love anyone, or known how to. My father was something else entirely. I don't know if I really did love him, despite what I said at the start. In fact I didn't like him. Anyway, a father is a very different thing. A practical matter, not an emotion. I was twenty-plus years old and I'd never been in love. It was laughable. Sometimes I brought a girl home. It wasn't hard to find one. Frolicsome, jolly students, or a completely different type: focused, apparently anxious about this nocturnal visit, as if it were something quite exceptional and rare for them. Or models. Or girls of ill-defined occupation, too idle to study or to do anything specific, waiting passively in cafés and clubs for something to happen that would change their existence, or at least provide the illusion of change for a couple of hours. This could be very nice, especially if the girl turned out to be jolly and knew the right way to behave, and when it was time to get lost. Sometimes I escorted them home, if we'd had a particularly nice time in those few hours together, sometimes I saw them to a taxi, and sometimes I didn't accompany them at all. But not even the nicest girl had ever left me with a sense of missing her. The time I'd spent with her counted, but beyond that there was no meter running. I avoided girls from my profession. There was no point in associating with them in that sort of way. There'd only be trouble later on, at rehearsals or recordings, because I knew from the experience of others – well, and partly from my own–that after things like that they always regarded themselves as entitled to make scenes if something went wrong because of their own ineptitude. No. It didn't bother me that my house was lonely and empty, with no one waiting for me. It was just that sometimes I didn't feel like going back there.

Right then I didn't feel like going home. To be frank, it did occur to me that if there were someone waiting for me there to whom I could talk about my father and Miss Hantz I'm sure I'd have been more eager to go home. But that doesn't really mean I was longing for someone to be there. Anyway, why *was* I so upset about it? Why should I care if my father made an idiot of himself? I decided not to waste any more thought on it, though in principle I hadn't dropped the idea of having some sort of discussion with the girl, though I still didn't know what shape it should take. I walked down Ujazdowskie Avenue towards Three Crosses Square. I fancied a glass of vodka. I am not a drinker, not in the least. I rarely drink, and reluctantly. But now and then, when there's something nagging at me like that from the inside and refusing to let go, I get the urge to knock one back. Then I calm down and can free myself of undesirable thoughts as easily as I can shake off someone who accosts me in the street. The simplest thing to do was to drop in at the club, but I didn't want to; there I'd immediately run into someone or other from the trade, and have the same old conversation, either on professional matters, or even worse and more hopeless. On Mokotowska Street, opposite the Hybrydy Club, there was a second-rate bar, always packed and noisy, its clients bursting with the impatient desire to throw as many shots as possible down their throats at high speed; the entrance was up a few warped, wooden steps. I turned into Wilcza Street and then walked down Mokotowska in that direction. Outside the bar stood a taxi, with a young girl beside it. She seemed to be arguing with the driver, who leaned out of the window and said: 'I've told you already, I'm going off duty, I'm not taking you to any station.'

'But I'll miss my train,' said the girl.

'That's no concern of mine. It's not as if I've agreed to be at your beck and call.'

The girl was holding a small bag; she was tall and slender, with dark hair falling on her shoulders. She emanated indecision and helplessness, and that moved me. I went up to them.

'Can you really not drop her at the station?' I asked, thinking to myself: Why am I butting in when it's none of my business?

The driver must have had the same thought, because he said: 'What's it got to do with you?'

'Nothing, it's just that if the young lady might miss her train, she needs some help.'

'Really? Then give her a piggyback and take her there yourself.'

The girl looked at me with large round eyes – I can't remember if they were green or brown, but she looked inquiringly, as if hoping I really would do as the driver suggested.

I felt a surge of anger. It was definitely anger because of my father's affairs, especially his dalliance with that singer, but it sought an outlet in this unexpected squabble. I have a reputation for great self-control, but nobody knows how often I start to seethe and boil inside, or how much it costs me not to explode and to avoid unnecessary rows. But here in the street among strangers I didn't care what anybody thought.

'It's odd how taxi drivers always have the same boorish manner,' I said. 'Are you all in league, or what?'

The driver lunged forwards. The girl moved closer to me. She was scared.

'You – private entrepreneur, taking an honest cabbie's fares,' he said, using an adjective I won't repeat, 'I'll show you boorish . . . You . . .'

Filled with rage, he had no idea what to do next. I turned to the girl and said: 'His insult is most unfair. I'm not a private entrepreneur. I don't own a car, and I've never had one.'

The driver can't have been particularly bright, because now he was plainly wondering whether what I had said was a new insult and how he should react. The girl was almost leaning against me.

'Please drop it now,' she said. 'I'll be too late for my train anyway. There's no point in making a fuss.'

'All right,' I said. 'He can get lost, and we can go in here for a quick drink.'

The girl hesitated, while at 'He can get lost' the driver lunged forwards again – it looked as if he were trying to jump out of the taxi.

'All right,' she said. 'Let's go in.'

She took me lightly by the sleeve and pulled me towards the wooden steps. The driver opened his door. A militia patrol was coming down Mokotowska Street with paternal nonchalance. The driver shut his door and drove off. He stopped a dozen metres further on and watched us ascend the steps, then drove off nervously and abruptly.

There was no one but men in the bar. There were no small tables, just high ones at which one stood. The men standing there looked like a uniform grey mass. At times it was hard to distinguish where the human mass ended, and where its astral body began: thick clouds of smoke mixed with dense kitchen steam. Everyone was self-absorbed, and nobody took any notice of the girl's entrance, despite the fact, as I noticed in the dim light of the bar, that she was pretty, if not stunning. People go to bars of that kind in an effort to ward off their cares and worries for the time being, including the ones that result from casting glances at women.

I was looking around for a free space when the girl pulled at my sleeve. She looked intimidated.

'I'd better go,' she said. 'Thank you . . .'

I shrugged.

'As you wish. You're late for your train anyway, but I never urge anyone to do anything by force.'

'These days it's very rare for a man to stand up for a woman,' she said, and stood scrutinizing me. It seemed she didn't feel like leaving.

'What time's your next train?'

She didn't answer. She became pensive, drifting off in her thoughts, as if anxious about something. We stood like that a while, because I too had suddenly started to think about my own affairs again. Finally I nudged her. She started, as if abruptly awoken, and smiled.

'I think I could stay a while, but I'm not all that fond of vodka.'

She slowly sipped some red wine, while I had plain vodka, the worst kind, with the red label.

'Have you ever thought about the fact that mankind is very lonely?' she asked, and was immediately embarrassed. 'That's a stupid question, isn't it? You must think I'm a typical silly goose.'

'No, why should I? There are no stupid questions, just stupid answers. For instance to the question: "How can a pretty young girl feel lonely?" one might give a wise or a stupid answer.'

She didn't let herself be disconcerted. She grew serious, and again her thoughts drifted off somewhere far away. I admit that these mental wanderings of hers were starting to irritate me. They seemed to have an effect on me.

'You've never been a pretty young girl,' she said, 'so you don't know anything about it. It's so easy to say "a pretty young girl" to someone who hasn't a clue about all sorts of things.'

She surprised me. I was expecting her to start simpering at the phrase 'pretty young girl', rather than respond that way. I thought I'd better take her more seriously.

'No,' I said. 'I don't know a thing, and besides, I pick people out when I need them, people of the kind I need. But I've never yet felt there was anyone missing, or the need for anyone in particular.'

The girl made a face as if seeing something strange but unconvincing for the first time ever. It was a determined look.

'You've never pined for anyone?'

A man stopped in the doorway of the bar and started to look around. After a while I recognized him. It was our taxi driver. He spotted us and rejoiced, as if he'd found some dear friends. He began to push through in our direction.

'No,' I said. 'I've never pined for anyone.'

The girl made almost exactly the same face again.

'And you've no idea what's meant by pining for someone?'

'No. At any rate, not in the sense in which those words are used in songs and sentimental poetry.'

The driver reached us. He was very pleased with himself.

'Excuse me for disturbing you,' he said.

'Please go away,' said the girl.

'Just a second. Please be so kind as to shut up, Miss. I'm not here to see you but this gentleman.'

'Please go away, or I'll call the militia.'

'The militia? But why? I just want to have a brief chat with the gentleman. We started to talk, and it occurred to me that somehow it doesn't seem right not to finish, so I parked the cab and came here. Would you spare me a moment of your time, please, sir?'

The girl grabbed me by the hand.

'Please tell him to go away, or better still call someone.'

'Who?' I asked. 'There's nothing wrong with him wanting to have a chat with me.'

I glanced at him and said: 'Not every conversation should be held in front of the ladies, should it?'

He wasn't as dim-witted as I'd thought. He understood, and cast me a look of esteem, which pleased me. It's curious how some of the business that happens between men, though brutal, is better and more honest than some of the apparently tender business that occurs between a man and a woman.

'It goes without saying,' he said. 'Let's go and have our chat. I won't take up much of your time.'

I eyed him up. He was smaller than I was, but stocky, and he looked fit.

'Let's go,' I said.

The girl was now looking mistrustfully at both of us.

'If you're not back in five minutes I swear I'll call the militia,' she said. She was a little perplexed and didn't understand us, but I liked the idea that she was worried about me.

'Well, give it ten,' I said. 'Please stay put and don't go anywhere.'

'And if anyone accosts you, smack him in the gob,' added the driver, more and more pleased with himself.

As we descended the steps, I went first, but he tripped me up and I fell onto the pavement. People turned to look, and a fat man stopped.

I got up and brushed off my clothes.

'That's not the done thing. Not nice,' I said. 'And people are stopping, the militia might come, and then what? Or is it that you're afraid?'

He was confused, and even took my offensive question on the chin.

'As God's my witness, I don't know how that happened. May I die on the spot if I did it deliberately. You've had a drink already, that explains it. You tripped over my foot of your own accord.'

'All right, let's go.'

We went into the first gateway. It was the courtyard of a gutted house, ideal for our purposes. We didn't fight for long. I was weaker than he was, but much more agile, and I knew a bit of judo, which he didn't. The poor guy probably worked long hours and had no time for exercise. I got a pretty good smack on the jaw, and he got a punch on the brow and another in the belly. Then I managed a dodge, threw him over my shoulder and held him down so he couldn't move.

'I think we should end it there. Our strengths are more or less equal and there's no point in bashing away any more. Besides, I didn't mean to insult you, it just came out like that,' I said, addressing him informally.

'All right,' he said. 'If we're going to behave nicely, that's fine. The name's Heniek. And I can apologize to the lady.'

Everything in him began to relax towards a need to observe the minutiae of social form. I let go of him, and we started to brush ourselves off.

'Would you like a drink?' I asked.

'Why not? Always possible, when someone is courteous enough to offer and the wheels are parked. And I'll take the opportunity to apologize to the lady.'

'Better not do that – for the sake of the social ambience, let's not return to that matter at all.'

'Really? You think so? If you say so, then so be it, very well and good.'

I seemed to have become an authority for him, as if my manner of speaking impressed him.

I have never been able to remember exactly what happened after that. To this day bits of it still come back to me out of the blue. Maybe I got so very drunk because of the blow to the head inflicted on me by Heniek; at any rate, for the first time in my life I got so sloshed that I lost the plot entirely. I remember us traipsing around with Heniek for a while longer, and being in a strange flat somewhere. Then the girl and I were left on our own, we went down to the Vistula, we saw the sunrise, and we were lying on the grass; I said all sorts of nonsense, like the things my father had spouted with reference to Miss Hantz. That night by the Vistula I must also have said (because something of the kind comes back to me occasionally): 'Now I think I know what pining is. It's exactly the feeling I have right now. That something is there, but will be gone one day, and won't ever return.' I don't know how such piffle could have stuck in my head, but it's a fact that it did, and that now and then it comes back to haunt me, among other memories of that night. But at the time I'd lost the plot, so totally and utterly that when I woke up the next morning the last thing I could remember, and that foggily, was the conversation with my father.

I woke abruptly and couldn't get a grip on reality. I could see the curtain in the window, the highly familiar curtain with yellow flowers on a blue background, but it didn't seem to be my one; what's more, the entire room seemed alien, nothing seemed to be mine, not even me. In the first instance I knew nothing about myself, apart from the fact that I was lying in the familiar, yet strange surroundings of my bedroom, I had no memory of the past, or any idea about the future. It was a while before I realized I wasn't alone. I became aware of a presence, close by, and heard regular, quiet breathing. I turned around. There was a girl sleeping next to me, lying on her stomach with her hands raised above her head, like Kim Novak in that thriller when the baddie aims a revolver at her and cries: 'Easy now, baby doll'. She was pressing her cheek to the pillow, but I couldn't see her face, which was turned aside, shielded by her dark, tousled hair. I wondered who she might be – I had absolutely no idea. By the door stood an unfamiliar travelling bag. On the bedside table lay hair clips, a suspender belt and one stocking. The second one was lying on the floor, alongside various other things of the kind that are usually removed in a great hurry, whether out of unbridled impatience, or embarrassed desire to get it over with quickly, and to end up in an unambiguous situation where nothing is like the daily routine of putting on and taking off one's clothing. But none of it reminded me of anything or was like anyone. Suddenly the girl moved, sat up on an elbow and turned her face towards me, but it was shielded by a curtain of dark hair, so I couldn't see her features well enough to find out if it was someone I knew.

'Who are you?' I asked. The girl fell back onto the pillow and must have gone to sleep at once. I thought that was probably a silly question, whoever she was, and glanced at my watch. It was ten to eleven, and suddenly I remembered about La Hantz, my father and his anniversary. My rehearsal with the young singer was meant to be at eleven. If I were late, she might not wait but would take off.

'The rehearsal doesn't matter, but I can't let her sit down at the birthday lunch as the lady of the house or something of the kind. Who could the girl be?' I wondered. 'Never mind. She probably won't steal anything, or run off and slam the door. And even if she does, it's all the same, as long as the Hantz girl doesn't escape.' I leaped up, washed and shaved, dressed and ran out of the house. Before leaving I peeped into the bedroom again and looked at the girl asleep behind a curtain of hair. Something seemed to flash through my head, something that wasn't nasty or embarrassing, but on the contrary, more like the memory of a beautiful painting I'd once seen in a gallery. But I hadn't time to stop and think about it, nor was my mind clear enough to hold, question and identify the memory.

I was ten minutes late, and I waited another fifteen for Miss Hantz. She arrived fresh and fragrant, radiating a carefree atmosphere. The rehearsal went badly. I wasn't thinking of the song. I was thinking of the singer and my father, but I had no idea what to do about it. My head ached, as did my jaw and my left leg. I wanted to accuse her of being out of tune, but I was the one who was off-key, I kept making mistakes, and finally she said: 'Hey, what's up with you today?'

'Nothing,' I said, and closed the piano lid. 'I've got one hell of a hang-over. The rehearsal is at an end.'

Miss Hantz was pleased.

'That's great,' she said. 'I wanted to shove off early today anyway, don't you know? It's a special day for me, I have to get ready, don't you know?'

I felt dead beat, and started to think doggedly about going home; I was totally indifferent to the business involving my father and this girl. Let her go and get ready for the role of lady of the house at that idiotic party.

'Come at the same time tomorrow,' I said.

'All right. Bye, darling. Take care.'

She waltzed off, but stopped in the doorway.

'Aha,' she said. 'Your old man invited me to that do of his. I'd love to come, but I can't. Would you be so good as to apologize to him for me?'

I got up and approached her. It must have looked dramatic because I saw amazement on her face.

'What do you mean, you can't come? What do you mean, I'm to apologize for you?'

'Listen,' she said, 'you shouldn't drink too much. Go home, go to bed and sleep it off. But maybe you're right, that would be silly. I'll call your old man and explain it to him. You have no idea how much I like him. But you know what, my boyfriend's flying in from Paris today. He was going to come in a week, but he's arriving today. He was pining for me so badly. You know what that's like, don't you? But off you go. Go home and go to bed.'

I didn't feel like going home any more, I wasn't thinking of home.

'Wait a moment,' I said. I wanted to demand an explanation, I wanted her to tell me in detail the whole story of her liaison with my father, but suddenly I realized she couldn't tell me any story of the kind, because she didn't know it.

'Of course,' I said. 'Of course I'll tell my father, and I don't think you need to call him. He's sure to be very sorry. He likes you too.'

'All right, then, bye, darling,' said Miss Hantz, reassured, and flew from the room.

I found my father in an excellent mood. He opened the door whistling. Dr Kornaszewska was bustling about in the kitchen – not someone I'd expected to find at my father's house at all. She was a handsome personage of over forty, a musicologist – when I was at the conservatory I used to go to her lectures on the history of music. She greeted me with indeterminate, joyful and overfamiliar shrieks. My father said: 'I don't think I have to introduce you to each other.'

He said this meaningfully and playfully, which made me feel queasy.

'You don't look your best,' said my father.

'I could do with a drink,' I said.

'Zosia,' called my father, 'take off that apron and come and join us. Mrs Ciechowa will be here in a moment and she'll take care of the kitchen. There's still time until lunch.'

Dr Kornaszewska came in, and tried to be even sweeter and even more conspiratorial. I drank the whisky my father poured for me. There was always whisky and other such things in this house.

'Miss Hantz asked me to apologize but she can't come,' I said.

'Miss Hantz?' asked my father, frowning. 'Oh, the little singer. An amusing girl. I once took her to the theatre on my ticket. She was standing there waiting for someone to take her, and Zosia couldn't go that time, because some Soviet musicologists had suddenly arrived.'

'Her boyfriend's flying in from Paris today,' I said, still with a faint shadow of hope. 'So you were at the theatre with her? Not the cinema?'

'At the theatre. And I invited her. You know, our dignitaries enjoy the company of singers and actresses of that sort. It rejuvenates and refreshes, and all that.'

'Oh, Henryk,' giggled Dr Kornaszewska inanely. 'How amusing you are.'

'Just the theatre?' I asked. 'Not the cinema? You didn't go for a walk? Or take her out to supper?' I said this quietly, to myself really, and my father asked: 'What's that you're mumbling?'

'Nothing. I'm singing to myself.'

'He's probably had an idea for a song,' said Dr Kornaszewska, rushing to my aid. 'Another drop of whisky?'

'Yes, please, as many drops as will fit in the glass.'

My father was surprised, and pretended not to notice this lack of respect. Dr Kornaszewska giggled again just in case, and they started up a jolly conversation, jumping from topic to topic, until they stopped at their memories of old, pre-war movies.

I felt a void inside. I felt as if I'd lost a close friend. I realized that the vision of my father being involved in such an inappropriate and stupid association, and the prospect of something like a scandal at his birthday party, like a modernized version of that romantic epic *The Leper*, made him human. I had grown fond of this affair, which made up for the deadly dullness of his literature. Now I felt cheated. I reckoned I had the right to smash up his entire flat – minibar full of refined drinks, trendy modern furniture, last year's *Paris Match* and all – and I regretted the fact that solicitude and customary but artificial conventions were stopping me from doing it.

'That must have been one of the first films I ever saw,' said my father with a kind of smile, which on his face I found new and puzzling. 'I went to that film with an aunt. I remember. I think it must have affected my entire life. I had a tragic experience. A shock. The film was called *In the Shadow of Brooklyn*. Such a stupid title, I don't know why, but to this day it makes an impression on me. Somehow I have a strange, wistful feeling whenever I hear or say it.'

I was listening.

'It was about a boxer. He took to drink. Then . . . I can't fully remember, but there was a girl. There were people chasing him. The girl saved him. Somehow they fell in love, and various other things happened, but then he got drunk again and was lying in the gutter, but she found him and leaned over him, and then he said: "Who are you?" And just imagine, quite out of the blue my aunt decided the film was unsuitable for a child, and she took me outside. I cried – in fact, and don't laugh, I'm still upset about it, sometimes I try to imagine what happened next, after he'd been lying in the gutter, she'd been leaning over him, and he'd asked her: "Who are you?"'

I raced out, ignoring their astonishment, which did its best to chase after me. Everything came back to me, all the details that my father would never remember. The girl, the fight with Heniek, tramping about Warsaw, the sunrise over the Vistula and the happy time I'd had in my sad home. For the first time ever my father had given a simple, beautiful and truthful description. And that was the first story of his to make an impression on me, to move me.

I entered my flat, but as I crossed the threshold I knew I wouldn't find what I'd suddenly started to desire. The flat had been wonderfully tidied, it was clean and cosy, but there was no one and nothing there; right before my eyes the warmth and tenderness that man is constantly fleeing and constantly pursuing evaporated and were gone.

The mirror in the bathroom had a sentence written slantwise across it in red lipstick: MY NAME IS EWA, IF YOU PLEASE.

'*W cieniu Brooklynu*'
Published as part of the collection *W cieniu Brooklynu* (Czytelnik, 1973).

MAREK NOWAKOWSKI

1935–2014

Marek Nowakowski was a prolific author of short stories and micro stories, essays, sketches, memoirs and plays. Several of his works were adapted for television or cinema.

In his youth he worked as a miner, as well as serving two prison sentences at a labour camp. In the mid-1950s he studied law at Warsaw University but didn't qualify.

He wrote about officially ignored areas of life, people from the 'social margins' living in the seediest Warsaw suburbs; his main characters are often at odds with the law. One of his best-known characters is Benek Kwiaciarz – 'Benny the Florist', a colourful conman so named because he buys flowers for the many women he pursues.

In the 1980s Nowakowski's work fell foul of the communist censors and was published abroad by the Paris-based Instytut Literacki, then smuggled into Poland and distributed in photocopied form. The most famous of these works are his impressions of the martial law period that began in December 1981; published in English as *The Canary and Other Tales of Martial Law* (see *Further Reading*), these snapshots of everyday experience show the huge gap that had grown between real society and the imaginary country depicted in the official communist version.

In the 1990s he continued to take a satirical stance in several books that portrayed the social reality of the period of political and economic transformation, notably in *Prawo prerii* (*Law of the Prairie*, 1999); he was not the only author of the day to depict liberal capitalism as simply a new embodiment of systemic violence. He also wrote memoirs of Warsaw in the past, and sketches mocking the absurdities of life in People's Poland.

The story that follows is an example of his attitude to the state of that country, which he defined with the metaphor '*zgojenie*', meaning 'putrescence'. His black humour contrasts the traditional, jolly group activity of mushroom picking with the dog-eat-dog power structure within a socialist-era company, where back-stabbing is the norm.

Antonia Lloyd-Jones

'When the Glow of Dawn Appears . . .'

Translated by Antonia Lloyd-Jones

The coach bumped over the potholes. This was the worst stretch of the city's main thoroughfare. The road surface was being replaced here, and only a narrow strip, full of pits and puddles, had been left for the traffic. They were passing a petrol station. At the back of the small building there was a yard with a garish sign: 'Cosy corner for self-service repairs'.

Władek, the driver, looked out of his cab and said in a hostile tone: 'Self-service repairs! What'll they think of next? Just try doing your own repairs!' Probably hungover from Saturday night, he had bloodshot eyes and stubble on his chin.

At the sight of a large sign that popped up on the wall of a defunct brickworks he merely spat. 'The culture and aesthetics of the workplace are our prime concern', it said.

'Yes . . .' agreed Engineer Jundziłł, who was sitting closest to the driver. 'There's too much of that sort of literature everywhere. Too much. It may look all right at first glance, but there's something wrong with it. I rode in a taxi,' he recalled, 'where there were eight signs saying things like "Don't spit", "Don't smoke", "Don't slam the door", "Don't dirty the seats", "Don't open the windows", so I travelled along feeling as if I were in prison. Nothing but prohibitions. And how neat all those little signs are, made of metal, or varnished . . .', he whined ridiculously in a lilting eastern accent.

The managing director could hear this speech. In fact, Jundziłł had turned around and was seeking approval in his eyes. But the MD didn't pick up the thread. He was immersed in *The Field Guide to Edible and Toxic Mushrooms*.

'Cab drivers have a tough life,' said Władek, the driver, 'all sorts of bastards . . .'

By now they had driven onto the highway leading out of the city. Suddenly there was a rasp of brakes, and everyone bounced in their seats. Władek leaned out of his window. A Trabant had sprung from a side street and shoved itself just in front of the coach. If not for Władek's quick and steady hand, there would have been an accident for sure.

So he leaned out, his face red with rage, and screamed: 'Where the fuck are you going in that soapbox?!'

The man in the Trabant cringed behind the steering wheel. Władek, a typical Warsaw wide boy, always said something like that on such occasions. Even the MD covered his mouth with a hand.

'Praise the Lord,' said Władek, wiping the sweat from his brow.

By now the densely built-up suburbs were at an end. They were passing market gardens, dovecots and plots where new housing estates were being built. There were grey, pockmarked, box-shaped tower blocks, earth ploughed up by bulldozers, and cranes with their claws immobile in Sunday repose. A few of the blocks were already inhabited, with TV aerials projecting from their roofs, and there were children playing among the piles of bricks and prefab materials.

'And they say the birth rate's falling,' remarked Engineer Jundziłł, who didn't like children.

'As you folks can see, that's typical linear architecture, in other words it's along the transport route,' said the head of accounts, showing off his erudition, though the truly erudite fellow was the man he'd heard talking about it on television. He held forth some more, but no one was listening to him.

Once the fields and thatched cottages had begun in earnest, Zbrożek, the Socialist Youth Union activist, spread his hands like a skilled conductor and suggested: 'How about a sing-along?' And at once in a ringing voice well schooled at various jamborees and training camps, he began: 'A sweet little maiden went to the woods so green . . .' Some of the tour group picked up the tune and joined in, singing: 'There she met a hunter, a handsome fellow he . . .' while swaying to the beat.

But despite the choral singing, Engineer Dopierała, whose nickname was Onward-and-Upward, caught himself quite unconsciously humming the hymn: 'When the glow of dawn appears . . .' It had been in his head all morning, while he was shaving, and later too, on the way to the assembly point for the Sunday outing. So he stifled the insistent 'glow of dawn', but didn't sing the stupid 'sweet little maiden' either. He gazed out of the window. The weather was nice, autumnal; there was a bluish mist rising from the fields and dissolving. There were a few cars on the highway, some motorbikes and several cyclists, probably out to pick mushrooms too. A coach just like theirs had stopped on the hard shoulder, and was disgorging its passengers into the bushes on both sides of the highway: men to the left, women to the right.

'Maybe we should stop too . . .' said Władek, slowing down.

But no one had any such need.

Engineer Dopierała gazed at the landscape of fields and meadows. He saw some cows like piebald statues, a frisky colt and an old peasant leaning on a stick while staring sluggishly into space. Engineer Dopierała smiled at his neighbour in the next seat. It was his colleague Prawiczek, a friend since their days at the polytechnic.

'Nice weather,' he said. 'We'll have a change of air, won't we?'

Prawiczek agreed. At once Engineer Dopierała turned around and started talking to the MD about some new prototypes licensed from a Swiss company on which they were currently working.

'Yes, yes,' he repeated, 'you're right to point that out, sir . . .' And time and again he fixed those pale, clear eyes of his on the MD.

Prawiczek was furtively watching him, in endless amazement at his colleague's cold fluency, urbanity, wit and respectful agreement. It was his warm, resonant voice: '. . . without a doubt, one must make adjustments, I agree with you, sir, and what's more, the parameters . . .'

Run to fat and gone grey, with a face that expressed nothing, the MD nodded. And so they carried on their discussion.

Suddenly the entire group burst into thunderous laughter. On a field road they'd seen a runtish mongrel setting about his amours. He had waylaid a large bitch and was awkwardly trying to deal with her.

'He sure is randy!' cried Władek, pointing at the spectacle.

The bitch was angrily shooing the mongrel away, but he wouldn't give up. Everyone was laughing.

'Such is life, Miss Mariola,' added Władek with a fake sigh. This comment was addressed to the prettiest girl at the design office.

There she sat, as sullen and majestic as a film star. She cast him a look of disdain.

'Taxi dancer,' muttered Władek. 'Before the war women like that danced the *chechotka* on the table for well-heeled guests.'

The whole time Mariola's faithful admirer, Engineer Pawluśkiewicz, made puppy-dog eyes at her. He was thin as a rake, and although they were going mushroom picking, he was wearing a black suit, a white shirt and tie. He kept pressing chocolates on her, and there was a scent of Sunday-best eau-de-Cologne wafting from him. What a comical paramour.

Meanwhile the two oldest clerks from the accounts department had started up their eternal bickering.

'So you say you served in Grudziądź?'

'Yes, in the Eleventh cavalry regiment . . .'

'I don't remember any permanent unit there – at most you could have been at the school, the Cavalry Training Centre . . .'

'Do you remember Lieutenant Arciszewski?'

'My dear man, there were five officers by the name of Arciszewski.'

The quarrel was growing fiercer. Like obdurate cockerels, they kept catching each other out on various inaccuracies in their reminiscences, setting cunning traps for each other.

But this debate soon fizzled out too. The coach sped along the asphalt highway. Now they were moving along smoothly and softly. Heads began to droop in slumber. Some people had even started snoring. Only Engineer Dopierała, nicknamed Onward-and-Upward, wasn't dozing. He was sitting up resiliently and gazing out of the window at the autumn landscape, clumps of trees and black, ploughed earth. He found it both sad and depressing. He remembered his last business trip to England. Or rather a certain part of it, extremely clear and precise in his mind, as if recorded on videotape. Hardly any of his time in London had remained in his memory – the meetings at the associate firm, his bashful English, his stage fright, those guys, becoming familiar with the new measuring equipment, then roaming the streets with a city map, shopping at some cheap little stores, Soho at night . . . It was of no consequence and had almost entirely faded away. His memory of the trip was foggy and full of holes. Except for that weekend away. A young engineer named Walter had invited him to his private home. Walter had been to Poland once, to visit their design office. He was tall and tanned, smiling broadly the whole time. He remembered a bar in Warsaw. Ah, yes – the Crocodile. This Walter was the same age as Dopierała. And they seemed to feel mutual sympathy. Peers . . . The motorway, a Volvo ride beyond the city, a superb sports car. Walter drove in a relaxed but confident way. Well-tended landscape, clusters of small houses a bit like toys. It was autumn then too. But warmer perhaps. Finally they reached the place. A driveway, flowerbeds, lawns, tall trees; did he play tennis, asked Walter. Unfortunately he did not. Now he went to the Legia courts twice a week. He was getting quite good at it by now. A wooden house with a small porch, little columns covered in a purple vine. Behind the house there was a court – he could hear the patter of balls. It was Walter's children playing tennis. A dark interior, a hall, a fireplace with a real fire in it, the flash of flames, the rattle of ice cubes. Walter's wife, Kate, tall, very shapely, perhaps too thin. Both friendly, they praised his English, *You speak correctly, really correctly* . . . A neighbour or someone came too. A ruddy man, in plus fours. Older. He'd come in contact with the Poles during the war. At the battle of Tobruk. He was full of praise for them. And the whole time Dopierała had felt bloody awful tension, trembling, a sense of being lost, alien, unfriendly, ashamed, regretful . . . His hands had sweated. He'd kept insensibly wiping them on his trousers. That lot had talked about their earnings. They'd asked him questions. He'd replied. And what was his boss like? Then he had thought of his fierce, ruthless duel with the MD. He's a good boss, he'd replied, a superb professional, an organizer. *Fine, fine*, repeated Walter and the older man in plus fours. Was he expecting promotion? At the time he was almost certain of it. They'd already unambiguously implied it at the district committee. How had they put it? Ah, welcome, comrade director. Sort of as a joke, and yet seriously, because at the time the MD's days were numbered. But he couldn't tell the Englishmen that. Only that he was expecting it, he'd be transferred to another research facility to take up a post as manager. Once again they were pleased. *Great, fine, that's right* . . . They'd smiled at him, and he at them. And the whole time there was that brick wall, impenetrable, strong, irremovable. It pained him, insistently chafed and tormented him. Did he like light music or serious? Serious, he replied automatically. At once there was Bach from the stereo gramophone. Walter's wife beamed. She too only liked serious music. Walter showed him around the house, the bedroom, a bathroom, the children's rooms, another bathroom, the sitting room, the library. And this is the study, he said, smiling proudly. The carpentry workshop. In his spare time he amused himself with it. For relaxation . . . A cupboard, shelves, side tables. He nodded, admired and smiled when appropriate. Meanwhile the wretched, insistent depression didn't leave him for an instant. And he felt so old. Walter, though his peer, was like a puppy, still wet behind the ears. And he found this thought consoling. As he smiled broadly but duplicitously at Walter, he was thinking: 'What do you know about life, you twerp . . . ?' At last it was night, at last he was alone, in a room upstairs, the guest room, but for ages he couldn't sleep. Though he could sense peace surrounding his hellish inner turmoil, there was equilibrium in the air all around him, it came with the murmurs of the night . . .

He sat up even straighter, pressed his face to the window, and to chase away the exasperating muddle in his head, he quite unwittingly started humming 'When the glow of dawn appears . . .' Just as when they'd sung the 'maiden', it took him a while to realize he was humming. He instantly stopped, clenched his lips and surveyed the passengers. They were all asleep. He turned around and met the MD's eyes. He felt uneasy. They were attentive, piercing eyes. They looked at each other. At once Engineer Dopierała, nicknamed Onward-and-Upward, smiled like a robot, broadly and winningly. But seconds later he felt slippery metal in his fingers. Throughout his memories of England he'd been playing with the Ronson lighter he had bought there. The MD's gaze reminded him of it. He quickly put it in his pocket. The MD wasn't looking at him any more. He had closed his eyes. Or perhaps he hadn't been looking at all? And Dopierała had just imagined it? For a while he wondered about that.

They stopped on a side road between tall broadleaf forest and a pine copse. The sun was high in the sky by now, nature shone in its many autumn colours, and the sand felt warm and pleasant. Everyone thought the spot looked promising. Władek had driven about five kilometres away from the highway into the depths of the forest. The engineers, the technicians, their wives, the draughtsmen, the clerks from planning and accounts, the personnel manager and his assistants were all happy to get out and stretch their stiff legs and backs. The place was empty, with no other mushroom pickers within sight or hearing.

One of the engineers' wives recalled that last year in this very same wood they had picked a vast quantity of mushrooms.

'Even saffron milk caps,' she said, with a flash of excitement in her eyes.

She surveyed the scene. Towards the young pine trees seemed to be the right direction, and at once she headed that way, carrying a wicker basket. Several of the most eager mushroom hunters went after her.

Once he had finished tapping the tyres, Władek crawled underneath the coach to check something there. His outspread legs protruded comically.

And so the Sunday mushroom hunt began.

Some immediately headed deep into the forest. Others, mainly the young ones, stretched out comfortably on a sandy hill, tuned their transistor radios and argued about the suspension of the new Fiat chassis. They started calling for Władek the driver to come and arbitrate, but he was still busy under the coach. The chairman of the company council, an old drunkard, was already reaching for the bottle, but stopped when he met the reproachful gaze of the MD.

'I fully understand,' said the MD, 'but I think in the first place one should enjoy a little fresh air and exercise . . .'

And that was that. The chairman agreed and put the bottle back in his bag. Though actually who knows? He went into the bushes, so maybe he took a swig?

Surrounded by several admirers, Mariola went for a walk. The women saw her off with less than amicable glances. As she walked she swung her rear, and her high heels sank into the sand. The admirers picked a bouquet of ferns and leaves for her. They reached a large clearing where some little village girls were grazing their cows.

'What wonderful peace and quiet,' said Mariola, stretching out in a feline way. She was wearing large glasses, so-called goggles. Her high breasts stuck out, squeezed into a tight sweater. The little girls grazing their cows began a noisy quarrel. They yanked each other's plaits and screamed.

'That's shit!' one of them shouted. 'That's real shit!'

'That's not a nice way to speak,' said Mariola sternly. 'Yuk!'

'It is nice, if you please, Miss,' replied the child firmly. 'That's modern talk.'

Everyone burst out laughing. Only Engineer Pawluśkiewicz, who looked like an apparition in his black suit in the forest, took violent offence.

'Nasty little brat!' he said.

And on they went.

The final group to head off into the forest included the MD. With him went the chief designer and his wife, the accounts manager, the personnel manager and Engineer Dopierała. And a few paces behind came timid Prawiczek. Engineer Dopierała was definitely only there because of the MD. He wasn't really interested in mushrooms. On the whole he had little desire for this Sunday outing. But since the MD was going ... So he'd decided to do it. He'd called his fiancée and they'd made a date for the evening.

And so, walking beside the MD, while listening keenly to his thesis on the properties of materials they'd been sent and new indicators of their reliability, in the background Dopierała was considering how the whole thing with his fiancée positioned him too. She was a market gardener's daughter. And perhaps would soon be his second wife. He had divorced the first one two years ago. For a while he even imagined himself driving a red Volvo car. He rated that type of car highest of all. But it was just an embarrassing dream, and he only briefly allowed his imagination to indulge in such idleness. With energy and gusto he began to hold forth about a new measuring device based on laser technology, something he'd read about recently in an American technical quarterly. He had realized to his satisfaction that the MD had scant knowledge of these latest scientific and technical developments, so he was even more willing to shine on this particular topic.

Meanwhile the other members of their group had started to spread out, with their eyes fixed on the ground, seized by a rising passion for mushrooms, because the first specimens had just started to appear. The chief designer's wife found two small but extremely neat little boletes. The personnel manager looked most peculiar, walking along with his head bowed, as if following a scent, his face focused, like a bloodhound.

'A police dog,' said the accounts manager gloomily, who had spent a good couple of years in jail during the days of the personality cult. And he said that because the old personnel manager had been on the other side. But these days he was actually quite human and not a thorn in anyone's side.

The first mushrooms soon caught the MD's attention too, and Engineer

Dopierała – Onward-and-Upward – started staring at the ground. If at first they had just been out for a bit of a walk, while going on about indicators and prototypes, now they had stopped talking, and their eyes had begun to spy out mushrooms hidden on the forest floor. More and more often these were boletes and ink caps.

Then, in a clump of birches, Engineer Dopierała discovered a whole colony of red boletes. He was quite childishly overjoyed. He picked them and put them in a plastic bag.

'Ten!' he exclaimed.

'A fine haul,' agreed the MD.

They moved onwards. More and more often they bent down abruptly, either finding a trophy or being disappointed by the false charm of a poisonous mushroom. They solved their doubts on this question by consulting the booklet the MD had brought with him – *The Field Guide to Edible and Toxic Mushrooms*. So as they stood over a suspicious specimen they turned the pages until they found the relevant colour illustration.

'Unfortunately,' confirmed the MD.

'A sad mistake,' agreed Engineer Dopierała.

They found a false saffron milk cap, deceptively similar to a real one, but when they bisected the root with a penknife there was no blood-red stripe inside, which is always the hallmark of a saffron milk cap.

In the course of this quest a sort of playful duel arose between them. The MD turned out to be erudite on the basis of the mushroom field guide. But Dopierała was an expert too, except that his knowledge was practical. And these two schools clashed: the common names and the names used in the professional literature. So if on their trail they came upon a yellow mushroom with a ragged, irregular cap on a thin stalk, the MD would say, 'It's a golden chanterelle', and Engineer Dopierała would simply say 'a girolle'. And when they found a species buried deep in the sand, with a small green head, the MD called the mushroom a 'man-on-horseback', whereas Engineer Dopierała said it was a 'yellow knight'. At this point the MD thought a while, and added the Latin name of the mushroom: '*Tricholoma equestre*'. 'He's got a pretty good memory,' Dopierała had to admit.

Now they were walking along a narrow track, well-trodden by mushroom pickers. The ground was boggy and thickly carpeted with leaves.

'Look out,' warned Dopierała, 'slowly . . .'

And there under a young beech tree they both spotted a magnificent penny bun at exactly the same moment. It was a perfect specimen, just like the ones the weather forecaster Wicherek sometimes showed on television. Seized by the fever of discovery, both men ran up to the mushroom. And Engineer Dopierała was the first to bend down. He was just about to pick it, when suddenly his hand froze, and he instantly retreated. The MD, who had run up to the mushroom from the other side, froze too.

'Please, sir, go ahead . . .' said Dopierała, making a broad, welcoming gesture.

'But you were first,' replied the MD, withdrawing his hand from the mushroom.

'What do you mean?' said Dopierała. He stood up and took a step back from the mushroom.

They got caught up in a peculiar display of over-politeness, each yielding the prize to the other.

'Surely I didn't . . .' The MD tried to defend himself, but more and more feebly.

'But indeed, every second counts, like in a race.'

'But you . . .' said the MD, staring at the mighty cep with its spreading cap.

'No, you were first.'

'Well, in that case . . .' said the MD, finally giving way. He squatted down and gently pulled the cep out of the moss. His eyes glittered at the sight of it. 'What a beauty,' he said.

'As long as it's not a devil's bolete,' worried Dopierała. He plucked a small blade of grass from under the cap. He tasted it. 'It's good,' he said. And thought about the effects of losing to the MD. Because ever since his underhand campaign had ended in a fiasco, he hadn't been on a single business trip to their capitalist clients. Not one. But before then he'd been to Belgium once, West Germany three times, and England twice . . . Now it was just the eastern bloc. Usually boring old Bulgaria. The MD had grounded him . . . He clenched his lips vengefully. He was filled with bitterness, and at the same time with rising tenacity. It only lasted briefly, for a split-second, then he looked through half-closed eyes at the MD – tubby and balding, with the remains of curly pepper-and-salt hair. He was inspecting his trophy mushroom, smiling with delight as he stroked its cap.

This tenacity was as heavy as a stone inside him. And at the same time he had patience. So once again he smiled winningly and said: 'Wonderful. It must be a record. I don't think anyone else will find anything quite like it.'

The MD smiled back at him too.

'It's like a gift from you,' he said.

And timid Prawiczek, dainty as a young lady, crouched in the bushes, watching this scene as if spellbound.

Tired after exploring the forest for several hours, they settled under some large oak trees growing on a hill. The MD was hailed as king of the mushroom hunt. His penny bun was the largest of all the mushrooms picked that day.

So now that the matter of mushrooms was dealt with, they sat comfortably under the oaks. It was quiet and pleasant here. Everyone gazed at the russet-and-purple forest, rising in a wall ahead of them, while behind them stood a dark-green clump of young pines and a sun-warmed glade, all wreathed in a gentle autumn mist.

'Hey, look!' cried Mariola, pointing upwards.

A fluffy brown squirrel was flitting from branch to branch like a dancer. It kept stopping to cast rapid glances at the trippers from the Elektromot design office sitting below.

'What a nice little creature,' said Władek the driver. His vulpine, wideboy's face softened too. The animal slipped to the ground and frisked near the people. Now and then it sat up immobile, holding out its forepaws ahead of it. They watched the squirrel until it finally disappeared. Sitting in the shade of the oak trees, some of them even lying down, they felt good, autumnal and blissful.

'Memories cast a spell,' said Mariola suddenly. Her patient admirer, Engineer Pawluśkiewicz, gazed at her hopefully. But she was not looking at him. She was running her fingers through the bouquet of golden leaves and yellow ferns, which rustled softly.

'She's in love with an actor,' remarked Lesiak from Personnel spitefully, nudging Pawluśkiewicz in the back. 'A beau, an American, I've forgotten his name, dammit . . .'

Engineer Pawluśkiewicz wasn't listening. He was still gazing at the girl's pretty, rather doll-like face. This Mariola was sitting in a provocative pose. In a short miniskirt, she had her legs raised high, and there was a lot on show underneath. Władek the driver's eyes shone as he took a good look. Mariola was dreamy and absent, as if in a trance. Perhaps her romantic lover had appeared to her? He must have suddenly come and carried her away to some wonderful other world . . . She smiled shyly and sighed.

And so they had a lyrical sojourn on the hill beneath the oak trees.

As Prawiczek, a shy and quiet observer, watched the others, somehow he found them poor, moving and pitiful. They were pulling hard, trying to break free, but their chains wouldn't give way. And he was chained to the same line too; this blissful rest in the autumn sunshine was just a brief pause. He was reminded of Nicnowski Forest, where he'd been on his first student holiday with a girl. They'd lost their way in those woods, and had wandered around for hours and hours, feeling exhausted, while the forest kept expanding like a wilderness, until eventually it turned out they were going in circles. That Nicnowski Forest wasn't very big, just some woods, nothing really . . .

The MD was lying on the grass with his hands supporting his head, staring at the sky. It was pure and blue, with only the occasional fluffy little snow-white cloud. He thought of his small home town; his tailor father, the rattle of the sewing machine, his parents whispering at night – they wanted to send him to the Gymnasium for higher education. He could hear those whispers as if it were today, he could hear them making calculations and discussing it in great detail. And for a while the constant tension left him entirely. He felt light and free. The whirr of the sewing machine, the calm rhythm, order and continuity. It was hard to believe a time like this had arrived: no trace of the sewing machine, his home, his father, nobody.

And he thought about the years that had come later. They seemed barren and wasted. He felt old and helpless. At least there was a little more sunshine, just enough, no more, the autumn sun was good, mild, not harsh . . . He raised his head and met the cold, watchful gaze of Engineer Dopierała. He shuddered. The tension was back again.

A picnic was now getting under way. Bags were being unpacked, and the women were providently spreading cloths and setting out ham sandwiches, cheese, chicken, bowls of salad, hard-boiled eggs, pork chops, tomatoes and pickled gherkins. The men were fetching out bottles and thermos flasks. Small plastic mugs were being filled.

Engineer Dopierała, nicknamed Onward-and-Upward, was watching all this thrifty activity with a sense of disdain. What a load of crap, he thought. But not for an instant did the broad, sincere smile leave his face. This smile was there throughout the preparations for the feast. From a dark-blue bag marked 'Sabena' – the Belgian airline – he fetched out a bottle of rowanberry vodka in a little woven basket.

'You're always so stylish,' said one of the women.

Without noticing which one had said it, he bowed gallantly.

'May we . . .' began Władek the driver, and turned to the MD. 'Your good health, sir.' At once he fell into confusion. After all, he was driving the coach. He smiled hesitantly and explained: 'I'm just having a symbolic drink, sir, so to speak, just one sip and not a drop more . . .' But he drained his mug, the old fraud.

So began the Elektromot mushroom-hunt picnic, in the autumn sunshine, amid threads of gossamer that gently brushed their faces. Everyone was hungry, so they had an appetite, and the vodka was going down pretty well. The ladies coughed and took a sip at a time, while the men drank bottoms-up. Even Engineer Pawluśkiewicz mustered the courage to drink to Mariola. She smiled at him quite sympathetically.

The MD rapped his penknife against a plate and raised his plastic mug.

The chatter and laughter fell silent. All eyes were fixed on him. And this is what he said: 'I'd like to take advantage of this pleasant occasion to thank the company council for their fine initiative . . .'

The chairman of the council, by now in his cups, started to clap and shout: 'Hurrah! Hurrah!' Somehow he was silenced.

The MD continued: '. . . that's to say for organizing our Sunday outing, which has now reached such an enjoyable finale. These are just my own personal impressions. Here we are, colleagues, having a bit of a rest in the sunshine, outside in the lap of nature.'

Everyone cheerfully agreed.

'I'd like to wish good health to all those present and not present, good luck to every one of us, all the best to our construction office and its results, to new successes for the whole team and each individual.' He drained his plastic mug.

Applause. He'd said it very nicely. Engineer Dopierała stood up and clapped the loudest.

As Prawiczek watched the MD he wondered whether he really did wish them all good health, and whether he really did see nothing but a sincere, close-knit team surrounding him. Couldn't he see that Brzękowski fellow among those present, who in that memorable period had drummed up so much bitterness against him and competed with Dopierała to bring him down? Couldn't he see that nasty Jundziłł, who had so ostentatiously said: 'Well, that's the end of that, at last our backyard will be tidied up too . . .' while glancing provocatively at the MD?

That's what Prawiczek was thinking, and he felt completely lost. But a little later his attention was alerted by Engineer Dopierała's toast to the MD in reply.

'I would like . . .' his friend from college – nicknamed Onward-and-Upward for his rapacious career-mindedness – solemnly began, 'on behalf of our entire construction office, because I think I'll be representing everyone, I'd like to thank the comrade MD for the warm and cordial words he has addressed to us . . .' – here he made a slight bow and cast a glance at the MD – 'here, in this collegial atmosphere of relaxation, on this very successful outing, the strong ties binding our collective have distinctly and forcibly emerged, showing us its integration and its primary aim, so precious and important to every one of us. Here I should stress – and once again, in saying this I think I'll be representing everyone – the role of our chief, our good friend, who has succeeded in creating a genuine bond between us, and thanks to whom we can boldly claim to be the leading research-and-prototype facility within our electrical engineering industry on a national scale. Here's to our continued success, and to the very good health of our MD!' So said the silver-tongued Engineer Dopierała, gazing into the MD's eyes throughout.

And the MD stood there – during this toast he had risen to his feet – gazing back at him.

That was when Prawiczek was reminded of the past – of the ambiguous glances cast insolently at the MD. The whispering and smirking. The MD had kept up his end somehow, put on a brave face, but he had aged considerably in that time. There was the constant light trembling of the fingers as he drank his tea, making his teaspoon ring. And those messages that started appearing in the toilets. Someone had talent – that excellent caricature of the MD was repeated over and over. And in the midst of it all Dopierała was like a pig in clover, cheerful, bubbling with joy and energy. On the go the whole time, on the go. He'd drop in at the workshop, or the personnel office, apparently to check something, to correct an order, and he'd stop for a chat, people would surround him, and he'd talk with gusto. And then came that memorable meeting, people hounding the MD like hungry dogs, dumping the blame on him for all the shortages, complaints, imperfections, nastinesses and oversights. And through the whole thing there'd been Dopierała's smile. And that civic concern of his. Towards the end of the meeting he had asked for the floor. 'Comrades, the mistakes made to date must be eliminated, the atmosphere must be sanitized and the management streamlined, it's high time to speak up as loud as possible . . .' The MD's head bowed low. Those times in the canteen when Dopierała had clapped Prawiczek on the back and said: 'Well, old pal, new times, changes to be made, a purge, we might now say' – here he paused – 'perhaps I'll have some fun playing the role of MD, what do you think, will I cope?' The MD's tired, ashen face. Dopierała had leaped up and pulled out a chair for him. 'Here you are, comrade!' The grimace on the MD's face; by then it was hard for him to fake a smile. And so it had continued for months on end.

'Thank you, engineer,' Prawiczek heard the MD say. A soft tone, as if moved.

Once again there was applause, as they bowed to each other, and smiled. The circle of revellers watched them, smiling warmly too.

Engineer Dopierała modestly withdrew to one side, lit a cigarette and wiped sweat from his brow. At the same time he noticed Prawiczek's look. He could read disgust and revulsion in his eyes. So Dopierała smiled at him, asking with that smile for understanding, then took him by the arm and led him further off to one side.

'Do you think I really hate him?' said Dopierała, almost in a whisper, after looking around to make sure the wrong ears weren't listening. 'Why? That's bullshit . . .' His eyes sparkled with derision. 'I'm simply moving forwards, I'm playing the game, scoring points, that was a different time, when it was only possible by special means, so I took the opportunity, watch out for the enemy, we need our own people, et cetera, I took advantage of the situation, agreed, but those were the rules of the game, cynicism, you'll say – agreed, but my dear man, noble principles went bust long ago, they're bankrupt, on the trash heap, rotting away there, all that counts is special means . . .' he said, and pensively chewed a blade of grass.

Prawiczek watched him throughout with a sense of disgust, but something new had stirred in him too: fascination.

'That's how things were then,' Dopierała continued. 'It was a nasty time, I agree, but it left him in a weak position, you know that, and what's more he stuck his neck out, he kept sticking his neck out, I know, I know all too well, he acted in the name of common sense . . .' he said, pre-empting Prawiczek's protest, 'he fought to raise the standard of the research work, he made an effort to form connections with facilities in the West, to achieve sensible contracts and modern labour organization, he clashed with those men from the ministry, it's true, but at the time everything had turned against him, that's what happened, how could I not take advantage, if there's a match, you play to win, so I took advantage . . . But now with my toast that has made you feel so hostile towards me, I've paid tribute to him, well, did I speak badly?' He became pensive again, quite oblivious to the ants crawling all over his bare calves, which were exposed. 'Now the situation is different, his position has improved, he survived the storm, but that doesn't mean I've backed off – our boss is too old, he's tired, he's just an old stager, but nowadays we have new economic policies, computers, the future is creeping in, you know what I mean, new cliques are coming along too, hungry, rapacious, a new load of crap, our dear old boss won't be able to cope with all that, but personally I'm on excellent form, ready for take-off, ready to take aim, sniff out the conditions, you know what I mean –' He broke off.

They heard the voice of the driver, Władek. He was telling a story: 'This outing is nothing, it's all gone nice and smoothly, it's good to stretch your legs now and then, especially for me, always behind the wheel, but I remember when I drove at the Ministry of Heavy Industry and there was a two-day trip to Zakopane, we got there pretty quickly and we got plastered, at the hotel, then at a pub, wait a mo, the "Beacon" was its name, we went all the way, there weren't many women and we danced so much with each one that the next day they were hobbling around like on crutches, well, quite, the plan had been a trip to the mountains, you had to go, anyway, we all thought let's go for a bit of a walk, for a beer and that'll be that, but there was this Russki with us, a big cheese, a guest of the minister himself, coming up to sixty but he slugged back the hooch like anything, so we walked off into the mountains, reached a clearing where there was a hotel, and everyone had had enough by then, but the Russki wanted to go higher, what could we do, he was a guest, so we dragged on up the hill, we were all out of breath, but that Russki was like a tank, he was hardly panting, some of our lot had fallen by the wayside, others were gritting their teeth but soldiering on, because it was too embarrassing to conk out in front of a guest, I tell you, folks, it was Golgotha, somehow we got up there, a mountain with a cross on top, yes, Giewont, and Zakopane so tiny down below, and that Russki stands there, with his legs apart, in short trousers, baggy shorts, he wipes the sweat from his brow and says, "*Vperyod!* – onward!", what a tough nut! We had trouble explaining to him that there was no path onward,' said Władek, ending his story.

'That's right,' agreed one of the oldest employees, 'it's the sacred truth, people are that tough in Siberia, there was this one guy, ten men couldn't deal with him . . . And they drink like dragons . . .' Someone began to hum a wistful Russian song about prospecting for gold. Then came *chastushki* – little Russian couplets that tell a joke.

Władek the driver turned out to be best at these comic verses. He knew all sorts of funny ones. In a very merry state by now, he began: 'Uncle Vanya's no weak tick,/ Killed a man with just his . . .'

'Now, now,' the MD stopped him just in time.

During the *chastushki* the chairman of the council made a clumsy pass at one of the women. He had knocked back a few and tried to grab her breasts. But this lass from the front office was very sharp. She bopped him on the bonce. At once he drooped, having finally reached his alcohol limit.

Next there was some funny business involving Engineer Pająk's wife. She was a bit tipsy too, and suddenly, out of the blue, she stood on her hands, walked a couple of metres and fell. Everyone was amazed. Engineer Pająk began muttering.

She got up, with leaves and grass in her hair, and said: 'Sometimes I feel as if something were lifting me up on wings, I really do, usually when we go out of the city, to where there's water, a forest, except that my husband drives terribly slowly, I tell you, my darlings, amid nature, beauty, I get this feeling, and I walk on my hands, tralala . . .' And she, this middle-aged woman, began to hum.

People were giggling. Furious, Engineer Pająk was gesturing to her to shut up, but she stubbornly went on: 'Because I'm a cheerful person, but my husband can't sleep at night, it's not normal, he moans, the poor thing, there's something bothering him . . .'

At this point Engineer Pająk couldn't restrain himself and quite roughly pulled her away from the company.

At once Engineer Dopierała defused the nasty situation by raising a toast to her acrobatic display.

'A striking, graceful show,' he described it.

There was still plenty of vodka. Time and again someone pulled out a hip flask and poured a round. The revels continued.

Engineer Dopierała, who generally didn't like to drink, knocked a good deal back too. He drank to almost every one of them. He'd rapidly empty the cap of his thermos flask and light a cigarette as a chaser. Later he got hold of a mustard glass and used that to regale himself instead.

'Your good health, esteemed colleague,' he importunately accosted Engineer Jundziłł, although they were bitter enemies. Jundziłł did not refuse. He smiled wryly and they both drank up.

Then he sat down next to the people from the front office and Personnel. He told some jokes. The women squealed. His face was shining brightly now, and his voice kept getting louder as he told ever more spicy jokes. He drank 'Brüderschaft' with Mr Wichrowski. He began to embrace the personnel manager. Later on he drank straight from the bottle. Just as someone else was pouring himself a drink, Dopierała upped and seized the bottle from him. And greedily drank from it, swigging down the lot. He threw the bottle into the bushes behind him. Then he began pinching the council chairman, who was sound asleep. He meanly pinched his cheeks and pulled on his ears, while sniggering joyfully. But the old man was so well-oiled that he didn't even shudder. So this game soon bored him. He tried to get up. It wasn't a great success. Twice he fell to the ground, until finally he managed to haul himself to his feet.

There he stood with his legs spread wide, swaying. He ran his eyes over the assembled company.

'Gimme some vodka!' he screamed. The MD cast him a look of amazement. Someone handed him a mug.

'I . . . I would like . . .' drawled Engineer Dopierała, but the words were unclear and incoherent, as if having a hard time getting out of his throat, 'to raise a toast, what I mean is to . . .'

No one was actually listening to him. Each was occupied with something else. They were all in high spirits.

He clenched his fist and raised it.

'A toast . . .' he repeated, 'essential, as we strive jointly for our results to . . . the hard work and effort . . . the wonderful prospect ahead . . .' he said, but had no more words beyond that. He stared into space and that was all. He felt something shift in his head, he actually had a physical sensation of it, as if the screws that had been keeping a tight lid on his secrets, everything that really mattered and that should never be said aloud, had suddenly given way, and it had all started to scramble out insistently from underneath. For a brief moment he was aware of that shift, but after that it was just an unbridled torrent. And wham, he hurled the mug of vodka forcefully to the ground.

'This drinking is absurd!' he roared. 'These toasts are all screwed up, a load of rubbish, just empty, stinking words, claptrap, rotten drivel, what does it mean, it doesn't mean a thing! Can't you understand that?'

The noise of the party began to die down. They stared at him in amazement. Now they were listening closely.

'We oil our tongues with this Vaseline-speech, mwah, mwah, all lovey-dovey, but with a stab in the back, yes, a stab, straight to the heart . . . But these stinking speeches are always regurgitated for any occasion in a flash, it's all so sweet, and happy, and wonderful, everything's better and better, just as it was in the past, I'm in your hands, dear brother, I beg your favour, my esteemed friend, but they're looking daggers, they're eyeing each other up, one has already dug a pit for the other . . .' He all but howled, dog-like, in a shrill tone. 'Do you understand . . .' he said in English, though it wasn't clear to whom, because he kept rolling his eyes around the circle of revellers listening, and carried on, as if blind to everything, 'justice, faith, it's all gone up in smoke, it was over and done with a bloody long time ago, and so was I, dammit, all that studying, the effort to learn English, the headphones, the conversation classes, climbing the bloody ladder, step by step, the indicators and parameters, the projects and prototypes, but all you really need here is the special means, how to get him from behind, how to hold the sonofabitch in a nelson until his spine starts to crack . . .'

His legs were giving way and he was finding it hard to keep his balance; after drawing one leg back, he frenziedly began to knock over all the bottles, thermos flasks, plates, salad bowls, mugs and dishes set out on the napkins.

'Rubbish!' he screamed. 'Rubbish!' And having kicked around the picnic set, he sobbed: 'I am innocent!'

Everyone stood gaping with their mouths wide open, seized by idiocy as they stared at him. What would he say next . . . ?

But Engineer Dopierała – Onward-and-Upward – said nothing more. Something began to yank inside him, he crouched, straightened, and crouched again. His cheeks puffed out dangerously and he only just managed to press his mouth shut with a hand. He ran off to one side.

At this point the MD's eyes flashed with something like satisfaction or derision. Perhaps he was taking note of an essential observation for the future.

Mr Wichrowski scowled with disgust and glanced at the MD. He always sided with him. And Władek the driver burst into gales of laughter.

'He's snapped,' he said.

He stared at Mariola's tapering legs. This Mariola was sitting shamelessly. Her legs were raised high, and her skirt was very short, a miniskirt – everything was on view.

'It happens . . .' said the driver after a pause, once he'd awoken from his staring. 'When I was in the army, there was a fellow like that who bet he could drink a litre with some solid snacks in an hour, but he only got down half, eating like a wolf the whole time, and then he brought it all up. I eat as few snacks as possible,' he concluded.

The autumn sun was starting to hide behind the high forest wall on the other side of the hill. The golden leaves were turning grey in the waning daylight. There was moaning and groaning coming from the nearby bushes. It was Engineer Dopierała vomiting. Worried about him, the merciful Prawiczek went into the bushes with a thermos of tea. Engineer Dopierała, nicknamed Onward-and-Upward, was lying on some withered leaves, kicking his legs because his guts were in such agony, and holding his stomach with both hands.

Prawiczek offered him the thermos.

'It's unsweetened,' he said, 'it helps . . .'

'A temporary indisposition,' said Dopierała, trying to smile rakishly. 'Onward and upward . . . But they define the direction . . .' But he didn't finish, once again his stomach churned, and he began to cough. Just then Władek the driver sounded the horn in the coach. The mushroom hunt was over.

'Kiedy ranne wstaja zorze . . .'
Published as part of the collection *Gdzie jest droga na Walne?* (Państwowy Instytut Wydawniczy, 1974).

.

KAZIMIERZ ORŁOŚ

1935–

Orłoś began his literary career in the late 1950s, when – despite the thaw that began in 1956 – Poland's writers were still expected to toe the political line. The stories he published in the 1960s were well received, and he began to write radio plays too. But in the 1970s his work fell foul of the commun-ist censors, and for publishing *Cudowna melina* (*The Wonderful Drinking Den*, 1973) with the émigré Instytut Literacki in Paris, he lost his job as an editor for Polish Radio and was banned from publication in Poland. He continued to publish his stories and novels abroad, only becoming officially accepted again after 1989 when democracy was restored.

The communist authorities' objection to his work was that it often criti-cized the political system obliquely, by depicting a world devoid of moral foundations, where people were indifferent to the suffering of others. But he also did it through direct parody; for example, *The Wonderful Drinking Den* is about an idealistic town council chairman who tries to curtail the corrupt practices of the local Party apparatchiks, but fails miserably and is despised for refusing to take bribes or drink.

In a footnote to the story that follows, Orłoś remembers Leszek Płażewski, a writer he befriended in the 1960s.

'Leszek was a raconteur,' he writes. 'Whenever we met he told stories about people he'd known (often socially marginalised) and incidents from the past. Orphaned in childhood, he was raised by his grandparents and spent the war and the postwar years in a Warsaw suburb. I never forgot his story of how his grandfather stalked the thief who'd been stealing fruit from a tree in their small garden. The thief turned out to be a friendly neighbour. I wrote "The Golden Pear Thief" without knowing that Leszek had written a story titled "Who's Stealing the Fruit?" Despite the obvious similarities, there were also essential differences. We discussed the matter. I gained his permission to publish my story, which all these years on I dedicate to Leszek's memory.'

Antonia Lloyd-Jones

The Golden Pear Thief

Translated by Antonia Lloyd-Jones

In memory of Leszek Płażewski

From early childhood I was brought up by the Majewskis – my mother's sister Helena and her husband, Uncle Edward. My mother had died when I was three years old, and my father was killed in the war. In 1948 I reached the age of twelve.

We lived in Ożarów, on Ogrodowa Street. The house was wooden, built by my uncle, on his post-office clerk's salary, in 1939. I remember the brown walls and the trees in the garden – apple, pear and plum trees that I used to shake, while sitting on the branches.

I went to the local school and played football with the other boys in the meadows, and that was the course of my life. The life of Auntie Hela – fifteen years older than my mother, always full of cares and only occasionally able to laugh heartily and at length – and that of Uncle Edek – sixty years old, white-haired and hunchbacked, in the soldier's jacket and four-cornered cap missing the eagle motif in which he had returned from the front in 1939 – ran along their own tracks, as if in parallel to mine. I can only remember a few events. For instance that my uncle often went about in backless slippers on his blue feet. He had a slight limp, a stiff left leg and leaned on a cane. Shrapnel from a German bomb had shattered his knee. He dragged the leg, and seemed to throw it upwards whenever he walked faster.

Today I'd say my aunt and uncle were god-fearing, honest people, if those words still mean something. They lived in poverty, on the post-office pension and on what my aunt sold at the market – in spring, summer and autumn. I used to help her to carry the goods there before going to school, usually fruits and vegetables from the garden.

Next door lived a locally well-known physician, Doctor Jabłoński. His was a different world, at which I gazed with envy and admiration. A large, stone house, with bright walls, and a German DKW car in a garage under a walnut tree, which in those days testified to wealth, so Auntie Hela said. A well-tended garden, mown lawns, a maid and two small children taken for walks and cared for by a nanny. The doctor's wife was a brunette, whom I remember in a pink dress with a low-cut neckline, reading books while sitting on a deckchair. I often heard her laughter through the fence.

Spiteful people used to say that Doctor Jabłoński was a careerist fraud, but Uncle Edek respected him because of the profession he practised. Before the war doctors had enjoyed particular esteem. Whereas according to my aunt he was a pseudo-doctor, not fully qualified, just a paramedic who had taken advantage of the chaos following the war to gain a doctor's diploma in a crooked way.

He belonged to the Party and supported the communists, proof of which were the red flags hung out by the gate to his property on the First of May and the Twenty-Second of July. What's more, apparently he worked at a military or Party clinic.

Uncle Edek, by contrast, was an enemy of the Party and the current regime, which he often stressed in conversation. In defiance of the authorities he hung out a red-and-white flag on the Third of May – Poland's traditional Constitution Day – until a militiaman he knew from the local outpost gave him a warning. 'There might be trouble, Mr Majewski,' he had said curtly. From then on Uncle Edek talked even more often of the government as Moscow-run. And he'd said that if Grandfather Piłsudski were still alive, he'd have driven all that riff-raff out of Poland.

'Including your friend the doctor!' Aunt Hela would put in her three-pennyworth. 'And everyone like him!'

My uncle, as I have said, did not share his wife's antipathy towards the neighbour. On meeting Jabłoński by the gate, for example, as he was getting into his car, he always said 'Good day to you, Doctor'. And he'd set two fingers to his cap. But the neighbour didn't seem to notice my uncle at all. He ignored his presence. He simply disregarded a disabled ex-serviceman. Sometimes he replied with a nod, but he never exchanged so much as a sentence. He'd drive away from the gate in his shining DKW without a word.

I admired that car in particular. Many times when the door of the garage under the walnut tree was open or when the doctor had left the car outside, I would be standing by the fence. The DKW had a retractable roof made of thick oilcloth. On hot days it was folded back. I would gaze at the black mudguards, the bright, nut-brown bonnet, and the silver radiator with the badge saying 'DKW'. Stretching on tiptoes, I would stare at the black leather seats, the mahogany dashboard with dials whose purpose I didn't know. From a few paces away I could catch the smell of lubricant, petrol and hot seat leather. Later, as I fell asleep, I'd imagine driving with the doctor along Ogrodowa Street, under the trees, in the sunlight that shone through the leaves. The girls from our class would be walking along the pavement and they would see us riding along. In my thoughts I admired Doctor Jabloński, although he took no notice of us.

And so it would have continued until Uncle Edek's death, which came a few years later, if not for certain events. In September 1948 – I remember the date well – my uncle noticed that the pear tree, speckled with large golden Clapp's Favourites, dripping with juice, to which on warm days wasps and hornets came flying from all over Ożarów, was unexpectedly losing its fruit. Each evening he'd count the fruits on some of the branches, and next morning he'd count them again. There were always fewer pears. Even odder, our piebald mongrel Azor never barked, though we knew he ran around the house at night. My uncle started to suspect my pals, who knew the dog. I rejected this theory with indignation. Meanwhile the sweet pears continued to go missing. To our amazement, from one night to the next the branches were ever more stripped.

I remember the nightly conversations on the topic.

'Those boys are stealing them,' said Uncle Edek. 'Darek's pals!' He pointed a finger at me.

'It's not true, Uncle! I don't have pals who are thieves!' I protested.

My aunt wasn't particularly interested in the matter, though she should have been, because she was selling fewer pears at the market.

'You've counted those pears over and over until you've got in a muddle! You'd do better to fix the electric light in the hall.'

On coming home from school I'd started doing the same, counting the pears. Amid the buzzing of wasps, I'd stand there craning my neck.

I'd bite into a pear and let the juice trickle down my chin as I drew a finger along the branches.

After several September nights on which someone continued to steal the fruit, my uncle decided to catch the thief. To this end he planned to lie in wait for the culprit in the garden. I remember my aunt advising him against this nocturnal escapade.

'What for? You won't get enough sleep, and someone will beat you up. Is it worth it for a few pears? You know what times are like, Edek.'

But my uncle was adamant. I remember him gathering up a torch, his cane and a small stool to sit on, putting on the army coat he kept in the wardrobe – because, as he put it, 'Once we've passed Saint Anna's day/ Morn and eve are cold and grey' – and taking up his position behind the gooseberry and currant bushes, a few steps away from the pear tree.

We know what happened that night from Uncle Edek's account. Next morning, at breakfast, he told us the whole story. The kitchen windows overlooked the garden, so as I ate my porridge, jangling my spoon against the plate, I could see the tree and the gooseberry bush behind which my uncle had lurked. He said that around midnight he had noticed some-one coming across the fence from the Jabłońskis' plot. At the same time Azor had run up to the stranger and greeted him. It seems he was given a tasty morsel.

Uncle Edek hadn't waited any longer: shining his torch, with his cane raised and a cry of: 'Stop, thief!' he had emerged from behind the bushes and, energetically throwing his stiff leg ahead of him, had approached the thief. On the way, as he told us, he lost one of his slippers. His sock began to be soaked with dew. There beneath the pear tree, with a stool in one hand and a bucket in the other, stood Doctor Jabłoński – the neighbour. In his pyjamas, a detail my uncle never forgot, and a sleeve-less waistcoat.

'Doctor Jabłoński, is that you?' asked Uncle Edek, illuminating the figure with his torch.

'Yes, neighbour,' confirmed the doctor, after a brief silence. 'It is I. Please don't shine that light in my eyes.'

The further conversation, according to my uncle's account, went as follows:

'What are you doing here at this time of night?'

'I'm looking for my child's ball – it must have fallen into your garden,' replied Jabłoński, once again after a brief silence.

'A ball?' said my uncle in amazement. 'At night?'

'So it happened,' said the doctor, looking around. 'But I can't see it. Oh well, it's not here!' Then he had ended the conversation by saying: 'Good night, neighbour.'

'Good night,' said Uncle Edek. And lit the way for Jabłoński as he went back over the fence. He placed a foot on the stool he'd brought and crossed to the other side. It seems there was a second stool waiting by the fence on the Jabłońskis' side of it. The doctor leaned over the fence posts to collect the other one from our side, and disappeared beyond the walnut tree. That was the last my uncle saw of him before returning to the house.

'He was looking for a ball,' he said at breakfast. 'What do you think of that, Hela? Maybe there really was a ball? It's possible, isn't it? I simply can't accept the idea that it's him! That it could be him!'

'He's the thief!' said my aunt, laughing. 'It's obviously him! A doctor, a gentleman, but actually a common thief! He liked the taste of our pears! That's the truth.'

For a long time my uncle refused to believe it.

'Can it be possible? Can it be possible?' he kept saying.

But the golden pears stopped disappearing from that night on, so gradually the truth began to get through to Uncle Edek. Until irrevocably, for once and for all, he lost his respect for Doctor Jabłoński. He stopped bowing to him and saying 'Good day to you'. And he no longer argued with my aunt when she referred to the doctor as 'not fully qualified' or 'that paramedic'.

However, the story does not end there. Unexpectedly it came to a new clash. Uncle Edek was painting the little garden gate next to our main gateway when the doctor's DKW stopped beside him. It was a warm day, the hood was down, and we saw a whole company inside: the doctor's wife in a straw hat, two other women, also in low-cut summer dresses (the three of them happened to be laughing out loud at that moment), and in front, next to Jabłoński, an officer in uniform – a major or even a colonel. He was sprawling in his seat, saying something to the women in the back. They were on their way home from the city.

Jabłoński hopped out to open his own gate. He stopped beside my uncle, who was concentrating, in silence, on coating the garden gate in oil paint. He had leaned his cane against the fence. He didn't even turn his head or glance at the doctor. We could hear the women's laughter and the hum of the DKW in neutral.

'What's this?' said Jabłoński, stopping beside us after opening his gate. 'Neighbour, don't you recognize me? Aren't you going to greet me?'

And then my uncle – plainly in a bad mood that day, at the sound of this company in the car behind him, the jokes and laughter, and surely remembering his encounter with Jabłoński that night, simply shot from the hip: 'I don't say "Good day" to thieves.'

I remember the way they fell silent in the car. Jabłoński leaned over Uncle Edek. He was a tall, solidly built man. A white shirt, blue eyes, a ginger moustache. And there was my uncle, in his old four-cornered cap and slippers on his blue feet, sitting on a stool, painting the gate.

'What did you say?' we heard.

'I don't say "Good day" to thieves,' repeated Uncle Edek.

'Are you referring to me?'

'Who else? Who stole the pears from my garden?'

Jabłoński said nothing more, he just got into the car. Only Mrs Jabłońska shouted: 'How insulting! Janek, that man has insulted you!'

The DKW drove away – the doctor moved off so sharply that gravel sprayed from under the wheels. Once on his property, outside the house, they shouted something. We heard raised voices – of the major, the doctor and those women. Uncle Edek hurriedly finished his painting, took his cane (the paints, brush and stool I carried for him) and we went back into the house.

'Well, Hela, I called a thief a thief!' he said with satisfaction. And poured himself a glass of juniper liqueur from a carafe that was standing on the sideboard.

My aunt did not share his good mood.

'As long as you haven't brought trouble on yourself. He's sure to be a vengeful fellow.'

My aunt's words soon turned out to be true. A court summons arrived. Jabłoński was accusing my uncle of defamation. He demanded an apology in the newspaper and a donation of a thousand zlotys to the Society for the Friends of Children. 'As compensation for calling the plaintiff a "thief" in the presence of third parties,' Uncle Edek read in a whisper, 'thus damaging his good name and demeaning him.'

'You brought it on yourself,' said my aunt. 'Where are you going to get a thousand zlotys?'

'But what can they do to me? The truth is that he stole our pears. Didn't he?'

'Do you have witnesses? Who saw him? You and who else? Go on, say it: what about Azor? Then call the dog as a witness!' And my aunt started laughing.

There were two or three hearings. At the local court, where Uncle Edek went in response to each summons. Always in his four-cornered cap and his army coat. He'd walk down the court corridors, dragging his stiff leg and looking for room number twelve or thirteen. Jabłoński himself never showed up once. His plenipotentiary, a fat lawyer named Dera, asked for a judgement in keeping with the plaintiff's application. The case, as he deduced, prompted no doubts.

'Before witnesses, in public, the defendant called the plaintiff a thief! With no grounds to make that claim!'

'What do you mean, "with no grounds"?' Uncle Edek interrupted. 'So who stole my pears?'

'Please do not interrupt,' the judge rebuked him. 'The defendant will present his explanations later.'

Finally the case was deferred with the aim of questioning witnesses at the next hearing. Then someone fell ill, and then the lawyer wasn't there. My uncle went to the court each time and came back with nothing. He told us all about it. He had an infinite belief in justice.

'Do you have witnesses?' asked the judge at the next hearing. An elderly man with white hair, so my uncle thought he'd be on his side.

'I saw him myself, Mister Judge.'

'Your Honour,' the judge corrected him.

'I lit him up with a torch, Your Honour. He was in his pyjamas. With a bucket, come for my pears.'

'All right then, but did anyone see this incident apart from the defendant?'

Uncle Edek thought a while.

'Well, no, just the dog. But the dog can't talk, Your Honour.'

The judge smiled and moved on to questioning the witnesses for the prosecution.

'Both the ladies who were in the car said that I called a man of an unsullied reputation "a thief". Mrs Jabłońska testified that I shouted "You thief!", and that I threatened to hit him,' my uncle told us. 'Can you believe it, Hela?'

'What is the defendant's final request in conclusion?' asked the judge.

'A just decision,' said Uncle Edek and left the room, without waiting for the verdict to be announced.

The letter came two weeks later. My uncle sat down at the kitchen table and began to read out the document in an undertone. The defendant was to repay the court costs and issue an announcement in the newspaper apologizing to the doctor. There was nothing about the thousand zlotys for the children's charity.

'Well, I never,' said my uncle once he had finished reading, 'I'm to apologize to a thief!'

Aunt Hela wasn't surprised.

'Didn't I say? It's always like that with thieves! If you suspect an innocent man he won't take offence, he'll just laugh. But try calling a thief a thief. At once he'll take you to court. And he'll win, because they always win. You're old, Edek, didn't you know that? Were you really counting on law and justice?'

'*Złodziej złotych gruszek*'

First published in *Życie*, no. 170 (2000), here from the collection *Powrót* (Wydawnictwo Literackie, 2020).

MICHAŁ WITKOWSKI

1975–

Michał Witkowski made an indelible splash on the Polish literary scene in 2004 with the publication of his debut novel *Lovetown* (translated by W. Martin, 2010) – the first Polish literary work to emphatically feature not only homosexual characters and themes but a distinctly camp – or as he would say, *przegięta* ('bent') – writing style. For all of the furore over its publication, which has been tied to increasing LGBTQ+ visibility in Poland, *Lovetown* was also an investigation into the experience of Polish homosexual men – and by extension of Polish society as a whole – before and after the abrupt transition in 1989–1990 from communism to neoliberalism.

The short story 'Fare-Dodging to Paradise', written in 2003, provides a glimpse of another moment in recent Polish history: the fallow period in the early 2000s, when unemployment had risen to its highest post-war rate of nearly 20 per cent, GDP growth was at 2 per cent and the wellspring of capitalism seemed to have run dry. All that would change, of course, when Poland joined the European Union the following year and EU money started pouring in. But the three lads our protagonist-author observes on the train back to Wrocław from Międzyzdroje – where he'd no doubt been cruising the nearby beach featured in *Lovetown* – can't even imagine that yet.

In recent years, social media has revolutionized Witkowski's work, providing him with digital stages for his persona, laboratories for forms of writing and author–reader relations. On Facebook and Instagram, he presents as a glamorous, gender-bending fashionista; on YouTube he delivers readings of his published works, discussions of Polish culture and society and 'videobooks', which are 'entire novels "artistically" dramatized with sound' that he records himself. Some of his works are only available to followers directly as e-books; while others are shared first with subscribers, digitally, before appearing in print, as with his well-received *Wiara. Autobiografia* (*Faith: An Autobiography*, 2023). In this, his most recent book, Witkowski describes experiences previously fictionalized in novels – such as *Eleven-Inch* (translated by W. Martin, 2021), which reimagines in fanciful, ribald and lurid relief the lives of Eastern European rent boys in Western Europe just after the fall of the Wall.

W. Martin

Fare-Dodging to Paradise

Translated by W. Martin

'Welcome to E-Plus!' my cellphone squeals cheerfully – since the route from Międzyzdroje to Wrocław runs right along the border, my phone keeps switching over to German providers. It's already dark and the train is practically deserted. A few hours earlier a certain well-preserved, well-upholstered older lady had informed me that she wasn't afraid of me, of sharing a compartment with me. But that in general, she was afraid. Nowadays, they rob and murder you in Poland, there are no standards left. I look glumly at the scenes passing by outside, dilapidated cargo sheds with broken windows, fallow fields, decaying shacks. And now that I'm by myself and have many hours to go before Wrocław, I feel uneasy. A miracle that I thought to bring my serrated bread knife, which I have in my rucksack along with my sunscreen and beach towels! I stick my hand into my bag on the seat beside me and sit there like that. If someone comes in, let them think I'm keeping my hand warm, seeing as how those wankers haven't turned on the heat. Poland these days has a big problem, I think, riding the train like that with my hand in my rucksack – basically, all I've done for the past month is travel and write at the Ministry of Culture's expense. I stand up to have a cigarette, lean out the window, look around, where on earth are we . . . ? Krzyż Station, the station of the *Cross*. For a moment I think of Stanisław Czycz, of his book *And* – what was it he said in that story about a cross?

The conductor comes to check tickets. How often had he already checked those tickets of mine, he just can't get enough of them, he probably enjoys sighing:

'Ah, ah, Międzyzdroje, Międzyzdroje . . .'

The taxi drivers sigh when they take me home from the station to Psie

Pole, the ladies at the counter sigh when I ask for information or buy tickets for holiday spots: ah Krynica, ah Zakopane, ah Stargard, even ah Ustrzyki Dolne . . .

I sit, I get up for the window, I go out into the corridor, light a cigarette, look out at the picturesque lakes and breathe in the smell of pine forests, leaning out the window; then I sit down again, hand in my bag – knife. Another round with the tickets, sighing, ah Międzyzdroje . . . we stop. The last of the sandwiches eaten. Slowly it's getting on for three in the morning, drizzle outside. The train suddenly lurches to a halt, as if someone had pulled the emergency brake. I stand up, open the window, what was that?

Brzeg Station. This is Brzeg Station – I do the megaphone myself because it's deathly quiet and somehow the quiet is making everything weird. A place so poor it can't even afford melancholy. Utter bankruptcy of material. Trashed all over, broken windows, everything rusted, a kind of nineteenth-century barrack abandoned by everyone but the playing crickets and the blustering wind. A single yellow lamp-post, steps heading down, remains of a bench and a remnant of lawn. I lean out even further and look, but beyond the station there's nothing. What a delusion, everywhere the electricity's been cut off, only the lamp at the station hasn't gone out. I feel uneasy being alone in the compartment, in the dark, with my hand in my bag. Now there's a jolt, maybe the carriages are being uncoupled? And a drawn-out wail like the sound of wolves, electric wolves. In the dark I light a cigarette; in the light of the match I touch my nose to the windowpane, and all of a sudden, I see – a handful of adolescents coming straight at me, across the dark station. And so, mindful of the words of that gazelle in her golden years, I grasp the knife handle tighter with my hidden hand and calmly puff on my cigarette, crossing my legs at the knee.

Wouldn't you know it, they're coming this way, and just guess, good people, to which carriage and to which compartment they're headed . . . They're young men, ranging from sixteen to thirtyish, their faces betraying origins in Brzeg, but I wouldn't want to describe them from memory for a forensic artist, physically and sartorially they look nothing alike. The youngest, whom the rest of the company calls 'Kid', wears his hair messy, tips peroxided and spiked with gel, the way people in seaside resorts did three seasons ago. Tracksuit bottoms, an outlandish shirt, gold necklace around his slender collarbones, on his finger a signet ring. His eyes are dull and rheumy and his teeth are yellowish too, since he smokes cigarettes. If you have seen an individual fitting this description, please notify the police at the nearest station. The next one up age-wise is a grifter type, but his body is no longer as fresh as the kid's, it's marked with all kinds of scars and cuts; he's dressed like someone from Brzeg on their way to Wrocław to go to the disco. Polo shirt with palm trees. He keeps winking and cracking little jokes – just like a grifter. The oldest one, on the other hand, who is overweight and balding, seems quite sorted: calm, earnest, dressed in an ordinary dark jacket. Anyway, they sit down in the seats across from me and look restlessly out the window to see why the train is still standing, as it should have left the station ten minutes ago. Maybe they've uncoupled us? I lower my lashes, look demurely out the window and examine my nails on just one hand as the other is in the bag, holding the knife. My fingers tap around in the dark, lightly scraping against the plastic, I'm making myself a little house in there right under their window. And through those lashes of mine I follow their every movement reflected in the glass. Soon, however, I drop all my precautions and even pull my hand out of the bag. I light a cigarette as calmly as possible, even offer them some from my pack, as I can hear what they're saying, and slowly I work out their whole bleary-eyed, low-budget story with no chance of an Oscar. This is what I learned.

We're moving. At one point the Kid starts squirming nervously, winking at the others and gesturing in other ways, poking, to say he really wants to talk but doesn't know if he's allowed to in front of me. They looked like conspirators. At first, they were all whispers and innuendoes, then after a bit, my presence evidently no longer an obstacle, they started a conversation from which I gathered the following.

There'd been a booze-up at the Kid's place earlier, and there they were in Brzeg knocking back until three in the morning out in the gazebo. In order to cheer them up, Grifter started telling them about his various adventures, mainly in Wrocław, how he used to pick up whores there, how many girls he'd been with, how cosmopolitan life was there, in the big city, all night long. Then suddenly, the decision: Let's go! Let's go to Wrocław right now, there's still time, we can still paint the whole town red! And in their drunken determination they decided to go and go they did. Thing is, they had no money, but they were dead set on making the trip, and they probably robbed someone. But they didn't say that directly, it's just that any time someone mentioned money their moods took a nosedive, then the fat one piped up and said they'd give it back somehow, not to worry about it.

The conductor comes in and takes my ticket, ah, ah, Międzyzdroje, Międzyzdroje . . . oh, when I get my holiday, oh, oh, Ustrzyki . . . maybe Kudowa . . . And then to them he says:

'Have your tickets been checked already?'

'Yes, sir!' they answer in unison and with straight faces, but the barefaced lie hovering over their heads pointed down at them.

Then Grifter starts fidgeting and says: My friend, come with me for a second, I want to tell you something. He goes out to the corridor with the conductor, showing us with a wink how he'll sort it all out, smooth it over. As soon as he's out, the Kid says to the fat one:

'But when I start banging, you ain't getting none of it, I'll let you watch, though . . .'

'We'll see about that . . .'

'Aw, it'll be ace, right?'

'When we get there, we'll see . . .' Fatty is clearly pretty sceptical about the whole excursion.

The train trundles along. The guys are silent. Then the Kid asks again about some detail of the night to come and Fats again responds sceptically.

And there I am, constructing whole apostrophes to them in my head, which go something like this:

'O, village lads of Brzeg Dolny, a town that can't even afford melancholy, have you gone completely bonkers? Maybe you're so insatiably horny you imagine Wrocław as some kind of twenty-four-hour City of Debauchery, another Amsterdam? Maybe you're headed to that mirage of yours, that photo-mural hastily conjured up in yon gazebo, to smash your young noggins right through it? Speeding off with the money you no doubt stole, no doubt from your elderly mothers, into the smoke, into the fog, into that cold morning of yours? And where will you be headed this Tuesday morning, back to bumfuck nowhere, when at any moment the day will be breaking at this time of year? And where even at the height of the weekend, at six p.m., to have the whole night ahead of you still might mean having nothing at all. As Zamoyski tells us: "The republics of the future will depend on how their youth are raised."'

In the meantime, we overhear a scuffle between Grifter and the conductor: No, no, no, you have to pay. Fatty pulls out all their money and pays, but now they'll be flat broke in Wrocław. He says, 'We can go to this strip club I know', and the Kid's eyes glint like gold plate . . .

We arrive. The train station is deserted, except for the homeless people sleeping in the corners and a lone cleaner with a machine for cleaning floors. I walk behind them. They've sobered up. In the main hall they notice me and say:

'Oh, there's our mate from the train . . .'

Fats looks over at the kebab stand: 'I could really do with a bite to eat.'

I walked out, ditched them. I'm fed up with our delusions, which keep bursting, and that Wrocław mirage of theirs with the palm tree and the parasol in a cocktail glass has already vaporized into a fine mist. Outside the train station it's getting light, the birds start singing, the cold intensifies, the air is sharp and fresh. This is that margin between the still-unfinished night and the day not yet begun, when things wholly unexpected can occur – after all, it's easy to guess what a day or a night might bring, but there's no knowing what to expect from this neither-here-nor-there.

I get into a taxi. Ah, Międzyzdroje, Międzyzdroje, Międzyzdroje, the driver sighs: Now, a holiday, that would be nice, maybe after the night shift, good thing it's almost morning . . .

'*Na gapę do raju*'
Published as part of the collection *Fototapeta* (Wydawnictwo W.A.B., 2006).

JACEK DEHNEL

1980–

Jacek Dehnel is a prolific poet, novelist, essayist, translator and painter.

His first novel to win critical acclaim was *Lala* (2006), a fictionalized portrait of his grandmother and the anecdotes she told about the family. His work covers a wonderful range of original ideas, including, to give just three examples: *Saturn* (2011), a novel based on theories about the life of the Spanish painter Goya, and his imaginary toxic relationship with his son; *Fotoplastikon* (*Photoplasticon*, 2009), a collection of old photographs found at flea markets, each equipped with a thought-provoking ekphrasis; or most recently *Łabędzie* (*Swans*, 2023), a work of non-fiction combining family history, a true crime story and a very personal memoir.

He has written eleven collections of poetry, and his many translations from English include works by Faulkner, Dickens, Larkin, Wilde and F. Scott Fitzgerald. With his husband, Piotr Tarczyński, he also writes historical crime novels under the pseudonym Maryla Szymiczkowa.

'I've never been to a brothel, but when I wrote "Olaf Tintoretto" I was going to be a painter rather than a writer,' he says. 'He's based on a real person, a strange, pale youth with a Scandinavian name. Reticent, and emotionally erratic, like many adults raised in a children's home, he seemed closest to his dog, an extremely randy German shepherd. He befriended a female artist twice his age, who dressed eccentrically in black suits with white bows, and was always half-cut. They went for dog walks together and had long conversations under the stars. I tried flirting with him, and drew his portrait, but nothing came of it; he liked being adored, but kept his distance. Eventually he broke off relations, complaining that he felt "used", and as "compensation" was keeping the CDs I'd lent him. Twenty years later, he emailed to say he was in Warsaw and wanted to give them back. We met at a café, he apologized, and we had a short, awkward conversation. Now I find all this more interesting than a made-up Italian brothel. But in those days I hadn't the language to describe it.'

Antonia Lloyd-Jones

Olaf Tintoretto

Translated by Antonia Lloyd-Jones

Yes, I think I can safely say that we all laughed at him that afternoon when he arrived at Signora Albacini's house, lugging two shabby suitcases behind him, oh yes, there was nothing desirable about him, or at least so we thought at the time, with that tousled hair and that skinny face, those child's lips that looked disgraceful on a fully grown man, but what sort of a man was he? No more than twenty years old, standing in the doorway like his peers when they came on their first visit to blush and lose their virtue; there he stood the same way, looking scared, shifting his cases now and then from one spot to another, because he was on the threshold where everyone kept jostling him and screaming at him to bloody well get out of the way, why were his eyes popping out of his head like that, never seen women before? Give him one of the girls, she'll soon show the lad enough to make him see stars.

In thunder and fury but all smiles Mama Albacini came downstairs to this scene, raging that her siesta had been interrupted, just like every day; Signora Albacini's siesta started after lunch and ran for an indefinite time, until something important occurred and she had to be woken up – a client making a fuss, a group excursion from the garrison or a visitor like this one with suitcases – if nothing happened all afternoon, the signora would get up after dusk, hot and sweaty from her feather bed, her eyes agog in her red face like two ravioli filled with black stuffing, and so here she came like every day, in thunder and fury but all smiles, with her dog and her parrot, pirouetting down the stairs with a gilded balustrade – the pride of the house – bellowing juicy oaths and greetings from top to bottom.

Mila and Maria were sitting on the sofa in their transparent negligees,

269

like two she-cats, while every client gaped at their *tette*; they were sipping something from cups, those *tardone*, coffee or tea, what do I care; fat Lola, sprawled in an armchair, occupying its entire soft seat upholstered in purple plush, laying out cards for patience on a little table, or possibly reading a newspaper, the devil knows, I can't remember after all these years; the rest of the girls were walking up and down, brushing against the leaves of the palms growing in gilded pots and against the knees of the menfolk, like every day and every night, though perhaps it was different, the only thing I remember is him, for Poppea and I were nudging each other, and I said what's that lad doing here who looks as if he's just emerged from under his mother's skirts, then she said he must have those skirts in his suitcases, because he seemed afraid to walk about the world, and I said maybe he's got his revered mummy in there, cut into bits, you can expect anything from fellows like that, with their innocent little faces, and just then the signora shouted above our ears, Who do you think you are, royalty? Get to work, there are clients waiting, get moving, *signorine*, get a move on!

So we got moving, we strolled up and down, to and fro, sheer perfection, very graceful, while remaining able to hear what that *pischello* wanted, and the signora paced across the room in her flounces and ribbons, dogs and parrots, paying compliments to Judge Gattorini, Dr Tosti and all the regular clients, whom the fancy had taken to pay us a visit on that particular day, and so, lumbering from one to another, she finally lumbered towards that lad who, gradually pushed aside, shabby suitcases and all, had found a haven under one of the palms and was staring at us with his eyes wide open; if one of us smiled at him or blew a kiss, he dropped his head and blushed red as a beetroot – even redder when the signora reached him in all her purple-and-gold splendour and boomed at him: 'So what are you doing here, my little sugared almond?'

He all but quaked in his boots and began mumbling an answer, but there was little to hear, what's more he had a poor grasp of Italian, so we went closer, and found out he was a priest, straight from the seminary, but they'd chased him out for arguing with the parson that he shouldn't sack the organist because although he was a drunk he had a heart of gold, but the parson had sacked him, so the young man had called him names, and he was terribly ashamed, on top of which they'd expelled him from the parish and the bishop had stripped him of all his rights, so now he couldn't say Mass or take confession, altogether a priest like this was useless; he had nowhere to live, because when they found out at home, guess what happened, so now he went from town to town, painting the walls in the richer houses, because he did know how to paint, and in those suitcases, which we had jokingly said contained his butchered mamma, he had paints; he started opening one to show us, but the signora told him to close it and not be silly.

At this moment it occurred to me that indeed he was the image of a *pretino*, a cleric who's still knee-high to a grasshopper, but already wants to turn back; what a pale little face, his hair combed any old how, to a point where I pitied him for standing up for that organist and being driven out; then the signora noticed me and Poppea standing there, so she chased us away and we heard nothing more, just snatches, that his name was Olaf, he was Norwegian, and that he didn't need much, just enough for paints, victuals and laundry, any corner to sleep in, and a few *centesimos*, if you please, though even without that he'd get by; he'd paint anything that needed painting, not naked women, that was not appropriate, but flowers and birds, absolutely, and he could do portraits, he painted cupids best of all, because they were suitable for churches as well as for a place of this kind.

At this the signora laughed heartily, and asked a few questions, then finally she clapped her hands and said, loud enough for us to hear every word halfway down the room, Very well, if heaven was sending us a priest, or half a priest perhaps, we weren't going to deny him, let him stay here while there are walls to be painted, he might turn out to be a dauber, in which case he'll never forget Signora Albacini's house because she had acquaintances who'll tear off the parts for which he had no use in life, come on, Alcina, clear the junk out of the laundry and get Lola to help you take it to the attic, do a bit of tidying up in there, chop, chop, we have a new lodger, the most reverend half-a-priest Olaf straight from Norway, and if any of you girls seduces him she'll answer to the Holy Father in the Vatican himself, come on, you too, Maria, show him the way upstairs.

And so we took him in at our house, the best bordello in San Luca al Mare, anyone will tell you – anyone who knows a thing or two, and not those *finocchi* who go to Augusta's, to Bella's and to Stinking Paola – we took in that unfortunate flaxen-haired Norwegian, with two cases full of brushes, paints and books and very, very few pieces of clothing, we took him in, and he thanked us over and over, blushing and apologizing for being so uncouth, but he wasn't used to worldly life, he said, not like us, such fine ladies, and he blushed again, then, seen off by our jokes and laughter, he meekly went to the garret, to a tiny room behind a partition, with a hard bed and a cast-iron sink in the shape of a shell, peeling plaster and the smell of damp walls, lye and soap, he went so meekly, contrasting so greatly with the golden staircase and the walls lined with red velvet, casting such mistrustful glances in all directions, that it was simply unbelievable.

From then on, dozens of times a day we would pass his little room, well, we didn't just pass it, obviously, almost every one of us peeped in, started talking, or at least whistling outside the door, upon which he would raise his eyes from his prayerbook or the large sheets of paper where he was sketching the designs for his frescos, and mutter 'God be with you', 'The Lord bless you', or 'Praise the Lord', then he would drop his gaze to the lines of verse or the lines of drawings again, as if nothing else existed, and then he would pray, he prayed all night long, at first on the floor, but later the Signora told us to fetch him a prie-dieu which had ended up in this house, God alone knows how, so we lugged it from the attic and gave Olaf a surprise, and that was the first time we saw him smile; it took six of us to carry that prie-dieu, each of whom was delighted by that wretched smile, and we only had to catch each other's eye to start snorting with laughter like piglets, enough said!

Three days later he started on his frescos, deploying a ladder and paints in the room the signora had chosen, where he locked the door and worked all day, then another day, and another, but we couldn't see a thing, not even through the keyhole, because he'd blocked it, on purpose, the crafty swine – we thought we'd go mad with impatience, none of us knew what to do with herself, and the signora was dissatisfied that we weren't sprawling on the sofas but walking about the hall chatting to the clients, but what else could we do with such curiosity, we tried to take him this and that, supper and breakfast, we lurked by the door, but he was as fast as a gecko, he'd open it, squeeze through and close it, so we couldn't see a thing, just some brightly coloured patches, and what good was that to us? while he, the cheeky boy, smiled at the sight of us running around in all directions whenever he emerged from his room in his stained smock with a bunch of brushes to wash.

Finally on Saturday – I have no idea why I can remember it was a Saturday – he came to the signora in his best clothes (he only had two outfits, one dirtier, for painting, the other cleaner, for grander occasions) and said he had done enough by now for her to tell if he were a painter or a dauber, to which the signora said yes please, she would like to see; she drove the dog off her lap, rose from her armchair and shouted for Alcina to summon us too, so we could all inspect the immortal work of our Norwegian *pretino*, our pale, flaxen-haired half-priest, and see for ourselves if he really had the balls for the job or was only fit for daubing holy pictures, and she bellowed it so loud that every one of us heard, from the cellars to the attic; Alcina didn't have to run upstairs, we were all by the door to that room in an instant.

The signora went in first, scrutinized the walls from floor to ceiling, cleared her throat and said, well, that's really something, I must say, the boy clearly knows his profession, this parrot is life-like, no matter if he won't paint naked women, the clients will like this too, after all my *casa* isn't like that Bella's or Augusta's, not to mention the others, here we've no need to fling it in their faces, this is taste, this is style, this is elegance, in short: La Casa Albacini, it's plain to see that only the best clientele comes here, those who appreciate frescos like these, bah, clients who know about art and culture, educated and learned people, etcetera, etcetera, and as a parting gift you'll get a few lira more, you'd even get one of the young ladies, but what can one do, such is the situation, you don't know what you're missing, my boy, and then she went up to him, pinched his cheek, and said maybe he does know, and he went red and dropped his gaze.

There's no need, no need, I said, standing beside him, the boy knows a lot about painting and that's the holy truth, and we all looked around, delighted, nudging one another and laughing, until the rest of the girls were sooner done with their clients and came racing in to see what was afoot, while the boy continued to stand there, as shy as on day one, listening to all the raptures and jokes; we simply couldn't take our eyes off the walls, the signora too, who didn't drive us straight back to work, although there were plenty of gentlemen, like every Saturday, but just muttered and smiled, as if totting up how many clients would come to us from the other houses as soon as they heard what elegance there was here, not just red velvet and golden stairs but painted rooms with parrots, cupids and garlands of roses wherever you turned your gaze.

Because we knew at once that our *pretino* would cover the walls and ceilings with decorations not just here, at the end of the corridor, but everywhere else too, little bows and roses, baskets of fruit, cupids with rosy buttocks and rosy cheeks, and he began that very afternoon, then every day – not counting Sundays, remember to keep the Sabbath sacred – he painted one room, then another, each girl's bedroom, the passages, the staircase, wherever there was no purple velvet; and he never finished anywhere, that's for later, he'd say, for later, the most beautiful things have to be in place, the background and frames can come last, we know angels appear against a blue sky, don't we, not a violet or an orange one, to which we said, for sure, any fool can paint a sky, and we laughed like mad.

Finally he and his ladder moved to the ground floor, where he painted the entire entrance in bouquets of narcissi and daffodils, and little monsters with the heads of people, the wings of birds and the rear ends of lions, or with horse's heads, human bellies and the hoofs of an ox, enough to make you split your sides; he'd start at dawn and stop at dusk, so drained he could hardly keep upright, but he'd drag himself up to his cubbyhole, wash, kneel at the prie-dieu we'd lugged from the attic, and pray, almost nodding off as he did so, once we even found him in the morning, frozen, rolled in a ball, after falling asleep at those prayers. What a hard-working lad – said the signora – and gave him a few *lira* now and then for small expenses, though he said there was no need, God will requite, he was doing well among us, and may the Lord Jesus bless us all. So he started to paint the large *salone*, which involved a lot of work, though only high up, close to the ceiling, because below that the walls were hung with velvet.

Up there he ran a row of circles, calling them either medallions or *tondi*, and there he painted each of us in turn, first of all the signora, in a golden frame, in her best dress, pearls and a cameo brooch, looking very respectable, like a real lady; she sent for a hairdresser specially to do her hair and tie the ribbons – she looked so beautiful that now we joked she might marry a handsome young *cavaliere*, and she laughed that after all these years in the profession you know what *furfanti* men are, she'd never marry, but she'd nibble a piece of fresh marzipan, and she roared with laughter, making the hairdresser jump up and warn her she'd spoil the whole hairdo, and was only to laugh when it was finished.

So first he painted Mama Albacini, then us, one after another; Maria and Mila, those moth-eaten she-cats pushed in ahead of the others as usual, but he chose me, so I was painted at the start; like all the girls I put on my best dress and did my hair, I didn't send for a hairdresser of course, but I did look truly pretty, and I doused myself in scent, not that it would show in the painting, but for him, to make it nice for him to paint me, I don't know how it came about, but I went to him as if to a lover, in rustling silk, my beads rattling on my neck at every step, my hands trembling as if it were the first time, although he was only to paint me, and I didn't care if I were prettier or uglier than others on the medallion, as long as he looked and looked at me, without end, as long as I could breathe in the smell of him, the smell of paints and prayerbook.

Down the stairs I went, like bride to groom, amid the rustle of silk and the rattle of beads, fragrant with ambergris and musk, while upstairs everyone was either working or sleeping off last night, the signora was having her sacred siesta, and the house was as silent as the grave, there were no new clients, just the occasional groan of bliss from one of the old ones, or a girl shrieking – some of the men liked that, while others liked the opposite; so he and I were alone, I asked if I looked all right, he blushed and said I looked very pretty, he dropped his gaze, so I laughed and went up to him, I poked him in the ribs until he began to stagger and dropped his head even lower, red as a beetroot, so I came closer, I raised his chin with my fingertips, he didn't even dare pull free, I slipped my arm around his waist and gently, very gently kissed him, for now my lips were dripping with honey and my breasts were like two fawns.

Then it was just as usual, like every time, with every fellow, except that it was completely, entirely different, because he was like a small child, he kept breaking away from me, but when I tried to leave, he pressed his cheeks to my breasts and said no, I must wait a moment, it was a terrible sin, he might not be a priest in the eyes of men, but in the eyes of God he was, and he had taken a vow of chastity, he had never sinned with a woman before, and this was a disgrace, but after a while he kissed me again, awkwardly, like the typical whelp who arrives at this house and stands in the doorway, crumpling his cap in his hands, and it's obvious what he wants, but he was a quick learner, very quick, suddenly he rose up and fell on me, clenching his teeth and squeezing his eyes shut, and began to weep, he wept copiously, out of rage at having sinned, no, not regret, but rage, and he pounded me on the chest with those little priest's and painter's hands of his, so I almost burst out laughing, but I held back, then he calmed down, as I gazed above him at the blank space on the wall where he was to paint me.

He painted the portrait rapidly, irascibly, slap-dash, and so it all began, from then on we saw each other every day, but I rarely snatched as much as a kiss from him, to say nothing of more, because he was always on that ladder, the place was always full of girls and clients, and even if I did, he was terribly sulky to begin with, scowling and pulling free, glancing at his prayerbook and wriggling like an eel, losing his temper and shouting at me, though he shouted quietly, in a whisper, not at all angrily, but somehow so endearingly that I felt a sweet sensation from head to foot, because I knew he was about to yield to me, we'd run off to an empty room, to his room, to mine or somewhere else, and we'd throw ourselves onto the bed, onto the rug, wherever, and once again he would breathe heavily in my arms, once again he would clench his teeth, once again he would weep, then I would console him, and he would only calm down when I smothered him in kisses and rocked him like a child.

The house was crowded in those two months because we had so much traffic it was like the entire garrison had been given passes and had come to us day after day at full strength, *finocchi*, chaplain and all – everyone wanted to see what new thing our saintly Norwegian had painted, while he sat on his ladder, modestly dropping his gaze and blushing, while each man joked, both Dr Tosti and Judge Gattorini, that maybe he wasn't quite so saintly, eh, young ladies, surely you must have taught him a thing or two, the only boy in the class, and first-class it is too, we have to admit, but come here, my dear, let me give you a hug, well then, have you girls been misbehaving with the *pretino*, he must have seen the heavens open and the heels of angels when you girls set about him; and then of course all the gentlemen went to our rooms with us, because they hadn't come to a museum, but to Signora Albacini's, all of them in excellent spirits, and they left us each a generous gift on the bedside table, so the girls grew even fonder of Olaf, even those harpies Mila and Maria, those syphilitics in transparent negligees.

But it wasn't just the clients who were different; we were different in those days too, festive and drowsy; as for me, I spent days and nights on end simply waiting for that angry cleric with hands that smelled of whitewash, paints and prayerbook to let me near him, that greedy boy with the mobile tongue that ran around my body like a golden lizard – I kept peeping into his little nook, I kept looking for him in the rooms he was painting, and there were more and more of them, I was amazed how many there were, because before then I hadn't even noticed, but either he wasn't there, or smeared in red, blue and green paint he was balancing on the ladder close to a ceiling, or one of the girls was with him, sometimes two, or even three, it varied, so there was no chance of fulfilling my desire.

And then one day, in the heat of noon I happened to go from his empty little room through the entire house, peeping through all the keyholes to see where that blessed rascal might be, that half-baked dauber, for whom my fawn-like breasts were bleating, to use a quotation from his favourite tome, until I stopped outside what was once the Emerald Room, but was now to be called the Peacock Room; I peeped through the keyhole and I had a fit – there he was, I could see him, covered in blue and green stains, against the blue and green fans of the peacocks' tails, I saw him in all that angelic glory amid sunbeams and puffs of cloud, with his eyes raised upwards . . .

And beside him Poppea, my best friend Poppea, picking up cherries one after another from a large glass fruit bowl, and saying: So, little boy, you'd like a cold cherry, would you?, I'm not surprised, in this heat, here you are – and she crushed it against his cheek, the juice went trickling down his neck and onto his chest (thanks to the heat he was working half naked), then she licked off the sticky red streaks, crushed another cherry against him, and another, and so on without end, surrounded by all those green peacocks with blue tails and blue ones with green tails, until I cried out in horror, Poppea leaped up, raced into the corridor and screamed that what business was it of mine, what had tempted me to spy on her, my best friend, was it that I had no trust in her, was that why I'd sneaked up to spy on her through the keyhole?

To which I said fine care she was taking of the little priest, but I had taken care of him earlier, and she should look after her fat-as-an-ox baker, who might yet marry her, or her thin-as-a-rake Judge Gattorini, whose breath stank from a mile away, but she shouldn't take up with my *ciccino*, then she grabbed me by the hair, and I grabbed her, the girls came running and tried to drag us apart, but in vain – we had changed into fiery viragos, defending ourselves as hard as we could, scratching and kicking, screaming at each other, until one of the other girls wanted to go and wake the signora, but as soon as she realized we were fighting over Olaf, she stopped, as if rooted to the spot, and screeched at us that we could murder each other in cold blood but the boy was hers, and would remain hers, so we'd better not waste our energy, and that was when the real trouble began.

Now it turned out we'd all had him, some only once, others several times, though I don't know the truth, because girls sometimes tell even bigger lies than boys about things like that; Mila and Maria were raging like hellfire – at others for stealing him from them, and at each other, out of jealousy – they swept the floor with those transparent negligees of theirs that meant their tits were on show, but also that we could see how saggy they were; by contrast fat Lola was silent, but we knew that a woman with her appetite for the men would not have let him go, just like Poppea, who admitted it at once, competitively, saying they'd done it several times, and he was pretty good, for such a young lad, which was the holy truth, because indeed he was pretty good, until finally one of us hit upon the idea of telling the signora – what a scandal!, and besides he must belong to one of us, because if the girls were going to fall out over him, life would be impossible.

But before Signora Albacini had descended the stairs in thunder and lightning, hurling curses in all directions, we had managed to reach a consensus that private interests were out of the question, Olaf was common property, and each of us must have a bit of him, twice a month, let's say, anyway, we shouldn't overtire him, as it was he was looking pale, so we'd write out a rota, just let him try to protest, and that was the end of it; in fact fat Lola was dissatisfied because she was emotional, but we all knew what she meant, and even those slappers Mila and Maria agreed, so Gianna flew to the office for paper and pen, when Francesca came running down the stairs in floods of tears, followed by Signora Albacini, fulminating that it was all in vain because Olaf had gone.

He must have overheard our conversation, probably thanks to those two *baldracche* who squeal like old hags, so their voices carry through padded walls; he must have taken fright now that everything was revealed, and had escaped through the Raspberry Room, packed his paints and brushes at high speed, his few items of clothing and his books, then fled outside by the back stairs, I bet he was red with shame, as red as a beetroot from the seminary kitchen, and had gone off who knows where, probably to another city; we couldn't tell how he'd be received there, because our Mama Albacini had a heart of gold, but not all the *signore* are like that, not to mention the police, the judges and so on, but he had left us, and also his unfinished frescos, though he could have done so much more good work, that's what we said, until evening fell for good and more clients arrived; each one inquired about Olaf, and with tears in our eyes we told them he had gone away to Rome because his rights had been restored.

And he disappeared. Suddenly alone and tired of everything, we heard nothing more about him; we paced the painted rooms, we stroked the brightly coloured parrots and the cupids with ruddy cheeks, now and then each girl began to cry, even those sluts Mila and Maria in their transparent negligees, every single one of us, even the signora came down from her room more quietly than usual, halting on the bottom stair, as if waiting for someone, until one day fat Lola came running from the city, where she had seen this girl at the Tazza Bianca, a very fashionable café, high style, and this girl, Paola, had told her that she and all the other girls at her *casa* had been sighing for a saintly painter fellow, but then they'd found out he'd done just the same to the young ladies at Signora Flora's establishment in Milan, and at Mama Giuseppina's in Brescia, as well as at three nice little bordellos in Rome and one in Reggio di Calabria; in Bari he had screwed the girls at two taverns on the docks, and in Naples he'd had all Signor Maurocci's boys, leaving the smell of old books and unfinished frescos of great beauty behind him everywhere he went.

'What a bold young *cavaliere*, I must say, the little sugared almond, it's a pity I'm too old for such young colts, now I'm sorry I didn't take a nibble of that marzipan too,' responded Signora Albacini, then rose from the table, moved back her chair and said some more, but her voice gradually faded as she went upstairs for her afternoon siesta – all purple-and-gold, with her dogs and parrots, wreathed in clouds of melancholy.

'Olaf Farbiarczyk'
Published as part of the collection *Rynek w Smyrnie* (Wydawnictwo W.A.B., 2007).

WOMEN BEHAVING BADLY

WITOLD GOMBROWICZ

1904–1969

While he is best known for his novels, plays and literary diary, Gombrowicz began his career writing short stories. Most of them were published in *Pamiętnik z okresu dojrzewania* (*Memoirs from the Time of Immaturity*) in 1933; a slightly different constellation of stories appeared as *Bakakaj* in 1957; Bill Johnston's English translation, *Bacacay*, was issued by Archipelago Books in 2004. 'The Tragic Tale of the Baron and His Wife,' however, never made it into these short-story collections. Initially published in the daily *Kurier Poranny* in 1933, it was included in Gombrowicz's collected writings.

In 1933, Gombrowicz, a law degree in his pocket, was in no hurry to get a steady job. He was a regular in Warsaw's literary cafés, where he proudly presented himself as a member of the country nobility. To the other artists and leftist intellectuals he must have looked odd, but this was a strategic move: the mores of the landed gentry seemed anachronistic even in 1930s Poland, allowing young Gombrowicz to stand out. Visiting his relatives in the country, meanwhile, he would change his pose and show off his urbane taste, leading the servants to wonder why the young gentleman ate so very little and never joined in the hunting. Unlike many men of his class, moreover, he did not take advantage of the female members of staff. Instead, one domestic employee reports, he would get up around noon, almost surprised that the rest of the household had already lived through half their day, then loiter around the house and garden until the evening, and finally he'd settle down to write and smoke in bed until the early hours. It is quite likely that the present story was written during one such visit.

In the 1950s Gombrowicz, exiled in Argentina, wrote essays exploring local notions of masculinity and femininity. Discussing sexual mores he regrets that 'principles' in South America 'tend to ossify and formalize. Appearances prevail over spirit, form takes the life out of the content. Women ought to be taught that even this so-called decency, if it is misunderstood and applied superficially and schematically, can turn into the number one enemy of decency.' Perhaps this plea for a more relaxed and humorous approach to the principles of sexual decency can shed light on Gombrowicz's provocative treatment of the same subject in his short story from 1933.

Tul'si (Tuesday) Bhambry

The Tragic Tale of the Baron and His Wife

Translated by Tul'si (Tuesday) Bhambry

The baroness was a charming creature. The baron had taken her from a family of high principles and had no reason to mistrust her, despite the fact that the tooth of time had already gnawed into him quite deeply . . . And yet a disquieting element of grace and charm lay dormant within her, which could easily complicate the practical application of the baron's *imponderabilia* (since the baron was a bit of a stickler). One day, after a period of conjugal life graced with the quiet bliss of marital duty, the baroness came running to her husband and threw her arms around his neck. 'I think I ought to tell you this. Henryk has fallen in love with me . . . Yesterday he declared himself to me, so quickly and suddenly that I had no time to stop him.'

'And are you in love with him, too?' he asked.

'No, I don't love him, because I have pledged my love to you,' she replied.

'Very well then,' he said. 'If you are in love with him but do not love him because it is your duty to love me, then my esteem for you doubles and I love you twice as much. And the young chap's suffering is a well-deserved punishment for his weakness of character – losing his heart to a married woman! Principles, my dear! Should he ever make another declaration of love, tell him that you also have a declaration to make – but of principles. A man of unshakeable principles can walk through life with his head held high.'

But soon after, the baron received some dreadful news. Henryk had no pluck in him whatsoever. Spurned by the baroness, the young man took to drinking and carousing, then he became melancholic, nothing interested him anymore, the world lost its charm and he seemed to be at death's door. According to widespread rumour, his imminent demise was due to unrequited love. 'Fine doings, these!' said the baron to his wife. 'Here we are eating canapés while he can't get anything down . . . Do you realize? . . . Because the image of you is preying on his mind. I wonder what he sees in you. I've been living with you for all these years and I've never had any feelings for you that could be called violent. In any case, this is a serious business and I am surprised to see you looking so well, knowing that wretch is suffering because of you.'

A week later he was in an even fouler mood. 'Well, bravo!' he sneered. 'You should be proud of yourself! Your charms have proved most effective – Henryk has one foot in the grave.'

'What can I do about it?' she replied with tears in her eyes. 'I never led him on, I have no reason to reproach myself.'

'Good grief! You are the cause of his hopeless state, your arabesques, your curves and features are the germs eating away at him.'

'What can I do? He's gone mad. Do you know what he suggested the day he declared his love? Divorce!'

'What? Divorce? You're not a strumpet yet, are you? Yes, of course you'll get your divorce, but you know when? – when I die, when I breathe my last, while still professing the same unshakeable principles.'

'And what if he dies?'

'Dies!' exclaimed the baron furiously. 'That's blackmail, for which I refuse to break my vow to keep you until my dying day!'

The baroness suffered bouts of terrible anguish. The last thing she wanted to do was to act unethically, and yet her heart bled at the thought of Henryk's misery. Besides, the baron, a member of many societies, had developed a distinct aversion to her. He simply could not bear to look at her beauty. Her bodily functions started to disgust him. One day he asked her: 'How about a bread roll?' And when she declined, he laughed with ferocious scorn: 'Ha ha, he is at the point of death, and she is unable to eat a bread roll.' As she floated around the house, gracefully swinging her hips, as she smiled wanly, as she slept, or combed her hair, all he saw in her actions was shameless cruelty and dark eroticism. One time she tried to show him affection. 'Pray do not touch me,' he shouted. 'You hellcat! A fine mess you've got me into. Not another word out of you. Now I see that a morally responsible man should never get involved with someone else's carnality, under no circumstances whatsoever.'

'Right!' the baron continued. 'It can't go on like this. This morning I heard that he made an attempt on his life. Are you even capable of grasping that to push a man into suicide is far worse than to strangle him with your own hands? That unprincipled whippersnapper is going to ruin us as well as himself. I have made up my mind – we cannot burden our conscience with such an awful responsibility. If there is no alternative – too bad, I give you my blessing, I'll jolly well go along with it; and now you, in the name of higher necessity, go ahead and play your part – do as your filthy womanhood dictates.'

'Darling!'

'Too bad! Could I have foreseen when I married you that one day you would be forced to choose between murder and adultery?'

'If there really is no other way out, and if you believe it's the right thing to do, I'll go along with it,' she said. 'As for my part, I will find it hard, but as God is my witness, I am entirely blameless.'

'Ptooey!' said the baron.

At this point the young man started to recover. The baroness, however, was visibly wasting away. Her domestic life was hell on earth. Her husband required her to dine apart at a little table and had her use a special set of tableware. One day she accidentally touched him. 'You are besmirching me,' he said with cold indifference. 'Look here! You touched me; now I must interrupt my reading and go to the bathroom to wash.' He frequently blurted out the insulting word adulteress. At four o'clock he would take out his watch: 'Now then,' he would say, 'it's time for you to go, don't be late for your wanton philanthropy.' She tried in vain to explain that she was innocent. 'There is one thing I ask of you,' he replied. 'Please refrain from introducing an atmosphere of indulgence and tolerance of sin into this house. Otherwise we might as well invite common prostitutes for luncheon – after all, it is God's honest truth that they are just as innocent.' The distraught baroness tried several times to break off her reluctant affair, but each time the young man threatened to kill himself, and it was clear that this was not mere rhetoric.

'No,' said the baroness, 'I cannot bear it any more. My life has become unspeakable torment. I have fallen into atrocious sin – but why? Because I am alluring. No one can understand, without personal experience, how strange it is in moral terms to be alluring. I am fed up with it. I shall disfigure myself, only I'm not sure if Henryk will be able to cope with it.'

'That's more like it!' her husband exclaimed enthusiastically. 'This might indeed plunge Henryk into madness, but our sorry plight requires us to take certain risks, and besides, we will prepare him for it. And to prove that I, ever the loyal husband, always stand by you when it comes to the moral burden, I shall disfigure myself, too.'

'You won't have that much to do,' she replied.

They went to their rooms, and soon there emerged two hideous scarecrows. The baron hugged and kissed his wife. 'And now Henryk must be prepared for this blow.' So he wrote the following letter:

Dear Sir,

It is with great sadness that I must inform you of my wife's frightful accident. One of her lovers, in a fit of jealousy over an admirer who had recently ceased to be a platonic friend, threw vitriol in her face. The poor woman has lost the charms that she was so good at putting to use all around her. Please come and take a look at her. Nota bene: *in my attempt to rescue her I, too, was horribly maimed.*

'There, we have done our duty,' he declared.

It looked as if Henryk would go insane, but the news of his lover's unfaithfulness gave him strength. He got over his feelings, which could not withstand that monstrous sight. The baroness, however, started to sink fast, and it soon transpired that the cause of her pernicious anaemia was her love for Henryk, which erupted with elemental strength following the end of the affair.

'Is there a curse on my house?' cried the baron. 'Here she goes again!'

The dying woman asked to see Henryk and the doctors endorsed her wish. 'For God's sake,' the baron whispered to Henryk, 'she is ready to die with a declaration of sinful love on her lips.' 'Have you gone mad?' he shouted at his wife. 'In your place I would prefer to enjoy a clean conscience. I don't think you realize how dreadful you look. And as for the lover who used to burn for your body, he has been scorning and disdaining you ever since you disfigured yourself for his sake. Break it off and you will soon recover and return to the world of principles.'

'This time I won't be fooled,' said the baroness, and expired.

The two men were left alone with the corpse.

'She perished as a victim of duty,' said the baron. 'I hold you responsible for her death.'

'It's your wife,' replied the young man. 'It's your corpse.'

'Dramat baronostwa'

First published in *Kurier Poranny* (1933), later included in some editions of the collection *Bakakaj*.

MARIA KUNCEWICZOWA

1895–1989

Kuncewiczowa is one of the chief Polish female authors of the interwar and post-war years, a writer of novels and autobiographical prose. Born in Samara, Kuncewiczowa (née Szczepańska) grew up in Płock, Warsaw and Wrocławek, the daughter of a schoolteacher. She trained as a singer but switched to studying literature.

The story that follows, 'Covenant with a Child' (1927), is regarded as her literary debut. Originally published in 1926 in the women's weekly *Bluszcz*, its graphic portrayal of childbirth and early motherhood – including the experience of breastfeeding from the perspective of an educated young woman struggling physically and psychologically – provoked scandal among traditional readers, many of whom withdrew their subscriptions, prompting the collapse of *Bluszcz* and its split into two separate journals.

Kuncewiczowa shows that motherly love is not necessarily instinctive, as assumed by the patriarchal view of motherhood, but constructed over time as the child develops and a relationship becomes possible based on mutual acceptance, the essence of the 'covenant'. Contemporary literary critics found her style too 'metaphorical' or 'excessive', but her more experienced contemporary Zofia Nałkowska (1884–1954) encouraged her to perfect it.

The story launched Kuncewiczowa as a writer of psychological prose. Her most famous novel is *Cudzoziemka* (*The Stranger*, 1935), an empathetic portrait – inspired by Kuncewiczowa's own mother's personality and thwarted career as a violinist – of a psychotic wife and mother whose early experiences make her feel constantly alien.

Dwa księżyce (*Two Moons*, 1933), parts of which were previously published, portrays the double life of the Vistula town of Kazimierz Dolny (where Maria and husband Jerzy Kuncewicz eventually settled) both as the home of permanent artisan and Jewish communities and as the summer playground of visiting artists and bohemians.

From 1962 to 1968, Kuncewiczowa taught Polish literature at the University of Chicago, having emigrated in 1939 to France, then Britain and finally the United States. She is the editor of the anthology *The Modern Polish Mind* (1962). In 1969 she returned to Poland.

Ursula Phillips

Covenant with a Child

Translated by Ursula Phillips

I

She was at home alone.

Noisy footsteps were dying away in the hallway; her husband had already run off down the street to his uninteresting male affairs; waves of words, laughter and kerfuffle vibrated still in corners of the apartment. But the waves promptly subsided as the subterranean waters of silence broke in their place.

The rooms filled with twilight. The furnishings – washed of alien life amid the grey inundation – regained their own aspect. The clock, which a moment ago was still a duplicitous zealot working the treadmill, boldly embarked on the path to eternity. Liberated from their plight as utensils, tables shook their spines – like a flock of crows spreading its rule over an oak tree. Silk cushions puffed themselves up on the sofa and hyacinths exuded pink.

Teresa descended into the afternoon solitude as into a bath. Not only did she feel that her husband had left, but that all amatory matters, kisses, thrills, had likewise deserted her. A stream of silence slowly encircled her body, saturated with life, and – soon – in the four rooms, only the clock persisted in its purpose and only the hyacinths blushed.

Teresa, like an island engulfed by sea, forgot about herself. And was happy. Disembodied voices reached her from the courtyard, like echoes of catastrophes raging somewhere in countries of which no one had heard. The clatter of *droshkies* and roar of motor cars stormed the house – like spuming billows dancing at the foot of a cliff. Stretched out on the sofa, Teresa closed her eyes and sank entirely into the green stars pulsing beneath her lids.

Yet from the direction of the ceiling, which was like the ocean's epidermis snatching air from an alien world, came a summons: a slight shock, a lightning bolt of sound. Her fourth-floor neighbour had struck a key – the note brushed aside the waves of silence and plunged to its very bottom, as far as Teresa's heart. Awakened nerves therefore rang the alarm and turmoil rippled at once throughout the apartment, tracing circles initially small, then ever wider, as objects stood to attention and awaited the human touch.

The man on the fourth floor began to truly play. But it was impossible to tell, really, if it were a man or young girl; a careerist spitting out his final reverie or a married woman who'd never had an affair. Someone sad, but full of disgust, had sat down at the piano and given vent to their thoughts on the black and white keys ... First came a question. It was this, the foray in sound into all adjacent worlds, that touched Teresa. So brimming was it with tears, so ripe and grave, it was first to set sail beyond the edge of silence ...

It sank in. Having ruffled another's silence with a question, the player did not wait for answers; all the sooner did he blurt into empty space his own anguish.

Disgruntled passages (a kind of senile peevishness) rained down, marked every few bars by a red pause, like a memento of youth. They showered abuse, unending abuse, lighting up wounds in passing.

Such passages were meant to be conciliatory, meant to fraternize with fate; menace, however, always shrieked in their final word.

At last, they drifted away.

Desolation cast its evil eye. The man (or maybe girl?) entered the *largo*. It was like dust, finely powdered offence, quotidian mournfulness – it rumbled at length in passages and then was gone! Now a voice of wisdom piped up, as if the source of all echoes, and slowly but emphatically spoke from heart to heart. Argued with people according to human law and addressed purely divine judgements to God. Then it summoned everyone by name.

A particular chord clearly stated: Teresa. She understood and opened her soul unprotestingly. She wished to hear, receive the confidence and find a remedy ...

Thus she lay relaxed, eager for mercy, open to any feeling.

The person above the ceiling began to talk like an anguished friend.

Saying embarrassing things, confessing the most painful longings; seemingly a young woman conscious of and hungry for love, she wept to the rhythm of a waltz; then again, amid the volatile *rubato*, he revealed the face of a man who'd defeated an enemy and was watching for who might crush him with an imperious foot.

At one moment the notes laughed provocatively – as if a lady were toying with her lover; later, a *cantabile* of truly tomboyish confidence suddenly burst into bloom ...

Inexpressibly vivid and eloquent, these things hovered before Teresa, tapping on her senses like birds outside a windowpane on a frosty day. She gazed at them without batting an eyelid – calm, though initiated ... Not a single nerve gave way to vagabonds.

Until her shamed conscience reacted: 'Why so hard, disobliging soul? Why not respond to the complaint? Maybe tomorrow, you'll want to play your own injury, and no one'll lend an ear to your complaint ...'

Teresa deepened her readiness; she longed to the brink of tears to warm to this parley with an unknown person. In the tenderest of words, she called upon kindness to fully ignite within her ... Her intentions bustled on the surface like ants – while the interior remained happy and cool.

Then the fourth-floor neighbour broke into a frenzy: thoughts sped to fingers and crawled meaninglessly up and down the black and white keys. Absurd exclamations ran hither and thither, sobs convulsed, and laughter slid off arpeggios like beads off a string.

Blood drained from the melody; only hollow sounds remained, rattling and knocking against each other like tiny skeletons. Finally, the din ascended to an unbearable fortissimo and shattered into millions of discords.

The pianoforte fell silent.

Teresa listened intently for a time, wondering if the strings might not whimper, treated so inhumanly by human hands. Then – rested and refreshed – she rose from the sofa; nail file in hand, she walked across to the window.

A street lamp stared her in the eye, a street lamp blushing like a young girl, encouraging and confidential. She smiled at it warmly as at a dear sister, and herself stopped still in a glow of the healthiest bliss.

*

'The laundress, ma'am,' fluttered the words of the maid. A head of rough curls thrust itself into the room.

'You said you'd talk to her yourself, it's none of my business . . .' A shrug of the shoulders, eyes galloping around all corners of the room, and the door slammed shut. After a while, the laundress entered.

A professional conversation struck up, not devoid of social digressions or even arguments of a political nature. Teresa – her hair drenched in sunset blood – sat against the backdrop of the window like a Renaissance lady crammed by an antique dealer into a modernist frame. The laundress was clamouring by the wall.

'As for the gauze, no need to worry your head, ma'am, we have to add a bit of soda, but as for that gauze, nothing more to say . . .'

The poor woman was minuscule, with bird-like face and kangaroo belly. Her glance so rinsed in steam and tears that nothing but faint blue smears loomed in the wells of her eye sockets. These eyes played no part in the oratory of her lips: they were always, invariably pleading for something. Irrespective of whether the laundress was cursing the high cost of living or forswearing the bleaching powder or whispering denunciations against the kitchen, her pupils would tirelessly plead. And this with a cry, with boundless exultation, with a prayer. No one knew what the two long-faded little blobs craved so insistently; you could only vouch that covered by their lids, or even lifeless, they would go on whining. On the other hand, Teresa had never heard a single word of request from Mrs Kwiatkowska's *mouth*.

This person preferred instead to render favours. 'As an exception and only for Miss Brońcia,' would she come to launder clothes on Hoża Street, although her favourite ironing service was located on Złota. Sometimes she would return from this ironing service with two extra handkerchiefs and often agreed to eat ham for supper instead of sardines. Now she was offering to iron the starched garments in person.

Evidently, much depended on Teresa accepting this proposal, since the saliva squirting from between the woman's teeth shot as far as the centre of the room, while the tip of her nose crinkled like a dog's. Yet the sentences spluttered forth briskly in the style of native Cracovians with no thought even of persuasion.

Teresa glanced at Mrs Kwiatkowska's 'waist', whereupon she declared: 'You need the money.'

Indeed. The woman was in her eighth month. Her 'overcoat' gasped for breath under the strain, as her swollen fingers did up the final button by force. Blown into the shape of a gander on stunted S-shaped legs, the woman threatened any moment to overflow her banks like a spring river. What's another month when the tortured body squeals for relief!

Soon Granny would be needed, with medicines and nappies, as well as an alembic for the partner in crime.

. . . Meanwhile Teresa's offended gaze stubbornly sniffed catastrophe in the contours of the mother-to-be. For the hundredth time, her eyes returned from the ravaged torso and skinny shoulders to the revolting profusion of the belly. An entirely material bitterness flowed from this staring – a bitter disgust smacking of quinine . . . The laundress seemed like a cephalopod, a monster from a bad dream stifling all life's joys with sticky tentacles. It had already devoured the hyacinths; in a moment it would suck the remaining red from the sky and slime the carpets with its touch.

Teresa shrank into an armchair, brows drawn like black pencil-strokes, and vowed: 'No. A thousand times I don't want it.'

II

The wallpaper was whiter than white, the bed comfortable. In a jug on the table stood a bunch of gladioli, by the wall two potted chrysanthe-mums. Propped up by pillows, Teresa was reading.

Outside the window, little birds – mischievous yet diligent – were tending their homesteads. The ordinary working day was progressing smoothly, like an old dance-leader, unaware even he was cutting capers as he walked down the street.

The heedless sun was smashing again into the same windowpane as yesterday; the same cooks were yelling on other staircases; on this same street corner a (different) tram conductor was again annoyed, as usual; while Górszczak bore to school the same shudder before his classroom test (except that yesterday it was a different schoolboy, Rontalerczyk).

Reinvigorated, fresh clouds were scudding across the sky, although they'd gone to sleep the previous evening black from soot and sorrow. A fisherman sat down on the Vistula shore; gazing lovingly at the water, he stroked with his free hand a sagging willow branch that had once maimed the arm of a drowning man. Pet dogs barked from floor to floor. Sometimes a whistle could be heard faraway, faraway, and you could see how the travellers were nodding their heads for another night in a carriage. You could see too what a long road the trains, the small boys, the Vistula and all those ordinary working days had before them. The road itself was lapping against the wheels, against feet and waves – like the moving walkway in the stacks of the Louvre; and so, people were running and little birds were tending their homesteads.

Teresa lay in her hospital room, watching for when a bizarre pain would suddenly swoop on her petrified self. For long months, alien life had been ruling the roost inside her, but now when it was supposed – according to the old plan – to violate and reject her – she was so distracted, so preoccupied anew with the most terrible wonder, like someone who'd seen a dead man in the hour of his death yet believed in his demise only after the funeral. She lay listening out for when alarm bells would ring in her own body, for when she would have to defend herself against her own innards. Footsteps were running up and down the corridor, a male voice was holding forth on the far side of the wall; a smell of fried food wove around the window, while the chrysanthemums stared at everything with a pitying grimace.

No one was by the bedside where two beings – one powerless and the other as yet unborn – were dozing, waiting for the order to lock horns in the fiercest of battles. Neither anger nor fear nor anyone's love made up for the sadness at Teresa's bedhead, her body and will about to rage in the hideous labour of childbirth. Thus there came a moment when the solitary woman turned her eyes towards the chrysanthemums and for the first time in her life, gratefully accepted pity.

The night that set in led Teresa down a purple path into the very core of the wilderness, into the most savage backwoods. Life's grim brother – physical pain – leaned his face over her mouth. Migraine sufferers, consumptives draped in elegant plaids, young ladies betrayed by lovers and parents of prodigal sons stayed behind somewhere in the wheatfield; new companions came out to meet her: lionesses, tropical gales, deadly jungle heatwaves and wounded soldiers. The forest wall parted and from behind the flowering lianas, hell peeked out. Fire slowly slavered her legs with its hissing tongue; in the midst of the flames flashed the eyes of Saint Joan and thousands of witches – eyes acknowledging the secret of torture for the first time. A Sioux warrior sorely mangled by an enemy tomahawk jabbered away in brotherly words as all dog, wolf and tiger souls drew close. Teresa's womb, like a monstrous lens, was sucking in every cruelty of the world. Inspired, desperate, it stamped its nakedness on the doctors' pupils.

Between heaven and earth only one thing persisted – life swollen to death. And into Teresa's brain – blue-black from torment – there entered the bloody truth of the body. And also, the truth of loneliness. For amid the circle of watching eyes, she lay lonesome as an Arab corpse on the sands of the Hoggar Mountains.

As she chewed silently on her pain, sweeping her half-dead pupil over faces, the nurses' carefree thoughts settled on her forehead, neck and breasts. They might have seemed like butterflies dancing above a carcass. And their foreignness was like a black Apache scarf that throttles screams, hope and terror. In the electric light, the professionals leaped up and down like evil personified, frolicking shamelessly on the roads.

At some undefined hour, the lightbulbs began to dim; a branch floated out of the livid blue of the world and nestled its slender body against the windowpane. The first creature free of gall. And so, Teresa's whole being rushed out through her eyes towards the sweet stranger. But the little branch hissed like a snake, twisted into the shape of a whip, and began lashing in thousands of strokes at the woman's hips and hands. Evidently, outside the window there was no mercy either. The birthing woman withdrew her eyes in shame from the morning twilight and shut herself – snail-like – inside her shell of pain.

She was not allowed to suffer, however, in passive resignation. Active torture was demanded – in the manner of a conflagration, which, in devouring all barriers, also consumes itself. No trace of request was there in the doctor's eye: he issued orders and threats. A hirsute paw prowled among her bodily swoons like a scorpion among weeds! While the Furies in white coats – impatient and rabid – set Teresa on the child, like hounds set the hunter on a wolf.

When, breathless to death, baited to squalid madness, monstrous and blind with terror, she tried to slide from her bed of torture like a stream tumbling headlong into the abyss – iron claws, ominous-looking forceps and bulbous cylinders of iodine loomed out of the twilight . . .

The mob of executioners lay silently poised, in order at the given watchword to yank her womb with a dozen teeth and tear it to steaming shreds of meat. Then, beneath her shell of agony, a scream began to swell: it bulged, prised open the shell . . . till it burst like a massive ulcer, spattering words like pus. The shriek spread in corrosive torrents on the livid waves of the dawn, it stung, frothed, spat – stormed, abated and whimpered puppy-like. Teresa was covered in a scalding shroud of blood.

At that moment the lamps finally acquired the semblance of irises pale from sleeplessness. And at once the pain grew lazy, like a broken string, and sticky – like birch tar. Thick black fluid flowed from one vein to another. People stepped aside, something was crying in the corner, shrilly, glassily. Apparently, the child had been born. Teresa was already asleep.

III

A baby *striga*, a little vampire, took up residence in Teresa's home. A creature grafted onto life like a splinter into flesh.

In moments of calm yet intense pulsation of the domestic organism, when the day swelled with juices and, so it seemed, the air was coalescing around Teresa in the form of a cocoon so that she might dwell – serene – amongst her furniture, dresses, books and most intimate thoughts, a scream would suddenly erupt from the tiny gutta-percha face. Vicious, like the swipe of a birch, the scream would tug at any hour. Like a hen sparrow, the mother would take wing and fly to the basket, which was – entirely like that French *boîte à surprises* – an eternal source of convulsion. Always identical – resentful and insistent – the child's shriek never explained in human terms if it were demanding a feed, raging under pressure from some pain, signalling its desire to touch the ceiling with its fist or simply cursing its wet nappy.

The voice from the basket brooked no discussion, required immediate and efficacious intervention. Like a pendulum jolted by a careless hand, it gained in ferocity with every second, stirring itself up and soaring ever sharper, ever wider into the air, until it culminated and lapsed into the tick-tock of regular obstruction.

And if only it were possible not to shudder at the touch of the arrogant summons, if only one's entrails did not get in such a twist under the scourge of incomprehensible emotions!

Teresa – albeit reluctant and wronged – circled day and night within the orbit of the screaming basket. Her cherished 'wants' and 'don't wants' had fallen by the wayside irretrievably. The era of brutal musts had dawned. (It had begun to bleed, like an open wound, in the bottomless chasm of that night when Teresa came to know the truth of the body. And also, the truth of loneliness.) Teresa did not like at all the little *striga* with the sardonically twitching cheeks, and yet it came about, in and of itself, that the *striga*'s scream regulated every moment of its mother's life according to its own inscrutable whims.

And – what was stranger still – the person who felt mutinous even at a distance of several rooms from the child, when faced eye to eye with her persecutor, gazed at it in all humility.

From then on, time was compartmentalized in accordance with a mammal's innate needs. During excursions into town, in the course of carefree conversation or in between one actress's tirade and another, Teresa would suddenly feel the tug of certain unfamiliar knots in her own veins or guts, a tug which said: the *striga* is calling for food. Like a somnambulist, she would redirect her steps at once towards the screaming magnet.

It was as though the umbilical cord had not yet snapped between herself and the little creature: each more violent spasm of its body pulled the mother towards it with organic force.

The child had cast an evil spell on her whole life. Whatever Teresa undertook turned to disaster and led in the end to her servicing that 'box of surprises'. Many times, the mother sought to rise to her former level of existence, forfeited because of the catastrophe; through restless activity, she longed to repair the breach between former and more recent times.

She attempted to sing. Scarcely had the melody managed to imbibe warm blood, however, scarcely had her vocal cords begun to quiver and fully resound – when in the pit of her larynx, where song was withering and moan beginning, at that very acoustic point, a scar not yet sufficiently healed would suddenly come to life, a scar left by the roar of 'that night'. Of course, her throat then ceased at once to vibrate with sweetness, and her heart filled with acrimony.

There came a day so innocent, so disarming in its simplicity, that Teresa consented to a game of tennis.

In the middle of the park, at the bottom of a green well (the chestnuts' shade was like a green well), shone the court. A young man strode out to meet her like a tiger weighed down by its own strength; he approached slowly, lazily stretching his leg muscles, or steel cables, hot from the sun. Like two Nikes waiting on Hermes, two girls wafted in his wake.

In their raised arms, the rackets resembled a kind of prankish weapon created for joke contests. The girls' breasts were firm and diminutive.

Play began. Balls flitted immediately above the ground like swallows. Hermes was in no hurry to chase them unduly; rather he kept the interlopers at bay with a slight ripple of his shoulder.

Despite this nonchalance, the projectiles smiting his multi-stringed shield bounced back furiously to their point of departure, keeping the boisterous energy of the girls in suspense.

Just as the young man's movements were frugal and adapted to every blow with machine precision, so the embattled Nikes gambolled like children. As they leaped in the air, their skirts flew up like butterfly wings, then – in moments of acceleration – clung tightly to their supple limbs and hips.

These tosses, squats, bends, flights and spins made up an enchanting frieze which plainly extolled beyond words the charms of youth.

Teresa stood on Hermes' side of the net; little therefore remained for her to do in the field. All the more greedily did she stare at the girls. To her their gestures were the commonest refrain of her own life until recently, an unconscious lure that naturally embraced her figure like the folds of a dress; lifting an arm or bending a knee was enough to strike a spark of beauty off those limbs. Now the mother's body was overawed, stripped bare of its self-assurance, wholly saturated still with remembrance of its wounds.

Running around the court seemed to Teresa a pleasure amputated forever from her muscles and nerves. She would approach the ball with a dignified step or try to extend the length of her arm by twisting her waist. She hated herself for such actions and thought despairingly of the infinite torments of old age.

At home – in rare hours of quiet (the *striga* did sleep sometimes) – bent over her needlework, Teresa would suddenly feel a discomfort unknown to her previously; her breasts would grow heavy and spill out of her brassiere. Her beautiful breasts, those adorable daisies – so desired by a man's eyes and mouth, so carefree – Teresa's breasts had become an alien thing, an object of crude utility; become the mammal's prey. She knew that whenever an especially insistent howl burst from the basket, she had to grasp the pink charms in her palms and let the glutton's lips pull clumsily on what had known no other touch but caress. Besides, they were already new breasts – not those opal dreams barely conspicuous between her undulating upper arms, but screaming magnolia blooms bloated with pride and milk.

All her dresses had been widened, as Teresa – with death in her soul – carried the hateful luxuriance of her body around the world.

Once at a *thé dansant* ... She forgot everything. A handsome dancer held her in his arms. Old youthful pleasures return. And so, music kisses her lips with hot breath. Rhythm restores suppleness to her limbs; and the steely sweetness of male thighs fondles and excites. Joy alone, satiety alone, the silky rounded 'yes' alone, speaks everywhere: in the eyes staring from behind the champagne haze and in the flesh-coloured gleam of lamps, in the scent of perfume – heavy as an odalisque's braid – and in the foolish foxtrot melody. In the heady malmsey of dance, Teresa felt the armoured carapace of her crippledom dissolve. She had regained herself.

During one of the Boston numbers, her partner clasped her tight. And ... the barely realized happiness scuttered away at once: her breasts – instead of tensing in delight – ached as if wounded. They were no longer her own property (affection and endearment) – they were swollen fruit, food for the voracious mammal. Immediately she understood the dictate; she abandoned the handsome dancer and began pulling on her gloves as fast as she could, sadly contemplating the long road home.

At this time, Teresa's attitude to people changed radically. Her heart hardened and nerves stiffened. Before the birth of her child, anyone else's pain had seemed to the healthy woman, stranger to all suffering, a wrong for whose righting there could never be enough smiles and gifts. Now, when she bore on her hips a network of pearly veinlets, each with hieroglyphic meaning commemorating an inhuman contraction – now, the evils suffered by her fellow creatures seemed events without substance. Teresa demanded for herself countless gifts, tendernesses and sacrifices, so that they might soothe the cruel wrong done to her body.

IV

Months went by. The baby grew fat. Became rosy and cheerful. The *striga*'s mask fell from his countenance – and the happy face of Teresa's only son was revealed. Most importantly – amid the deluge of screams emanating from the basket, certain sounds of fixed tonality stood out and had power to redirect the mother's panic towards strictly known activities.

The little fellow gradually lost the bad habits of his pre-mortal existence and began to cast human glances at human beings. To Teresa's relief, the hostility and urgency brought into the world from a nursery teeming somewhere at the bottom of a volcano gradually gave way to the child's sunny goofiness.

With every passing day, the little creature shed his exoticism along with his red skin. And the human child appeared less and less like an Ashanti fetish and more and more like Jędruś.

Indeed . . . Only after six months did the boy's name begin to acquire traits of verisimilitude. His mother learned to dress her son in it as in his first woollen bootees – for it was already clear that the infant wished to stay in the family and that these little legs would soon be walking the earth.

The grim grotesquery absorbed shades of pastoral. And so, peace slowly returned to the home routed by Teresa's catastrophe.

In time a new chair stood by the table – high but also diminutive – and upon this throne Jędruś would celebrate over his bowl of rice *kasha*. No ritual of the adult world could compare with Jędruś's rice-eating ceremony. Never did lover follow with such exasperation a woman's hand unbuttoning her dress; never did huntsman encompass with so fierce a gaze the distance between his gun barrel and a bear's great bulk, as when Bobo stubbornly subjugated every movement of the full spoon to his eyes.

Caught in the clutch of the chair, the little body would strain towards the *kasha* as the heliotrope flower strains towards the sun; the dark irises, black from almost religious horror, would be eating the rice before the baby mouth managed to capture its victim. The child's whole being: cheeks, saucy tuft of hair in the middle of his head, tiny hands helpless yet – despite the dimples – impassioned, legs, little nose dilated from effort – everything lay in wait for the rice with tiger-like ferocity, and dollish comicality.

A great smacking noise would emanate from over the plate; Nanny would blush, while Teresa – like a bee on a July afternoon – brimmed with sweetness to the point of exhaustion. As the *kasha* vanished from the bowl, so Jędruś's gaze would soften, the tension relax in his person and various whims begin – like tiny cloudlets – to scud across his face. Not those peevish ones born of itchy gums, hunger or hatred towards the great moss-grown body of the night; no – rosy-coloured whims, light and airy, and immensely funny. Sprawled after the banquet on his back, the little fellow digested the food effortlessly. Satiety, like a velvet ball, enclosed his body in a world of smiles. His twitching limbs resembled a dancing fountain; arms and legs cut capers like spurts of merriest water. Jędruś's eyes then expressed joy akin in its spotless purity only to sunlight.

That happy glow, that sparkling fever of health blossomed and quickly faded, however, as Bobo dropped off to sleep. His baby face, bright as a flame a moment ago, would darken and assume an expression of puppet-like rigour. Deep reflection and reasons of state would settle between his brows; his little nose, slightly dilated, was already blabbing something about passion; whereas the whole adorable drollery of babyhood, unblemished silliness, sweetness and indolence wove wreaths around Jędruś's mouth. ('A pink rosebud,' Nanny would say.) Breath pulsed silently between his lips – the winged heart of a daisy . . .

And never did the world's richest lady wear such soft silks nor the most splendid Oriental prince kiss such smooth skin, so soft and smooth were the two red ribbons fastened into the smile on Jędruś's face.

Leaning over the sleeping child, Teresa was lost in a spell that sucked her in like a chasm swallowing a torrent. Happiness stronger than orchid scent gushed from the child's sleep, as stimulating as mountain air; rapacious happiness so sweet she felt faint. The mother would walk away from his cot more physically drained than after a night filled from shore to shore with caresses.

Thanks to this wondrous torture of eyes and nerves, Teresa first fell in love with her son.

Jędruś's second summer arrived and found him running about on his own two legs. The feeling of organic bond with a creature as irksome as a tumour on the brain had finally passed from Teresa. She felt like a human being again.

She was still not the beautiful woman of two years ago, but she'd at least ceased to be a breastfeeding female. A certain promising – though for the time being superficial – perspective had sprung up between herself and the child.

Jędruś, like a young hazel shoot, had split off from his mother and was burgeoning farther and farther from the trunk. It was possible to forget about him for an hour and then return, not to the howling basket in which hunger impertinently clamoured, but to a wobbly-legged little being cleverly fighting his own way through the tide of events.

In Jędruś's brain, the insect of curiosity was breaking free of its casings and titillating his senses with its ticklish wing – senses still blunt as a puppy's nose. The little boy would sniff, look around him, toddle about, touching things with pointer-like zeal yet moth-like clumsiness.

His most developed organs for registering impressions were his tongue and that 'pink rosebud'. And so, whatever entranced his eye – some delicious red colour recalling a rooster in all its glory, or some round or lively shape – it was at once subjected to the taste test.

And if, God forbid, the object couldn't be dribbled over thanks to its ungraspability or enormous size, then heartfelt resentment, disappointment and remorse would erupt from the little man's innards, intermingled with a stream of sobs. The first resistant gesture of the Unknown. And first suffering flowing from ideal impulses.

Meanwhile a heatwave – like a rat charmer playing on his bucolic panpipes – was leading people out of town in their droves and into the dappled courtyards of freedom, between lacy walls of shade. The weary swarm, thousands of legs aching from their march along city pavements, hurried but hurried towards roads as fragrant as warm wholemeal bread. Thousands of heads were raised above the earth, their brows facing the wind, so as to feel the touch of its palms wet from its sport with the sea.

Just as urgently, Jędruś was teaching his feet to walk through grass. Lifting his big toes like a snail extending its tentacles and retracting the rest, he would charge through the meadows like a three-zloty-a-ride railway, of which you could never be sure when it would run out of steam and when accelerate unawares. His heels and rocking head rushed after him as fast as they could. He was still inseparably by Teresa's side, but his presence had shed its nightmarish qualities. His needs had grown regulated, freed of any mystery; he allowed himself to be simply cultivated like a cheerful bush in a girl's flowerpot.

He was served above all by the sun. So, Teresa often peeled the dolly rompers off her son's body and let him run naked amongst the mullein and chicory.

His infant nakedness would then pamper the eye more vividly than the flowers, as it wheeled amid the greenery shaped like an exotic animal of the monkey family, or like a rococo putto. The agility of his person, and especially the unbridled hunger of his hands, recalled the mannerisms of the splendiferous Bandar-log monkeys. Whereas his form, as if moulded from separate rolls of fat and agleam with porcelain glaze, was cherubic.

Certain twists of his torso, flexions of his hand and upturned pupils gave him a semblance of holiness in the style of Boucher. The child appeared predatory, like a disciple of black-and-gold Bagheera diving among the lianas, yet at the same time adept at the arts of gavotte and antiphon recitation. For the backdrop to Jędruś's games with nature was equally suited to the lightning grabs of the Bandar-log system as to a dancing rococo assumption into heaven.

Whatever the boy had in mind – attacking a spray of lupin or dissecting a cockchafer, or excessive courtship of a fly, or some *rondo capriccioso* with a bread roll in hand – the grass, clouds, bright sunlight and sticky-sweet air (that monstrous robe of the earth's great body) always clung fondly to Jędruś's figure with the grace of a child's pinny.

When the little fellow wallowed in a cluster of thyme, laughing copiously, or a hawthorn branch caught hold of his hair, Teresa, as she observed her naked son's progress, soon ceased to differentiate between what was the child's hand, what a woven braid of leaves, what the little man's joy and what the smile of a plant.

*

Somehow during this time Teresa began to like herself again. Her hips and breasts, through which had passed the cosmic wave of birthing, returned to their previous, almost maidenly forms. Hardly a visible trace remained of the luxuriation of her organism, of her nurturing profusion, just a softness in her general outline and strengthening of certain muscles.

The sole conspicuous trace was the shift in her worldview to its rightful place – that place which Jehovah had marked with a bloody stain in the brains of the first married couple.

Everything that troubled her imagination was laid bare. All basic human truths unveiled their countenances – only death remained, and before it an endless chain of repetitions, reminiscences and supplements to things she'd already come to know.

As the young woman sat in the grass, squeezing tight her eyelids, and her child's chatter reached her from close by, she would see a perfectly closed circle in her thoughts on life.

Twenty-something years ago she herself had been born; countless springs and autumns followed, all of which begged for patience, with finger pressed to lips, and promised reward. Throughout that whole preparatory period, the little – and ever bigger – Teresa would run from closed door to closed door trying to break into life. In the meantime – without knowing anything about it – she was living, while whatever lay behind the doors was seeping away between the chinks, and in the sanctuary of rewards more and more space was taken up by emptiness.

As her senses took shape and her stock of knowledge increased, so the command to wait outside the door grew more impossible with every day. At last, the time of Eros arrived.

Like seasonal flowers, her yearnings budded, unfurled and wilted – both the accepted and the rejected. Man stepped out from behind a street corner and stood in her path. Like a hawk – first love swooped on her heart, foolish and more torturous than physical pain. Followed by a second, hatched already from the chrysalis, romantic, totally locked in word and gaze, ignorant of the body, rapturous and happiest. Later there was ballroom love; spiteful as a lizard and elusive: a masked lady scheming viciously, yet ravishing.

Things were still happening, however, before closed doors. Eventually, an affair erupted in a great blaze. Girlish. Boyish. An affair with no final card. But so thrilling, so close to some extra-human truth that when the conflagration fell to ashes, Teresa was left groping by a closed door exhausted and almost incurious.

Then she got married. With total scrupulousness, she began to crack the sour kernel of marriage; and one day, at some hour, she perceived that the doors had been left behind and that she was already living in a house of adults. As she cast her eyes around her new abode, she knew in her heart how little – beyond the threshold of mystery – remained to be known . . .

For during the time of Teresa's struggles on the doorsill, life had drained away through the walls like water from a swimming pool. Only now was the waiting woman dazzled by a vision of receding waves, which washed over her body and were that life. To her boundless amazement, it became clear that what passes unnamed every hour is precisely the revealed mystery; clear also that the whole stream had almost run dry. Yet in the most secret recesses of her home, an impenetrable wellspring still throbbed: the enigma of childbirth. Out of the corner of her eye, Teresa followed the pulsations of this enigma: she had no desire to penetrate its chaos – afraid to glimpse at the bottom a worm of ugliness. Meanwhile the spurned wellspring proved to be the crater of a volcano, spewing lava and drowning Teresa against her will in flames of agony. She had given birth to a son. And so, the circle had closed.

The mother stared calmly at the path down which she had to walk towards death. Stared at this path ruddy from the sun, grey from ordinary weekdays and drunk from Sundays. She saw a crowd hastening along the path together with her as far as the spot where a black stone marked an end to all treading and trudging.

The whole dust of this path as well as its whole vulgar necessity were intimately contained within Teresa's heart – until recently so velvety, so fastidious and utterly regal. She felt neither heaviness in her heart nor revulsion in her gaze – only the way that same purple stain, with which Jehovah had marked the brains of the first married couple, was swelling with blood.

V

Trees strayed farther and farther from people, retreating into the thicket of their own affairs, incomprehensible to mortal eye.

In spring they'd been close to everyone, vulnerable, young, stretching out their limbs full of trust to passers-by. You'd be walking through the forest on brotherly terms with the oak or underage hazel, as the transparent golden-green web imparted a feeling of unconcern. As if oaks, people, snakes and hares were a family of devoted friends . . . !

The weeks had moved on, however, and the sun changed its sleeping pattern. Animal and plant existences grew more complex and condensed.

Sensing their own power, trees began to stare haughtily at passers-by. Even a fox – cowardly in April – now, at the end of summer, would stab the Voyt's back with sneering eye from behind a bush. An uncompromising spirit settled on boundary strips, thickets and branches. Having emerged long ago from the downy chaos of spring, fleshy kernels now hardened into fruit in the blazing August conflagration. The forest denied access to people; shut itself totally in these orgies, in some kind of titanic labours and bloody struggles.

From time to time, pinecones struck the rambler on the head; lesser woodland creatures would leap out suddenly at intruders and vanish again with a silent chuckle into the ferns – satiated with human trembling. Leaves took on the appearance of metal blades, grasses injured hands, while heifers turned their soft and foolish horns on herdsmen.

Something was happening everywhere between the sky and the globe's perspiring skin; something was happening in a hurry, in pain and suffering, in the early-morning tumult and in the horror of night. Existences were being formed that wouldn't ripen on earth, while owls barked to the moon of crimes that trample brushwood and muddy watery deeps.

Teresa meanwhile glided amid an avenue of evenly clipped hours, sensing how beyond one or other wall of her peace, a thousand herbivorous and carnivorous existences were at loggerheads, goading one another, wrangling and dancing, divine or simply cannibal. Before her, she had her saffron-coloured path and square metre of free air to left and right; above her head, the Unknown, and underfoot the constant trembling of the earth.

Teresa was alone. Unsure of her fate, like a seagull caught in a net, she was lost in the straight avenue of trees like an ant on a parquet floor, and constantly greedy for signals from the alien world to fill her road with red light, like semaphores.

And so, it sometimes happened that in such a pale moment, Jędruś would stop at the mouth of the path and approach his mother from the other pole of events.

He would come towards her from afar, from his own conquered domain; come unhurriedly, diminutive, yet master of his own steps and sovereign creator of his own diminutive affairs. For an hour or two there'd be no sign of him; chill waves would gather around Teresa, when suddenly the little fellow would burst – like a cry – into the realm of silence.

Imagine then the mother's rapture and amazement when her son came towards her *from the world*, from beyond the green wall, out of the ring of broiling heat and clamour.

He would stamp on the shells of snails and on thousands of striped and spotted torsos, wound the stalks of plants with his tread, brandish his wicker wand, hide his trophies in an undiscoverable hole, take a drubbing from every stone along the way, and – mocked by golden orioles, barked at by the neighbours' dogs – come alone with his bruises, full of joy.

Teresa revelled in the sweetness of these sudden encounters with her child, to whom she was no longer always necessary. Confirmation of the beginnings of Jędruś's emancipation made him especially dear to the young mother.

Between herself and her son, a gentlemen's agreement of 'fair play' was starting to clarify – a *voluntary covenant* was dawning, still as misty as a web of blossoming apple boughs, yet as everlasting as the fragrance of that rosy web.

And thanks to Jędruś's hunting expeditions into the wild backwoods between the melon patch and box hedge . . . thanks to Jędruś's irruptions onto the path and his confidences, Teresa forgave some almighty power (some benefactor or executioner) for the violence inflicted on her will during the memorable night of his birth.

And – more importantly – Teresa managed to get over and consign to oblivion those successive months of maternal exertions around the hideously alien creature, grafted onto life like a splinter into flesh.

Affected by certain of her warrior son's glances, she was even haunted by the suspicion (or rather timid hope) that her womb had not been an accidental gateway through which Jędruś had made his first entry into the world.

And that maybe in the bizarre country whence her parents had once led herself, making some sign – unbeknown to themselves, assiduously captured by the angel of destiny – that in this country of unborn people, maybe the present-day Jędruś and present-day Teresa had already spent long eternities together in mutual understanding.

In October, as God punished the trees with nakedness for their August conceit, so Teresa felt keenly her own nakedness under the casing of her mink coat. Hips, knees, breasts and temples were aquiver, reminding her of their existence. Twisted into a capricious arch, her mouth was on fire. Music, ordinary everyday smiles, words without substance and books read long ago suddenly cried out to be embraced.

Into the arena stepped her husband in the role of gladiator. His wife observed that this gentleman had wide shoulders, that his fondling was painful and that she could have a lot of it. A salty rivulet of blood had seeped into their marriage. Teresa ceased to comprehend what her husband said at table, and also neglected to wear her long-ribboned nightcaps. She no longer lay down for the night like a coquettish corpse in her coffin, but waited anxiously by the door with her hair hanging loose.

She understood the fascination of ugliness, the temerity of the lowliest submission, comprehended wherefore an angel would always turn his back on woman and why Christ the Wise would always forgive her.

Pleasure warped Teresa's feelings as fire the limbs of a witch burned at the stake: they tensed in a martyr's dance; and then the frenzy of nerves had within it a heroic onrush of yearning. It seemed it would only take one wave of blood and the mystery would spatter at last into a thousand splinters and the core – happiness – be unhusked. The object of fervour, however, remained slippery, like a glass ball; fury trickled in streams over cool walls, yet the core of the mystery grew even more tightly sealed.

Then equanimity descended on their faces; stripped of yearning, the body sank readily into imbecility. How sweet to forget about shame, to nestle one's cheeks into the beast's shaggy mug, feeling oneself the sister of she-wolves, mares, speckled guinea-hens! The minutes trundled by dull and inane like pumpkins; the room was full of incubuses, lizards, some kind of velvety birds of prey and far too fleshy lips.

Teresa would dream a heavy daydream and wake from it in despair like a nun who'd succumbed to the moon in her reveries. By her bed stood Thursday or Monday and dangled two eyes of stone above the stubble-field of fondling.

And one day it so happened that Jędruś – instead of some Thursday – crept into the room clutching his teddy bear. Chattering away in bird-like words, asking questions. Not, of course, about her impressions of the night before nor even why Mummy hadn't yet had breakfast. He asked about something funny.

From that moment on, Teresa's desires – scarred by bloody wheals of shame – cringed like whipped dogs, while the olive oil of calm spread over the surface of all her nights. Her days duly gained in transparency and pulse. Life again shone with elegance like a salon whence the bed had been removed.

In the course of the third winter of Jędruś's existence, motherhood ceased to be for Teresa a 'state of emergency' – it became a 'civil state' no more troublesome than possessing a lifetime annuity.

The child had been sucked into life like a tumour rendered harmless.

And so, countless things swirling outside of home: people, motor cars, politics, artistry, animals and flowers – their collisions, their voices – were once again coated in colour visible to the eye.

People were summoned especially eagerly. (Motor cars were too dear – though their screech from afar brought happy thoughts of wealth. Artistry strolled around the park like an offended prince, keeping forgiveness for a lover's dying hour. Politics yelled directly in one's face, belching garlic and Four Thieves vinegar. Not all animals knew how to be of service, whereas flowers followed people of their own accord, like poodles.)

And so, Teresa had lots of dresses made and let her heart rush to the door every time the bell rang, vying with the maid.

Old acquaintances returned and brought with them new. The hours spent with Jędruś were restored to their former lord and master – her hairdresser.

Gentlemen and women occupied the most beautiful chairs in the apartment, dinners lost track of their proper time, evenings grew tentacles extending as far as midday; the telephone became the most important personage, whereas a face began to be necessary only at dusk.

First one man then another declared himself to Teresa. Not his love, however, only 'What was most important', only 'What they punch one another in the face for'. They danced. The fauns in Łazienki Park buried their horns under caps of snow. Kisses froze on lips, and melted only in ballroom warmth, bathing some dances in sweet dew.

As Jędruś in his dreams was greeting his summer companion – a cow named Zazula – his mother was greeting her 'table' at a *café dansant* with the friendliest of smiles.

Waiters, drivers, doormen and dance-leaders remembered her and bestowed their liking. Meanwhile the country schoolmistress in her ugly village far from the railway track, or the bookkeeper's assistant at the butchers' trade union, counted her name amongst those exquisite words fragrant of tuberose, words which in the *Warsaw Courier* signify glamour, unattainable luxury, beauty from beyond the seven seas.

Teresa began to have migraines, while her taste deepened through all gradations to reach almost Gallic finesse.

Throughout this whole period, she dabbled not at all in thought. Observations and opinions, however, would ooze out from under the stamp of consciousness in an uninterrupted stream, and permeate the source throbbing in her soul. Unfathomable were the flights of impressions, strange indeed – their landings.

And so: after an evening spent in the clasp of scores of dance partners, whiled away in the parlance of hummingbirds – Teresa would fall asleep, having a startlingly vivid image of the universe manifested for the first time in her brain.

Another time, amid feverish dress fittings, irrefutable social truths suddenly unravelled out of the lustre of silk charmeuse. Designations that until recently had flown on the rustling wings of intuition acquired the weight of stones.

Distances became fixed as the flickering riot of ideas cooled in the form of dogma. At the same time, Teresa grew admirably adept at the art of juggling masks. She already knew how to deck brutal people in lacy face masks, while sensitive filigree types she clothed in dreary colours, turning them into mastiffs.

Whenever she acted thus, constantly surrendering to the influence of events – Jędruś would walk by in the far distance, intertwined hand in hand with Janek and Hanusia. Jędruś had managed to form friendships. He no longer stalked game single-handedly – he had companions. He behaved sensibly, with decisiveness and grace. Often his clipped little voice would reach her ears, fine-tuned to the tones of an army major.

In town they were dancing, for the carnival lasted a long time and the value of the currency had gone up but the price of mayonnaise come down. A man attached himself to Teresa . . . Passable but nothing special. Black-haired, lanky, beautifully dressed.

Attached himself like a mascot, like a riff from the foxtrot-shimmy 'Je cherche après Titine'. Teresa grew used to this man being with her every-where. As she put on her ballroom dress, she also put on the mascot. During the least rhythmic of activities, the man would leap out of thin air like a tiresome melody. Once he sat on the carpet and Teresa gazed into his eyes.

She felt someone's palms clasp her ankles above her feet. This was not so terrible. But immediately afterwards the man uttered the words: 'I love you', while Teresa could still see into his eyes.

Only now was it terrible.

Something turbid and slippery in the man's eyes clearly said: 'I hate you; I'm about to bite you with poisoned teeth and you'll die from the wound. I despise you: I'm about to kiss you and my kiss will slap you like a hand. I'm begging; I'm about to stretch out my arms, and the foul stench of my rags will encircle your head.'

The words 'I love you' flapped about in his mouth like a bird trapped in a cage, while his hands slithered around the seated woman's legs like a couple of slow-worms.

Teresa fled screaming from the room.

Unbelievably nauseous and loathsome days ensued. Days with acned faces.

Teresa swam in abhorrence. Even flowers looked at her askance.

Some sort of vermin floated up from the bottom of her memory, gnaw-ing at all her thoughts, until no rubbish remained.

The incident seemed beyond blame and beyond what she deserved.

*

At exactly this time, Jędruś was going through his building-block phase. Crouched amid the rubble of red and white bricks – he was creating.

His chubby paw wandered with deliberation over the piles of material.

Suddenly, it would swoop on a chosen object and return as fast as possible with its prize to the 'tower', whose rather bulky fabric was laboriously rising from the ground.

In these hours of construction, Jędruś's brow expressed no less gravity than once did the countenance of Leonardo, bent over his flying-machine designs.

This is how Teresa found her son one afternoon. She stood sadly behind him, watching him build his beautiful castle.

To show the boy kindness, she asked: 'What are you building, Jędruś?'

The little fellow raised his head and began talking animatedly: 'For you, Ummy, I'm always building a house.'

And so, without a moment's hesitation, Teresa wrapped all her heartaches in sunny cheer as in a veil – and entered her son's house to dwell there forever.

'Przymierze z dzieckiem'
Originally serialized in *Bluszcz* (1926), then published as part of the collection *Przymierze z dzieckiem* (Wydawnictwo Jakuba Mortkowicza, 1927), here from *Nowele i bruliony prozatorskie* (Czytelnik, 1985).

MAGDALENA TULLI

1955–

Magdalena Tulli has won a number of major awards for her novels. She is also the author of plays, a well-received children's book, and translations from French and Italian of writers including Marcel Proust and Fleur Jaeggy.

Her writing is rich and refined, sometimes described as postmodern. Identifying some of her literary influences, the American critic W. S. Merwin noted that: 'the originality of Tulli's writing is not lessened by representing a family tree that includes Michaux, Kafka, Calvino, and Saramago.' The *Los Angeles Review of Books* described her prose as 'astonishing in its beauty and leaps of imagination'.

Four of her short novels have been translated into English by Bill Johnston, who describes her debut, *Dreams and Stones* (1995) as follows: 'It's a novel about objects and about ways of seeing and explaining. The only actual character is the narrator, whose rather pedantic voice is our only clue to his existence.' From the start, Tulli was hailed as a new and distinct phenomenon in Polish literature, the representative of a certain anti-prose, dedicated to breaking the laws of traditional fiction.

Her next two books, *In Red* (1998) and *Moving Parts* (2003), have identifiable plotlines, but the narrative wanders between them. According to Johnston, 'Tulli gradually introduces narrative, though she does so in a very tentative and self-aware way (this is why she's sometimes accused, wrongly, of writing "meta-fiction").'

Her fourth book, *Flaw* (2006), can be read as a universal parable, yet the fate of the Jews in the Second World War is a clear point of reference (Tulli is of Italian-Jewish-Polish descent). However, the refugees who feature in the book are only ever referred to as 'the Others'.

Born to a Polish-Jewish mother in Warsaw, Tulli spent much of her childhood with her father in Italy. This unusual family background appears in the novel *Włoskie szpilki* (*Italian Heels*, 2001, not yet translated into English). Largely autobiographical, it marks a change of direction from her earlier style.

Antonia Lloyd-Jones

Red Lipstick

Translated by Antonia Lloyd-Jones

She called me out of the blue in mid-February, after a very, very long time. She hadn't been in touch for at least three years. And suddenly she felt the desire to go to the cinema with me.

'To an old Swedish movie,' she said. 'To the shopping mall. Before the film we can go and look at pretty things, and after it we can have something nice to eat.'

To the shopping mall and an old Swedish movie? Shops before, a meal after? Last time a similar programme took up our entire day. I hadn't forgotten the minor unpleasantness right at the end, so I wanted to tell her I wasn't coming. For the first time in the history of our acquaintance. But this hesitation was short lived. For all these years it was she who had called me, I had never called her. That was why I had never refused. And was I going to refuse now because of something trivial that happened three years ago?

'I'll come and fetch you in the car,' she told me. 'Wait downstairs, I'll be there in half an hour.'

She was late. Enough time for me to get frozen, because it was the chilly, damp, grey end of winter. I had started to think she wasn't coming when a car stopped by the kerb. She opened the passenger door for me. I got in.

'You look great,' she said. She'd been prone to dark rings around the eyes before we finished high school. Now it was much worse. She glanced in the mirror. 'Don't be shocked. I don't sleep well.'

We slowly drove across some half-frozen puddles. Suddenly she stopped. She started rummaging in her handbag and searching the glove compartment. She apologized to me: she'd have to go home for her glasses.

'You've got them on your nose,' I remarked. But no, she didn't mean those ones, they were tinted and she only wore them for driving. We turned round and drove down some narrow little streets lined with villas. I stayed in the car, parked outside her beautiful house. I'd seen the inside before, three years ago. She got out alone, a little disappointed that she wouldn't be showing it to me again. She disappeared for quite a long time. When she came back, she put a dark-green crocodile glasses case into the glove compartment on my side.

'These are for the cinema,' she said. 'But the ones for near sight must have stayed behind on Marszałkowska Street. We can drop in there. It's almost on the way.'

She had a flat on Marszałkowska Street in a lovely pre-war building, on the first floor. I used to go there in our schooldays. At primary school. At high school we weren't best friends any more. We just sat together at the back of the classroom for physics and geography and played battleships. She always won. I might have started to suspect she was cheating. But it never entered my head. She always won, and that seemed quite natural to me. I remember her mother well. As soon as we arrived she would stick her head out of the kitchen and call: 'Aren't you hungry, girls?' When she died I saw the announcement in the paper. Her father was dead too. He had a grand state funeral.

'So where exactly do you live? In the villa, or on Marszałkowska?' I asked.

She wondered what to say.

'I have a studio flat in Ochota. I usually sleep there. Because it's quiet. But I can't live there. I'd get claustrophobia. At the villa I have space. And a bed with a special mattress that prevents backache. But it's not possible to sleep there.'

'Why not?'

'Faint undertones.'

'The neighbours' washing machine?'

She cast me a glance across the steering wheel, piqued; after all, we weren't talking about a flat in a high-rise block.

'Yesterday it was quiet, so I decided to stay, and I even fell asleep for a while. It's a lottery, you never know when it'll start and when it'll end. At dawn I had to give in. It was cold, sleeting. I got into the car and went to sleep at Ochota.'

How dreadful, I thought. And she probably can't put that bed in the studio flat because it's too big.

'What about Marszałkowska?' I asked.

'Marszałkowska!' she laughed curtly. 'You can hear every single tram, every bus, every car. I can recognize the make by the sound of the engine. It's as if I could see them all. As if they were driving through the middle of my bedroom. They're not even quiet at four in the morning.'

Her ennui was infecting me. The mistress of so many beautiful properties without a roof over her head. In her place I'd look for a quiet flat on a peaceful street.

'I've been looking for one like that,' she assured me. 'For some time, believe me.'

By a miracle we found a place to park. She had just disappeared inside the gateway when a bird made a mess on the windscreen. If it was a pigeon, it must have been an extremely big one. The stain was pink, white and grey, with a dark tone and an extended tideline. That's all we need! I thought, with strange weariness, evidently caught from her. Just as in our schooldays, in adult life she always infected me with her impatience, her boredom, her frustration. But while she surrendered to these emotions impulsively and frivolously, I felt obliged to build positive relations between her and the world. As if I were responsible for reality and rather ashamed of it.

Involuntarily I kept glancing at that stain, until suddenly my hand opened the door and my body got out of the car. I reached into my handbag, took out a paper handkerchief and set about cleaning the windscreen. Just a barely visible trace of tideline was left, which refused to come off, because it had had time to dry out a bit. All right, I thought, that'll do. I pulled the handle – the door wouldn't budge. It was jammed. I tugged for a while, with increasing energy, in vain. I gave up. By the time she got back, I was frozen again. She aimed a furtive glance at me. Was she wondering why I'd got out of the car? Did she think I was trying to escape? But hadn't been quick enough?

'What have you done to the door?' she asked, yanking the handle on the driver's side a couple of times. Nothing, I tried to say, but the word stuck in my throat. I tugged at the handle on the passenger side.

'Better leave it,' she said firmly.

I felt guilty and unhappy. Here was the worst thing that could have happened to me in this car; without meaning to, I had broken something. Why on earth had I cleaned the windscreen instead of sitting quietly in my place? I thought with despair. She waved the remote a few times, did some more tugging at the handle, waved the remote again, and tugged again.

The door gave way, but I felt no relief, I still had the same turmoil in my head and my heart.

She tossed another glasses case into the glove compartment, also crocodile, but white.

Once again we drove through the puddles. A thin layer of ice cracked beneath the wheels, and water splashed.

'I always forget to ask you how your kiddies are doing,' she said, overtaking a bus. It was true, she always forgot to ask me about them. Probably because she had none of her own.

'Fine. He's at university, and she still has to pass her final school exams,' I replied.

'Ah,' she sighed painfully, and was silent for a moment. Time flies. It makes no exceptions, not even for her. 'Husband still the same?'

Still the same. For her it was hard to imagine. She'd been married three times. Two divorces and one funeral, which I'd heard about from gossip. From the last of her husbands she had inherited shares in a major chain of perfume stores. She lived off them. Because she'd finished with the theatre long ago. At the height of her success, just after reaching thirty. She'd got as far as playing the lead in a well-known film. I'd seen it. During the bedroom scenes I had instinctively looked away. After that she had refused all further offers. She hadn't acted again. Why not? I have no idea. I'd always forgotten to ask her.

She parked outside the shopping mall, changed her tinted glasses for the long-distance ones (green crocodile), and then took the third pair (white crocodile) out of the glove compartment. For a while she had two pairs on her nose, but then removed one. Through the glasses for near sight she inspected the front windscreen, where there was still a sign she couldn't decipher: the outline of an island. She didn't speak – it was a matter between her and her car. She pressed a button and the pistons threw up a shot of wiper fluid. The wipers came on for a while, moving to right and left. Then she inspected the glass again, and shook her head with resignation.

'We can go,' she said.

The car park was iced over. Halfway across, the phone in her handbag rang. She extracted it hastily. She slipped. I quickly grabbed her by the elbow, otherwise she'd have fallen headlong. She scowled and tore free of me. The phone went on ringing, not a tune, just a plain intermittent signal, sounding quite insistent.

'Yes,' she said. 'No, I can't. I'm at the cinema. No, alone. Good. We'll meet this evening. Yes, at Marszałkowska.'

Something had changed. I noticed the radiant glow of triumph on her face, quite unmistakable. I didn't know the circumstances. I could only guess she'd been waiting for that call, probably for days.

And then she suddenly started talking about perfume. About the perfume that was the hit of the season. It was called Heart.

'It's the scent of spring,' she said. 'I've had enough of the winter.'

Heart, a red flask with a flashy silk bow on the seal. I remembered it, thanks to the adverts.

The chain of perfume stores in which she had inherited shares didn't have an outlet in this shopping mall.

'Come on,' she said, gently pulling at my sleeve. 'Let's take a look at the competition.'

She wants to choose a new perfume for a new romance, I thought. She's got a date with someone this evening and wants to smell of this scent of spring.

The perfume shop was crowded, even for a Saturday. But I saw the Heart perfume from some way off, on display right in the middle of the shop. She reached for the tester and stuck a strip of card moistened with the scent under my nose. I found the fragrance banal. Freshness, of course. A slight sweetness and a hint of lemon. In a word, lemonade. I reached for the perfume that stood beside it, then the next one. I liked those ones more. I offered her a strip of card.

'No, no,' she said. 'They won't do.'

None of them would do.

After the fifth or sixth sample the smells merged into something characterless. She must have been having sensory overload too, because she didn't buy anything. We left the shop, and almost at once I noticed the aroma of coffee, a sign that my sense of smell had returned. We sat down at a small table, intending to order two small espressos. There was a Saturday crowd at the café too. For ages none of the waiters approached us.

'Now let's see what your perfume smells like at the second attempt,'

I said, taking the bunch of cardboard strips from her. But she was no longer sure which one had Heart on it.

'I think it's this one,' she said.

'No, that's Acqua di Gioia. This is Mademoiselle. What's this?' I offered her a strip that smelled slightly bitter. 'I don't remember sniffing that.'

It was a mystery. Before we'd ordered coffee, I nipped back to the perfume shop and sought out the saleswoman.

'Bitterness at the second try,' I said. 'What is it?'

She sniffed the cardboard strip.

'Heart,' she replied without hesitation.

By the time I got back to the table she'd forgotten about perfume. She seemed as if on tenterhooks.

'Let's go somewhere else.'

'It'll be the same everywhere, it's Saturday. Anyway, we've got enough time.'

In silence, she stared at the tabletop.

'Can you hear that?' she asked a little later.

It was quite loud, I'd have had to be deaf not to hear it. Snatches of music mixed with the hubbub of conversation.

'No, no. Listen carefully.'

In fact there was something else hidden within the noise – a very low, constant, monotonous buzz.

'It's just sounds,' I said. 'Probably the air conditioning. Or some sort of refrigeration appliance.'

She glanced at me with a look of suffering. Then we tried to find a place where there wouldn't be any noise, so she could have her coffee in peace. Because she slept badly at night, and absolutely had to have coffee, otherwise, she told me, she'd fall asleep in the cinema. We came upon a small self-service bar. She picked up the coffee and tea menu, then started looking for her near-sight glasses. She took everything she had out of her handbag. She put it all down on the table: two phones, some thick face cream and a lipstick.

'May I?' I asked, picking up the lipstick. Dark red, an upmarket brand of course.

She added some crumpled chocolate bar wrappers and a pile of ATM receipts, three bunches of house keys and two different sets of car keys, a pair of pliers, a sailor's knife and finally the green crocodile. The white crocodile was lying in the middle of the table, open and empty. She remembered that she must have left the glasses somewhere by the perfumes. She put all the mess away again. This time it was she who went back to the perfume shop.

'I'll be right back,' she said. 'Order the coffee while I'm gone.'

Viewed from behind, she hadn't changed at all, she looked just as she did in our high-school days, and was even wearing similar trousers. At school the boys revolved around her from a distance, like planets around their star, elliptically. She turned them down without mercy. The teachers treated her with respect, though she gave them plenty of reasons to have it in for her. She was difficult, she refused to study. Or to play the piano. I was endlessly told how talented she was, which was always mentioned in the same breath as a reprimand which ended up sounding like an involuntary tribute. She had no trouble getting into drama school. Possibly because her father was the dean of the drama faculty. But probably not only that.

I stood in a very short queue for coffee, then drank it at a small table, then spent another quarter of an hour feeling bored over an empty cup. The glasses had been found but her coffee had gone cold, so she pushed it away and fetched herself a fresh, hot cup, followed by another one – she must have been terribly in need of sleep.

'Do you remember?' I said. 'At high school you had a dark-red Helena Rubinstein lipstick, just the same as now. After class you used to paint your lips in the cloakroom. For that student who came to fetch you on a motorbike.'

She laughed, but didn't take up the subject.

I went out with a boy in the parallel class. He looked at that red lipstick as if bewitched. I found out the meaning of helplessness. She lured him away from me quite nonchalantly, leading him on and keeping him at a distance. We were both unhappy all the way up to our final exams.

She wasn't in the mood for reminiscence.

'I must use the toilet,' she announced, getting up. The toilet was at the end of a long corridor, which one entered from the main passage between the exclusive china and the diving gear. I stood in this corridor, waiting for her again, while a long queue wound past me, and now and then someone came out. But she had gone inside and all trace of her was lost.

'Finally,' I rejoiced when she showed up again after a long while. She shook her head.

'What were you doing in there all that time?'

'You might not understand,' she said in anguish. 'The partitions are so thin that you can hear everything. The crowd waiting to come in, strange women peeing next door, someone trying to sit a child on the loo . . . I need another toilet, something cosier. Perhaps there'll be one at the cinema.'

I pressed the handle of the door marked with a wheelchair symbol.

'Here you are,' I said. 'Try this one.'

She cast me a look of gratitude and disappeared inside. Once again I waited for all eternity. I was reminded of our time in the junior classes when I had to hold the door shut for her in the school toilet because there weren't any bolts. The thought that someone might look in while she was peeing horrified her so much that she'd have preferred to suffer through the whole of the next lesson. 'Lavatory lady!' the big girls, who came to smoke in there, called me. I wouldn't have known how to explain to them why I agreed to it all. But how come I didn't even impose conditions? And now? What am I doing now?

I walked away from the door, left the corridor, stopped outside the china shop and was looking at the display when she grabbed me by the arm.

'There you are!' she cried angrily. 'Why couldn't you have waited?'

'I was waiting here,' I calmly replied.

'I thought I'd never find you. You had a great idea, and I was so pleased. Comfort, peace, soft Mozart from the speakers.'

'So what's your problem?'

There was a look of reproach in her eyes, but not ordinary reproach, the kind an ordinary person can express, but concentrated reproach of murderous strength, the very essence of reproach. The two divorced husbands and the third one who died must have been familiar with this look.

'You disappeared! When I came out, you were nowhere to be seen. You left me on my own. You simply ran off!'

But for her, casting a look like that one was no great art – after all, she used to be an actress, it occurred to me, and all of a sudden I sniggered. We couldn't have lost each other, we both had phones. I was laughing, at the murderous reproach in her eyes, at the door with no bolt in the school toilet and at myself. She fluttered her eyelashes – she'd always had extremely long ones. At first she didn't know how to react. What do you do when your tragic monologue makes the audience laugh? Leave the stage? Go on with the show, pretending nothing's wrong? As a spectator, I had let her down. But then she began to laugh too, and we laughed together for a while, as we rode up the escalator. The people coming down were looking at us. They could see two middle-aged women, old friends having a great time out shopping. She surrendered, I thought. She won't do that to me again.

We were late for the cinema, but only by a couple of minutes.

On the phone, when she had promised an old Swedish movie, she hadn't said it would be THAT movie. We'd seen it together in the past, in another world, a hundred years ago, playing truant.

She bought the tickets and refused the banknote I had put on the counter.

'You paid for the coffee,' she said. Yes, for her coffee that had gone cold and been rejected.

We entered the auditorium at the same time as the nurse, she on the screen, we from the back of the hall. The nurse closed the door behind her.

'How are you feeling, Mrs Vogler?' she said.

'Where are we sitting?' I asked in a whisper.

She pointed to the middle rows. It was almost empty. Before the nurse had admitted that she didn't know how to deal with Mrs Vogler, the rebellious star, I heard a noise beside me. I turned around. She was asleep, with her head tipped back. The two coffees hadn't helped. She was woken by raised voices. She gazed vacantly at the screen, then at me. There was a short scene featuring a quarrel, soon over. Then I heard the whistling noise again.

'Did you sleep through the whole film?' I asked, once we were sitting in a restaurant at a table covered with a white cloth. There were even more people here than there had been in the café downstairs. But it turned out she had foreseen this, and had made a reservation by phone.

'I remember how badly it shocked me,' she said, examining the menu with her glasses balanced on her nose. 'At the time I could sense the touch of a genius, but watching it on the screen I felt all at sea. Mrs Vogler was an actress, living the sort of life I dreamed of in those days, but she'd dropped it! There must have been a suicide attempt in the background, hence the hospital. Had she sunk into depression? Or perhaps it was a rebellion? What a disturbing enigma for me at the time. Years later I realized where I stood, and I did the same thing as she had . . . I'll have the spinach tortellini. And for the main course . . .' she said, turning the menu over, 'trout.'

'I'll have the tagliatelle with pesto,' I told the waiter. 'And trout.'

'White wine with that?' he asked. 'I can recommend the Queensland white, an Australian wine. Excellent.'

'Yes,' I nodded. She nodded too, her gaze rather absent.

'And for dessert?' he asked again.

'We'll put that off until later,' she said. 'We don't know if we'll have room.'

Something occurred to me.

'Why exactly did we leave the perfume shop without buying any?'

She smiled and reached into her handbag. She brought out a red flask with a silk bow, without the box, which puzzled me. Yet after leaving the perfume shop she'd put the entire contents of her bag on the table in the coffee bar. And I hadn't seen the red flask there. But there was something even odder too.

'May I see?'

Unbelievable. There was a piece of thick transparent tape attached to the bottle, the remains of a security tag. The actual security tag had been ripped off with a sharp instrument. A sailor's knife, perhaps?

'You stole it,' I whispered.

She smiled again.

'I don't support the competition.'

It almost sounded natural, but it wasn't the entire truth.

'And why do you carry pliers around with you?' I asked. 'To steal from clothes shops?'

'Pass me the salt?'

She added lots and lots of salt. She won't eat it, I thought. Or she'll salt herself to death.

She put down the salt cellar.

'The pliers come in handy for all sorts of things,' she explained.

We clinked glasses, but she didn't even wet her lips. Anyway, the wine wasn't too good. If she knew that, why hadn't we ordered a different one?

And if she didn't drink at all, why pretend? In fact I couldn't remember what had happened three years ago. Had we ordered wine or not? In the old days she hadn't liked the hard stuff, that I did remember.

The pesto, green with basil, smelled superb and was hellishly garlicky.

'You'll be driving me home later,' I reminded her. 'Can you bear it?'

She shrugged.

'Garlic doesn't bother me. So what did you think of the film?'

'You chose it because once upon a time it shocked us.'

She began to laugh.

'We were young. Half Mrs Vogler's age. Now we're older than she was. We know twice as much as she does. I know almost everything. It's written on my forehead. Take a good look at me.'

'And that's why you slept through it.'

'You kept nodding off too,' she said. 'You probably thought I hadn't noticed. You don't complain of insomnia. I might have assumed you spent half the night quarrelling with your husband. You're a good couple, but sometimes you quarrel half the night, you can't stop, and you both feel like jumping out of the window. Right? And the children lie in their beds, listening in terror.'

Right. I had spent half the night quarrelling with my husband. Of course I'm familiar with the menace of the family idyll, which comes at the cost of a hundred rotten compromises. She had never agreed to rotten compromises.

'You prefer to get divorced,' I remarked. 'Get divorced or . . .'

'Or what?' she asked sternly.

I dropped my gaze.

'Or become a widow,' I said quietly, my heart pounding.

She burst out laughing again.

'Try coming up with something better than that,' she replied.

I was silent. I wound the penultimate ribbon of pasta around my fork, raised it to my mouth and swallowed. Goodness knows why, but there before my eyes stood that door with no bolt and the big girls smoking in the toilet. The pasta stuck in my throat. I looked around helplessly and swigged at my glass. And that was when I came up with something better.

'You drank,' I said. 'That's why you're not drinking. A close relationship is something you can't bear without alcohol. It doesn't really surprise me when I know you can't even pee without special conditions. Watch out, since you're just getting into a new romance. It seems to me as if you live in this world like a china doll. How odd that you haven't broken yet.'

'I have broken,' she said, looking me in the eyes with hatred. 'Can't you see that I'm entirely stuck together with all-purpose glue?'

A man came in and bowed as he passed our table. I was sure I'd seen him somewhere before. On the screen perhaps, or in a colour supplement. She casually returned his nod across her empty plate.

'Who's that?' I asked.

'That man? A friend, an actor, a nice kid.'

The waiter brought us the trout. The trout smelled lovely too.

'They took me straight from the funeral to the detox ward,' she said once he had moved off. I hadn't heard about that. What I knew from gossip was that her husband had left her all his property, passing over his ex-wife and children.

Is it possible to put someone in an ambulance without their consent? Like in a soap opera?

'The paramedics from a private clinic were waiting in the car park outside the cemetery. My husband's brother had arranged it in secret. My husband loved me very much, if you want to know. I spent the first ten days in detox climbing the walls. The drying-out treatment took three months. I lasted a year until my first setback. Then I had three months more in detox, but this time of my own free will. I came home last week.'

Even as he was dying, he had organized a rescue mission for her.

'"My husband loved me very much"!' I repeated. 'How like you, how typical of you that is! You think you're the centre of the universe and you've nothing to offer anyone. Do you remember how you stole my . . .'

She interrupted me abruptly.

'What are you on about? After that you married him anyway.'

And what if I tried to tell her that the betrayal, the lies and misery had become a part of my marriage? She'd just have laughed. She certainly wouldn't have been able to tot up all her betrayals and lies, but then they hadn't brought the world to an end.

It had just grown terribly old.

A well-known television presenter bowed to us from a distance; she had probably retired by now.

'And what about him?' I asked.

'Who?'

'The man you've got a date with this evening. Will you tell me who he is?'

'No,' she replied, smiling to herself.

It crossed my mind that for her I was something like a chair or an umbrella stand, nothing more. I was dealing with a monster. With a satisfied monster, gearing up for a pleasant evening.

'You were fed up with waiting for the phone to ring. You only needed me to help you stop thinking about it, because you were falling to pieces. But you got back your self-confidence when he did actually call.'

'And so what?'

'I hope it gets you nowhere. I hate you.'

Silence fell. The words had been said, I couldn't unsay them, the cards were on the table. But she was no innocent victim. She leaned over her plate and slowly dug around in it with her fork. Then she raised her eyes. She looked at me very benignly.

I've shaken her, I thought. She has realized she went too far. She hasn't got any children, her husbands have gone. She gets her strength for life from the past. And I am part of the past.

'I don't think it will get me anywhere,' she said. 'It's like with the perfume. Hard to refuse, although my sense of smell's not . . .'

Perhaps now she'll finally start to talk to me without posturing.

She broke off. But picked up the same topic at a different point.

'It's true, I used to drink. And I took pills. Resulting in structural changes to my brain. Most of all I regret losing my sense of smell. Apparently I'll never get it back again. My hearing is all right. What I hear best are the noises I can't stand. I can't see at all well, but it's better that way. Glasses only when necessary. On top of that it feels as if I have no skin. Every touch is painful.'

'Yes . . .' I said, with a lump in my throat. 'Yes . . .'

'But I have something,' she added after a long while, 'that other people only get on their deathbed. Too late for them to be able to appreciate it.'

The waiter took away our plates. She ordered a crème brulée and an espresso. I made do with a cup of tea, hot and bitter. I drank it slowly.

'What do you have in mind?' I asked at last.

'No illusions,' she said, tucking into her dessert. 'I know the senses lie. Our world doesn't exist. Matter consists almost entirely of a void with some sort of particles wandering around in it. You probably think a cup is a cup, a table is a table. You imagine the border between you and me to be something incredibly substantial. But this entire world is like one big cloud of something that's hardly there at all. And this something that's hardly there never stops overflowing from the future into the past. From nothing into nothing.'

The senses lie, something cried out within me, nothing could be more obvious. I felt a pain as if the world had suddenly turned into a void. Yet it hadn't ceased to exist from one moment to the next. There was nothing sudden about it. Such is its nature. No wonder, since it was created out of nothing. Can something really be created out of nothing? Of course not! In a way we are not here at all, the thought went spinning around my head. This is the life I have given my children.

'You're not going to drink that, are you?' I asked, reaching for her glass with a shaking hand.

She waved at the waiter to bring us the bill.

'Together or separately?' he asked.

'Separately,' I said.

'Don't be silly. I know you two haven't any money.' She smiled, sure that her perfume shops were better than our jobs. The waiter smiled too, discreetly. Just as he had three years ago. Though that was a different waiter and a different restaurant.

'*Czerwona szminka*'
Published in the anthology *Zachcianki* (Świat Ksiązki, 2012), text modified by the author for this anthology.

MISFITS

.

MARIA DĄBROWSKA

1889–1965

Like much of Maria Dąbrowska's fiction, the short story 'Miss Winczewska' has its roots in the author's personal experience. In 1925 her
husband of fourteen years, Marian Dąbrowski, a major in the education wing of the Polish Armed Forces, died unexpectedly. The following
year, Dąbrowska and her sister-in-law funded and organized a library
for soldiers at the Citadel military base in Warsaw. Some years later, her
experiences in this endeavour became transmuted into 'Miss Winczewska',
which was first published in the short-story collection *Znaki życia* (*Signs
of Life*) in 1938. By that time Dąbrowska had acquired great renown in
Poland thanks to her expansive novel cycle *Noce i dnie* (*The Nights and
the Days*, 1931–4), the work for which she remains best known. Her short
fiction bears the same stamp as *The Nights and the Days* – a penetrating,
intelligent, generous emphasis on personality and relation, along with a
superbly well-controlled, precise use of language, especially in its emotional
palette. In 'Miss Winczewska', she paints a subtle, multi-faceted picture
of the title character, by turns ridiculous, pitiful and strangely moving. In
counterpoint to her heroine, she offers a second character in the form of
a thinly disguised self-portrait (Natalia Sztumska's last name amusingly
recalls Dąbrowska's own maiden name, Szumska), an authoritative figure
who wavers between righteous indignation, sympathy and belief in the
possibility of improvement. As always in Dąbrowska's writing, the whole
is brought to life not only through its psychological believability, but also
through the brilliant use of convincing detail (the creaky, echoing stage
next door to the library; the huge dog that fetches a rock instead of a
ball). The setting too is rendered with masterful authenticity, from the

unpredictable sentries at the Citadel gate, to the deserted tearoom the two women visit for lunch. The main focus, though, remains the fascinating duel between the exasperating and the exasperated, between powerlessness and power – yet also between condemnation and compassion.

Bill Johnston

Miss Winczewska

Translated by Bill Johnston

In mid-June, right before she was to leave for her vacation, Natalia Sztumska decided that rather than delegating the job to one of her assistants, she personally would carry out an inspection of the soldiers' reading room located inside the former citadel.

This reading room did not fall directly under her authority. Natalia worked in the head office of the Association for the Cultural Welfare of the Soldier, while the citadel was in this regard the responsibility of the association's local branch.

For some time, however, there'd been reports that the person appointed to oversee the reading room was not up to the task. Yet whenever Natalia had broached the matter to the local people, she found everyone busy organizing some official breakfast or tea, or regimental day, or field Mass to celebrate the presentation of the colours. Each time she visited, some major or captain was standing by the desk of the branch president, and together they were anxiously realizing that they'd omitted some detail, that something or other had not been ordered, someone or other hadn't yet been invited. The officer would exclaim excitedly: 'We may still have time!' and snatch up the telephone receiver, while the president, a handsome, charming woman with heart problems, would take advantage of the pause, lean over to Natalia and quietly, so as not to interfere with the instructions being shouted into the phone – instructions that seemed to fill her with an intense solemnity – would beg her to set aside for the while the delicate subject of what was known as the citadel reading room.

'Please believe me,' she would say, 'we're overwhelmed by all there is to do here. Just at the moment it'd be too much for us to add the citadel to our agenda. At the present time our library inspector couldn't possibly

337

fit it in, the poor woman's already doing the work of three people. In a little while, right after the Twenty-Eighth Regiment's celebration, we'll sort the place out.'

But after that celebration, another immediately needed to be organized; then three whole new cultural centres were opened. In the end, Natalia couldn't wait for the right circumstances to come along; she woke up one morning with the realization that she herself had to intervene, bypassing, so to speak, the official channels.

From that point on, whenever she had a free moment she would visit the citadel cultural centre during the opening hours of the reading room to observe the work there. She noticed numerous irregularities, while each encounter with the librarian left a disagreeable and at the same time slightly comical impression, the essence of which was for the moment hard to pin down.

The librarian's name was Regina Winczewska. She was not professionally trained but was, as the expression goes, a social activist, and had even been decorated, so people had believed she'd be able to handle the work.

After several trips to the citadel, and a multitude of explanations from Miss Winczewska that did nothing but raise further doubts, Natalia informed her one day that tomorrow she would come in the morning and the two of them together would conduct an inventory of the collection, and a review of the lending slips and the statistics of reading-room use. She ordered the lending of books to be suspended for two days.

The following morning she rose early, and by a quarter to eight she was already boarding the tram so as to be in place by nine o'clock, as they'd agreed over the telephone.

There had been a rainstorm in the night, after which the temperature dropped significantly. At the crossing where the tram stop was situated, a strong wind battered and roared from around the corner. In the drab, cloud-covered sky only a handful of paler gashes and scars shone with a faint gleam. The outlines of the apartment buildings looked fresh and a little stern. The pavements were still wet.

In the tram, Natalia kept thinking about Regina Winczewska. She recalled some of the silly answers the woman had given to her questions, and she thought in alarm that probably, as a result of the actions she was now taking, it would be necessary to remove this unsuitable employee. She didn't know if she would have the strength for the task. She felt comfortable only around things she could approve of; in any conflict she had a tendency to concede that her opponent was right.

She was roused from these reflections when she noticed the tram had filled up. It had been empty to begin with, but since a certain stop it had become crowded.

With other people's dresses and overcoats right next to her face, Natalia pressed as close to the window as she could and watched the indistinct, broken reflection of the tram moving across the display windows of ever smaller shops with ever more garish signs. From time to time, against her back, her shoulders and her knees, she felt the press of other passengers getting on or off.

After a time the crush of people eased. The tram had passed the city limits. On either side of the street were the green lawns and frail bushes of the new park, and further on there appeared, also green, the rounded fortifications and sloping flanks of the former citadel. Finally the tram pulled up at the terminus. The driver noisily unscrewed the steering handle and carried it away with him.

The last remaining passengers jumped down from the platform. Inside the now deserted carriage a little girl was pretending she didn't want to get off. Her mother called to her: 'Come on, be good!' The girl turned away contrarily and looked out of the window with a smile.

To get to the citadel you had to cross a footbridge over the railroad tracks. The footbridge was old and the wood it was made of had turned dark, but the steps leading up to it had been fitted with fresh metal plates and a couple of rotten boards had been replaced.

Natalia was pleased to see this. The last time she'd come this way she'd been worried that no one would think about sprucing the footbridge up. Yet here the time had come and someone had taken care of it.

Evidently the right time comes for everything, she thought, as she gazed at the gleaming metal plates beneath her feet. Maybe Winczewska's time will come too, and I'm hurrying it along unnecessarily?

Down below, a train was slowly rumbling along the track. It was barely moving. You could hear the loose clatter of the wheels and the puffing of the engine. Two boys elbowed their way past the pedestrians and ran to the parapet to watch the train. To the right of the footbridge a soldier was lying down below in the luxuriant grass, leaning on one elbow and reading a newspaper folded in four. On the other side two grimy workers were squeezing through the gap between the handrail of the steps and the fence that separated the railway from the street. In this way they were trying to bypass the footbridge and cross directly over the tracks instead. The entire handrail tilted from their effort; in the end they made it through.

Natalia came into the avenue of large trees that led to the citadel gate.

The wind was less gusty here; the trees swayed ponderously with a monotonous, drawn-out soughing.

Just beyond the gate there was a small vaulted room where passes were issued. A sergeant with a chestful of ribbons sat at a massive registry book. He was writing out a pass for an old woman in a checked headscarf.

'Last name?' he asked.

'Name and address?' he then said, turning to Natalia. She told him, and began to search in her handbag for the identity card that was usually required. This time, however, the sergeant did not ask for it. In fact, generally speaking, sometimes he did, sometimes he didn't. It was the same with the soldier standing at the entrance to the bridge over the moat. On some days he wanted to see her pass only when she was leaving the citadel, but occasionally he'd also require it as she entered.

Potatoes and vegetables were growing good-humouredly in the bed of the moat. In a corner right by the gateway a huge elderberry bush grew, its disks of white flowers reaching as far as the bridge's handrail.

Passing through the second, interior gate, Natalia followed a walkway of disagreeably uneven flagstones towards the temporary home of the reading room. Her heart was beating. She was increasingly dreading the conflict with the librarian that awaited her.

The entrance to the centre consisted of a handful of boards sloping from the threshold to the walkway. The boards were rotten and full of holes, while the threshold itself was nothing but a splintered, jagged remnant. This woeful sight stirred something like a combative spirit in Natalia.

The broad staircase, however, made her feel more conciliatory. It was freshly washed. The large door painted the colour of bull's blood that led into the centre stood open. You could reach the reading room either through the studio apartment where the librarian lived, or across the stage of the little auditorium. Natalia chose the latter route; as she moved forward, she again felt up to the challenge of the struggle for the reading room.

The auditorium was decorated with tattered white-and-red paper bunting and with portraits of state dignitaries by amateur artists who had given their subjects gloomy and frightened expressions. The ceiling in this place of intellectual entertainments was leaky, and after the rainstorm the previous night there was a puddle on the floor.

Natalia mounted the stage via a bench serving as a step. The hollow boards echoed beneath her footsteps. The thin walls of the stage were painted pink, with a devil's trail in flowers. To the side, an upright piano stood by a stiff painted hanging.

From the stage you had to climb back down some exceedingly steep steps to the door that led to the reading room behind the wings.

This spacious chamber was divided in two by a thin partition that did not reach all the way to the ceiling. A door-shaped cut-out in the partition was blocked by a table on which there lay, evidently freshly prepared: the reading-room inventory register, the hasped catalogues with their covers curling upwards, and the shallow cardboard trays containing the lending slips. At the back of the room there was a low ash-wood cabinet of the kind that serve as immemorial archive repositories in offices. The librarian was absent.

Natalia went up to the table, looked across the room, and saw a cabinet standing at right angles to the other one, forming a kind of small office space. The doors of both cabinets were open wide; books lay in disorder on the shelves. Natalia had the feeling there were strangely few of them. She picked up the lending slips to see how many books were on loan, but the card at the front bore the number ten. The slips were not in order. They'd simply been stuck in the trays completely haphazardly.

Natalia passed between the table and the cut-out in the wooden partition into the interior, took off her overcoat and hat and hung them on the handle of a half-open window, from which there was a view of the green flank of the battlements and, closer by, some tall acacias in bloom. The wind was shaking the trees, and when their branches bent back a little, beyond them you could see the cloudy sky. For a brief moment Natalia was unable to tear her eyes from those tiny little dishevelled leaves and the budding flowers whose ever-so-light clusters thrashed back and forth.

She couldn't help being amazed at how much strength and resistance there was in something so slender and fragile.

'Like in people,' she found herself saying, then all at once she grew impatient.

There isn't a living soul in here, she thought dispiritedly.

She cast an abrupt glance towards the door. At that moment, on the other side, someone began plonking on the keys of the piano, while a voice straining for an alto register sang out:

> 'If not today then tomorrow
> Girl, you are going to be mine.'

Natalia jerked open the door and saw Miss Winczewska over at the piano. Her grey-brown dog Linda lay next to her, her long muzzle resting on her paws.

Miss Winczewska jumped up and skipped towards Natalia.

'How is that possible?' she exclaimed. 'You're here? That can't be. How on earth? Which way did you come? Linda and I went to meet you. But we didn't see you. It isn't possible.'

'Yet here I am, however improbable it may seem to you, madam,' said Natalia, feeling herself turn pale with irritation at this greeting.

For a while, Miss Winczewska was unable to comprehend how they'd managed to miss one another on the way.

'It's of no consequence,' said Natalia, at the same time fending off the dog, whose tongue she had unexpectedly felt licking her face. 'Down,' she muttered, removing the dog's paws from her shoulders.

'She knows you! She knows you!' Miss Winczewska cried. 'Linda! Stop dancing! Look at that, madam – she's dancing for joy!'

The dog was indeed performing something like a dance, turning in a circle, and barking as she did so. Then she stopped, pricked up her ears and seemed to be gauging the impression she'd made.

It made Natalia want to laugh. She turned to the window so Miss Winczewska would not assume her visitor's approving smile was directed at herself.

'Let's get down to work,' she said, still looking away. 'We won't manage to finish everything today as it is.'

'Let's get down to it!' Miss Winczewska repeated enthusiastically.

As she bustled about she went on:

'I always take Linda along with me whenever I can, because I'm worried she'll not get enough exercise. You see, madam, she's in the family way,' she said with shy pride.

Natalia had composed herself by now, and took a seat at the table.

'For goodness' sake, let's leave the dog out of it,' she said loudly and frostily.

'My Lord,' Miss Winczewska said in surprise, 'you're talking to me as if I were a child.'

Miss Winczewska was an extraordinarily small person, and as mobile as a little spider. Her frail legs were not visibly crooked, but seemed just shy of being actually straight; and because they were so thin, they looked as if at any moment they might bend and break before your eyes. Her face was dark-complexioned, long and narrow, and gaunt as could be. Her top and bottom front teeth were missing; her smile revealed pale gums the colour of strawberry pulp. Her lustreless, ink-black shock of hair appeared to be crushing her insubstantial figure, that seemed wasted before its time, as if by fever. Her dark eyes had something scorching about them, like two burning drops of sealing wax.

Before beginning work, several times Miss Winczewska scurried back and forth between her apartment and the reading room, while the indefatigable dog accompanied her to and fro.

Natalia began by checking which books were on the shelves. She read the book's classification number from the catalogue, and Miss Winczewska, at the shelf, reported whether the book with that number was there, and if so what its title was. As they did this Natalia noted that the reading of the titles did not go smoothly. Miss Winczewska stumbled over the most well-known, classic authors' names, and made mistakes with the titles of masterpieces that are as much a part of any civilized person's life as combing one's hair and washing. She furthermore seemed oblivious both to her own mistakes and to Natalia's surprised, embarrassed glances. She scuttled briskly from one shelf to the next, hopping onto the stool that served in lieu of a ladder, and startling her dog with the stool as she whisked it from one place to another.

'Fetch the ball,' she would command with a stamp of her foot, while she worked. 'Fetch now! Oh, you little mother!'

The dog jumped up heavily, barked, and then danced in a circle again.

'Look, madam! Look!' the librarian repeated in delight. 'Oh, you little hero,' she added, with a meaningful look in Natalia's direction.

'Yes indeed,' she went on, patting Linda with the book she held in her hand, 'we actually got a medal for bravery – in the market square in Katowice.'

Natalia already knew the story of Linda the dog. During various visits to head office Miss Winczewska had managed to recount more than once the tale of how the aforementioned dog had run thirty kilometres in a deep frost in order to warn the Silesian insurgents that her mistress had been locked up by the Germans. How she had subsequently led the rebels to the gate of the prison, and how everything had ended with both heroines being decorated in the Katowice market square.

Natalia, however, was not of the opinion that one could run a library on the basis of this heroic myth. She was disconcerted and angry at herself for not knowing how to neutralize the valorous dog and that past heroism weighing so heavily on everything. It could not in fact be done.

'I've heard that story before,' she said coldly at the mention of Katowice.

'Heavens,' Miss Winczewska said, shocked and saddened. 'I don't understand . . . Once again you're talking to me as if you thought I was nothing at all.'

In response, Natalia gave the number of a book, then after a pause said as calmly as she could: 'I'm annoyed because you're reading the titles as if this were the first time you were hearing of these books and these authors.'

'The first time?' Miss Winczewska said in the tone of surprise you hear from common women when, in the middle of a shouting match, they stand abruptly with arms akimbo. 'Goodness me! The first time! I don't know how you can even say such a thing.'

And she assumed an expression that suggested she failed to comprehend what she was being accused of, but only felt indistinctly that she was in some danger. At the heart of her expression and of the way she took offence was a sort of prudent caution and a sly, almost animal-like watchfulness.

Is she simple-minded maybe? Natalia wondered to herself.

But Miss Winczewska was apparently beginning to get the point, and she manifested it in the only way she knew how. While working on one of the subsequent books she said out of the blue: 'I recently suggested this one to Jóźwik. He's our best reader. He was so grateful. "Your recommendations are always so good, ma'am," he said.'

Natalia met her words with silence.

Before long they came to the science section and Miss Winczewska tried her new method again. In checking one of the classification numbers, after a moment's reflection she read out the title: '*Research into Organic Creatures on Earth*, by Józef Sapalski.' She then exclaimed: 'Oh, excellent. I've been meaning to set this aside to read. I've wanted to for a while, because I don't know this one.'

Natalia gave her a long look.

'This one you wanted to set aside?' she asked. 'Wouldn't it be better to start with Mickiewicz?'

Miss Winczewska said nothing for a moment, her eyes straying around the walls, as if she was unable to comprehend the immensity of the peril she faced. In the end she said in her usual way:

'Heavens above! How can you talk like that. As if I didn't know Mickiewicz!'

'Come along now,' said Natalia. 'We should move on to the missing books.'

'That part'll be easy,' Miss Winczewska said cheerfully. 'We've done the most important job, and as you see, madam, everything is in order.'

Natalia lit a cigarette as she studied the strange librarian closely.

'Are you putting on an act,' she asked, 'or do you really not know what's most important here?'

'Goodness gracious – that tone again?' Miss Winczewska said in alarm. 'What do you mean, an act? I've never put on an act in my life. I know everything perfectly well,' she said a little uncertainly.

'And you really haven't noticed that only a third of the books are on the shelves?'

'What of it,' Miss Winczewska replied, recovering her aplomb. 'They're out on loan.'

'Out on loan?' Natalia said with a sour smile, for she had the worst forebodings regarding those missing books. 'Let's see how things stand with them being on loan. Bring the lending slips, please.'

A kind of panic showed on Miss Winczewska's face. Playing for time, it seemed, she suggested they go and get something to eat. It turned out it was two o'clock already.

'I'd have them bring you lunch from the mess,' she said, 'but I don't know how good it would be. The regimental tearoom, though, has really nice cold cuts. The meat is fresh every day. As for me, I don't need to eat at all. A person really lives by work alone.'

Natalia maintained a hostile silence. Right now she had no desire whatsoever for even the briefest and most superficial social contact with Miss Winczewska. After a moment, though, she changed her mind. Perhaps if they took a break and ate together she'd be better able to figure out what kind of person the librarian was.

So they went.

During the short walk to the tearoom of one of the regiments that occupied the citadel, Natalia hardly spoke at all, while Miss Winczewska's talkativeness intensified considerably.

It soon became clear that this hour of repose was an hour of triumph for Miss Winczewska, who now had the advantage over Natalia, since she knew the way, knew where things were, and could direct the other woman's steps.

'Watch out, madam,' she called, 'there's a hole here. Walk around this way. It's a short-cut. You're probably surprised the place is so deserted? The men are at the firing range. Oh yes, if you want to run a cultural centre you have to know everything!

'Oh, I hope my Linda will have cool weather like this for her hard days,' she sighed. 'German shepherd bitches don't do well in the heat in general, all the more so when they're pregnant. And she's due any day now . . .'

The dog was indeed big and heavy; all the same, she ran about in high spirits, poking about in courtyards and bushes, stopping attentively in the middle of the street, running far off, then returning obediently to heel.

'Yesterday I thought it was about to happen,' Miss Winczewska prattled on, 'but I counted up from when that husband of hers visited her, and I realized it'd be another two weeks. Oh, look, madam! Look!' she suddenly shouted. 'There's Linda's husband!'

Holding Natalia back, she pointed excitedly to a fine-looking German shepherd in a muzzle, which passed by its supposed wife with indifference, bounding stiffly towards some previously spotted goal.

'Then the puppies will be thoroughbreds,' Natalia blurted out despite herself.

'Of course. What did you expect?'

On the mustering ground, which was surrounded on all four sides by barracks, a group of soldiers were sitting on a bench in front of the guard-house, while one of their comrades stood nearby sounding reveille, facing each direction in turn. The bottom of his tunic, the colour of brown clay, had wrinkled into a little upturned frill beneath his belt at the back.

In the tearoom, another soldier in the same uniform was slouching at the counter, behind which a server in a stained white apron was bustling about. Cheese, cigarettes and chocolate were laid out in the glass display cabinets on either side of the countertop. In the window a cat slept amid empty bottles, next to a pot of wild strawberries sprinkled with sugar.

'Let's go through here, it'll be nicer,' said Miss Winczewska, and they passed into a second room. This too was almost empty. A lone corporal sat sideways at one of the tables. One elbow resting on the tabletop, the other on the arm of his chair, he was staring at his interlocked fingers. There was no trace of any food or drink on his table. After a short while the corporal stood up, stretched, and moved away. By the door he paused for a moment to light a cigarette.

Natalia ordered tea and a slice of bread, while Miss Winczewska helped herself to two smoked sausages, a portion of mustard and two slices of cake, along with a quarter pound of scraps for the dog.

'What was I saying when we came in?' she asked, spreading mustard on the sausages, then turning to the cake. She couldn't remember, so she embarked on a new topic.

'You might be worried that the butter isn't fresh. But I'd smell it a mile away. I've been terribly sensitive to bad fats ever since the Germans fed me pure margarine. And black coffee.'

Her voice trembled.

'Seventeen days, ma'am, on black coffee. Can you imagine it?'

And once again there followed the account of her heroic educational work, the Germans' entry into Katowice, her imprisonment, and so forth. When it came to the moment where Linda fetched the soldiers, who disarmed the German guards and broke open the gates of the prison, Miss Winczewska's voice failed her and she burst into tears.

'Here,' she said, wiping her eyes and rooting in her handbag. 'This is a photo of me from those times, right after I was freed. See how I look. A shadow, a ghost, not a human being. And there's Linda.'

Natalia gazed at the photograph without a word, while Miss Winczewska talked on.

'I just wish you could have seen how people loved me there in Katowice. They did everything they could to keep me, but like a fool I insisted on moving here. Why I did it, I couldn't say. I've got it coming here. I was warned from the get-go that they'd tear me to pieces. And they will. The women will,' she added meaningfully, ever bolder.

Then, wiping the tears from her blazing eyes, she began again:

'Me, though, I don't give a hoot about that. I go on working and pay no attention to the rest. And I work so hard. People ought to learn about things in detail before they pass judgement. For instance, see those flowers on the windowsill? That was all me. If it wasn't for my influence there'd be nothing there. I don't even know why I have such an influence. Officially I don't have anything to do with this tearoom, but ask the server and she'll tell you how I look out for everything here. Now, for example, there's a new commanding officer and he was going to sack the server. But I wouldn't let him. "Colonel," I said, "you can't do that to people, you have to get to know them first." Because I might be one thing or another, madam, you don't know me yet, but I can't bear to see an injustice done. That's why people respect me everywhere I go. Only a person that judges with their eyes alone might think I'm the superficial type. The new commander was like that to begin with, he'd go on about this and that and the other, then when he finally saw, he said: "And there I was thinking you only like to joke around, because you're so cheerful, yet you've done so much here." And I said to him: "Colonel, anyone who's lived through as much as I have, they have to treat life seriously."'

She stopped talking and ate the last slice of cake. Linda was roaming around the room, sniffing about, slinking under tables and into corners. Natalia was finishing her tea. In the other room, the server said to the soldier: 'I love listening to sad music. That's just how I am, I can't bear to hear anything happy.'

Soon Miss Winczewska resumed her chatter.

'I wish you would come see one of our shows someday. The shows I put on, this one corporal – that reader of ours – he said to me: "Madam, since I discovered the centre, I've stopped going into town." Though believe me, madam, organizing a show like that is a nightmare. One time, one of them came with a – you know – well, in a word, a hussy. But I put a stop to that. Right away I went and hung up these signs: "Clothes don't make the person!" "Treat your entertainments with respect!" "Keep the cultural centre pure!" And to her of course, I said: "Off with you!" They were going to ban the man that brought her, but I said, "No, gentlemen! She's the guilty one, because a woman should always remember her dignity."'

Her eyes glowed like burning caramel at these words, and a dark flush lingered on her bony face. She swallowed and rambled on.

'Honestly, you've no idea how hard it is to deal with soldiers. The worst was the orchestra; in the orchestra every musician was corrupted, so to speak . . . if I hadn't sorted them out, I don't know what would have happened. Whereas now? They're the best patrons, the best lads . . . And they're always so glad to play for me. Whether it's for a film, or a dance, I never need to worry,' she boasted, as if she wanted to get it all out while they were still at lunch.

Natalia rested her head on both hands and continued staring intently at Miss Winczewska.

Frankness is so completely ineffective against a person like this, she was thinking. What good would it do to tell her how I feel about her blather? Though actually, how *do* I feel about it? I myself couldn't say.

Meanwhile, after a longer pause Miss Winczewska leaned forward and said in a discreet undertone:

'I'm writing a play. A library play, to encourage people to read. A play with a purpose. A simple thing. I can't help it,' she added with a sigh. 'I have an artistic nature. Though it's hardly surprising, I come from an artistic family—'

At this point Natalia broke in.

'We should go,' she said, 'it's time to get back to work.'

'We should go,' the librarian agreed energetically. It wasn't clear how she interpreted Natalia's long silence. On the way back to the reading room she was ever so sociable, as if she and Natalia were two friends who'd had a delightful lunch together.

'Oh,' she said, looking at Natalia's black and white outfit, 'I love it when everything's chosen so the colours all go together. I really like what you're wearing. I ought to think about having something like that made for myself. My clothes are all worn out.'

Natalia glanced sideways and saw that the expression of cautious watchfulness had entirely disappeared from Miss Winczewska's face. She looked serene and as if already comfortable in her new circumstances.

Natalia felt her face change colour in anger at this sight.

'You ought to be thinking about the lost books,' she said sourly.

Miss Winczewska furrowed her brow.

'Dear Lord,' she grumbled, as if at a major disloyalty. 'You're starting again. What lost books?'

The state of affairs that became apparent as the work progressed turned out to be worse than Natalia had feared. A great deal of time was spent on simply sorting the disorganized lending slips. When Natalia expressed her surprise that the slips hadn't been put in order before her arrival, Miss Winczewska said: 'It's just a few silly little slips that have got mixed up, and you're making such a fuss about it. I'll fix it in no time.'

Yet she couldn't manage it. Very soon she muddled up the slips again. Natalia had to do the job herself.

In the meantime, Miss Winczewska strove to keep up the friendly atmosphere that she evidently thought she'd earned by her confidences in the tearoom.

'How do you manage to keep your hair so nicely styled like that?' she asked. 'I wish mine would stay in shape without a permanent wave. I mean, I don't have time to go all the way into town from here just for the hairdresser's, and so I end up looking like a scarecrow. Though I don't have any great ambitions in that direction, it's true.'

In a different tone, she twittered to the dog:

'My little married girl, my poor little thing, my heroine! Fetch, fetch the ball!'

The dog bounded across the room and brought from the corner not a ball, but a large grey rock that she dropped with a clunk on the floor.

When Natalia looked up at the sound, Miss Winczewska explained with a smile:

'She had a ball but she chewed it up. I had to bring her this rock . . . Do you know she reacts to numbers? When the soldiers are counting off, she always pricks her ears up and barks. "Listen, Linda! One! Two! Three! Four!" See how she jumps and yelps. It's true madam, isn't it, that she's reached the first level of being human, because she's made a sacrifice? . . . There in Katowice. I mean, for a dog to run thirty kilometres in the cold like that to save someone . . . And my Linda, who's so delicate . . .'

Natalia gave her such a cold and piercing look that Miss Winczewska fell silent.

For perhaps the first time in her life, Natalia felt a sort of urge to pound her fist on the table and shout insults. She'd always believed that only fear made people cruel. Since she was a child she'd been terrified of spiders and earwigs. When she saw one of those creatures near her, and she couldn't run away, she had to kill it, closing her eyes and perspiring from disgust and fear. Now she realized that the sight of double-dealing foolishness also spurred her to cruelty.

Bristling from the effort to control herself, she informed Miss Winczewska that it was clear from the work they'd done that the books missing from the shelves had all, one after another, either been written down incorrectly on the lending slips, or were overdue, or had long ago been returned by the borrowers and had vanished without a trace.

'Right away you're saying "without a trace",' Miss Winczewska complained, taken aback and upset.

'Well, if the books are crossed off on the borrower's card and not checked out to someone else, and yet they're not on the shelf, how can I trace them?'

'My Lord,' the librarian responded indignantly. 'I'm saying, the books are out on loan, while you keep asking where they are.'

After a moment, Natalia composed herself somewhat and in a calm voice attempted to explain to Miss Winczewska that under her system, or rather the disorder of her way of working, this wretched reading room would go to rack and ruin. At this point Miss Winczewska began to push back openly and desperately. She claimed that the opposite was true, the reading room was thriving, since you couldn't even imagine how things had been here before. With the colossal amount of work involved, a person could make a couple of mistakes, surely that was understandable. But even so, almost everything Mrs Sztumska was angry about was certainly the work of the previous librarian.

'You keep saying books are overdue. But what about this book, for instance? True, it says it was borrowed in January. But there's no year next to the date. It must have been a year and a half ago. Actually, I can tell perfectly well from the handwriting. See, that's not my writing. I write my accents like so, while hers go the other way. You can tell at once.'

'And this is also not your handwriting? And this? And this?' asked Natalia, showing her places where someone had written a January date with the current year.

Miss Winczewska peered solemnly at the slips.

'Well, yes, I won't deny that. Though . . . the day looks like it's in my writing, while the month has a different accent. But I won't argue. Who's there?' she suddenly exclaimed, listening intently. 'Excuse me, I need to go and see.'

She and the dog hurried out together. A moment later they came back.

'There wasn't anyone,' announced Miss Winczewska. 'I was convinced somebody was knocking.'

A short while later, as Natalia was poring over her notes, Miss Winczewska spoke again.

'Sorry, I have to go and check whether our professor isn't by any chance here to give his lecture. I told him it had been cancelled, but who knows, he might have come. Everyone likes to visit. Even when there's nothing on, they still come and spend time here.'

When Miss Winczewska had gone, Natalia looked around, sat up straight, sighed and rubbed her face with her hand.

The light in the room had changed. It had become warmer, had acquired a glow. Natalia looked unthinkingly out of the window. Outside, the sky had cleared. At this very moment the acacias were bathed in sunlight; they looked as if someone had suddenly dipped them in golden olive oil. The wind was easing and at times the trees were still. Then, however, it returned, shaking them back and forth.

Miss Winczewska came back with the news that someone called Michał had done a poor job of cleaning the lecture-room floor.

'Maybe it's true that soldiers can turn their hand to anything,' she complained, 'but not one of them knows how to scrub a floor with a wet brush.'

On the outside of the building, here and there the slamming of doors was heard. Before long someone began to walk across the auditorium. The steps ceased for a moment, then echoed on the boards of the stage. There was a resonant thud of the lid on the piano keyboard being opened, and immediately afterwards there came the sounds of skilled practising.

'You hear that, madam?' exclaimed Winczewska. 'Cezary's come to practise. He's in the orchestra,' she added in a confidential whisper. 'He studies at the conservatory. I wish he'd play some proper music for us.'

She cracked open the door that led to the stage.

'Cezary!' she commanded. 'Play something proper!'

Cezary, however, kept inexorably working on his exercises.

Miss Winczewska said exaltedly:

'I've been to the conservatory.'

'If you please, can you finally restrict yourself to answering my questions?' Natalia suddenly retorted.

'Lord in heaven,' said Regina Winczewska in consternation. 'No one's ever spoken to me like this in all my life. You keep treating me like I was a naughty child. I know I don't look it, but I'm almost forty.'

'You act as if you were four.'

Miss Winczewska abruptly began to cry.

'I don't know, really. You're just disrespecting me.'

'You're disrespecting yourself,' said Natalia, embarrassed and at the same time finding it hard to maintain her composure. 'A single one of these errors that are so abundant here disqualifies you, and on top of that you're beating about the bush and you won't own up.'

A flash of hope passed across Miss Regina Winczewska's frightened face.

'Not own up?' she said animatedly. 'No one can accuse me of that. Me, not admit to my own mistake? It's just that certain people won't look closely at a situation. If you'd only look closely, you'd see that, yes, there are mistakes, but it's nothing so very serious . . .'

'How exactly am I supposed to look closely?' Natalia was imprudent enough to ask.

The librarian shook her head vigorously and hastened to reply:

'It seems to me you started off wrongly, madam. Me, I'd have begun by writing out on a separate sheet of paper . . .'

Natalia stopped listening to what Miss Winczewska would have written out on a separate sheet of paper. She had immediately realized that she'd unleashed from its lair a fearful and invincible beast: the reasoning of a foolish person. It strikes every weapon from your hand, whereas it possesses only a single crippling means of attack of its own: the pulling of wool over your eyes. She sensed that if she now gave Miss Winczewska free rein to share her ideas, she would never sort things out with her. She overcame her incipient doubts and, not believing her own voice, said firmly:

'I'm not asking about that. Please stop talking.'

And all the way till eight in the evening the work went on in a silence broken only by Natalia's brief questions and Miss Winczewska's reluctant, resentfully polite responses.

Natalia did not work faster in this atmosphere of offended quiet, but she felt it was more appropriate, and she regretted not having brought about such a situation sooner.

Turns out she simply needed a good shouting at, she thought to herself.

Afterwards, however, there remained an unpleasant aftertaste, like the uncovering of a hidden vice. Natalia now had the feeling that everything in her that contained kindness and friendliness was false, since she was capable of raising her voice at someone like that. She justified it to herself by saying that you can't be easygoing with everyone. Each person is kind to some, unkind to others. Circumstances determine whether they're the one or the other.

All the same, something continued to trouble her; she couldn't help stealing sidelong glances at Miss Winczewska, though she herself wasn't exactly sure what they meant.

Winczewska, meanwhile, after refraining from speaking for quite some time, asked softly:

'I'm terribly sorry. I just wanted to ask, because I've forgotten . . . Should I be writing with a fountain pen, or can I use an indelible pencil?'

Natalia looked at her without anger.

'Just write it all down,' she said as gently as she could. And she suddenly realized with a jolt that the inner feeling of unease that was bothering her, was the fear that she had hurt Miss Winczewska badly.

The latter, as if noticing the change in Natalia's disposition, raised a finger and said, listening closely:

'I hear the roosters crowing. Oh, I hope the weather's going to clear up. Maybe it will.'

Natalia's voice was once again stiff.

'Four-hundred-and-ninety-seven?' she asked, and on receiving the reply: 'Borrower's card number 23,' she checked that book number 497 had been recorded on that card, then crossed out. The borrower had returned the book and it ought to be in its place on the shelf.

It was not, of course. Natalia checked in the inventory register to see which book had disappeared in such a way.

'Van Eeden,' she read. '*Little Johannes.*'

She recalled reading that book one hot day, lying on the grass by a flowering snowball bush. She smelled the scent, saw the colour, and heard the melody of that holiday from so very long ago.

That copy of *Little Johannes* had also gone missing.

Tearing herself away from this memory with an effort, Natalia read off the next number. Others followed.

One book had been taken out a year before and never returned. By the lending date, there was a note in the previous librarian's handwriting: Shot himself.

Natalia again looked to see which book had been kept out for such an awful reason. It was *A Man and His Dog* by Thomas Mann.

She remembered in sorrowful surprise that at about the same time this unfortunate man had borrowed the book, she herself had been lent it by a female friend. She'd read it lying in a hammock in her relatives' delightful suburban garden. She'd then passed it on in turn 'just for the day' to one of her friends, and now she realized suddenly that she'd never asked for it back.

As the review of the lending slips progressed, Natalia's irritation abated completely, and the silent librarian, who appeared even smaller than before, now seemed to her a creature worthy in the highest degree of pity.

Natalia had no difficulty at all in interpreting the other woman's sighs, and her responses delivered in a reedy murmur, as contrition and an acknowledgement, finally, of her errors.

That's all that matters to me, she thought to herself. It's a question of one's attitude to what is wrong. The wrong itself is neither here nor there.

And she felt more and more sorry for Miss Winczewska.

What do objects, books, really matter, she thought, next to the fate of a poor wretched person. After all, what does she have, this poor

Winczewska? A she-dog, and the illusion that she's surrounded by men – young men – who need something from her. And if one of them should reach out his hand not for a book, but for her herself – be it Michał who doesn't know how to scrub a floor, or Cezary who refuses to play proper music, then good Lord, it's hardly surprising if such a pleasure is more precious to her than all the libraries in the world. Or if, on the other hand, the poor woman is longing in vain to experience the thing without which, life is not life . . .

Yes indeed, Natalia was fully aware of the value of such pleasures.

She wanted to say something to Miss Winczewska to console her. She almost wished to apologize for her own brusqueness; to beg her for a little goodwill, ask her just to concentrate a bit harder.

Her anger was further mitigated by the fact that she could already see a concrete task before her: she had a clear vision of what needed to be changed and corrected here, what instructions should be issued. Anger has a place only while you're criticizing. When you actually get down to work, you sense within you an almost divine strength; you're not afraid to labour alongside the worst, most foolish person, you're confident you can make anyone good and clever.

Natalia wanted to convey this confidence to Miss Winczewska after they'd finished for the day. Yet she didn't know how to express it.

Tying her scarf around her neck she said coolly and officially:

'I'm going to come here daily. I won't leave for my holiday till we've finished the inventory, and I'll give you jobs to do for the entire summer. I won't say anything about what I found here. But if everything isn't put in order by the autumn, you won't remain here a single day longer. Up to that point you'll be dealing with me. Not as somebody from central office, but with me personally. With me.'

Natalia suddenly went red with embarrassment as she heard the pride that sounded in that 'With me'.

She was about to leave, but Regina Winczewska stepped in front of her.

'You won't tell on me?' she asked breathlessly. 'Don't go saying bad things about me . . . You'll s— . . . You'll see, everything will be fine. I'll do it all. I'll find everything . . . I'll redeem it all myself.'

As she spoke, she thrashed about like a fly stuck on flypaper yet still buzzing.

Natalia wagged her finger at her. Miss Winczewska snatched hold of the hand threatening her, then Natalia's other hand, and kissed them elatedly. She drew them to her chest, which was hard and lean as a board, and at the same time extraordinarily hot. Natalia flushed. 'That's enough,' she said and shook her finger again from the doorway.

Miss Winczewska ran after her, followed by the dog.

As they crossed the stage, the soldier playing his exercises stood up and bowed, then sat back down and, without interrupting his playing, watched until Natalia, the librarian and the dog had left the auditorium.

At the stairs, Miss Winczewska and the dog turned back home.

Natalia set off on her own.

The street was deserted and clearly little used; weeds grew between the flagstones of the pavement. Seeing no one around, Natalia immediately began to hum loudly to herself. As she did so she made a vague movement with her hand, and even skipped along for a few steps like a little girl.

'What am I doing,' she whispered, almost bursting into laughter; it was only when she came out onto the bridge over the moat that she curbed these manifestations of a crazy joyfulness.

It was at this moment too that she realized what she was happy about. She was happy because Miss Winczewska had not been offended, she'd kissed her hands, she'd shown contrition and a willingness to improve. And the world around was also full of joy. The wind had died down. The sky was clear and unsullied, as if it had never once been touched by a shroud of clouds. In the stillness, the slight chill in the air could not be felt. The green of the moat and flanks of the citadel was already in shadow. Only the tops of the tallest trees were bathed in a ruddy glow. Far away, the harmonious buzz of the city could be heard as it glittered in colours of fleshy pink and violet.

Along the side of the street, cutting across the view of the city, a crimson tram passed by, its windows ablaze with the golden gleam of the sunset.

'It's like one of those evenings when I was little,' whispered Natalia in delight. And, as if endowed anew with the receptive sensibilities of her childhood years, she stood on the bridge and gazed insatiably into the fresh greenery in the moat. Then, all of a sudden, she was assailed once more by misgivings.

'How could I have let myself be taken in like that,' she said virtually aloud. 'It was nothing but a classic ploy of small-time wrongdoers, little people introducing confusion into the air around them. There was even a historic legend, as there always is in such cases.'

No, no, she thought. My anger was righteous; my anger was righteous.

She sought to rekindle it, set it alight again. Yet instead of righteous anger, a powerful sympathy was burgeoning uninvited in her heart.

Tomorrow, she consoled herself, more things will come to light that'll make me lose my temper again. At that point I'll tell her that I wanted to let her keep her job, but I can see it isn't going to be possible. And I'll send a report of the inspection to central office, and submit my recommendation that the Winczewska woman be relieved of her duties.

She's throwing dust in our eyes . . . what of it?, the thought emerged from beneath her resolutions. After all, there are animals that, when cornered, emit a noxious odour. Is it their fault? They're just trying to defend themselves and stay alive. And in some ways it's reasonable, they have a right to exist.

Natalia was often troubled by the notion that wrong can never be uprooted, nor can it be fully made good. Rather, it's cancelled out somehow, equalized by right things, which are found in the same abundance throughout the world. Yet this balancing process is not perceived at the level of an individual human existence, and those who witness the sowing and reaping of wrong do not get to see that dimension of justice.

Still, whether they see it or not, a poor wretch has no other choice than to sow right or wrong. But what is the right or the wrong actually supposed to be with regard to Miss Winczewska?

Grab her by the scruff of the neck, force her to work hard the way anyone should, straighten out that befuddled head of hers somehow or other. Don't let her rest. Just don't let her rest, till everything is clear as crystal. Whether that's right or wrong, I don't know how to do things otherwise, Natalia reflected, her thoughts as if aflame.

And the desire to accomplish this feat overwhelmed her for a moment, with a thrilling power that was almost like the rapture of someone in love.

All at once she realized how it would all end. The reading room would more or less function, Miss Winczewska would regain her self-confidence, and only then take offence at what had happened today. At the association there'd be a big to-do about how Natalia had ignored official procedure, forcibly taken charge of the citadel reading room, and was ruling the roost there; Miss Winczewska would create a new legend for herself.

Well, so be it, Natalia thought to herself, superstitiously accepting the notion. The sacred law of the collective demands it. After all, that law exists in order to protect the small and the weak. And no doubt it must be so.

Immersed in her musings, Natalia didn't notice that she had walked through the gateway.

'Pass!' the soldier shouted after her.

She turned around, and presenting the pass to the dark outstretched hand, said:

'Sorry, here it is.'

As she left the confines of the citadel, she saw her tram waiting to begin its route. She quickened her pace, broke into a run.

She hopped onto the car just as it was setting off. Jerked by the movement, she staggered and dropped down out of breath into the first seat she came to.

Across from her sat a man in a workman's jacket. He was holding a bunch of white stock in his lap. His head drooped heavily.

Where on earth can he be taking those flowers? Natalia wondered. I feel so sorry for him. What does it mean that I feel sorry for everyone?

Through the windows, for a brief moment as the tram turned towards the city the huge ruddy disk of the sun appeared above a strip of violet haze.

The conductor tapped Natalia on the shoulder.

'Ticket, madam?'

'Panna Winczewska'
First published as part of the collection *Znaki życia* (*Signs of Life*), 1938.

BEATA OBERTYŃSKA

1898–1980

Beata Obertyńska grew up near Lwów as the daughter of a poetically gifted mother and an engineer father, surrounded by their writer and artist friends. Her mother taught her the discipline needed to put her natural poetic talent and imagination to effect. She and her siblings enjoyed devising and performing plays for their domestic theatre. In 1919 her brother, Ludwik, was killed during the Ukrainian–Polish war, the archetypal hero dying for Poland.

In 1918, Beata married landowner Józef Obertyński, but they proved unable to have children, and the marriage fell apart. For the rest of her life, Obertyńska was deeply devoted to her sister's children. Independent and creative, she belonged to the lively literary world of the interwar years and soon built a career as an acclaimed poet. In the 1930s she acted professionally.

When the Red Army invaded Poland in 1939, her world collapsed. Many Poles were deported to remote wastelands. Arrested in July 1940, Obertyńska was imprisoned in a series of dismal, crowded cells. Transported by cattle car, she ended up at Vorkuta, the grimmest Soviet prison camp north of the Arctic Circle. When Germany attacked the USSR in 1942, the Poles were released and could travel south to join 'Anders' Army'. After a harrowing journey, Obertyńska reached the mustering point, and became a lieutenant in the Women's Auxiliary Service.

During the journey south with the army through the Middle East, she was tasked with writing a memoir of her ordeal. The result, *W domu niewoli* (*In the House of Slavery*, 1946), bears testimony to the atrocities of the prison camps and the lies of Soviet propaganda. Throughout her tribulations she continued to write poetry, often shaped by her experiences.

Reunited with her sister and brother-in-law, she settled in London, where they lived together for the rest of their lives. Obertyńska refused to set foot in socialist Poland. She continued to write, publishing poetry, short stories and other fiction, including a Gothic novel. Her sister, Lela Pawlikowska, became a society portrait painter, specializing in portraits of children, including one of the three-year-old Diana Spencer.

Although 'Babka' is about an uneducated village woman, it expresses Obertyńska's own sense of loss and nostalgia for the Poland of her youth.

Antonia Lloyd-Jones

Babka

Translated by Antonia Lloyd-Jones

The woman to whom I'd like to dedicate this recollection was far from being a famous personage. Famous personages are usually distinguished by the fact that they habitually make sure in advance, and in person, that they will be remembered posthumously. The way they do it is by starting to be famous during their lifetime.

But nobody knew Walentyna Buczko. Naturally, her son, with whom she lived, knew her. So did several of his friends, and so did we (their next-door neighbours), two or three Englishwomen, the grocer, the milkman and the cat. I can quite boldly rule out the postman. Who on earth would have sent Walentyna Buczko a letter?

In saying nobody knew her, naturally I'm leaving out her former friends and 'countrymen' who lived in the small village she was from – I don't even know its name – near Grodno, or Białystok. Such people were of no consequence any more. All that was like something from another dimension – from another planet, quite simply from a previous incarna- tion. Walentyna Buczko's sole, chafing reality was England, and the fact that London is not a small, godforsaken hole outside Grodno or Białystok; as she put it, 'Lord God Almighty! You'll never see the end of it!'

The first time I saw her in the street in front of me – like a narrow, solemn pillar of wool, with her eyes fixed on the pavement – I hadn't a shadow of doubt that she was Polish. Especially the headscarf! Thick, with several layers, black wool, folded at each temple and at each jawbone too, tightly crossed under the chin and tucked into a black overcoat. No bright colours. No feather duster stuck in the hat. Nothing plastered on the face – so definitely not an old Englishwoman!

'You're Polish, aren't you?'

'Yes, thanks be to God, missy, Polish!' she confirmed with delight, avidly inspecting us with her small, friendly eyes. The frown and the ominous set of her toothless mouth that had struck me a moment ago was gone without trace. 'Oh, how lovely to meet folks from home! Do you ladies live nearby?'

'Yes, right here . . .'

'I live at number fourteen. In the *suteren*. What they call the "basement". There are lots of Poles in this neighbourhood. So sometimes there's someone to chat to. For I don't know a word of English, missy. And somehow it's clear to me I'll die with nothing but Polish. I'm . . . too old. Or too dense. But so what?' She smiled knowingly. 'In heaven they understand Polish anyway, probably better than the language spoken here, and in the shop I get by with signs . . . Pardon me, ladies, but what parts are you from?'

And so our friendship began.

We usually met on the short stretch between our gateways and the grocer's or the baker's, at least on weekdays. On Sundays we shared a longer walk to church. I don't know if it was her eyesight, her hearing or her legs that were failing the old girl by now, or perhaps it was just the speed of the traffic that frightened her, but suffice it to say that crossing the road was always sheer torment for her. So she often aimed for the same time as we did. Tightly clutching one of our elbows, she would forge over the crossing at a trot, with her knees bent low, as fast as possible – anything to get to the opposite pavement.

'And why hurry all the time? In the past nobody was ever in such haste and it was better. If it weren't for the traffic an old person could go to vespers a good many times on their own . . . But as it is, it's impossible to push your way through this thicket, where you can't even tell who's hooting and why!'

At church Walentyna Buczko had her own regular seat. Not one with a metal plaque, of course, but one that even without a plaque was never occupied, because it was the worst seat in the entire church. Just below the swinging door that opened non-stop and kept banging shut, causing an endless stream of cold air to flood that back pew – a seat so far from the altar that I doubt whether her tear-filled eyes could see the priest at all. Possibly the candles. Luckily she didn't need to hear the sermon; she wouldn't have understood it anyway.

'It's my only consolation – the church. But this one is too big. It's clean and rich, true, but I preferred our ones. Wooden. If a church is smaller, the Lord God is that much closer . . . But praise the Lord for this one too. In Kazakhstan there weren't none. All that time!'

And as if wanting to make up for those years, the toughest period in her exile, she would remain in church for two or three Holy Masses, sometimes in a row, resigning herself in advance to the danger of crossing the road on her own. But sometimes she left at the same time as we did.

And it was on those occasions – on the way to church or on the way back, during our long chats outside her gate or ours – that I learned Walentyna Buczko by heart, just as one learns a tune or a poem one has no way of noting down; I learned her consciously, carefully, well aware that I was 'recording' on the tape of memory, that I was catching, preserving something unique.

The tales told us by 'Babka' – as we called her, meaning something in between 'the old girl' and 'Granny' – charmed us by being compellingly vivid, and we were equally enchanted by her language – full of mistakes and distortions, full of foreign loan-words and peculiar syntax – something I shall try to recreate in the monologues cited below as accurately as I can, but which without her facial expressions, gestures and emphasis will be neither complete nor faithful. Possibly something even worse will happen – she will cease to be herself.

Babka liked to talk. In fact, talking was the only thing that brought her any relief. The only way to expel the poison that chronically festered inside her – her constant concern for Poland and for the Church in Poland, her sympathy for the people suffering there, her yearning for her native land. This was always the bottom line, the background, the source, the beginning and the end for her. She was already so steeped in this torment, so exhausted by waiting, so childishly irritated by England and so helpless in everything, that sometimes she almost choked. Condemned to solitude for days on end, she hungrily lay in wait for one of the 'folks from home', to have at least a chinwag with them. So the trade was in both directions: hers was relief at talking, and for the other person there was the gain of listening.

But she never imposed herself. She had incredibly sensitive intuition and knew perfectly well whether our 'folks from home' had time right now, or were in a hurry.

'Well, well . . . This is all we have today . . . Just enough time to praise the Lord. I won't keep you,' she'd say, giving me a friendly nod as I passed the prison bars of her basement trapdoor. 'God be with you, missy, God be with you.'

On the other hand she was grateful and full of relief whenever she could pour out her heart, and then she would bid us farewell with a special formula, very much her own.

'Thank you, madam, for my having seen you . . .'

I don't know how Babka comported herself in the past. For all I know the proximity of Grodno or Białystok or wherever it was had ousted the last of the traditional costumes from her native village long ago. Now – after all those years in the wilderness, wandering in Asia, Africa and then Europe again, during which she had often had to accept gifts from international charitable organizations – apart from her headgear, there wasn't a shadow of folklore left in her. Against the streets of London, her black costume and the headscarf she wore, both winter and summer, stood out incongruously.

She had enormous hands, worn hard and dry by work, lumpy with arthritic growths, and her feet must have been even more outsized. She put them down flat, the entire sole at once, the way one puts down an iron. Walking alongside her, it always felt as if those great black boots of hers probably weighed more than the rest of her scrawny body. In the manner of a nun, she usually slipped her hands into her sleeves, and in a similar way, as she walked, she looked from above at the pavement just ahead of her. Walentyna Buczko was like a member of a third order.

There was something remarkably nun-like about her entire behaviour in church. She went numb. She switched off. She was like a house with the blinds down. Centripetal, seeing no one, she sat up straight in that back pew, looking dignified, never moving an inch. Never leaning her back against it, never with her elbows hooked on the rest in front, with her eyes fixed on the distant altar, probably without blinking. Out of pure reverence and concentration.

There she is in my memory – a small, immobile post, standing beneath a pillar with a dignity and devotion for which I cannot find words. A matt-black droplet against the motley coloured mush of the more distant pews, in whose blackness and stillness was solidified all the suffering, injury and bitterness, all the yearning and all the grandeur of the chronic, distressing, perhaps expiatory penance for which God had chosen, judged and destined her.

Naturally, she was quite unaware of this. She was one of those wonderfully simple, humble souls, whose own greatness is forever unfamiliar to them.

To many other issues she had a very well-formed, though special approach, typical of minds that are left to discover and construct the world for themselves.

'Learning, I didn't have much learning ... Only reading and writing, and a little of that arithmetic. On occasion later in life I were sorry to be so benighted. But missy, the Lord God knows what He gives a person. Maybe if I'd gone further into those books I'd have found a place in my mind to store all the rubbish from them? Don't books leave lots of rubbish in your mind? Different folks learn differently. This one this way, that one that, and you don't make it all out at once, for where are you to get the insight when you're young? Perhaps I were better off after all: not being learned, but not going daft from too much wisdom either ...'

Despite this mistrustful approach to knowledge, Babka loved to read. Her eyes were already weak by this time, so she'd borrow a book and keep it for weeks, but she always asked for 'something good to read' again. She said that in her youth she'd got into the habit of books. At the local manor, 'their countess' (could it have been Kossakowska?) had a lending library for the village, and one could take out a new book every Saturday. She'd done plenty of reading in those days! In winter. In the evenings. Aloud.

'There were two things I liked, missy. Besides the church, because the church takes first place of course. Reading, and weaving kilim rugs. Our village produced lots of kilims. I remember that as soon as I sat at the loom I'd forget the whole world ... We made beautiful kilims. Brightly coloured. Large. Flowers, or some other pattern. Each woman who wove had her own design. From her mother, or her grandma, or from even further back. And each stuck to the one style for good. It ran in families. And some knew how to dye the wool too. The old people best of all ... Those kilims were beautiful. There were one I'd woven myself, and that night, when the deportation happened, I ripped it off the wall and threw it on the sledge. We were ready to move off when I raced into the house for that kilim! In case of frost. For there was frost. I lived off it for three months at the settlement in exile later on. For the life of me, I were so sorry to sell it! Like a part of myself. But what could I do? Some nights I still dream about that kilim. And for sure, it'd be jollier for me in that basement if I'd brought it all the way here. Just to look at. Just for the memories. In England they don't make kilims. Here everything's from the shop. Ready-made. On a plate. Not like at home, where everyone makes their own – for themselves – in their own way . . .'

'Can you please tell me, missy, what on earth is going on? The English folks ain't done me no harm, but somehow I don't like them at all. They're so foreign, for the life of me! Our fellows, even if they're strangers, have something about them that makes them a friend at once. But those folks? They seem polite. I can't say. But what are you to do, when you can't feel the heart in them? And it makes a person take a crooked view of them too. What's that about? In all justice, if it weren't for their grants we'd have to live from hand to mouth here. But they give the money. Not very much, but they give it. But a person remembers nothing at all, except that it's not Poland here! How are they to blame? And thanks to the grief and the hurt – you know what, missy? – I don't like nothing about this England . . . Not the people, nor the church, nothing. At home, in the village, as soon as I went past the fence – the road ran right under my cottage – the main road – then I knew there were plenty of space, a view and enough room, I knew there were something to look at, and that's the truth, our village was large and beautiful – but this London – dear madam! It's so small, so cramped, so – may God protect us – so narrow in all directions! There's nothing to please a person here. And worse. It breeds anger in him. Do you know that, missy? I'm sorry to say it . . . What harm has the English grass done me? But I don't even like the grass here! Just because it's not ours. Not Polish. Not our own. God Almighty! When I bring back the memories! The sight of the young grass at home in the spring! It was under the gooseberries that it first came up, so I remember . . . You'd want to stroke it, just for being so new. But here? Here the grass isn't green, the salt isn't salty, nor the sugar sweet! And that's why something's gone wrong in a person. Not by choice, he's just not granted otherwise . . . And that's why there's the struggling. And the petitioning. And the anger . . .'

And it was true. Babka had periods of blind rebellion, bitterness, total immersion in pain. And others when she was full of mature resignation, when she surrendered, and found meaning and purpose even in things beyond her understanding. Sometimes she struggled for whole weeks on end, like a wretched linen sheet withering on the fence that the wind will not let live in peace; even if it settles down for a while, it'll be sure to spring up again to flap even harder. Yet her humble returns from the open sea of rancour and petitioning God involved moving persistence, compulsion and indomitable loyalty to the same site of a returning wave. She wanted to walk away, but she could not. She raged, frowned, and was overcome by bitterness – then fell face down, onto the one, safe shore she knew, once again resigned to all and ready for anything.

'Glory to God the Almighty, thanks be to the Lord! What would a person do if He weren't there? He'd waste away – he'd go to ruin, with no consolation or blissfulness . . . But He's there! Praise the Lord – He's there! And though in your distress sometimes you might bite Him, He'll never drive you away. A dog sometimes bites the hand that feeds him. Out of stupidity. And a person is not always wiser than an animal, though he has an eternal soul and though the Lord Jesus died for him on the cross. But the Lord God is patient . . . What is He to do? He won't do away with everyone at once, for He has pity. So He waits. Oh my. For the better among us to come to their senses. I speak for myself, I know it. I must expect great patience from the Lord God, otherwise woe is me! And if only I were better in old age! When I am not! For so it is: I remember, when I were still in Poland, when I were young, at home, when the Bitter Regrets Mass came, or when I prayed the Way of the Cross – madam! Many a time I thought my heart would break, I felt so sorry for our Lord Jesus! Now – here – in this exile, whenever I pray the Way of the Cross – do you know what? I weep! So much! I weep so much that sometimes I can't see the Stations – but I weep for myself! For no one but myself! So bad has a person become because of all this pain. A person fails to remember how much He suffered for us, he fails to remember Him, but only thinks of himself! Oh my. How can one treat the Lord God without patience? He won't execute everyone at once. He has pity. So He waits. What is He to do?'

'I am simple and not learned, missy. Except they taught me to read and write (and to keep a smallholding, though that's of no use in England now, is it?). I may be dim, but sometimes I do some thinking for myself. How can I not think when I'm alone for days on end? My son's at work, and I'm in the basement, like I'm in a grave, not a word to anyone . . . So sometimes, of an evening, I go out and sit by the pavement. With my rosary. My only gain is to say my prayers. But you can't protect yourself from thinking – even if you wanted to. And there's no good comes of that thinking! When there's such heaviness in the heart, it's better for the head not to think. For wherever you start, you'll always come back to one thing. Why has all this happened to us? Mighty God! What have they done to our poor Poland? What sort of an authority have they handed it over to? To forbid children to learn about God? To shove priests into prison, like somewhere in Russia? And why has such divine retribution come upon us? For what reason? Are we really so much worse than others? Have we really antagonized God so much that He has had to scowl on us like this? Surrender us into such hands? I've seen enough of Russia that I don't need to say a word! Now it's as though all Poland has been sent into exile! But for what? For sure, everyone's a sinner. Everyone's guilty. But if everyone is, then what about all these people?' With a sweeping gesture she pointed at the street. 'For them, the war has been and gone. They bled like everyone else. Their streets took quite a beating, it's true. But it came to an end, and now there's peace. Nobody was driven out of their home. Nobody scattered them about the whole world like, with your forgiveness, dung in the spring. And not just for a year, or two, or three. Let it be five! But for such a long time it becomes unbearable! Hard as you try, you can't hold out for so long and keep a kind heart.'

'For it's like this, missy: I weren't rich at all. Anyone who says otherwise would be lying. But I weren't no landless tenant neither. There was the cabin – you could even call it a cottage, because it had stone walls and a tin roof, and it stood on the main road – there was a garden, not large, but with a picket fence, and behind the cabin there was an orchard. I had this one pear tree in it – "young ladies", they called them – such a fine tree that one year when it had a good crop, every branch had to be supported with a prop, and even so the props snapped. The people in the village were familiar with that pear tree of mine. So were the fruit farmers from the town. Oh my! And so were the wasps! Mighty God! The wasps guarded it better from

the local boys than a dog. It was a very excellent pear tree . . . I had a good
piece of field, but far from the house, at the very edge, by the forest. It was
a half-hour walk, though maybe at harvest or when there was going to be
a storm it was shorter. I were almost twenty-three years old when I were
widowed. With two children. My husband was very weak in the chest. He'd
work as if there were nothing wrong, but he'd cough and cough, he got as
thin as a rake, until one day coming up to the spring he died. May the Lord
grant him eternal rest . . . He wasn't a bad man – I can't say any more than
that he was fourteen years older than I and had that weak chest . . . His
mother and I were left alone to keep the smallholding. Madam! Fancy what
it means for two women to run a whole farm, with little ones still in the
cabin! His mother was already getting on in years, but she was robust and
carried herself straight, like a young woman. There was a horse. There was
a cow. We always fed two pigs: one for sale, the other for the winter, not to
mention the poultry. We had some. As did every cabin . . . But there were
only ever two pairs of hands to do the work and two pairs of eyes to do the
minding. If the neighbours hadn't helped us there'd have been trouble with
the harvest. But they did help. Fair exchanges. Everything as it should be
between households. In neighbourly fashion. A courtesy for a courtesy . . .
It was tough. I'm not complaining – God forbid – but the work had no
reason to complain about me either . . . A person never got enough sleep,
sometimes not enough to eat . . . Not that we went without – there simply
wasn't the time or the thought. And so just the two of us kept it all going.
My mother-in-law and I. But she was a rare woman, you won't find her
type with a candle in daylight . . .'

Somehow that round lump of a face, old and tired – with no eyelashes
or eyebrows and with yellow, glassy skin, like the peel on a baked apple –
emanated a huge range of expressions, and of such power!

She was silent. For a long while the sunken scar of her mouth flickered,
and as she focused her thoughts, between the folds of her brow something
kept moving, laboriously but consciously. She shifted to a different tone.

I think a similar change takes place inside an organ when the organist
changes register. When from a brighter tone the music is to drop into a
gloomy, more solemn one . . .

*

'In the countryside they say: *Husband's mother, strife and bother*, only that,' she began slowly. 'They plainly don't speak the truth. Because nowadays in all justice I can attest that everything good I have learned in my life was from her. On the farm and at church and in the house. For she was wise, you won't find another like her! Where did she get it from? God alone knows. But maybe it was from Him, because she couldn't even read. The oldest men in the village used to come to her for advice. The chief himself. If anyone were going to tell the truth to someone's face, or to their conscience, if anyone needed reconciling, or if there was a match to be made in God's honest way – she was the one! As for spinning, baking the best bread, healing, helping with a birth – I don't even need to say. She could do everything . . . And what beautiful kilims she taught me to weave! And what lovely songs! At church she knew all the hymns better than the organist did. Even hymns that no one else knew any more. Ancient. Long ones. The loveliest for Lent. All her wisdom came from the Lord God. Oh my. Without the Lord God, we have nothing. And we'd pray for the souls in purgatory too . . . I remember as if it were today. We'd go into the field – just the two of us, at daybreak, when there was still dew on the boundary strips, drops the size of peas, and skylarks so high up you could hardly hear them, whenever we went into the field like that – and we had to go out before dawn to reap all the day long – before we touched the work, his mother always knelt on the bare earth, so she did, she told me to kneel and then out loud she recited the "Angel of the Lord" for the dead who worked before us on this piece of land, and said this land was theirs . . . She was very mindful of the souls of the dead . . . very much so. I had such great respect for her that when she died – because I weren't so old when she died, and they still wanted to marry me off – I wouldn't hear a word of it. As if it would come to that, as if as soon as she closed her eyes I'd start looking around for a man to fill the cabin! Oh no! Anyway, how could I have thought of such a thing at the time? It was around that time that my daughter began to weaken. In the chest, like her father. Oh, madam! How I wept for her! How much I spent on doctors – and then what? Somehow on the Feast of Our Lady of the Rosary she reached the age of sixteen, and on the eve of the Ascension we held her funeral. Sixteen years old! In her bloom! So full of life! And into the ground . . .'

*

If Walentyna Buczko had known how to cry, at times life would certainly have been easier for her. But she couldn't do it. She could *no longer* do it. Her eyes – small and bleary like the eyes of an old dog, hidden beneath her puffy, lashless eyelids – looked as if they had been bankrupt, in terms of tears, long ago. Every emotion showed in her through a trembling of the chin and a sudden, blotchy redness around her drooping mouth. Weeping in the past had left her with the habit of hastily wiping her nose with the tail of her scarf, tied under her chin. Now it was just a sort of shorthand, a conventional gesture, a symbol.

'Dear madam! What a child she was! I can hardly speak. As an infant, and around the house, and in her illness. She was so patient! Even when she could hardly breathe she never complained. She didn't want to show me. That's what she was like. And as for her death, missy, she foretold her own death to the very hour, I give you my most sacred word. "Don't cry, Mama," says she, "I won't die today. Our Lady has told me it won't be today." How can I know if that was a delusion brought on by fever, or for real? "When was she here?", I ask. "Just now. She was standing here, at the foot of the bed," says she. "And she gave me this, look," she says to me. I look, but there's nothing there. I can see the child is cradling her fingers to show me something, like someone scooping water in both hands . . . But there's nothing to see. "She gave me a rosary. So lovely. All of gold," says she. "Look, Mama, it's sending a bright light right across the ceiling," she says. But where, where can I, sinful as I am, see anything of the kind? I can see nothing, because the tears have blinded my eyes. "Don't cry," she says. "By Ascension Day I will be in heaven. But I shall only die on Saturday. On Saturday night." And so it was. Word for word. I thought I would weep out my soul for her. The graveyard was just beyond the village. On a hill. It was a pretty graveyard. A little overgrown, perhaps, but sloping nicely towards the sun. I buried her beside her father. Oh my. One beside the other. And I put up a gravestone with a cross and added an inscription. All that's due to the dead. And every year from then on I cut the grass around the grave with a sickle myself, and whitewashed the cross, so it shone from afar. At some point in the second spring, as I remember it – that's to say, as she died in August, by March the next year – I planted peonies on the grave. I dug up a bush from in front of the window and planted it on the child's grave. Let her have it! The most beautiful thing I had. But also because it was the peony of all peonies! Such beauties! One big bouquet when it bloomed. So whenever Corpus Christi was coming, the priest knew in advance that no one but Walentyna Buczko would decorate the entire altar from her garden. A whole altar from one bush! It was pink, semi-double and scented! Like a rose! The child liked to gaze at that flower in life, so let her enjoy it after death too, that's what I said to myself. Quite so! And for a long time she enjoyed it. It's terrible to think what sort of people there are in the world! How evil and base. Some time – not two years had gone by – I came to the graveyard, I looked at the grave – and my legs almost gave way. Christ the Lord! My peony had been ripped from the grave and stolen! Have you ever heard the like? From a graveyard! Stealing from a grave! To think they did not fear God. I tell you, madam, I fell face down into that fresh pit, I were out of my mind for weeping. I thought no one on earth could be as unhappy as I. First my husband, then his mother, then my daughter, and last of all the peony! In his grief a person muddles everything. When things are so hard for him, when the Lord God does nothing but lashes and lashes him, he ends up not knowing what matters and what doesn't. Now that He has fully pressed me to the ground, I wouldn't weep about a silly bush, I wouldn't find the tears inside myself. I've cried them all out. To the last drop. In Kazakhstan, in India, in Africa and lastly here, in this England, in this basement . . .' She waved a hostile hand towards the steps disappearing into the damp abyss beyond the pavement.

'What is it about a person that means on home ground everything's different? I weren't rich at all. And I had to work hard. I had no experience of youth, nor of joy, nothing but work and more work . . . Well, true, there was the church! That was my entire escape, my consolation, my joy. But although I weren't rich I were respected even so. Because by the time my mother – my husband's mother – died (I won't say I ever had her wisdom, God forbid!) I'd learned so much from her that afterwards they respected me too. And that in turn taught me to respect myself! You see what a person is like? But then the whole farm stood behind me, that piece of field and the house and the livestock I looked after, and my son who was already going to school – so I were the sole mistress, so to speak. So I were. As you know, missy, now they came to me for advice. Were they really going to ask me too what to do and how? And I – on home ground – said straight to their faces what was on my mind – to each one, even the chief – and I feared no one and asked no one for charity – off my own bat, somehow I were so wise that today I can hardly believe it. Because here – oh, missy! – I'm so dim that I can't say a word! You go here – they don't understand. You go there – they stare at you like a calf staring at a new gate. Here's a bag lady, they think. And how are they not to think it? All this makes me sit quietly in this cave, and it's a good thing if I get any work from anyone. Darning, patching, sometimes I put together some belts for a shop, which I've learned to do quite well now. And so it goes, month after month, year after year. I ain't seen a crop – like in a field – for eight years now! Not a single little blade of wheat! In the past, at the start, when I were in the hostel, I did have a small garden plot. Now there's nothing, just concrete and more concrete, concrete wherever you move, still wet too. Oh, missy! I give you my most sacred word. Many a time it has occurred to me' – at this point she would lower her voice and glance at me furtively, inquiringly, almost suspiciously, before continuing – 'perhaps I'm already in Purgatory? Perhaps this is no longer life? Perhaps I've long since been doing my penance after death? That I would understand. If this is penance, so be it. But like this?'

'Did you not read in their English papers what will become of us? Shall we ever return to our beloved Poland or not? Will they ever free it from that grip, or have they betrayed it for ever and ever amen? Sometimes I feel so homesick I can't look it in the eyes. Either let me die or let me go home! Let there be an end to it. I probably haven't got long to go now anyway, one way or the other. Seventy-one years old. I'm old. But oh my God! How I'd like to go back! If only for half an hour! Just enough to run around everything, see it all, touch it with my hand. I think things will only be as good again in heaven. Even in winter, though our winter is long. But so what, when the house was protected, the windows were sealed with moss and there was plaited straw right around the door to stop the draught from the hall blowing underfoot. It was nice and warm. Well, the days were short. But as soon as the thaw came, the hens started pushing their way into the sunshine by the window, so the room was darker because of them – then we knew spring was coming. Even an early one. However many springs you have behind you, you feel joy at each one, as if it's the first. Nothing but joy. Oh my. And when our beloved Easter came! When everything was whitewashed after the winter, the windowpanes washed, the floors scrubbed, when a person had been to confession – there was nothing but sky and sky! So light. So good. So nice. And then there were the bells too – oh, madam!'

She stalled; for a while she couldn't speak for emotion. Because happiness typically only makes one happy at first hand. Something of the kind must have occurred to her too.

'If only a person were capable of doing things differently, missy. He thanks the Lord God Almighty for all that's good, but as soon as he's looking back at it from behind he weeps. Why? Because it's gone? It was bound to go. Everything has its end. But I'll tell you the truth, missy, sometimes it's sweet to have a cry for the good things. Oh my. It's worse for those who have nothing to weep for. But I do have something to weep for and to remember. I'd be lying if I said I hadn't. Sometimes I walk about the house in my thoughts as someone else would use their legs. And I feel both good and bad. I myself don't know how. I remember how I'd get up early in the morning . . . The windows are still misted, but if it's a cold night the weather's more certain. First thing – the fire. Summer or winter – first thing. It's ready, laid yesterday, you just have to put a match to it. The ash pan is clean and the kitchen properly swept. Just as it should be. However late it is, I would never, ever go to bed until everything's clean and in order. Then it's easier to get up for the day too. While Mother was alive, we'd start saying the Hours at once. Over our work. Each at her own task. Sometimes I'd be in the stable, she'd be in the room, but with the window open, so we could hear. Later she'd be in the shed going for the kindling and I'd be in the loft, going for the hay, but the boards weren't so soundproof, and again we were separate but together . . . So, as I remember, we'd often weave our way through the entire house with those Hours, like a woollen yarn! Both household work and praise for the Lord. Each on our own, but together. And it was happiness. And although it was work, it was joy. Because work is happiness too. Sometimes I think it's the greatest happiness – work. As long as you're on your own ground. And working the land. In the countryside people are different. More sincere. Not so loath towards God's commandments as those in the city. Not so giddy. Not in such a hurry. For in the countryside it's like this: either a person works, or he waits. Surely? He sows, then waits. He plants, then waits. There can be no kind of hurry about it. If he's working, he's doing what the Lord God Almighty foretold from the start: "By the sweat of your brow will you have food to eat", He says. And that's all right. So he works. And as he waits again, first he exercises patience, and second, he has more time to examine God's world. A man from the city is where – where? He neither sees nor knows, or has any thoughts . . . Anyway . . . perhaps he does have some thoughts, but they're different. City ones. In the city they think like this: you want flour – you go to the corner shop. You want barley – you go to the corner shop. The corner shop – that's their entire wisdom. But having to think how and what – God forbid! They only know how to buy. In the village it's not like that. In the village you can learn from anything. You take a bean pod, for instance. Beans like any other. To one man it's nothing, to someone who doesn't look and doesn't know that everywhere, at every step there's something to bow to the Lord God for . . . To someone like that it's nothing. But a man who has worked hard to grow those beans and has sweated – he knows! He shells the pod – my God! But who painted this bean like that? Each one different. Each one dappled. Blue and black and white. What little beauties! A painted egg is so much bigger, so you must toil all the more for it to come out neat. A large seed is just as beautifully designed as the smallest. All by itself. By order of the Lord God Almighty. By His will and reason. Oh, my!'

'So what's the truth, missy? There are bad people. And if they're bad they should be punished. But why doesn't it work the other way? Why doesn't a person who's good here on earth have a good life? I am old now and have seen enough. And I can see that not just the bad suffer, missy, not just the bad . . . But few people – the good ones – are protected from divine retribution. As for heaven – I can't say. In heaven everyone will have their just reward. But why don't people understand that down here? Why are people so blind that they can't see none of the injustice around them? Because justice exists – it has to – but it's different, unknowable, not for human dimness. How can that not be so, when the Lord God rules everything? Surely? The Lord God to his own, man to his own. Why, why, nothing but why and for what? If only the Lord God would give man a different understanding, everything would be easier. I'm not saying easy, but a little easier. Man seems to know all this – but he doesn't! Over and over he keeps trying to explain it all to himself, as if to someone else. For that is the greatest thing, but it's hard – never to ask the Lord God why on earth this is so, and why on earth that? It's enough that He knows. But who among people is so wise that in his pain he doesn't press Him in his own cause? Perhaps only the Blessed Virgin. She alone never asked. Not for anything. Well . . . but she was She! And what are we?'

I no longer remember exactly when, but around late spring we all noticed that Babka was looking very unwell, moving with more difficulty, falling silent more often while talking as she endured the surges of emotion that came over her. In short, that she was in a bad way.

One day, her son approached me at the bus stop. 'My mother is waning,' he said. 'She hasn't got up for a week now. She has some mending ready to be returned. Perhaps you'd drop in . . .'

I did drop in. Or rather down. Eight concrete steps down. And then, well below the street, there was a nook full of rubbish bins, mostly with open lids. A sweetish odour was wafting straight into the basement's one and only window, which for this reason was always tightly shut and solidly barred.

This basement was a deep, dark space crammed – like all cheaply furnished rooms – with heavy pieces of trashy furniture, hideous, yet giving an impression of comfort and affluence. There was a fireplace of course. Above it a clock, and on the clock a metal outcrop representing a hunter with his kill, a chamois. In the corner stood a folding bed, pretending not to be there. There was definitely no brightly coloured kilim, sold in Russia during the tough and hungry times that Babka still had dreams about.

Babka didn't live here, in the formal part of the basement flat, but in the furthest depths of it. Her room must once have been a bathroom, a damp, narrow toilet with no trace of a window, just a ventilator grille in the wall, ropes for drying the washing, and the rhythmic kiss of water dripping from on high into the sink.

Lying in bed, Babka looked different, as though she were half the size. And she was – she wasn't wearing a hundred layers of beneficent wool or a black headscarf. She was like a pathetically tiny little seed husked out of a thick shell.

She was pleased. She thanked me for coming. 'Do sit down.' She was worried it was a stool and not a chair. A couple of times she went back to the fact that the work she was returning wasn't 'necessarily as perfect', but it was impossible to do otherwise.

'My strength has gone, missy. I can't eat, or sleep or move. Something aches inside me whenever I eat. The doctor?' She waved a heavy hand. 'How can the doctor help when a person's old and worn out? A tree loses its leaves too. A field blackens too, when the world goes into winter . . . It wouldn't be hard for me to die now, but I wish I were on home ground. And I wish I could have our sort of burial, and could lay my bones in my native earth . . . A couple of years ago I still had hope in God. I thought that if a person begged for a Polish grave . . . Plainly I were too great a sinner. Plainly I petitioned God too much. I wanted to turn things to my advantage – to have it my way – as I wanted – not His. A person is old and stupid. Stupid until death. And if he were born four times into the world he'd be stupid four times. By regarding himself as wise. Off his own bat. Only when death is looking him in the eye can he see that all the wisdom in the world is the Lord God! And that what He wants is for the best. All my life I knew that, but so what? Did I think I were better than others, or that I'd be granted a better death than those who didn't know? Oh, missy! If not for God's mercy and the intercession of Our Lady on our behalf, I'm afraid to think! A person lives in this world as if he were to remain in it forever. He should know that one day the end will come, but he lives as if he's blind. He thinks, "I have time". "I have time," he thinks. And it's true, he does. Just enough for God's point to be proven . . . Well, a person is blind. So life flows through his fingers like water. And only when death is pressing him hard can he finally see. Then he sees it all. Both his own blindness and his own stupidity and his own sins, the ones he didn't want, and the ones he gathered more than anything. And now there's no time to make amends. For how? For when? Seventy-one years I've had! Seventy-one years!'

And as if only now realizing for the first time in her life what a big chunk of time that was, she rocked side to side, and with the gesture of every Jesus, the Man of Sorrows, rested her cheek on the palm of her hand.

'And who justifies himself? Who will remain? Almighty God! Without Your mercy we are nobody!'

*

Some time later, on my way home from the office, I found Babka by the gate. She was waiting for me. This had never happened before. There she stood, serious, silent, flushed with confusion, her chin quivering. Nor could she speak immediately. And it was only then, after all those years of knowing her, that I found out there were still some tears left in the poor thing.

She had come to say goodbye. She was going into hospital. For an operation. She knew she wouldn't survive it. She had come to bid me farewell, to say thank you and to apologize.

She spoke slowly, in a tone of incredible gravity. She was solemn, focused, intense. As 'in the hour of death'.

No. She wasn't at all afraid. Not of the operation or of dying. Let God's will be done. His sacred will in all things. Clearly this was her destiny. In exile. Let this too be to His glory. For her sins. And for Poland.

Her hands were cold, light, as if weathered. And it was only the alien, characteristic intensity of the look in her eyes that still wanted, in parting, to confirm something, to say more, to bear witness to something . . . Something of vital importance.

Following the operation, she died in hospital after a few short days, but after more than a dozen long years of extreme, deeply felt suffering.

Walentyna Buczko. Nobody.

Thistledown blown by an ill wind all the way here from Poland.

Nobody. Torn by the roots from her native soil, an ardent, faithful heart, tossed live onto concrete, onto stones, onto alien ground.

Nobody who was known about at all.

A few people at Kensal Green or some other London cemetery. A bunch of flowers and the hollow rattle of earth hitting the coffin.

Walentyna Buczko. A simple, penniless woman from outside Grodno or Białystok.

Grant her eternal rest, O Lord . . .

'Babka'
Published as part of the collection *Ziarnka piasku, Opowiadania i nowele* (Wydawnictwo Veritas, 1957).

EDWARD REDLIŃSKI

1940–2024

To Edward Redliński any aspect of the Polish national mythology could be satirized with glorious irreverence and great humour. He started his career as a journalist, but was fired from the Warsaw weekly *Kultura* for criticizing the Party authorities in Białystok, the region he was from.

His writing could be said to belong to the rural literature genre, but it reflects the Polish countryside through a very distorted mirror. His collection of stories *Listy z Rabarbaru* (*Letters from Rhubarb*, 1967), from which 'Birches' is taken, show village life as primitive and brutal, if not blackly comical. His novella *Konopielka* (1973; the title is the folkloric name of a malevolent sprite) is about a backward village where the locals are confronted with modernization as the socialist authorities try to drag them into the twentieth century. Efforts to introduce literacy and mechanization are alien to the peasant mentality, and produce absurd results. Redliński achieves the comedy through exaggeratedly grotesque characters and bizarre colloquialisms.

From 1984 to 1991 Redliński lived in New York, a period of his life that he called 'researching capitalism by means of participatory observation'. Inevitably, Polish immigrants to America became a target for his satire, notably in *Szczuropolacy* (literally *Rat-Poles*, 1994), which shows Polish newcomers living in 'rat-hole' apartments and being incapable of starting a new life; confronted by the reality of the alien, materialistic, unwelcoming USA they revert to stereotypical Polish behaviour, or rather Redliński's literary version of it.

Equally provocative was his fantastical novel *Krfotok* (1999; the title twists the word '*krwotok*', meaning 'haemorrhage'), in which he distorted history by imagining, retrospectively, that an all-out war with the USSR erupted in 1981 instead of the imposition of martial law. Once again, this was Redliński's vehicle for describing the Polish national character as he saw it, and for debunking sacredly preserved traditions.

Although three of his novels, including *Konopielka*, were adapted into films, his work has been woefully overlooked in English translation.

Antonia Lloyd-Jones

Birches

Translated by Antonia Lloyd-Jones

I've been jealous of my older brother Witek for as long as I can remember. He picks the apples before they're ripe and doesn't get worms. He loots Bosak's strawberries and his hand doesn't wither. He steals eggs to buy sweets and doesn't go to hell. 'He's a devil, not a child,' our mother complains. 'He'll grow up to be a thug,' our father frets. He often takes off his belt and thrashes Witek on the bum, and Witek bawls his head off. Meanwhile our mother keeps drumming it into his head: 'Just look – your brother Pawełek doesn't get belted. Be like Pawełek.'

My status as the good son has lots of pros, but far more cons. For instance, I can't pass a catechism test with just a C, I'm supposed to get an A, or at least a B. While I'm grazing the cows I swot up on the seven deadly sins, the corporal works of mercy, and what angels are . . . And it's not all right for me to use swearwords. On the roads I look out for blind people so's I can do a good deed: escort them across a footbridge, show them the way, cheer them up with a kind word – at least once a week. Father Andrzej, who sets these rules, is about thirty, and he's a very active man, always in a sweat. We sit in the gloomy nave on pine benches. Father Andrzej casts an eye over the rows. As he strips a twig with his slender fingers, he lectures us: 'Some children are cruel. For example, they catch a fly, and what do they do to the poor fly? They tear off its little wings, its little legs and its little nose. You can't be doing that, dear children, it's a sin! The fly suffers dreadful torments! You can kill a fly, but – wham! Do it with a single blow, painlessly.'

Ugh, life . . . A buzzing fly lands on my forehead. It crawls across my nose and neck, and creeps under my shirt. It crawls down my sleeve and out onto my palm. I move my hand and it flies off. It's back again. Oh yes – a single blow, he said. So ... thwack! The echo clatters around the empty church, and Father Andrzej goes purple. He runs up and lashes me on the calves with his willow switch, but it's as if he were lashing my fervent heart.

'You little rascal,' he scolds me, 'I'll teach you to make fun of the priest.' And whack, whack goes his switch. He wipes off the sweat. 'And now: the seven deadly sins!'

My teeth are chattering as I start to list them: 'The first sin is pride, the second is avarice, the third is impurity ...'

Jacek, the manageress's son, asks in a businesslike way without the slightest tremor: 'Please, Father, what is pride?'

The organist's son wakes up. He opens his mouth. Not to yawn. He has a question.

'What's impurity?' he asks.

Jacek knows: 'Impurity is filth.'

The priest claps his hands for silence. Since the best pupils are asking, he'll explain.

'Dear children, you're asking about impurity. All right ... I'll tell you. You see, naughty boys have these games ... They play with themselves, or sometimes with little girls ...'

You could hear a pin drop.

'They play with themselves in private, secretly. Because they're ashamed. And if they're ashamed, that means what they're doing is dirty.'

It's as if I could see the Stolarski boys!

'The Lord God does not like dirty games and dissolute children. Later they'll grow up to be thieves and thugs. And thugs go to hell. Now children, who's going to tell us about hell?'

No one shows willing. We're all looking at our hands resting on our knees. It's my opportunity to put things right.

'In hell there's fire and red-hot pitch,' I declare. 'The devils stand there with pitchforks and prod you in the back. They have sharp pincers and they pull you by the ears with their pincers. They throw sinners into the pitch ...'

At school the teacher fights against telling lies.

'Children, lying is the ugliest thing on earth, you must always tell the truth. All misfortune comes from the fact that people don't tell the truth. It's also very wrong to talk during lessons.'

There are two sixth-formers sitting on the back bench 'after lessons', as a punishment: Gutecki and my brother Witek. They're supposed to be doing an assignment, but I can see they're covering their mouths with their hands and whispering to each other. I raise my hand.

'Please sir, Witek keeps talking all the time.'

The teacher summons Witek. He tells him to hold out his hand. He gives him seven whacks with a ruler and sends him home.

I spend the next two hours in a state of eager excitement. I count the fastest, I write things out the quickest, I draw the neatest.

But there in the woods, lying across my path is Witek, using his satchel as a pillow. At the sight of me he gets up.

'You spy! You sneak! Fancy ratting on your own brother!' He lets me go ahead and every few paces he kicks me in the bum. 'You dirty swine! Take that! And that!'

When I turn around and remind him about hell, he hits me on the back of the neck with his satchel.

'Hell? You idiot!'

The most rewarding place for carrying out my salvatory mission is the meadows beyond the wood. In autumn the farmers from Rabarbar and Bruki harvest the second crop, and as soon as the grass has grown back a single centimetre we drive the cows there for the last days of the grazing season. We light a bonfire, we bake potatoes and carrots, and we play a thousand games. The stray cows trail among the smoke-wreathed willow trees. There's no harm done, the fields are empty, because the winter crops sprout later. For us it's like life on the steppe.

The Stolarski boys rule the roost – if only because their herd includes the stud bull. His name is Juan. Juan has a metal ring through his nostrils and lets even Kazik, the smallest of the Stolarskis, lead him by the nose. He doesn't eat much, he just moos all the time – sometimes in a deep tone, sometimes a high one.

The Stolarskis are first-rate daredevils: they gallop on the cows, jump around the fattest willow branches like monkeys and walk on their hands. In the spring their mate, Leszek from Warsaw, who since the war hasn't had a home or parents and works as a cowherd at Sztecki's place in Bruki, takes baby crows from their nests. He hurls them against a tree, killing them without pain, and tosses them into an ant heap. The crow parents fly down and scream. A few days later Leszek pulls out the clean white bones. The Stolarskis have even better ideas. They pump up frogs through a straw, then stomp on them to shoot their insides out. And Leszek drinks milk from the cows: he crawls under their bellies on all fours and sucks like a calf.

And I, the apostle of the catechism, traipse around after them, shocked by the baby crows, and even more disgusted by the way they treat the frogs. As I watch it all happen my eyes grow gigantic and my hair goes even more yellow with horror.

Sometimes half-witted Beetrot drives the cows to the fields – she works as a cowherd for the farmers, just like Leszek. She's about forty but mentally five times less, so she lets various jokes be played on her.

The Goździowa sisters, Maryśka and Zośka, keep on the sidelines of the gang. They dance, jump a rope, sew themselves gloves for the winter, and play hide-and-seek. I often play with them and that's how I got the nickname 'the girly king'. But who cares! One time Zośka patched my trousers with red thread, and Maryśka laundered my shirt in a puddle, then dried it out over the bonfire.

We have the biggest laugh with Beetrot. Sometimes she comes along in high-heeled boots – one's black, the other's brown with a top. Once she wove some twigs into her plaits and pretended to be a tree. All summer and autumn she sings Easter songs, usually 'Today a merry day has dawned'. She composed a song herself, which we like very much:

> Black is the flower, sad is the world,
> So's your heart, my darling girl,
> Oh my darling, say goodbye,
> Save your tears, do not cry.

She sings if there's an audience or not. She sits herself under a tree, taps out the beat with a stick and wails to every point of the compass, in a voice as deep as a bloke's.

One time she tried to scare Witek, who often tricks his way out of herding the cows, by saying the Lord God will punish him like old Sołowiej: 'In his youth Sołowiej tied a rag around his leg, ha ha, to fool his father into thinking he was injured, ha ha! And you know what? His leg withered away. The Lord God, the Lord God metes out justice!' she finished off, to the tune of the folk song: 'All the little fish sleep in the lake . . .'

Witek, being Witek, instead of repenting, dragged Beetrot among the willow trees. How he boasted afterwards! He even said he'd throw a hot potato in *there* for her. But the Goździowa sisters don't think it's possible.

Even better at these things are the three Stolarski brothers. It's embarrassing to say it, but they make love to their Friesians. They even drill holes in the ground with sticks and make love to the earth.

I took action against these vile practices.

During my confession, I told Father Andrzej what happens when we're grazing the cows. He broke into a sweat and started asking about the details. 'Did you try doing that with the earth too?' 'No,' I said, without lying, to the whole church. 'And did you try it with this Beetrot?' 'No!' 'And what about these Stolarski boys?' 'Yes, they get at the Goździowa girls too.' By now the priest was gasping for breath.

'For shame,' he said to me through the grate, 'for shame. Tell them to come to confession next Sunday. And go to Bruki, tell Stolarski to guard his children against Satan. Will you go? Now say: God be merciful . . .'

I've become a saintly youth. I am possessed by the sweetness of my covenant with the priest and with the Lord God. Every night I say one Our Father, one Hail Mary, and one I believe in God per person. I pray for everyone I know: for the Stolarski boys, Beetrot, the Goździowa sisters, my father, my mother and Witek, I'm down on my knees for half an hour. My mother steps around me on tiptoes. 'He'll be a priest,' she confided to Mrs Sołowiej, I heard her myself. 'He's been touched by the grace of God,' she explained with pride.

One Sunday I went to Bruki. Mr Stolarski and his wife were having their dinner, but the boys weren't back from the meadow yet. 'Whose are you?' they asked curiously. I replied I'm Kosy's boy, from Rabarbar. 'What have you come about?'

So I told them what Bolek, Antek and Kazik get up to with the baby crows and the frogs, and what Bolek does with Beetrot. I also hinted at the cows and the earth. Mrs Stolarska got upset. 'Mother of God! My boys?' Her husband was tapping the marrow out of a bone against the windowsill. He burst out laughing.

'All quite normal . . . I was just the same. This one must be a bit touched in the head. Fancy forbidding the boys their fun. Let them enjoy themselves while they can!'

I began to tremble.

'You Stolarskis will all go to hell! The whole family!'

I also dropped in at Mrs Goździowa's to tell her to guard her daughters against the Stolarskis. 'Sonny,' she said emotionally, 'come here for a kiss . . . May God requite you, sonny.' And she gave me two zlotys.

I burst into tears at what Stolarski had said.

'I'll have it out with him, the great ox!' she exclaimed.

Maybe she did, because not a week went by before Stolarski rode his bike over to our place. He offered my father a cigarette, they lit up and talked of this and that. Finally he asked about me. 'Józek, thrash the child that's ruining my reputation. Goździowa's been drivelling all over Bruki that Stolarski's a filthy pig, that my kids are swine, and that I've been getting at her girls, and the like. Your kid was in Bruki, mouthing off.'

My father isn't stupid and he took no notice of such prattle. If the folks in Bruki don't like Stolarski, it's definitely not my fault. But now honour won't let me go near the Stolarski boys. And it's November, I could do with the warmth of a big bonfire. My father won't let us burn things under the aspen trees. I peep from behind the bushes and watch the gang playing. For example, I can see the Stolarskis leading Maryśka and Zośka into the shelter. Later the girls are padding out their dresses with hay. They walk round and round the bonfire, then go back into the shelter with Beetrot. They do some moaning and crying, then they come out with a fake baby: a dolly made of straw and twigs. Then they dig a hole in the ground, line it with grass and lull their dollies to sleep. And the boys are baking potatoes and carrots on the fire.

They played at houses. They drew walls, stoves and beds on the ground. Then they pretended to have a quarrel. Zośka said to Kazik: 'You dirty fucker!' To which he said: 'You're no better!' and slapped her in the face. They quickly made it up and played at baking bread.

I heard Bolek talking about his mum and dad: he said he didn't sleep until midnight and heard everything. The rest of them were all ears! Especially the Goździowa sisters and Leszek, who hasn't got a father or mother.

As if that wasn't enough, Bolek took the boys aside, into the bushes. He said he was a real bloke now, and he showed them. They went pale.

They started trying to do it themselves, but it didn't work. I ran out of my hiding place. Shame, shame on you!

At confession I kept these performances a secret.

My father said today is the last day I'll graze the cows. Winter's coming.

Now it's winter. Witek has made himself skis out of staves. I'm reading about cowboys and about love. I decided to shorten my prayers by half, but to say them more carefully. In zoology the reproduction of mammals is coming up. I know the chapter about rabbits by heart. I wonder if Mrs Kowalska will tell us about it and if she'll go red. She teaches the first year.

We've had that lesson. Mrs Kowalska told us to read it to ourselves and write a summary at home. She dodged it.

Today they handed out our reports. I went into the seventh class. My marks are average.

Seventh class. The head teacher, Mrs Kalinowska, caught me reading *Nightmares* under the desk, and as a punishment she sat me next to Leonka. Leonka has the biggest bust at school, bigger than the teacher's. She's been held back for a third year in the seventh class. She has no idea what an equation is. Or why you read from left to right. In the breaks the boys grab her by the head and pull at her bust. I'd like to do it too, but how do you do that? What if instead of defending herself, she just drops her hands? What then?

Something happened. The Stolarskis again. This time it was Kazik, the youngest, who's doing his second year in the seventh class. He plotted with the others, and as soon as Mrs Kowalska went out, they caught me and Leonka and shoved us together. There were ten of them squashing us, while Leonka and I pushed each other away with all our might. She grabbed me by the hair and yanked it, the idiot, as if I were pushing her of my own will. Kazik Stolarski kept shouting that I couldn't feel a thing because mine's tied up. They drove the girls away and told me to show it, they knocked me over by force. I managed to get my foot free and kicked Kazik on the nose with my heel as he was trying to unbutton my flies. That made him bleed, so now perhaps they'll get off my back.

They have.

What do they know . . . I'm planning to run away from home, to real people who don't get up to such vile behaviour. To clever, brave, noble people. I'll just finish seventh class and as soon as it's June I'll run away.

I want to know what there might be beyond the horizon to the west. In every direction all I can see is black forest; only to the west does the sky come in contact with a bare hill. There's a simple tree growing on the hill. It's round, maybe it's a pear tree . . . Or maybe an oak? I keep reading about oak trees in books, but there are only alders, birches and pine trees in our local woods. And some smaller trees too, like aspen, rowan and viburnum. The prettiest tree is the birch. Oh, how I love birches. I don't know why, but they seem modest, bashful. They're tall and white, with little green heads. The tallest one grows on the hillock by the ditches. When the cows go to lie down under the aspens, I climb to its highest branches to see what's visible beyond the lonesome oak tree.

You can see a large valley, something like meadows by a river. That's probably the Narew. And the tower that twinkles on the sunniest days must be a church. What church is it? Maybe in Suraż. Or Łapy. Or perhaps it's the Palace of Culture in Warsaw itself? No, that's impossible, it's too far to Warsaw. I've never been to Warsaw. What sort of a city is it, actually? There's so much written about it. Grzesiek Dąbrowski studies in Warsaw. He says that in Warsaw the people have more refined manners, on a higher level. I think I'll run away to Warsaw.

I often climb the birch tree. It's not tricky – you just have to tie your feet together with your trouser belt. Then you wrap your knees firmly around the trunk and use your hands to pull yourself up. The birch tree has white skin, well, slightly yellow, as if it has a tan, and in places it's bumpy. It smells of sap. Birch sap has an indescribable taste. In April, if you bang a nail into the lower part of the trunk, next morning greenish liquid will start to trickle out, as sweet and cool as if it's from the centre of the earth. I know it's barbaric to damage a birch tree. But every spring I try. Then I glue up the hole with clay.

I stood under the birch tree again. This time the sun was setting directly opposite the solitary oak tree, and the dome of the tree was set against a purple disc. There were elongated clouds burning in the sky like never before. It was muggy. I undid my belt and put it around my feet. I climbed upwards, faster and faster. Below me the clover crunched in the cows' mouths. I looked up into the sky – there was something strange happening to me. As if from the white trunk, from somewhere around my knees and belly intoxicating tension were rising. The world began to sway, to shake along with my birch tree. With the last scrap of my willpower I managed to make a few more movements upwards, my hands were growing numb as I grabbed the top branch and pressed my sweating face against the bark. Somewhere nearby a lapwing gave a shrill whistle. My fingers opened. I tumbled headlong.

'Brzozy'
Published as part of the collection *Listy z Rabarbaru* (Ludowa Spółdzielnia Wydawnicza, 1967).

SOLDIERS

ZYGMUNT HAUPT

1907–1975

Wilfred Owen, the British poet of the Great War, said of his own poems: 'My subject is War, and the pity of War. The Poetry is in the pity.' This sentiment echoes powerfully as one reads Zygmunt Haupt's story 'A Headless Rider'. In terse, lapidary sentences Haupt recounts two otherwise unrelated wartime experiences – the discovery of a peasant love letter written in doggerel, and a headless body lying by the roadside – that have in common precisely the pity and poetry of wartime. Haupt – writer, artist, architect – himself served in the Polish Army during the 1939 campaign against the German invasion, and later in the war also in the Polish forces based in the United Kingdom. He eventually settled in the United States, where he worked for the radio broadcaster Voice of America. 'A Headless Rider' was included in Haupt's 1963 short-story collection *Pierścień z papieru* (*Ring Made of Paper*), first published by the émigré Kultura publishing house in Paris. For many years after his death in 1975, Haupt was a forgotten figure in Polish writing, a fate that befell many Polish-language writers working outside communist Poland. *Ring Made of Paper* was finally reissued in 1999 at the instigation of writer Andrzej Stasiuk. Since then, Haupt's brilliant, hypnotic prose has been winning over increasing numbers of admirers. He has been compared to many other authors – Bruno Schulz, Isaak Babel, even Marcel Proust – but any such comparison belittles Haupt's achievement. The hyper-realistic way in which personal memories are brought before our eyes; the extraordinary incorporation of folkloric scholarship and ancient art amid the brutality and devastation of war; the jagged, rhythmic, almost dream-like language – all these are Haupt's own, and he remains a unique author not just within the Polish tradition but far beyond.

Bill Johnston

A Headless Rider

Translated by Bill Johnston

Christ be praised.

From far away, not from near, I'm writing these words to one so dear. At the table now I sit, the letter I'm writing lies on it. Down from on high a falcon flew, one of his feathers to me he threw. You in the middle, me to the side, our hands reach out to be unified. You're up high and I'm down low, between us two the water does flow . . .

It was a time of great solitude. In the beginning our arrival was often unexpected, and at such moments life could still be observed at first-hand taking its course. But our steel, our guns, the way we burst upon the scene, the clamour we brought and the roar of our engines, were like the coming of a storm, like a bolt of lightning on a sun-drenched afternoon. Then there was the artillery lumbering heavily over the pot-holed roads, and the ammunition wagons laden with shells, the hubs of their wheels catching on the corners of buildings and tearing the bark from living trees, forcing their way through orchards when the roads were filled with carts as the people fled in desperation, in fear and panic. Hands would be feverishly lashing the straps of the harness to the swingletree, while the women called their children to them in a loud wail as they carried out chests, pictures of saints snatched down from the walls, pillows, and a moment later there was the same empti-ness and abyss that we always brought with us. The flies alone tapped against the windowpanes, and chickens cowered fearfully in the corners of the farmyards.

As time went on, however, we would find the places of our incursions already abandoned by their inhabitants and deserted. Houses left to their own fate, their doors gaping open. Walls, furniture, bedding, pantries, cattle wandering in their enclosures, apples hanging pendulously from the branches of their trees, tools, cradles, dough rising in the kneading trough, sewing machines, laundry and pots drying on the fence: everything was left to the mercy of the emptiness. There were no people.

This time, on the table, there were untouched plates of food. They hadn't even begun to eat when they'd abruptly packed up and fled in disarray. There were dumplings on the plates, already long cold, slices of bread, some cabbage in a pan. Time frozen in mid-stride. Something had arisen between us and the people who had until a short time ago given life to this house, something had separated us from them irrevocably. That emptiness of a peasant cottage nevertheless had something lofty about it, as if our irruption, our unceremoniously taking possession of the place, was somehow unreal, insignificant and in fact transitory, and so deserving of a forbearing pity. From outside the window came the sound of the guns being emplaced: the artillerymen were mercilessly cutting down cherry trees in the orchard and pulling up the stakes of the fence so as to open up the near ground to the barrels of their ordnance. It would soon be evening.

Evening fell, someone lit a kerosene lamp – a kitchen lamp with a brass reflecting plate – and stood it on the map spread out on the tabletop, from which the plates with the untouched dumplings had been cleared. Through the window, beyond the crest of a hill, there was the glow of fires: one, two, a third.

I was ashamed of the way we'd taken charge without a by-your-leave of those walls, on which there hung a row of fly-specked religious pictures with dried Easter palm fronds tucked behind their frames. In the corner of one of the picture frames someone had stuck a prim family photograph taken at some fair; when I leaned in to take a closer look, I noticed an envelope poking out from behind the frame. I reached for it embarrassedly, as if I were reaching into the depths of someone else's life.

It was a love letter.

The letter began with a formula: *Christ be praised. From far away, not from near, I'm writing these words to one so dear. At the table now I sit, the letter I'm writing lies on it . . .* In a plain, clumsily formed script that inclined laboriously to one side, the words of the letter flowed. The couplets followed one another with a rhythmic, monotonous exactness. At places, amid the doggerel, I was taken aback by a strange assonance.

You in the middle, me to the side, our hands reach out to be unified . . .
The writer of the letter did not encounter any particular difficulties; he
employed the crutches and scaffolding of ready-made, familiar, hieratic
words. With them he poured out his feelings and dammed them between
the sluice gates of conventional, accepted expressions. He didn't hesitate
for a moment. After he placed a full stop at the end of each sentence he
had no misgivings, he did not regret a thing. Before the ink had even dried
on the sentence he'd written, it became something natural, self-evident,
solid as a fossil. He was writing his beloved a letter, but it could just as
easily have been a magic sign cut into the bark of a tree, or chiselled in
stone, or twisted into a wicker cord, or a statement made in a court of law,
something that had unchanging, definitive worth, like the words spoken
in an oath.

You're up high and I'm down low, between us two the water does flow . . .
I would wash your feet, wash them again, and drink the dirty water then . . .
Let us not laugh, out here people have established, hieratic canons, ways,
patterns for dealing with such things. They've been studied by specialists,
collectors of the flickerings of human life, pedants and conservators, all
tireless in their zeal, their urge to compile, catalogue, footnote. Volumes
of periodicals, yearbooks of scholarly journals contain innumerable quan-
tities of such magical texts. A snoop would have been disappointed to find
nothing sensational in the letter. He wouldn't even have been able to make
fun of it, because the poetry of this missive from a young country fellow
to his chosen one presented too complex a cipher.

Anyone who has happened – with tragic deliberateness, stubborn determination and repugnance to the point of nausea – to set about writing a
love letter, is well aware how many unspoken emotions from the extraordinary physiology of love gather when one looks at the pages one has
written: the simulation, imitation, the set phrases, even the most select sentences, noted and borrowed from exceptional masters of language. After
all, how can you express something that uncoils in you like a spiral spring,
or that is like breathing stopped momentarily by a sudden recollection,
or the pain experienced when you unconsciously dig your fingernails into
the palm of your hand, or that rings out like distant footsteps, brings the
scent of forgotten flowers, the call of birds, is hazy like objects seen in
mist? It's to no avail.

That evening, at dusk, in the dark cottage a country lover – 'the best-looking boy in the village', unseen, since he was in black 'town' clothes – in his outstretched hand, over his cap, was handing me a love letter in laborious awkward handwriting to his dear one, by this gesture appointing me a special emissary, messenger of love.

Without warning we were ordered into action, instructed to move off in pursuit of something or other. One of us, standing up quickly from the table, accidentally knocked over the peasant lamp; it rolled briefly across the tabletop, then fell to the ground and shattered. The blue and yellow flame rose up and began to creep along the floor. In ordinary circumstances this would have been an incident of a different magnitude and would have rendered the situation extraordinarily powerful. Whereas here? I remember that, as simply as you would squash some mud under your sole, or step on a wad of spit, with a few stamps of my boot I trampled out the light. It perished under my foot in a crunch of glass, as if I were grinding the flames of hellfire into the floor.

Then we tumbled out of the cottage, because we'd been told to head out.

At the entrance to another village, close to a wretched calvary, lay the body of a soldier next to his horse. There was a signpost nearby announcing in orderly letters that this was DISTRICT OF . . . ZAGADKA VILLAGE. 'Zagadka' meaning mystery; but there was no mystery here, only twisted tin roofs lying on the ground, scorched trees and avenues of chimneys lining the road, poking up into the sky above the stoves and hearths of kitchens; all the rest was ash, charred ruins, from which thin spiralling wisps of smoke still rose into the evening air, while the entire area was coated with a layer of ash as fine as sea foam. In the settlement the only thing to have survived was the trembling surface of the water in the well.

We often came across the bodies of soldiers. At dusk they stood out clearly against the grass darkening in the glow of evening, because generally the corpses had been stripped of their uniforms and above all of their boots. Their shirts and long johns were left to cover their mangled remains, being all that was left to show that until recently they had belonged to the living world. For this was no longer evident from their inert arms, their ashen fingers with bruised nails that had a rim of grime beneath. Nor from their grey faces, their blackened lips, their sharpened noses, lustreless hair, in the dirty whites of their inward-turned eyes.

Whenever I came upon the dead – upon lacerated, mute cadavers still striving in a last clown-like contraction of the limbs to imitate life – I was filled with hatred, contempt, savagery. As I mentioned, in almost every case the clothing had been removed from these bodies.

Between the hinterland – the region of chaos behind the lines, paradise of crooks, cowards, drifters, stragglers, who shifted for themselves there, forcing their way into abandoned houses, breaking into shops, stuffing their pockets with food, fruit, boxes of matches, loud and wordy men who take cover from air raids in hallways and cellars, thieving and raping, talking utter nonsense or with high cunning distorting the already terrible truth – between here, then, and the line of battle, or whatever it should be called, there was always a neutral zone, a no-man's-land, a precinct of impersonal, hollow fear. In such places there live and prey creatures – beasts – that are born from darkness, that in place of eyes have burning green tinder, instead of hands have claws and hooks, that call to one another in an incomprehensible tongue, in grunts and hissing whispers. They travel neither in packs nor singly but in twos and threes; they appear in the most desolate locations, moving confidently, as if following a string, as though they were led by a special sense of smell to places where death has recently – with a crashing and grinding and cackling – scattered the fragments of human meteorites. With an effort it's possible to pull off army boots fresh from the depot, still freshly tanned with yellow chrome and with the hobnails on the soles still blue. Belt buckles can, with a struggle, be unfastened. Afterwards, beneath the sky, that in the night-time draws so close to the earth, the bare, hateful human remains now lie.

Next to the body of the horse – swollen beneath the girth of the saddle, whose leather flaps had already been cut off – lay the body of the rider. It was the body, also stripped, of a youngster, as could be surmised from the officer cadet's piping on the epaulette of the torn field jacket he was still wearing. It was this white-and-red twisted cord that indicated the age of the soldier; for where the head should have been, there was nothing. A nearby shell crater explained what had caused the disfigurement. The headlessness of the body made an extraordinary impression. Rather than human remains, these seemed to be something not of the visible world, something brought from beyond its borders – the absolute foreignness of a death that is not of this earth. A nothing, a dust-covered human trunk without a head, as if in mockery of its terrible sacrifice.

Our imagination has produced the world of mythology, of monsters that are not reduced but augmented; we have created complex morphologies, a horde of new species, centaurs, harpies, griffins, chimaeras, with the most bizarre combinations of torsos, tails, wings and talons, as if the simplicity and purposefulness of nature's patterns were not enough. In cunningly realistic designs, thighs become overgrown with plumage and end in claws, the scales of sirens and chimaeras gradually merge into outer skin, the hydra flicks its snakelike tail, the sphinx grips with its lion's paws and proudly thrusts out its hard female breasts; even the sanctuary of St Anthony beneath the branches of a tree has been spattered like an ordinary chicken coop with droppings by the harpies. A different mythology is revealed to us in the displays of natural history museums, where there are dusty piles of the humps, plating and excrescences of palaeological finds, traces of their fingered paws left in sandstone, and the calcified membranes of wings transported here in massive blocks of stone. Each of these two mythologies multiplies, blends, joins forms, combines in innumerable variations. Yet there is a further mythology that functions in the opposite way, by reduction and omission. The mythology of art, that imitates life, but involves diminished configuration, omits details; that uses primitive composition, outlines; that limits things to their essence, to accents, applying a kind of amputation that is undertaken deliberately, with purpose. Is the muteness of a painting, the blindness of a poem, the deadness of a sculpture, not evidence of this reduced mythology that expresses itself in abbreviations?

A headless rider: in my conflicted, protesting mind I compared him to a certain sculpture – a woeful piece, whose pathos is so very pathetic – which, with wings plucked free of feathers like a goose's, springs from a lichen-blotched fragment of the bow of a marble ship on the landing of a staircase in a great museum. This figure is tiresomely reproduced in every art-history album, in encyclopaedias and guides, handbooks and engravings. With its fluted folds clinging to its breast, belly and thighs, it is by now so familiar and trivial it's hard even to imagine that at one time it must have borne a head on its marble neck. Any reconstruction, any conjecture, any attachment of such a head to this sculpture recovered from the rubble-strewn earth, would add nothing, would detract, rather. Indeed, perhaps it was not the goddess of victory at all, perhaps it was the angel of death, or Aurora, or an evil spirit, given wings to disguise it? Perhaps on its shoulders it had the head of a lizard or a falcon; perhaps its missing arms bore not laurels, but a sword, or lightning bolts or nothing?

On the outskirts of a burned-down village, beside a ditch, by a cattle path, lay a human body, stripped of its boots, slipping away into non-existence, genderless still in its youthfulness: Nike of Samothrace, a headless rider.

'*Jeździec bez głowy*'
Published as part of the collection *Pierścień z papieru* (Instytut Literacki, 1963).

TADEUSZ RÓŻEWICZ

1921–2014

Tadeusz Różewicz was nominated several times for the Nobel prize in literature for his vast body of poetry, collected in more than forty volumes and translated into at least forty languages. But he also wrote short stories, stage plays and screenplays.

Before the Second World War, he and his older brother Janusz shared a great love of literature and both wrote their first poems. When the war erupted, Różewicz had to work in a German factory, but then joined Janusz in the Home Army, and fought as a partisan in the forest for more than a year. The autobiographical story that follows makes reference to this – his wartime alias really was Satyr.

The poetry he wrote at the time was inspired by a fighting spirit and a belief in victory at any cost, but the horror of the war changed his attitude. Janusz was captured, tortured and shot by the Nazis in 1944. Badly affected by his experiences, Tadeusz faced the impossible task of 'creating poetry after Auschwitz': 'I was full of worshipful admiration for works of art . . . but at the same time, there grew within me a contempt for all aesthetic values,' he wrote.

His first post-war collection, *Niepokój* (*Anxiety*, 1947) was seen as controversial, brutally honest, stark poetry, that in the era of Socialist Realism was attacked as 'nihilistic'. But as Czesław Miłosz puts it, Różewicz was 'one of the key moral voices of post-war literature'.

From 1956 he wrote avant-garde plays, bringing the 'theatre of the absurd' to Poland in the tradition of Beckett and Ionesco. With his younger brother, film director Stanisław, he also wrote screenplays.

Unlike his poetry, very few of his short stories have appeared in English translation. One of his best known (though not yet translated) is

'Wycieczka do muzeum' ('A Trip to the Museum', 1959), a chilling depiction of a tourist outing to the Auschwitz museum that reflects public indifference to the horror of the Holocaust by being told in the voices of the tour group.

Antonia Lloyd-Jones

Comrades in Arms

Translated by Antonia Lloyd-Jones

It was mid-January, 1962. That day I'd spent several hours in the reading room at the Book Club and emerged into the street feeling dazed. I'd consumed so much printed matter, so many words of various kinds, that I felt as full as I would after a heavy meal. As I hopped off the tram outside my house I heard a shout: 'Satyr!' I'll react to the sound of that word to the very end of my days. If I hear it out of the blue, it shakes me to the core. An old man came up to me whom I didn't recognize. He was wearing a baggy grey coat. It was shapeless, creased and mud-stained. He also wore a beret, but not a soft one – it was stiff and bulbous, like a pudding bowl. Under the dirty black bowl there was a pale, puffy face.

'Don't you know me?'

'No, I don't,' I replied. 'What do you want?'

I didn't ask: 'What can I do for you?' I didn't say: 'Excuse me, but . . .' I didn't want to be polite. I didn't like the stranger. At first glance I felt antipathy towards him. He came up very close.

'Don't you recognize me, Tadzio? We were in the forest together.'

'I don't remember.'

'In Alek's unit, remember?'

He knew the alias of the commander I'd served under as a partisan. I took a close look at him. I couldn't recall his face.

'Don't you remember? You and I transported the wounded to a forestry lodge together. That small guy, remember? He'd been shot through the leg.'

A distant, hazy, younger face began to break through the features of the crumpled one before me. I remembered a sandy road amid dwarf pines, and a peasant cart with three wounded partisans on it. I remembered a boy in a navy-blue school jacket with a rifle slung casually over his shoulder, 'barrel pointing down'. And wheels creaking. The whole overexposed image flashed through my memory and dissolved. Then it came back to me: that was the boy I couldn't stand. He hadn't liked me either. There had been a natural aversion between us, as between certain species of animal. In fact we were only in the same platoon for a few days, then I'd lost sight of him for the past twenty years. And now here he was, standing in front of me, saying: 'You see, Tadzio, I've got a problem . . .'

'I hear you, sir.'

'What's up, brother, don't you recognize me by now?'

'I remember . . . But what's this about?'

'Finally! Brother . . . you're my only salvation . . . my saviour. I'll tell you the whole story.'

'How did you find me here? How did you know I live here?'

'Because there's a guy from R. here, and he told me, and I've heard that you make films . . . so I looked for you here through the registry office . . . In a nutshell, brother, I've had a sort of . . . adventure. I was travelling on business. And I fell asleep on the train, and when I woke up my briefcase containing all my official documents was missing, and so was my money – such bad luck! I spent the night at a militia post, left in the morning, and was reminded, by the radio, that you live here, so I started to look for you, and thank God, I've found you.'

'You must have been drinking before the journey,' I said, scrutinizing him.

'You know what life can be like, Tadzio . . . my saviour! They stole my briefcase and my official documents, and all my money, so I've nothing to get me home . . .'

'How much?'

He thought about it, but didn't name a sum . . . He was looking at me.

'I'll reimburse you as soon as I get home, I'll send it by post. Wait, here you have my ID card. Oh – you can write down my address just in case.'

Yes, now I remembered. Not just from the unit. This man had always disgusted me. We couldn't bear each other. Though we had only ever exchanged a few words a couple of times. He's found his saviour, who makes films, I thought; all right, I'm curious to know how much he'll try to touch me for.

'Yes, Tadzio, it's such bad luck . . . not part of the plan, and I did have a drink. I haven't forgotten that you live here because this one guy told me, and I went to see these friends in the capital, you remember Romek, he's a doctor, he's climbed very high, brother, he's a surgeon, and his brother tours all over the world with an orchestra, but as for me, brother, I slog away in an office at the cooperative, anyway, I'm changing jobs. Wait, I've got my ID card. Here you are . . . you can write down my address . . . In any case, I'll send it straight back to you by post as soon as I get home, but write down the address, then you'll know where I live . . . I'm married, I've got two daughters, but you're married too, so I've heard, congratulations, in short, you're doing well, a fellow's pleased to see that his pals have gone far, well, our People's Poland isn't so motherly to everyone, is it? In fact, I thought of looking for you through your mates at the radio a while ago, when I needed a second witness to vouch for me, I'd found that doctor, you remember, with the pot belly, the one who took a bullet out of Bluey's balls, wow, that guy was lucky, I was going to look for you via the radio to be my witness, because I needed two to get into the old combatants' association, but I found a second person, Kiliński, the younger one; the older boy was going to the polytechnic, so I did my best to give him some extra enrolment points that way . . . Did we fight, Tadzio? We sure did. But various people did various things, didn't they? We're owed something, aren't we? We sure are. If you like, I can vouch for you too . . .'

'All right, all right, I don't need any witnesses . . . Tell me how much you need, I have to get back to work.'

'Five hundred,' he said, but at once corrected himself, 'as much as you can, brother, every zloty is my salvation, my saviour . . .'

'I won't give you five hundred, two hundred will be enough to get you a ticket home and a hot dog, and you'll still have something over for a beer.'

'Thank you,' he mumbled, and put the money away in his pocket. He held out a hand to me. 'Well, goodbye then . . . As soon as I get home I'll post it to you . . .'

'Bye.'

We exchanged a firm, manly handshake.

When I got home, only my younger son was there. My wife wasn't back from the institute yet, Granny had gone to buy milk, and the older boy was at a friend's.

'I was looking out of the window and I saw you talking to a man.'

'Ah, so what did you see?'

'He had a long, muddy coat, I saw that. He spent ages chatting to you.'

'We haven't seen each other for twenty years.'

'Twenty years?'

'Eighteen, perhaps.'

'So who was he?'

'A pal.'

'Such an old guy? Why didn't you invite him in?'

'Well, I didn't. But maybe if he comes . . . He's one of my "comrades in arms", you see. We were in the forest together . . . Anyway, I only saw him there once.'

'In the partisans?'

'Yes.'

'It's a pity you didn't bring him in, because right now, in our class at school we're looking for old insurgents, prisoners from the Nazi torture cells, partisans and heroes like that to tell us about their exploits. What a pity your "comrade in arms" didn't come in, I'd have written it down at once. But what did he want from you?'

'Oh, nothing much . . . we talked about old times.'

'Did he have a nickname?'

'An alias? Yes, he did.'

'What was it?'

'Black Lion.'

'You're kidding! Black? That old guy in the long coat and the beret? Black Lion? Why black?'

'That was his fancy and that was his name. Each man chose his own alias . . . There were lots of Lions, Wolves and Thunderbolts.'

'But no Giraffes or Kangaroos?'

'You little squirt, are you making fun of the heroes?'

'I'm not making fun of anyone. The giraffe is a very beautiful animal.'

'All right, bye for now, I must get on with my work.'

My son went to fetch the wooden box of toy soldiers that he kept under his bed, and I sat down to work. I set about correcting a poem I'd found in some notes from 1950. It was about a book with a broken spine. The book had a hole in its leather spine. When I opened the green cover, a piece of rust-coated metal flew out of its white spine. It was as if a mouthful of metal from a bomb had been bitten off by the explosion. I'd bought it at a second-hand bookshop, in a major city that had suffered a dreadful siege and bombardment. I've been writing and correcting this poem for about fifteen years now, and I can't finish it. I'll give it the title 'Book with a Spinal Injury' or 'Book Wounded in the Spine'.

From the bedroom I could hear shouts, shots and commands. It was my younger son playing at his own war.

'Towarzysze broni'
First published in *Odra* (1970), then as part of the collection *Próba rekon-strukcji* (Zakład Narodowy im. Ossolińskich, 1979).

TADEUSZ BOROWSKI

1922–1951

From a Polish worker's family, Tadeusz Borowski completed high school in 1940 in the underground school system that operated during the Nazi occupation. He went on to the underground version of Warsaw University to study literature, while working as a night watchman and for the black market.

He was also writing poetry, in a very different tone to his contemporaries; turning his back on the resistance movement, he rejected the idea of Polish martyrdom but presented the Poles as slaves at the mercy of the indifferent forces of history. He himself was a victim of fate when he accidentally fell into a trap set for resistance members by the Gestapo; he was arrested and sent to Auschwitz, where he spent two years. Transferred to Dachau, he was liberated by the Americans and lived for a while in Munich, where he wrote his stories about the Auschwitz camp.

A selection of these stories was published in 1948 as *Pożegnanie z Marią* (*Farewell to Maria*), and caused controversy by showing that in a concentration camp the distinction between victims and criminals is unclear; the camp philosophy was the survival of the fittest, and morality was irrelevant. The narrator, named Tadeusz, is good at surviving and remains emotionally detached from the horrors he witnesses. These stories are perhaps the harshest testimony to the cruelty of the Nazi camps.

Yet Borowski was a profound moralist, outraged by the way the genocide was swept under the carpet as soon as the war ended. 'Fatherland' portrays the period when the American liberation had begun, and demonstrates his attitude. Seeking an ideology that would change the world for the better, he embraced communism, but was soon disenchanted. At the age of twenty-nine, he took his own life. His suicide came as a shock to political and literary Warsaw, but was probably the result of ideological disappointment and a complicated love life, as well as a self-destructive streak.

All his stories are now available in Madeline G. Levine's excellent translation, collected as *Here in Our Auschwitz and Other Stories* (2021).

Antonia Lloyd-Jones

Fatherland

Translated by Madeline G. Levine

Obviously, I thought, were it not for me, working in the *kommando* would make him swell up from hunger. The men from the uprising were actually intelligent and thoroughly resourceful fundamentally, but they were growing accustomed to death too easily; they had been taught that it is beautiful to die for the Fatherland. Among us, in our small, hard camp, they were like frightened bunny rabbits; towards the Germans, they were as disgustingly accommodating as toilet seats; among themselves, as greedy as worms for every bit of carrion; and when they were on their own, they had no idea what to believe in, they were as dazed as a child on a merry-go-round. When our boys pulled their leather boots off their feet and drove them barefoot into the mud and snow, they imagined that the sky was about to fall. They were losing their ability to comprehend the smiling logic of the world, and so they were dying peacefully. When they boasted of their ignorance, I thought immediately about the gas chambers.

'I've always had that proverbial woman's luck (you won't believe me, of course), but after all, I've only stumbled once in my life. I survived this whole stupid regime abroad; however, right before the war, I don't know why myself, I decided to leave Turkey and return to my husband,' a woman who was snuggled in the corner of the purple, plush-covered bench was explaining politely.

'What did she say now?' the young soldier with an albino's white hair and red, freckled cheeks, wanted to know. His legs in their carefully pressed trousers were stretched out against the plush. Out of boredom, he was combing his hair with his big hands, which were covered up to the wrists with colourless fur.

'She regrets that she returned to Germany,' I interpreted for the soldier.

The woman looked at the albino from under her long lashes and wrinkled her round nose, its shadow wandering over her face as she smiled. The train slowed down on the curve, stopped for a moment under a signal, and pulled, clanking, into the station.

'I don't regret that I came here; war's a very interesting thing,' the albino, who was wearing an American uniform, remarked. He spread out an illustrated weekly magazine on his knees, and after taking a good look at the legs, thighs and breasts of a girl lounging in an unambiguous pose on its two glossy pages, rolled it up and gave it to the woman. She thanked him and started mechanically looking at the pictures.

'Wouldn't you really like to go home?' I asked the soldier.

The platform was almost empty; evacuees, driven away from the express train by military police in white helmets, shuffled over to a freight train without a locomotive that was standing on a siding. The darkening cloudless sky shone through the ribs of the station lobby's burned-out roof.

'In Europe there are white girls, a lot of white girls, you know,' the albino said, and stretched out his muscular, sweaty hand. 'Look at what blue nails I have.'

'What's he saying now?' the woman asked anxiously, locking and unlocking on her belly her slender suntanned fingers with bands of lighter skin from the rings she used to wear.

'He's saying he's a Negro and he likes white girls a lot,' I interpreted for the woman. I didn't need to find an outlet in daydreams, I thought; it was necessary to trust one's herd instinct. It was necessary to go along with the entire camp; German villas were wide-open for liberated camp prisoners; the women washed their feet for them out of fear and went to bed with the former prisoners on demand. The stupid and the sensible were equally starved. But the stupid raped peasant women they happened upon, and brought onions and meat to the camp. The sensible stole clothing, watches and gold, and mistresses showed up on their own. Why, then, did I drag myself mechanically around the camp, mocking both the one and the other? Was I expecting some kind of morality? If I'd enriched myself, then I could be making use of my capital now; after all, I'm one of the sensible ones. For years on end I dreamed of liberation, and when it came, I was as flustered as if I were impotent. If I'd only been able to describe it!

'Tell them they should pay for your services in this erotic transaction,' a man from Warsaw said in Polish. He was sitting comfortably in the other corner of the compartment, his legs spread out lazily, and was looking out at the empty corridor. He yawned with boredom, took some cigarettes out of a pack, and held them out to the woman. She felt around in the cigarette case with her fingers, and, having selected the one she wanted, not too firm and also not too crumbled, she asked for a light. The car swayed, and the train, finally emerging from the demolished station, moved slowly alongside the burned-out railroad workshops. Rusted, warped railroad tracks stuck out between half-destroyed walls; bent metal sheets, burned through, lay in piles, and shells of locomotives that had been exploded by bombs towered over them. Near the walls and along the railroad track there was a green meadow riddled with bomb craters in which murky, filthy water had collected. The train rode across a high viaduct from which one could see a red city that looked as if it had been flayed, and then, gathering speed, it emerged onto a railway embankment beyond the outskirts of the city.

The albino with the blue nails took a pack of cigarettes wrapped in cellophane out of his pocket, broke the seal, tapped his finger on the bottom of the pack, dug out one cigarette and offered the rest to the woman.

'I like her; she's not as persistent as the ones in France,' the soldier said, and encouraged her with a gesture to take them. The woman put the cigarettes in her handbag and shrugged her shoulders with joyless sympathy. Her feet were propped on the radiator pipes; her legs were graceful and in thin stockings that lent a darker colour to her skin, as if she were suntanned.

'Beautiful, really beautiful,' I said seriously to the woman, making an explanatory gesture. She had wide lips, painted red in the American fashion, and fine, grey, cosy wrinkles under her eyes, which gathered around her nose when she smiled. Her blonde hair fell onto her shoulders in gentle waves. She was dressed unfashionably and seductively; she wore a light-blue shaggy coat and under it a see-through pale-pink embroidered dress, without any décolleté, as was the style in Germany during the war, with navy-blue silk that clung tightly to her body shining through it.

'You'd better leave that woman alone,' the albino with the blue nails said impatiently, understanding my gestures. It was becoming hotter and hotter in the compartment from the radiator. The albino unfastened his wool shirt and displayed his hairy, freckled chest under it, as white as the skin underneath a woman's brassiere.

'Naturally you like them,' the woman confirmed with understanding. 'Before the war, I was a classical dancer, but now ... Maybe I'll perform in the American officers' casinos. But you know, my husband ...'

I have been born again, I thought; I can begin to live again. From my former life I still have my name, the number on my left forearm, a German uniform and experience. Now, I could get together a little bit of money if that guy would really let me in on it. I'll live with him for a couple of months, then I'll cross the border into France or go to Italy to join the army; transports are leaving all the time by truck across the Brenner Pass. I could enroll in a university in Paris, Bologna or Rome. So why, then, have I sat here for so many months? I should have left immediately when we were still being welcomed with open arms and open pockets. And have I already got to know this country and this people so well that I can leave them now? I won't be able to describe them faithfully; I always construct characters and landscapes from the same elements; I could make up a short, uncomplicated list of them. True, I could just as well have lied, using the eternal devices that literature has grown accustomed to using to support the pretence that it is expressing the truth, but I don't have the imagination for that. Besides which, I also thought, I don't know either Italian or French.

'Are you going to take her?' I asked the albino in the unbuttoned shirt.

'Oh, I don't know yet; I only have two days of leave and I'd like to, but I don't know of any private room in the city, a *Zimmer*, understand,' the albino answered, and went back to his magazine. His right cheek was flushed; you could see the white design from the plush headrest stamped into his skin.

'Soldier, I have a room,' the man from Warsaw said in awkward English and blocked the aisle with his legs.

A thin, hunchbacked man with gold spectacles, dressed in Tyrolean fashion, opened the compartment door and said, 'Ah, but there's room here with you.'

'*You, go out*,' the albino said, looking indifferently at the man in the gold spectacles.

'*Der Herr* says there's no room in the compartment,' I translated for the thin man.

He looked at my German uniform and said in a soft voice, without any sign of impatience, 'You understand that my wife is seated in this compartment.'

'You just found her now?' I asked ironically.

'Ah, what can you know? I was looking for her through the whole train,' the man said.

'Why doesn't he leave?' the American soldier asked and, placing two fingers in his mouth, let out a long, piercing whistle, like a locomotive coming round a bend. Equally piercing whistles answered him from the neighbouring compartments.

'I beg you, please don't say anything to him,' the woman said with feeling. She extracted from her bag the cigarettes that she'd got from the albino and gave them to the man. She implored him, 'Peter, go away, really go. You think you're . . .'

The man stretched out his hand, but the American soldier took the cigarettes out of the woman's hand and said firmly, '*No!*'

'You can see, it's occupied,' the man from Warsaw said indifferently, and slammed shut the door to the compartment. The train rode through a bombed-out station, passed long chains of burned freight cars and crowds of people with bundles waiting on the platform, and again emerged onto the embankment that cut through the valley. In the valley, darkness was descending, and we looked down at the patches of dark grass as if from a moving cloud. The hilltops burned with a western, metallic glow; in the hollows lay stony coarse violets and reddish snow, and lower down, on the gentler slopes, grapevines shone red, while small cottages, enveloped in a gentle evening mist, glowed dimly in the light from the sun as it set behind the mountains.

She ought to have survived, I thought; if only they sent her to work for a *Bauer*. The German countryside didn't kill people immediately, although it sucked and devoured a person alive like a spider. If she wound up with a stupid or greedy farmer, she might have contracted tuberculosis, syphilis or a child. What about a factory? She had never really grasped what physical labour is like, and carrying German rails and cement had already killed more than a million people, even those familiar with work. Most likely, she died in the city, but if she survived, she was probably sent to a camp; after the uprising, transports of women passed through Auschwitz and Ravensbrück.

'Ask her why she gave him the cigarettes,' the soldier said angrily. He stood and lifted down from the luggage rack a shiny briefcase with a Gothic monogram. He pulled out a thick chocolate bar, broke it, offered some to the woman and put the remainder into his pocket. The briefcase was stuffed with canned goods, biscuits in translucent wrappings and two bottles of French wine.

'The stranger asked me for cigarettes,' the woman lied and looked at me inquiringly.

I translated her words faithfully for the soldier and added, 'Do you have a lot of cigarettes? Or maybe you know someone among your acquaintances who'd like to sell some goods?'

The albino rummaged in his briefcase and extracted a crushed pack in cellophane. He unwrapped it and offered it to us. I said that I don't smoke. The man from Warsaw took two, winking, slipped one into his jacket pocket and crushed the other one indecisively between his fingers. Now the train was travelling near an airport, which was situated on a plain nestled against a sparsely forested mountain slope. Endless rows of four-engine planes, their motors covered, stretched across the field. In wooden huts raised up on tall stilts, sentries were walking back and forth, back and forth. The train passed tents and buildings at the edge of the airport and entered a terrain of wetlands overgrown with reeds.

'Tell him that I'll buy any quantity of cigarettes, gold, cameras, postage stamps and, you know, in general,' the man from Warsaw said. The soldier listened attentively, wrinkling his white eyebrows.

'I followed right behind the front-line troops, so I do have a few things,' he replied. 'Will you find me a room in the city?'

The man from Warsaw smiled broadly and pulled a piece of paper and a fountain pen from his pocket. He began to explain the route to the soldier, making use of some dozen English expressions that he had learned from trading with the army. The woman and the soldier bent over the paper attentively. I went out into the corridor, slamming the compartment door behind me. The train thudded and rocked rhythmically. Only the fleeting telegraph poles and the landscape revolving on an invisible axis indicated that it was moving extremely fast. Inside the compartment, the man from Warsaw leaned back more comfortably against the plush, covered his head with his coat, and began to nod off. The albino with the blue nails sat down next to the woman and placed his hand on her knees. The woman twisted her head with annoyance, but didn't protest more violently than that. I lowered the window. I felt a damp, cool wind on my face mixed with the suffocating, oily smoke from the locomotive spreading out across the field like sticky down.

I wonder, I thought, if all women smell alike. They use different perfumes and wear differently cut dresses, but does an ordinary female body bathed in hot water always smell the same? In the summer, the Jewish women smelled of stale blood; they wore padded Soviet uniforms and then they went to the gas and smelled like burned fat. If she went to a camp, I followed my thoughts, she almost certainly didn't survive the evacuation. Of course, they might not have discovered that she was Jewish; fortunately, the Talmud doesn't require that women be circumcised; after all, how could it be done? But in Ravensbrück right before the war's end Aryan women also went to the gas. She could have had swollen legs or scabies; she could have got chilled and contracted dysentery; she might simply have become very thin, she was always worried about keeping her figure.

The German with the gold-rimmed spectacles emerged from the next compartment and came down the corridor, somewhat stooped and walking with a slight limp.

'Would you by any chance have a cigarette, friend?' he asked, stopping near the window with his back to the compartment.

'I'm from a camp,' I said to the German. I gave him a friendly smile and patted my pockets.

'Yes, we're all well off now,' said the German. He said that he is a technician by profession and that now he has to do physical work; during the war he was enrolled in the party. That's of no help now to either him or his wife. He spent three years in the west building fortifications, but he took shrapnel from a bomb; they had to operate on his leg and groin.

'That doesn't help us either,' he added with a faint smile.

I'll have to wait and get rich, I thought. I'd like to describe what I experienced, but who on earth will believe a writer who uses an unknown language? It's as if I wanted to convince trees or stones. Anyway, I wouldn't be writing out of love of the world; I'd write out of hatred, and that's not popular. I wonder what I would do if I found out that she is alive after all? I don't know, I thought cautiously; too often in my mind I undress women whom I see on the streets.

It was already completely dark when the train pulled into our station. The few streetlamps shone with a yellowish glow on their high poles and didn't illuminate the road at all. The station buildings covered the platform with an even darker shadow.

People's shouted greetings, footsteps, the shuffling of packages on concrete, and the railroad workers' whistles all could be heard on the platform. Soldiers were jumping noisily out of an American express train, throwing their military bags onto their backs and climbing the stairs to the embankment that separated the train station from the city located high above it; they loomed up for a moment at the top of the embankment, brightly illuminated by a streetlamp, and then immediately disappeared in the darkness. Their youthful laughter, shouts and whistles reached us from far away. The man from Warsaw jumped straight down onto the ground from the car and took his small suitcase from me. The American soldier with the blue nails carefully lifted the woman down from the high step and took his briefcase from her. She slipped her hand under his arm, and, calling goodnight to us, they clomped up the wooden stairs and disappeared behind the embankment with the other people.

'We don't have anywhere to sleep today,' the man from Warsaw said with satisfaction. 'We'll go to a certain friend of mine, only it stinks a little of broads at his place, you know?'

'Did you make a deal with the cowboy for your room?' I asked as we crossed the platform. We handed our tickets to a controller wearing a cap with official stripes and headed for the stairs.

'The main thing is to establish contact and trust with someone,' the man from Warsaw said coolly.

'Why did you give it to him for nothing?' I said angrily. 'We ought to have taken her, a completely fresh woman, though maybe getting a little stout.'

'Didn't you see that she's older?'

'Of course, I like older women!'

'How could I know, my dear, you've always insisted on the opposite,' the man from Warsaw said, surprised.

'You always know only what's convenient for you,' I said belligerently.

The locomotive whistled and the express moved on. The brightly lit windows of the carriages slipped past the platform, the burned-out buildings and freight cars, and vanished inside the trench.

'Man, if only you'd put together some dollars, you'd have so many of them here! You wouldn't have enough life or desire!' the man from Warsaw said, shrugging his shoulders dismissively. We walked slowly over the gravel. Right near the steps we passed a cripple who was dragging a large backpack and a suitcase and supporting himself with a Tyrolean walking stick. He hopped up the stairs clumsily, lifting his stiff leg.

'Did you by any chance notice, gentlemen, which way my wife went?' he asked when we emerged onto a dark street that ran among the ruins.

'No, we didn't by any chance see her,' I answered.

I thought: I really like these deserted German cities, slowly decaying like carrion in the wind and sun. Whoever has smelled crematorium smoke can appreciate the beauty of the cellar-like smell of German ruins that no one has touched. I like these people who, waiting for what will happen as if for trains that pass them by, wear out their old clothes, ideas, women. I could wander without rest through the burned-out streets of these cities and constantly experience anew many hours of happiness. Does there still exist in this world another country that could be more of a fatherland to me?

'Of course, I did see your wife,' the man from Warsaw said haltingly. He walked on a couple of steps in silence, then added, 'She went off with the Negro. What a woman! *So eine Frau!*'

He laughed maliciously and bent his elbow as an expression of his admiration for the woman.

'A pity,' said the cripple. He crossed the road with us, stepping heavily under the trees, dragging his leg over the withered, rustling leaves.

'A pity,' I answered.

'You wouldn't by any chance have a cigarette?' the cripple asked the man from Warsaw.

'I don't by any chance have a cigarette,' the man from Warsaw answered patiently.

'Goodnight, gentlemen,' said the cripple, touching his hand, in which he held his walking stick, to the brim of his Tyrolean hat with its white bit of edelweiss.

'Goodnight,' said the man from Warsaw.

The German with the gold-rimmed spectacles turned away and, dragging his leg, started across the street. I called after him in a sing-song voice, 'Goodnight, goodnight!'

The man from Warsaw erupted in a high-pitched giggle. I started whistling loudly and out of tune until the echo carried down the empty street. I rubbed my hands together maliciously and struck him a blow across his shoulder blades with the flat of my hand.

'*Ojczyzna*'
First published in *Zeszyty Wrocławskie* (Zakład Narodowy im. Ossolińskich, 1948).

TADEUSZ KONWICKI

1926–2015

Tadeusz Konwicki was born near Wilno, then in Poland, now Vilnius in Lithuania. He was a novelist, screenwriter and film director, well known internationally.

After clandestine high-school studies during the Nazi occupation, from mid-1944 he fought in a Polish Home Army partisan unit, against both German and Soviet troops. After the war he moved within the new borders of Poland and went to university. At first he wrote Socialist Realist stories about heroic workers building socialism but was soon disillusioned by the new regime, and was associated with the opposition for the bulk of his career.

His first novel, *Rojsty* (*Marshes*), was written in 1947 but withheld by the censors until 1956 for its extremely negative portrayal of partisan soldiers, compromising their heroic image. The story that follows is in the same vein, based on Konwicki's own experience, and shows the reality of war rather than a patriotic ideal.

In 1956 he started writing screenplays for other directors, as well as writing his own. Despite being banned from publication, he continued to write novels about the reality of People's Poland that were published unofficially. Several exist in English translation, including *The Polish Complex* (1979), in which Konwicki's regular first-person narrator – a parody of himself – stands in a queue on Christmas Eve to buy Soviet goods that never arrive, discussing with other would-be shoppers why the Poles are eternal slaves, unable to create a strong state of their own but constantly invaded and occupied. The man behind the narrator says he wants to shoot him for betraying the cause of freedom for Poland; he represents the author's own conscience, and their conversations describe the moral dilemmas of life in such a rotten country.

Though set in more-or-less recognizable reality, Konwicki's writing is often surreal, using flashbacks, dreams and his narrator's double to question himself and his surroundings. *A Minor Apocalypse* (1979) also satirizes failure to live up to the national ideal; this time the narrator's opposition-member friends want him to self-immolate outside the Palace of Culture as a form of political protest, but he wanders the city with a can of petrol, unable to commit to either cause.

Antonia Lloyd-Jones

Corporal Billygoat and I

Translated by Antonia Lloyd-Jones

'Squad, stand easy . . . and fall out!' crowed Corporal Billygoat, in a voice that betrayed it had only broken lately.

And at once, off duty now, he slapped Dragon on the back and said: 'Hey, brother, go find out what's for dinner.'

Dragon eagerly set off for the nearby farm buildings where we were having our break that day. The thick blue smoke rising from the chimney of the cottage where our commanding officer was billeted was giving us the hope that today's dinner would make up for the last few days' lack of food.

Meanwhile, idly swaying from side to side (he always had his legs bent at the knees, which made him look as if the chair had just been removed from under him), Corporal Billygoat went over to a pile of crumpled straw and, with a low grunt, sat down. Then he cheerfully surveyed the squad surrounding him. The lads idolized him – or so at least it was said.

'Why are you all standing there as if you're at a wedding? Onyourarses-sit! Aren't your legs aching? Maybe you want some more drill?'

Corporal Billygoat was a fine fellow. Maybe just a bit too sharp. Though that probably came with obeying the rules – he was a great stickler for the rules. Even after the longest march no one could lie down without roll-call and prayers. An hour before going into action he was quite capable of putting the platoon through his favourite drill. Truly, that drill was enough to put the keenest men off walking a step further. In any case, none of us had much faith in it – why did anyone need to know how to march in swarm formation if the first random ricochet could finish him off? Whereas Corporal Billygoat felt wonderful during drill. He would choose a hilly site for our exercises. He would take up position on a natural rise and strike his crop against his boot tops as he shouted the commands in a shrill voice:

'Fan out, men!'

'Take your positions!'

'One by one, at a jump, forward march!'

Here, regrettably, I must add that Corporal Billygoat's one weakness was that wretched shrill voice of his, totally at odds with the gravitas of the rank he held (leader of the first squad, sometimes deputizing for the commanding officer). Apart from that, Corporal Billygoat was, to make no bones about it, the typical, all too familiar martinet of an NCO. Perhaps only slightly odder, because he was very young, and operating within the particular conditions of a partisan army. Several times since, from the distance of many years, which has galvanized me to take a more critical view of Corporal Billygoat, I have often wondered whether his entire attitude was actually a pose, adopted from something he happened to have read. But these thoughts may also have been prompted by the events I'm going to describe.

The sun was already brushing the threadbare tops of the pine trees, and there was a stink of sweat-soaked foot wrappings on the air. We were sprawled about on the grass beside the corporal's pile of straw, none of us in the mood for talking, because it was quite stuffy, and a man becomes terribly idle in such a sultry atmosphere. Corporal Billygoat slowly pulled off his boots, then unwound his foot wrappings, sniffed them in disgust and spread them out on the grass. As the foot wrappings lay steaming, suddenly the corporal said: 'Well, boys, what if the war were to end right now?'

We made cheerful but non-committal noises. For what could we say? It was often mentioned, but if it were to happen, we wouldn't actually have known the whole thing had started – 'the whole thing' meaning civilian life, as lived at peace. Damn it all, we had grown up during the war and we'd got used to it.

Corporal Billygoat's question was awkward. And yet I ventured to take up the debate.

'To tell the truth, sir, I've had enough of the war by now,' I said.

Billygoat gave me an indulgent look. I passed in the unit as a duffer – the intellectual sort who can't even carry out a food patrol properly, 'Because it's a pity to take the last hen,' as I had excused myself once to the corporal.

Billygoat disdainfully scratched his chin, on which the first few hairs had managed to push through, resembling gingery down.

'Bonehead' – such was the pseudonym they had given me, despite my desperate protests – 'you're an arse. 'Cause you're afraid of everything. Can't do this 'cause it's a pity, can't do that 'cause you'll go to hell . . .'

I kept silent, in keeping with military form, while Billygoat turned his drying foot wrappings over. There was no sound, just a crane calling from somewhere in the marshes.

'You don't win war by being kind-hearted, brother. If you don't blast the bastard first, he'll finish you. That's the basic principle of war. We don't take any prisoners here.'

His final words stirred the interest of the squad. I had already withdrawn from the debate, for in this situation what could a man say who until recently had recoiled at the sight of blood?

'So what if we were to take prisoners, sir? What would we do with them?' asked Mollusc timidly.

Corporal Billygoat didn't lose his temper. He didn't even show ironical surprise, but raised his right hand and motioned with his index finger, as if pulling the trigger of a rifle.

'We'd rub them out.'

'Shoot the bastards,' retorted Wiktor, famous among us for his courage.

'Sir, let's have Chaffinch or Bonehead blow away the first Kraut we capture,' cried Blackbird, and the squad roared with laughter, making some anxious dogs respond with barking from the farm buildings.

Corporal Billygoat stretched his legs out and began keenly examining his dirty fingernails. We all knew he was on the verge of telling a story. I moved up, and lounged on the corporal's straw, perhaps overstepping the mark, but he didn't notice that, and after a glance at the yellow sky, he began his tale.

'Last summer, when I was still in Thunderbolt's unit, three of us went to the highway. We were bloody short of guns in the company and there were nothing to eat. I was itching to get my hands on a Luger. So off we go, I'm leading the way. It's quite hot, so we stop at this village for buttermilk.' (Corporal Billygoat always told his stories in great detail.) 'Then we follow the borders of the fields to reach the highway. The corn ain't been harvested yet, so we get up really close. We lie down in these bloody prickly juniper bushes. There was a ditch full of water by the highway. We were thirsty. So Pinetree – he was a brave lad – he crawls into it and drinks the rainwater. We lie there for an hour or so. Until we hear an engine . . .'

The corporal broke off his narrative and started fumbling in his pockets. He took out an old pipe tobacco tin and began to roll a cigarette. Some cows were lowing on their way back from pasture.

Snorting smoke, Billygoat continued his story.

'So we look, and there from around the bend comes a truck, mottled all over. Meaning an army truck. I lob a grenade onto the highway, my mates blast a few shots at the engine, and we jump out into the road. The cab doors slowly open and, brother, two arms slide out. I look and there's this dream of a wristwatch. So then we drag out two Krauts. Nothing special in the vehicle, just a bit of fuel. They got tins of food in the cab, a rifle and a sub-machine gun, the ones I've got now. We stripped the Krauts right away – those bastards were quaking with fear something dreadful. Pinetree says: "Slug 'em, sir?" I just wink, and he drags one of them by the shirt and off into the bushes. The German starts moaning, but Pinetree says: "Zum Kommandant". I grab the other one and off we go the same way too. Just one blast from the gun – it was primed. We set the lorry on fire. Pinetree lugged the tins back with us. We counted – there's seventeen of 'em. It was just a shame about the truck. Great vehicle, but not much use if the cylinders are shot through . . .'

Corporal Billygoat was done, and looked around at the lads, who were silent. After a pause Chaffinch asked: 'Sir, what about the watch?'

Billygoat stretched out a skinny arm, and there on his wrist we saw a bright nickel watch on a metal band, the first time we'd noticed it.

I don't know why – somehow I always blurted things out at the wrong moment – but I said: 'When is it so . . . like, er . . . killing prisoners . . .'

The lads exchanged glances and snorted with laughter. Corporal Billygoat laughed the longest. And then he grew serious and said: 'Yes, brother, you don't fight a war with books.'

I wanted to speak up again, but the corporal fell back supine and suddenly sighed: 'Huh, I could do with a nice piece of arse . . .'

The conversation moved on to girls, and being no expert on this topic, I limited myself to listening. In any case I felt quite intimidated, and had no desire to take further risks.

But Corporal Billygoat was feeling pleased with himself, laughing in a rather squeaky tone that startled the swallows trying to get under the thatch of the barn outside which we were lying.

Our unit commander was a lieutenant not much older than we were. In fact, he was just a boy. He did look quite impressive – he was very tall, with huge black eyebrows, a massive hooked nose and rather bovine eyes. He was very concerned about the unit's moral standards (not even Corporal Billygoat dared to curse or start up an indecent conversation in his presence), and generally he ran the unit in keeping with the rather literary rules of the gentleman commanding officer. He was also very strict. I don't know if I can repeat this, but according to Wiktor, who had been in another unit with him somewhere else, our commander had quite a tragic past. At the end of his cadet training the top brass organized a combat mission for some of the novice cadets, including our commander, as one of the most promising officers. The aim chosen for the mission was to destroy a German Stützpunkt – a fortified strongpoint, which was held by the Lithuanians. The Stützpunkt was situated in one of the many manor houses in the area. That night the small unit, on their first mission, crept up to the estate's outbuildings. The first men to go inside the manor house were to be our commander and a close friend of his. Their task would be to terrorize the Lithuanians, who would be taken by surprise. The rest of the unit were to provide back-up, and to occupy the remaining estate buildings. True to plan, our commander and his friend went up onto the porch of the house and stood outside an open door, through which light was falling. They were close enough to hear the Lithuanians' voices. As it was their first mission, they were all extremely excited, which is quite enough to explain what happened next. Our commander's friend was the first to race through the open door, shouting: 'Hände hoch!' There was a burst of gunfire, and minutes later when our commander's friend came out again, in the total chaos our commander mistook him for a Lithuanian (they were wearing German helmets). A short volley of shots rattled from his Soviet PPD (a fine automatic, the commander's pride and joy) and then he heard his friend groan: 'They fucking got me,' before slumping into the darkness. The mission was a success. But one more birch cross was put up in the Gojcieniszki village graveyard. He was the only man killed during the mission. Apparently our commander had lost his mind for several months after that, but somehow his madness had abated and he had started to lead his own unit. He had been unlucky. The story wasn't at all original, and Wiktor may very well have made it up, and yet the young commander's permanent sadness and strictness lent some credence to the story. I was personally connected with the commander by some ties that were hard to define. At the start we had had a number of conversations. But in time this had come to an end, because the commander never allowed himself to distinguish me for that reason. Instead he was more demanding, and often punished me for various offences, which he called 'Bonehead's oafishness', whereas I did not want to create the appearance of imposing myself, and began to keep away from him.

So next morning my surprise was all the greater when, shortly before dawn, while I was on watch by a broken fence, staring at the rose-pink sky, the commander came out of the cottage, relieved himself under a lilac bush and slowly walked up to me.

'Well then, Bonehead, all quiet?' he asked, buttoning up his flies.

'All quiet, sir,' I said, straightening my hunched shoulders in military style.

'It seems we haven't had the chance to talk lately, Bonehead. The way it goes I'm permanently exhausted and can't pull myself together.'

I looked closer, and sure enough, I could see a fog of weariness in his eyes.

'I'm not doing too well, sir, I'm afraid I'm a bit of an oaf,' I started clumsily justifying both him and myself. 'I'm no good at the requisition patrols. It's like . . . bloody hell, like waging war on women. Because if there's action, at least everyone's shooting, so then I shoot too. And, apparently, I'm a coward,' I added after a brief hesitation.

I was expecting a protest, a denial on the part of the commander. But he gave me an almost hostile look, very harsh, and said: 'Don't you forget that I demand more of you than the others. You've got to overcome your intellectual complex. The fact that you don't want to take anyone's boots away isn't an ethically justified gesture of honesty. Don't forget this is war, and this is your unit. Any moment of weakness ricochets back on all of us.'

By now the sun had cut its way out of the purple strip of forest and was shuddering in the red mist. The day promised to be blazing hot.

'Yes, sir,' I agreed in soldierly manner.

The commandant fixed his bovine eyes on me and stared for a while. Then he pulled his belt up and began to chew his nails. He knew he'd never be able to convince me. In any case, the point of our dispute was something we couldn't easily define.

Now in an official, if not a hostile tone (or maybe it just seemed that way to me) the commander asked: 'Who's on watch after you?'

'Chaffinch, sir!' I said, clicking my heels.

The rifle was weighing me down, so I shifted it to my left shoulder.

The commander slowly walked back to the cottage, and I felt as if I'd broken an expensive watch.

Then roosters began to crow somewhere nearby, the cattle mooed as they were herded out of the barns, and a dishevelled girl carrying a bucket walked past the fence, heading downhill to a small well. Her shirt was open, making it easy to see her wobbling breasts. She laughed at me stupidly and lustfully. What a bitch, I thought, and angrily turned to face the cottage, where I could hear the rap of wood being chopped to light the stove. Then Chaffinch dragged himself outside, sleepy, sour and shivering with cold.

'Screw the bloody watch,' he muttered. 'Just make sure they replace me on time,' he muttered as I got myself ready to leave.

For an hour I dozed at the table, still conscious, but then I crashed on the straw and fell asleep.

When I awoke, the sun was high in the sky. The merciless heat had wrung large beads of sweat out of me. I raised my head. Beyond a rainbow of dust my comrades were sitting at the table, eating. The stink of small wooden tubs full of pigswill hung in the air. The dirty, sweaty housewife was clanking cooking pots on a large stove. Flies buzzed.

'On your feet, men!' joked Corporal Billygoat as I sat up, yawning, on the straw.

'Come and get your blinis,' Chaffinch invited me.

The squad was busily slurping away. Billygoat amicably drew up a bowl of blinis for me. I was hungry, so I set about eating.

'Tuck in, lads,' said the corporal, wiping his greasy chin. 'We deserve a good rest. Looks like it's quiet round here. We can sit in peace. This evening when it cools down we'll do some exercises,' he added.

'Corporal,' argued Wiktor, 'couldn't we call it a day now? It's so bloody hot it's probably going to rain.'

'It won't do you lot any harm to get some air in your pants. Are you an army or a bunch of civilians?' raged the corporal at such overfamiliarity. Then he rolled a cigarette and went to get a light.

After breakfast we went out into the yard. The sun was blazing down so hard that we even took off our shirts. At once there was a delectable sound of lice being squashed.

'Fuck this bloody war,' said Wiktor. 'The lice bite worse than the Germans. And whose fault is all this? Those bastard Krauts. Shoot the whole bloody lot of them and there'd be peace.' Furiously he hurled a stone against the side of a kennel, in which a moth-eaten mongrel was dozing.

But the Germans were far away, the district was quiet, and soon we were sprawling on the grass, adroitly avoiding the chicken shit thickly strewn about the green yard.

For a while I stared into the heated sky, then lazily shifted my gaze to the ripening fields. Blackbird was on watch by the fence, wiping the stream of sweat that was pouring from under his helmet (on the commander's orders we had to wear helmets; Corporal Billygoat made sure the order was obeyed). Past the fence, another guard was standing outside a second cottage, the one where the commander was billeted. Sometimes a breeze would briefly arise that did little to cool our burning bodies.

Corporal Billygoat appeared in the doorway of the cottage with a girl, the one I'd seen that morning.

Then I must have dozed off a while.

I was woken more by instinct than by any particular noise. I looked up and saw Blackbird come running from the fence. His helmet was bouncing comically on his sweaty head. I felt a wave of anxiety. The other lads began to look up nervously as well. I noticed Billygoat in the doorway, on his own now, after getting up in a hurry.

'Germans,' was all Blackbird could gasp breathlessly . . .

We were dumbstruck.

For some seconds there was such total silence that Blackbird's panting brought the danger closer. We hastily jumped to our feet. I suddenly felt sick and almost keeled over. But the lads had already raced indoors. As I was running into the cottage Corporal Billygoat appeared in the doorway again, hurriedly loading his sub-machine gun. Inside the boys were silently turning the straw over to fish out the guns they had tossed there carelessly.

After some feverish clattering we ran outside again. As usual, I was the last. It seemed I was never quick off the mark.

Blackbird was already kneeling by the fence with his rifle to his eye. Slightly to one side of him, Corporal Billygoat was crouching under a lilac bush. We stealthily ran up to the bushes dividing the yard from the country road. I remembered my rifle. The butt was already slippery with sweat from my hands. I loaded it. The clank of the bolt was so loud that I thought it had caused an echo.

'Quiet, you bastard,' whispered Billygoat angrily and leaned forwards.

I heard a German voice.

A split second later, through a gap in the undergrowth I noticed a head in a grey forage cap about ten metres in front of me.

After that I couldn't keep track of the rapid sequence of events.

It seems Billygoat leaped out from under the bushes screaming: 'Hände hoch!'

Several other voices instantly repeated this order in various tones. Before the astonished Germans – only two of them – had had time to make a move, the lads had torn their weapons from their hands. As I crawled out of the bushes (last again), Wiktor was patting down the Germans' pockets. They stood with their arms raised, as if trying to check which way the wind was blowing. Their eyes expressed utter amazement and terror. Corporal Billygoat stood with his braces down in the middle of the road, brandishing his sub-machine gun. The rest of the lads, a dozen half-naked ragamuffins, surrounded the captives. My hands were shaking. I wanted to say something.

'Where are their weapons?' I asked.

There was no answer. Just heavy, rapid breathing. Then I noticed the two Mausers in Chaffinch and Blackbird's hands.

From the Germans' pockets Wiktor proceeded to remove some packets of cigarettes, boxes of matches, a wad of letters, wallets with documents, folding knives and some smaller items that I couldn't see. Then he undid their cartridge belts.

'That's all they've got, sir,' he reported.

Corporal Billygoat straightened his braces and thought for a while. Then in a voice that was almost calm he said: 'Escort them to the cottages.'

Wiktor pointed the barrel of his Mauser towards the cottages and ordered: 'Quick march!'

Not understanding, the prisoners turned on the spot and began to walk backwards in the direction indicated. They were still holding their hands hesitantly overhead. Wiktor prodded the one on the left with the barrel of his gun.

'Schnell!'

It was almost pitch dark in the cottage after coming in from the sunny yard. The prisoners sat down on the straw in a corner. Slowly they lowered their hands and gazed anxiously at the circle of men surrounding them. Through the window I saw Billygoat running to the commander's billet. It was still unbearably quiet.

'Blackbird, why have you left your post?' I asked, to break the silence, and my own voice gave me a shock.

The prisoners glanced at me in terror. I felt sorry for them. Blackbird went back on watch. The housewife and her children were trembling by the stove.

By the time the commander arrived with Corporal Billygoat we had almost entirely calmed down. Wiktor had even tried to make a joke, saying: 'Chaffinch, I can tell you got scared,' and then sniffing the air. But nobody laughed.

The commander took a look at the prisoners and told them to hand over their documents. I went closer, ready to help, though I didn't know a word of German.

The commander turned in his hand a little green booklet, on which it said 'Soldbuch' in Gothic script. Then he opened it and read out: 'Erich Knothke.'

The straw rustled. It was one of the prisoners moving about. With some difficulty the commander translated the data from the army booklet. Obergefreiter – or Lance Corporal, born in 1925, conservatory student. The other NCO was a tailor by profession. The booklets smelled of sweat and army cloth. Flies buzzed against the windowpanes. The prisoners sighed in the corner.

Gradually we returned to our normal occupations. Wiktor and Chaffinch went outside, while Signal stood by the prisoners. He would keep watch on them. Corporal Billygoat even put his sub-machine gun down on a bench.

On his way out the commander said: 'Keep a close eye on them.'

And that was all.

Corporal Billygoat gazed at the prisoners for a long time. Finally he stood up and approached them. He made signs to tell them to get undressed. They blinked, failing to understand. 'Schnell,' Billygoat urged them. Suddenly the younger one began to sob. They held out their hands, begging for something. They thought there was going to be an execution. Corporal Billygoat started explaining, half in German, half in Polish and partly in sign language that he only wanted them to swap clothes because his soldiers were in rags. They understood, and quickly began to strip off their uniforms, while feverishly trying to explain something. They were clearly expressing their readiness to hand it all over in exchange for their lives.

Later, when we assembled in the yard, while the prisoners went on sitting in the cottage in torn rags under guard, Billygoat appeared, in spite of the heat, in a German NCO's jacket. He seemed quite proud.

In fact all of us were feeling a certain joy. And a little anxiety. After all, they were our first prisoners. We were pleased. But as ever, I stupidly blurted: 'Sir, what are we going to do with them? We'll let them go this evening, won't we?'

Corporal Billygoat laughed out loud. Several others joined in. For a while he examined the flashes on the epaulettes of his new, ex-German uniform and then suddenly, as if wearily, he said: 'What? You know that – they get rubbed out.'

I realized my arm had gone numb. I turned onto my other side. Somewhere crickets were chirping. I felt sorry for the prisoners. I always had been sentimental.

'Bang, and the head explodes,' said Wiktor, snapping his fingers, and laughed unpleasantly. I was afraid of him. A red-legged rooster strode across the yard. Dinner time was approaching.

We ate our dinner out of doors. I was pleased about that. I couldn't bear the sight of the prisoners hunched in the corner. By a lucky turn of events I wasn't tasked with guarding them either. The sun continued to blaze down on us. Still in the uniform, Corporal Billygoat smeared the bulging beads of sweat across his brow. The dog lay lifelessly by its kennel. 'When will they do them in?' I wondered, as I gazed at the black hole of the window. The first small clouds were starting to appear on the horizon. The soup was impossibly hot. The conversation dragged along idly. Then we lay on the grass.

After recent events the exercises Billygoat had announced probably wouldn't happen. The hens were moving their heads in a comical angular way. I was feeling anxious about the evening ahead.

Corporal Billygoat turned lazily from side to side, and then calmly, as if spontaneously, as if he'd only just remembered, said: 'Hey, Bonehead, go and give the prisoners something to eat.'

I moved slowly on purpose, to avoid showing too much eagerness, in the hope that the corporal might yet rescind the order. In no hurry, I walked over to the dog and scratched him on his bony side. Panting fast, he glanced up at me from a festering eye. As I entered the cottage I felt the gaze of the lads on me. I tried to listen, in case they said something. But they remained silent.

Inside it was almost chilly. The prisoners were sitting still in their places. The guard was playing with the safety catch on his automatic. I didn't look in their direction. I fetched two plates of soup from the housewife and put them down in front of the prisoners. Then I went back for some bread. The prisoners livened up. The younger one, from the conservatory, began to whine about something. His eyes were damp, but I couldn't understand what he was saying. I guessed he was afraid. I looked out of the window. The curtains were rippling in a light breeze.

'Nicht Tod,' I lied. 'Essen, then nach Hause,' I said, pointing at the bright rectangle of the door.

They looked at me mistrustfully. I smiled again.

'Essen.'

They believed me. The younger one said something else, but in a calmer tone this time. Then he reached his bony white hands out for the plate. They ate in silence. The younger one just slurped away, while the Unter-offizier occasionally smacked his lips.

Noiselessly, to avoid attracting the prisoners' attention and to escape their eyes, I slipped outside. It was quiet. A shadow of cloud slithered across the ripe corn and brushed soundlessly against a linden tree.

I lay down on the grass beside my comrades, and there we remained for ages, measuring the time by the narrow shadows of the clouds.

The day was still extremely hot, but luckily it was drawing to an end. A flock of crows gathered above the woods, debating loudly, and then flew off into the colourless sky. Then they reassembled, and the noise of their cawing muffled our heavy breathing.

Corporal Billygoat was sitting on the threshold, his right hand shamelessly fiddling with the girl's breasts. Occasionally he laughed and cast a glance at the squad flopping on the grass, to see if anyone had noticed his love-making. But the lads were dozing. Somehow I felt anxious. I was afraid of the evening.

Wiktor was on guard by the fence.

At some point I heard footsteps. I raised my head. The commander was coming over to us from his billet. He had a jacket thrown over his sloping shoulders.

Quickly I got to my feet. Roused from their slumber, the lads looked up. The girl disappeared into the darkness of the cottage, and Corporal Billygoat came the other way.

'So what about the prisoners?' asked the commander.

'They're sitting quietly, sir,' replied Billygoat. 'They've been given dinner.'

The commander stood lost in thought. As we stood around them in a circle, my hands began to shake. The commander smoothed his hair.

'Billygoat, your squad will shoot the prisoners this evening,' he said firmly but quietly. I felt myself flush. Corporal Billygoat shifted from foot to foot and noisily swallowed his saliva.

'Yes sir,' he said softly and neutrally.

'You'll draw lots. The two who draw the marked lots will shoot the Germans this evening when we're on the march.'

We said nothing.

The crows cawed alarmingly in the yellowing sky.

'All right, Billygoat, get on with drawing the lots!' snapped the commander.

Billygoat stirred, then straightened up and said: 'Yes, sir!'

Then he slowly walked towards the cottage. We followed him. The commander stood up straight in the middle of the yard. There was a moist breeze from the meadows. I shuddered.

We stopped outside the cottage. The corporal went inside. We could hear his footsteps and the rustle of straw. Soon he came back out with a page torn from an exercise book. Somewhere nearby cows were lowing.

The corporal addressed the commander, asking: 'Do I have to prepare a lot for myself too?'

'Yes.'

Billygoat slowly tore the sheet of paper into eleven strips. I leaned against the door frame. Then he licked the stub of a copy pencil, and on two of the strips he drew a crooked cross. There was total silence.

The commander was standing still with his eyes closed.

The corporal rolled up the strips of paper and tipped them into his greasy four-cornered cap. Then he stirred them with a finger. We all went up to the commander.

The first to draw was Chaffinch. As he unrolled the scrap of paper and glanced at it, his eyes hardened. We didn't ask him the result. Then other hands plunged into the cap in turn and drew out more scraps of white ruled paper.

I stepped back to the outside of the circle, counting on someone else drawing the fatal lot before me. But I couldn't keep still. I could feel a tight knot in the pit of my stomach, a familiar sensation from school. The lots were drawn in turn by Wiktor, Blackbird, Ploughshare, Button, Mollusc, Antek and Signal. Then Dusky went up. I held my breath. But he too tossed a blank scrap of paper to the ground. I turned round to face the fence. My hands were shaking. Now it should be Corporal Billygoat's turn to draw, and to take out the slip of paper with the clumsy cross.

But I heard him saying irritably: 'Who hasn't bloody well drawn yet?'

I realized that mine was a lost cause. He was counting on the same thing as I was.

I went up to the circle. My comrades stepped aside in silence. The commander watched calmly and malevolently. As I reached into the cap, I noticed that Corporal Billygoat's lips were quivering. Or maybe I just imagined it?

The ticking of Billygoat's watch was loud, very loud in that silence.

I unrolled the slip of paper. A wave of heat flooded over me. The paper was marked with a cross. I made an effort to smile.

Billygoat asked calmly: 'Well, so there's no need for me to draw?'

The commander nodded.

'Ts-ts-ts-ts-ts,' cried the housewife, calling in the piglets. The dog began to bark by its kennel.

Without looking at us, the commander said: 'So Chaffinch and Bonehead will carry out the execution. Chaffinch can use the corporal's sub-machine gun and Bonehead can have my Luger. Once we're on the march the corporal will explain the rest.'

And he slowly walked off to his billet. We saluted.

Then gradually normal conversation took off again, perhaps more animated than usual. Everyone, except for me and Chaffinch, was overjoyed. The corporal sat down on the threshold again.

I couldn't gather my thoughts. I lay down on the grass, and listened to the blood pulsing in my temples. That brought me relief. I also avoided looking in the direction of the cottage. I felt stifled, even though the sun was sinking on us.

I lay there for ages, trying my best the whole time not to think about anything. I kept shifting my gaze to a different spot. I tried focusing on trivial things that would keep me from looking at the dark rectangle of the window that linked us with the prisoners. And yet time dragged very slowly. The yellow sun was bursting and turning red, getting ready to leap into the blackening horizon. I thought about other metaphors to describe the sunset. But my gaze kept creeping like a thief towards the cottage. I was sweating. I don't know if I was feeling for the prisoners. I was just afraid to put an end to life. We had always valued life.

Then the cows came home. Earlier than usual, because the unit was to have a drink of milk before leaving. The piebald cows with drooping udders mockingly gazed at me with the eyes of the commander. The air was muggy.

Totally at their ease, my comrades were listening to Wiktor's jokes. They had shifted the whole business of the prisoners onto me and Chaffinch. I suddenly felt thirsty. I walked around the house in search of a bucket, but didn't go inside. Something rustled in the raspberry bushes, and I could hear squealing. It was Corporal Billygoat lustfully violating the girl. I walked downhill to the well. A crane let out an alarming screech. I leaned over the side of the well and saw an almost childlike face, which the wrinkles of water were twisting into a grimace of laughter. Quickly I turned away, and without drinking any water, went back to the yard. The sun was now touching the line of the forest. The cry of the crane rang out from the marshes again.

An hour after sunset the liaison officer came from the commander. We'd be marching out in fifteen minutes. We gathered up our kit. I hung an ammunition belt over my shoulder and put on a knapsack filled with bullet pans for the Degtyaryov machine gun. My rifle felt strangely heavy. We led out the prisoners. They scanned the sky, bright amid the falling darkness, and they were uneasy. Blackbird and I guarded them. They made signs to ask if they could go now. I shook my head. They were starting to guess what was up. The younger one burst into bitter tears. The Unteroffizier was silent. The younger one tried to ask if he could go to one side. I shook my head. I showed him he had to relieve himself on the spot. At gunpoint he lowered his trousers and began to do his business. I turned away from the stink. He hadn't even the right to shame.

Then we went to the commander's billet. The two other squads were already standing there in readiness. They stared in curiosity at the ragged prisoners with bare heads. Corporal Billygoat kept order in the uniform from which the Unteroffizier's insignia had been freshly unpicked. It was getting cold.

I kept far away from the prisoners. The commander came out of his billet and disappeared at the head of the column. We got moving. We were seen off by prolonged barking from the dogs, answered by others yelping in the distance. The sky was going dark and the first stars were twinkling. Then Orion floated up, to be our guide that night. The Great Bear, our compass yesterday, remained to one side, behind us. We came onto a sandy road that was at once surrounded by forest. In my knapsack the ammunition in the machine-gun pans sang monotonously.

Once swarms of stars were crowding the sky, indicating a time of roughly an hour before midnight, the order went to the front: 'Head of column, halt!' The column halted. My heart missed a beat. I knew this was it. But I didn't move from the spot, as if hoping they'd overlook my presence and manage without me. But I could already hear Corporal Billygoat's hushed voice: 'Where's Bonehead? Bonehead! Bonehead!'

I stirred myself.

'Here,' I whispered, using a hand to quieten the ammunition rattling in my knapsack. I walked up to the corporal. He sought my hand and stuck the Luger in it. By the faint light of the stars I noticed that the hairs on his juvenile chin were trembling. I was shocked by the gravity of the moment.

'There you are,' he whispered hesitantly.

He walked off, but immediately returned. He said nothing, but as he turned around, he waved a hand and muttered: 'It's loaded.'

I drew level with the column. At once against the background of the sky I recognized the bare heads of the prisoners. Chaffinch was already there too.

'I'll take the musician,' I told him.

He didn't reply.

Somewhere nearby Corporal Billygoat's watch was ticking insistently.

I tugged the younger prisoner by the sleeve. He understood. He tried to kneel down, weeping and grabbing me by the hands. I pushed him away.

'Zum Kommandant,' I explained.

He didn't believe me.

'Zum Kommandant,' I repeated, and dragged him along. I hid the Luger behind my back and noiselessly released the safety catch.

I told him to walk ahead, and we went in among the trees. He was snivelling the whole time. I was afraid of him, even though he had no weapon and very soon he was going to die. I couldn't stand it any longer. I raised the Luger. At that moment the prisoner turned around and looked down the barrel of the pistol. He stepped back and shrieked – 'Aaaaa . . .' – and without aiming, I pulled the trigger. A streak of flame touched his forehead. In the final split second his white sneering teeth shone in the dark. Then the top of his head disappeared, his body began to sway, and like a balloon deprived of air he wilted to the ground. On my way back I felt springy moss beneath my feet. A short volley clattered from the sub-machine gun. That was Chaffinch. As I was nearing the column, a startled tawny owl cackled. I squatted down in shock, and then quickly retook my place in the column. I tossed the rifle onto my back. Nobody came to get the Luger. I handed it forward to the front.

Then came the question: 'All in order?'

We were silent.

Then someone said in an angry tone: 'In order.'

We set off. I felt total emptiness inside, like the corpses that had remained there in the moss. I began to laugh nervously. Somebody took the rifle from me. A voice said: 'Fucking hell.'

To one side I noticed that someone was hurriedly tearing off his jacket. German metal buttons flashed and a uniform floated down onto the road behind us. A shadow in a white shirt joined our column. At the rear behind us a shapeless patch remained on the road: the discarded Unteroffizier's uniform.

Poetic Orion tirelessly guided us onwards amid the clamour of vigilant grasshoppers.

'Kapral Koziołek i ja'
First published in *NURT. Literatura Nauka Życie*, no. 2 (Robotnicza Spółdzielnia Wydawnicza Prasa, November 1947) here from *Wiatr i pył*, a selection of uncollected texts (Czytelnik, 2008).

MAREK HŁASKO

1934–1969

With a scowl, a cigarette hanging out of his mouth and an attitude to match, Marek Hłasko became one of the quintessential rebels of 1950s Poland, known as much for his fiction as for outrageous tales about his stormy, largely unhappy life, which came to a premature end in 1969 owing to a lethal mixture of sleeping pills and alcohol.

Born in Warsaw, Hłasko left school at sixteen and worked briefly as a lorry driver, an experience that would furnish material for his early stories. Encouraged by positive feedback from established authors he contacted, he made his publishing debut at the age of twenty. His unflinching portrayals of ordinary people's daily struggles were well received by the communist literary elite, who helped to quickly make him a household name, although his gritty, increasingly individualistic approach rarely conformed to prescribed standards. The story titled 'The Soldier' comes from Hłasko's prolific period in the mid-1950s and explores themes present in much of his work: love, loneliness and the scars left by war.

A keen observer with a sparse, brutally beautiful style, Hłasko became the voice of a new generation disillusioned with the harsh realities of life in post-war Poland. His meteoric rise brought him huge print runs, a flat in Warsaw, film adaptations and the permission to spend a few months in Paris, in 1958, at the invitation of the Polish Literary Institute, which soon published his two new short novels. During his absence, a vitriolic smear campaign against him suddenly made him a persona non grata in his own country. After the Polish authorities failed to renew his passport, he began a peripatetic existence, moving between France, West Germany, Switzerland, Israel, the United States and elsewhere. He continued to write, work on screenplays and publish abroad. Whether in Poland, Israel or the USA, his hard-boiled, disillusioned protagonists often live at the margins of society, drinking copiously, loving impossibly – and hoping for something against all hope.

Eliza Marciniak

The Soldier

Translated by Eliza Marciniak

It was July 1945, and people were still surprised by the silence: it made them anxious and they didn't trust it. Two months after the last shots had been fired, peasants would stand in front of their houses, shading their eyes with their hands to gaze at the cloudless sky; flocks of birds in flight still inescapably brought to mind approaching planes, and Jews in the towns still hid their faces, with terror in their eyes.

The soldier walking beside the woman said, 'Were we afraid? It's a hard question to answer. They say that courage sits on a chair of fear. But does it really? I don't think so. You see, being there, you had to choose. You had to choose, even if it was just to know where you stood before dying. Sometimes fear came and made you shrink. Fear came even in our sleep. Sometimes we'd be eating, far from the front line, and all of a sudden I'd feel afraid. Each of us had moments like that; some woke up in the night screaming. At those times they were like little children . . .'

The soldier broke off and lit a cigarette. They had walked out of the town; the last shabby houses and garden plots were behind them now, and they were walking along a narrow path among fields. The sun was in their eyes; the warm earth smelled of hay and fresh milk. The soldier was silent. The woman walking beside him looked at his hard, stern face; she had waited for him for many years and hoped he would finally stop talking about *that* and say something more ordinary – about the weather, the sun or the earth. She imagined that as soon as he said the first words of this sort, he would finally stop going back to his memories, and then both he and she could manage to forget it all. She clenched her fists and mentally tried to suggest various words to him; she knew he loved her, so he should be able to guess her thoughts.

But the soldier was saying, 'There was this fellow in our battalion: he was a farmer and all he dreamed about was going back home to work on his land. The one thing everyone knew about him was that he was afraid. He was very afraid, and his fear spread to others; that sensation is more contagious than typhoid fever and much harder to cure. I overheard people quietly wishing him dead, and now I understand that was cruel, but back then I wanted to live and that man carried death inside him. He was afraid, so afraid that his eyes looked white all the time. But in the end he died like a hero, no, like a whole battalion of heroes! One day we were walking through a village. All the people were fleeing, their horse carts loaded, driving their cattle through the streets; the sick and old people were sat on top of the carts, dying. I remember one man carrying a plough over his shoulder. They were running away, leaving their houses and their land intact. In the places where we'd fought up to that point, there was no trace left of the houses and the earth had been ploughed up three times over. Here it was still unspoiled and the corn was just coming up. You understand? We were retreating, and this soldier knew that we were giving up that land without a fight, at least for the time being, and that those who came after us would poison and ravage it. That's when rage swelled inside him. And this wasn't even our country; it was very far away from here. He never left that place, but he fought like the devil, like a hundred devils. I remember we used to call him Grzesio, but I don't even know if that was his real name . . .'

He pulled the head off a thistle, put it on his palm and blew at the seeds. A warm wind was in his eyes, making him squint. The dog he had brought back from the war was running ahead of them; it had funny ears and a short tail and was called Grenade. The woman hated this dog and would close her eyes whenever it came running and nuzzled up to her, licking her hands. The soldier had brought back many things: a piece of shrapnel that had landed an inch above his head, a flattened bullet that had once been lodged in his leg, brass ashtrays made from sawn-off shell casings; his cigarette case was made out of aluminium sheeting from a shot-down plane. The woman ardently wished that some strange thief would turn up at their flat and take all of that away. She could not bring herself to poison the dog and destroy those things; she had waited for the soldier for many years and through many sleepless nights thought how everything he brought back would be dear and precious to her. But now he was farther away than he had been when she would gaze out of the window at the dark sky, imagining the day of his return. Farther away and different from the image she had carried in her heart. As the sky grew lighter she would think, 'Will he return? Is he alive? Is he wounded or is he all right?' Sometimes an alarming thought entered her mind: being far away from her, would he fall in love with someone else? But she would immediately chase that thought away and repeat, 'Will he return? Is he alive? Is he all right?' In the courtyard below her window, there were boys playing war day after day; their high, reedy voices filled her with hatred. They had wooden machine guns, wooden sabres and paper hats. One day, when she realized that the children were pretending they were executing Jews, she swore to herself that as soon as he came back they would leave that building forever. Now they had walked out of the town to look for a place where they might build their new home. In the fields, sheaves of harvested corn shimmered like gold. The dark skeleton of a windmill loomed in the distance: a stray bomb had shattered its sails and torn off its roof.

The soldier noticed the windmill and said, 'You see that? It reminds me of a story another soldier once told me. It was back in 1939. The Germans were coming, in huge numbers. Our men were retreating towards the woods. And then two tanks appeared out of the trees, cutting them off. That soldier and a few others hid inside a windmill, and from there they started blasting away with their machine guns. Then bang, the windmill got hit, but somehow nobody was hurt, except their eyes were plastered with flour. They ran blindly, under fire, and imagine this: nobody was hurt. But that soldier said he would never touch bread again, bread or anything that smelled even remotely like flour. You see, comical things happen in a war too.'

'When this windmill got hit,' the woman said quietly, 'many women and children were sheltering inside, and every single one of them died. They were down-to-earth country women and they had taken shelter inside a windmill because they thought the enemy wouldn't bomb windmills – because that's where bread is born, and bread is a sacred thing. But they all died.'

'Bah!' the soldier replied. 'It must have been a very light bomb and it hit from the side. That's nothing. The Americans were organizing air raids with thousands of planes! And each of those planes could drop a few tons of bombs. It's hard to even imagine what happened out there! After a bombing like that, nobody had any idea where the houses or the street *used* to be; the devil himself wouldn't be able to work it out. People trapped under the rubble could take a week or more to die. And God only knows how long they might lie there still, before somebody digs them out and buries them properly.'

They had come to the top of the tallest hill around. The town was off in the distance and now, in the setting sun, its blackened roof tiles appeared golden. Church spires gleamed and a luminous glow filled the sky above the cupola of the town's only Orthodox church. Over the distant forest the sky was already growing darker; a river ran through the valley below them, and fog was rising from the fields. It was a beautiful spot; the birds sang louder and more freely here, and one could breathe more deeply.

The woman said, 'This is where we will build our house.'

The soldier said nothing. He stood on the hill looking in every direction. He turned to face the forest. Then he looked down into the valley, furrowing his brow and moving his lips, as if calculating something. He shielded his eyes with his hand and surveyed the area for a long while. Then suddenly his stern face lit up and he smiled broadly.

He grabbed the woman's hand and, pulling her close to him, exclaimed, 'Well, I'll be damned! What a great spot for defence! Just think, all you need are three medium machine guns, a few grenade launchers and that's it. You could defend yourself for weeks! Let's imagine the attack is coming from the forest . . .'

'No!' the woman cried in despair. 'No!'

The soldier flinched and the light went out of his face. And then for the first time since he'd returned from the war, he saw that there was grain growing out of the earth, that people had ploughed it, that they were working on it without killing each other; he remembered that the earth is not only a grave but a source of life too. And suddenly, for the first time since the day he'd returned from the war, he felt exceedingly tired. He realized he was old and very alone.

'*Żołnierz*'
First published in *Po prostu* (1955, nr. 14), here from the collection *Pierwszy krok w chmurach* (Agora, 2014).

SURREALISTS

BRUNO SCHULZ

1892–1942

Bruno Schulz is renowned both for the intense poetic style of his writing and the tragic circumstances of his death in the Holocaust. He flashed on to Poland's literary scene in the 1930s with two collections of fantastical short stories. In 1942, during the German occupation of Poland, he was shot dead by a Gestapo officer in his hometown of Drohobycz (now Drohobych, Ukraine). Often likened to Franz Kafka, Schulz has inspired writers across the world with his unique imagination, but also with the legend of a great work lost in the war – an unfinished novel called *The Messiah*.

Schulz was born into a Jewish family in provincial Drohobycz, then part of the Austro-Hungarian Empire. His eccentric father – who would become a character in his stories – ran a textile shop. After the First World War, the region became part of a newly restored Polish state. Drohobycz was colloquially known as 'one and a half cities' for its mixed population of Poles, Jews and Ukrainians.

Schulz initially aspired to be a visual artist, making his living as a drawing teacher at the Drohobycz gymnasium school. From the early 1920s, he began exhibiting his own work, which obsessively featured masochistic erotic representations of stunted men prostrating themselves at the feet of imperious women.

Schulz's writing experiments began in the same period, but his first short story collection – *Sklepy cynamonowe* (*Cinnamon Shops*) – would not be published until 1933. Written in an exuberantly metaphorical style, the stories forged a kind of private mythology, imbuing the everyday world of Schulz's childhood and family with visionary imaginative power. He followed up with a second volume – *Sanatorium pod klepsydrą* (*Sanatorium under the Hourglass*) – in 1937. The Second World War cut short his career and then his life, brutally extinguished along with most of Drohobycz's Jewish community by the German occupiers.

After an initial period of anonymity in post-war socialist Poland, the inimitable inventiveness of Schulz's language eventually established him as an enduring classic of modern Polish literature.

Stanley Bill

My Father Joins the Fire Brigade

Translated by Stanley Bill

In the first days of October, we returned with Mother from a summer resort in the neighbouring province of our country, in the forested basin of the Słotwinka River – a region permeated with the springy murmur of a thousand streams. With our ears still filled with the rustle of alders interlaced with the chirping of birds, we travelled in a large old landau carriage, its enormous hood bulging like a dark, roomy inn, squashed in among our bundles in its deep, velvet-lined alcove, while colourful images of the landscape fell in through the window, page by page, as if shuffled slowly from one hand to another.

Towards evening, we came to a windswept plateau – a vast, astonished crossroads of the country. The sky hung deep and inspired above those crossroads, revolving at its zenith in the colourful rose of the winds. This was the most distant toll-gate of the country, the final bend before the expansive, late landscape of autumn opened up down below. Here was the border, and here stood an old, rotten border post with a faded sign playing in the wind.

The great wheel rims of the landau grated and dug into the sand; the chatter of the flashing spokes died away; only the great hood dully resounded as it flapped darkly in the crosswinds like the ark stranded in the wilderness.

Mother paid the toll, the toll-gate boom creaked up, and the landau drove heavily into the autumn.

We drove into the withered boredom of a great plain, into a pale and faded blusteriness that opened its blissful, vapid infinity over the yellow horizon. A late, towering eternity arose from that faded horizon, blowing across the plain.

Like an old romance novel, the yellowed pages of the landscape turned ever paler and ever more insipid, as if they were to meet their end in some great dissipated void. In that dispersed nothingness, in that yellow nirvana, we could have driven on beyond all time and reality, staying forever in that landscape, in that warm, barren blowing of the wind – a motionless stagecoach on enormous wheels, stuck amidst the clouds on the parchment of the sky, an old illustration, a forgotten woodcut in a quaint, scattered romance – when suddenly the coachman yanked on the reins with the last of his strength, steering the landau out of the sweet lethargy of those winds and turning into a forest.

We drove into a thick, dry fluffiness, a tobacco-like shrivelling. Soon it was as cosy and brown around us as the inside of a box of Trabucos. In that cedar semi-darkness, we clattered past trunks of trees as dry and fragrant as cigars. As we drove, the wood became darker and darker, smelling ever more aromatically of snuff, until at last it locked us in, as if inside the dry body of a cello that the wind had dully tuned. The coachman did not have any matches, so he could not light the lantern. The horses panted in the darkness, finding their way by instinct. The clatter of the spokes slowed down and became muted, as the wheel rims turned softly through fragrant pine needles. Mother fell asleep. Time passed, unaccounted, forming strange knots and abbreviations in its flow. The darkness was impenetrable and the dry soughing of the forest roared over the hood, when suddenly the ground hardened beneath the hooves of the horses into a cobbled road; the carriage turned on the spot and came to a halt. It stopped so close to a wall that it almost scraped against it. Across from the open door of the landau, my mother was groping about for the front door to our building. The coachman was unloading our bundles.

We entered the great, branching entrance hall. It was dark, warm, and cosy, like an empty old bakery after the oven has been put out in the morning, or a bathhouse late at night as the abandoned tubs and pails cool off in the dark in a silence measured out by drips. A cricket was patiently unpicking illusory stitches of light from the darkness, a faint thread from which it did not grow any brighter. We felt our way to the stairs. When we had reached a creaky landing at a corner, my mother said: 'Wake up, Józef. You're dropping on your feet. Only a few more steps now.' Senseless with sleepiness, I nestled more closely into her and fell fast asleep.

I could never find out from Mother afterwards how much had been real of what I had seen that night – through closed eyelids, overcome with drowsiness, falling into silent oblivion – and how much had been the fruit of my imagination.

A great debate was unfolding between Father, Mother and Adela, the protagonist of the scene – a debate of fundamental importance, as I now surmise. If it is in vain that I guess at its still elusive meaning, then the fault lies with certain gaps in my memory, the blank spots of sleep, which I strive to fill with guesswork, supposition and hypothesis. Dazed and unconscious, I kept drifting off into dull oblivion, while the breath of the starry night, scattered across the open window, fell upon my lowered eyelids. The night breathed in pure pulsations and then suddenly threw down a transparent curtain of stars, peering down from on high into my sleep with its old, eternal face. The ray of a distant star trapped in my eyelashes spilt its silver over the blind whites of my eyes; through the crack between my eyelids, I could see the room in the light of a candle tangled in a muddle of golden lines and zigzags.

Perhaps the whole scene really took place at some other time. There is much evidence to suggest that I witnessed it only some time later, when we returned home one day after closing up the shop with Mother and the shop assistants.

On the threshold of our apartment, Mother let out a cry of astonishment and delight, while the shop assistants were dumbstruck with awe. In the middle of the room stood a splendid brass knight, a veritable Saint George, made enormous by a cuirass, the gold bucklers of his spaulders, and the whole jingling paraphernalia of polished gold plate. With admiration and joy, I recognized the bristling moustache and beard of my father sticking out from beneath the heavy praetorian helmet. The breastplate rippled on his agitated chest, and the brass rings breathed through the gaps like the body of an enormous insect. Augmented by his armour in the gleam of golden metal, he looked like the Prince of the Heavenly Host.

'Sadly, Adela,' said Father, 'you have never had any understanding of matters of the higher spheres. Everywhere and always you have thwarted my plans with your outbursts of mindless anger. But now, clad in armour,

I laugh in the face of your tickling, which once brought me, defenceless, to the brink of despair. Helpless fury now moves your tongue to a pathetic volubility whose crudeness and vulgarity is mixed with dim-wittedness. Believe me when I say that it fills me only with sadness and pity. Devoid of any noble flights of fantasy, you burn with unconscious hatred for everything elevated above the commonplace.'

Adela looked Father up and down, her eyes filled with utter contempt. She turned to Mother with an agitated air, weeping tears of annoyance in spite of herself: 'He's taking all our juice! He's taking all the demijohns of raspberry juice that we cooked up together in the summer! He wants to give it all to those wastrel pompiers. And to make matters worse he has been showering me with impertinences.' She sobbed briefly. 'Captain of the fire brigade – captain of the bandits, more like it!' she cried, aiming a baleful look at Father. 'The place is crawling with them. In the morning, when I want to pop out to the bakery, I can't even get through the door. Two of them have fallen asleep on the threshold in the hallway, blocking the exit. On the staircase, there's one lying on each step, fast asleep in their brass helmets. They invite themselves into the kitchen, shoving their rabbity faces in those brass cans of theirs through the crack in the door, sticking up two fingers like schoolchildren and whining imploringly "Sugar, sugar" ... They tear the bucket out of my hands and run off to carry the water, dancing and simpering around me, as if they were wagging their tails. And all the while they leer at me with red eyelids, licking their lips repulsively. It's enough for me just to glance at one of them for his face to puff up in red, shameless flesh like a turkey. Imagine giving our raspberry juice to them!'

'Your vulgar nature,' said Father, 'defiles everything it touches. You have sketched out an image of these sons of fire worthy only of your own vapid mind. As for me, all my sympathies lie with that unhappy breed of salamanders, with those poor, disinherited creatures of fire. The only fault of that once magnificent breed lay in their submission to human service, that they sold themselves to men for a teaspoon of miserable human fare. They have been repaid with contempt. The dim-wittedness of the plebs is boundless. Those delicate creatures have been led into the deepest decline, into total degradation. Is it any wonder that they do not care for the bland, vulgar provender prepared in a communal cauldron by the school caretaker's wife for them and the town prisoners? Their palate – the delicate and prodigious palate of fire spirits – demands dark and noble balms, aromatic and colourful fluids. And so on that festive evening, when we shall all sit in celebration in the great hall of the town's Stauropegion Institute at a table laid in white, in that hall with its high, brightly illuminated windows throwing their light out into the depths of the autumn night, as the town outside teems with thousands of lights, then each of us will dip his bread roll into a cup of raspberry juice with the piety and discernment so characteristic of the sons of fire, slowly sipping the thick and noble liqueur. In this manner, the inner essence of the fireman is restored, regenerating the richness of colours that the whole tribe projects in the form of fireworks, rockets and Bengal lights. My soul is filled with pity for their misery, for their guiltless degradation. If I have accepted from their hands the captain's sabre, it is only in the hope that I might succeed in lifting the tribe out of its decline, leading it out of humiliation and unfolding above them the banner of a new idea.'

'You are entirely transformed, Jakub,' said Mother. 'You are magnificent. But you won't be going anywhere tonight. We haven't even had the chance to talk since my return. As for the pompiers,' she said, turning to Adela, 'it does seem to me that you are motivated by prejudice. They are nice boys, even if they are wastrels. It is always a delight to behold those slender young men in their fetching uniforms, just a little too tight at the waist. They have a great deal of natural elegance about them, and it is touching to see the ardour and enthusiasm with which they are ready to wait on the ladies at the drop of a hat. Whenever my parasol slips from my hand on the street or the ribbon of my shoe comes undone, one of them always comes running, filled with fervent solicitude and eagerness. I haven't the heart to disappoint their ardent intentions, and so I always wait patiently for him to reach me and come to my aid, which seems to make him very glad. As he walks away after the commission of his knightly duty, he is surrounded at once by the gang of his companions, who engage him in lively discussion about the whole incident, prompting the hero to re-enact it in mime. If I were you, I would make the most of their gallantry.'

'I regard them as freeloaders,' said Teodor, the senior shop assistant. 'After all, we don't even allow them to put out fires because of their childish irresponsibility. It's enough to see how enviously they stop before a group of boys tossing buttons against a wall to judge the maturity of their rabbit-like minds. When the wild shriek of play echoes in from the street, you can be almost certain when you look out of the window to see those beanpoles charging about among the whole gang of boys, entirely pre-occupied, almost unconscious in the clamour of the chase. At the sight of a fire, they go mad with joy, clapping their hands and dancing like savages. No, they're no use for putting out fires. We use the chimney sweeps and municipal police for that. Which only leaves games and folk festivals – in which they are unrivalled. For example, in the so-called storming of the Capitol, at the crack of dawn in autumn, they dress up as Carthaginians and lay siege to the Basilian hill with an infernal uproar. Then they all sing "Hannibal, Hannibal ante portas".

'Towards the end of autumn, they become lazy and languid, falling asleep on their feet. By the time the first snow falls, they can't be found for love or money. A certain old stove fitter once told me that while repairing chimneys he finds them attached to the inside of the flue, rigid as chrysa-lises in their red uniforms and shiny helmets. They sleep upright like that, drunk on raspberry juice, their insides filled with sticky sweetness and fire. Then he hauls them out by their ears and marches them back to their barracks, drunk with sleep and unconscious, through autumn morning streets coloured with the first light frost, while the passing street rabble throw stones at them, and they grin their embarrassed grins, filled with guilt and bad conscience, staggering along like drunkards.'

'In any case,' said Adela, 'I'm not giving them any juice. I didn't ruin my complexion in the kitchen boiling it up so that those wastrels could drink it all.'

Instead of answering, my father raised a whistle to his lips and blew it hysterically. As if they had been listening at the keyhole, four slender youths burst in and lined up against the wall. The room brightened with the gleam of their helmets, while they stood to attention, dark and tanned under their bright basinets, awaiting orders. At Father's signal, two of them took hold of each side of a large wicker-encased demijohn, filled with purple fluid, and, before Adela could stop them, they raced down the stairs with a clatter, carrying off the precious loot. The remaining two made military bows and then disappeared after the others.

For a moment, it seemed that Adela might be roused to an act of insanity, such was the fire that had engulfed her beautiful eyes. But Father did not wait for the eruption of her anger. In a single bound, he reached the window-sill and spread his arms. We ran after him. The market square was brightly sown with lights and teeming with colourful crowds. Beneath our building, eight firemen had stretched a huge sailcloth out into a circle. Father turned back to us once more, shining in all the glory of his armour, silently saluted us, and then, with arms outstretched, as bright as a meteor, he leaped out into the night, which burned with a thousand lights. It was such a beautiful sight that all of us clapped our hands in delight. Even Adela, forgetting her rancour, applauded the leap, performed with such elegance. My father hopped down jauntily from the sheet, jangled his metal carapace, and took his place at the head of the squad, which marched off in twos in a long, winding column that slowly disappeared down a dark channel through the crowd, the brass tins of their helmets shining.

'*Mój ojciec wstępuje do strażaków*'
Published as part of the collection *Sanatorium pod Klepsydrą* (Wydawnictwo Rój, 1937).

LEOPOLD TYRMAND

1920–1985

Leopold Tyrmand, novelist, writer, editor, sports journalist and jazz critic, was a familiar and stylish figure (famed for his colourful socks) in Warsaw in the first years after the war. He was a journalist at this point, but soon fell foul of the authorities in the early 1950s, and his uncompromising anti-communism and struggles with censorship meant that by the mid-1960s he had moved to the United States, where he spent the latter half of his life building a reputation as an arch conservative political commentator.

At the time the story that follows was written, however, Tyrmand was still a journalist in Warsaw, his home town. He had led quite an adventurous life by then. Hailing from an assimilated and comfortably off Jewish family, in the 1930s he studied architecture in Paris, which is where his passion for jazz was kindled. When war broke out, he ended up in Lithuania, writing for a communist publication. In 1941, he was arrested by the NKVD, but managed to escape en route for the gulag. He then volunteered for labour service in Germany, of all places, as he was able to pass for a Frenchman and worked, among other things, as an agricultural worker, translator, waiter and hotel clerk. At the end of the war, Tyrmand found himself in Norway as a press correspondent. It was this Scandinavian stint that provided him with the material for his first stories, including this one, which were published after his return to Warsaw in 1946. Many of them have remained in print ever since.

He is probably best known for his diary (*Diary 1954*), written in the early 1950s 'for the drawer' (that is, in the knowledge that immediate publication was unlikely), when he was struggling to get published, and for the thriller *Zły* (1955, translated as *The Man with White Eyes*). Set among the criminal world of post-war Warsaw, it became an instant bestseller. His other great claim to fame is for introducing American jazz to a Polish audience. In fact, he was the founder of Poland's oldest jazz festival, which continues to this day.

Anna Zaranko

The Bicycle, or Morality's Revenge

Translated by Anna Zaranko

This is a completely improbable story and had I not witnessed it very directly, I would never have believed it myself. It began as I was crossing the great hall of Stockholm's Central Station at a leisurely pace, when some quite down-at-heel fellow approached me and said in a plaintive voice: 'Help me, kind sir, not a morsel has passed my lips today . . .' He stretched out a suitably dirty hand for alms as he spoke.

'Sir,' I said in astonishment, 'have you not confused your lines of latitude and longitude a little? I am not in the habit of daydreaming, and you, sir, look to me like a regular Warsaw beggar, which in view of both the national aspect of your person and your profession, constitutes rather a rare phenomenon in Sweden.'

'Indeed,' the beggar gave a somewhat melancholy smile, 'and hence I rarely importune Swedes. I look out for foreigners and attempt to address them in their native tongue. Sometimes I'm mistaken, but on the whole, it makes an excellent impression. In your case, sir,' here he made a bow of some refinement, 'I had the sincere pleasure of addressing you in the language of our mutual homeland. The newspaper poking out of your pocket and the provocative glance that you direct at everything you see in a foreign station revealed the truth to me.'

Sure enough, a Warsaw newspaper was still stuck in my coat pocket. As for my glance, I did not feel affronted, since in the conviction of almost every Pole aggressiveness passes as an asset. On the other hand, this beggar with a Voltairean hero's powers of reflection and the gestures of a man of the world was of keen interest to me. He was very seedy, true, but his shabbiness had a certain style, as though cultivated deliberately. It did not seem to me, however, that this incontrovertible finery was meant to be a feature of the trade; it emerged rather from indifference to his role, an artistry of sorts that characterizes the sophisticated in everything they do. The fellow had evidently told himself at some point: 'Now we shall take up beggary for such and such a time,' and would therefore do anything to ease its tedium. I don't deny that circumstances might have driven him to it, but nonetheless, the fundamental principle remains the same.

'My dear sir,' I said with as much nonchalance as I could muster, 'I have three hours before my train departs, as I am only passing through Stockholm. Would you care to take a cup of coffee with me?'

'Dear God,' he said with faint irony. 'I am moved by these manifestations of fellow feeling. I hope, at least, that you are not prompted at this point by national solidarity.'

'You are right. After the last war and its migratory consequences, I rather avoid manifestations of national solidarity when abroad.'

'And are you not embarrassed to sit down in a café with me?'

'My dear sir, the very fact that I gave you no alms is proof enough that I am no superficial slave to convention. In Warsaw, I might perhaps have hesitated in such a situation. In Stockholm, I am sure that my novel company is only to be envied.'

'You have convinced me,' he said, with another faint bow, and a moment later we were walking in the direction of Kungsgatan.

In an elegant tearoom, we were welcomed, as I had expected, with curious glances. I studied my companion in full light. He must have been well over thirty and had the face and eyes of someone who was no stranger to thought. It was a matter only of what kind.

'Well then?' I said expectantly.

'Naturally,' he replied, drawing deeply on his cigarette, 'I might have foreseen it. The curiosity of a consummate old collector of interesting stories, eh? Well, I have nothing to hide – on the contrary, such a café confession might afford me some relief, perhaps even good advice.'

'The outbreak of war,' he began, 'found me in Gdynia, where I was director of a certain highly prosperous business. I don't claim that the business was of any greater economic than social significance, and social only in a very limited sense. Oh no, let's be frank: the economic gravity of my concern was negligible. What, after all, can a small, clean and indolently managed tobacco shop mean in the turnover of a great port? Even the fact that one could always obtain contraband tobacco from anywhere in the world in this shop was not the crux of the matter. Tobacco-smuggling, a minor shortcoming in terms of prevailing regulations, was a harmless, charming façade. All the senior officers of the Gdynia port police got their supplies of "Camels" and "Abdullas" at my shop, patting me knowingly on the shoulder. "If yours was the only kind we had to deal with . . ." they would say, with indulgent smiles, as I celebrated the ritual of selling a smuggled pack of cigarettes to the authorities' most dangerous representatives.

'Behind the shop was a small, nicely arranged room, of which my favourite detail was its thoroughly well-stocked library. I loved those books, bound to them as I was by numerous ties. The pages of some concealed bills of lading worth millions, freight transfers constituting the wealth of every kind of financial centre in Warsaw, Budapest, Prague or Vienna, and routes and collection points for goods of limited cubic capacity but worth a lifetime's earnings. *Des affaires louches*, you, sir, might say, as they do in France in such cases. Indeed, but that's not all. My affection for books had also a touch of purest gratitude for things intangible. From these books I derived faith in myself and the legitimacy of my practical principles. And on the basis of these, I built my ethics and morality, my worldview. It wasn't complicated, this worldview of mine, and certainly nothing novel. It simply constituted a system perfectly justifying all the instincts, impressions and arguments that stemmed from my earliest years, and most importantly – stamped all I had been doing for many years with the seal of logic and righteousness. What had I been doing, you might ask? That's simple: I stole. I stole in the most ordinary way in the world and with remarkable virtuosity. You must admit, too, that the most gorgeous library could be assembled of books justifying and even glorifying thievery.

'I will confess that sometimes I wondered at myself regarding the source of this passion of mine for inner validation of my own actions. I was the son of a Warsaw shopkeeper from Krucza Street. I went to a good high school, and supposedly stood out on account of my intelligence and talents. Throughout my youth, I could see a clear incongruity between my father's life and his dreams. He wished to grow wealthy through the scrupulous and honest trade of imported groceries. His desires seemed praiseworthy to me; the means of realizing them came across as a profound misunderstanding. When I looked around, I easily ascertained that everyone stole, restrained to a greater or lesser degree by fear or lack of competence. For a short while, I wondered if this was a good thing, if the fault lay in the structures of interpersonal relations, but I quickly concluded that it was not a fault at all, but the essence of life, and that it wasn't bad, but actually very good. I came to believe in the doctrine that living beings mutually devour each other and applied it to my observations. As a result of these reflections, I understood that stealing was a result of civilizational progress, a superior form of gaining the upper hand over one's fellow man and destroying him, that it was the privilege of the cleverer and more astute, and a nobility of sorts. The growing complexity of forms of theft – there's the true history of civilization! Honesty for me was the religion of the weak and of little value. I resented Nietzsche for drawing back midstream without ever formulating this truth.

'I left my family home presently and became famous as one of Warsaw's most nimble-fingered thieves. I worked alone and soon the capital's entire criminal world knew me. Warsaw jewellers trembled at the mention of my moniker; I was elusive, and considered the police who stalked me to be opponents whose aim was not to protect the property of others, but to destroy me as their rival in combat. I relished the feeling of personal power. In time, I abandoned stealing and took up fraud on a grand scale. I came to the conclusion that it represented an even higher degree of development, the mathematical antithesis of honesty, full of thrilling, mental effort. The speculative essence of the great scandals of the time seemed to me equal to pure philosophy, and I revelled in it intellectually and creatively. I settled in Gdynia as a small tradesman and quiet Epicurean. My way of life, after all, natural and unaffected – peaceful evenings with a book and elegant parties for a select group of friends, a fine collection of antiques and innocuous sedate pastimes – earned me a good reputation in the town. Presently, my business grew to gigantic proportions. The little tobacconist's shop became the centre of a network encompassing Rotterdam and Lulea, Bahia-Blanca, Saigon and Marseille. Obviously, I became more than just a rich man; I could afford myself the luxury of not keeping a wife, and frequent contemplation in a comfortable armchair with a bottle of smooth sherry.

'War destroyed it all. I felt deep disgust for politics and politicians.

I regarded their activities as the most brutish kind of crime. All force aroused my abhorrence. It contradicted the progress of civilization, of which the greatest embodiment for me was the skill and finesse of the thief or swindler. Politics brought crime in its wake, and crime was regression, a backward march in the direction of the Stone Age. I had always despised crime, violence and murder and strove to keep my hands clean of them. Everything in me seethed at the sight of the Germans who perfectly personified the politics of crime. Had I undertaken anti-German operations in these new circumstances, I would have descended, with time, to the role of a Janosik, that legendary Slovak highwayman, a role that had always struck me as cheap and melodramatic. It was easy for me, therefore, to move to Sweden.

'Obviously, I was still a very wealthy man. I had a sizeable fortune in Sweden, a beautiful villa and all the accoutrements of a comfortable life. At first, I studied my new surroundings keenly for a while and came to the conclusion that fate could not have placed me better. Sweden seemed to me like some mission territory, just waiting for my arrival and activity. I also quickly honed my conviction that the proverbial honesty of this country's inhabitants was a false, coerced discipline that constituted an antiquated muzzle on the path to developing a genuine life. With light-hearted zeal, and convinced that I was amusing myself rather than working, I set about organizing a black market in Sweden. Certain successes – in the sense of profits – were there to be achieved, but they were the outcome of limited speculation among the large group of political and war refugees that had arrived in Sweden at the beginning of the 1940s. The few hundred Swedes who had let themselves be drawn into the realm of illegal stock-market speculation did not amuse themselves for long, with the exception of the few who were completely ruined and for whom a return to their points of departure became impossible. When the currency-trading circuit completely lost its appeal, I set about rebuilding my smuggling contacts; I adapted them to wartime conditions and created a black market for goods. After an initial period of success smuggling medicines, spirits and expensive tobacco, after a few deftly organized diamond and drug booms and busts, I ascertained with interest that a substantial majority of Swedish society was not interested one jot in the black market. I lowered my prices to a minimum, consequently suffering enormous losses. I wanted to imbue the ordinary Swede with a desire for original Scotch whisky, and to set the average Swedish woman aglow with the hope of obtaining original Coty perfumes for a song. The surveys that I conducted in conversation at every opportunity showed me that my efforts were going down the drain, that grey Swedes did not want all these things in the least, that they were deeply indignant about people who sabotaged government prohibitions, considered their activities to be harmful, and believed that since the state had decided not to import certain things – the citizen should forgo them for his own good.

'This satisfied, bovine honesty that limited itself to possessing the small but permitted thoroughly infuriated me. I could not conceive how one could content oneself with what was given and not desire what belonged to another. The legalism of the Swedes seemed to me tragically excessive, and their honesty – the ultimate foolishness. I determined to wage a life-or-death battle against the habitual ethical climate that prevailed in this country. I withdrew into my abode and for whole days at a time in my study I devised gigantic battle plans against rectitude. At last, the plan was ready. I was determined to provoke a universal crisis of mutual distrust, beginning with a series of shocking thefts to torpedo and blow the lazy peace of this land sky high. I worked out a detailed schedule of action. In the seclusion of my villa, I practised and trained in preparation for the astonishing actions that were to appal and incite revolution in Swedish public opinion.

'As a little training exercise in the field, before embarking on the action proper, I decided to rob a small jeweller's shop on one of Stockholm's main streets. Here, I must inform you that at one time I was an unsurpassed master of shoplifting, popularly known in Warsaw as *szopenfeld*. My exploits back in the home country and my guest appearances abroad in Europe's greatest capitals were the talk of every newspaper and the cause of attacks of melancholia among the chiefs of police concerned. The extraction of four pearls from the Parisian house of Duval et Duval was my work, a deed that set several heads spinning among the jewellers' dynasties on the rue Rivoli. The craft of *szopenfeld* found its champion in me, whose destiny it was to transform it into Great Art. The famous academy of larceny at Straszun Street in Wilno, whose graduates called the shots across three continents in the criminal world, offered me the chair of the theory of *szopenfeld*, with a fee of one thousand dollars for a cycle of lectures. I refused, but I did deliver one address before an audience of professors for which I was awarded a doctorate *honoris causa* from that now defunct institution. The president of the Belgian police sent me a private letter, full of expressions of astonishment, after I'd robbed a few of the wealthiest diamond cutters in Antwerp. After a guarantee of absolute immunity, I engaged in a two-hour conversation with him, upon which he presented me with his photograph bearing the dedication: 'To a Grand Master from an old detective' and we remained firm friends. Armed with these traditions, I set off for my training session as for a pleasant long-neglected pastime. I even eschewed all appurtenances, I didn't take a car, I dressed casually. I was careful only to acquire a passport with a false name, got on my bicycle and, whistling to myself, I rode along the bustling streets of Stockholm. On reaching the spot, I parked my bicycle on a little square at the intersection of Queen Street and Apelbergsgatan and with my hands in my pockets I turned onto the main road. I opened the door to the shop and entered, to exit in the company of two policemen. Yes, yes, only then did I truly understand the relativity of all values. A kindly, pink, gormless little ignoramus, a third-rate Stockholm jeweller, turned out to be my first vanquisher. He'd noticed a lightning gesture, a gesture more fleeting than the waft of a breeze and faster than light, a gesture that the most consummate sleuths could only dream of noticing. Next, with the help of a nimbly drawn revolver, he forced me to put up both my hands, briskly closed his shop and quickly contacted the police. Those five minutes of fortune's vicissitudes cost me eighteen months in prison in all, but they taught me the power of relativism.

'I made use of the time of seclusion that my failure had cost me in fundamental rumination. Once again, through careful analysis of my life and deeds, I tested their validity and the validity of their premises. I remembered the times of my early youth, when I began to discover the intoxicating taste of transgression. The long-forgotten moments of first misdeeds and first thefts came back to me. I recalled the pleasure I'd already taken as a child when, unnoticed by anyone, I could wipe my snotty nose on someone else's fresh towel or, when visiting acquaintances, I would clean my shoes with their most beautiful curtains. Through these memories, I conjured up the incomparable joy that flooded my heart after the deft appropriation of some object, regardless of whether it was the tie of an incidental companion in a swimming-pool changing room, or a gold bracelet from the counter of a jeweller's shop. On each of my several hundred days of prison, I strengthened my faith in my own power, superiority and autonomy, while every evening I fell asleep on my prison bunk in the blissful conviction that I was right, and with the clear conscience of a person who has chosen his own path in life. Hence, when I came out of prison and realized that in the meantime my servant had sold the villa and disappeared without trace, I bore him no ill-will. I considered him to be a plucky individual who, knowing much about me and not wishing to inform the police of my real name and standing, had also taken his chances in the most appropriate manner possible. As for me, I had to start all over again. I was, however, full of the energy and inner joy that a clear life goal provides. Owing to my considerable sense of sportsmanship, alongside an indispensable *esprit de revanche*, I determined to resume my activities by thoroughly clearing out the jeweller with whom I still had an account to settle. With this aim in mind, I disguised myself superbly – a talent I've not yet mentioned – and set off, full of the joyful spirit of battle in a just cause. Crossing Queen Street slowly, at a certain point I found myself faced with a completely unexpected phenomenon. Imagine, if you will, that my bicycle, which I had ridden to this self-same square twenty months before, was standing there, leaning against the rack, in the very spot in which I had placed it with my own hands. I came closer, rubbing my eyes in astonishment, but the fact proved as real as could be. My bicycle stood before me, a little rusty from the rain, and dusty, but the very same. You should also be aware, sir, that it was a beautiful bicycle, the best English make, very expensive and stylish, and equipped with every possible enhancement: a dynamo, indicator lights, reflectors. What's more, in the pannier bag – you know, here in Sweden they have these side-bags – in this bag, then, I had left 500 kronor in small notes. I remembered about the money, left over from some trip or other, while still in prison. Now, with trembling hands, I unfastened the bag and trembling inside I took out the 500 kronor and a few other trifles, like a gold cigarette case and a lighter of the same.

'What a blow! A slap as salutary as it was devastating. Five-hundred kronor was the monthly salary of a reasonably paid official in those days.

In my situation, such a sum could prove salvific as substantial seed capital. But on the other hand, these same 500 kronor, lying for twenty months in the very centre of a busy street and undisturbed by anyone – this was a blow to my concept of life. I stood over the bicycle, not knowing what to do. My rapacious energy for battle, energy for vengeance and conscious endeavour yielded to some kind of violent disintegration. After ten minutes I decided to take the money and the bicycle, another ten and I'd come to the conclusion that this would be the greatest of my life's disasters. I knew very well that I could not rise to an encounter with my jeweller that day. Eventually, I left everything as it was. 'It's impossible,' I repeated to myself, 'today, tomorrow or the day after, some sensible person will turn up who will take it all . . .'

'From then on, I came to the corner of Queen Street and Apelbergs-gatan every day. I was incapable of any kind of undertaking. I lost all sense of purpose, and what follows from purpose – faith in one's own strength. I was afraid that my nerves would fail me should I embark on any kind of action and that I'd break down like a novice. I'd stand about the street for hours at a time, staring at the bicycle like someone hypnotized. I began to hate it. A kind of silent battle ensued between us, a terrible struggle between the bicycle and me. I abused it, as one abuses a personal enemy in one's thoughts while standing at a distance of several paces from him. "You swine," I'd say, "I could smash you into a tiny heap of old iron, but no, after all, I'm no fool; your fate is to be stolen, together with the cash deep in your bag . . ." I trembled at the thought that it might end up tidied away by the city council, and that they would make an announcement in the lost and found columns in the newspapers. I would open the morning papers with alarm and every day I'd ascertain with immeasurable relief that it had not happened. At night, I dreamed invariably that I could see a hunched figure stealing towards the bicycle: with quick furtive movements, he removes the money from the pannier, looks about on all sides, jumps on to the saddle and races away, in fear of pursuit. I would wake up, full of blissful joy that all was in its proper order, that once again the world revolved about the sun and not the other way around, as it had done for these past few days. I would jump up and run to Queen Street to check that the bicycle was indeed there, on the spot, contradicting the most mar-vellous dreams. I attempted to escape it. I would flee to the furthest ends of town, to remote, half-deserted parks, I would sit on benches and construe precise and foolproof plans for magnificent thefts. I would jump up from the bench full of new vigour and optimism and rush back to town. Then my feet would turn of their own accord always onto that same path at the end of which loitered the solitary, rusty, blackened bicycle. Once, I decided to take a trip away from Stockholm. I bought a ticket and boarded a train. A minute before departure I tumbled out of the station like a madman and raced to that luckless corner. Suddenly it seemed to me that it was all over, that the bicycle had gone, that I couldn't leave without knowing of this great victory. But the bicycle was there. And the money too, the cigarette case and the lighter.

'Slowly, the reserves of money returned to me upon leaving prison ran out. I was incapable of earning a living, I, a poor wreck of a human being for whom the whole of humanity and his view of it had suddenly fled the earth for the moon and there turned upside down. *Et, me voilà*, as the French say.'

He finished, lit a cigarette and smiled at me. Irony vied with despair in this smile. I felt greatly confused. What to say to someone who has lost his illusions? It made no essential difference that here was a strange phenomenon of illusion lost *à rebours*; the very fact of losing the ground from under one's feet, the loss of one's own view of the world, is tragic enough and can lead to catastrophe. This poor man had overdone negativity somewhat, but he was hardly the first in the world to do so. Worse were the overly far-reaching conclusions that he had drawn from his initial pessimistic assertions, but that was a question rather of individual destiny.

'Excuse me,' I said tentatively, 'but did you never consider that people might be honest for, let us say, completely altruistic reasons, out of a mere sense of moral equilibrium, from a simple consciousness of good and evil, or perhaps even due to an impulse of the heart?'

He gave me a long look. The despair in his eyes was clearly subsiding, leaving pure irony.

'That's good, what you just said. Yet you yourself do not believe it. You simply want to believe it. You gather a little bouquet of clichés with which you wish to persuade me, while achieving the exact opposite of what you intend. Do you think that human honesty can be justified somehow? Do you imagine that without fear of punishment, any bunch of humans could possibly understand the concept of honesty at all?'

I felt quite uncomfortable.

'You know what,' I said, 'please show me this bicycle. I would love to take a look at it myself. It will lift my spirits.'

He bowed his head in disgust. I paid and we emerged onto Kungsgatan, which was brightly lit. Passing the entrances of banks and the rich displays of jewellers, my ragged companion cast a seasoned hunter's glance at them. We turned into Queen Street. Approaching the junction slowly, the beggar leaned forwards, straining to see. He turned pale and his lips began to tremble. He grabbed my arm and whispered: 'It's gone!'

Nearing the little square, empty at that hour, I could see the plainly empty, multi-bicycle rack. Something strange was going on with the man beside me. He was shaking and his hands were fluttering as though in a fit of shivering.

'A cigarette, please,' he whispered, feverishly. 'I'll give you a thousand in return. In a month's time, I'll hold a banquet in your honour at the most expensive restaurant in Stockholm. The bicycle obsession is over! I have won! I have triumphed! Tomorrow, I will start afresh. So, I was right, in the end. In a week's time, I shall be one of the wealthiest men in this accursed and stupid country. I invite you to my mansion, I shall send you the address forthwith. We will drink sherry and discourse by the fireside on the eternal, immutable, human Thief . . .'

A figure emerged from the dark wall on the opposite side of the street. It crossed the street and headed straight in our direction. It was a tall, burly man in some kind of uniform. He came up and touched his cap. Then he said a few words, from which I gathered with difficulty that he was asking us what we were looking for. My companion was silent.

'A bicycle,' I said, in my broken English. 'Our bicycle was standing here.'

The Swede began to explain something. Amid the rush of words, I ceased to grasp anything. With astonishment I ascertained only that the beggar was backing away, looking at the Swede with eyes full of alarm. Suddenly he turned, and began to run. In a moment he had vanished from our sight.

The Swede was utterly dismayed. Luckily, he knew a little German. Stammering with concern, he asked what had happened to my companion.

I felt very foolish since I did not know how to explain. In any case, I circled my finger at my forehead a few times, an international sign for the same phenomenon. It did not enlighten the Swede much and he continued to be upset. He was the night watchman of this district and as it turned out, even the hypothesis of a slight derangement on the part of the fugitive reassured him not one bit.

'But why did it disturb him so,' he repeated, 'when I told him the bicycle was ready to be picked up? Not even a madman should be flustered by such news. Because you see, sir, it was I who took the bicycle. I was sorry for the vehicle, it had stood here so long, I thought: I'll take it and clean it up. I don't know why the owner doesn't come and fetch it, but when he does, then at least he will find it in good order. While I'm on duty, I don't have much to do at night in any case, so it will occupy the time. There was some cash in there, a cigarette case and lighter, but everything's here, you'll find it in its place.'

'Would you tell me please,' I said after a moment's silence during which the Swede shook his head without stopping. 'Honestly: the bicycle has been standing here a long time, no one has claimed it, it's rusting away in the rain . . . Did it never occur to you simply to take it?'

'No.'

'But why? Can't you explain why you didn't?'

'That's very simple.' The Swede smiled broadly. 'Why, the bicycle isn't mine.'

'*Rower, czyli zemsta moralności*'
Published as part of the collection *Gorzki smak czekolady Lucullus* (Czytelnik, 1957).

STANISŁAW LEM

1921–2006

Well read in biology, physics, chemistry and philosophy, Stanisław Lem was the father of Polish science fiction. The genre gave him a degree of freedom from the communist censors, and his highly inventive mind allowed him to use it for philosophical exploration.

He was a prolific author of novels and short stories, many of which have been translated into dozens of languages including English. Partly because of two film adaptations, his best-known novel is *Solaris* (1961, available in translation by Bill Johnston), about a planet covered by an apparently lifeless ocean that exerts a strange influence on the scientists who go to research it, causing them to bring their subconscious images to life; thus they are haunted by ghosts from the past. Ultimately this unsettling story is about the transitory nature of human existence.

Lem was Jewish and survived the war in Lwów under a false identity, but was never willing to talk about his wartime experiences. Since his death, his biographers have identified many of his most significant ordeals cryptically disguised within his fiction. Often described as a futurologist, he was remarkably good at predicting future technological advances, including e-books, smartphones, virtual reality, AI and the internet, of which he took a pessimistic view, predicting that it would cause trouble.

Though fascinated by technology, he refused to use a computer, but he did have an electric typewriter, the only kind that existed with Polish fonts, made by an East German firm called Robotron, which went bust. With no ribbons available any more, this machine, like many others that he collected, became yet another piece of out-of-date technology cluttering the Lem household. He loved cars, and was especially proud of his Mercedes, in which he drove his wife and son on family holidays abroad.

His talent for writing disturbing stories that make us question our existence was equalled by his skill as a comedian. 'An Enigma' illustrates his incredible imagination, erudition and ability to play with language.

Antonia Lloyd-Jones

An Enigma

Translated by Antonia Lloyd-Jones

Father Tynkan, Doctor of Magnetics, was sitting in his cell, creaking a bit – having deliberately failed to oil himself in an act of self-mortification – and was busy studying a commentary by Chlorophantus Omniscius, paying special attention to his famous Part Six, 'On the Creation of Robots'. He had just reached the end of the verse about the programming of the Universe, and was earnestly examining the pages of colourful illuminations that showed how the Lord, having taken a special liking to iron above all other metals, breathed the Spirit into it, when Father Chlorian quietly entered the cell and stood shyly by the window, for fear of disturbing the great theologian in his meditations.

'How now, my dear Chlorian? What do you have to tell me?' asked Father Tynkan shortly after, raising his limpid, crystalline eyes from the volume.

'My Father and Master,' said Chlorian, 'I have brought you a book, inspired by the urgings of Satan, newly anathematized by the Holy Office, and written by the vile Lapidor of Marmaggedon, known as the Halogenite, with descriptions of the lewd experiments he conducted in an effort to controvert the true faith.'

And he placed before Father Tynkan a slender tome, already bearing the stamp of the Holy Office in the appropriate manner.

As the venerable Father wiped his brow, a little rust fell from it, sprinkling the pages of the book, which he picked up briskly with the words: 'Not vile, not vile, my dear Chlorian, but unfortunate for having gone astray!'

As he spoke, he leafed through the book; seeing the titles of the individual chapters, including 'On Softies, Softlings and Pallid Softcentres', 'On Intelligent Dairy Products', 'On the Genesis of the Mind from the

Mindless Machine', he smiled faintly, but benevolently, and then casually said: 'Both you, my dear Chlorian, and the entire Holy Office, whom I respect and admire, take a wholly misguided approach to matters of this kind. What do we really have here? Imaginary bunkum, pure balderdash, bogus legends, reheated for the umpteenth time – all on the theme of these sponge-bodies, jellymen, or pasty-faced squidglings, as the other Apocrypha say – the so-called Aspicians, who in days of yore allegedly created us out of wire and screws . . .'

'Instead of the Lord on High!' hissed Father Chlorian, shuddering.

'Anathematizing everything to the left and right will not have much effect,' Father Tynkan benignly continued. 'As a matter of fact, did not Father Etheric of the Phasotrons adopt a wiser position three decades ago, when he said that this is not an issue for theology, but for natural history?'

'But Father Tynkan,' said Father Chlorian, almost choking, 'preaching this doctrine *ex cathedra* is prohibited, and the only reason why we have not condemned it is the saintliness of its author, who . . .'

'Calm down, my dear Chlorian,' said Father Tynkan. 'It's just as well it hasn't been condemned, because it doesn't sound bad at all. In Etheric's view, even if we accept that once upon a time there really were some sort of soft beings, who supposedly created us in their workshops, and then annihilated themselves, that does not in the least contradict the supernatural origin of the spirit. So by the will of the Lord, who is almighty, those simple pallidones could have been the tool of the genuine creation – thus He entrusted to their hands the construction of the steel folk, who after the Last Experiment would raise their voices in songs of thanksgiving to Him. Indeed, I believe that an alternative attitude, categorically denying such an eventuality, smacks of appalling heresy, for it goes against the Scriptures by denying His omnipotence.'

'Nonetheless, Father Tynkan, the doctor of holy theology Cyborax has pointed out that the work titled *The Jellicles* by the pallidologist Tourmaline, on which Father Etheric based his study, contains not just theses that are an affront to reason, but also blasphemies against the faith. For in this work it is said that the Aspicians did not produce their progeny on the basis of standard designs, with the involvement of reprostruction engineers, by the only natural method, meaning assembly from prefabricated parts, but without any training or documentation, in a wanton manner, with no consideration whatsoever. But how on earth could such designless offspring be possible? If it were illegal, or made, for instance, according to a plan that hadn't been approved by the relevant authorities at the Department for Demographic Industry, that I can understand – but without any documentation?!'

'It is strange, I admit, but where is the blasphemy in that?'

'Forgive me, Reverend Father, but I in turn am amazed that you cannot perceive it . . . If they could do something *stante pede, ipso facto, ex tempore,* which for us requires the completion of higher education, elaboration by a committee and computational expertise, then every one of them must have had a command of reprostruction equal to the knowledge of our cyberneticists, PhDs and even senior professors of computer science at their fingertips! Can that really be possible? How could any pipsqueak produce progeny out of nowhere? How on earth could he know what to do? That would mean the alternative to gaining a diploma is producing offspring without any knowledge at all, just like that, with a push and a shove – I can hardly force the words out of my mouth. Because that would mean ascribing to them the potential for *creationis ex nihilo* – making something out of nothing, and, by that same token, the power to perform miracles – that is a property of the Lord alone.'

'You are saying that they were either geniuses of conception, or miracle workers?' said Father Tynkan. 'But according to the pallidologist Dialysius, although they did not produce their offspring in consultation with a learned assembly, nor did they do it singly, but in pairs. This is where I discern their expert specialization! The evidence is to be found in words that have survived on the pages of burned library books, where they appear to use paired forms of address: "Bello", "Bella" – surely it was meant to be "Jello" and "Jella"? And thus *semper duo faciebant collegium multiplicationis* – they always multiplied in a council of two, do you see? They sought privacy in order to consult each other, to discuss the technical drawings, and perform the essential multiplication. They must have conferred on the concept, because without carrying out the conceptual work, conception would be impossible, as the etymology plainly implies, my dear Chlorian. They must certainly have agreed on the design before starting to assemble the micro-components – how could it have been otherwise? Planning and making a rational being, whether hard or soft, is no mean feat.'

'I'll tell you what I would rather not live to see,' declared Father Chlorian, his voice trembling. 'Reverend Father, your line of thought has taken a dangerous path! Just another step, and you'll be telling me offspring can be produced not at the drawing board, by testing prototypes in a laboratory, with the highest concentration of the spirit in the metal, but in a bed, without any templates or training, at random, in the dark, and quite unintentionally . . . I implore you – I warn you, this is not just meaningless twaddle, this is the incitement of Satan! Father, come to your senses . . .'

'Do you think Satan would put himself to all that trouble?' replied the stubborn old fellow. 'But never mind the arcana of child production. Come closer, and I'll let you in on a secret that you might find reassuring . . . Yesterday I learned that three chemistants from the Institute of Colloids used gelatin, water and something else too – cheese, I think – to build a blancmange that they're calling the Jelloid Brain, because this blancmange can not only solve problems of higher algebra, but has also learned to play chess so well that it won against the head of the Institute. As you can see, it's quite futile to insist that no thought could ever be sustained in gelatinous matter, and yet that is the rigid opinion of the Holy Office!'

'Zagadka'
Published as part of the collection *Zagadka. Opowiadania* (Wydawnictwo Iskry, 1996).

SŁAWOMIR MROŻEK

1930–2013

Sławomir Mrożek was internationally famous as a writer of absurdist plays that satirize the totalitarian world and the helplessness of the individual in the face of institutions and systems. He also wrote numerous short stories and novellas, and drew cartoons.

After graduation, in the 1950s he wrote satirical texts for the press, radio, theatre and cabaret. His surreal humour was soon apparent, sending up bureaucracy and what Miłosz defines as 'the specifically Polish mixture of industrialization and backwardness, sophistication and parochialism'. For instance, in his story 'The Elephant' (1958), concerned about their lack of one, the directors of a small-town zoo make their own, inflatable elephant, but the wind blows it away and treetops puncture it; their disillusionment prompts some child witnesses to become hooligans.

His first play, *The Police* (1958), established his reputation. It satirizes the secret police, which has to invent crimes to keep itself going, and despairs when there's only one political offender left. He turned towards 'absurdism', writing plays that centre on two or three people cast into an existential dilemma. In *Out at Sea* (1960), three elegant shipwrecks sit in a raft debating which one should be eaten by the other two; in *Tango* (1965), a young man tries in various peculiar ways to impose order on his dissolute parents and grandparents, but fails; driven to impose a reign of terror, he's finally deposed and murdered by his mother's proletarian lover. *Tango* encapsulates Polish intelligentsia attitudes over several decades, and satirizes various approaches to political organization: through tradition, an ideology, fascism or revolution.

In 1963 Mrożek emigrated, and spent much of his life in France. He returned to live in Kraków in 1996, but emigrated again in 2008.

In 2002 he had a stroke, resulting in aphasia, which he overcame by writing *Baltazar* (2006), a remarkable autobiography. Free of his usual humour, it describes his childhood, his youthful reasons for embracing socialism and his problems with alcohol in the early 1960s.

Antonia Lloyd-Jones

Last Words

Translated by Antonia Lloyd-Jones

I

Basically I'm a philosopher. But my work titled *On the Nature of Everything* has not brought me fame, because I've never written it. My poems have been published in several academic journals with a readership limited to the editors' immediate circle. I had a little more success with some stories that appeared in the more serious pornographic magazines. It was only my television series, in other words a fictional story produced in episodes, that made me famous. The title of the series and the opinion of the more discriminating critics are two things I shall pass over in silence, but if I mention fame or, to be precise, popularity, it's only because it was thanks to this popularity that one day I found myself in a high-security prison visiting room, face to face with Tomasz, known as the Zombie, a mass murderer.

Tomasz the Zombie had been sentenced to death. The protests of those who opposed the death sentence on principle and the appeals of the defence counsels were still in progress, but the date when the sentence would be carried out had already been fixed; the chances of it being changed or even deferred were very slim. Tomasz had killed professionally, as a hired assassin, from early youth and for many years before he was caught for the first time. He'd been given a long prison sentence, then released early for impeccable behaviour, but had immediately returned to his former activities. Caught a second time and given a life sentence, then released again – though a little later than before – thanks to the ruling of psychiatric experts, he was soon up to his old tricks, which were quite variously interpreted. Some regarded his deeds as ordinary crimes, while others saw them as an indictment of society for raising Tomasz the

Zombie badly; they demanded the immediate, radical, political and economic transformation of this same society. Yet others regarded Tomasz's doings as curious symptoms of the psyche in action, deserving understanding. Only those directly involved, in other words Tomasz the Zombie and his victims, expressed no opinion.

Tomasz was caught a third time and sentenced to death. The sentence prompted as much outrage as applause, yet the court had little chance of making any other decision. Apart from the proof against him, which was so self-evident and copious as to be tediously repetitive, the defendant – without alacrity, yet without the least resistance – not only admitted his guilt (a fact that obviously could not be taken into consideration as evidence for the prosecution) but supplemented the existing evidence against him so precisely that the most skilled of his defence counsels were helpless. What's more, Tomasz's incorrigibility filled those in favour of the re-education of criminals through leniency and persuasion with discouragement, if not deep depression. And for those judges who might have been inclined to impose a milder sentence it was an insurmountable obstacle.

It was to be the first execution for many years, during which time liberalism had kept a firm advantage over other political outlooks. Regardless of the essential arguments – concerning the justice system, and indirectly social philosophy and pragmatism in general – it stirred a sensation of another kind, inferior in nature to the purely intellectual or moral one.

Thanks to, or rather as a result of, the extraordinary spread of entertainment news, or news entertainment, or to put it in a nutshell, showbusiness, in other words because of the existence of a powerful news-and-entertainment industry and of demand for its products, the chance of a spectacle as thrilling as the execution of Tomasz the Zombie could not possibly be missed, either by demand or supply. The rights to broadcast it on television, record it on video or audio tape, and the distribution of the relevant cassettes were bought by the most competent companies, and with growing excitement several hundred million potential viewers were looking forward to witnessing the death of Tomasz the Zombie.

Tomasz, however, had not apparently been spoiled by fame. Here before me sat a man who was not so much modest as detached from the sensation he provoked. He seemed fixed on some object of his cogitations that had nothing in common with the general excitement or with the anxiety of a great actor. A man of few words, his reticence arose from an innate inability to form sentences, though – should one wish to sketch his portrait in subtler style – it could have been explained by self-restraint. So the conversation would have been difficult, if not for the presence of the lawyer.

The three of us were sitting in large armchairs upholstered in perfect imitation leather. I sat expectantly, the lawyer sedately, and Tomasz the Zombie with that special property of people who sit in exactly the same way on any surface and in any circumstances.

'Tomasz wanted to see you without fail,' said the lawyer.

'Why?'

'Tomasz has to utter his last words before . . . you understand. Just before . . . Tomasz would like his last words to be as fitting as possible. Because they'll be his last.'

'That is understandable.'

'He needs professional help. He'd like his last words to be suitably composed. Both in terms of form and content.'

'But why should it be me who . . . ?'

'Tomasz is a great fan of . . .' Here the lawyer named the television series I had written. 'He believes you are the one and only person on whom he can rely.'

'But . . .'

'The fee will be very high. Thanks to sales of the reproduction and broadcast rights, part of which income is due to him, Tomasz has become a rich man.'

'However . . .'

'Do you need some time to decide? Unfortunately time is of the essence, for reasons that I don't have to explain. You must make up your mind immediately.'

I had nothing against the money. But another motive demanded consideration. Whatever form of creativity I had plied until now, even the ones I wasn't proud of, I had always done it under my own name. Anonymity did not appeal to me.

'Before I answer . . . What's the general idea, the message that your client would like to convey to the public?'

'That will depend on you.'

'But they're not my last words!'

'No. But you have an entirely free hand. My client trusts you. He says you're the only man who can do it.'

'But do what?'

'It.'

'Meaning what?'

'Say it.'

'Say what?'

The lawyer was losing patience.

'If we're approaching you as a professional, surely we can expect . . .'

He broke off, because just at this moment Tomasz the Zombie stood up and started walking slowly towards me. I felt uneasy because – though a quite unnecessary thought in this situation – it had instantly occurred to me that for rather a lot of people the sight of Tomasz the Zombie approaching them had been the last thing they ever saw.

Tomasz the Zombie leaned over me, and without a word first he pointed at himself, and then ahead of him, into the distance far beyond the prison walls, a gesture that encompassed everything between him and infinity.

'Agreed!' I cried in a blinding flash.

2

When Tomasz the Zombie made this gesture of non-verbal communication, I realized that this was something more important than any of my previous undertakings. Only my unwritten work, *On the Nature of Everything*, could be equally ambitious, but with the one difference that it had to be written in philosophical language, while Tomasz the Zombie's last words had to be drafted in colloquial speech. At the same time these words of mine – because they would be mine, only under the name Zombie – would reach the widest public and would be paid the greatest attention. To get to speak and to be listened to – that could be done, with a little persistence, skill and good luck. But to be listened to carefully, with the greatest attention, to be fully heeded, is a very rare event that doesn't happen to literary professionals at all, but to the leaders of nations and religions, and then only at watershed moments in history. The literary professionals can only dream of such attention, or delude themselves that the public takes that much notice of them. Tomasz the Zombie's last words gave me a unique opportunity.

We signed the contract that very day at the lawyer's office, and then I found myself back at my hotel. Before the receptionist had had time to inform me that someone was waiting for me, two gentlemen got up from behind the potted palms. One of them had a document file in a light beige colour.

'May we talk?'

'Yes, of course.'

'Not here.'

They chose a café several streets away from the hotel.

One of them spoke, with the document file on his lap. The other was silent. I soon interrupted the first one.

'How do you know that Tomasz the Zombie's last words belong to me?'

'That's beside the point.'

Asking such an unnecessary question reflected badly on my intelligence. Once I left the lawyer's office but before I reached the hotel, the lawyer would have had enough time to inform them. Realizing the redundancy of my question, I was satisfied with the evasive reply.

When he had finished talking, without a second thought I refused his offer.

'We can discuss the rate of remuneration. It is by no means non-negotiable,' said the man who'd been silent until now.

'That's not the point, but do you gentlemen really think I could agree to such a proposal?'

'But my colleague only offered an idea by way of experiment. The Zombie doesn't have to say "I'd rather die than give up" as he drags on one of our firm's cigarettes. He could say something completely different, though of course with the same general drift.'

'No.'

'Please give it some more thought.'

And paying the bill, they left me a business card, adding: 'We'll be ready for your answer whatever the time of day or night.'

As I entered the hotel again, I cast a careful glance around the potted palm area. Yet among the people gathered there I didn't spot anyone with a document file of any colour or shape. Without delay I packed up my things and headed for the airport. Sitting in the waiting room, I gradually lost sight of my immediate surroundings. Although I was not yet in the secluded place where I was used to working, my impatient mind had already set off in search of the Ultimate Last Words of its own accord, slowly at first, but gathering speed as it moved away from the reality around me. Only its periphery was reacting to the signs sent by the real world, but that was enough for me to end up on the plane as a passenger at the right moment and in the appropriate manner.

When the drinks were brought round I was asked which one I wanted. I didn't want anything to drink. Instead of a bottle and a glass, I laid a sheet of paper on the little shelf in front of me. My plan was to write the first of the last words on it. What should it be? A great deal depended on the beginning. My pen hesitated over the paper.

'Let's get straight to the point,' said the man sitting to my left.

'Are you talking to me?'

He opened a document file of a dark, coal-grey colour.

'We have the contract ready, all that's left is to fix the sum to be paid.'

'But what's this about?'

He gripped the neck of the bottle standing before him and turned it so that I could see the label. It was beer.

'No!' I shouted, and leaped from my seat. But my safety belt threw me back into it.

'The Zombie only has to say "Aaaah", just "Aaaah", nothing more, with the right intonation of course, a sort of sigh of pleasure, you get it? And he could wipe his mouth with the back of his hand, while holding the bottle in the other. Please sign here.'

'No, I won't!'

'Bravo!' said the man sitting to my right, opening a dazzlingly yellow file. 'We have a far more interesting offer for you. Tomasz the Zombie will hold up a pill . . .'

'What sort of pill?'

'Our pill.'

I undid my safety belt.

'For headaches. Then . . .'

I stood up.

'Please let me pass.'

'With no words, you see, without any "Aaaah", he swallows it.'

'Please let me get past this instant!'

'And there's relief painted on his face. Perhaps a smile too.'

I spent the rest of the journey in the toilet, while someone banged on the door relentlessly.

3

The next day I was kidnapped. The men who approached me in the street and forced me into a car didn't make any offers. They said nothing throughout the journey to a remote farm, where they locked me in a rather dirty room with no view, in a basement opposite the boiler house.

Only on the day after that did a smartly dressed man come to see me, holding a black document file.

'What do you want?' I asked the moment he entered. 'What's it to be?'

'We don't know yet,' he replied, sitting down and laying the file on his knees.

'Cigarettes, beer or pills?'

'It could be cigarettes, or beer, or pills, or something else. We're waiting for offers.'

'You mean I'm waiting.'

'No. The decision will be ours. Once we've gathered a sufficient number of offers, we'll select the most profitable one.'

'You? Who are you?'

'Think of us as middlemen between you and the clientele. The clients apply to us on the basis of a tender, and we choose the one who makes the highest offer, then we pass the order on to you. You carry it out, and it's all done and dusted.'

Only now did I understand.

'Don't worry, there'll be no lack of offers,' he said, patting the file. 'We've got more than a dozen already, and that's just the start.'

'Oh, yes . . .'

'It's all the same to us who wins the tender. To you too.'

'To me?'

'Of course it won't be quite as advantageous for you as it would if you were working for yourself, without us. Instead of acquiring the whole sum, you'll get a percentage from us, quite a small one, I admit. But there it is, business is business.'

'But what if I don't agree?'

'Sorry?'

'What if I refuse?'

'I advise you not to consider that idea,' he said mildly.

Silence.

'Do you have any special requests?' he asked, looking around the basement. 'No? In that case . . .'

He glanced at his watch and stood up.

'I must be getting back now. Meanwhile, have a nice rest and don't think about anything. We'll inform you when we have something specific.'

4

So I'd been kidnapped, carted away, locked up and was under close guard. And yet in my situation this was a good thing. Good in a manner of speaking. Nobody could offer me any more proposals.

On the other hand, I couldn't propose anything either. Tomasz the Zombie's last words no longer belonged to me. They were to be dictated to me – I was now merely their formal owner. There was no chance of Tomasz the Zombie's last words being *my* 'Ultimate Last Words'. But I had only agreed to write them so that they would be *my* 'Ultimate Last Words'.

Ironically enough, better and better ideas kept occurring to me about how and what I could say to the world through Tomasz the Zombie, if only I had the opportunity. Though to tell the truth they weren't fully formed ideas, but an aura of ideas, a presentiment that now I would be able to carry this tentative start, this potential into effect. I could do it, if only I were allowed to.

So all my energy turned into helpless rage against the violence that was preventing me. Helpless, because I'd been kidnapped, imprisoned and put under guard, and could only wait until something or other was dictated to me.

That night I was woken by a question: 'Do you like penguins?'

At first I thought I was dreaming. But there was someone sitting on my bed.

'Who's there?' I asked.

'Do you like them?'

'Yes, I suppose so . . .' I replied, true to my conscience.

'What does "I suppose so" mean?'

'It means I'm in favour of them. At any rate, I have nothing against them. May I switch on the light?'

But my interlocutor had already done that for me. I was relieved to see one of the two men who were both guarding me and acting as servants at the same time. The other one was much older, which didn't mean he was old, or even middle-aged, but probably far more advanced in his criminal career. To see someone familiar, even if he's a bandit, is better than seeing a ghost. Even if he's gone mad or is drunk. I sniffed, expecting to smell the odour of alcohol. But I couldn't smell anything. So perhaps he'd gone mad?

'But what do you know about penguins?' he asked.

'Well, they're sort of birds and sort of mammals, actually they are birds, but they can't fly. They live in the far north . . .'

'No, in the Antarctic,' he corrected me sternly. 'Around the South Pole. And is that all you know about them?'

'I think so,' I admitted remorsefully.

'Well, yes, that fits.'

He became moody and pensive.

I didn't know what to do next. Get up and get dressed? Or maybe I'd better wait passively to see how things developed. Try not to irritate the madman. So I lay there quietly, keeping still.

'Nobody knows about them,' he said at last, bitterly. 'No one cares.'

Something began to dawn on me. I don't live in the modern world for nothing.

'Unfortunately,' I agreed, 'public opinion shows reprehensible ignorance.'

'Indifference. Who's worried about the penguins?'

'Nobody,' I confirmed, this time with deeper conviction.

'Quite so. No one cares about their fate, their habits, history and culture . . . It's an injustice. Do you find that acceptable?'

'Oh, no! If I myself am poorly informed, it's only because I've fallen victim to the manipulation, misinformation and institutional bureaucracy behind which the powers of imperialism and major capital are hiding.'

He beamed.

'That at least I don't have to explain to you.'

'Yes, that much is clear.'

'So do you agree that this can't go on any longer?'

'Not a second more!' I cried, jumping out of bed and reaching for my trousers.

'That one must act?'

'Without delay!' I cried, struggling with a trouser leg. 'The prejudice against penguins has gone unpunished for far too long. Enough is enough!'

'What do you suggest?'

I froze, with my head in my shirt. But I couldn't take the initiative myself, I had to proceed with caution.

'I wonder . . .' I said, diving out of the shirt and once again encountering the maniac's immobile, burning eyes. 'Maybe a battlefront for . . .'

'That will come later, but right now.'

'A front to put the right demands forward. For example . . . You say they live at the South Pole?'

'Nowhere else.'

'That's it! They've been forced to live in the most appalling conditions! Our first demand will be to return them to a temperate climate, if not a sub-tropical one. During my last stay in the tropics I myself found it quite depressing. But only now do I realize why. It's because there was not a single – not one! – penguin. "Penguins to Florida!" – that will be our slogan.'

I felt as if I were galloping ahead, but luckily he took no notice of that. He just brushed off my exaggeration with an impatient wave of the hand.

'Above all we must raise public awareness,' he said.

'But how?' I asked, pretending not to know what he was driving at.

'You can do it.'

'*I* can?!'

'The Zombie just has to say something about penguins.'

'How do you know that the Zombie and I . . .'

'I'm not supposed to know, my task is just to guard you. But I have ears.'

'So if you know, then you also know that it's impossible, and you know why.'

'Yes, I do. But only as long as you're sitting here.'

I kept quiet, not believing my own luck.

He moved closer and lowered his voice.

'I'll let you into the boiler house, and you'll sit in there until morning. In a while my colleague will be coming on duty outside, and I'll be off to bed. Tomorrow morning I'm to drive to the city for food. I'll drive the truck under the boiler-house window, and you'll come straight through the window into the truck.'

'Then what?'

'Then Tomasz the Zombie will say something about penguins,' he concluded triumphantly, and his eyes flashed with the brilliance of a just cause.

5

It wasn't the sort of beach where I'd choose to resettle penguins by way of recompense for the injury of many centuries of exile to the polar regions. A stony shore in a cold fog, a small fishing town devoid of industry or entertainment, and everything that goes with that, far away from big business, enterprising organizations and individuals. I chose it as a place of voluntary exile. Isolated but free, I sat in a rented room by a feeble stove, all alone with the last words of Tomasz the Zombie, meaning *my* 'Ultimate Last Words'.

They belonged to me again. I worked at a bare wooden table, with a calendar hanging opposite me. I had less and less time. Piles of scribbled-on paper littered the floor. And there was nothing on any of them but drafts, assumptions or general concepts. Everything I began instantly branched out, developed and grew but was never ripe enough. And even if one of my concepts finally seemed not just ready but worthy of forming the 'Ultimate Last Words' (and how could I know if it was worthy if it wasn't ready?) I still had to process its raw material into a short work, which had to be shaped, the shorter the better. So before I had even arrived at it, the second part of the task already looked to me like one of those grains of rice on which an artist in the Far East would sculpt an entire city, complete with pagodas and the suite of a maharajah on elephants.

Now I knew that the inspiration I had had during my imprisonment was illusory. The impossibility of realizing my task gave me a quite fantastic sense of its possibility. Yes, now Tomasz the Zombie's last words belonged to me alone, they were mine exclusively, but to change them into my 'Ultimate Last Words' was now as difficult for me as it had seemed easy when they didn't belong to me.

I had my first moment of doubt. What if I were to give up? Throw in the towel? I conquered my weakness, and worked on again. But the second attack was more serious and almost ended in my defeat. The fact that it didn't can only partly be ascribed to my heroism.

One night I had truly had enough. 'It's over, I'm not going to do it, I'm not capable.' A cloud of tobacco had long since been irritating my eyes, but now it seemed to settle on me, on the furniture and the walls in a grey layer. The black coffee was no longer having any effect, as if I were pouring it into a corpse. Suddenly I stood up, throwing off the blanket with which I had covered my numb, frozen knees. Like a sleepwalker, feeling full of squalid emptiness, the obscene pleasure of unconditional capitulation, I went down the stairs to the telephone in the hall.

I dialled the number, preceded by several area codes. It was to be a very long-distance conversation.

'Yes?' said the lawyer's voice in the receiver.

I said nothing. There was still time to hang up and take on the fight anew.

'Who's that?' he said, less impatient than unconscious at this time of night. I'd probably roused him from deep sleep.

I presented myself.

'Where are you calling from, where are you, and where have you been all this time?'

'Never mind that. I just called to say . . .'

'Do you know what day it is today? Do you realize your time's up?'

'Yes, I do. And I wanted to say that I resign.'

Silence. And then: 'What's that?'

'I'm backing out. I won't write Tomasz the Zombie's last words.'

'Have you gone mad?'

'Don't ask me the reasons. I just don't want to do it any more.'

Silence again. Then suddenly an entirely sober voice said: 'All right. But we still have clause three, paragraph E7.'

'What clause, what paragraph?'

'Of our contract. In case of non-fulfilment of the commission, by way of compensation, you pay . . .'

And he named a sum.

Now it was my turn to be silent, having in my turn come to my senses. It was more than my entire income for the past three years.

'Are you still there?'

'Yes.'

'I'll be expecting you at my office this coming Monday. With the completed text, of course. We can forget about this conversation. Goodnight.'

He hung up. So did I. I stood by the telephone mindlessly until a cold touch on my forehead awoke me. I had dozed off standing there, or else I had sunk into lethargy and my head had come to rest against the phone. I went back upstairs and immediately fell asleep, but this time lying down.

6

There were only three more days left. Not until 'this coming Monday', which had already passed, but until the execution. I had to count one day for the journey, and one for Tomasz the Zombie to get a rough idea of the text, which meant I had one day left to come up with something I'd failed to come up with during the past few weeks. One day and one night. Before I left the small town tomorrow morning.

After breakfast I went for a walk along the seashore. The sea was turbulent. An infinity of foam, spray and eddies, waves rising and falling, every shade from cobalt blue to dark silver, assaults and retreats, the roaring and shuffling of gravel rolled to and fro along the sloping shore – infinity in motion. We usually associate motion with a destination, a route without a destination is just the phantom of a route, but here was nothing but routes without any destinations, an infinity of routes and forms – but with no relation to anything except themselves, to anything beyond, beside or as well as – just a gigantic phantom. Even the solitude of a seagull related only to itself; self-contained and self-sufficient, it was a phantom of solitude. Slimy seaweed stuck to my rubber boots. Apparently I had emerged from the sea several billion years ago, but now I could no longer return to it.

How was I to find the last words? The heaps of scribbled-on paper lying over there behind me, within four walls not visible from here, but to the right of the angular church tower, near the chimney of the fish-processing plant, gave no more of an answer than the restless gurgling ahead of me. I had known for ages not to expect an answer from that direction. I had not gone down to the seashore to beg for anything, for any mercy free of charge. I simply needed some air.

Of course, I could give up without paying a penny, and I could even earn a fortune in the process. I didn't have to break the agreement at all – I only had to accept any one of the proposals I'd been offered earlier on. Give up on the 'Ultimate Last Words', but not the last words. After all, the Zombie's last words could be anything at all, but they wouldn't be the 'Ultimate Last Words'.

But I had to find the 'Ultimate Last Words'. Something greater than my own personal ambition had come into play. It was about settling a question as weighty as 'to be or not to be' – namely, 'to think or not to think'. And actually – weightier. Because 'to be or not to be' only appears to depend on what we decide – mainly one is or isn't regardless of one's opinion about it. Whereas the factor of free will plays a greater role in thinking or not thinking. And in any case, even our decision on the matter of being or not being depends first of all on whether we do or don't think about it, and only then, if we do think about it, what it is that we think.

To think . . . But what's the value of thinking if it's not taken to extremes, if it's just like the gurgling sea that lay stretched before me? Like movement in an infinite number of directions, but with no point of reference, like this energy-filled, infinitely various, but meaningless activity, like all this noise about nothing? What is the value of literature if it can't give a dying man the right words for his moment of death? Key words, answers, in short, the Ultimate Last Words. What is the value of our words, the billions of words that for billions of years we have already uttered, repeated and are still repeating, if at the ultimate moment a man can't say something ultimate? If at the moment of Totality he can only express a fraction, only the sum resulting from the number one divided by infinity? Never mind me, or my ambition, never mind the defence of literature. This was about greater things.

But I only had one day ahead of me, less than a day by now; amid the roaring, shuffling and whistling of the sea, like a shard of glass among leaves, alien to their nature, I heard the sound of the clock on the church tower. One o'clock, so there was only the rest of the day and the night left. Impossible for me to complete the task.

And what if I did have more time? I wished I could reduce those heaps of paper to their essence, and with this thought alone I kept multiplying and increasing them. The more substance, the more inevitable the essence. But why deceive myself? I'd never reach the limit from which I could turn back. So I had nothing but multiplying, increasing and wishing ahead of me.

At this, the seagull – immobile in the expanse until now, heedless of all but itself in its solitude, absent even for itself – vanished. At once came fluttering amid the waves and the seagull was back again, carrying something in its beak. No longer soaring, it was flying low over the sea, further and further away. Not the same seagull any more.

Away with this pile of paper. I'd been walking down the wrong path, and that was why I hadn't come to anything. I'd been building systems, accumulating arguments, seeking connections, motives and axioms. The systems could never be fully closed, the arguments were never enough, the connections kept coming undone, holes kept appearing in the principles, and the axioms were just words of honour. I'd been wandering a plain in the hope that my footsteps would form a pattern, a graph, a mathematical diagram, a formula for the universe. I had as much chance as a maggot dipped in ink and let loose on a sheet of paper. Here something different was needed. Not a flat plain, but a point, not in time, but a moment earlier than the moment, meaning not reason, but instinct was needed here. A flash, a vision, an illumination. It should have happened at once, but it still wasn't too late. The approaching night would suffice for me to complete the task.

I went home and took the now redundant calendar off the wall. I sat down and started to work according to my new formula. At dawn I got up from the table.

7

She was sitting in the visiting room, unreal but intense, with an unequivocal face and a very literal body. The sort of face one instantly ignores after a cursory glance, as one's entire attention focuses on the rest, which is not the rest, but the main part, because in such cases it's the face that's just a remnant of the body. The perfection of her figure was not to her credit, yet she usurped all the honours arising from this title, an arrogation that did not prompt any reservations. But at this particular moment she seemed unoccupied either by her life's one and only calling, or by the illustrated magazines she was flicking through nervously and mechanically. Not for long, because moments later she was only looking at me, then she came up and, uninvited, seated herself in the armchair beside me, her perfectly literal body on the perfect imitation leather.

'Are you a friend of Tomasz's?' she asked.

'Sort of.'

'Don't deny it. Tomasz has told me everything.'

'Meaning?'

'Don't pretend. You've come to see him. I know what it's about.'

'If you know . . .'

'I know, and I want to tell you the whole thing's nonsense.'

'Perhaps, in a way . . .'

'In every way. Tomasz knows perfectly well what he wants to say. Without you.'

'However, he signed a contract with me.'

'Nonsense. Tomasz has always known what his last words will be. And he'll say them regardless of what you've thought up for him. There's nothing for you to look for here.'

'Maybe. But I must stick to the agreement. Afterwards he can do as he wishes.'

'But I'm telling you to get out of here immediately!'

I looked around. The visiting room was like the reading room or the smoking room at a reasonably well-off club. Over the past decade they'd done everything to make prison life appear normal. If not for the guard discreetly stationed by the bar, it would be hard to spot the difference.

'Get out of here.'

'I will, but only when I've heard the same from Tomasz as I've heard from you.'

'Are you going or not?!' she shouted hysterically.

The guard by the bar shifted meaningfully.

'No.'

'All right, then sit there,' she said disdainfully and haughtily. 'It won't do you any good. Tomasz will only say what he wants to say.'

'So you know what he wants to say?'

'Sure I do.'

'I'd be keen to know what it is.'

'That he loves me.'

'Ah!'

'Yes! He has always loved me. And nobody's going to force him to say anything else. Neither you, nor your advisors. Nobody!'

'Of course. If that is his will . . .'

'He has always loved me, he loves me now and he will love me forever, even beyond the grave. Those will be his last words.'

'In that case . . .'

The door through which the prisoners were led into the visiting room opened. It was exactly like the door by which the visitors entered and exited, and so was the door by the bar, for the staff. The same fake mahogany. I stood up, and at the same time my interlocutor jumped up too.

Tomasz the Zombie came in, escorted by a guard. Then he stopped, turned around and went out again.

I glanced at the woman and found that for the first time her face deserved attention.

The guard returned, but without the prisoner. He came up to us, seeming embarrassed.

'Do you have a meeting with the Zombie, sir?'

'Yes.'

'The Zombie says he won't come in while the lady is here.'

The guard and I both looked at her.

'I'd like a word with you,' she said to me.

The guard moved away.

'Tell him to say it . . . You know what.'

I nodded.

'Please, I beg you.'

I nodded.

She turned away from the door and, with a smile that was worth at least as much as any of the proposals I'd had so far, added: 'I'll be waiting for you by the exit.'

Whereas I was waiting by the entrance. When Tomasz came in, from a single step away I fired seven bullets into his belly from a short-barrelled revolver known as a 'bulldog'. Perfect for such occasions, because it's high-calibre but small, so it doesn't pad out your pocket or arouse premature suspicions. Tomasz died without any words, just as I wanted.

8

If the Ultimate Last Words aren't possible, one should die in silence. The Zombie didn't understand that.

Though maybe I killed him for personal reasons. For the fact that I was incapable of thinking up the Ultimate Last Words. Fatally wounded literary ambition. Frustration.

Anyway, if they sentence me to death, it won't occur to me to utter any last words. No way, no how.

Because it's not impossible that I will get the death sentence. Indeed, the motives for my crime are sufficiently unclear to them for me to be acquitted. But they'd have to call off the show in which they've already invested so much money, and to which everyone has been looking forward. Whatever, if it comes to that, I won't make a fool of myself. I won't say anything inferior to the Ultimate Last Words.

That means I won't say anything.

I'll die without words.

Though perhaps . . . Maybe I can still come up with something? Maybe I'll manage it? After all, I've still got a little time.

'*Ostatnie słowo*'

Published as part of the collection *Opowiadania* (Wydawnictwo Literackie, 1981).

SURVIVORS

ADOLF RUDNICKI

1912–1990

Born into a Hasidic family as Aron Hirschhorn, Adolf Rudnicki was the youngest of seven children whose parents ran a tavern in a shtetl near Tarnów. After a traditional religious education, he underwent a crisis of faith; rumour has it that he shocked the company at his own bar mitzvah by making the comments of a non-believer.

Following army service, in the 1930s he moved to Warsaw, changed his name and began a successful literary career with the novels *Szczury* (*Rats*), about a young man escaping a stifling family background, and *Żołnierze* (*Soldiers*), about his military service. His work was praised by Witold Gombrowicz and he became a member of the lively literary scene. His novella *Niekochana* (*Unloved*), about unrequited love, was later filmed.

Mobilized in 1939, he was captured, but escaped within months. He sheltered in Soviet-occupied Lwów, moving to Warsaw when Germany attacked the USSR in 1942. Living on 'Aryan papers' – with a purely Polish identity – he actively protected other Jewish authors and artists. He had several close calls, but was the only one of his siblings to survive the war.

The horror of the Holocaust gave his work a new tone and a major mission to leave a testimony to the Polish Jews and how they died. His stories about the Holocaust are close to eye-witness reportage, but remain lyrical and psychologically effective. According to Czesław Miłosz, Rudnicki's collection *Żywe i martwe morze* (*The Living and Dead Sea*, 1952) 'explores the personal relationships between highly individualized characters caught up in the infernal machine: regardless of their virtues and vices, the Jews are crushed for the sole reason that they belong to a race condemned to die . . . Only a man of avowed duality, a Pole and a Jew, could grasp all the complex sets of relationships between Jews and Jews, Jews and Poles, as well as between the victims and their Nazi executioners.'

He also wrote about the post-war experiences of Holocaust survivors, as in the story that follows, which documents the sad truth that they were often made to feel unwelcome in Poland.

Antonia Lloyd-Jones

The Black and the Green God

Translated by Antonia Lloyd-Jones

Jakub Goldman had proposed to Flora about a week after they met; in this regard he was like others; the young people were getting married right away; marriage was one of the cheapest things in the world; no one was acquiring coats-of-arms or fortunes, but purely and solely suitcases, plus the set number of square metres of living space given by the state. Morals were extremely loose, despite which the young people were setting up home. They had no idea one could set store by marriage, or that one could set store by anything. They were tragic, without knowing it, they were tragic, with their immorality and easy marriages. They were producing children in such high numbers that the social workers were tearing their hair out. Although this generation liked to sound off, every superfluous word annoyed them, in fact they hated words, they'd been raised on formulae, and although they thought they hated formulae, they sought them everywhere, because they were too pervaded by technology, which relies on formulae. The young people couldn't forget that yesterday's death of tens of millions in cruel torment had a crude formula as its only justification, and they were sure that a formula of the same kind would be enough for the same purposes tomorrow. This awareness defined their attitude to life. The only gods before whom they bowed down without reservation were sex and sport.

Goldman and Flora both liked the idea that they were getting married. Flora saw it as an excellent lark, and she thought he felt the same. She was pleased he was so handsome, and that they made a perfect picture. They attracted attention wherever they appeared. She liked the foreignness of his looks, the colouring no longer encountered on our streets, she liked to look at him. 'And it's all mine,' she thought, not without trepidation, 'that black hair, those joined eyebrows, those puppy dog eyes, that nose, those helpless hands'. She found his hands immensely moving, and had to wrestle with herself not to kiss them – a woman never kisses a man's hands.

After the cataclysm of the Second World War, Goldman was alone, like most of the Jews, who, deprived of their families, lived in a closed, tight circle of their few remaining acquaintances. Flora was soon able to confirm that all Goldman's friends and associates were either leaving the country, or wondering whether to leave; they were too grief-stricken to make up their minds about anything. Though highly diverse in looks, to her they all seemed to have something in common. The fact that so many of them were leaving made it easier for the young couple to get married. Jakub's chemist uncle, 'old Goldman', was leaving too, and for the rest of his stay was living with acquaintances whose house had plenty of room because another occupant had recently left the country. Old Goldman was not like his nephew: he was tiny, he smiled like a demon, his eyes glittered constantly, and his head was too solemn for such a shrimp, too energetic, as if removed from a great, big body – it was just asking for a little pair of horns. At first he regarded Flora with animosity, but then he quite simply fell in love with her. From him she learned a few details about Jakub's parents; Jakub himself never talked about them.

Flora loved Goldman and wasn't upset by what was said about him at the theatre, that he didn't have what actors call the 'bloody hell factor', that he had nothing beyond intelligence and would probably end up as a second-rate director, or, definitely, a second-rate translator from foreign languages. She'd fall asleep and wake up happy, she felt as if she were water-skiing along a not very deep, but safe and jolly river. In this period she read the texts of the tragedians as if they were the work of pulp writers, and couldn't see the difference between them; tragedy was hunger, and after satisfying the most persistent of hungers – the hunger for happiness – she had nothing else to wait for.

If she hadn't met Goldman that evening, it probably would have happened the next day or a few days later at the theatre, because it turned out Wiktor had taken him into his company. In the very first few days she was witness to the following conversation between two of the pre-war actors, both middle-aged; the chasm between the pre-war and post-war generations was immense.

One of them said: 'They give each other mutual support.'

'Are you talking about Goldman?' asked the other. 'You're wrong, as usual. As usual you don't understand a thing, you don't know what's going on. The one and only anti-Semite at our theatre is Wiktor himself. It's that he's observing the rule of the first Jew, and as that's him, he doesn't want a whole crowd of them. He took on Goldman because he's harmless, because he's only just starting, he took him instead of . . . But that Goldman should have spruced himself up with a nice stage name.'

'Why's that?'

'Can't you understand why? A stage name is proof that the guy has buckled under, that he'll do his best to fit in.'

'Why make such a farce of it?'

'It's necessary! It is! People would scoff behind his back, repeating his real name on the sly; sometimes it would be printed in brackets in the press to keep the fellow in check, to rein him in if he gets too big for his boots. All told, if there's a stage name we've got the upper hand – because it was he who came to us. Goldman – try saying that name to yourself out loud. Can't you hear it? Straight away you've got a spoke in your wheels, you've got to jump across something foreign.'

'Perhaps.'

'Perhaps? Definitely, man! That Goldman has already made several serious mistakes. His father – well, that's too bad, no one chooses their own father. But why *Goldman*? So number one, we have the name *Goldman*. Number two: his voice is too harsh. Three: he's too good-looking, that hurts Joe Public's feelings! They don't like it, they don't like it when someone's too good-looking . . .'

As she overheard this conversation, Flora saw Goldman in front of her the whole time, telling her his first confidences. While the ghetto was burning, he told her, the whole city talked about nothing else: some were delighted, others horrified that people were being burned up. The only living beings that never spoke about it were the Jews themselves; not a word on the topic could pass their throats.

Suddenly the weather became inhuman in its beauty. The sunlight, the colours and smells made life impossible, and being in the city was unbearable. People walked about in a daze, constantly returning in their conversations to the weather, to memories of the summer, and to places where the sun could not be killed off by walls and workplaces. Flora and Goldman were both determined to go away, on a short trip to the town of K., for instance.

By now they had entered a time when there was no sweetness in the city to change ugly streets into gardens, though it was still beautiful, sunny and warm. The sun looked yellow and only had strength for about an hour at noon, then it went white, melted and cooled off; the evenings set in early, cool and deep. In the desert of the evening only the moon cried above the town.

To escape the threat of the inexpressible beauty of the evenings, to escape the chill and the desert they sought refuge at the Tourist Centre, the only bright, warm, safe place where they felt at home; the rest of the town – at night – was like exile abroad, at the end of the world. At the Tourist Centre they had meals both urban and rural: sour milk, bread and butter, white cheese, hot black pudding and apple compote. To reach the Tourist Centre, on the edge of town, they walked through empty little streets, plunged in impenetrable darkness, a journey that afforded them impressions they had never gained on the well-lit streets of the big city. On the way, huddling together, they felt aware of the union of two people as an elemental, natural refuge from fear and darkness. They felt it again later on, especially after the meals, as they returned home through the utterly deserted town, and their footsteps rang with a loud echo at the other end of the marketplace, as if someone were constantly following and aping them. They hurried down the empty little streets, making haste to be in the two small rooms they had rented; they were the last guests of the summer. Their skin went numb with cold in this summer-time accommodation, in a house within a garden by a river. There was not much furniture, no double windows, and the walls were thin. Goldman's little room had nothing but a wooden bed with a straw mattress and two chairs, on one of which stood a wash bowl; each morning they fetched water for themselves from a nearby well. But there was a huge number of portraits of kings and heroes hanging on the walls in the cheapest reproductions. In the other little room, which was darker, stood a wardrobe lined with apples, a large table surrounded by six armchairs suitable for anything but sitting; they must have been designed by a madman and made by another. The rooms were connected by a glass door, always set ajar. They slept in

Jakub's bed. The man took full advantage of his rights, going beyond the woman's desire. He took her with a softness at the bottom of which she could sense cruelty.

On their first evening, chilled to the bone, they had only just sat down, when in the doorway of the Tourist Centre the mighty figure of the Black God appeared, and lunged towards them with a shout. Flora hadn't seen him since that time. She realized it was he who had united them; if she had met Goldman at the theatre, the result might have been different. Wearing an anorak with the collar of a navy-blue sweater protruding from under it, and short plus-fours on his fat legs, the Black God looked like a prematurely aged boy. A little later it occurred to Flora: 'He's just the same as all the Jews – you could put your hand between his teeth and he wouldn't bite; maybe that's why some people like them.'

'Well, what's up?' he asked her. 'Well, how's life? All right?'

She smiled.

'No, don't say it's still too early for the divorce courts. One can see everything right away; the grudges and defects merely come into focus later on, but they're the same grudges and defects one could sense on the first day. The world was created on the first day, all at once.'

The Black God was born here in this town, then he had left, and now he had come back to say goodbye to it; he too was leaving the country. On that first evening he came with a local artist, Orywał, who painted saints. The saint-painter and 'Flora's Jews' were on the best terms immediately. They spent the whole evening drinking in each other's words, enjoying a good, warm and pleasant mood, and none of them wanted to leave. Late into the night Orywał told stories about the Queen of Sheba, who was in fact the Black God's aunt, a teacher whose name was Klara Segał. Her true nature only appeared once the Jews had been deported to the other side of the river, where they lived behind a wire fence. The local peasants often sneaked up to the fence bringing a loaf of bread, a pat of butter or a chunk of pork fat, in exchange for which they got clothes or the occasional piece of jewellery. One day, Klara Segał gathered her folks around her and made a long speech that started like this: 'Children, we are doomed, we don't know the day or the hour. Let no woman refuse a man, or man a woman. It is God's wish. I have told my three daughters to do the same.'

Late at night, the saint-painter and the Black God escorted them home.

On the way they didn't meet a living soul, not even a drunk; the fog was thick, biting, and they shivered with cold. Next day, when at breakfast in the cafeteria they met the Black God again, drinking milk, Flora felt as if they had never parted at all, as if she had met someone who'd been a friend for years.

As the Black God had come to bid farewell to the town, they said goodbye to it together. Together they went for walks, together they ate their meals, they hardly parted at all. One time he showed them the house where he was born. It was a small wooden villa on a low foundation, in the style of houses in the foothills rather than the local ones, though in fact there wasn't any local style; the poor wooden cabins were the most typical.

'I'm leaving,' he said. 'I think I'll find a crust of bread in the outside world. I have family, they'll help, they have a duty. Someone must do the dirty work for the poets, their own is too clean, which must be why there's so much meanness in them, so little character, reduced by a complete lack of definition of what they call their work, but luckily I'm not a poet, I'm an architect. I have decided to leave for two reasons. First, I want to avoid the putrefaction that's inevitable wherever something has come to an end, and where there are no young people. You can run the length and breadth of this country with a candle in daylight and you'll hardly find any young people of Flora's age. Wherever there's no youth, putrefaction is inevitable, and the old people are suspended in a void – they're doomed to pity, which is a base emotion. I think all the past wanderings of the Jews have been an escape from putrefaction. Second, I want to preserve my memories. One should not ignore one's memories, memories are a fine thing, of paramount importance. Here I have fewer and fewer memories, here I keep burying them every day.

'And I advise you, children,' he said, glancing at Flora, 'to do the same. They bake bread throughout the world. Goldman is young, and could change his profession, in fact he should, he absolutely should, and you, Flora, should help him to do it. Because here they'll eat him up; sooner or later, by means boorish and elaborate, crude and refined, before he knows it, he'll be devoured . . . Leave the country, it's better in a marriage for both partners to be foreign than just one,' he said, smiling as usual.

'When I was a boy,' he continued, 'I thought I had an answer for everything. Now I'm forty-five, and I know that I know nothing, and have an answer for nothing. I'm facing all the same questions that stood before my father. Whenever a figure from the past floats before my memory, a dearly beloved face, I say to myself: "So will none of it ever return?" Now I know: everything that was ever going to be has already been and gone. Every time I look at that stretch of water between the willows, I can't drive away my amazement that the landscape has remained unchanged, but the people are gone. It's as if a huge fish has shaken them off its back. But the huge fish has shaken off some, and not others.'

On Friday, their first evening, they were almost alone at the Tourist Centre, and their table was one of only three that were occupied; on Saturday evening a few tourists arrived, who are similar the world over, but on Sunday a considerable gathering was expected; a painting was due to be consecrated at the monastery. They were advised to secure themselves dinner elsewhere, as they might not get it at the centre.

So on Sunday they went for a long walk, had dinner at the manicurist's, and then headed at a slow pace towards the town, where it was as crowded as it was in the high season.

At one point the Black God stopped them. On their right hand lay an empty slope gilded by the sun, and above it they could see the delicate image of a birch grove against the sky.

'What are you folks looking for?' asked a peasant who was sitting on the slope, wearing a flat cap and a brilliant white shirt that contrasted with his tanned, crumpled face; he was peeling an apple.

'Listen, fellow, wasn't there once a cemetery around here?' said the Black God, whose face was worried.

'A Jewish graveyard?' asked the peasant.

'That's right. I think it's somewhere here,' said the Black God.

Hesitating to answer, the peasant stared hard at Flora.

'Isn't this the place?' asked the Black God.

'It's here,' replied the peasant slowly.

'Where?' asked the Black God.

'Right here,' said the peasant, pointing at the slope where he was sitting.

'Here? There's no sign of it . . .'

'We ploughed up the earth,' said the peasant, finally ceasing to stare at Flora with the hard eyes of a man used to taming animals, and skilled in how to force the earth, trees, livestock and women to produce for him;

this was not some urban commoner, but a peasant, in whom the Green God lived life to the full.

'It's here . . .' repeated the Black God firmly.

'We ploughed the earth, we need bread, people must eat,' said the peasant, smiling at Flora.

'People must eat,' repeated the Black God, also only addressing Flora. At once she remembered the pain in old Goldman's voice when, just before they left the city, he had told them that the ground where one-hundred-and-fifty-thousand victims lay buried had been appropriated for a sports field.

'What was done with the gravestones?' asked the Black God.

'They went to pave the street during the war. The Germans gave orders.'

'The Germans gave orders,' repeated the Black God.

'People often used to come here,' said the peasant. 'They'd take soil in little bags, as if from a sacred site. But very few come here now.'

'There's no one left,' said the Black God.

Then they walked towards the marketplace, not quite visible from here, yet they could already sense the hubbub and stench of a human throng, like at the approach to a stadium. On the exposed street the sun, though white and fading, still produced a warm, muggy atmosphere, which always gave Flora a headache; in this regard she envied her friend Klara her fantastic hats, which she hadn't the courage to wear herself. ('But you have the courage for things I'd never dare to do,' Klara would reply.) People began to pass them, with overcoats in hand or tucked under their arms, wearing sweaters and trousers held up by cords with their underpants poking out, while the women had bulging bags with small umbrellas protruding from them. Among both the men and the women the semi-rural type prevailed, fair and stocky, excessively bold or excessively timid.

As soon as they entered the crowd – on a small street before the marketplace, then in the marketplace itself – something happened to the Black God that Flora couldn't understand. His face was clouded with a sort of angry solemnity, as if someone had mortally offended him. Ostentatiously, with no regard for anyone, time and again he stopped, laid a hand on Flora's arm, and in a loud voice poured out everything he knew about the cathedral, the monastery, the local religious paintings and relics. He spoke in smooth, rounded sentences, stressing every vowel. Flora grasped that the crowd was looking at them – they were a rather garish, foreign stain. Sensing sweat on her brow, she listened to the Black God with a wry grin, her eyes fixed on the ground, as he, slapped in the face by his own colouring and otherness, by she knew not what, replied to every one of her *unspoken* words with a dozen of his own, as he parried every *intended* blow with a counter-blow, and replied to every *potential* insult with an insult, all under the guise of a lecture about the cathedral, the monastery and the religious paintings. 'But this is a clash,' it suddenly occurred to Flora, 'between the Green God and the Black . . .' She wanted to get out of the marketplace as fast as possible, where the crowd was at its thickest, but on the small streets beyond it the crowd was already thick enough for the Black God's rage and garrulousness to continue. He merely passed on to lecturing about the birds and the trees.

Later, once they were all back in the room, the Black God said to her: 'In a crowd like that I always feel as if they're going to come up and ask me: "Why did you crucify Him?"'

'Centuries of hatred,' she thought. 'Now it'll take new centuries to remove it.'

She made her way into the other room and turned the knob on the radio. But it wasn't the radio that deafened her, just the words that yelled wildly inside her: 'Kill the hatred! Kill the hatred and break free of its gods.' Deafened by this inner screaming, she stood over a crooked, wobbly little table.

'*Czarny i zielony bóg*'
Published as part of the collection *Kupiec Łódzki. Niebieskie Kartki* (Państwowy Instytut Wydawniczy, 1963) with the title *Flora i bogowie*.

IDA FINK

1921–2011

Ida Fink, née Landau, was born into a secular Jewish family. While part of the Polish intelligentsia, they also had a strong Jewish identity and were socially and culturally involved in both the Jewish and non-Jewish communities. At home they spoke Polish and German, rather than Yiddish.

When the Nazis invaded Poland in September 1939, Fink, a talented musician, was studying at the Lwów Conservatory with a view to becoming a pianist. The family were confined to the ghetto in her home city, Zbaraż (now Zbarazh in Ukraine), until she and her sister obtained false identity documents, which – along with their fair hair and looks regarded as not 'typically Jewish' – allowed them to survive the war. Her novel *The Journey* (1990) is a fictionalized version of the war years, and inspired a German television film. After the war she married Bruno Fink, the only member of his family to survive the Holocaust. In 1957, along with their then five-year-old daughter Miri, they moved to Israel, where they remained for the rest of their lives.

In the late 1950s Fink started to write short stories in Polish, based on her own and other survivors' experiences, choosing fiction as her preferred genre. 'Aryan Papers' is from the collection *A Scrap of Time and Other Stories* (published in English translation in 1989), and demonstrates the power of her subtle but forceful storytelling. These tales depict the everyday reality of the Holocaust, how people survived, or didn't. They also explore the ways in which the survivors remember and relate to their traumatic past.

Fink's interest in memory and how we bear testimony to shocking experiences led her to write *The Table* (1988), a play in which four witnesses describe events that occurred at the Warsaw ghetto's Umschlagplatz during the mass transport of Jews to Treblinka. The four accounts reveal the horror experienced by the Jews, but they are significantly different and contradictory, showing that while every testimony is vital, human memory is not unequivocal.

Antonia Lloyd-Jones

Aryan Papers

Translated by Madeline G. Levine

The girl arrived first and sat down in the back of the room near the bar. Loud conversation, the clinking of glasses and shouts from the kitchen hurt her ears; but when she shut her eyes, it sounded almost like the ocean. Smoke hung in the air like a dense fog and curled towards the roaring exhaust fan. Most of the customers were men and most of them were drinking vodka. The girl ordered tea, but the waiter, who had no experience with drinks of that sort, brought beer. It was sweet and smelled like a musty barrel. She drank, and the white foam clung to her lips. She wiped them brusquely with the back of her hand; in her anxiety she had forgotten her handkerchief.

Perhaps he won't come, she thought, relieved, then instantly terrified, because if he didn't come that would be the end of everything. Then she began to worry that someone would recognize her and she wished she could hide behind the curtain hanging over the door to the toilet.

When he entered, her legs began to tremble and she had to press her heels against the floor to steady herself.

'Good, you're here already,' said the man and took off his coat.

'A double vodka!' he shouted towards the bar, 'and hurry!'

He was tall, well built, with a suntanned face; his cheeks were a bit jowly, but he was good looking. He was in his forties. He was nicely dressed, with a tasteful, conservative tie. When he picked up the glass she noticed that his fingernails were dirty.

'Well?' he asked, and glanced at the girl, who looked like a child in her plain, dark-blue raincoat. Her black eyes, framed by thick brows and lashes, were beautiful.

She swallowed hard and said, 'Fine.'

'Good,' he said, smiling. 'You see? The wolf is sated and the sheep is whole. As if there was a reason for all that fuss! Everything could have been taken care of by now.'

He sat half turned away from her and looked at her out of the corner of his eye.

'Would you like something to eat? This place is disgusting but you must understand that I couldn't take you anywhere else. In a crummy bar like this even the informers are soused.'

'I'm not hungry.'

'You're nervous.' He laughed again.

Her legs were still trembling as if she had just walked miles; she couldn't make them stay still.

'Come on, let's eat. This calls for a celebration.'

'No.'

She was afraid that she would pass out; she felt weak, first hot, then cold. She wanted to get everything over with as quickly as possible.

'Do you have it ready, sir? I brought the money . . .'

'What's this "sir" business? We've already clinked glasses and you still call me sir! You're really something! Yes, I have everything ready. Signed and sealed. No cheating – the seals, the birth certificate – *alles in Ordnung!* Waiter, the bill!'

He took her arm and she thought that it would be nice to have someone who would take her by the arm. Anyone but him.

The street was empty and dark; only after they reached the square did the streetlamps light the darkness and the passers-by become visible. She expected that they would take a tram to save time, but they passed the stop and went on by foot.

'How old are you, sixteen?'

'Yes.'

'For a sixteen-year-old you're definitely too thin and too short. But I like thin girls. I don't like fat on women. I knew you were my type the day you came to work. And I knew right away what you were. Who made those papers for you? What a lousy job. With mine you could walk through fire. Even with eyes like yours. How much did your mother give him?'

'Who?'

'The guy who's blackmailing you.'

'She gave him her ring.'

'A large one?'

'I don't know.'

'One carat? Two?'

'I don't know. It was pretty. Grandma's.'

'Ah, Grandma's. Probably a big stone. Too bad. So you see, I noticed at once that you had a problem, but I didn't know that you would admit it right away. At any rate, it's good that you happened to find me. I like to help people. Everybody wants to live. But why the hell did you spill it so fast?'

'I didn't care any more.'

'That's just talk! You knew I liked you, didn't you?'

'Maybe. I don't know.'

'And why did your mother let the papers out of her hands?'

'They said that they wanted to check something and they took them away.'

'And they said that they'd give them back once she came up with some cash. Right?' He laughed. 'Was it always the same guys who came?'

'Yes.'

'Naturally. Once you pay the first time, they'll keep coming back. They must have been making a pile. How much time did they give you?'

'Till the day after tomorrow. But we don't have any more money – really. The money I've brought for you is all we have.'

He steered her through a gate and up to the third floor. The stairs were filthy and stank of urine.

'That means you want to leave tomorrow.' And he added, 'Send me your address and I'll come to see you; I've taken a liking to you.'

The room was clean and neatly furnished. She looked at the white iron bed on which lay a pair of men's pyjamas with cherry-red stripes.

If I throw up, she thought, he'll chase me out of here and it will all be for nothing.

'Please give me the documents, sir, I'll get the money out right away,' she said.

'Sir? When you go to bed with someone, he's not a sir! Put your money away; we have time.'

It probably doesn't take long, she thought. I'm not afraid of anything. Mama will be happy when I bring the papers. I should have done it a week ago. We would already be in Warsaw. I was stupid. He's even nice, he was always nice to me at work, and he could have informed.

'Don't just stand there, little one.'

He sat down on the bed and took off his shoes. When he took off his trousers and carefully folded them along the crease, she turned her head away.

'I'll turn off the light,' she said.

She heard his laughter and she felt flushed.

An hour later there was a knock at the door.

'Who's there?' he shouted from the bed.

'It's me, I've got business for you, open up!'

'The hell with you, what a time for business! What's up?'

'I'm not going to talk through the door. Do you have someone in there?'

'Yes.'

'It's important and it ought to be taken care of fast. They could steal it from under our noses, and it would be too bad to lose all that good money.'

'Get dressed,' said the man. 'You heard, someone's here on business. A man doesn't have a moment's rest! Don't put on such a mournful face, there's nothing to be sorry about! You'll be a terrific woman someday! Here you are, the birth certificates, the *Kennkarten*.'

He counted skilfully, without licking his fingers. She could barely stand, and once again she felt queasy. She put the documents in her bag, the man opened the door and patted her on the shoulder. The other man, who was sitting on the stairs, turned around and looked at them with curiosity.

'Who's the girl?' he asked, entering the room.

'Oh, just a whore.'

'I thought she was a virgin,' he said, surprised. 'Pale, teary-eyed, shaky . . .'

'Since when can't virgins be whores?'

'You're quite a philosopher,' the other man said, and they both burst out laughing.

'Aryjskie papiery'
Published as part of the collection *Skrawek czasu* (Wydawnictwo W.A.B., 2009).

PAWEŁ HUELLE

1957–2023

Huelle was born in Gdańsk to parents who met there after surviving extreme wartime situations. Both the city and the history of his family antecedents were major themes in his writing, and he had a great talent for processing past experience into fiction and plays.

Politically active as a student in 1980 he delivered Solidarity leaflets to factories by bicycle, an experience he later described in a short story. He went on to work in the Solidarity press office. His literary breakthrough was the novel *Who Was David Weiser?* (1987), about an enigmatic Jewish boy who has a mystical influence on his peers and then vanishes. In it Huelle showed his skill at weaving several timescales into a single plot, and also his sense of mystery. The identifiable settings in his work have contributed to Gdańsk's literary mythology; an old railway bridge that features in the novel is known as 'Weiser's Bridge'.

Extremely erudite, he made reference to the writers he admired, for instance in the novel *Castorp*, a prequel to Thomas Mann's *The Magic Mountain* – set in Danzig, as Huelle's native city was then called, or *Mercedes-Benz*, which pays homage to Bohumil Hrabal.

Though many of his stories are set in Gdańsk and the surrounding region, most of the places that he visited, including foreign countries, became settings for his fiction. In literary terms, he travelled in time as well as space, exploring the forgotten past when his area was home to the Kashubians (a Slav ethnicity that still has a strong cultural identity), the Mennonites or the ancient Prussians, and in his imagination the annihilated Jewish past was very much alive, as was the German community that once thrived in Danzig.

'The Cobbler' is a fine example; the Polish reader recognizes the name

Kosterke-Trzebiatowska as Kashubian, the story is set in Gdańsk, but with reference to its past, when the Germans were expelled following the war and the Poles were imported from formerly Polish cities such as Wilno, now Vilnius in Lithuania – Joachim's native city.

Antonia Lloyd-Jones

The Cobbler

Translated by Antonia Lloyd-Jones

The years went by quickly, like an express train passing a village station at night. Joachim saw Kosterke-Trzebiatowska through the window of his workshop. He had a memory of her from many years ago. She'd been young then, and fine in every way. He'd even been mildly in love with her. But now, as she emerged from number three in a wine-red apron, slightly stooping, in tracksuit bottoms and tennis shoes, and a beret covering her grey bun, now, as she took the first swing of her broom, now it was impossible to imagine her in any other form, from however long ago. The fact was that her present appearance gave an impression of timelessness, as if she'd arrived in the world like that.

The water began to gurgle in the kettle. Joachim would have switched it off if he hadn't forgotten about the stopwatch. He always pressed its oxidized button the moment Kosterke-Trzebiatowska started her journey. He liked to watch as she swept the asphalt pavement, which in hot weather bulged here and there, creating large bubbles. Whereas the winter left holes in it, which generally were not patched until someone broke a leg. Then the *Evening Coast* raised a stink, boldly asking what the district administration was doing. But now the spring had come. Following a mild winter there were no holes. Now and then Kosterke-Trzebiatowska set aside her broom and bent down to impale a dog-end on her litter spike. There were no exceptions: she had to inspect every item, even a soggy shred – like on a mushroom hunt – before tossing it into her pail. If the dog-end was a bit longer it made its way into her apron pocket. Joachim liked to watch this too. So he quickly started the stopwatch and took the kettle off the heat. Before the coffee emitted its aroma, he had time to get his half-filled notebook ready. For years he had been carefully recording all Kosterke-Trzebiatowska's results in these little notebooks. How many of them were there by now? He couldn't remember. The pile grew from one year to the next, and although he kept promising himself he'd count them properly, he never got around to it. Some of them had gone yellow like school exercise books that turn up in unexpected places – in a toolbox for instance, a chest of drawers or a kitchen sideboard.

Through the large windows of his workshop, which had once been a regular shop as well, Joachim could only see Kosterke-Trzebiatowska for two or three minutes. From outside number three she moved at her own pace to the little bridge over the Strzyża. There he lost her from sight, but he knew the exact route she took. She would go as far as Wybicki Square, and once she had finished her work she would walk back, tired but upright, carrying her pail, broom and spike like the kit that was no longer needed until the next battle. She only cleaned her own side of the street. The side where Joachim's almost inactive – in fact already lifeless – business was located she simply ignored. Only on Sundays and holidays was there no reason to start the stopwatch. All in black, summer or winter, with a black handbag on which the lacquer had cracked long ago, she would walk in the opposite direction, to the corner of Wallenrod Street. He knew this route of hers very well too. She would turn right and go straight on, all the way to the viaduct, which the trains rattled across at speed. Yes, under the viaduct she had to turn left from Wallenrod, then after the passage beneath the iron structure she'd go left again. From there along Czarna Street she didn't have far to go to the church. Joachim never went to Mass, or received the priest on his parish rounds, but a couple of times he had followed her, to see her in the Gothic interior full of golden ornaments, pictures and plaster figures of the saints. She would sit in the penultimate pew, take a rosary from her handbag, and as if the order of service were of no concern to her, she would finger each of the beads in turn while saying her prayers. Meanwhile her lips didn't move, not even when the congregation was reciting 'Our Father . . .' or their voices were united in song. Only upon the Elevation of the Host, when the altar boys rang their bells and incense smoke wreathed the presbytery did she put away her rosary to kneel like all the others, and like many she headed for the altar to receive the Body of Christ. From her face, almost stony and pale, it was impossible to read any emotions. She left the church rapidly, maybe to avoid standing in the long Sunday queue at the patisserie under the arcade.

The stopwatch ran at its usual pace. Gerhard Richter & Söhnen. Leipzig. By now it was the one and only object that in all these years still remained from the previous owners of the shop. Now Kosterke-Trzebiatowska must be sweeping more or less outside number five. Her speed became slower by the year. Meanwhile Joachim was remembering the time when, carrying his backpack, he had set off towards the Langfuhr district, heading for the address given him at the commission. The passenger trains weren't running yet. Once past the viaduct he was almost at the spot. He had gazed at the rows of houses in amazement. They hadn't been reduced to dust – as in the city centre – by heavy shelling and bombardment. On the façades he saw bas-reliefs featuring flower motifs or mascarons. Some of the buildings were topped with turrets, but not necessarily for decoration, since under their pointed spires small, possibly attic windows were visible. Some of the houses had balconies with wrought-iron semicircular railings. Hertzstrasse was almost deserted. Here and there behind a windowpane the drapes were drawn. The two small shops that he passed had tightly secured grilles, barring access to the inside. It was hard to find his bearings on the German map of the city. Finally he found Luisenstrasse, marked with an indelible pencil by the clerk at the commission. He turned into it and reached his destination. On the left-hand side of a door painted brown there was a tall, arched window. On the right there was an empty shop display. He saw the shop sign ('Couture Fashion Hats'), but he wasn't sure exactly what it meant. Once inside he realized it was a sort of tailor's and milliner's workshop. A piece of flannel was trapped in the foot of a Singer sewing machine, as if it had stopped working only minutes ago. On a long table lay finished and unfinished hats, army caps with an eagle badge, some for officers, scissors, patterns, tailor's shears and some lacquered peaks. Gazing at all this from the wall was Adolf Hitler. Before taking down the colour print in a solid frame, Jakub peeped backstage. The two tiny rooms with a kitchenette did not imply that the owners were well off. But what interested him most was the view from the window. In the yard between the walls of the houses ran a little stream enclosed in a stone channel, at most three metres wide, shallow but fast-flowing. Over it he saw the arch of a small footbridge with handrails, which connected some little gardens separated by the water.

Joachim finished his coffee. It was still too early for breakfast. His curd-cheese roll could wait. He glanced at the stopwatch. It was a strange device, not just designed for high-speed races. The first hand surely measured the seconds for sprinting. The next hand measured the minutes for relay races. The third one measured hours. To set it going, it had to be wound for far longer than a normal watch. All three hands were synchronized. For example, the reading might be one hour, two minutes and fifteen seconds. The inside cover was engraved with a proverb: *Si vis vitam, para mortem*. For quite a long time, before he opened his workshop, he didn't know what it meant. His first customer, Dr Szeliga from number thirteen, who ordered a pair of solid brown walking shoes, explained that it was a Latin proverb meaning: 'If you want to endure life, prepare for death'. The doctor was surprised by this wording. From his gymnasium on Dominikańska Street, right next to the church of the Holy Spirit, he remembered another version: *Si vis pacem, para bellum*, which translated as: 'If you want peace, prepare for war'. And what was a stopwatch of this kind doing at a milliner's studio? Maybe the person named Waschke, whose papers still lay in the chest of drawers, had been a sports referee? This of course they had failed to determine. But over a glass of weak tea that Joachim made on a primus stove, they had talked about pre-war Wilno, their native city. The doctor mentioned the Church of the Holy Spirit, where all the Mickiewicz Gymnasium pupils began their school year. The compulsory Easter confession took place there too. The doctor had had a consulting room on Gdańska Street. Joachim had had a workshop inherited from his father on Niemiecka Street, on the corner of Klaczka and Jatkowa streets. After the war the doctor was still a doctor, Joachim was still a cobbler, and from Wilno both of them had ended up in Gdańsk on the same street, the German name of which had been changed to Aldona. Wasn't that quite amusing in its own way? Joachim hadn't taken a penny from the doctor. The first customer is the first customer, he's to bring good luck. Yes, even if they had met before the war at his Wilno workshop – which was rather unlikely, because a doctor with a private practice would certainly have sent his maid to do the shopping – even if Dr Szeliga had entered his shop in person to collect his shoes, they certainly wouldn't have had a chat. About what? At most two or three sentences about shoe soles and grades of leather. Here – as equals – they were united by their former city, the most beautiful city there ever was on earth. Joachim was aware that since getting off the goods train to the strains of a Red Army concertina, this was his first reminder of the roar of the Wilejka river racing down from the Zarzecze district, the hill in Antokol, the steamships in the harbour and the gilded cupolas of the Baroque churches. His heart beat faster and he almost burst into tears. Normally he avoided reminiscing.

But where had Kosterke-Trzebiatowska got to by now? Could she be outside number thirteen, where Dr Szeliga had lived, and then died? It was probably too soon for that. She was more likely to be outside number eleven, where the opera singer Zofia Janukowska had practised her scales and arias to her daughter's accompaniment each afternoon. What a wonderful customer. She used to order court shoes, stilettos, autumn walking shoes and knee boots, quite often two pairs at a time, without ever quibbling about the price. Through Janukowska society people found their way to him. A shipyard manager, a theatre actor, the head of a union. One time a pre-war major from the Grudziądz Regiment came and ordered a pair of officer's boots; he couldn't get over his amazement that there was still a cobbler in Gdańsk who remembered the old military style.

Jakub thought of Kosterke-Trzebiatowska again. As she was in the past, when she still worked at the local brewery. The hands on the stopwatch were ticking precisely, but in his memory time moved in a different way: in layers, that stacked up on top of one another as shade or as light, but in a random order. Things and events from the remote past could float up to the surface for a trivial reason or for none at all, while something that happened a year ago could sink to the bottom of a deep well. By now eight minutes of street-sweeping had gone by. According to his calculations, at this point Kosterke-Trzebiatowska should be in between numbers nineteen and twenty-one. Where Samuel Lipszyc used to have his shop, the best men's tailor in the city.

Joachim started on his breakfast. Two rolls with margarine, curd cheese and cucumber. He'd first seen Kosterke-Trzebiatowska after the turret on Wallenrod Street had caught his eye. The Germans were still here then, though not in all the houses. They'd been ordered to share their apartments to provide accommodation for Poles. He couldn't remember any stories about fights or rows, but the fact that he'd been given a workshop and two rooms without their former residents was a stroke of luck. The

Germans made appearances in the streets – they had to go out for bread and milk. But on passing new arrivals, they lowered their voices or fell silent. Yes, on that occasion he'd seen two women, possibly a mother and daughter. Spring had washed the snow down from the faraway Brętowo hills, and the Strzyża, which usually flowed peacefully between the houses, had suddenly become fast and unpredictable. Mud-brown and turbid, it carried stalks, bushes and wooden objects. Its level rose by the hour, the cellars on Aldona and Grażyna streets had soon flooded, and the ground floors were at risk from it at any moment too. On top of that, rain was bucketing down. Dusk was falling. The water was already racing down the street, and the women were shouting to each other, in two minds whether or not to cross the little bridge. Joachim came out of his workshop with two pairs of galoshes. In broken German and sign language he tried to say he was lending them these rubber boots, he didn't want any money, but instead of crossing the bridge they turned back and disappeared. That was when he saw it – a light burning in the turret of one of the houses on Wallenrod Street. Dim and feeble through the streaming rain, but definitely a light. His eyes weren't deceiving him. Especially as all the windows in that house had been dark at night ever since he had come to live here. The street door was shut with security bars and a solid padlock, as well as a sign that said: 'No entry and no occupation of this site on penalty of a fine or imprisonment. National City Council.' Various things were said about it. One suggestion was that the house was to be occupied by Russkies. Or security service employees. Or that the wooden joists were in danger of collapse. From then on he went out each night to observe the turret. It grew from the roof like the chimney of a steamer, though not in the middle, but to one side. Quadrangular, with tiny windows, crowned by a tall spire. He waited patiently. The light did not appear. Maybe he had suffered a hallucination during the flood? He also wondered why the Germans had built these turrets. They weren't practical; by now he knew they weren't attics. And they weren't for observing the sky. In early May, he was standing outside his workshop to smoke a cigarette when the light appeared for about fifteen seconds and went out. Just like a lighthouse. He decided to investigate. He approached the empty house from the back. The door on the garden side had no security bars or threatening signs, but the handles refused to yield to cautious pressure. He went home, bent a bodkin in a vice to make a simple skeleton key, and once again, equipped with a torch, stood at the back door. The ground floor smelled of rotten timber and musty potatoes kept in a cellar. He climbed the stairs cautiously so they wouldn't creak. He shone the torch onto the apartment doors, or rather the nameplates. Wolf, Hoppe, Glinsky, Meyer, Hoffmann, Zelonka, Stroch, Elgenmayer – they had all gone by now in the first wave of resettlement, been killed on the front or were rotting in a Soviet camp. This thought occurred to him without satisfaction, but without sympathy either. What was to be found in these apartments? Only two on each floor, so they must have been large, with bathrooms. Pianos, dining-room furniture, sideboards, bedroom suites, bedside closets, ornate chandeliers, bookcases, rugs, larders, bathtubs, flower stands, prints and paintings. The door to the attic was open. Some dusty, mouldy laundry hadn't got as far as a mangle. He found a double-sided ladder. The trapdoor into the turret, which he had to push firmly from below, clattered open.

Joachim glanced at the stopwatch. Kosterke-Trzebiatowska definitely hadn't yet reached Wybicki Square, tightly surrounded by houses from the 1930s. They had no ornaments or turrets like the ones on Lelewel, Grażyna and Wallenrod streets. He added a dash of milk to his tea. He always liked the mixing moment, when the two colours rapidly created a third. It was odd, but he couldn't remember the shade of the shirts worn by his football club. They were brown. But brown like what? Autumn leaves? The veneer on his wireless set? The shirts worn by Śmigły Wilno were definitely brown like brandy. In 1933, or perhaps 1935, they'd thrashed the team from Siedlce. After that match Joachim had moved to Elektrit Wilno. At Śmigły there were lots of army men. They looked down on a cobbler, the son of a cobbler and the grandson of a cobbler. Elektrit trained and played its matches on Bouffałowa Hill. Śmigły played on Werkowska Street, on the other side of the Wilia river. Now, as he was measuring Kosterke-Trzebiatowska's speed again for the umpteenth time, certain events joined up in his memory. It was clear that he had started to lose customers ever since being rejected by the Gedania Club because of his age, though he hadn't been all that old yet. One failure brings another in its wake. The era of factory-made shoes was slowly but inexorably advancing. Even if they had to stand in long queues, people bought them because they were cheaper. But he still couldn't reduce his prices. He had nothing left but repairs: heels, soles, worn-out uppers. The last customer to order a pair of leather lace-up shoes was Mr Fox, the viola player from the symphony orchestra. Joachim went out of his workshop. Kosterke-Trzebiatowska was moving unusually slowly. He could see her silhouette more or less three-quarters of the way down the street. He could leave her in peace – the stopwatch was running reliably. He went and bought two teacakes at the patisserie under the arcade. On the way back he stopped at the house with the turret. A cloud of dust and the smell of pigeon droppings suddenly returned, as if he had only opened that trapdoor seconds ago. There he'd seen a woman, lying on a makeshift bed under a dirty quilt with no cover. As he stood before her, she covered her face with a pillow.

He spoke to her gently, in a hushed tone. When at last he saw her mouth, eyes, cheeks and brow he couldn't get over his amazement. She looked like Regina, as if she were her younger sister. When he heard the first words she spoke in Polish, he was instantly aware of a harsh German accent. She had taken him for a militiaman or someone of the kind. She was afraid of being arrested. Instead of talking about it, surprised by his own sudden practicality, he had asked her a few questions. How was she managing to get food? And how was it possible to relieve oneself here? She refused to talk about food. As for other needs, at night she went down to an apartment on the top floor, where there was a WC and running water in the bathroom. When he offered to bring food twice a week, she hesitated, then finally refused by shaking her head. He said he wasn't one of those people who inform. For several sleepless nights he thought about Regina, remembering their picnics and walks. To Three Crosses Hill and to Antokol. Also her visits to the workshop at the end of Niemiecka Street. Or to Zarzecze, where he had an aunt.

He hadn't been able to resist the temptation: one night he had filled his backpack with cheese, bread, jam and a bottle of tea, and had entered the empty house by the back door again. Once he had placed it all before the woman, he had wanted to have a conversation, but she had been unwilling to talk. The trapdoor was open and he already had a foot on the ladder when he heard sounds from below. There in the dark square he saw Kosterke-Trzebiatowska from number three, opposite his workshop. He only knew her by sight. They looked at each other mistrustfully, like two conspirators from two different organizations. Kosterke-Trzebiatowska unpacked her provisions and three jars of compote. Then they had walked a short stretch of the street side by side, in silence. Neither of them had even said goodbye.

Holding a small plastic bag containing the two teacakes, Joachim cast another glance at the turret. The metal-coated spire had long since become tarnished. The two little windows were boarded up. Plaster was falling off the walls of the house, which hadn't been renovated since 1945, revealing the bricks underneath. There was dark-green lichen growing in the gateway and around the gutters. The silted-up channel of the Strzyża poorly concealed various bits of rubbish: a pram with no hood, a chair warped by the water, a leaky tub and half a divan bed with its springs exposed. It crossed his mind that it was time to close the workshop and move somewhere else. But how was he to do it? A year after the war he'd been sent the confirmation of ownership for which he'd paid a lot of money. He'd had to pay the rest in instalments for ten years. The document turned out to be worthless. Everything had been nationalized, even the little shops. They never gave back the money. From then on he had just been a craftsman renting a site. It was a miracle the authorities had allowed him to stay here, raising the rent every few years. As he was entering the workshop, he looked down the street. Kosterke-Trzebiatowska had disappeared, as if she'd never been there. But he wasn't worried: sometimes she dropped by the shop on the square for milk. Then he deducted her shopping time by simply pausing the stopwatch. But that meant waiting outside to restart it when she reappeared at the top of Aldona Street. This time he didn't bother. He could always subtract five or six minutes from the total. In the dusty interior, which still smelled of leather and glue, he aimlessly rearranged his lasts and a pair of ankle boots no one had ever collected. The teacakes were for supper. He had already prepared his lunch – refried potatoes and soured milk. He thought about her, the neighbour from number three. When for some unknown reason they had fired her from the brewery she became their street cleaner. In those days she swept both sides. Now, in retirement, she only swept one. Joachim entered the small space that was his bedroom. Above the bed hung two pictures – of his father and mother. When the gendarmes had expelled them from Niemiecka Street, herding them and screaming, he hadn't had time to rescue his photograph of Regina from the chest of drawers. He had regretted it very much as he and his father walked to Zarzecze, to Aunt Helena's. He never knew his mother, who had died when he was two years old. And what about Regina? He couldn't think about her. He could never bring his fiancée to mind. Niemiecka Street, between the small and large ghettoes, often resembled a river. The Jews were driven along it. But first the Jewish owners had been thrown out of the rich shops on that street. Germans and Lithuanians had taken them over. His father had fooled himself into believing their workshop would be left in peace. It wasn't. There was no room on Niemiecka Street for the Poles either. Joachim sighed as he straightened the pillows and the bedspread. They had lived at Aunt Helena's until the end of the war, taking on various jobs.

He remembered the last group of German deportees marching along Wallenrod Street, carrying bundles or pulling wooden carts on their way to the station in Wrzeszcz. From the pavement and open windows onlookers shouted the names of concentration camps more than any other words. That day he had run into Kosterke-Trzebiatowska on the Strzyża footbridge. By now they knew they'd go to the turret that night. But the woman wasn't there. She had left the quilt, pillow, plate, mug and a few rags. Joachim wondered aloud whether she had gone with the Germans. That Kosterke-Trzebiatowska did not know, but she knew something else. It was the first time he had entered her room with a kitchen on the second floor. She made ersatz coffee. She served him biscuits. There was a group photograph, First Communion, taken in front of the church beyond the railway tracks. On the left, next to Kosterke-Trzebiatowska stood a little girl with a plait. Gudrun, her best friend throughout school, a good many years before the war, and after it too. She understood the inquiring look he cast her over the photograph. Her voice became hoarse as, in short, simple sentences, she described how the Russians had entered Wrzeszcz. This part of the district was where the wave of their fury had come crashing down. They hadn't set fire to the houses. No more grenades flew into the apartments. But for the women it was the same as everywhere else. They picked them out of the cellars, hiding places, cubbyholes and workshops. Gudrun had been in the wrong place at the wrong moment. She was walking down the pavement when a jeep came to a stop behind her. Three of them jumped out. They had their way with her in an empty apartment on the ground floor, and did up their army belts as they walked out of the gateway. But Gudrun had not left the house. Kosterke-Trzebiatowska had watched it all from opposite through an attic window. Her friend fled to the turret. Later, when there were no more Russians in the streets, she couldn't believe it. Something had shifted in her mind, as at a crossroads. Joachim didn't ask how Gudrun knew Polish, though far less well than her friend from First Communion. Nor did he say a word about the Lithuanians, Poles, Germans and Jews in the city he had left forever.

All this had been a very long time ago. Joachim tossed some diced onion into a frying pan, and once it had browned he added some boiled potatoes cut into slices. What was the point of his life? And was there a point to anything at all? He'd long since gone without good shoes. He, who had made so many court shoes for elegant ladies. So many men's lace-ups. He decided that now, as soon as Kosterke-Trzebiatowska was on her way back from the square, or came trudging along tired, stopping in their street to check if she'd done the job well, he decided that right now, before he saw her through the window, crossing the little bridge over the Strzyża, before switching off the stopwatch, he'd get down to work. He hadn't touched his lunch. He had no trouble finding his last, twine and bodkin. He still had a piece of yellow leather in the store cupboard, it was perfectly good, though he'd have to prepare the solution and the tub to soften it. It didn't take long. It was harder to get the pattern ready. After years working on repairs, he'd got out of practice. He couldn't decide whether to make himself a pair of ankle boots or something with a top. He remembered that on the day his fiancée was seized he had finished a pair of loafers for Professor Antkiewicz. Just then Mrs Mahoniowa had burst into the workshop. Her hands were actually trembling as she screamed that Regina had made the mistake of walking along Niemiecka Street. But that was the way she had gone, no other. The Lithuanian Riflemen had been goading along a column of Jews. Their uniforms, caps with death's heads, russet shirts and black ties surrounded the marchers like a swarm of dirty-green flies. Some German gendarmes and SS men brought up the rear. It was one of these who had glanced at Regina, shouted that she was a Jew and pushed her into the crowd under escort. In vain she denied it, in vain she waved her Lithuanian document, which clearly confirmed that she was a Catholic. In vain she took the cross from her neck, in vain she struggled with the SS man. Clouted by a rifle butt, she fell to the cobbles. Two of the riflemen picked her up and her fate was sealed. If only they'd intended to shut those Jews in the small or large ghetto. Then there would still have been a chance that somewhere near Szklana Street, Gaon, Klaczka, Rudnicka or Jatkowa streets Regina could have survived for a few days. After all, she was an Armenian, not a Jew. Something could have been arranged through one of their higher-ranking Lithuanian customers. But the Jewish columns were driven to Ponary. Everyone in the city knew what the riflemen did to them. Regina had at most three or four hours to live. In tears, Mrs Mahoniowa said that Joachim's fiancée had simply been in the wrong place at the wrong time. A few weeks later, when they were thrown out of the workshop and forced to pack in ten minutes flat, amid chaos and panic, Joachim hadn't taken Regina's photograph with him. Throughout the war he regretted it, and still did as he said goodbye to his father and Aunt Helena, who were to arrive in Poland on the next transport, but never got there.

Finally he decided on ankle boots. For rainy days in autumn he could always make himself a new pair with tops. The last time he had made himself boots was when he was still going to dances at the cultural centre in Kuźniczki. How long ago was that? He couldn't remember precisely. Maybe when they fired Kosterke-Trzebiatowska from the brewery? Once he had invited her to a dance. But she'd given him a look as if to say that men like him weren't the type who marry. Fundamentally she was right. Joachim was faithful to Regina, though he hadn't known her for long. Yet he had promised himself he'd never enter another relationship. And he had stopped going to church. True, at the dances he had cuddled some girl or other, he might even invite them home, which happened several times, but never one and the same girl. The pattern wasn't ready yet, but he had to think about the shape of the toes and the number of holes for laces. Once again he remembered Gudrun in the turret. So like Regina, but probably not an Armenian. Anyway, who could know? Only Kosterke-Trzebiatowska. Suddenly he realized that while working with his back to the window he might fail to spot her. Then today's timing would be pointless. He changed his position at the table. A cyclist came along the street. Then a woman walked by, pushing a pram. In fact, just as Gudrun was like Regina, he was like Gudrun too. He had spent all these years on the same street, shut in his own tower of time. Everything had its double, but they weren't exactly the same, like a pair of shoes he made to measure. The Germans hadn't been driven to Ponary. They had boarded goods wagons, just like the Poles who'd been expelled from Wilno. Joachim sighed. For the first time he felt sorrow. Perhaps he had wasted his life? If he had married and had children, perhaps it would have moved along a different, better track. Definitely not as monotonous. He hadn't even bought himself a television set. The old Pioneer only received one station now, Radio Warsaw. What's more it wheezed and crackled. During storms and rain it was impossible to listen to. He decided the toes would be rounded, not pointed. And he would make four holes for laces, that was best. Suddenly he saw Kosterke-Trzebiatowska. She crossed the bridge over the Strzyża, and shortly after disappeared through the door into number three. He switched off the stopwatch, but didn't record the result in the notebook as he leaned over his last. He didn't even notice her entering the workshop a little later. Instead of her wine-red apron she was wearing a yellow blouse and a chestnut-coloured skirt. She had shabby sandals on her bare feet. She fetched a bottle of home-made liquor from her bag and put it on the table.

'The shoes I wear to church have entirely fallen apart,' she said. 'There's nothing left to repair. I wonder if you could make me some new ones? I'll never find any like those ones.'

'Of course,' replied Joachim. 'Take a seat and I'll get my tape measure.'

She took the sandal off her right foot. While he was drawing its outline on a piece of cardboard, and then measuring the height of her instep, Kosterke-Trzebiatowska added: 'I've nothing to pay you with. That's why I brought the liquor. I'll bake you a cake. Every Sunday.'

Joachim nodded and brought two dusty shot glasses. He rinsed them in the sink, wiped them with a cloth and put them on the table. They sat facing each other. They each took a small sip, barely wetting their lips.

'Tell me, why do you clean our street? Everyone knows you don't get a penny towards your pension for doing it.' Joachim hid the stopwatch under a newspaper.

'Yes, if you can explain why you time me whenever I do it. Everyone knows it's pointless.'

They sat in silence. Each sunk in their own thoughts. For the first time a jet, rather than a propellor plane, flew over the city. The Strzyża went on flowing under the bridge. Joachim smiled at Kosterke-Trzebiatowska. Kosterke-Trzebiatowska smiled at Joachim. Time went on flowing, ever more slowly, as if now they were to stay like that forever.

'*Szewc*'
Published as part of the collection *Talita* (Wydawnictwo Znak, 2020).

MACIEJ MIŁKOWSKI

1980–

Trained as a psychologist, Maciej Miłkowski is a writer, literary critic, translator and teacher of creative writing in Kraków. He has published three collections of short stories: *Wist* (*Whist*, 2014), *Drugie spotkanie* (*The Second Meeting*, 2017), and *Trzeci Dzień Świąt* (*The Third Day of Christmas*, 2021), as well as a novel, *System Sulta* (*Sult's System*, 2019). An essay collection, *Anatomia opowiadania* (*Anatomy of a Short Story*), was published in 2024. His work has garnered acclaim for its subtle construction, wry humour and philosophical depth.

'The Tattoo', an exploration of Holocaust memory in transition-era Poland, was inspired by a reflection on the role of tattooing in the Third Reich. 'Assuming that a Holocaust survivor would probably never want to get a tattoo,' Miłkowski says, 'I began to wonder how far the popularity of tattoos today indicates a collective repression of this traumatic part of Polish history.' What is more, the story is set in Poland in the 1990s, soon after the collapse of communism. 'This was a very special time. All sorts of things began flowing in from the West – basic necessities as well as absurdly useless stuff. Every day something appeared on the market that hadn't existed the previous day. It was a time of tremendous opportunity: if you were in your twenties and in the right place at the right time, you could, overnight, become vice-president or deputy minister. When it comes to literary fiction, however, the 1990s were a time of missed opportunities.' Critics lament that no Polish novel has captured the essence of the year 1989. 'That's because back then, writers were busy looking forward, into the future. They should have been writing, not necessarily *about* 1989, but *in* 1989 – about anything at all.'

With its dingy everyday setting and luckless protagonists, this short story allows the momentousness of the historical past to emerge with remarkable poignancy.

Tul'si (Tuesday) Bhambry

The Tattoo

Translated by Tul'si (Tuesday) Bhambry

In those days we didn't even have our own office. We rented a tiny space not far from the city centre, on the ground floor, which we shared with a tattoo studio. Actually, at that point they weren't called studios yet – it was only a couple of years later that everything would be transformed into parlours, salons and studios. It was simply called 'Tattoos'. We were called 'Travel Agency'. Those were pioneering days, and we, like all pioneers, were naïve, unsophisticated and rather childish. We pretended that our hands were trembling with eagerness, yet for most of us the trembling was purely from good old fear.

The guy in charge of 'Tattoos' was called Skin and, at first sight, this nickname didn't seem particularly subtle, given that Skin was indeed bald as a coot and regularly attended to his baldness with an ordinary disposable razor. He often shaved in front of me – that is to say, he shaved his head, never his face. I don't know, maybe at the time he couldn't grow facial hair. There was a sink in the tiny back room, but our only mirror was in the front room (closer, in fact, to my desk than to Skin's), which was why his shaving routine usually involved him traipsing back and forth in front of me. He would dip and rinse his razor in the back room, then he'd come over to shave, performing peculiar twists and turns in an effort to see the back of his head in the mirror. He refused to accept that this just cannot be done if you've only got one mirror at your disposal. Besides these contortions, his other technique was to run his hand against the grain of his shorn hair. But more often than not, he still ended up asking me to reshave his scalp here and there. I would make him follow me to the basin in the back room, where I would do a few touch-ups. Looking back, I think he shaved in the office on purpose. He probably didn't have anyone to clean him up at home.

All the same, Skin and that nickname of his were quite suspicious. What fascinated me most was the fact that among the so-called mates who came to see him virtually all were skinheads, but evidently only where Skin was concerned did a spade get called a spade. In their eyes, Skin's way of being a skinhead must have been superior or primordial somehow. Their shaved heads were imitations; his was original and natural, even if it was forged over a chipped sink in a dingy cubbyhole with the help of my none too dextrous hand.

Did he actually do any tattooing there? I can't remember. He certainly had tattoos – as did the others. Every now and then he'd be sketching something (a 'pattern' – nobody used the word 'design' back then). But did he tattoo anyone? Not in the office, at least. It's possible that he only took orders there, performing the actual work elsewhere. Though I do remember some equipment for cosmetic torture lying around in the back room. So maybe he did? But how much of all this do I remember? It was probably an ordinary money-laundering business. That's what we'd call it now, but what about back then? There was already money around, I think (though it was still the kind that showed Copernicus, Chopin and the like). But was there dirty money yet? I don't know.

There were still Russki tanks around. And even if there weren't, they'd only have left recently and could still have returned at any moment. That was our free market – in the shadow of Russki tanks. People only breathed a sigh of relief when the man in the red pullover became president; the same man who had, just a short time before . . . Everyone breathed a sigh of relief because when he, of all people, became president, and the tanks still didn't come back, we could tentatively begin to think they might never return at all.

But that wasn't until a few years later, when our office had long ceased to exist. We lasted about six months. Then the headquarters in the capital went under, and so, as a matter of course, our branch went under too. I don't know how many tours I sold in those six months. Five? Seven? Lots of people came into our office, but they only came to ask if it was true that you could just up and go to Paris now. Yes, you could. And by coach. In those days people went everywhere by coach. Paris, Vienna, Italy, England, Greece, Spain. Twenty-four hours, forty-eight, seventy-two. Without air conditioning, without a toilet, but with meat loaves and jars of pickled gherkins down in the baggage hold. There was also a kind of soup in a carton, which was supposed to warm up mysteriously when you shook it. I don't know how it worked. I don't know if any of it worked at all – the soup or those famous tours. I never shook a soup carton, and I never went on a coach tour.

The coach would set off from the capital, arriving in our town a couple of hours later. They always started their journeys in the evening, in order to avoid losing a day – some tomorrow or day-after-tomorrow in Paris. As a result, the coach usually arrived here at some ungodly hour, like 4.30 a.m. Today, those rare holidaymakers would probably have been calling me in the middle of the night, but back then no one called, because there weren't any telephones yet. I mean, people had telephones, but at home, not in their pockets, and that's quite a different thing.

So there were no phone calls, and hardly any holidaymakers either. Everything worked according to the same plan in those days: you'd walk into a place, ask if this or that was possible, then you'd hear that yes, indeed it was, but in the end you wouldn't go for it anyway, because . . . well, how? Where? What? Who are we to show up like this? With our pickled gherkins? In Paris? So you'd walk in to see what was on offer – because everyone was asking if you'd already been – you'd put on the face of an expert, look around in disdain and walk out empty-handed. The saleswoman wouldn't even bother to get up. She'd be used to it. Sex shops were going under at lightning speed.

In other words, I had a lot of custom that led to nothing, while at Skin's custom was lousy but much more substantial. Skinheads would always come to see Skin on some business or other. They would leave immediately, taking him along with them, and soon after another pair of shaven-headed blokes would appear and ask if Skin was in. I would reply that he'd just left with two guys. 'With two skins?' they'd ask to make sure. I'd say yes, and they seemed to know who was who. They had their own codes. They managed without phones.

Skin and I had this agreement that if any customers came to see him when he wasn't there, I would show and explain everything to them, and he would do the same if it was the other way around. Only there was no other way around, because I was always there, while Skin was often out.

I had no flair for business, and was simply being swallowed by a bigger, hairless fish in the Darwinian lake of early capitalism.

Anyway, Skin went bankrupt a few months after we did. He didn't make enough money to cover the entire rent once our contribution was gone. There was no one to look after his office, or to tidy up the back and top of his head with a blunt razor over a dirty sink.

But until we duly wound up both our businesses, we had that one-sided gentlemen's agreement, and I even photocopied Skin's price list so I wouldn't have to keep running to his desk – though, honestly, I wasn't going to have much running to do. There were photocopiers already by then – the people upstairs had one. You'd insert a sheet of paper at the bottom, making sure it went in straight, and on top you'd slide a huge flap across. Like in the underground – a duplicator.

All this happened somewhere near the beginning. When the old system collapsed, I wasn't quite twenty. At the time, the catch was you had to be at least twenty to be anyone – if you were over twenty, you could be a company chairman, or a deputy minister. But if you weren't, you ended up in an office with Skin.

I divided my time into two parts, spending one half telling pensioners that yes, it was possible to go to Paris, and the other half dealing with Skin's eternal stubble. That's all I have to say about how I spent my time. But there was also the time-in-between, which usually stretched into long hours. With no Skin and no pensioners around, I'd immerse myself in this time-in-between, mostly reading the classics. I read all of Dostoevsky on that watch. A poor choice.

Besides reading the classics, I was also busy waiting. The whole country was busy doing the same thing. It was as if we weren't living life to the full, but with one foot on the brake. We were waiting for something, but for what? It was clear that everything around us was temporary and transitory, that something else was bound to emerge from it, that it had to transform into something else. No one knew if the Russki tanks would return or if we'd build a new economic superpower instead. But we knew that everything around us was a cardboard stopgap that would soon fall to pieces, one way or another. And so we were waiting, shirking life, convinced that life was yet to come; for now I must sit it out in this anteroom with Skin, but later I'm sure to be admitted to the ball.

And as far as life, macroeconomics, travel and tattoos were concerned, this turned out to be essentially true. But literature? What about literature? In those days I believed that we had to read the classics and dig through the tunnel of the transitional phase, bore through the Urals from Asia into Europe, stick it out until the time when we'd have nice clothes, nice interiors and exteriors, when it'd be like Paris over here, with croissants, wine and blue cheese, and we'd be sitting in a garret overlooking the Seine, which would by then have emerged from the Vistula . . . we'd be sitting there churning out novels, just like that.

But today I think that those were exceptionally novelistic times. Perhaps it was impossible to write without that garret, but we should have been taking notes. There was a novel knocking at our door in those days, knocking and banging at the gate, like in *Macbeth*, climbing into our bed of its own accord. And not just one novel either, but entire trilogies, tetralogies and sagas – entire libraries, epochs, genres, milestones, Prousts and Nabokovs. And I don't mean that we should have been writing about those times, singing the praises of the political, economic and cultural transformation. I don't mean we should have been writing about that turmoil – that's what I'm doing here, and no novel seems to be emerging. The point is that we should have been diving into it. Because that was a time of heightened perception, a sort of super-reality. We thought it was a time of suspension, but in fact it was a time for suspending. The walls were empty, with naked hooks protruding, and we should have been putting up one picture after another. Other fields weren't obstructed by similar delusions and inhibitions, which is why today we have, for instance, cars (or tattoos), but no novels. We missed our moment, reading the classics in semi-virtual travel agencies. It never came, but it went. The planets won't align like that again for another hundred years.

But what if I had to choose one unexploited situation – out of all the missed opportunities that haunt the dreams of a sluggish striker? One girl I failed to follow off the bus? One novel that came knocking at my gate?

I think I would choose one that came knocking not at my gate, but at Skin's – which actually boils down to the same thing, firstly because I was working as Skin's porter at the time, and secondly because Skin probably wasn't waiting for that kind of knocking with particular eagerness. Now that I think about it, if anything he was more likely to have been afraid of any sudden knocking.

'Hey, listen, if I happen to be out somewhere and a novel should need to be written, you'll deal with it, won't you?' Skin never told me to do that. But would he have needed to?

Skin was out. Into the office walked an old man, wearing a really stupid outfit. It suggested pre-war elegance, but was cobbled together from communist-era ingredients. He had a hat, naturally, as well as a suit and tie (or perhaps it was a cravat – no, actually, I don't think so). But all of it was ugly and cheap, made from indistinguishably dull, greyish-brown fabrics, factory-faded for lack of dye.

'I came to inquire about tattoos,' he said.

'My colleague is out,' I said. 'But I have his price list and catalogue somewhere here. Would you like to take a look?'

'The price list, please,' he said.

I showed him the list, which he studied carefully (while I studied him), but then he said, 'The item I was looking for isn't here.'

'What are you looking for? Are you thinking of getting a tattoo?'

'I have one already,' he said. 'When will your colleague be back?'

'I don't know, to be honest. But I can pass on a message. We have an arrangement, you see. I run this travel agency. If you wanted to go to Paris, for instance . . .'

'I've been to Paris,' he cut me short.

He's got a tattoo. He's been to Paris.

'So what can I, or rather my colleague, do for . . .' I tried again.

'It's not on the price list,' he said, 'but I know that it can be done these days. I'd like to have a tattoo removed. Would you ask your colleague if that's possible?'

'Yes, of course. How big is the tattoo?'

'I'll show you,' he said, and started to unbutton his jacket.

'Is it in a private place?' I asked, just in case.

'Moderately.'

He unbuttoned a shirt cuff and started to roll up the sleeve. Five digits on the forearm. A low number. He must have been in there for a long time.

'Do you know what that is?' he asked.

546

'Yes, I do.'

'I wanted to make sure,' he said, and I thought he was quite right to do so, because a guy like Skin, for example, definitely wouldn't have known. And perhaps it would have been better that way, if he were the one removing the tattoo.

'I understand,' I said.

'When my wife was still alive,' he said, 'I couldn't do it. She said we must remember. But as you might imagine, I remember perfectly well in any case. The thing is, I don't want to be buried with it. I'd like to stand before Saint Peter the way God made me, not the way Heinrich Himmler did.'

'I understand,' I said again.

'I doubt it,' he said, buttoning up his shirt and putting on his jacket. 'Please do ask your colleague. I'll drop by in a couple of days.'

'I will,' I said.

'I wish you good day,' he said (he couldn't have been a local), bowing slightly, and moments later he was gone.

And that's supposed to be a novel? No, not yet. The novel wasn't born until the following day, when I related the whole incident to Skin, and he, with the naïveté of a noble savage, handed me the missing piece of the puzzle. Because there's no such thing as an idea for a novel. To write a novel (or a short story for that matter), you need to have two ideas – both equally strong, equally developed – only then does it turn out to be just one idea after all, one bi-polar foundation.

I'd guessed right. Skin had no clue. Skin had seen nothing, which was why he was so authoritative. But in this instance he was my porter, not I his.

'What?' said Skin. 'Couldn't remember his old girl's phone number?'

'But it was only five digits,' I said. 'That's too short.'

'But you said it was an old guy, right? 'Cause before the war, you see,' he lectured me, 'hardly anyone had a phone, and that's why the numbers were short. Grandpa probably made a bet when he was pissed, and now he's having regrets. That's how it always ends. I have a rule that says I don't do it under the influence. I mean, I can't be drunk, and the client can't be, neither. Some people want to have a stiff one beforehand, but I won't have it. No way. 'Cause afterwards we don't give them their money back.'

'But can it be removed?'

'Not really. There's some sort of stuff you can inject, some sort of milk. It lightens it a little, but it won't go away completely. It'll show. He shouldn't have gone drinking. Besides, if it's well done, he can't ask for his money back. He should have had it done at a studio' – I guess we did have studios in those days – 'and not in someone's back room. Do you know if the old boy got it done professionally or, as they say, under field conditions?'

'Professionally, but under field conditions.'

'Well, then I don't know. Tell him nothing can be done. He's old, so what does he care? He won't have to carry it around for too much longer. And he won't be going to the beach, eh? Anyway, I don't remove tattoos. No one's ever asked me to do that. No wait . . . one guy did. And guess what. It was another old geezer. In Germany.'

'You went to Germany?'

'Yeah. For work. And there was this old German, a pretty decent guy. As soon as he saw my tattoos he asked me who'd done them, so I told him I did them myself . . .'

'You speak German?'

'No way! His Polish was top-notch. The only thing I can say in German is "*Heil Hitler!*",' said Skin, waving his hand not exactly like those people did, but in the end it's the thought that counts. 'And then he tells me he's got a tattoo too, but he wants to get rid of it.'

'Did he show it to you?'

'Yeah. He had some piece of shit near his armpit. Two letters, A and B. I told him you could hardly even see it, but he said they'd see it in the morgue, and he didn't want any fuss about his estate. Search me – it must have been someone's initials . . .'

'His blood group,' I said. 'A rare one, too.'

'Yeah, but what's the problem? And what estate? Can't a guy get a fucking tattoo? I know this one bloke, he's a company chairman now, and he's got a little pig on his arse, you know, the one from the Muppets, or the Moomins.'

'What did you say to that German?'

'I told him it can't be removed, but I could add a couple more letters from the alphabet, as a sort of cover-up, in case it was his first wife's initials or whatever.'

'Did he go for it?'
'Nah.'

At this point I should have got up and left, instead of staying there with Skin, waiting for bankruptcy. I should have said: 'Sorry, Skin, I'm out and unavailable. If anyone comes to ask if it's possible to go to Paris, tell them that it is, but that the Baltic coast is also very nice. I'm off. I'm off to look for that old guy of yours, and mine, too – not physically of course, but with a pencil and my notebook. I'll be back in three to five years. And as for you, why don't you go ahead and go bust, and deal with your own stupid hair, you shitty, badly shaven crook!'

I should have left, instead of waiting for the old man to come back, because of course he never did. He wasn't local. Perhaps he got it removed somewhere else. Or perhaps he died. It does happen sometimes.

Oh, yes. Today tattoos can be removed by laser. In Germany they must have been doing it for years. Without a trace. Only it's better to have it done by a doctor, not by Skin. I saw Skin in the street the other day. He's still bald, in case you're wondering. But what sort of novels are being written today, and what sort are knocking at the gates, that I don't know, and I probably never shall.

'Tatuaż'
Published as part of the collection *Wist* (Zeszyty Literackie, 2014).

Further Reading

This list generally refers to work from the period covered by this anthology, in English translation.

Anthologies of Short Stories Published in English Translation

Ten Contemporary Polish Stories. Ed. Edmund Ordon. Santa Barbara, CA: Greenwood Publishing Group, Inc. 1958, 1974. Reprint. Detroit, MI: Wayne State University Press. 1958.

The Broken Mirror: A Collection of Writings from Contemporary Poland. New York, NY: Random House. 1958.

Contemporary Polish Short Stories. Ed. Andrzej Kijowski. Warsaw: Polonia Publishing House. 1960.

The Modern Polish Mind. Ed. Maria Kuncewicz. Boston, MA: Little, Brown. 1962. London: Secker & Warburg. 1962.

Polish Writing Today, Ed. Celina Wieniewska. Harmondsworth: Penguin Books. 1967.

Russian and Polish Women's Fiction. Ed. Helena Goscilo. Knoxville, TN: University of Tennessee Press. 1985.

The Dedalus Book of Polish Fantasy. Ed. Wiesiek Powaga. Sawtry, Cambridgeshire: Dedalus Books. 1996.

Description of a Struggle: The Vintage Book of Contemporary Eastern European Writing. Ed. Michael March. New York, NY: Vintage Books. 1994.

The Eagle and the Crow: Modern Polish Short Stories. Ed. Teresa Halikowska and George Hyde. London: Serpent's Tail. 1996.

Chicago Review, 46.3–4. Special Issue on New Polish Writing. (Fall 2000.)

Contemporary Jewish Writing in Poland. Ed. Antony Polonsky and Monika Adamczyk-Garbowska. Lincoln, NE: University of Nebraska Press. 2001.

The Short Story in a Polish Context. Ed. Oscar E. Swan. Paris: Piasa Books. 2024.

Warsaw Tales (City Tales series). Trans. Antonia Lloyd-Jones. Ed. Helen Constantine. Oxford: Oxford University Press. 2024.

Individual Collections of Short Stories in English

The following collections, in English translation, are by authors who appear in this volume. Many of the authors have written short stories that have not been translated. Some of them have written novels that have been published in English translation, and individual short stories that have appeared in English-language journals.

For lack of space the translated novels are not listed here, but for readers who wish to explore, the novelists whose work does exist in translation include:

Jerzy Andrzejewski, Jacek Dehnel, Stanisław Dygat, Kornel Filipowicz, Witold Gombrowicz, Marek Hłasko, Paweł Huelle, Tadeusz Konwicki, Maria Kuncewiczowa, Stanisław Lem, Dorota Masłowska, Leopold Tyrmand, Olga Tokarczuk, Magdalena Tulli and Michał Witkowski.

The poets whose work can be found in English translation include: Jacek Dehnel, Julia Fiedorczuk and Tadeusz Różewicz.

The playwrights whose work can be found in English translation include: Sławomir Mrożek, Witold Gombrowicz and Tadeusz Różewicz.

There are also works of non-fiction (reportage or memoirs) available in English by:

Miron Białoszewski, Józef Hen, Margo Rejmer and Tadeusz Różewicz.

Short-story Collections Published in English by the Authors in This Anthology

Tadeusz Borowski
This Way for the Gas, Ladies and Gentlemen. Trans. Barbara Vedder. New York, NY, and London: Viking Press. 1967. Penguin Books. 1976, 1992.
Here in Our Auschwitz and Other Stories. In the Margellos World Republic of Letters series. Trans. Madeline G. Levine. Foreword Timothy Snyder. New Haven, CT: Yale University Press. 2021.

Further Reading

Maria Dąbrowska
A Village Wedding, and Other Stories. (Translator not named.) Warsaw: Polonia Publishing House. 1957, 1970.

Ida Fink
A Scrap of Time and Other Stories (Jewish Lives). Trans. Madeline G. Levine. Evanston, IL: Northwestern University Press. 1995.

Witold Gombrowicz
Bacacay. Trans. Bill Johnston. New York, NY: Archipelago Books. 2004.

Paweł Huelle
Moving House and Other Stories. Trans. Antonia Lloyd-Jones. London: Bloomsbury Publishing. 1994.
Cold Sea Stories. Trans. Antonia Lloyd-Jones. Manchester: Comma Press. 2013.

Jarosław Iwaszkiewicz
The Birch Grove and Other Stories. Trans. Antonia Lloyd-Jones. Budapest: Central European University Press. 2002.

Stanisław Lem
Tales of Pirx the Pilot. Trans. Louis Iribarne. New York, NY: Mariner Books. 1990.
The Star Diaries. Trans. Michael Kandel. London: Penguin Random House. 2015.
Memoirs of a Space Traveler: Further Reminiscences of Ijon Tichy. Trans. Joel Stern, Maria Swiecicka-Ziemianek and Antonia Lloyd-Jones. Kraków: Pro Auctore Wojciech Zemek. 2018.
The Truth and Other Stories. Trans. Antonia Lloyd-Jones. Cambridge, MA: The MIT Press, 2021.

Sławomir Mrożek
The Elephant. Trans. Konrad Syrop. Westport, CT: Greenwood Press. 1962, 1975. New York, NY: Grove Press. 1984. Reissued: London: Penguin Random House. 2010.

Marek Nowakowski
The Canary and Other Tales of Martial Law. Trans. Krystyna Bronkowska. London: Harvill Press. 1983. Also: Garden City, NY: Dial Press. 1984.

Adolf Rudnicki
Ascent to Heaven, Trans. H. C. Stevens. London: Dennis Dobson Ltd. 1951.
The Dead and the Living Sea, and Other Stories. Trans. Jadwiga Zwolska. Warsaw: Polonia Publishing House. 1957.

Bruno Schulz
The Street of Crocodiles and Other Stories. Trans. Celina Wieniewska. New York, NY: Penguin Books. 2008.
Nocturnal Apparitions: Essential Stories. Trans. Stanley Bill. London: Pushkin Press. 2022.

Short-story Collections Published in English
Translation by Other Polish Writers

Andrzej Bursa
Killing Auntie & Other Work. Trans. Wiesiek Powaga. London: CB Editions. 2007.

Natasza Goerke
Farewells to Plasma. Trans. W. Martin. Prague: Twisted Spoon Press. 2001.

Stefan Grabiński
The Dark Domain. Trans. Mirosław Lipiński. Sawtry: Dedalus Books 2013.
Orchard of The Dead and other Macabre Tales. Trans. Anthony Sciscione. Richmond VA: Valancourt Books, 2023.

Mikołaj Grynberg
I'd Like to Say Sorry, But There's No One to Say Sorry to. Trans. Sean Gasper Bye. New York, NY: The New Press. 2022.

Gustaw Herling-Grudziński
The Island: Three Tales. Trans. Ronald Strom. New York, NY: Penguin Books. 1994.

Urszula Honek
White Nights. Trans. Kate Webster. Brighton: MTO Press. 2023.

Zofia Nałkowska
Medallions. Trans. Diana Kuprel. Evanston, IL: Northwestern University Press. 2000.

Piotr Paziński
Bird Streets. Trans. Ursula Phillips. Detroit, MI: Vine Editions. 2022.

Andrzej Stasiuk
Tales of Galicia. Trans. Margarita Nafpaktitis. Prague: Twisted Spoon Press. 2003.

About the Translators

Tul'si (Tuesday) Bhambry grew up in Poland, Germany and India. She studied languages and literatures in the UK (London and Cambridge) and France (Tours) and holds a PhD in Polish Literature (University College London, 2013). In 2015 she won the Harvill Secker Young Translators' Prize and moved on to translate poetry and song lyrics, short stories and comics. She also translates non-literary writing, such as books in the humanities and social sciences, art museum catalogues and historical source texts as well as writings related to anti-discrimination and empowerment. She also works as an interpreter and moderator.

Stanley Bill is Professor of Polish Studies at the University of Cambridge. He works on twentieth-century Polish literature and culture, and on contemporary Polish politics. He is the author of *Czesław Miłosz's Faith in the Flesh: Body, Belief, and Human Identity* (Oxford University Press, 2021), and co-editor of *The Routledge World Companion to Polish Literature* (2021) and *Multicultural Commonwealth: Poland–Lithuania and Its Afterlives* (Pittsburgh University Press, 2023). He has published translations of Czesław Miłosz's novel *The Mountains of Parnassus* (Yale University Press, 2017) and a selection of short stories by Bruno Schulz entitled *Nocturnal Apparitions: Essential Stories* (Pushkin Press, 2022). He is the founder and editor-at-large of the news and opinion website Notes from Poland.

Sean Gasper Bye began learning Polish at university as a way of reconnecting with his roots. He translates mainly contemporary fiction and reportage, as well as historical texts and theatre. He has translated authors such as Małgorzata Szejnert, Szczepan Twardoch and Mikołaj Grynberg. His work has won the EBRD Literary Prize and the Asymptote Close Approximations Prize; and been shortlisted for the Warwick Prize for Women in Translation, a National Jewish Book Award, the Sami Rohr Prize and the National Translation Award. He also works as a mentor for emerging translators.

Jennifer Croft won a 2022 Guggenheim Fellowship for her novel *The*

Extinction of Irena Rey, the 2020 William Saroyan International Prize for Writing for her illustrated memoir *Homesick* and the 2018 International Booker Prize for her translation from Polish of Nobel laureate Olga Tokarczuk's *Flights*. She is also the translator of Federico Falco's *A Perfect Cemetery*, Romina Paula's *August*, Pedro Mairal's *The Woman from Uruguay* and Olga Tokarczuk's *The Books of Jacob* (a finalist for the Kirkus Prize). In 2023, she received an American Academy of Arts and Letters Award in Literature. She lives in Tulsa, Oklahoma, with her husband and twins.

Bill Johnston won the 2019 National Translation Award in Poetry for his rendering of Adam Mickiewicz's 1834 rhyming verse epic *Pan Tadeusz*. He also received the PEN America Translation Prize and the Best Translated Book Award (shared with the author) for his translation of Wiesław Myśliwski's 1984 novel *Stone upon Stone*. His most recent translation is Julia Fiedorczuk's poetry collection *Psalms*. He is currently working on a translation of Maria Dąbrowska's four-volume novel cycle *The Nights and the Days*. He teaches literary translation at Indiana University-Bloomington.

Madeline G. Levine, Kenan Professor Emerita of Slavic Literatures, began translating from Polish so her students at the University of North Carolina, Chapel Hill, could see for themselves how the radically different narrative approaches adopted by Miron Białoszewski in his *Memoir of the Warsaw Uprising* (1977; revised edition published by New York Review Book Classics, 2015) and by Ida Fink in *A Scrap of Time and Other Stories* (1987) each resulted in a stunning literary representation of the Nazi occupation of Poland and the Holocaust as it unfolded there. Other writings on the border between memoir and fiction followed: books by Bogdan Wojdowski, Hanna Krall and Wilhelm Dichter, ending with *Here in Our Auschwitz and Other Stories* by Tadeusz Borowski (2021). Levine has also translated four volumes of prose by Czesław Miłosz. For her 2018 translation of *Collected Stories* by Bruno Schulz, she received the Polish Book Institute's Found in Translation Award.

Eliza Marciniak is an editor and a literary translator. Her translations include *Swallowing Mercury* by Wioletta Greg (published by Granta Books in the UK and Transit Books in the USA), which was longlisted for the Man Booker International Prize 2017, as well as a series of classic Polish children's books by Marian Orłoń (published by Pushkin Press): *Detective Nosegoode and the Music Box Mystery*, *Detective Nosegoode and the*

Kidnappers and *Detective Nosegoode and the Museum Robbery*. She lives in London.

W. Martin is an educator, editor and translator from Polish and German. Publications include Michał Witkowski's novels *Eleven-Inch* (Seagull Books, 2021) and *Lovetown* (Portobello Books, 2010), Erich Kästner's children's book *Emil and the Detectives* (Overlook, 2007) and Natasza Goerke's short-story collection *Farewells to Plasma* (Twisted Spoon, 2002). Forthcoming are translations of Witold Gombrowicz's novel *Cosmos* (Fitzcarraldo Editions) and Hubert Fichte's ethnopoetic novel *Puberty* (Seagull Books). He is the recipient of Fulbright and National Endowment of the Arts fellowships, has had residencies at Yaddo and the Baltic Centre for Writers and Translators, teaches for Bard College and Pratt Institute and lives in Berlin.

Jess Jensen Mitchell began translating as a PhD student at Harvard University, in the hope of sharing the tragicomedy of Polish writing with English-language readers. She was chosen for the NCW's Emerging Translator Mentorship in Polish in 2022 and published her first translation – a short story by Dominika Słowik – in *Two Lines Journal*. She co-produces a podcast on literary translation and is finishing her dissertation on contemporary depictions of Upper Silesia, a region in western Poland known for its mining industry, distinct language and superb rail system.

Ursula Phillips writes on Polish literary history and is a translator of literary and scholarly works. She has been instrumental in introducing the work of Polish female authors from the nineteenth to twenty-first centuries to Anglophone readers. Translations include Maria Wirtemberska's *Malvina, or The Heart's Intuition* (1816), Narcyza Żmichowska's *The Heathen* (1846), Zofia Nałkowska's *Choucas* (1927), for which she received the 2015 Found in Translation Award, Nałkowska's *Boundary* (1935), for which she received the PIASA Wacław Lednicki Award in 2017, and Agnieszka Taborska's *The Unfinished Life of Phoebe Hicks* (2013, trans. 2024). She is also the translator of Jacek Dukaj's 1000-page alternative-history-cum-sci-fi epic *Ice* (2007), which is forthcoming.

Anna Zaranko's most recent translations from Polish include *The Peasants*, an early twentieth-century classic novel by Władysław Reymont, and Leo Lipski's *Piotruś*, a 'micro-novel' first published in 1960 and set in 1940s Tel Aviv. Her translation of Kornel Filipowicz's *The Memoir of an Anti-Hero* won the Found in Translation Award in 2020.

Copyright Information

Every effort has been made to contact copyright holders of material reproduced in this anthology. We would be pleased to rectify any omissions in subsequent editions.

ANIMALS

Irena Krzywicka, 'Love and Life in the Hen House'. Translation © Jess Jensen Mitchell, 2025. Text © The Estate of Irena Krzywicka. Originally published as 'Stosunki w kurniku', 1961.

Anna Kowalska, 'Horses'. Translation © Antonia Lloyd-Jones, 2025. Text © The Estate of Anna Kowalska. Originally published as 'Konie', 1960.

Kornel Filipowicz, 'Cat in the Wet Grass'. Translation © Anna Zaranko, 2025. Text © Aleksander Filipowicz and Marcin Filipowicz. Originally published as 'Kot w mokrej trawie', 1977.

Paweł Sołtys, 'Rysio the Cat'. Translation © Eliza Marciniak, 2025. Text © Paweł Sołtys, 2019. Originally published as 'Kot Rysio'.

CHILDREN

Jan Parandowski, 'The Phonograph'. Translation © Antonia Lloyd-Jones, 2025. Text © the Heirs of Jan Parandowski. Originally published as 'Fonograf', 1953.

Joanna Rudniańska, 'Her Sovereign Decision'. Translation © Antonia Lloyd-Jones, 2025. Text © Joanna Rudniańska, 2019. Originally published as 'Suwerenna decyzja'.

Olga Tocarczuk, 'The Green Children'. Translation © Jennifer Croft, 2025. Text © Olga Tokarczuk, 2018. Originally published as 'Zielone dzieci'.

Julia Fiedorczuk, 'Moss'. Translation © Anna Zaranko, 2018. Text © Julia Fiedorczuk, 2016. This translation of 'Moss' first appeared in